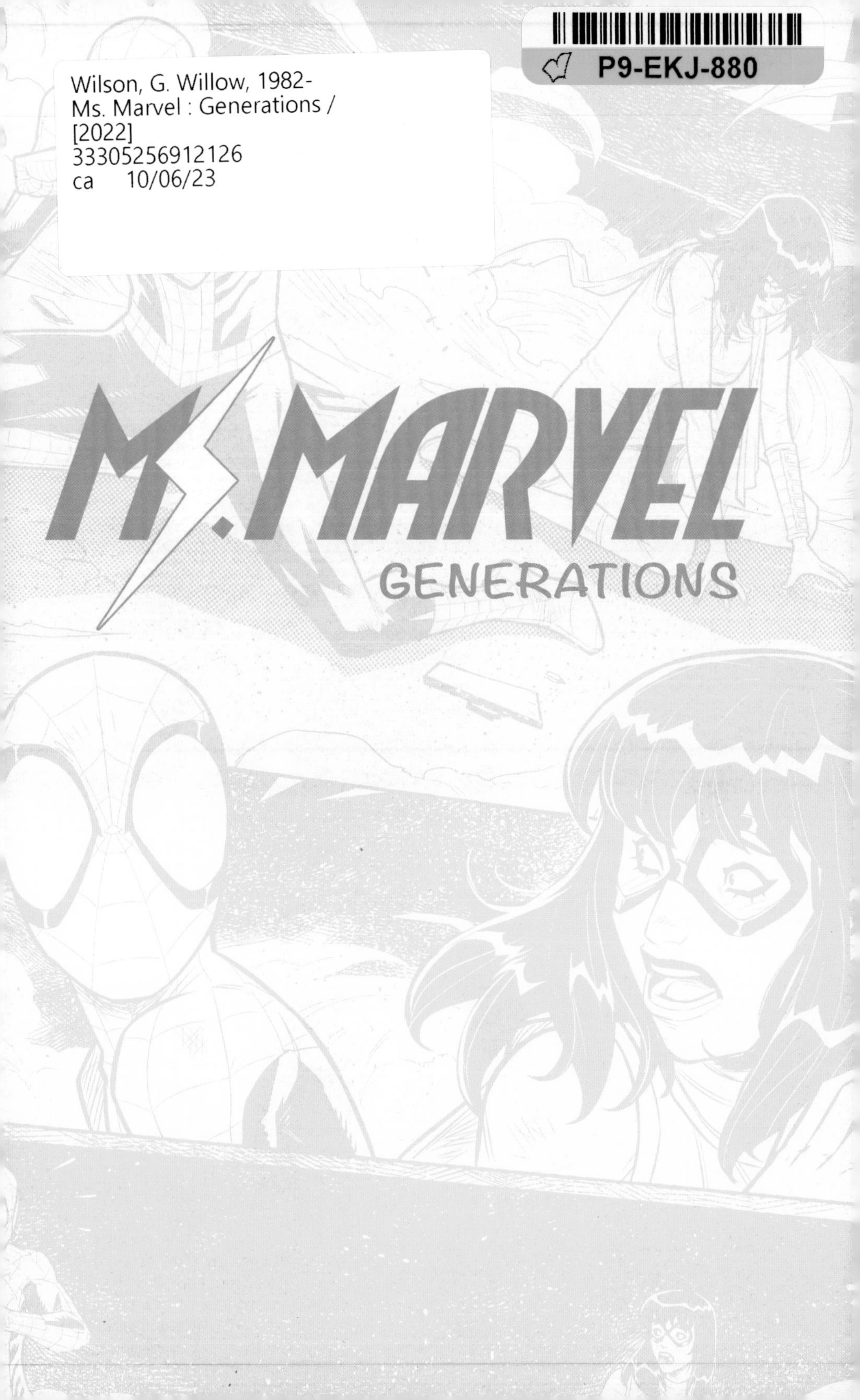

MS. MARVEL
GENERATIONS

PREVIOUSLY

After a semester abroad in Wakanda, Kamala's former best friend Bruno has returned to Jersey City. The stress of their confused feelings for each other — to say nothing of the super-hero shenanigans that left Bruno injured and inspired him to leave in the first place — has put a strain on their relationship. They're slowly learning to be friends again, starting with experiments to learn how Kamala's powers work, wherein they discovered her polymorph powers operate by sharing mass with herself across time. But what else does Kamala not know about her powers...?

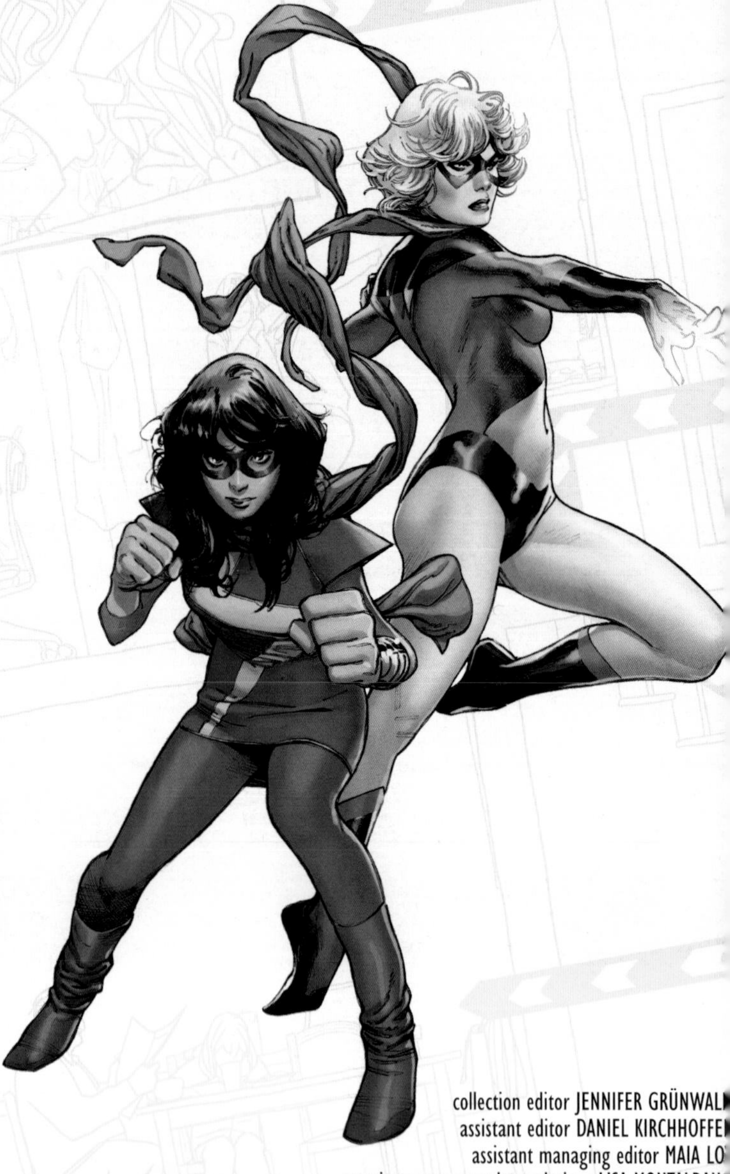

MS. MARVEL: GENERATIONS GN-TPB. Contains material originally published in magazine form as MS. MARVEL (2015) #36-38, GENERATIONS: MS. MARVEL & MS. MARVEL (2017) #1 and MARVEL TEAM-UP (2019) #1-6. First printing 2022. ISBN 978-1-302-94529-9. Published by MARVEL WORLDWIDE, INC., a subsidiary of MARVEL ENTERTAINMENT, LLC. OFFICE OF PUBLICATION: 1290 Avenue of the Americas, New York, NY 10104. © 2022 MARVEL No similarity between any of the names, characters, persons, and/or institutions in this book with those of any living or dead person or institution is intended, and any such similarity which may exist is purely coincidental. **Printed in Canada.** KEVIN FEIGE, Chief Creative Officer; DAN BUCKLEY, President, Marvel Entertainment; DAVID BOGART, Associate Publisher & SVP of Talent Affairs; TOM BREVOORT, VP, Executive Editor; NICK LOWE, Executive Editor, VP of Content, Digital Publishing; DAVID GABRIEL, VP of Print & Digital Publishing; SVEN LARSEN, VP of Licensed Publishing; MARK ANNUNZIATO, VP of Planning & Forecasting; JEFF YOUNGQUIST, VP of Production & Special Projects; ALEX MORALES, Director of Publishing Operations; DAN EDINGTON, Director of Editorial Operations; RICKEY PURDIN, Director of Talent Relations; JENNIFER GRÜNWALD, Director of Production & Special Projects; SUSAN CRESPI, Production Manager; STAN LEE, Chairman Emeritus. For information regarding advertising in Marvel Comics or on Marvel.com, please contact Vit DeBellis, Custom Solutions & Integrated Advertising Manager, at vdebellis@marvel.com. For Marvel subscription inquiries, please call 888-511-5480. **Manufactured between 7/29/2022 and 8/30/2022 by SOLISCO PRINTERS, SCOTT, QC, CANADA.**

10 9 8 7 6 5 4 3 2 1

collection editor JENNIFER GRÜNWAL
assistant editor DANIEL KIRCHHOFFE
assistant managing editor MAIA LO
associate manager, talent relations LISA MONTALBAN
vp production & special projects JEFF YOUNGQUIS
svp print, sales & marketing DAVID GABRIE
vp licensed publishing SVEN LARSE
editor in chief C.B. CEBULSK

MS. MARVEL
GENERATIONS

Ms. Marvel #36-37
writer **G. WILLOW WILSON**
artist **NICO LEON**
color artist **IAN HERRING**
cover art **VALERIO SCHITI** & **RACHELLE ROSENBERG**
letterer **VC's JOE CARAMAGNA**

Ms. Marvel #38
story **G. WILLOW WILSON**
writers **G. WILLOW WILSON** (pp. 1-9), **DEVIN GRAYSON** (pp. 10-12),
EVE L. EWING (pp. 13-15), **JIM ZUB** (pp. 16-18) & **SALADIN AHMED** (pp. 19-21)
artists **NICO LEON** (pp. 1-9), **TAKESHI MIYAZAWA** (pp. 10-12),
JOEY VAZQUEZ (pp. 13-15), **KEVIN LIBRANDA** (pp. 16-18)
and **MINKYU JUNG** & **JUAN VLASCO** (pp. 19-21)
color artist & bonus page **IAN HERRING**
cover art **SARA PICHELLI** & **JUSTIN PONSOR**
letterer **VC's JOE CARAMAGNA**

Generations: Ms. Marvel & Ms. Marvel #1
writer **G. WILLOW WILSON**
artist **PAOLO VILLANELLI**
color artist **IAN HERRING**
letterer **VC's JOE CARAMAGNA**
cover art **NELSON BLAKE II** & **RACHELLE ROSENBERG**

Ms. Marvel Team-Up #1-3
writer **EVE L. EWING**
artist **JOEY VAZQUEZ**
with **MOY R.** (#3)
color artist **FELIPE SOBREIRO**
cover art **STEFANO CASELLI** &
TRÍONA FARRELL
letterer **VC's CLAYTON COWLES**

Ms. Marvel Team-Up #4-6
writer **CLINT McELROY**
artist **IG GUARA**
color artist **FELIPE SOBREIRO**
cover art **ANNA RUD** & **EDUARD
PETROVICH**
letterer **VC's CLAYTON COWLES**

assistant editor
**SHANNON ADREWS
BALLESTEROS**

editors
**SANA AMANAT, MARK BASSO,
ALANNA SMITH** & **CHARLES BEACHAM**

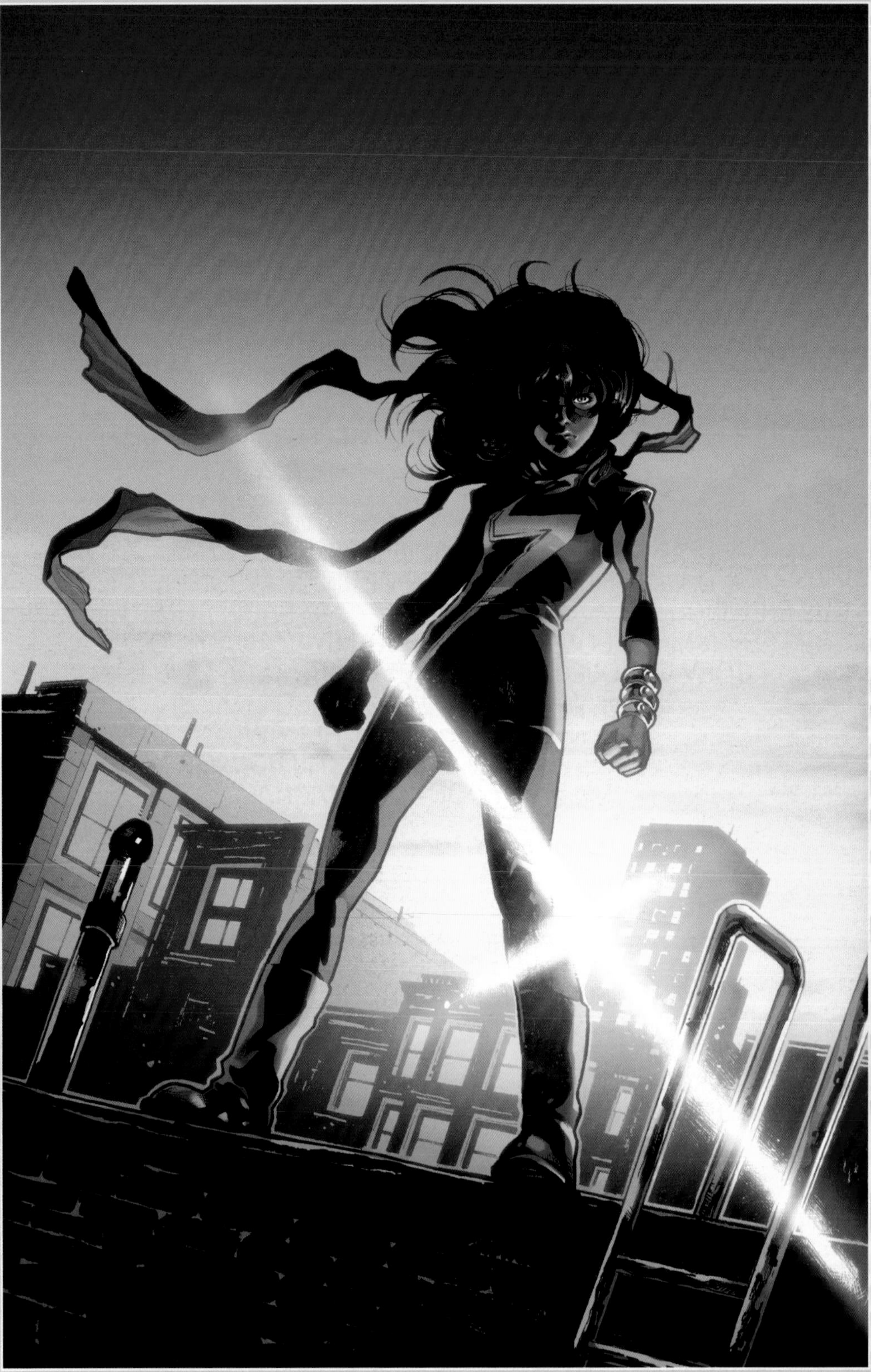

MS. MARVEL #36

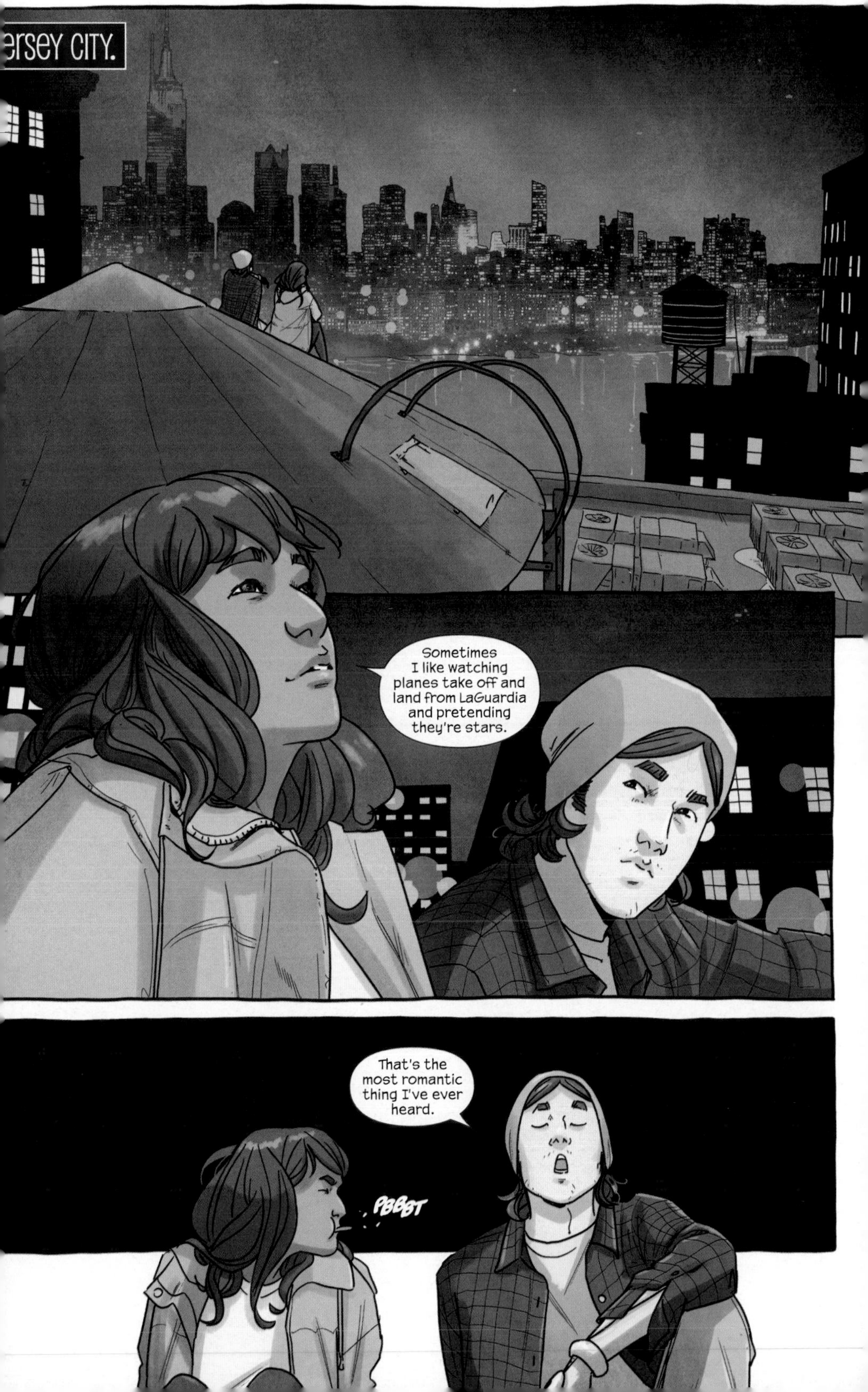
ersey CITY.
Sometimes I like watching planes take off and land from LaGuardia and pretending they're stars.
That's the most romantic thing I've ever heard.
PBBBT

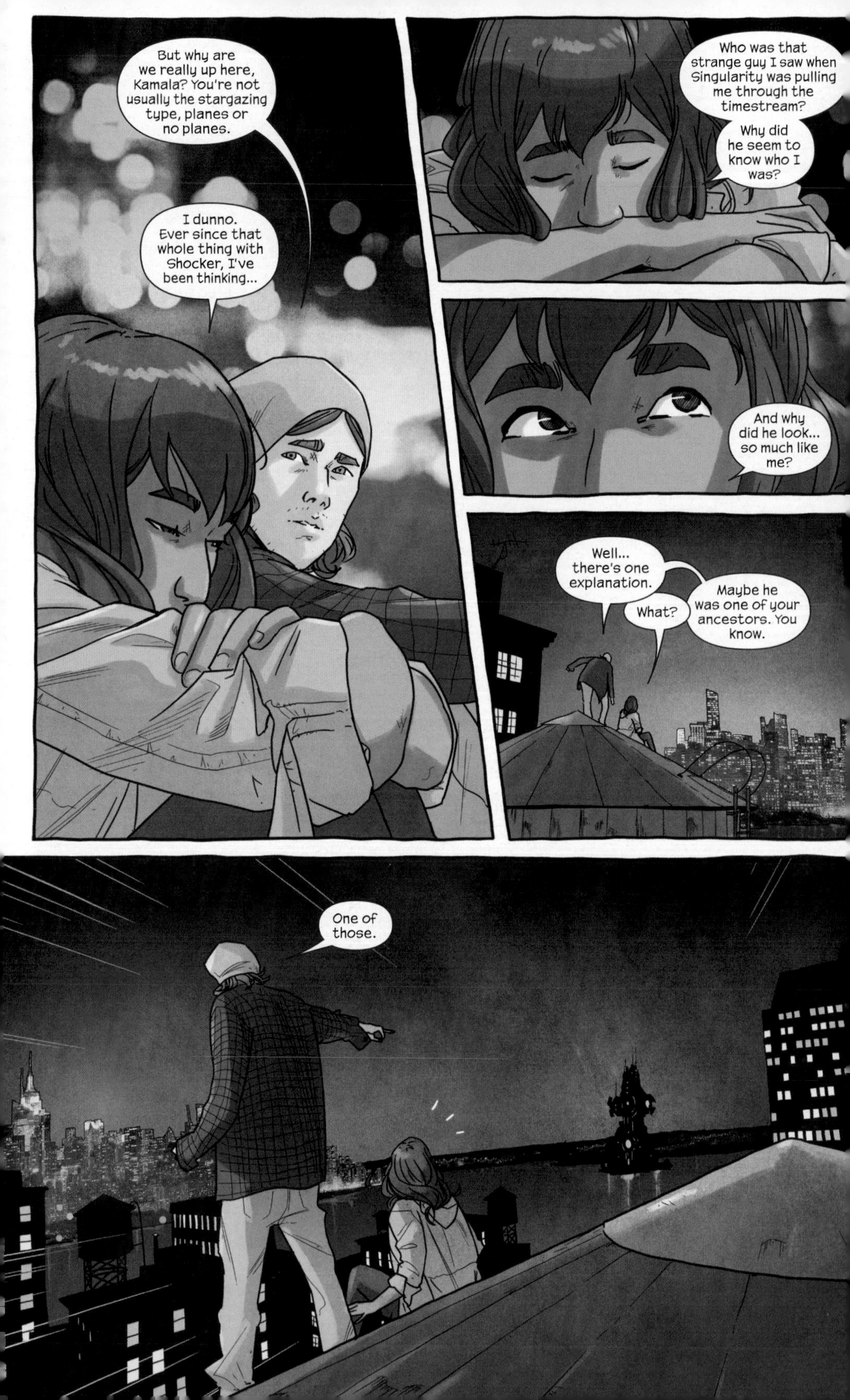

But why are we really up here, Kamala? You're not usually the stargazing type, planes or no planes.
I dunno. Ever since that whole thing with Shocker, I've been thinking...
Who was that strange guy I saw when Singularity was pulling me through the timestream?
Why did he seem to know who I was?
And why did he look... so much like me?
Well... there's one explanation.
What?
Maybe he was one of your ancestors. You know.
One of those.

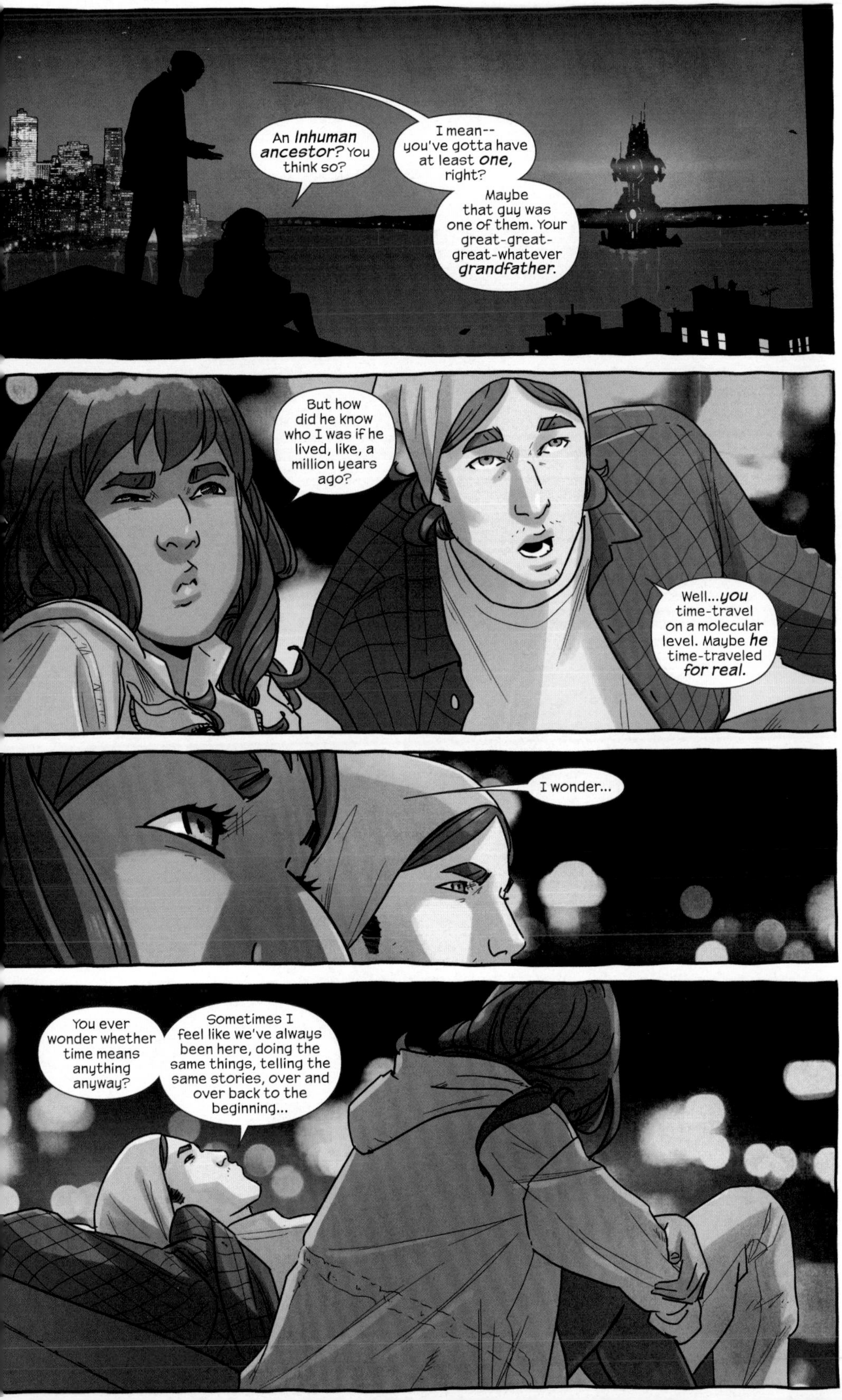
An *Inhuman ancestor?* You think so?
I mean-- you've gotta have at least *one,* right?
Maybe that guy was one of them. Your great-great-great-whatever *grandfather.*
But how did he know who I was if he lived, like, a million years ago?
Well... *you* time-travel on a molecular level. Maybe *he* time-traveled *for real.*
I wonder...
You ever wonder whether time means anything anyway?
Sometimes I feel like we've always been here, doing the same things, telling the same stories, over and over back to the beginning...

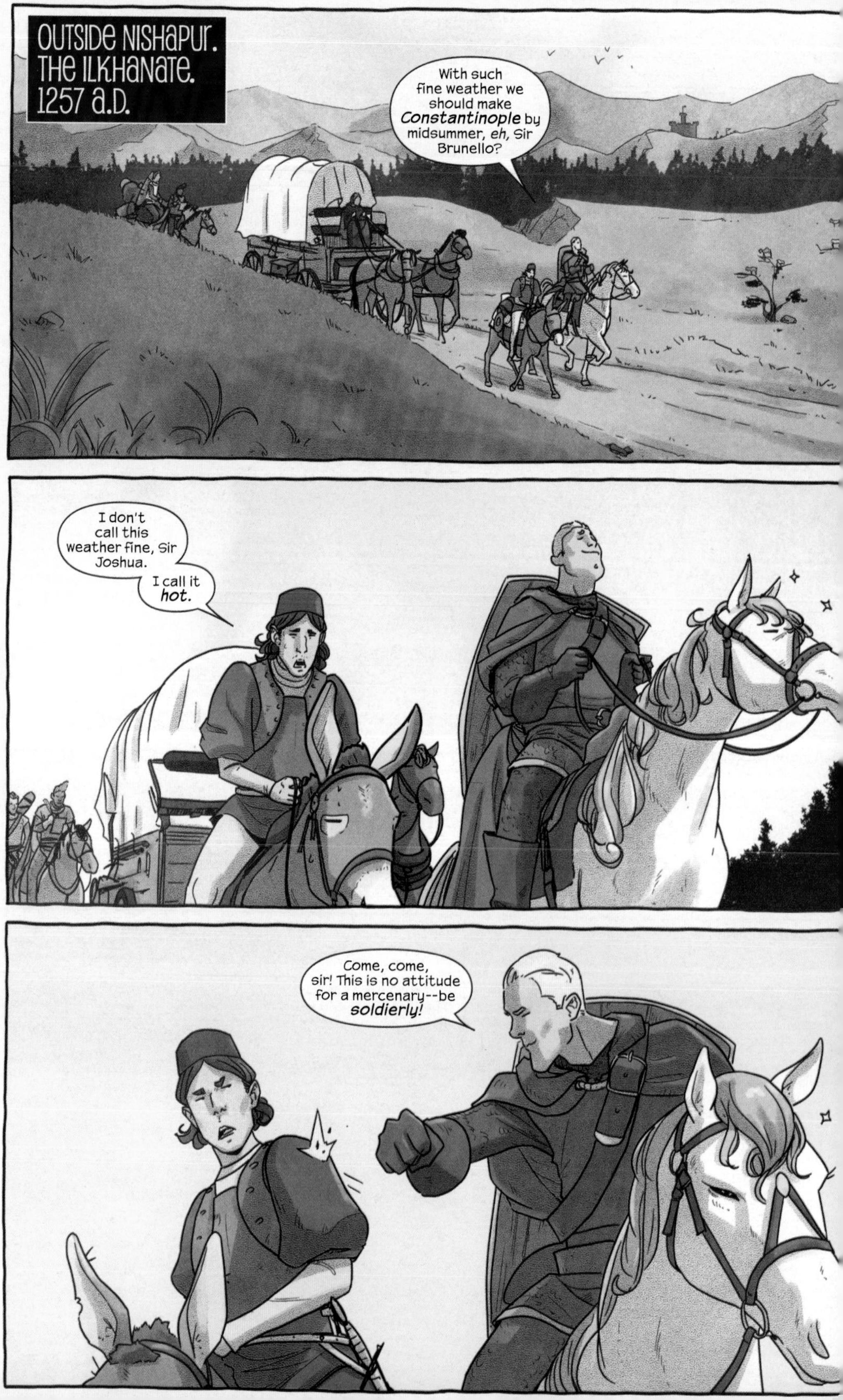
OUTSIDE NISHAPUR. THE ILKHANATE. 1257 A.D.
With such fine weather we should make *Constantinople* by midsummer, *eh,* Sir Brunello?
I don't call this weather fine, Sir Joshua.
I call it *hot.*
Come, come, sir! This is no attitude for a mercenary--be *soldierly!*

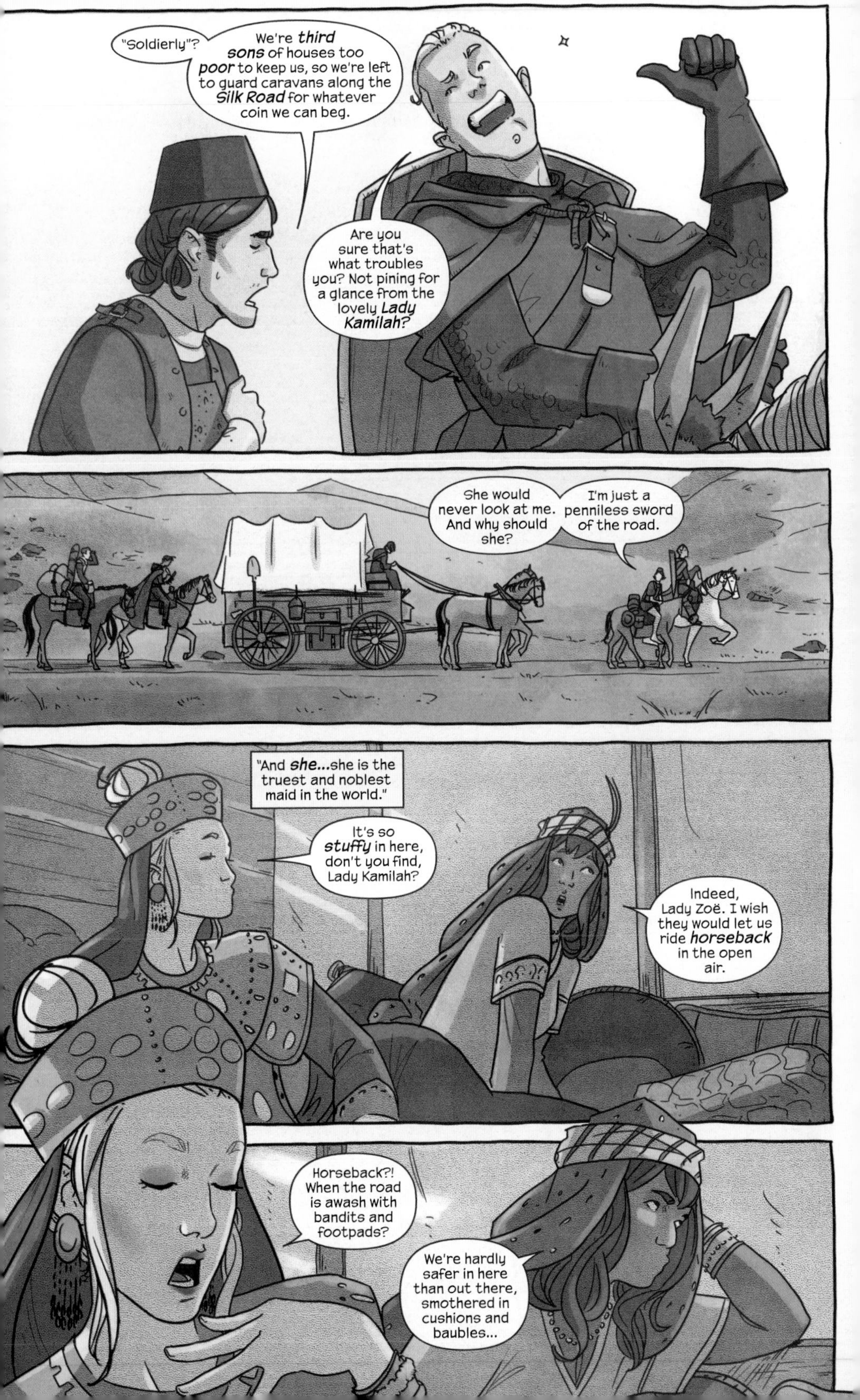
"Soldierly"?
We're third sons of houses too poor to keep us, so we're left to guard caravans along the Silk Road for whatever coin we can beg.
Are you sure that's what troubles you? Not pining for a glance from the lovely Lady Kamilah?
She would never look at me. And why should she?
I'm just a penniless sword of the road.
"And she...she is the truest and noblest maid in the world."
It's so stuffy in here, don't you find, Lady Kamilah?
Indeed, Lady Zoë. I wish they would let us ride horseback in the open air.
Horseback?! When the road is awash with bandits and footpads?
We're hardly safer in here than out there, smothered in cushions and baubles...

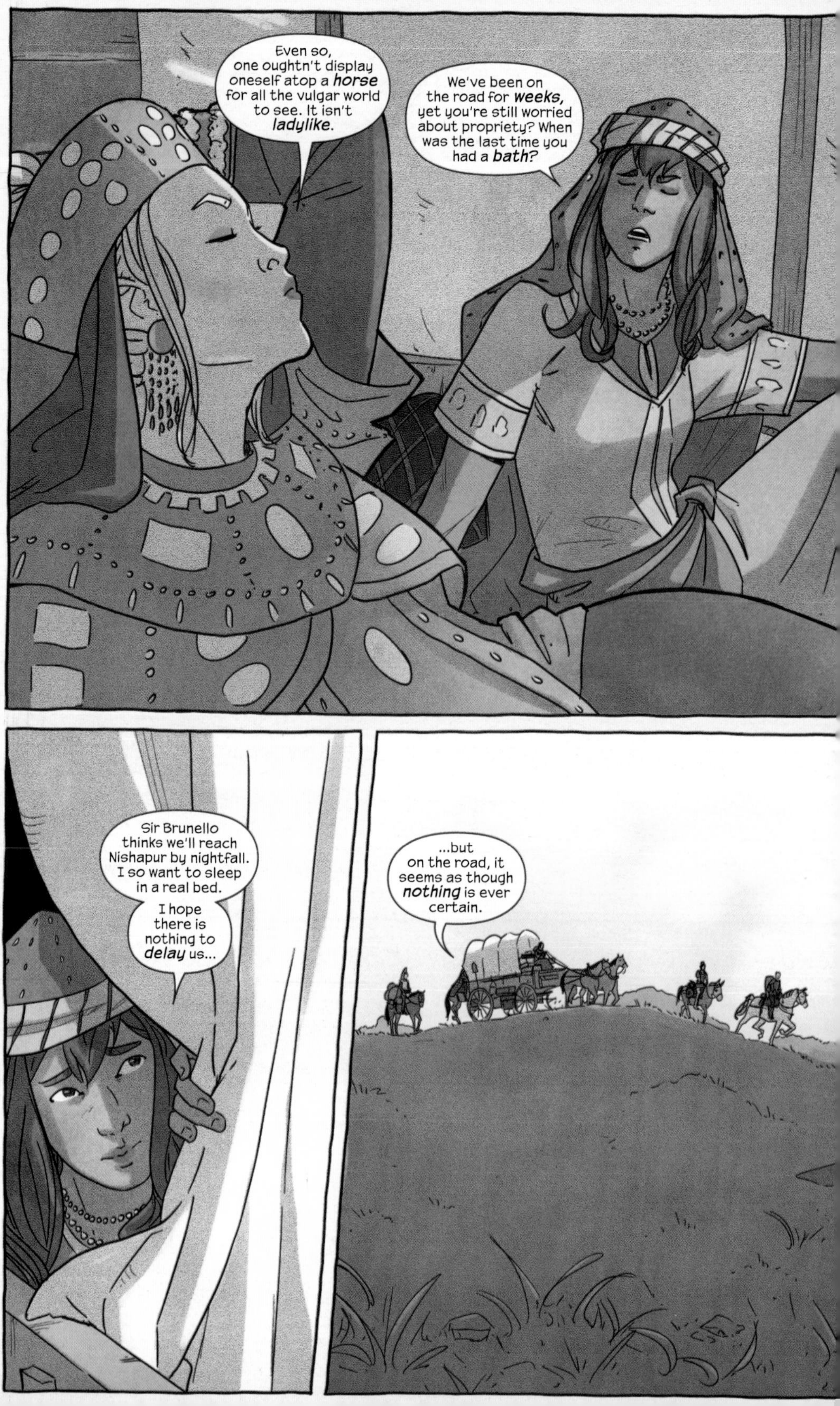
Even so, one oughtn't display oneself atop a horse for all the vulgar world to see. It isn't ladylike.
We've been on the road for weeks, yet you're still worried about propriety? When was the last time you had a bath?
Sir Brunello thinks we'll reach Nishapur by nightfall. I so want to sleep in a real bed.
I hope there is nothing to delay us...
...but on the road, it seems as though nothing is ever certain.

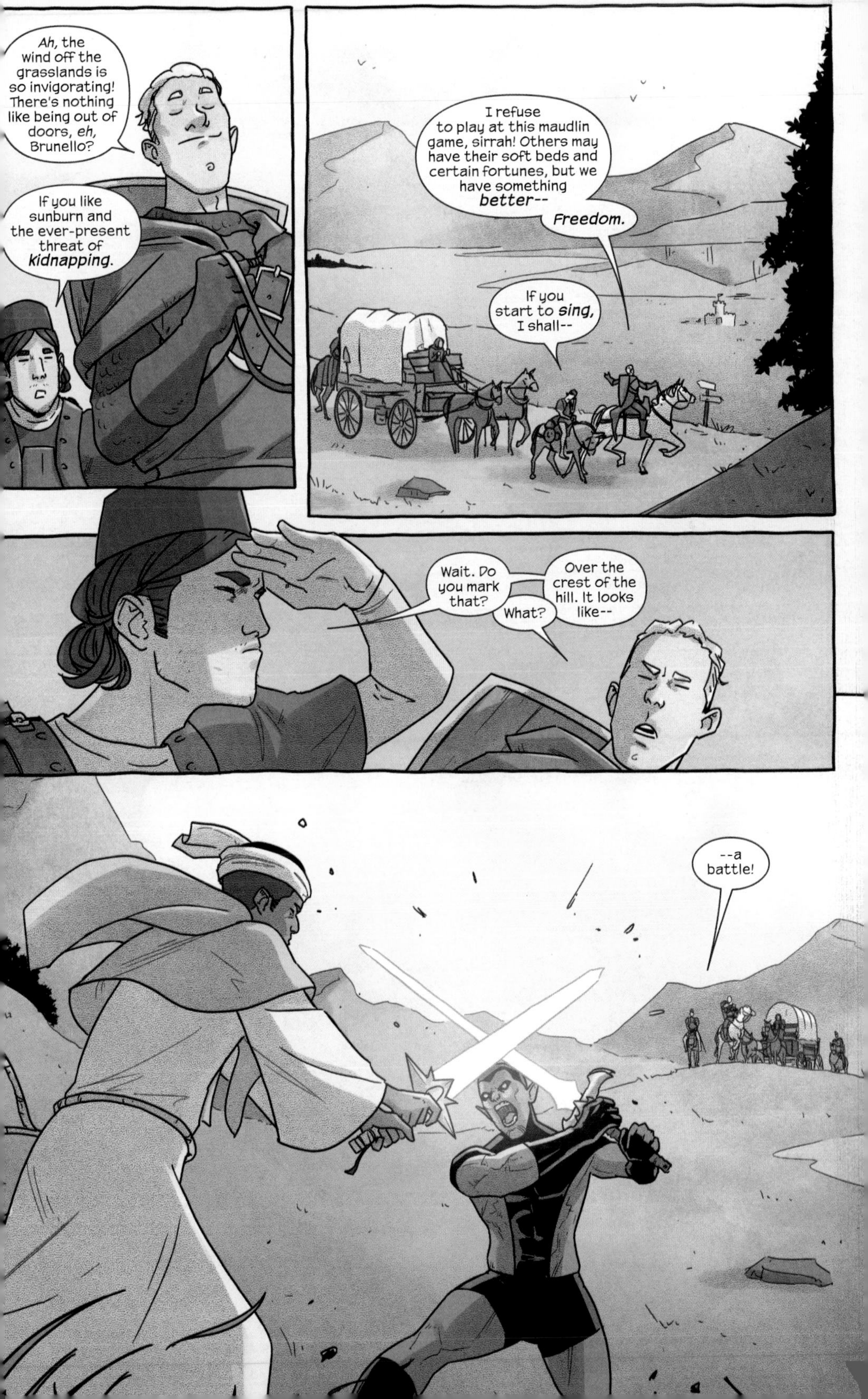
Ah, the wind off the grasslands is so invigorating! There's nothing like being out of doors, eh, Brunello?
If you like sunburn and the ever-present threat of kidnapping.
I refuse to play at this maudlin game, sirrah! Others may have their soft beds and certain fortunes, but we have something better--
Freedom.
If you start to sing, I shall--
Wait. Do you mark that?
What?
Over the crest of the hill. It looks like--
--a battle!

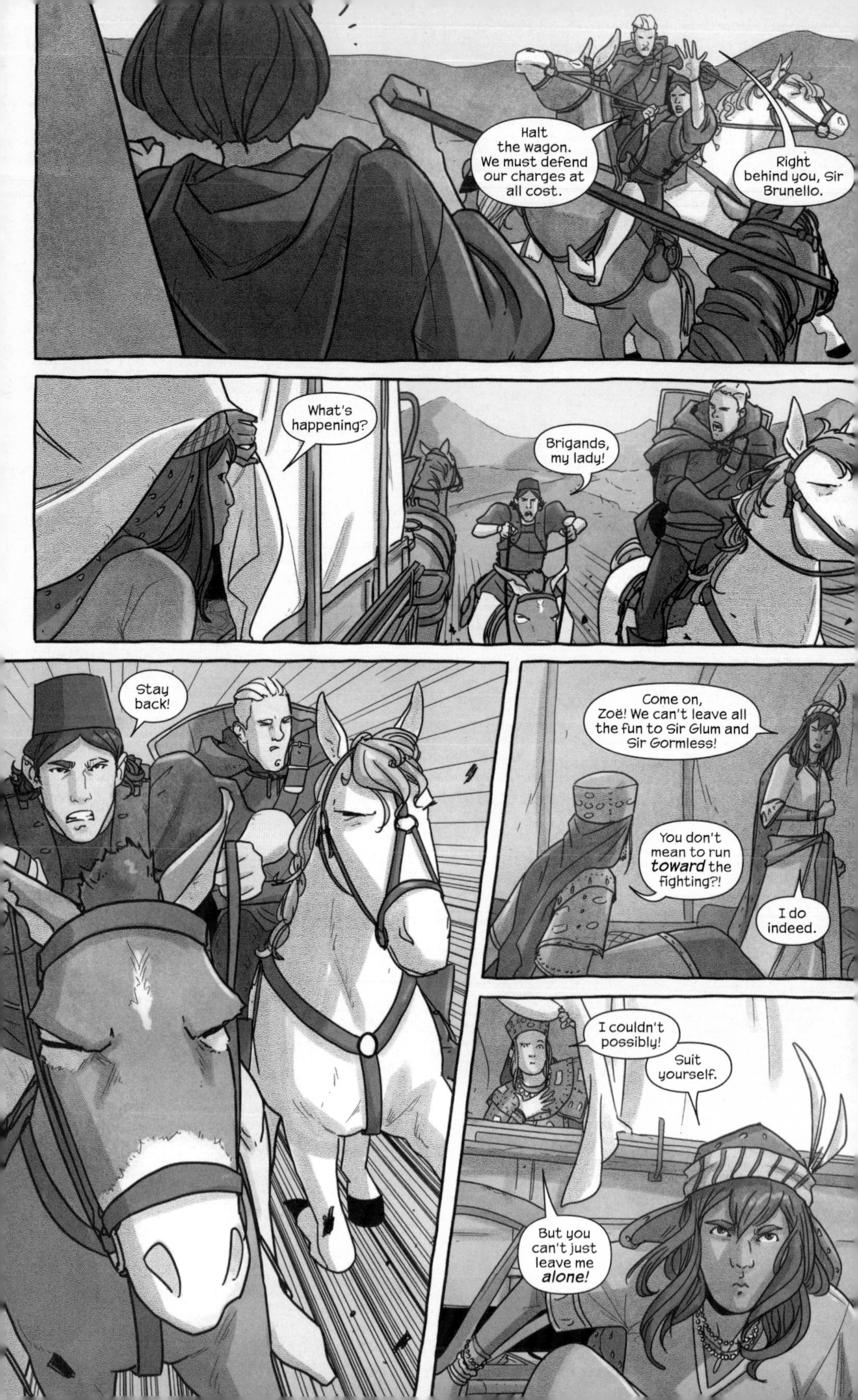

Halt the wagon. We must defend our charges at all cost.
Right behind you, Sir Brunello.
What's happening?
Brigands, my lady!
Stay back!
Come on, Zoë! We can't leave all the fun to Sir Glum and Sir Gormless!
You don't mean to run **toward** the fighting?!
I do indeed.
I couldn't possibly!
Suit yourself.
But you can't just leave me ***alone!***

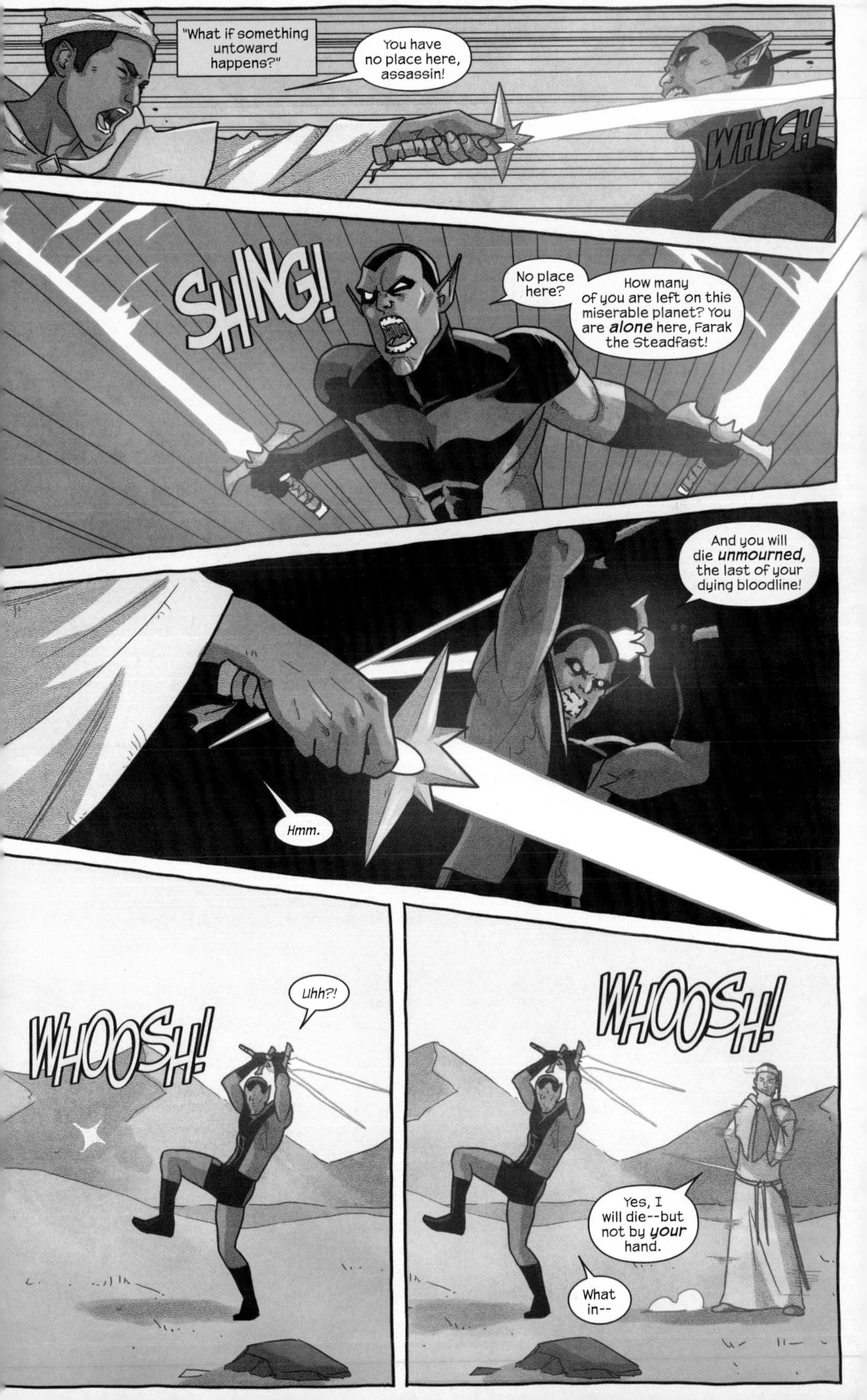
"What if something untoward happens?"
You have no place here, assassin!
WHISH
SHING!
No place here?
How many of you are left on this miserable planet? You are *alone* here, Farak the Steadfast!
And you will die *unmourned,* the last of your dying bloodline!
Hmm.
WHOOSH!
Uhh?!
WHOOSH!
Yes, I will die--but not by *your* hand.
What in--

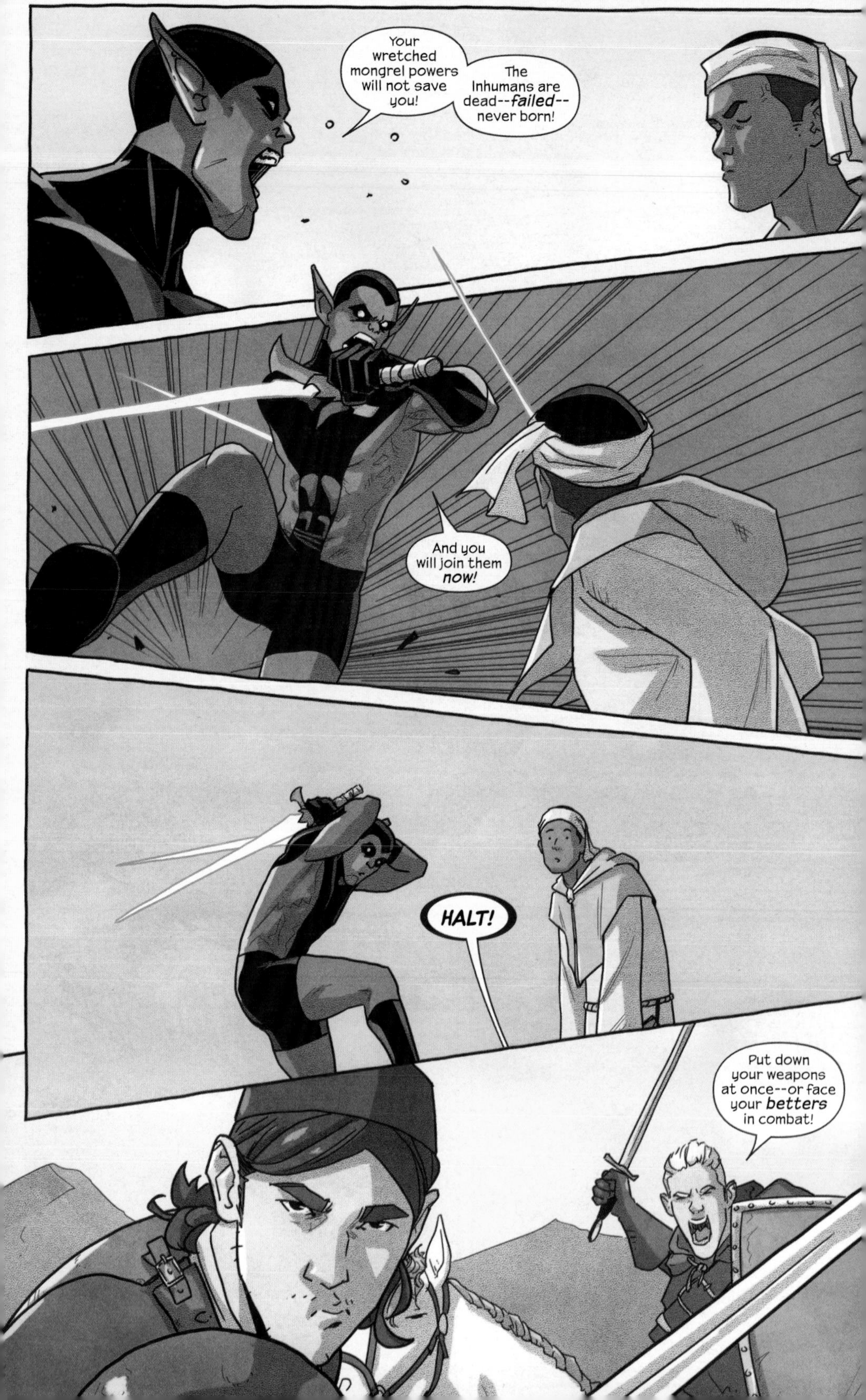
Your wretched mongrel powers will not save you!
The Inhumans are dead--*failed*--never born!
And you will join them *now!*
HALT!
Put down your weapons at once--or face your *betters* in combat!

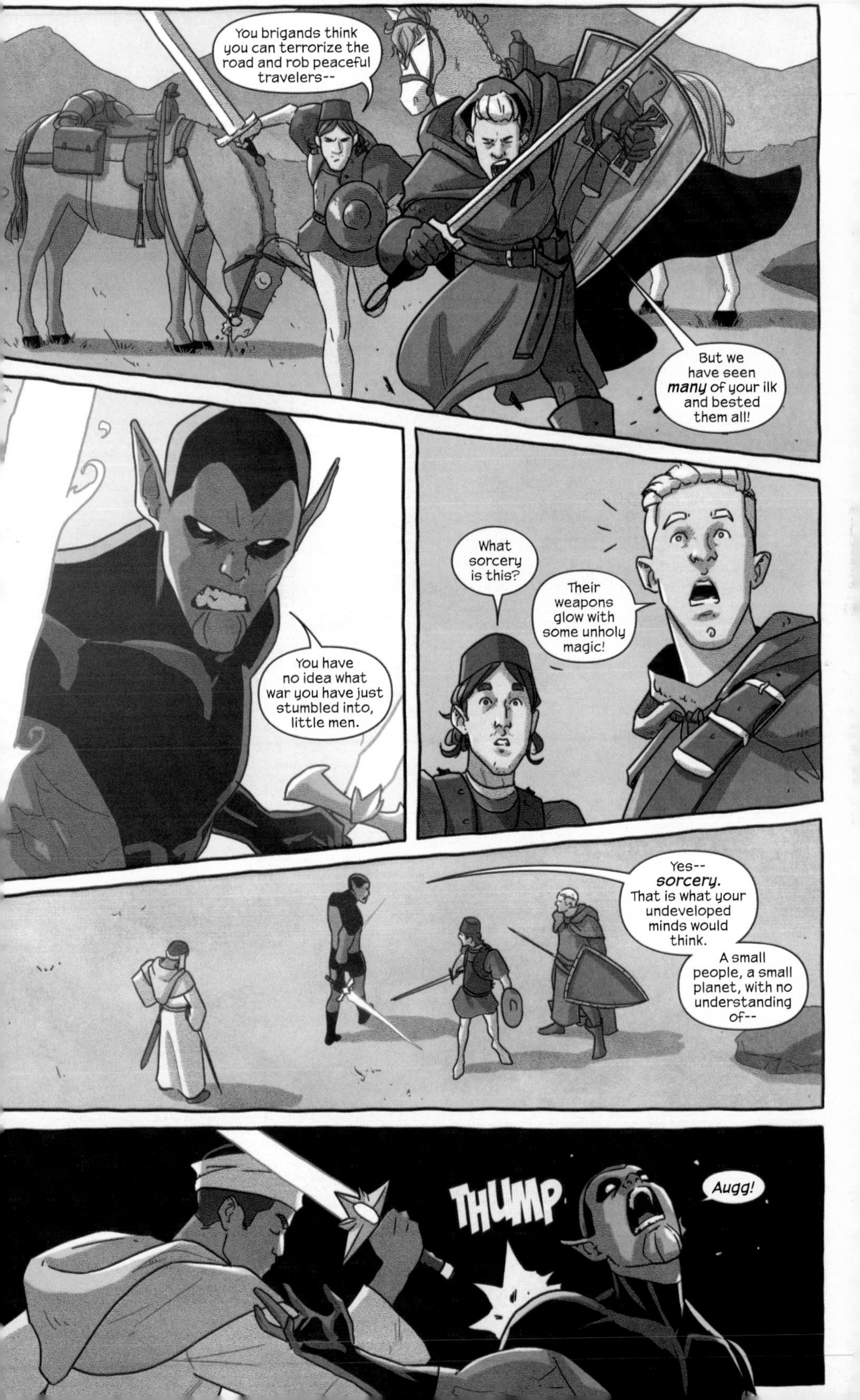
You brigands think you can terrorize the road and rob peaceful travelers--
But we have seen *many* of your ilk and bested them all!
You have no idea what war you have just stumbled into, little men.
What sorcery is this?
Their weapons glow with some unholy magic!
Yes-- *sorcery.* That is what your undeveloped minds would think.
A small people, a small planet, with no understanding of--
THUMP
Augg!

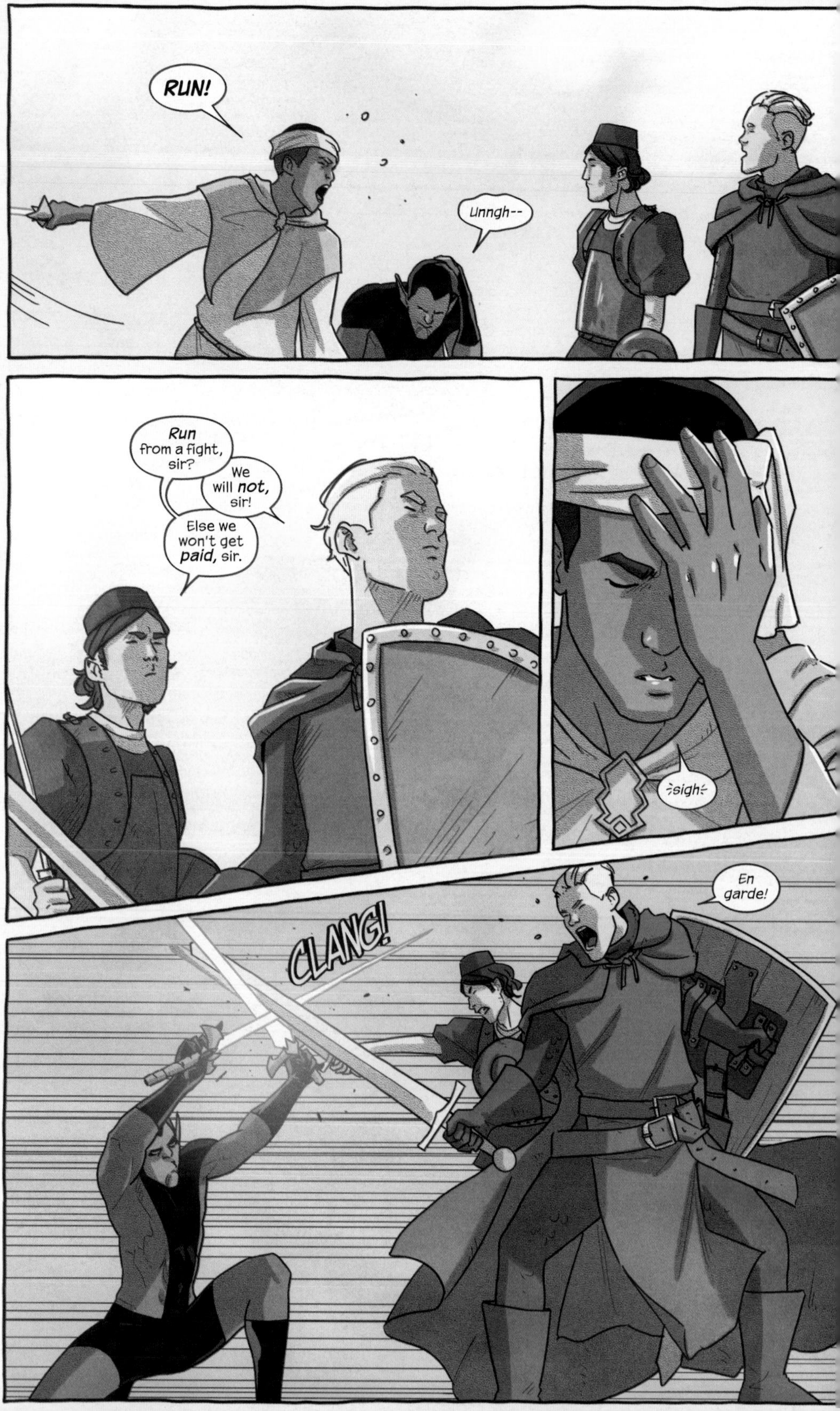
RUN!
Unngh--
Run from a fight, sir?
We will not, sir!
Else we won't get paid, sir.
sigh
En garde!
CLANG!

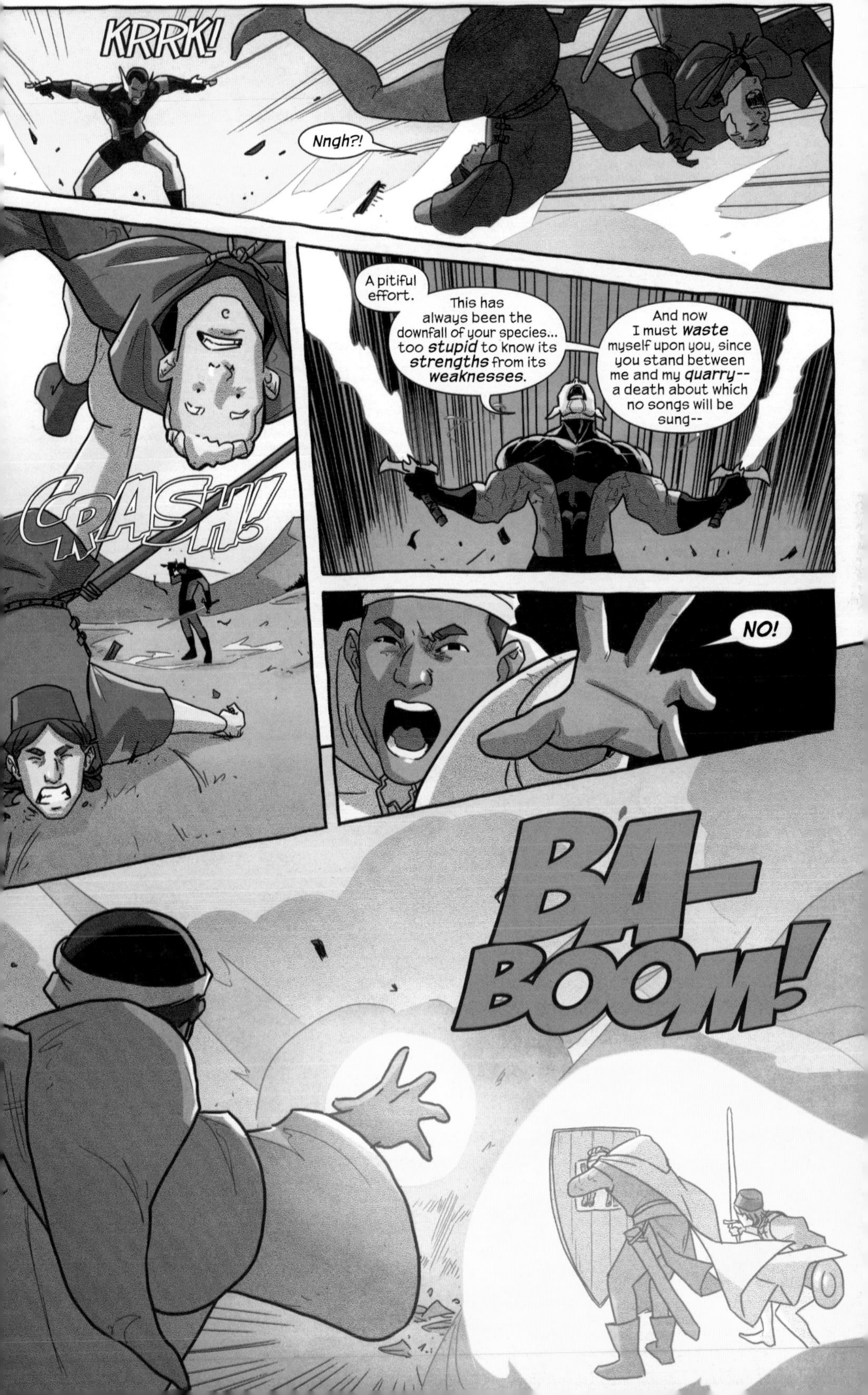
KRRK!
Nngh?!
CRASH!
A pitiful effort.
This has always been the downfall of your species... too stupid to know its strengths from its weaknesses.
And now I must waste myself upon you, since you stand between me and my quarry-- a death about which no songs will be sung--
NO!
BA-BOOM!

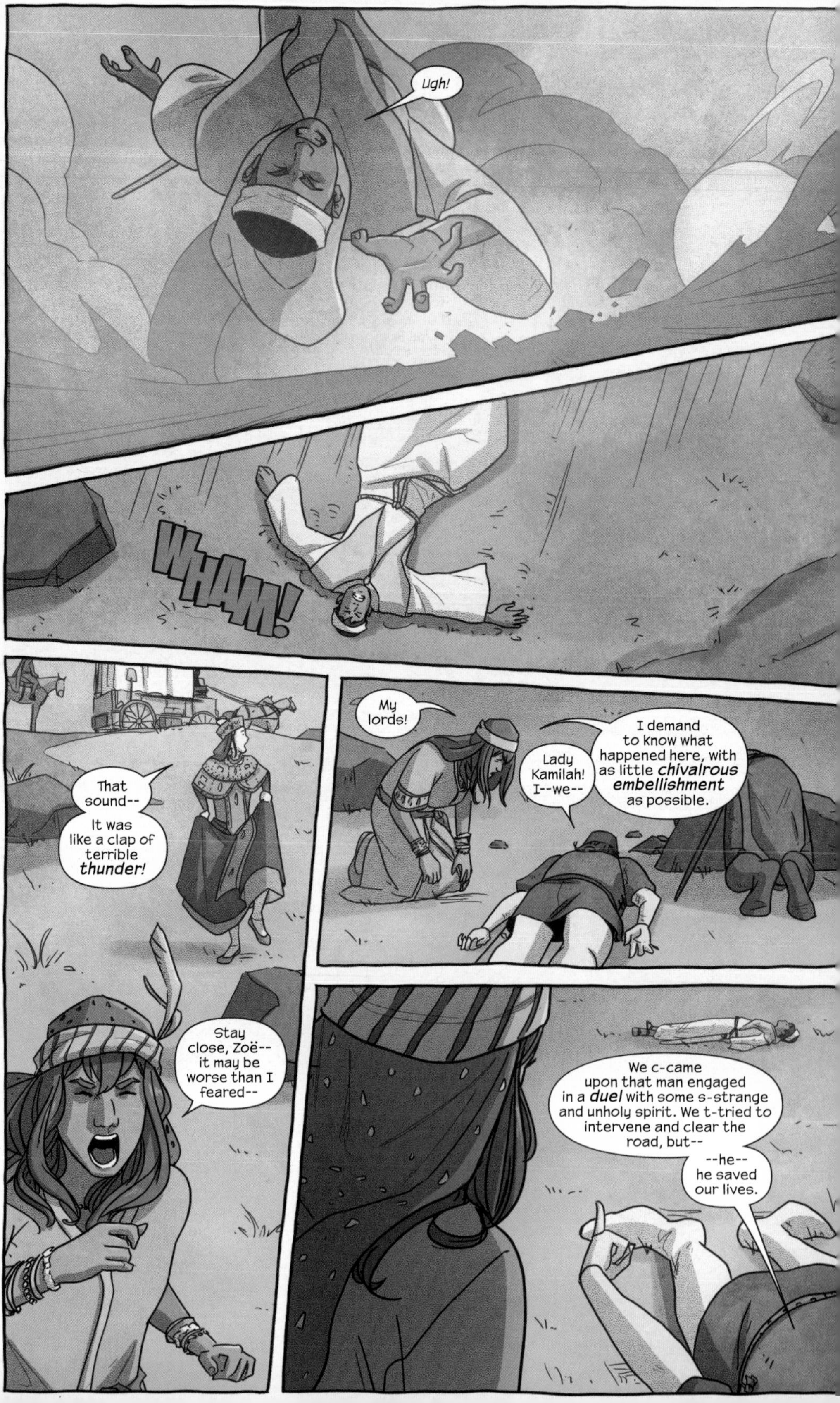

Ugh!
WHAM!
That sound--
It was like a clap of terrible *thunder*!
My lords!
Lady Kamilah! I--we--
I demand to know what happened here, with as little *chivalrous embellishment* as possible.
Stay close, Zoë-- it may be worse than I feared--
We c-came upon that man engaged in a *duel* with some s-strange and unholy spirit. We t-tried to intervene and clear the road, but--
--he-- he saved our lives.

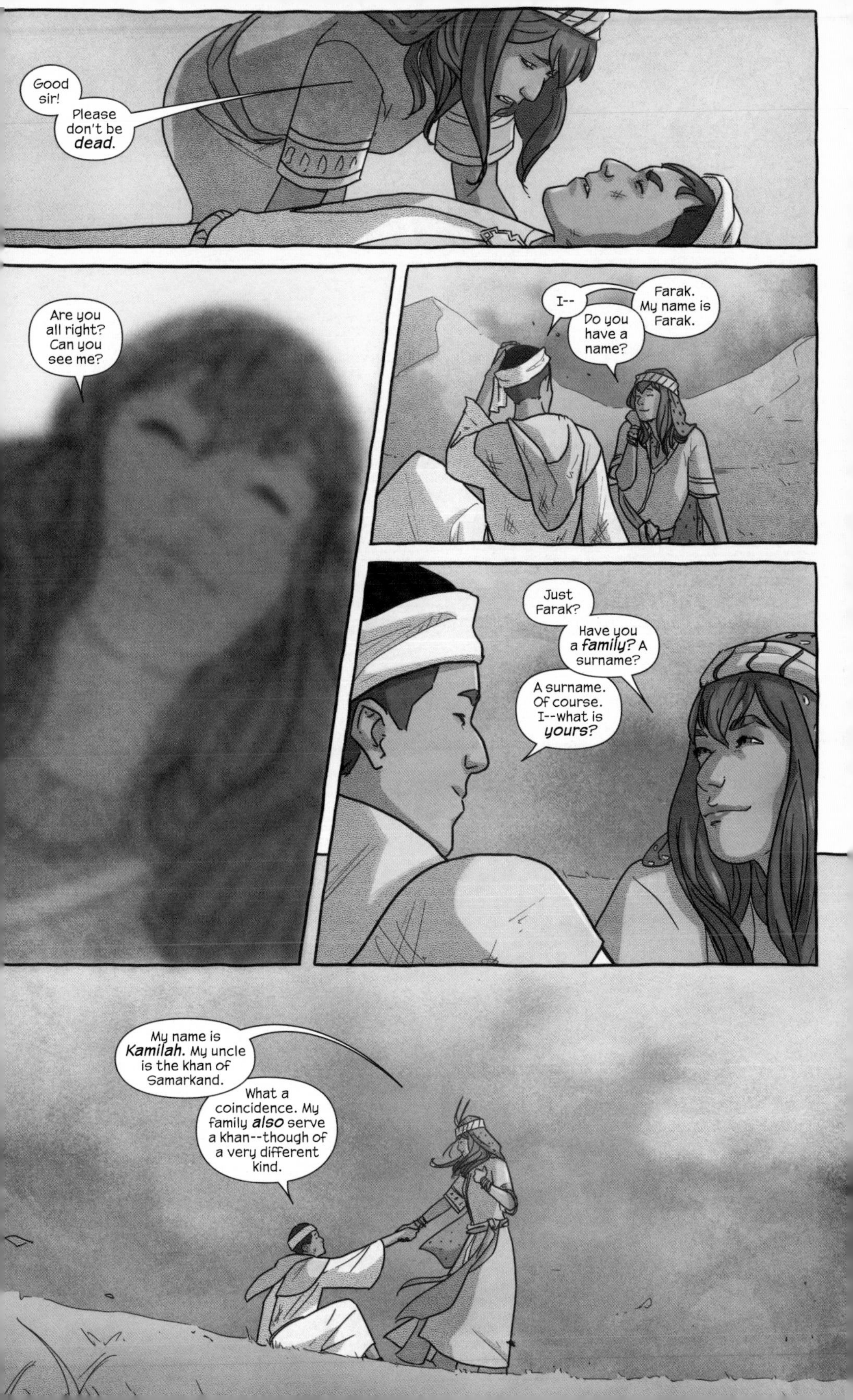
Good sir!
Please don't be *dead*.
Are you all right? Can you see me?
I--
Do you have a name?
Farak. My name is Farak.
Just Farak?
Have you a *family*? A surname?
A surname. Of course. I--what is *yours*?
My name is *Kamilah.* My uncle is the khan of Samarkand.
What a coincidence. My family *also* serve a khan--though of a very different kind.

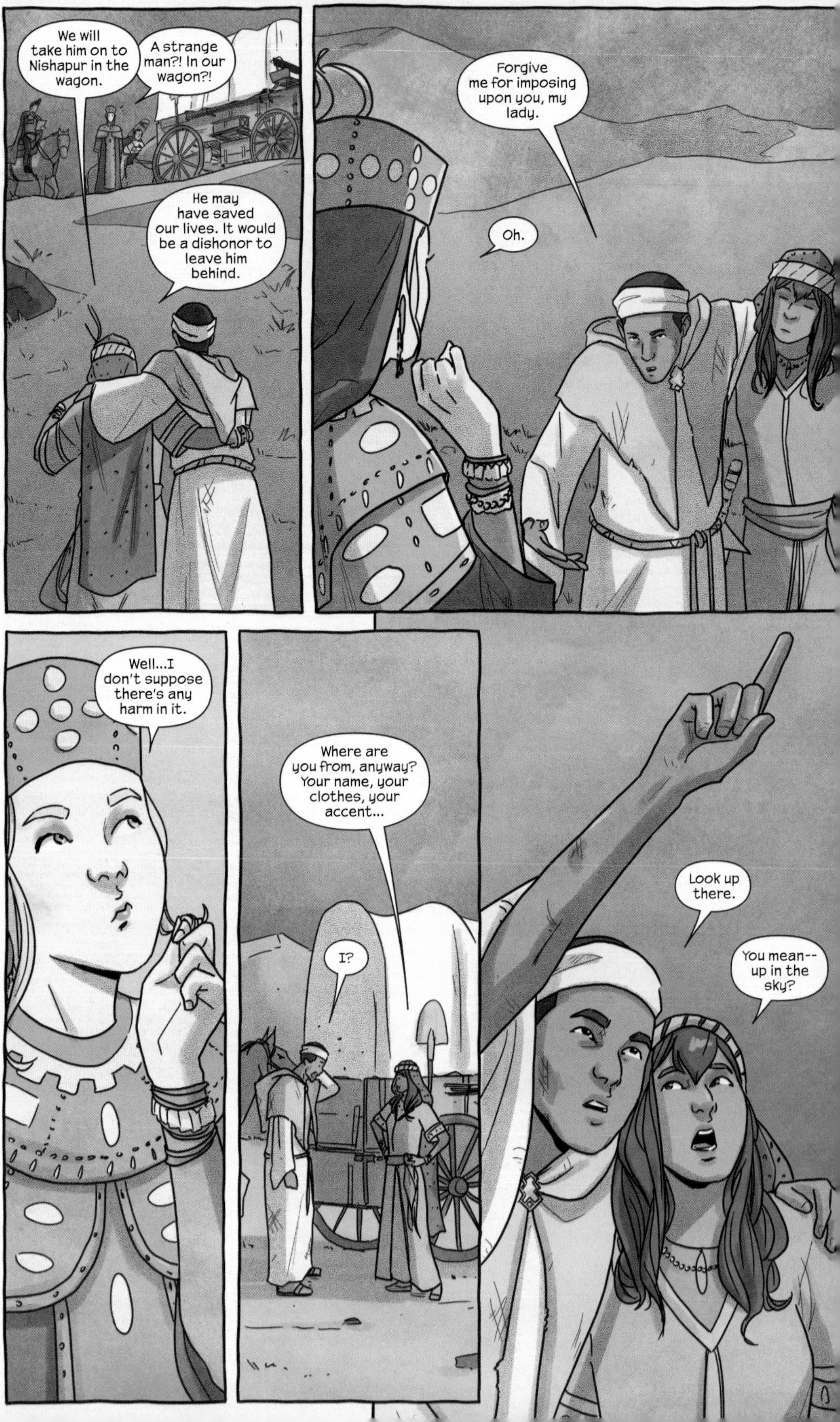
We will take him on to Nishapur in the wagon.
A strange man?! In our wagon?!
He may have saved our lives. It would be a dishonor to leave him behind.
Forgive me for imposing upon you, my lady.
Oh.
Well...I don't suppose there's any harm in it.
Where are you from, anyway? Your name, your clothes, your accent...
I?
Look up there.
You mean-- up in the sky?

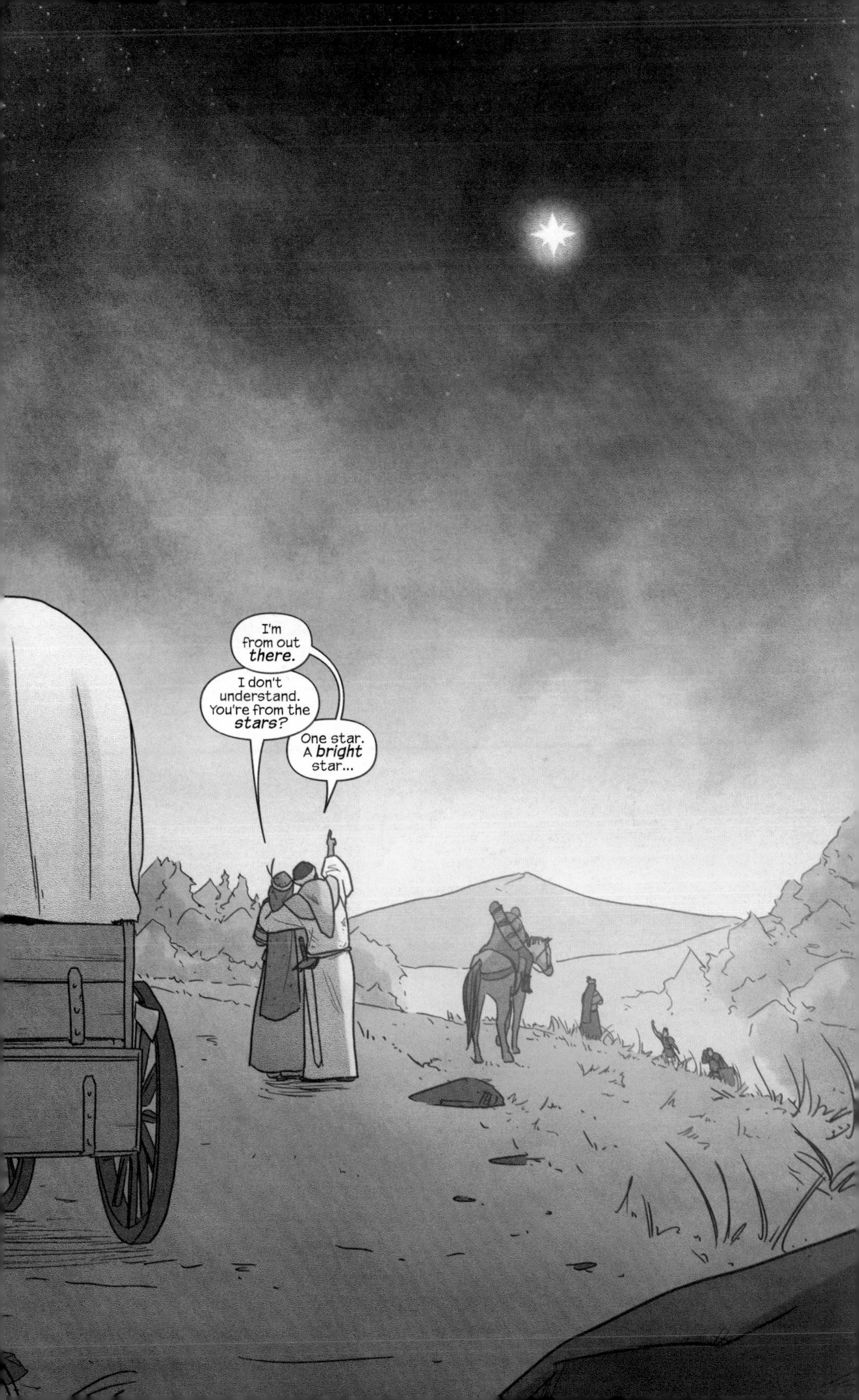
I'm from out there.
I don't understand. You're from the stars?
One star. A bright star...

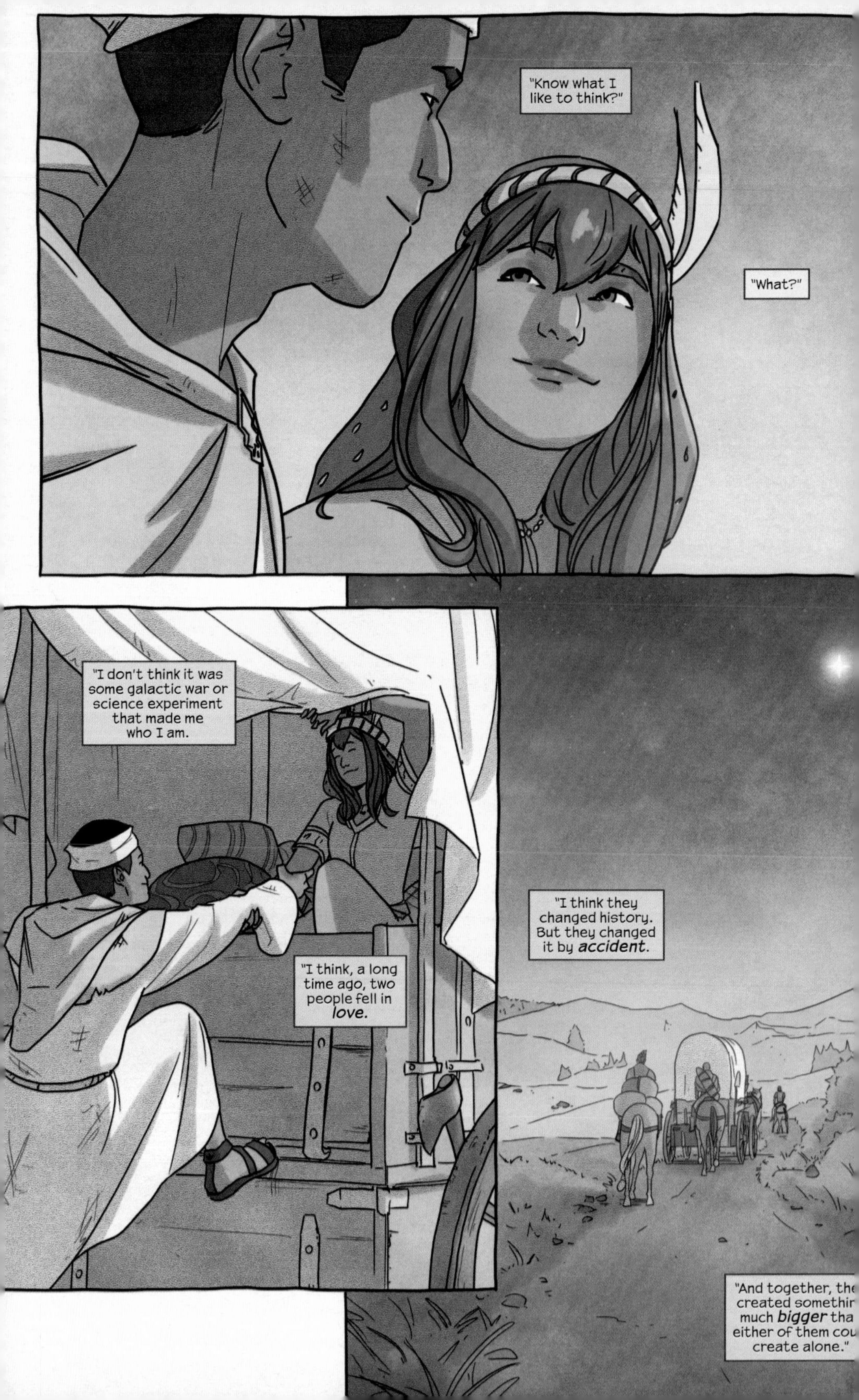
"Know what I like to think?"
"What?"
"I don't think it was some galactic war or science experiment that made me who I am.
"I think, a long time ago, two people fell in *love*.
"I think they changed history. But they changed it by *accident*.
"And together, the created somethir much *bigger* tha either of them cou create alone."

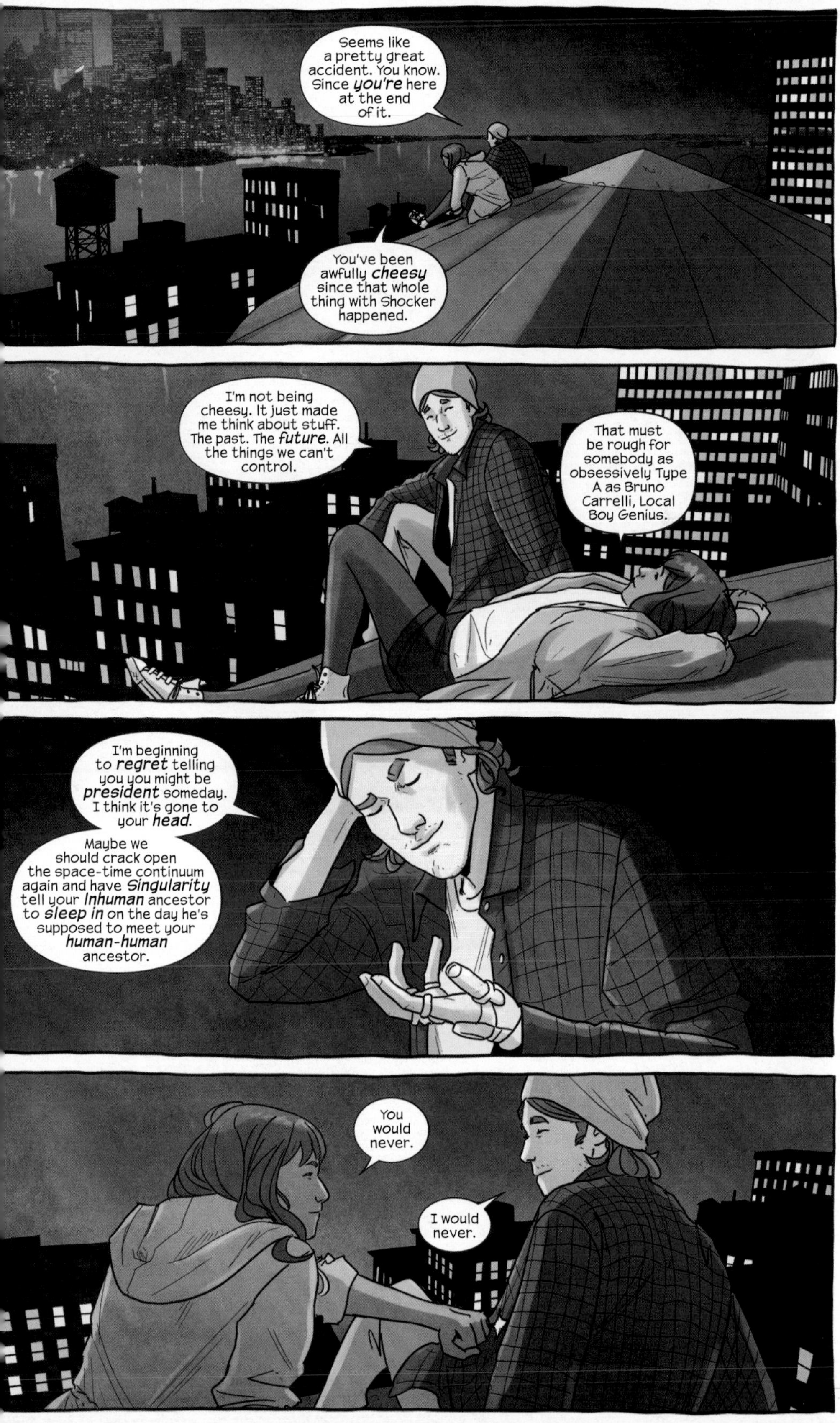
Seems like a pretty great accident. You know. Since *you're* here at the end of it.
You've been awfully *cheesy* since that whole thing with Shocker happened.
I'm not being cheesy. It just made me think about stuff. The past. The *future.* All the things we can't control.
That must be rough for somebody as obsessively Type A as Bruno Carrelli, Local Boy Genius.
I'm beginning to *regret* telling you you might be *president* someday. I think it's gone to your *head*.
Maybe we should crack open the space-time continuum again and have *Singularity* tell your *Inhuman* ancestor to *sleep in* on the day he's supposed to meet your *human-human* ancestor.
You would never.
I would never.

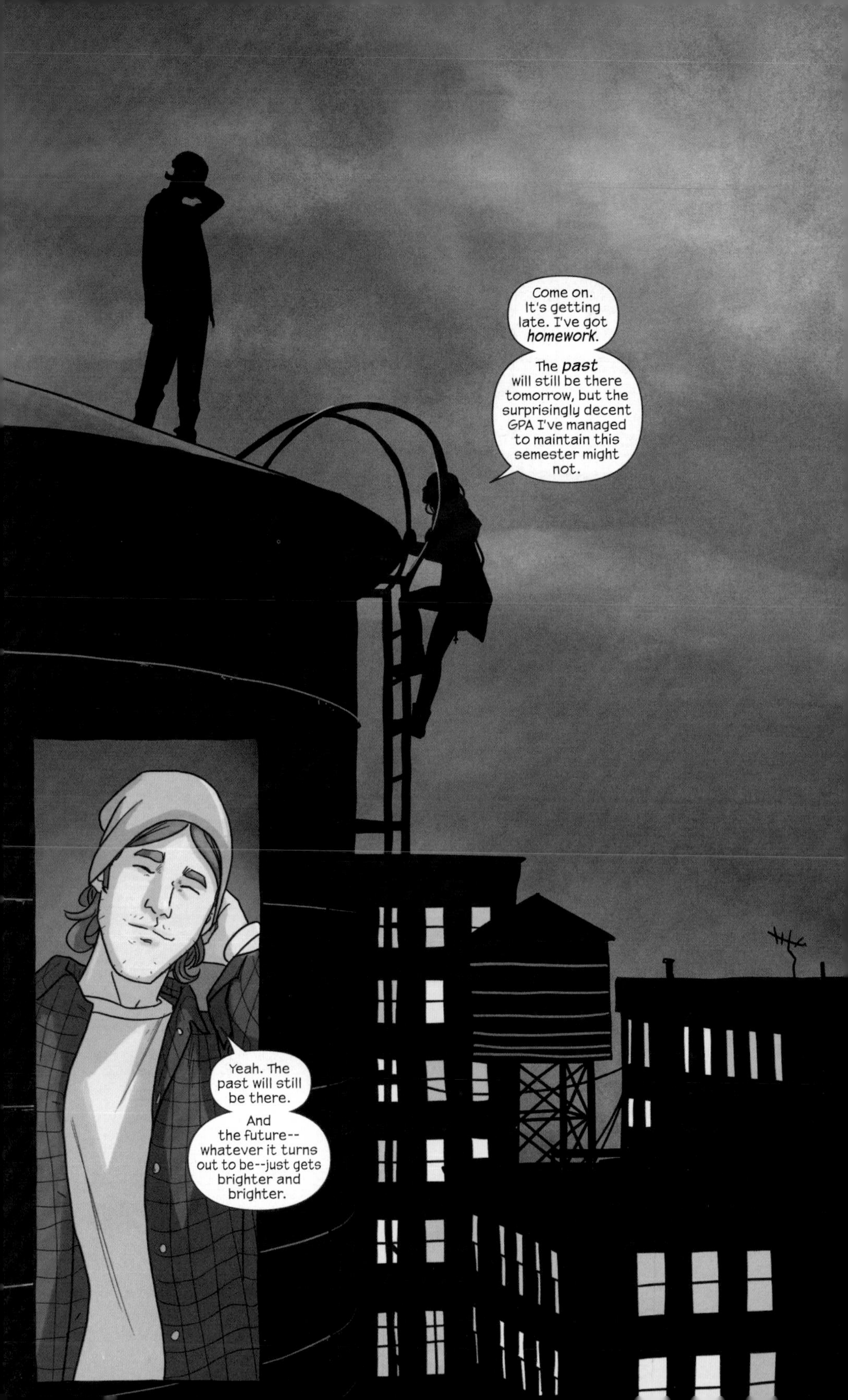
Come on. It's getting late. I've got *homework*.
The *past* will still be there tomorrow, but the surprisingly decent GPA I've managed to maintain this semester might not.
Yeah. The past will still be there.
And the future--whatever it turns out to be--just gets brighter and brighter.

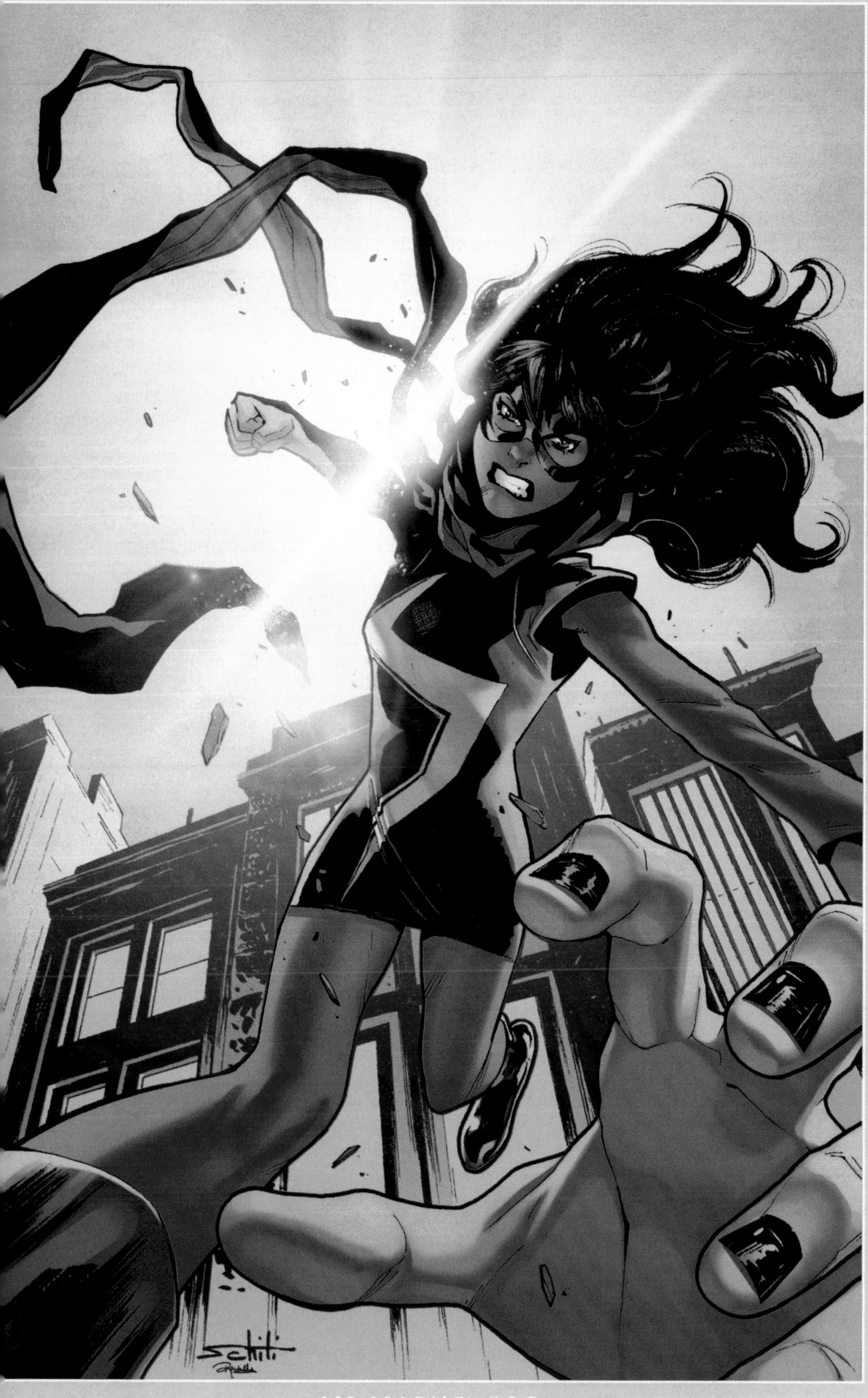

MS. MARVEL #37

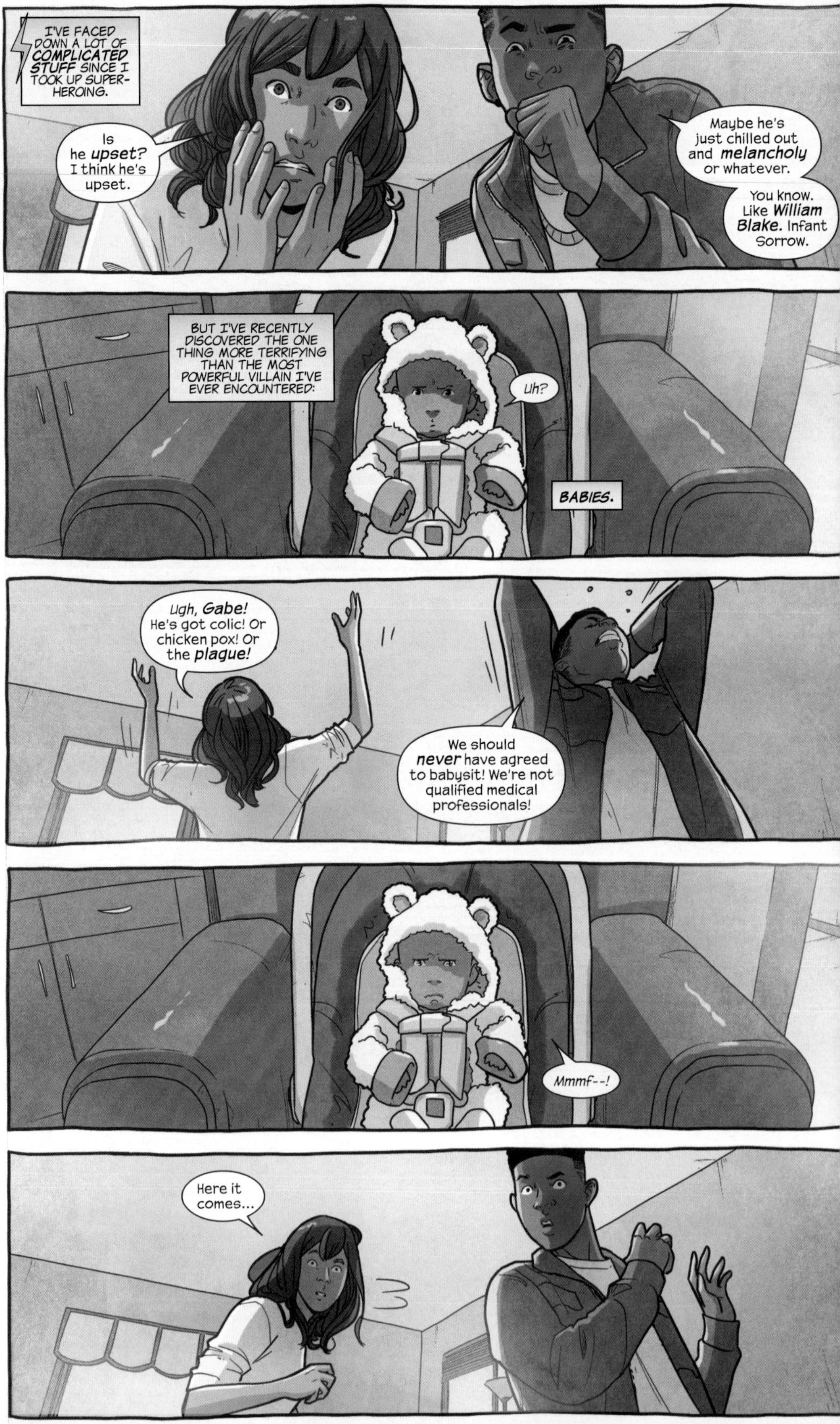

I'VE FACED DOWN A LOT OF COMPLICATED STUFF SINCE I TOOK UP SUPER-HEROING.
Is he upset? I think he's upset.
Maybe he's just chilled out and melancholy or whatever.
You know. Like William Blake. Infant Sorrow.
BUT I'VE RECENTLY DISCOVERED THE ONE THING MORE TERRIFYING THAN THE MOST POWERFUL VILLAIN I'VE EVER ENCOUNTERED:
Uh?
BABIES.
Ugh, Gabe! He's got colic! Or chicken pox! Or the plague!
We should never have agreed to babysit! We're not qualified medical professionals!
Mmmf--!
Here it comes...

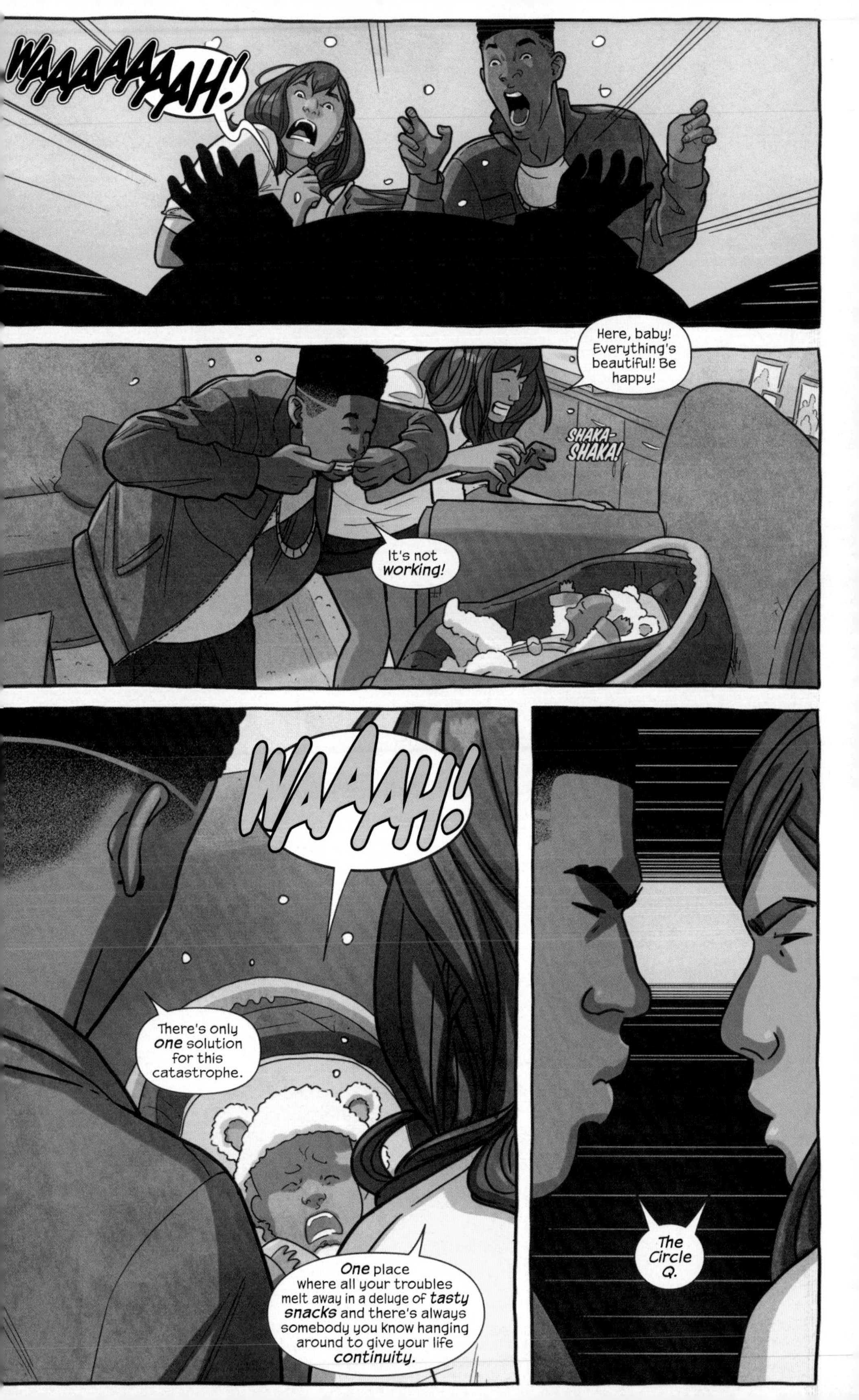
WAAAAAAAH!
Here, baby! Everything's beautiful! Be happy!
SHAKA-SHAKA!
It's not *working!*
WAAAH!
There's only *one* solution for this catastrophe.
One place where all your troubles melt away in a deluge of *tasty snacks* and there's always somebody you know hanging around to give your life *continuity.*
The Circle Q.

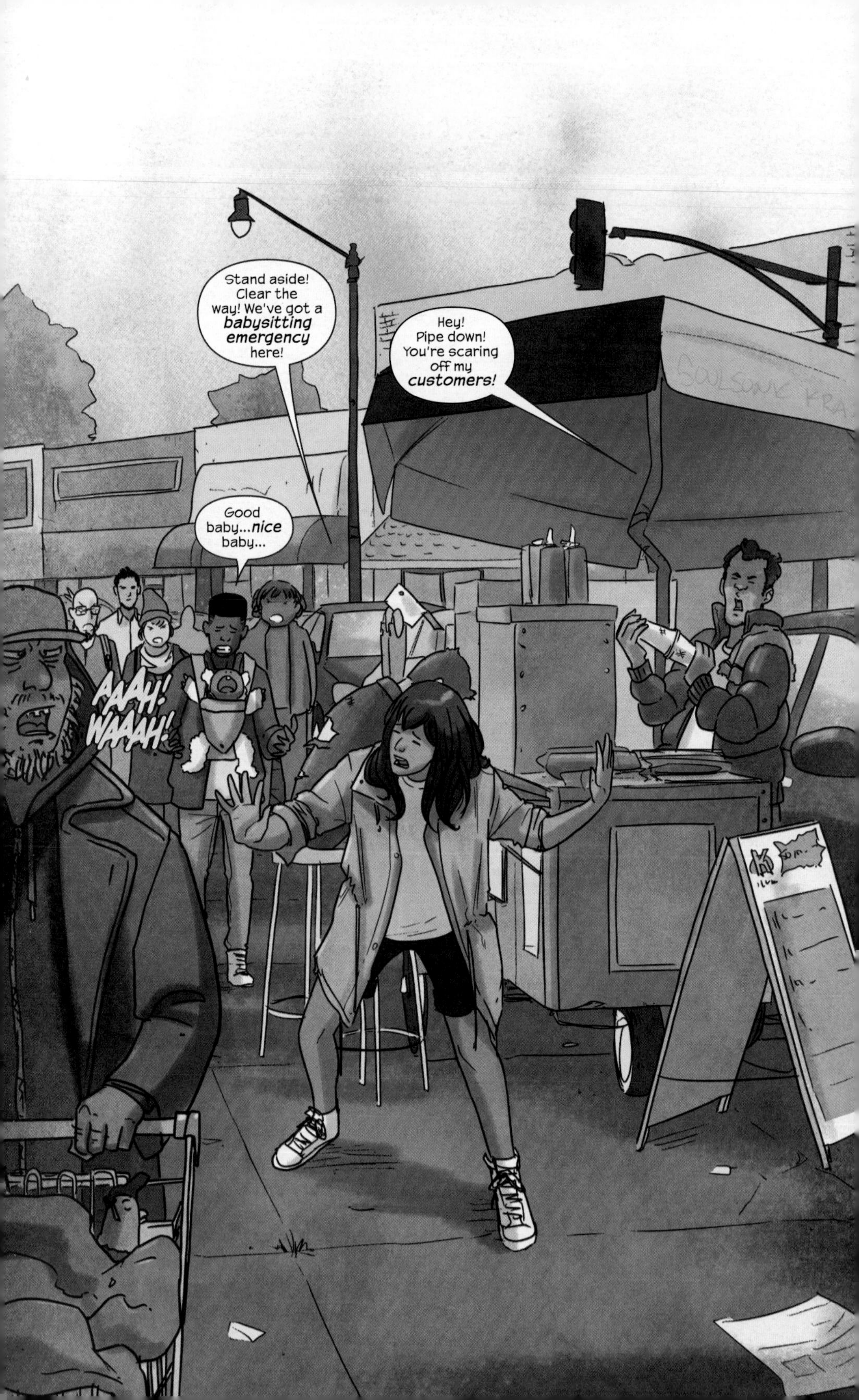
Stand aside! Clear the way! We've got a ***babysitting emergency*** here!
Hey! Pipe down! You're scaring off my ***customers!***
Good baby...***nice*** baby...
AAAH! WAAAH!

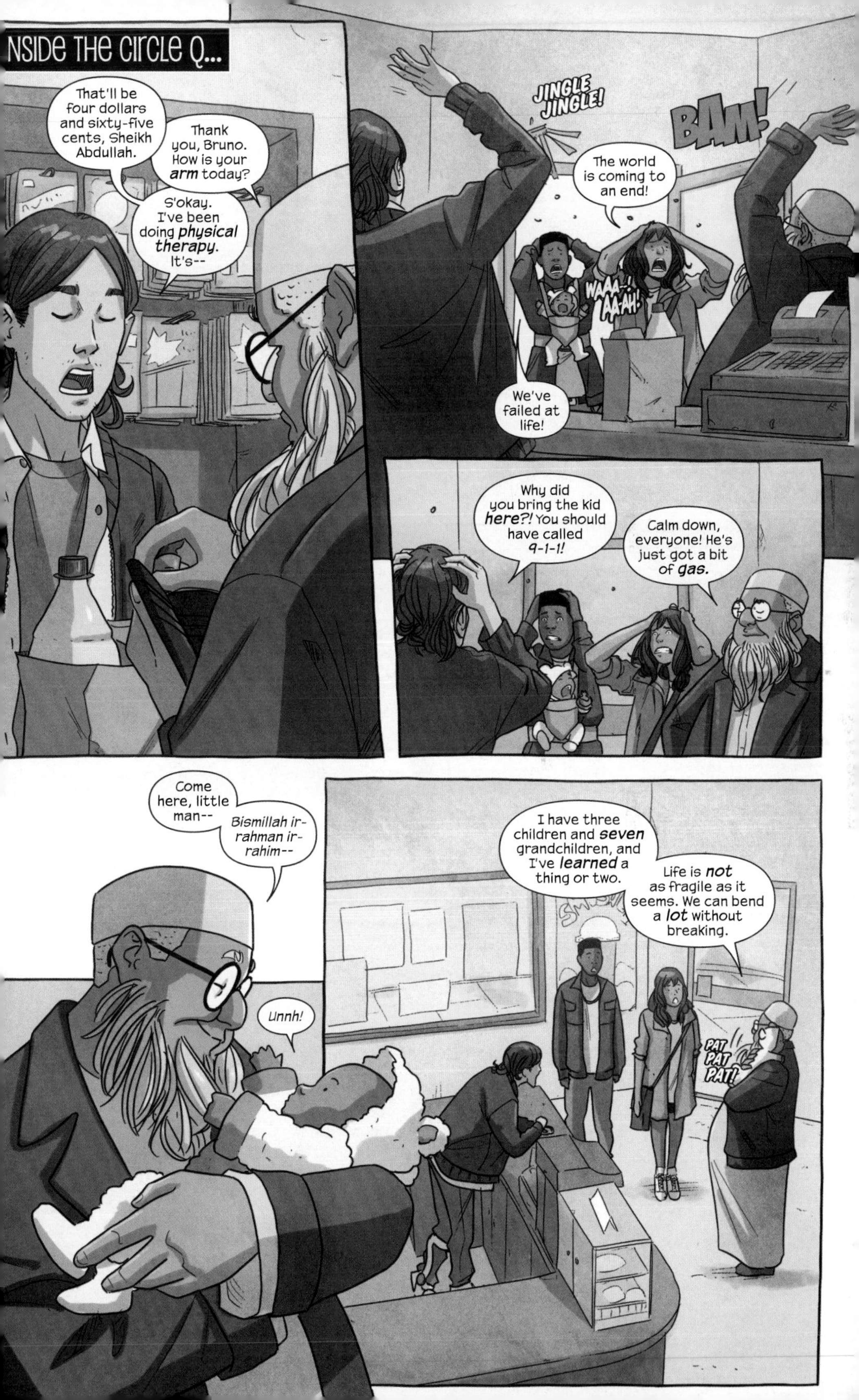
NSIDE THE CIRCLE Q...
That'll be four dollars and sixty-five cents, Sheikh Abdullah.
Thank you, Bruno. How is your *arm* today?
S'okay. I've been doing *physical therapy*. It's--
JINGLE JINGLE!
BAM!
The world is coming to an end!
WAAA--! AA-AH!
We've failed at life!
Why did you bring the kid *here?!* You should have called *9-1-1!*
Calm down, everyone! He's just got a bit of *gas.*
Come here, little man--
Bismillah ir-rahman ir-rahim--
Unnh!
I have three children and *seven* grandchildren, and I've *learned* a thing or two.
Life is *not* as fragile as it seems. We can bend a *lot* without breaking.
PAT PAT PAT!

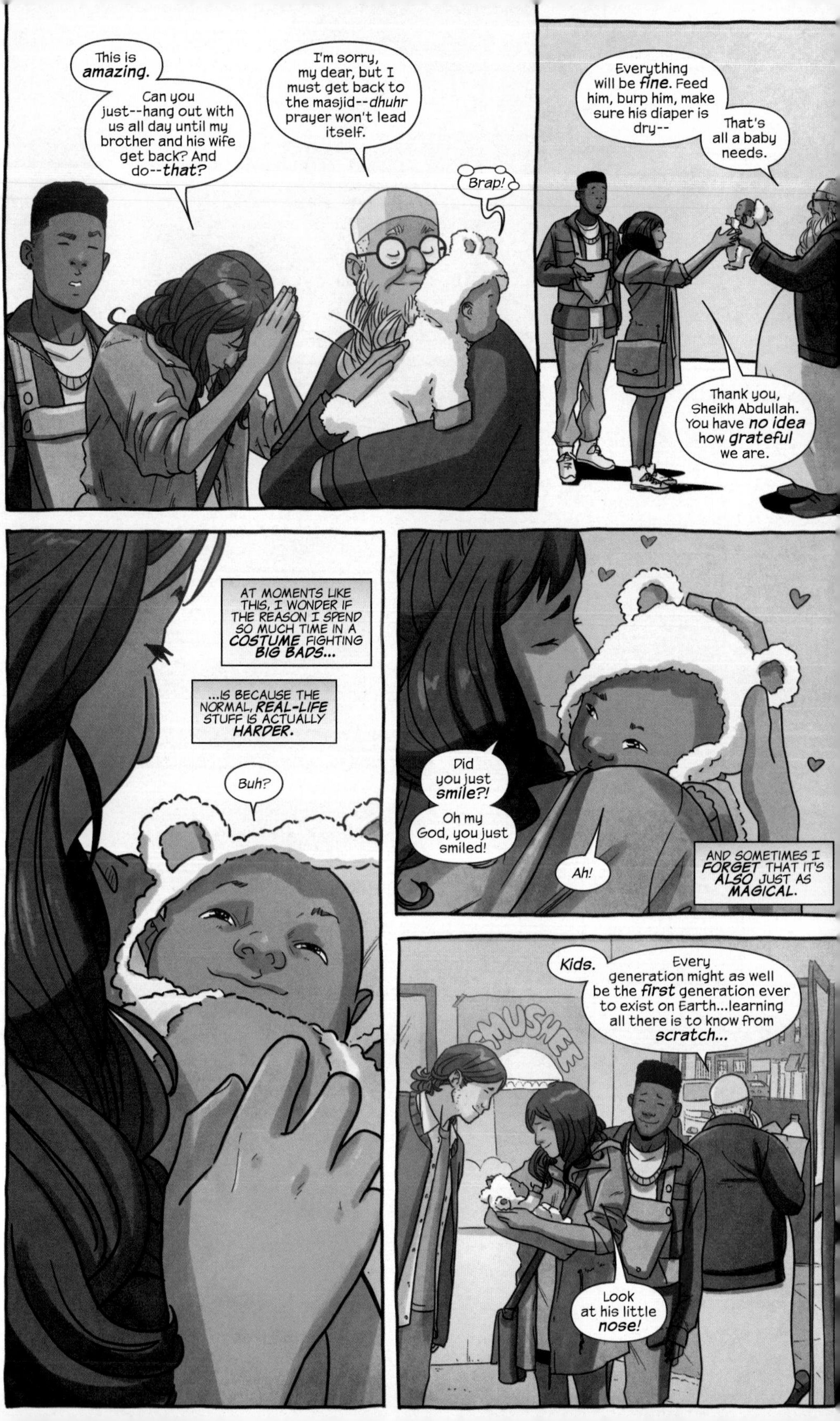
This is amazing.
Can you just--hang out with us all day until my brother and his wife get back? And do--that?
I'm sorry, my dear, but I must get back to the masjid--dhuhr prayer won't lead itself.
Brap!
Everything will be fine. Feed him, burp him, make sure his diaper is dry--
That's all a baby needs.
Thank you, Sheikh Abdullah. You have no idea how grateful we are.
AT MOMENTS LIKE THIS, I WONDER IF THE REASON I SPEND SO MUCH TIME IN A COSTUME FIGHTING BIG BADS...
...IS BECAUSE THE NORMAL, REAL-LIFE STUFF IS ACTUALLY HARDER.
Buh?
Did you just smile?!
Oh my God, you just smiled!
Ah!
AND SOMETIMES I FORGET THAT IT'S ALSO JUST AS MAGICAL.
Kids.
Every generation might as well be the first generation ever to exist on Earth...learning all there is to know from scratch...
Look at his little nose!

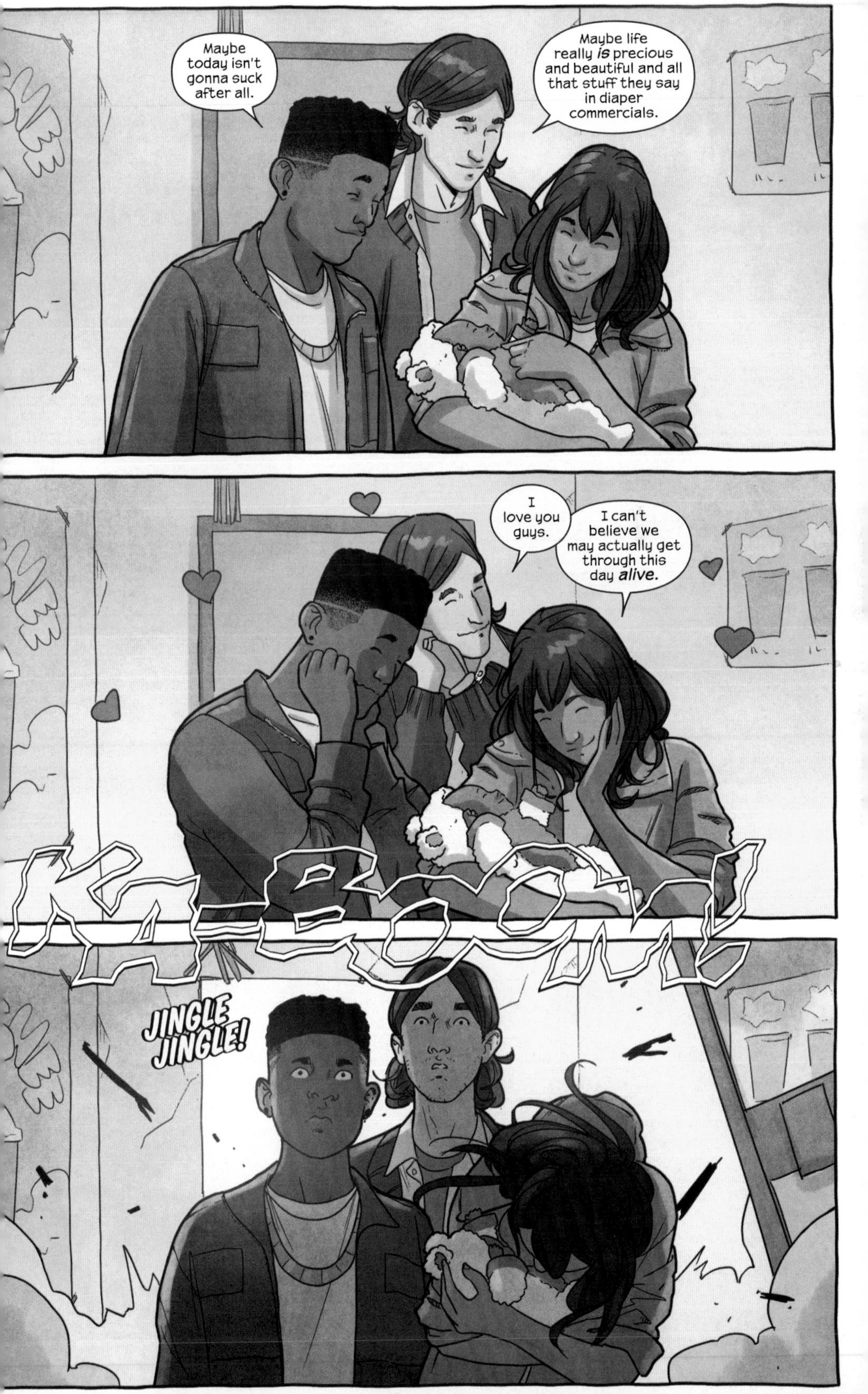
Maybe today isn't gonna suck after all.
Maybe life really *is* precious and beautiful and all that stuff they say in diaper commercials.
I love you guys.
I can't believe we may actually get through this day *alive*.
JINGLE JINGLE!

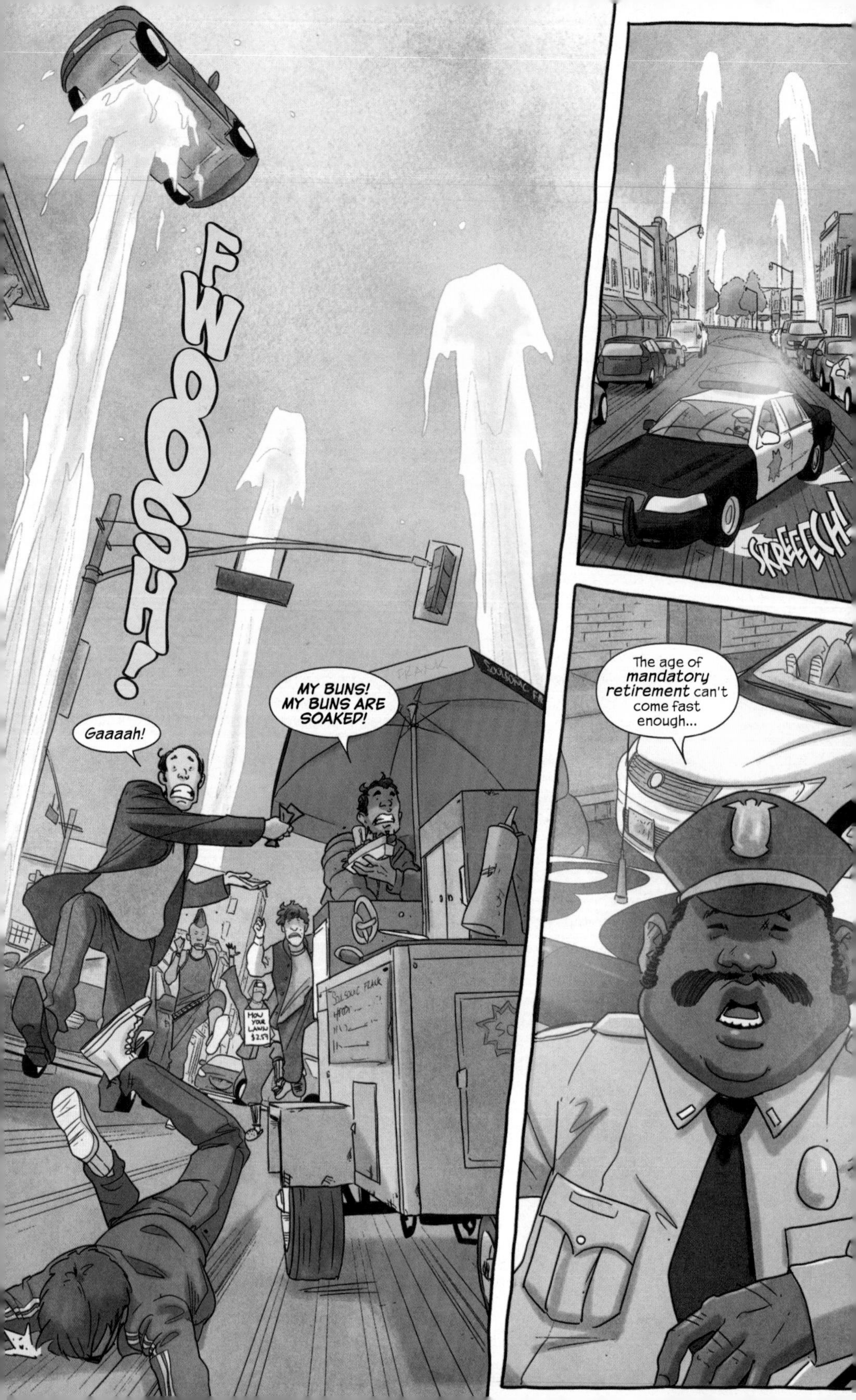
FWOOSH!
Gaaaah!
MY BUNS! MY BUNS ARE SOAKED!
SKREEECH!
The age of *mandatory retirement* can't come fast enough...

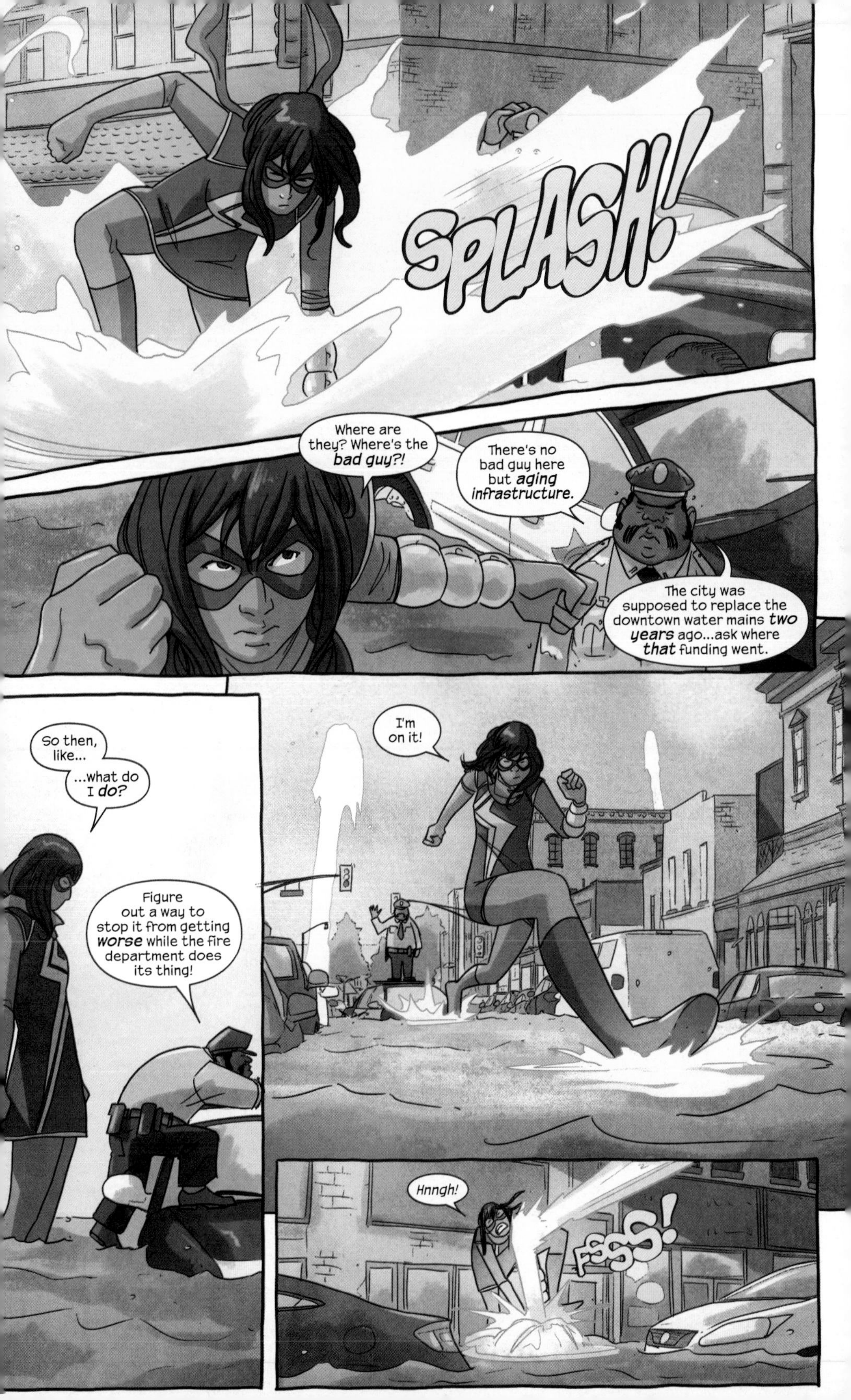
SPLASH!
Where are they? Where's the bad guy?!
There's no bad guy here but aging infrastructure.
The city was supposed to replace the downtown water mains two years ago...ask where that funding went.
So then, like...
...what do I do?
Figure out a way to stop it from getting worse while the fire department does its thing!
I'm on it!
Hnngh!
FSSS!

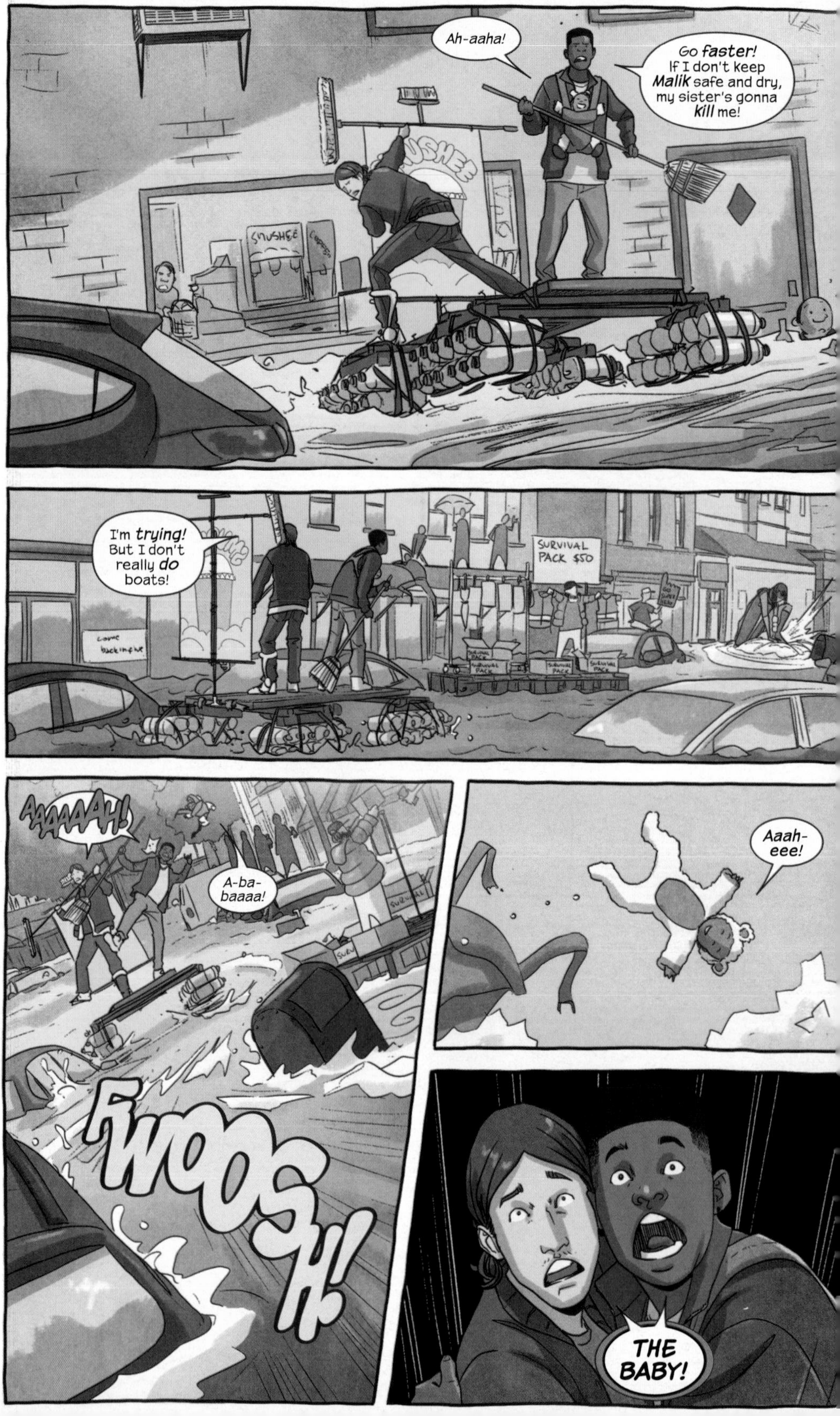
Ah-aaha!
Go faster! If I don't keep Malik safe and dry, my sister's gonna kill me!
I'm trying! But I don't really do boats!
SURVIVAL PACK $50
AAAAAAH!
A-ba-baaaa!
FWOOSH!
Aaah-eee!
THE BABY!

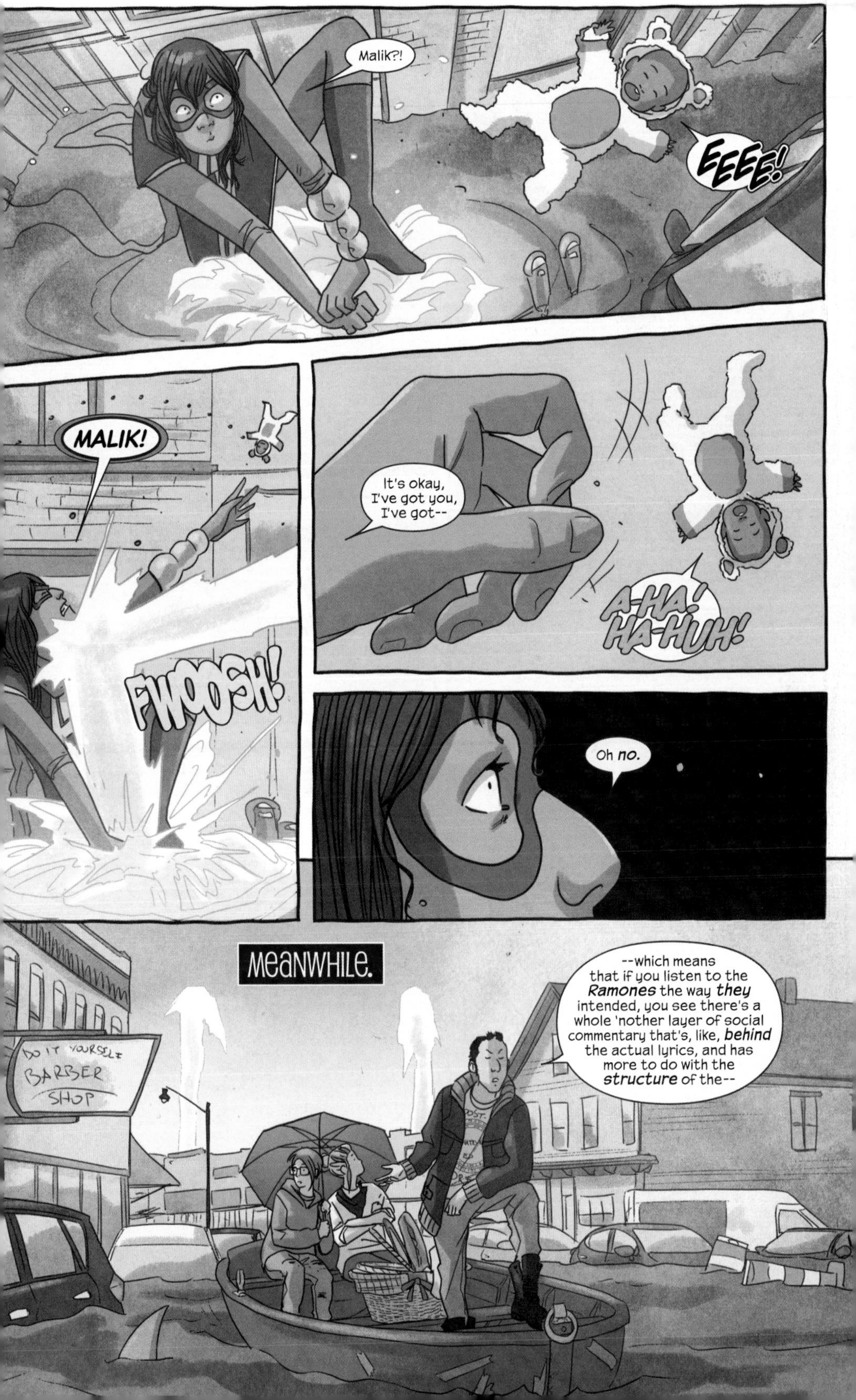
Malik?!
EEEE!
MALIK!
FWOOSH!
It's okay, I've got you, I've got--
A-HA! HA-HUH!
Oh no.
MEANWHILE.
--which means that if you listen to the Ramones the way they intended, you see there's a whole 'nother layer of social commentary that's, like, behind the actual lyrics, and has more to do with the structure of the--
DO IT YOURSELF BARBER SHOP

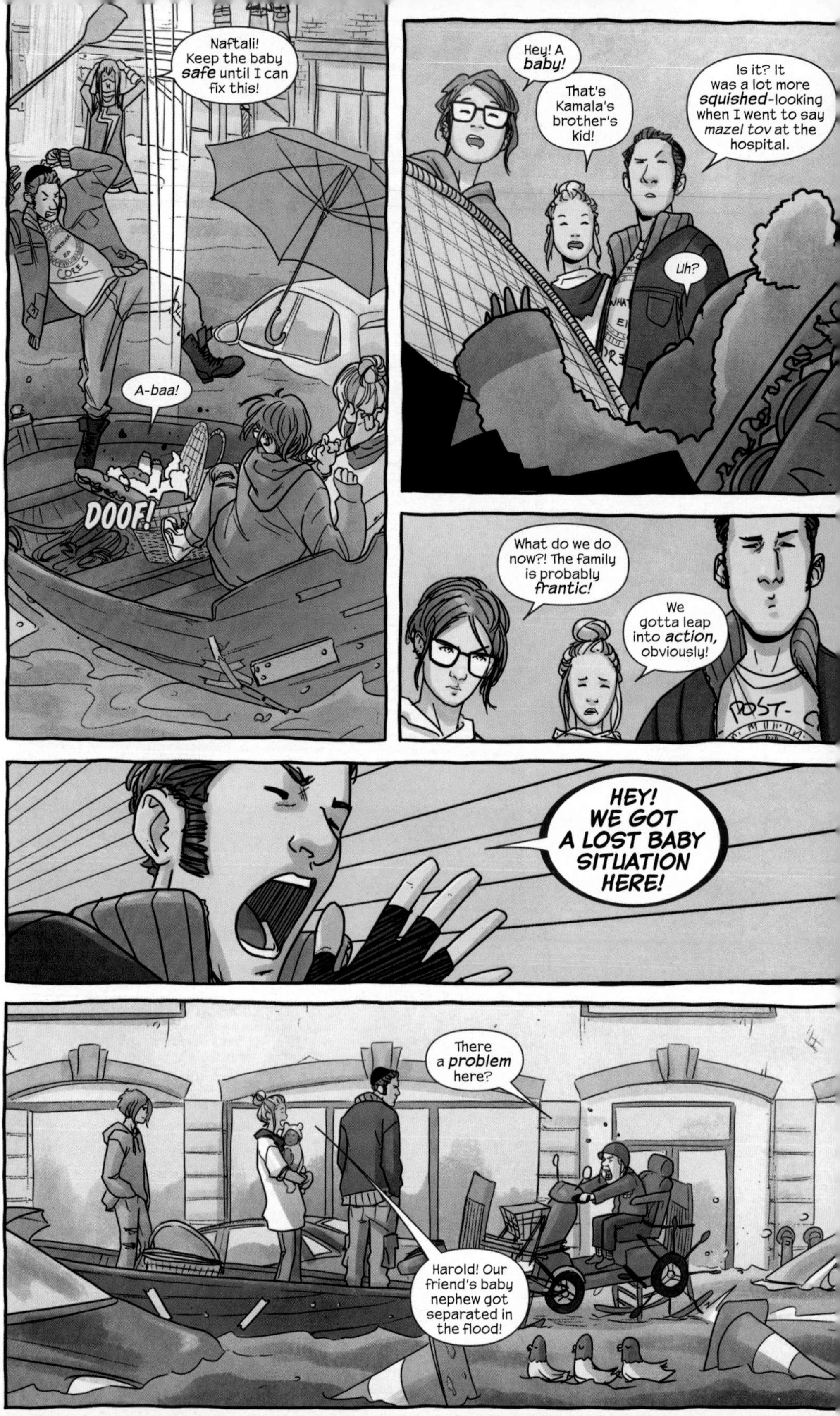
Naftali! Keep the baby safe until I can fix this!
A-baa!
DOOF!
Hey! A baby!
That's Kamala's brother's kid!
Is it? It was a lot more squished-looking when I went to say mazel tov at the hospital.
Uh?
What do we do now?! The family is probably frantic!
We gotta leap into action, obviously!
HEY! WE GOT A LOST BABY SITUATION HERE!
There a problem here?
Harold! Our friend's baby nephew got separated in the flood!

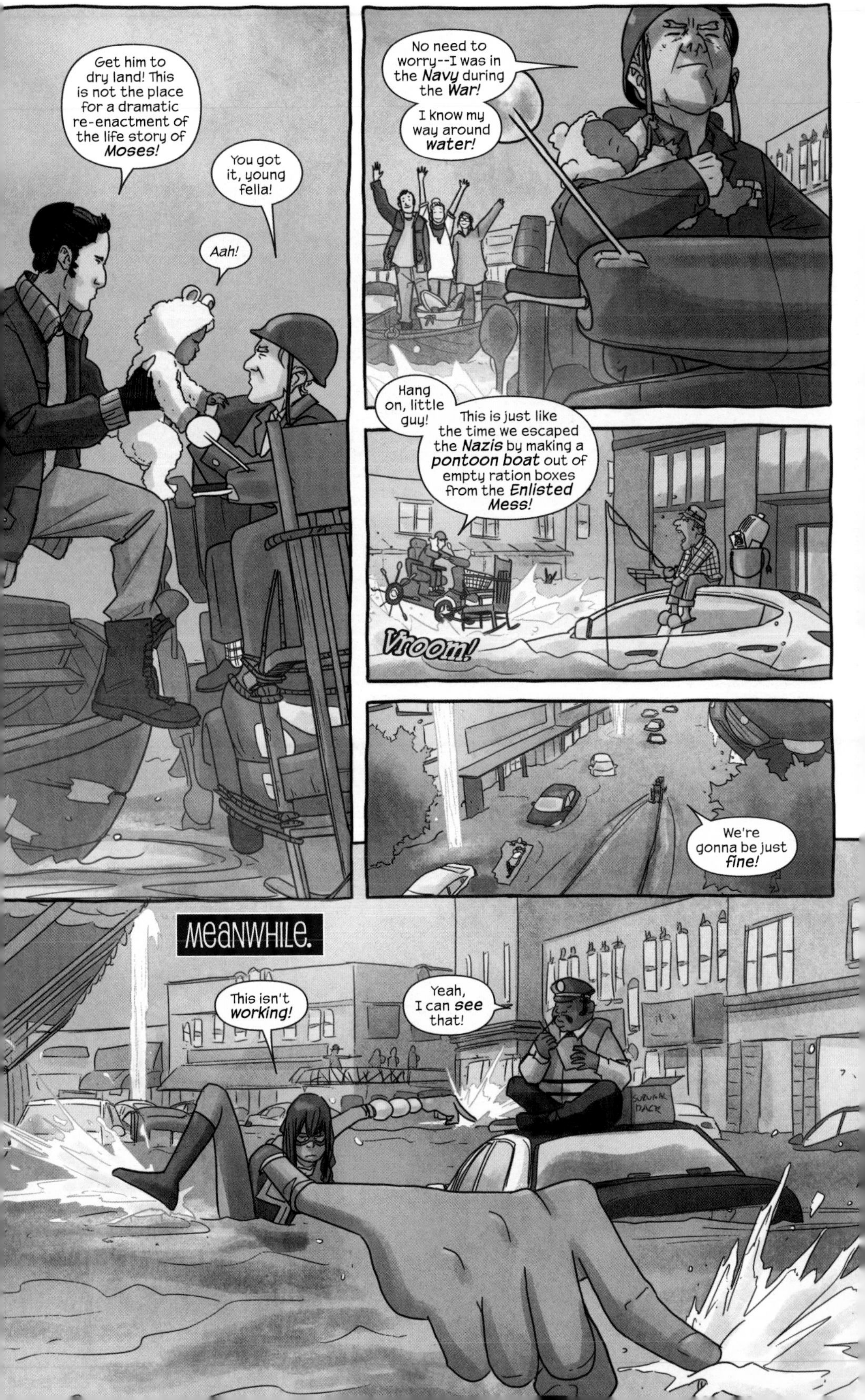
Get him to dry land! This is not the place for a dramatic re-enactment of the life story of Moses!
You got it, young fella!
Aah!
No need to worry--I was in the Navy during the War!
I know my way around water!
Hang on, little guy!
This is just like the time we escaped the Nazis by making a pontoon boat out of empty ration boxes from the Enlisted Mess!
Vroom!
We're gonna be just fine!
MEANWHILE.
This isn't working!
Yeah, I can see that!
SURVIVAL PACK

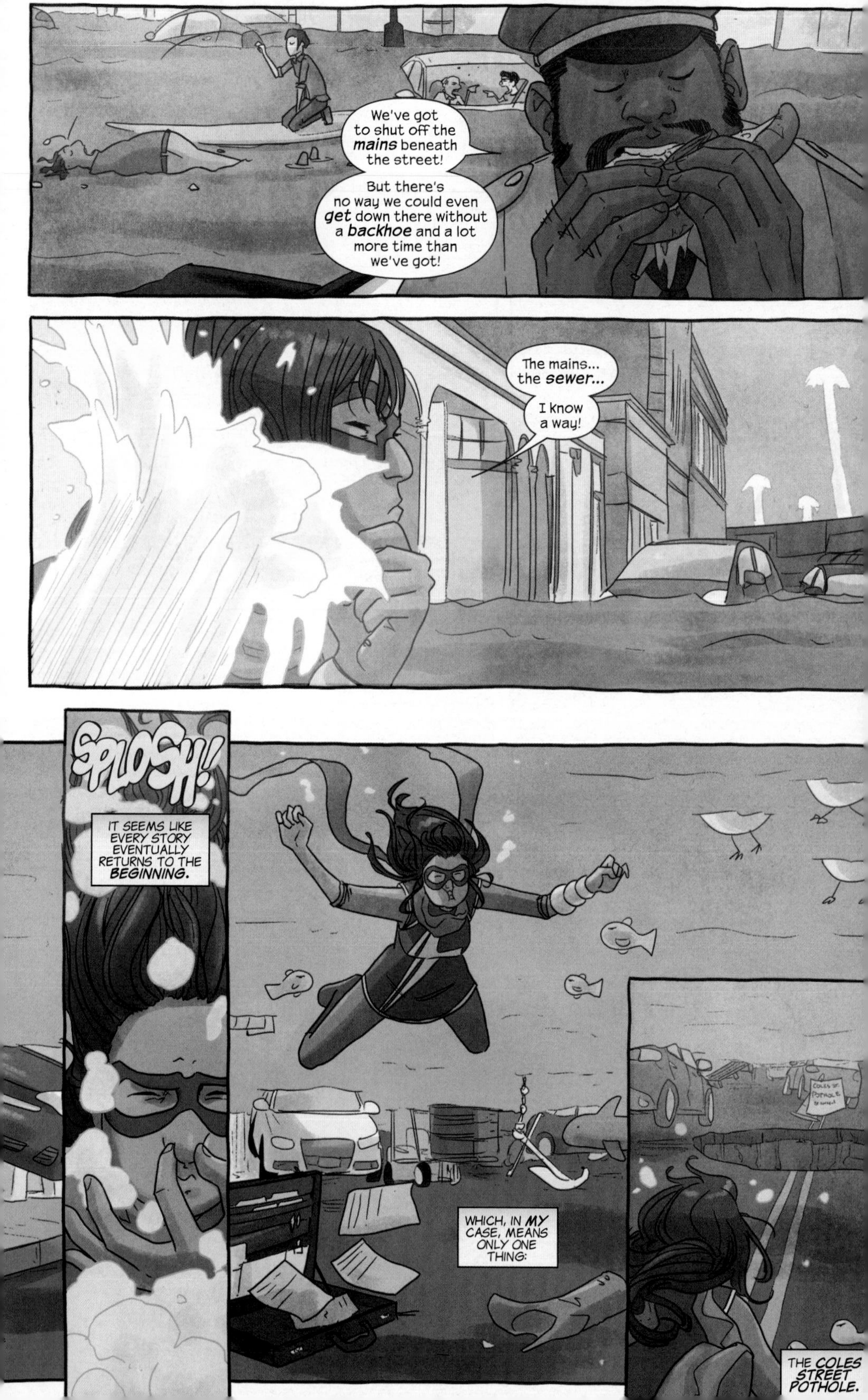

We've got to shut off the *mains* beneath the street!
But there's no way we could even *get* down there without a *backhoe* and a lot more time than we've got!
The mains... the *sewer*...
I know a way!
SPLOSH!
IT SEEMS LIKE EVERY STORY EVENTUALLY RETURNS TO THE *BEGINNING*.
WHICH, IN *MY* CASE, MEANS ONLY ONE THING:
THE *COLES STREET POTHOLE.*

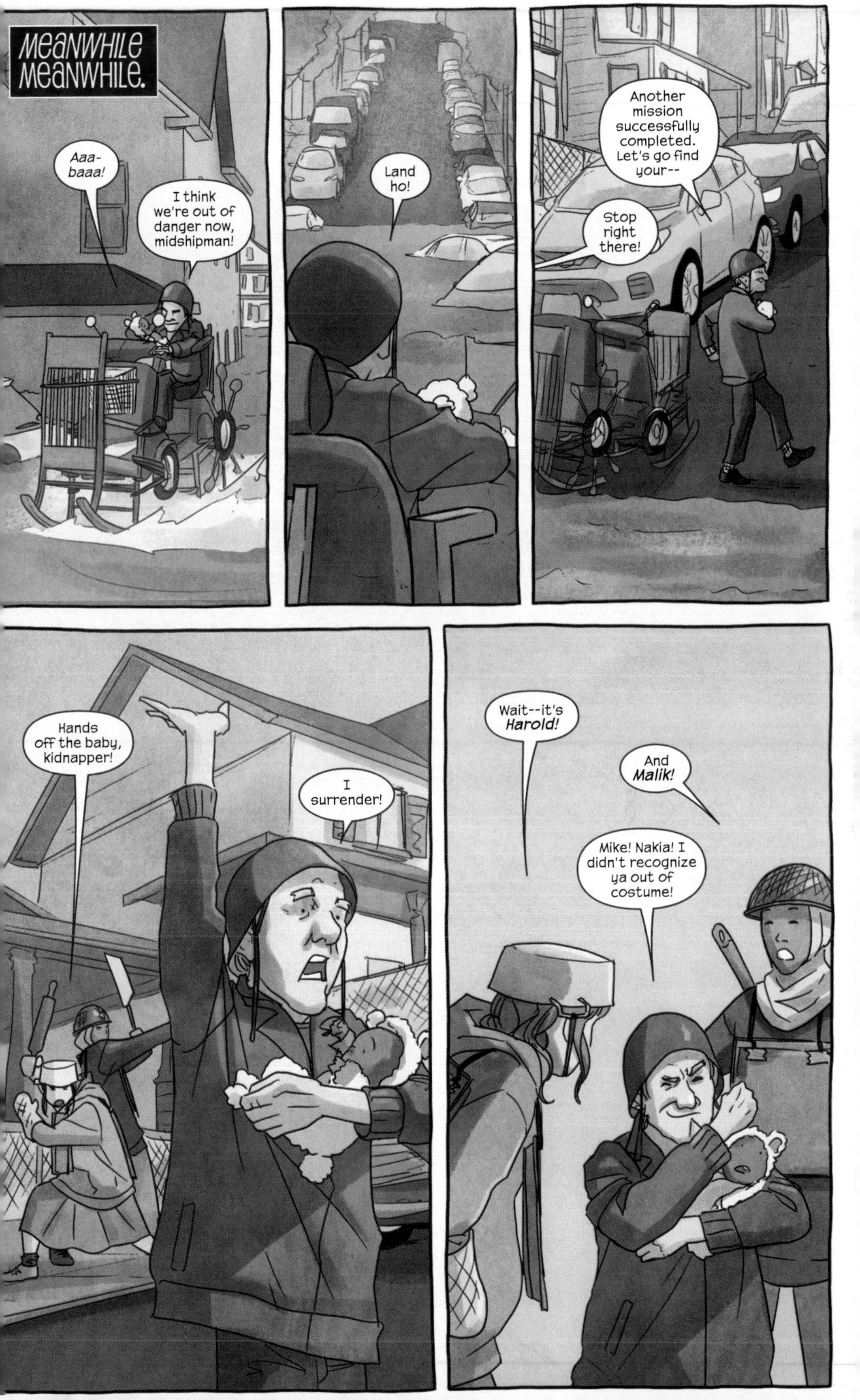
MEANWHILE MEANWHILE.
Aaa-baaa!
I think we're out of danger now, midshipman!
Land ho!
Another mission successfully completed. Let's go find your--
Stop right there!
Hands off the baby, kidnapper!
I surrender!
Wait--it's Harold!
And Malik!
Mike! Nakia! I didn't recognize ya out of costume!

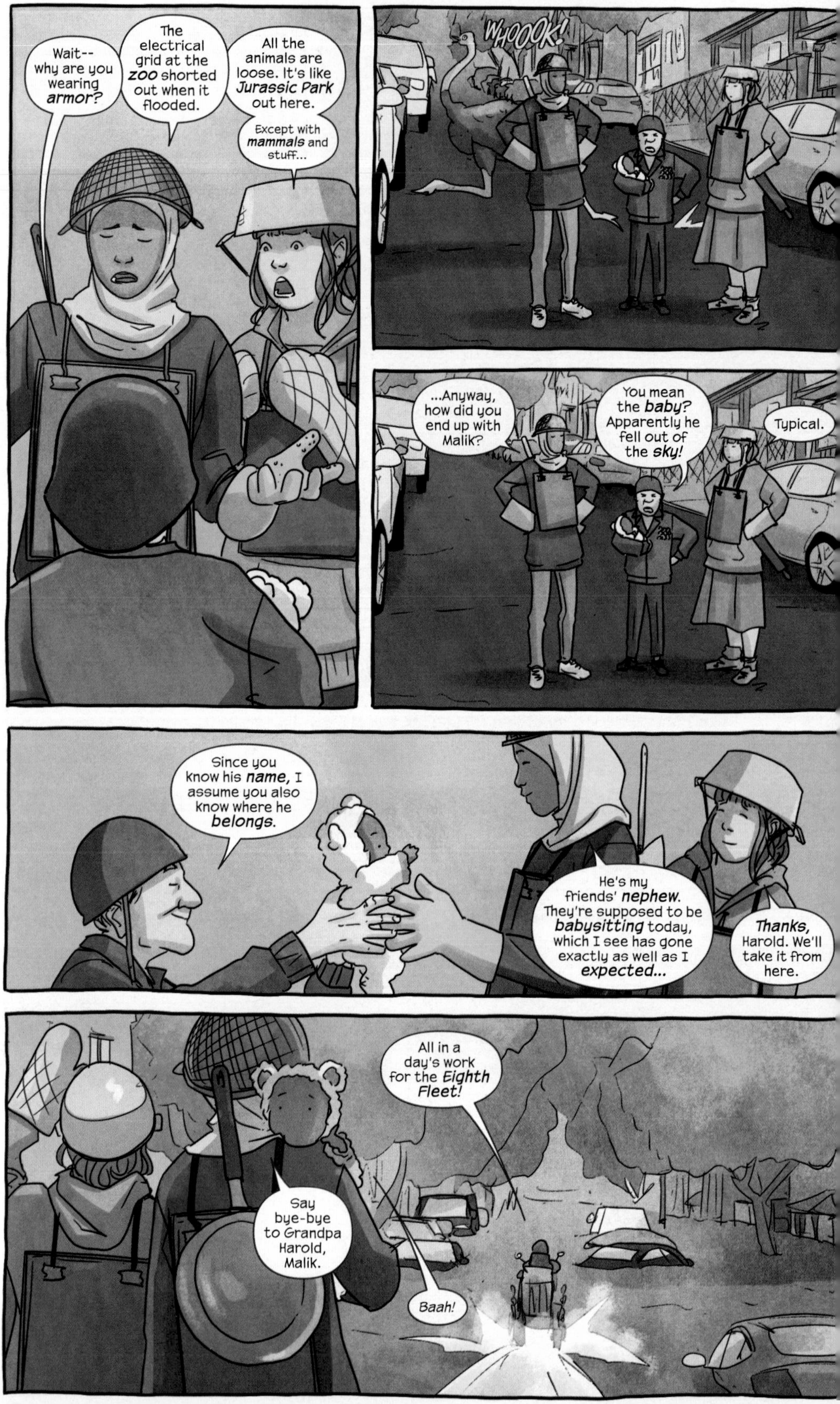

Wait-- why are you wearing armor?
The electrical grid at the zoo shorted out when it flooded.
All the animals are loose. It's like Jurassic Park out here.
Except with mammals and stuff...
WHOOOK!
...Anyway, how did you end up with Malik?
You mean the baby? Apparently he fell out of the sky!
Typical.
Since you know his name, I assume you also know where he belongs.
He's my friends' nephew. They're supposed to be babysitting today, which I see has gone exactly as well as I expected...
Thanks, Harold. We'll take it from here.
All in a day's work for the Eighth Fleet!
Say bye-bye to Grandpa Harold, Malik.
Baah!

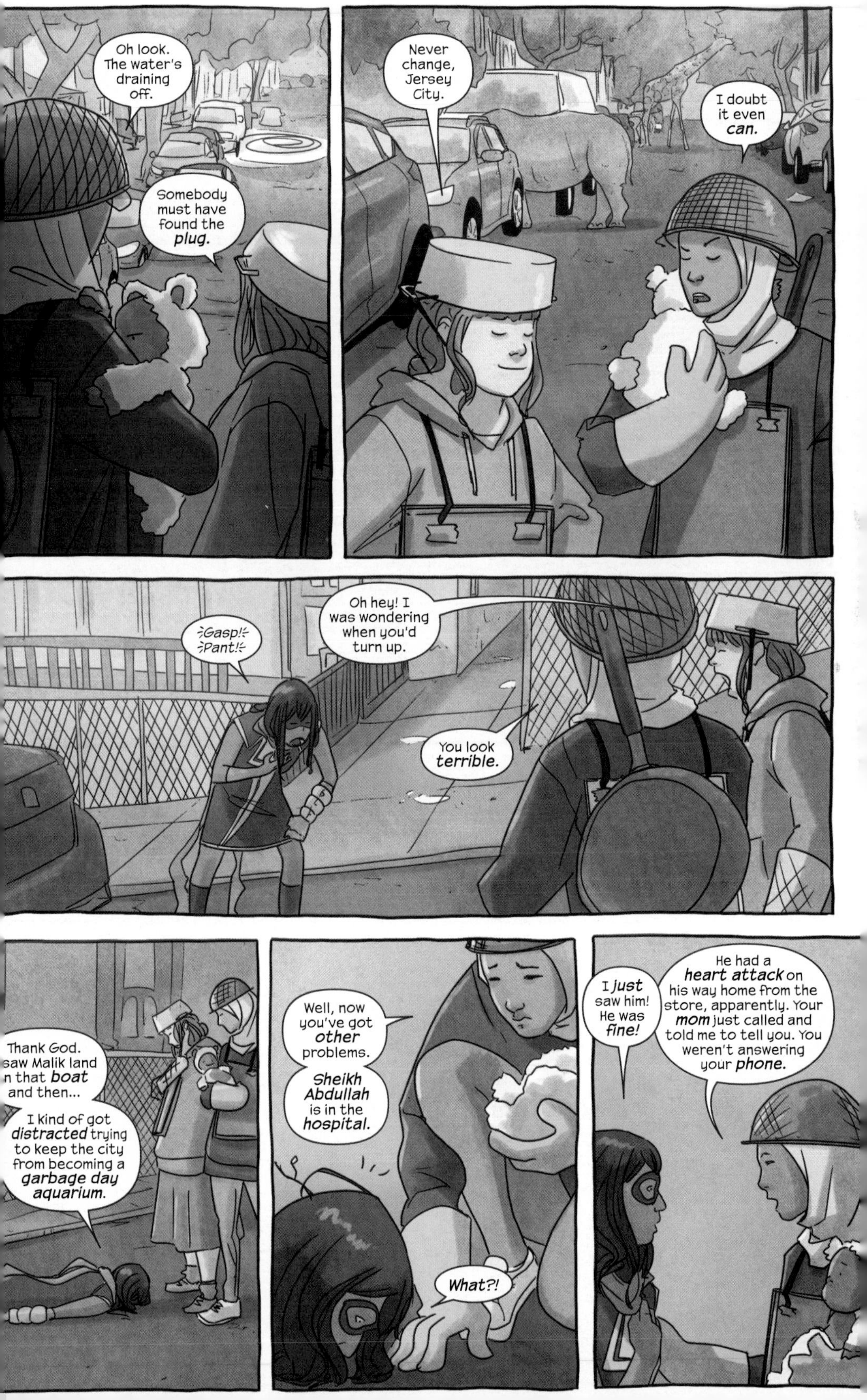
Oh look. The water's draining off.
Somebody must have found the *plug.*
Never change, Jersey City.
I doubt it even *can.*
Gasp! *Pant!*
Oh hey! I was wondering when you'd turn up.
You look *terrible.*
Thank God. saw Malik land n that *boat* and then...
I kind of got *distracted* trying to keep the city from becoming a *garbage day aquarium.*
Well, now you've got *other* problems.
Sheikh Abdullah is in the *hospital.*
What?!
I *just* saw him! He was *fine!*
He had a *heart attack* on his way home from the store, apparently. Your *mom* just called and told me to tell you. You weren't answering your *phone.*

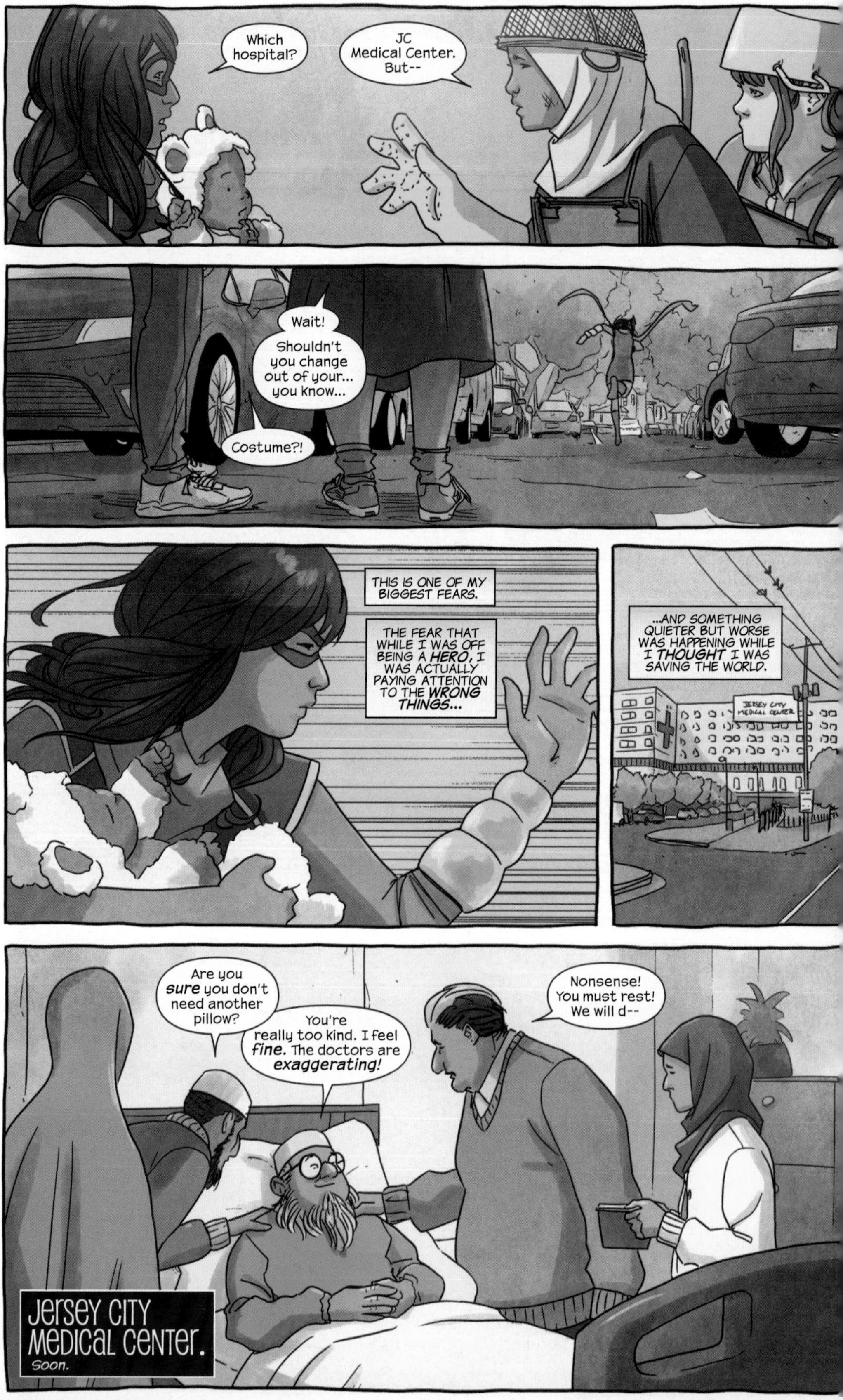

Which hospital?
JC Medical Center. But--
Wait!
Shouldn't you change out of your... you know...
Costume?!
THIS IS ONE OF MY BIGGEST FEARS.
THE FEAR THAT WHILE I WAS OFF BEING A HERO, I WAS ACTUALLY PAYING ATTENTION TO THE WRONG THINGS...
...AND SOMETHING QUIETER BUT WORSE WAS HAPPENING WHILE I THOUGHT I WAS SAVING THE WORLD.
JERSEY CITY MEDICAL CENTER
Jersey City Medical Center. Soon.
Are you sure you don't need another pillow?
You're really too kind. I feel fine. The doctors are exaggerating!
Nonsense! You must rest! We will d--

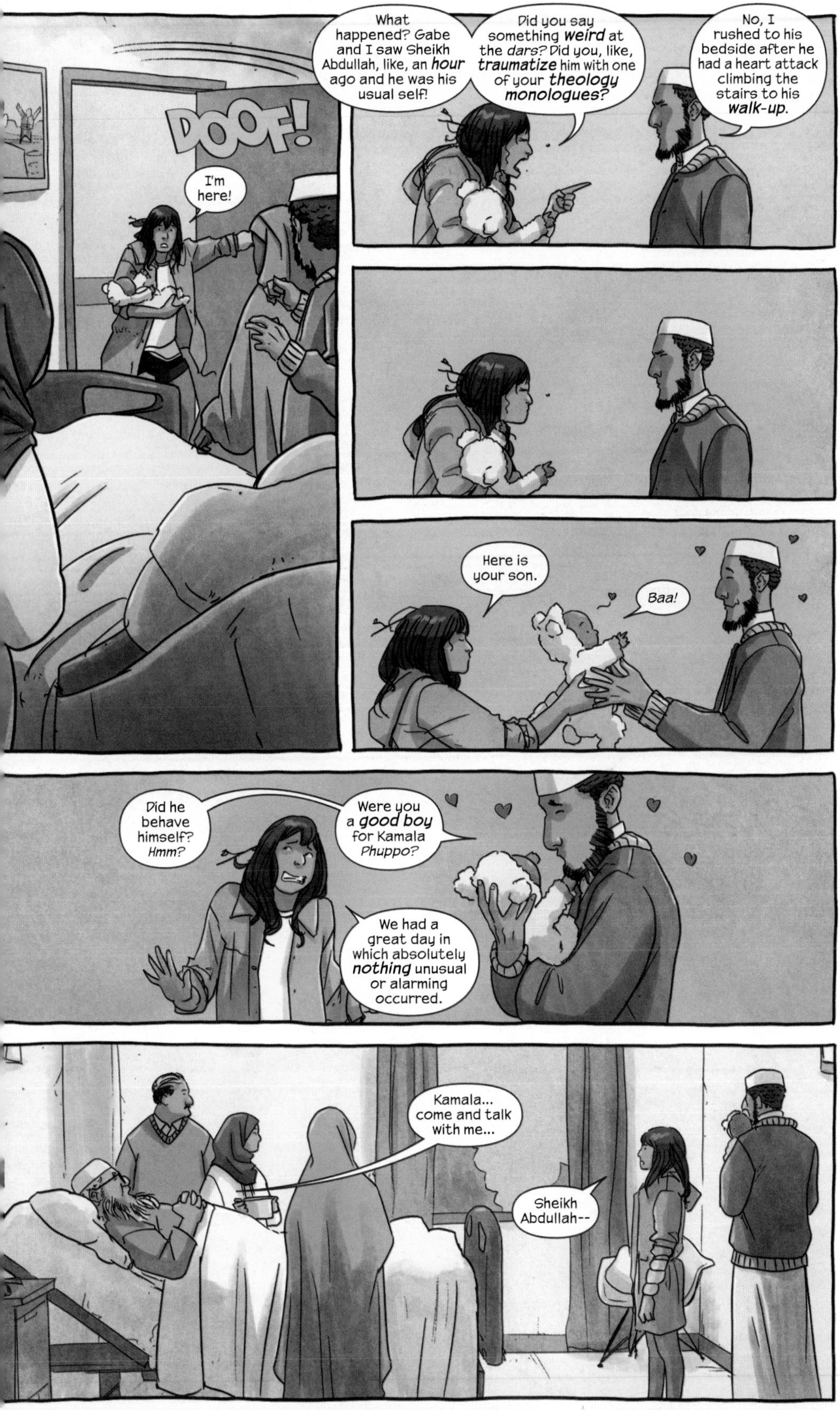
DOOF!
I'm here!
What happened? Gabe and I saw Sheikh Abdullah, like, an *hour* ago and he was his usual self!
Did you say something ***weird*** at the *dars*? Did you, like, ***traumatize*** him with one of your ***theology monologues***?
No, I rushed to his bedside after he had a heart attack climbing the stairs to his ***walk-up***.
Here is your son.
Baa!
Did he behave himself? *Hmm?*
Were you a ***good boy*** for Kamala *Phuppo?*
We had a great day in which absolutely ***nothing*** unusual or alarming occurred.
Kamala... come and talk with me...
Sheikh Abdullah--

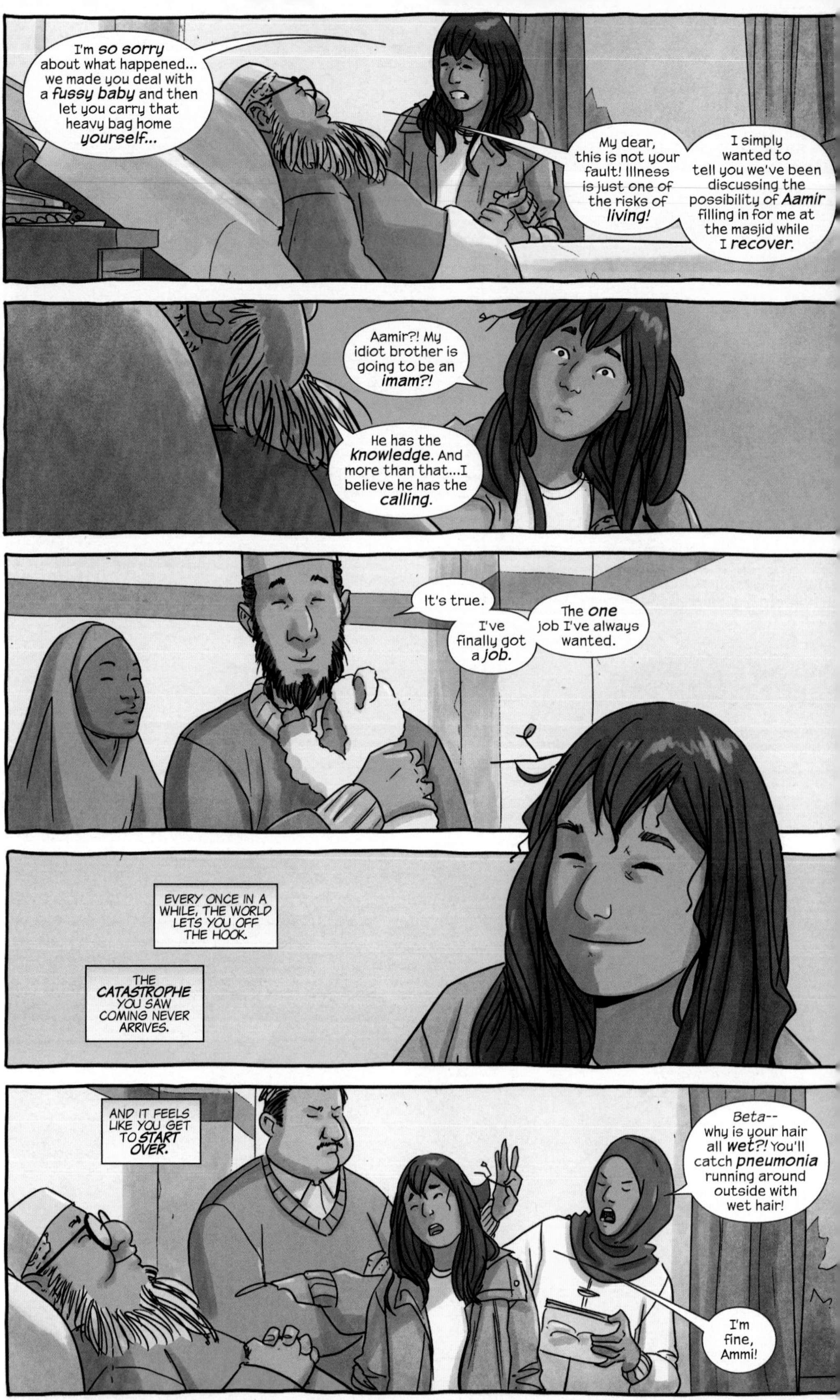
I'm so sorry about what happened... we made you deal with a fussy baby and then let you carry that heavy bag home yourself...
My dear, this is not your fault! Illness is just one of the risks of living!
I simply wanted to tell you we've been discussing the possibility of Aamir filling in for me at the masjid while I recover.
Aamir?! My idiot brother is going to be an imam?!
He has the knowledge. And more than that...I believe he has the calling.
It's true.
I've finally got a job.
The one job I've always wanted.
EVERY ONCE IN A WHILE, THE WORLD LETS YOU OFF THE HOOK.
THE CATASTROPHE YOU SAW COMING NEVER ARRIVES.
AND IT FEELS LIKE YOU GET TO START OVER.
Beta-- why is your hair all wet?! You'll catch pneumonia running around outside with wet hair!
I'm fine, Ammi!

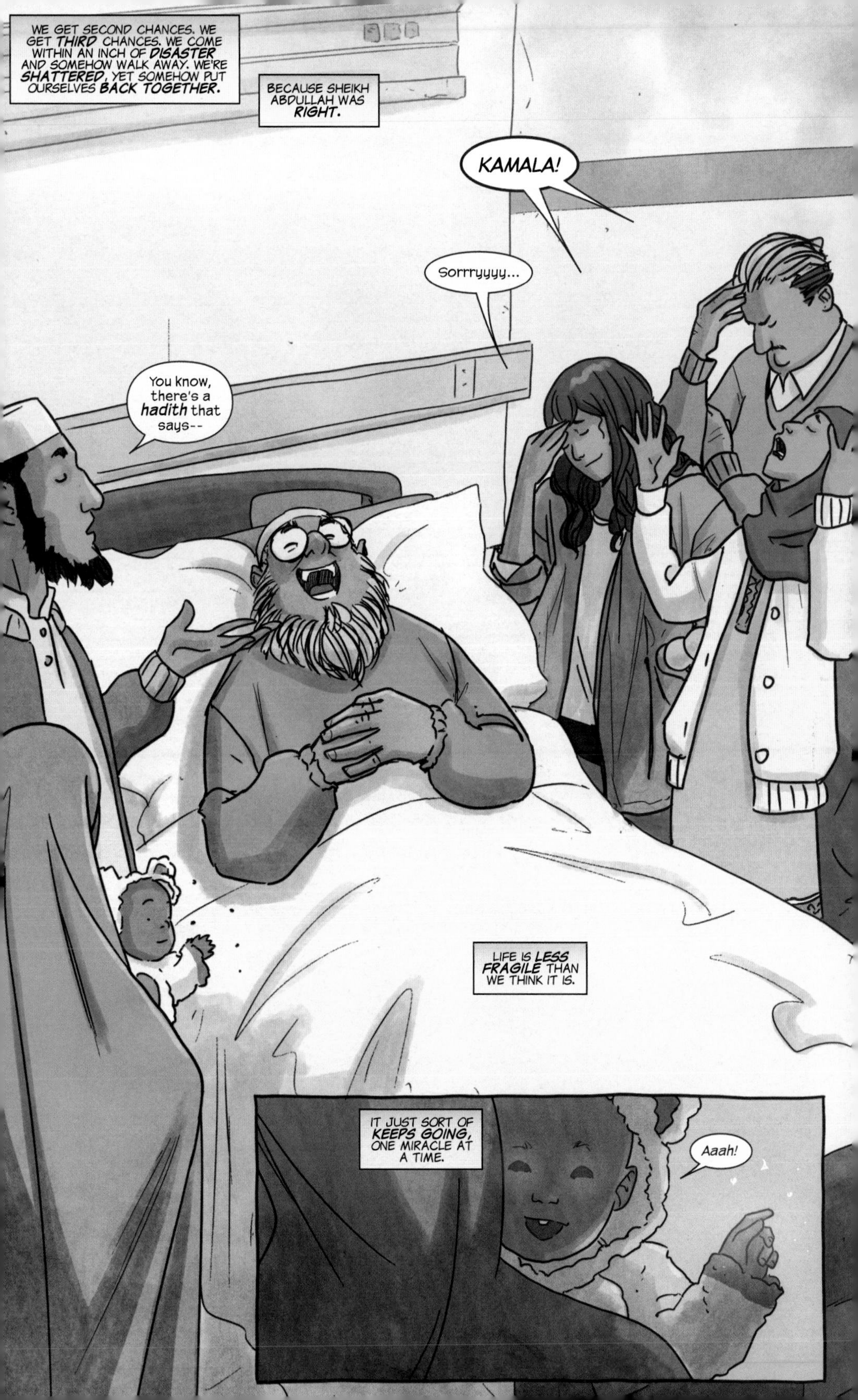
WE GET SECOND CHANCES. WE GET THIRD CHANCES. WE COME WITHIN AN INCH OF DISASTER AND SOMEHOW WALK AWAY. WE'RE SHATTERED, YET SOMEHOW PUT OURSELVES BACK TOGETHER.
BECAUSE SHEIKH ABDULLAH WAS RIGHT.
KAMALA!
Sorrryyyy...
You know, there's a hadith that says--
LIFE IS LESS FRAGILE THAN WE THINK IT IS.
IT JUST SORT OF KEEPS GOING, ONE MIRACLE AT A TIME.
Aaah!

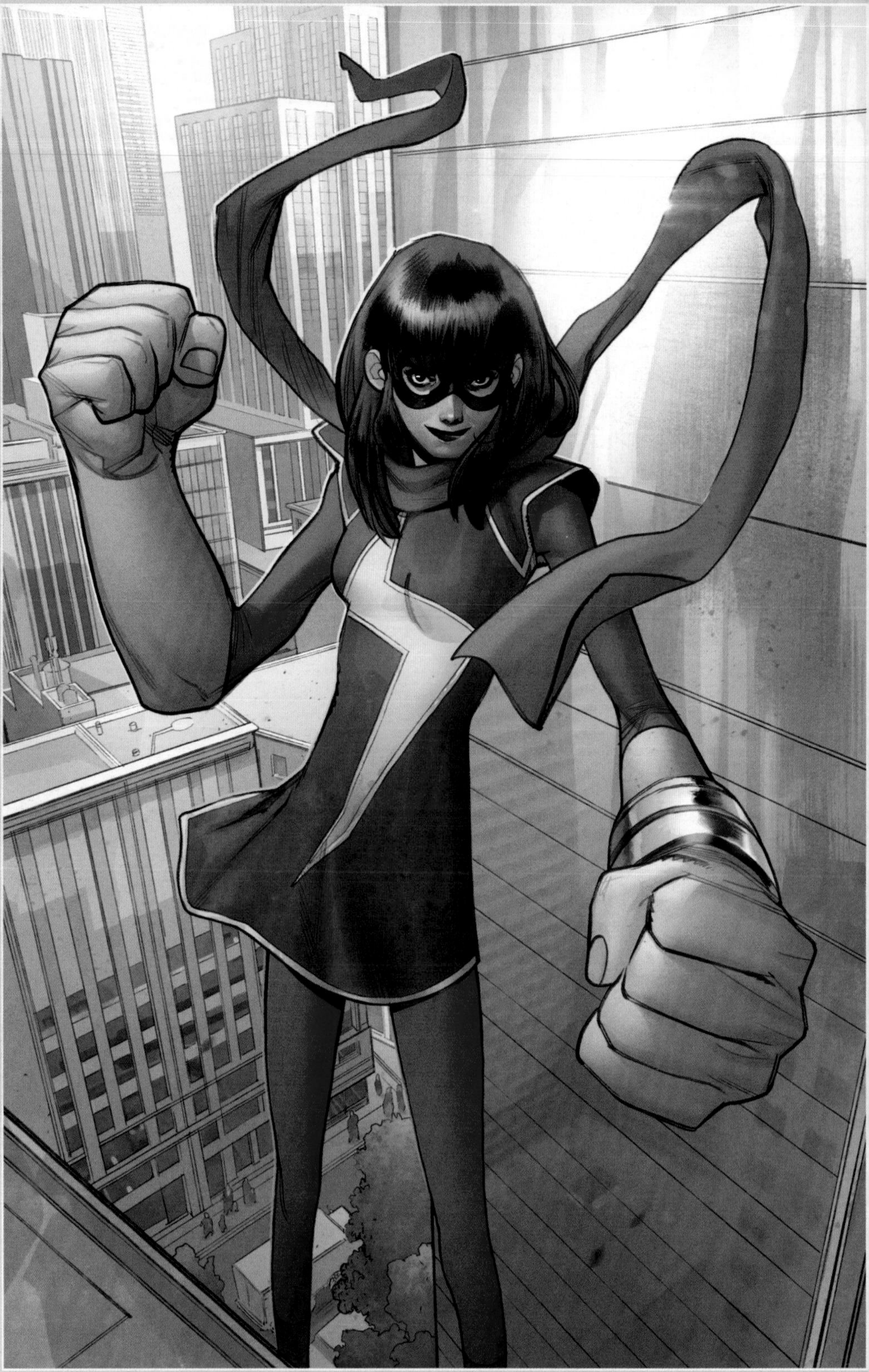

MS. MARVEL #38

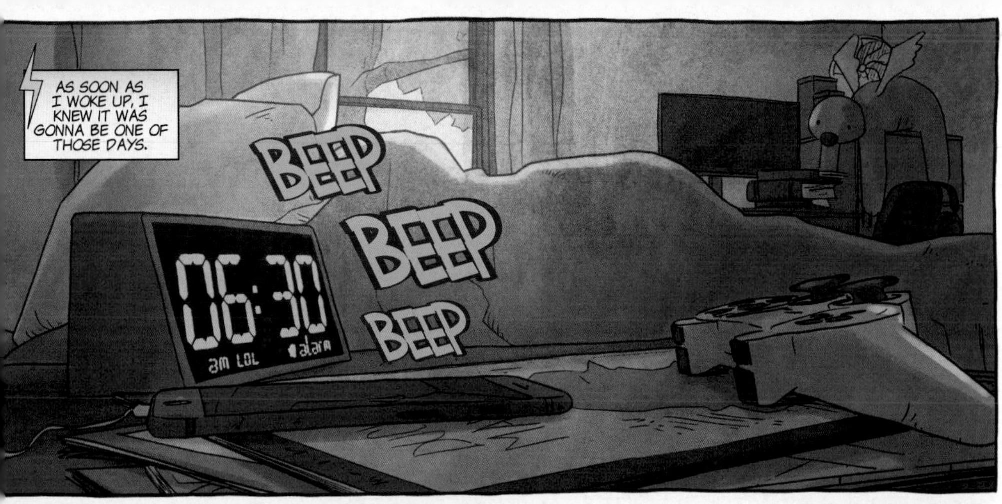
AS SOON AS I WOKE UP, I KNEW IT WAS GONNA BE ONE OF THOSE DAYS.
BEEP
BEEP
BEEP
06:30
am LOL
alarm

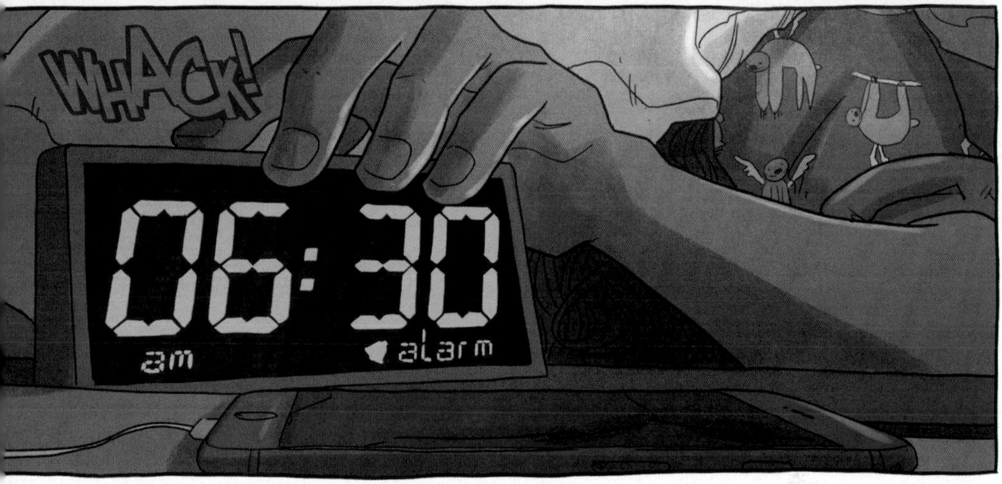
WHACK!
06:30
am
alarm

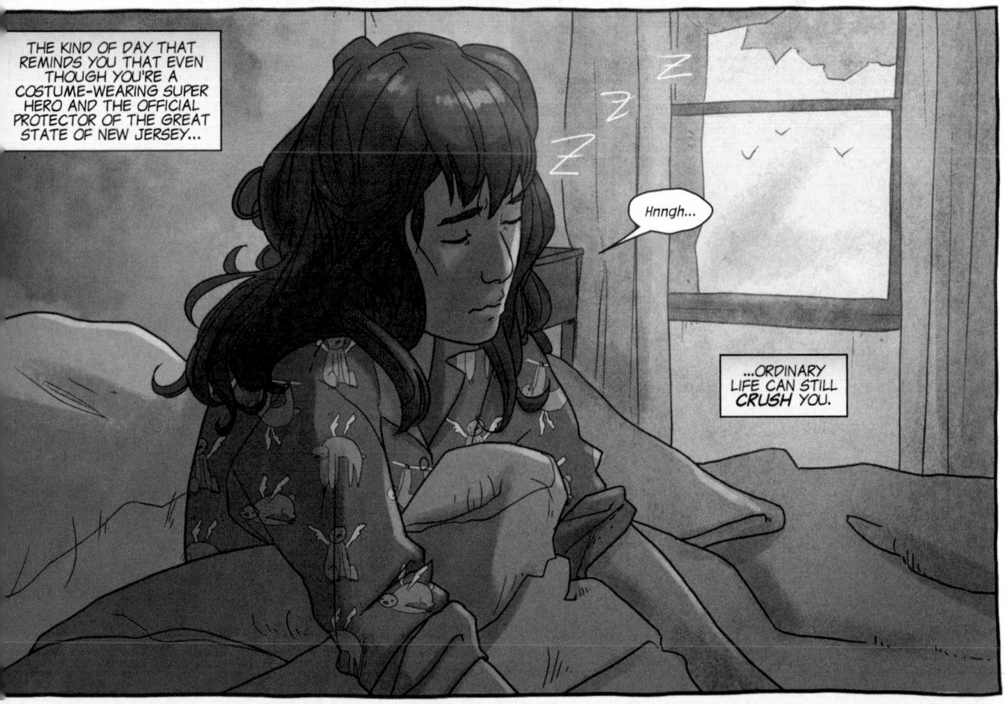
THE KIND OF DAY THAT REMINDS YOU THAT EVEN THOUGH YOU'RE A COSTUME-WEARING SUPER HERO AND THE OFFICIAL PROTECTOR OF THE GREAT STATE OF NEW JERSEY...
Z
Z
Z
Hnngh...
...ORDINARY LIFE CAN STILL CRUSH YOU.

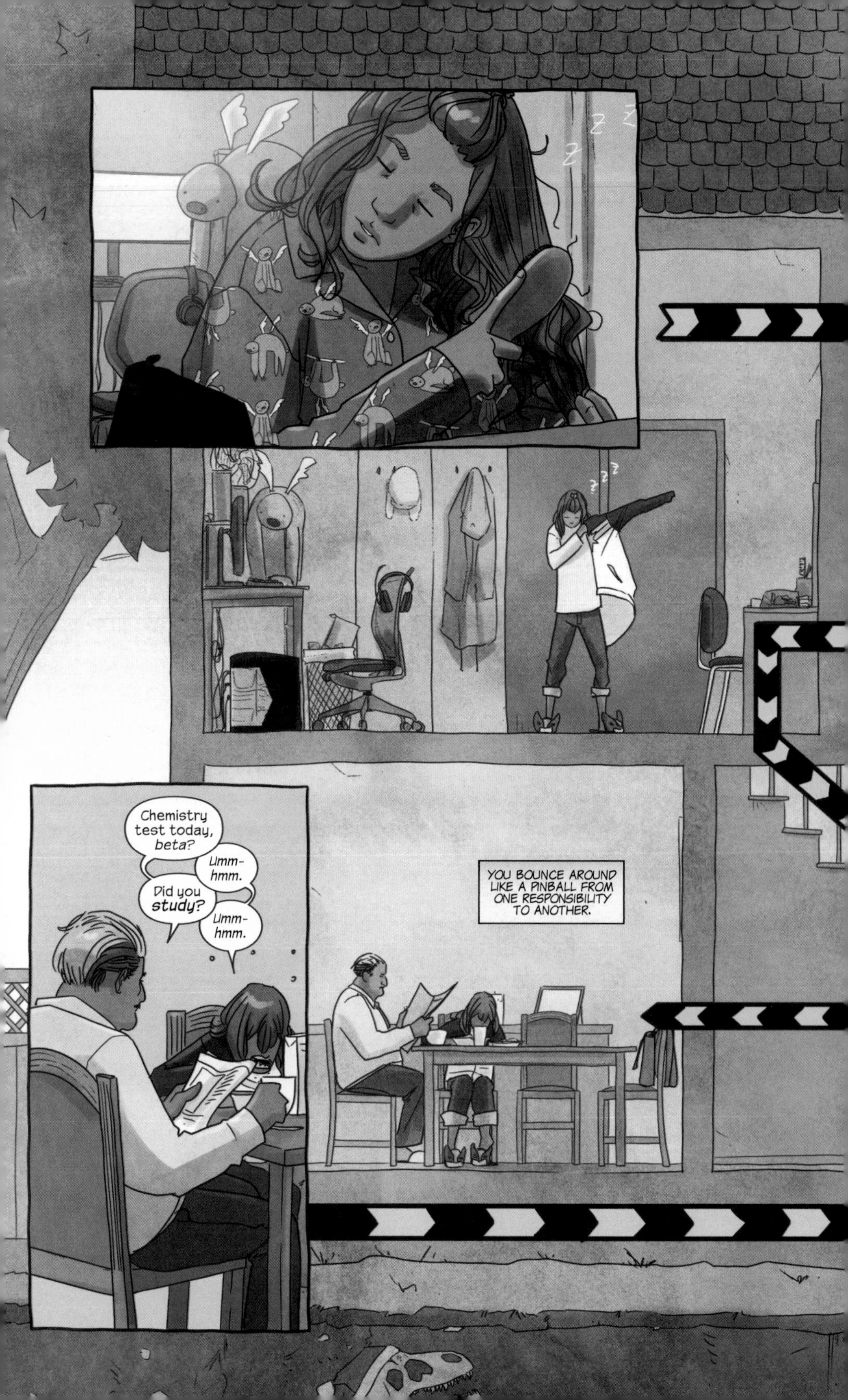

Z
Z
Z
Z
Z
Z
Chemistry test today, beta?
Umm-hmm.
Did you study?
Umm-hmm.
YOU BOUNCE AROUND LIKE A PINBALL FROM ONE RESPONSIBILITY TO ANOTHER.

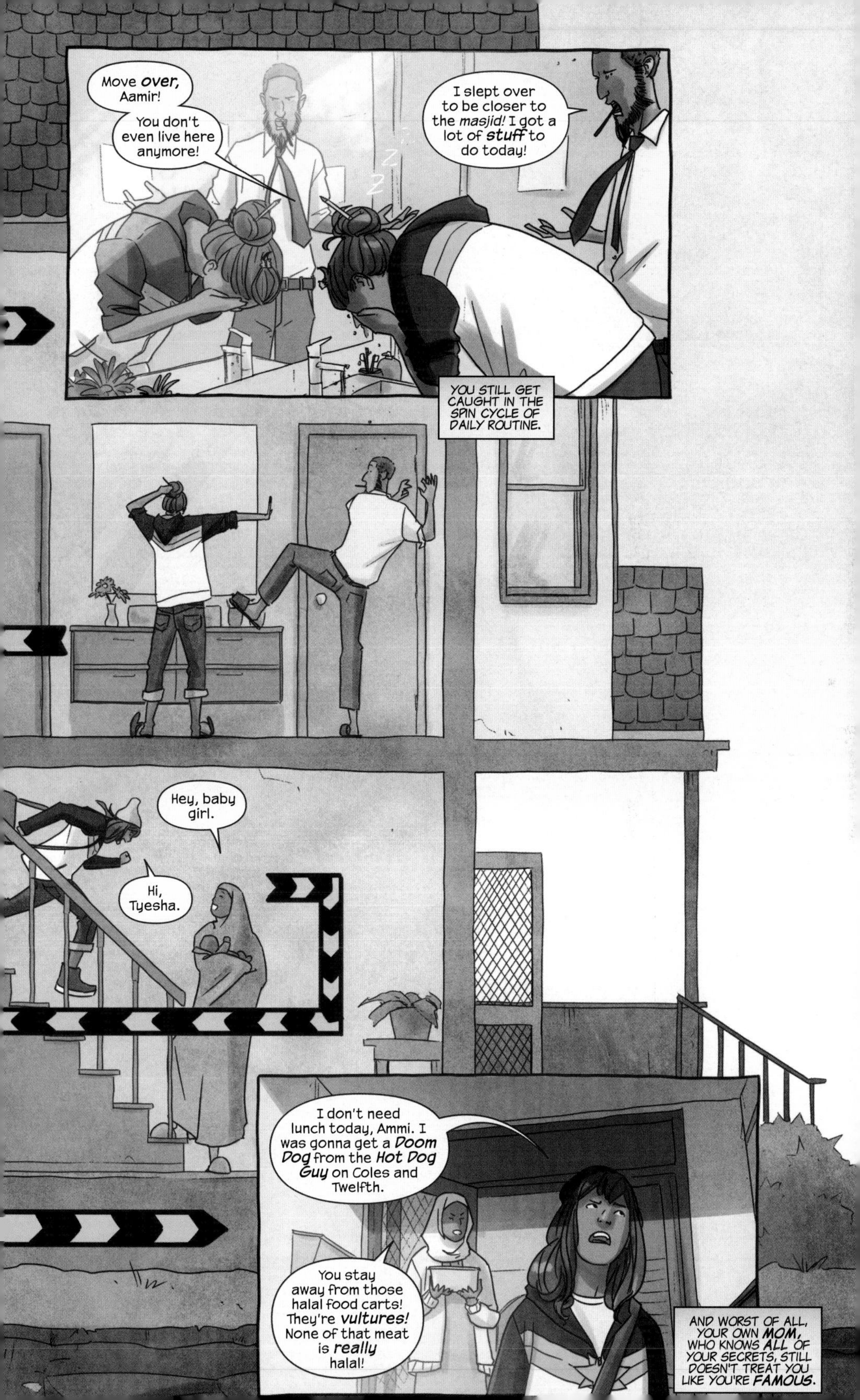

Move over, Aamir!
You don't even live here anymore!
I slept over to be closer to the masjid! I got a lot of stuff to do today!
YOU STILL GET CAUGHT IN THE SPIN CYCLE OF DAILY ROUTINE.
Hey, baby girl.
Hi, Tyesha.
I don't need lunch today, Ammi. I was gonna get a Doom Dog from the Hot Dog Guy on Coles and Twelfth.
You stay away from those halal food carts! They're vultures! None of that meat is really halal!
AND WORST OF ALL, YOUR OWN MOM, WHO KNOWS ALL OF YOUR SECRETS, STILL DOESN'T TREAT YOU LIKE YOU'RE FAMOUS.

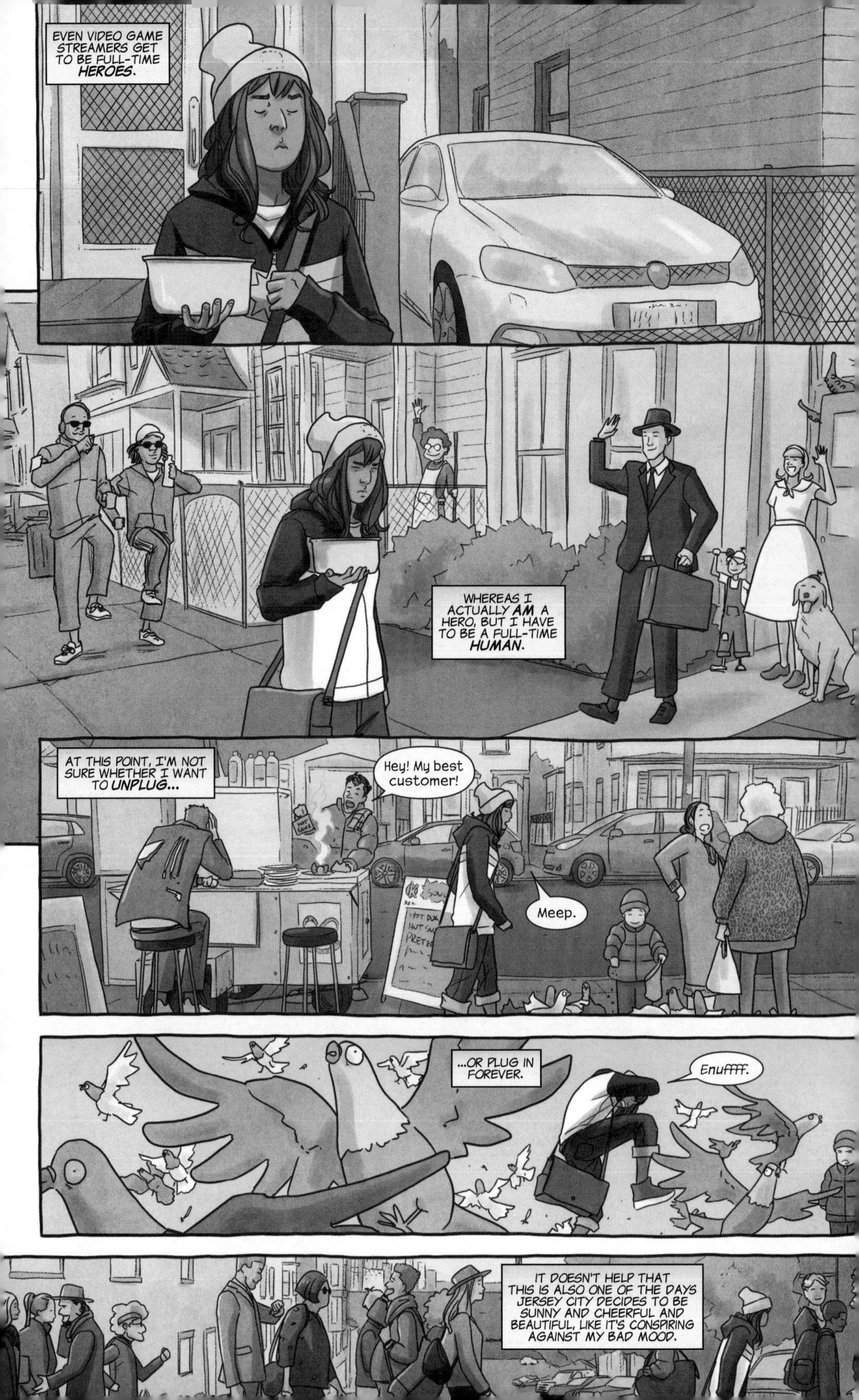
EVEN VIDEO GAME STREAMERS GET TO BE FULL-TIME HEROES.
WHEREAS I ACTUALLY AM A HERO, BUT I HAVE TO BE A FULL-TIME HUMAN.
AT THIS POINT, I'M NOT SURE WHETHER I WANT TO UNPLUG...
Hey! My best customer!
Meep.
...OR PLUG IN FOREVER.
Enufffff.
IT DOESN'T HELP THAT THIS IS ALSO ONE OF THE DAYS JERSEY CITY DECIDES TO BE SUNNY AND CHEERFUL AND BEAUTIFUL, LIKE IT'S CONSPIRING AGAINST MY BAD MOOD.

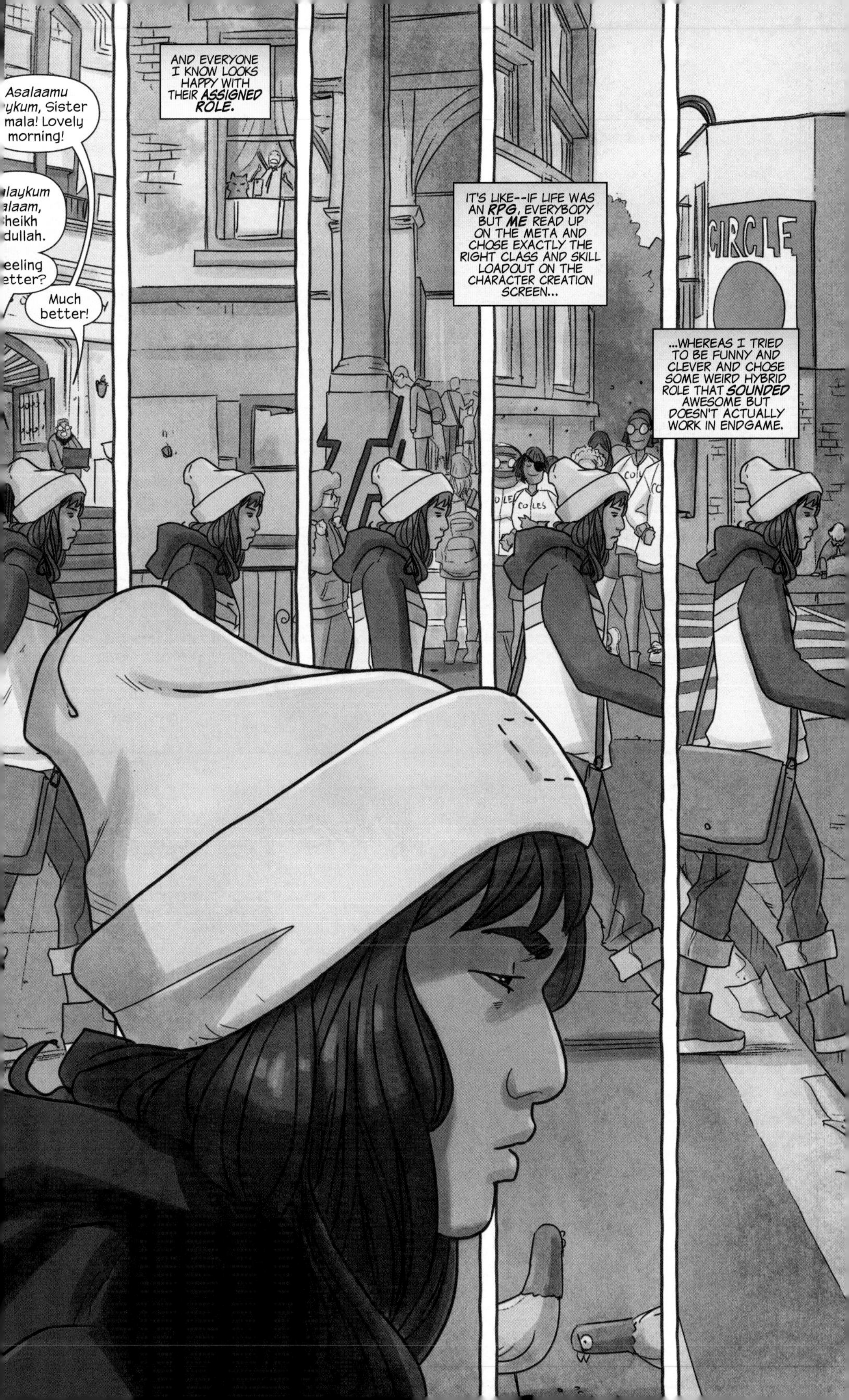
Asalaamu ykum, Sister mala! Lovely morning!
laykum alaam, Sheikh dullah.
eeling etter?
Much better!
AND EVERYONE I KNOW LOOKS HAPPY WITH THEIR ASSIGNED ROLE.
IT'S LIKE--IF LIFE WAS AN RPG, EVERYBODY BUT ME READ UP ON THE META AND CHOSE EXACTLY THE RIGHT CLASS AND SKILL LOADOUT ON THE CHARACTER CREATION SCREEN...
...WHEREAS I TRIED TO BE FUNNY AND CLEVER AND CHOSE SOME WEIRD HYBRID ROLE THAT SOUNDED AWESOME BUT DOESN'T ACTUALLY WORK IN ENDGAME.
CIRCLE

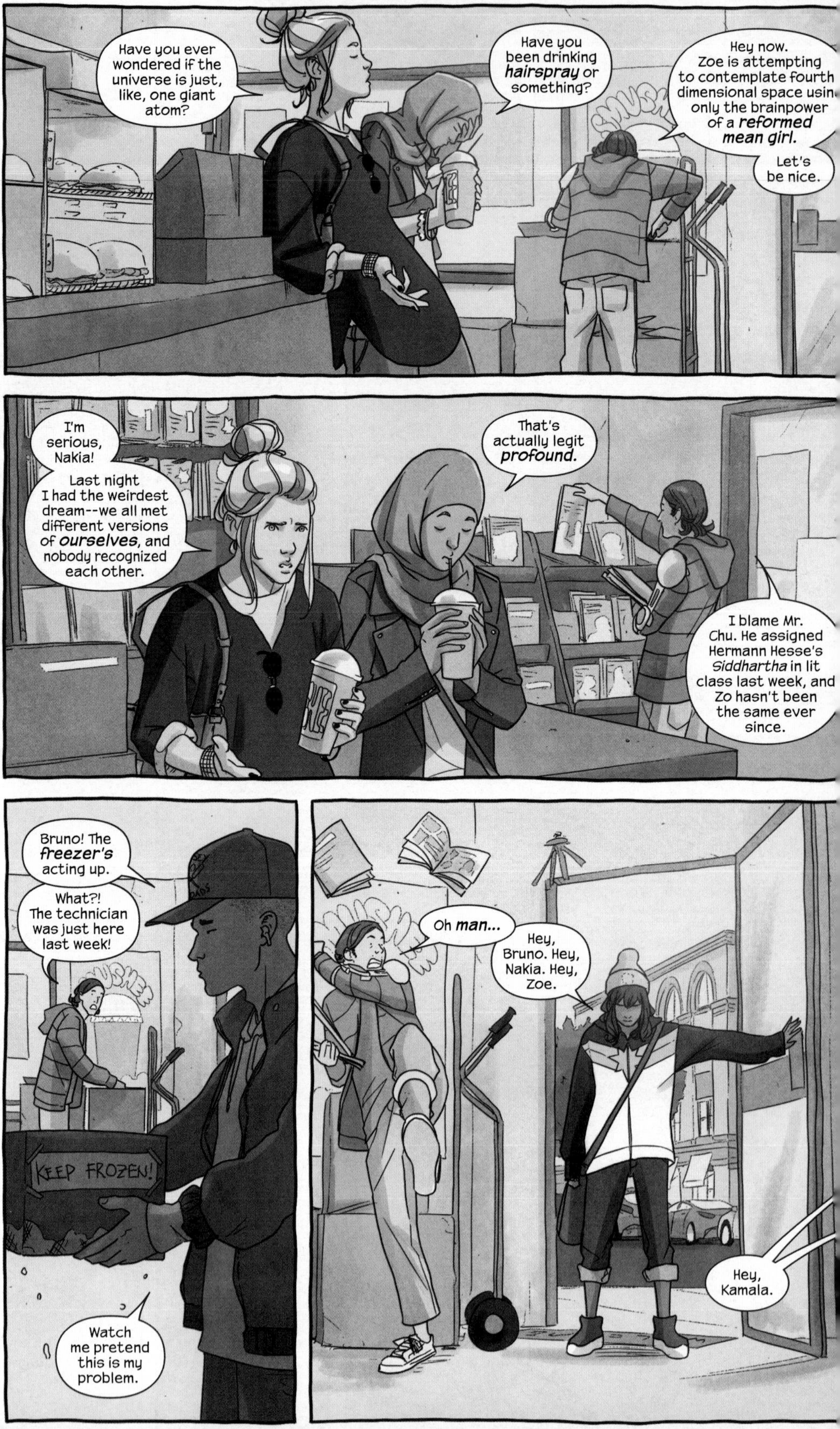
Have you ever wondered if the universe is just, like, one giant atom?
Have you been drinking *hairspray* or something?
Hey now. Zoe is attempting to contemplate fourth dimensional space using only the brainpower of a *reformed mean girl.*
Let's be nice.
I'm serious, Nakia!
Last night I had the weirdest dream--we all met different versions of *ourselves*, and nobody recognized each other.
That's actually legit *profound.*
I blame Mr. Chu. He assigned Hermann Hesse's *Siddhartha* in lit class last week, and Zo hasn't been the same ever since.
Bruno! The *freezer's* acting up.
What?! The technician was just here last week!
KEEP FROZEN!
Watch me pretend this is my problem.
Oh *man...*
Hey, Bruno. Hey, Nakia. Hey, Zoe.
Hey, Kamala.

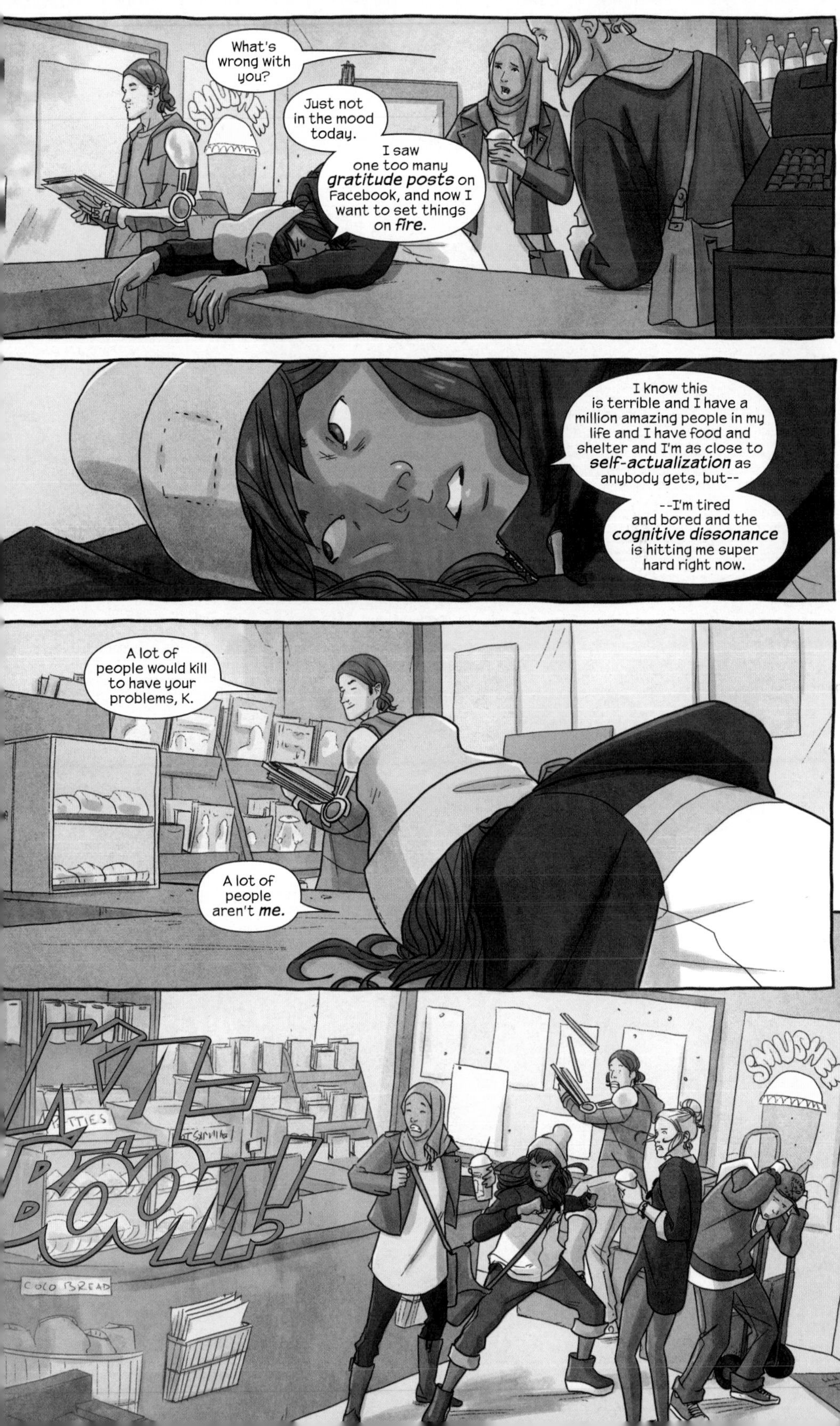
What's wrong with you?
Just not in the mood today.
I saw one too many gratitude posts on Facebook, and now I want to set things on fire.
I know this is terrible and I have a million amazing people in my life and I have food and shelter and I'm as close to self-actualization as anybody gets, but--
--I'm tired and bored and the cognitive dissonance is hitting me super hard right now.
A lot of people would kill to have your problems, K.
A lot of people aren't me.
KA-BOOM!
PATTIES
COCO BREAD
SMUSHEE

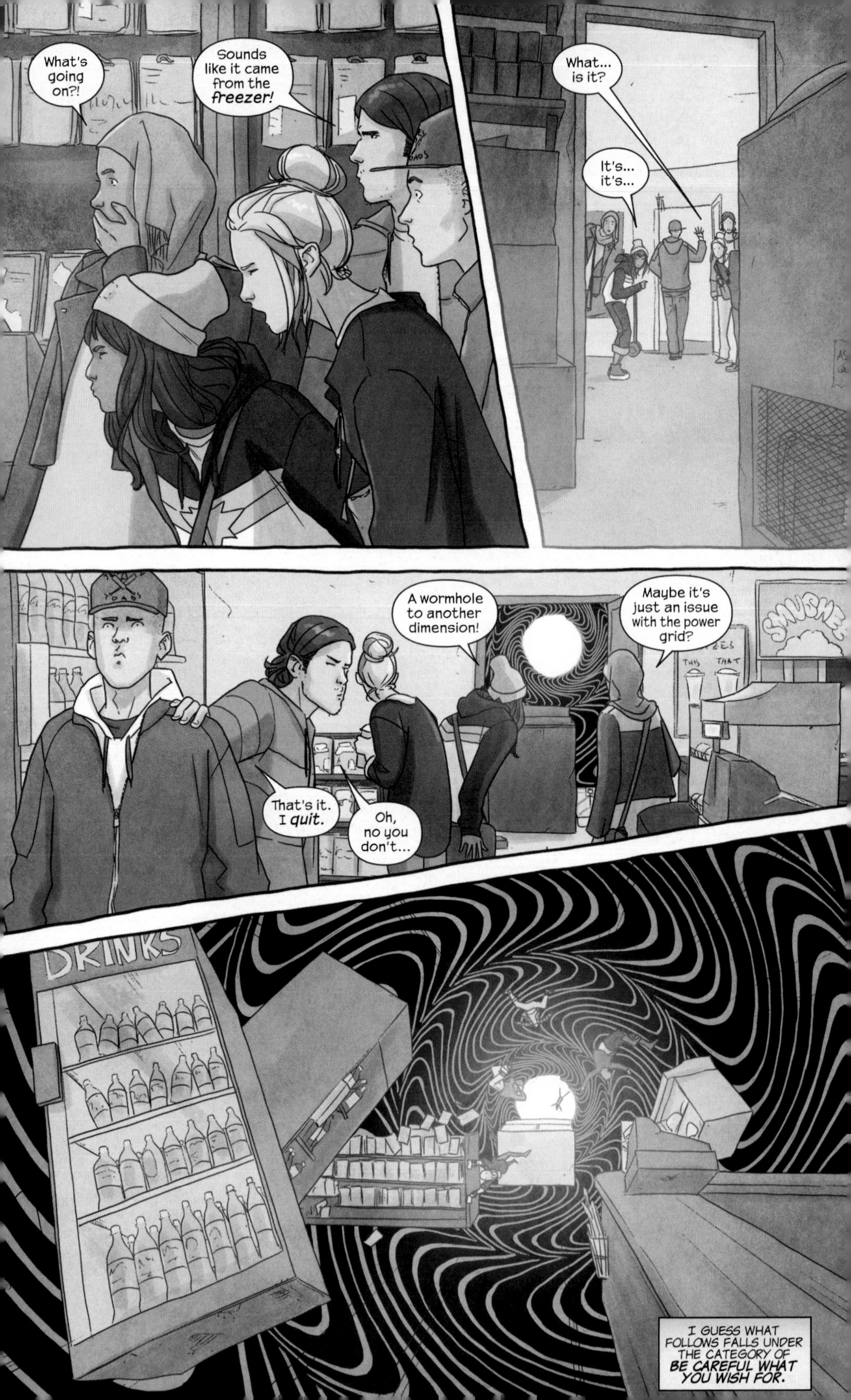
What's going on?!
Sounds like it came from the *freezer*!
What... is it?
It's... it's...
A wormhole to another dimension!
Maybe it's just an issue with the power grid?
That's it. I *quit*.
Oh, no you don't...
DRINKS
I GUESS WHAT FOLLOWS FALLS UNDER THE CATEGORY OF ***BE CAREFUL WHAT YOU WISH FOR.***

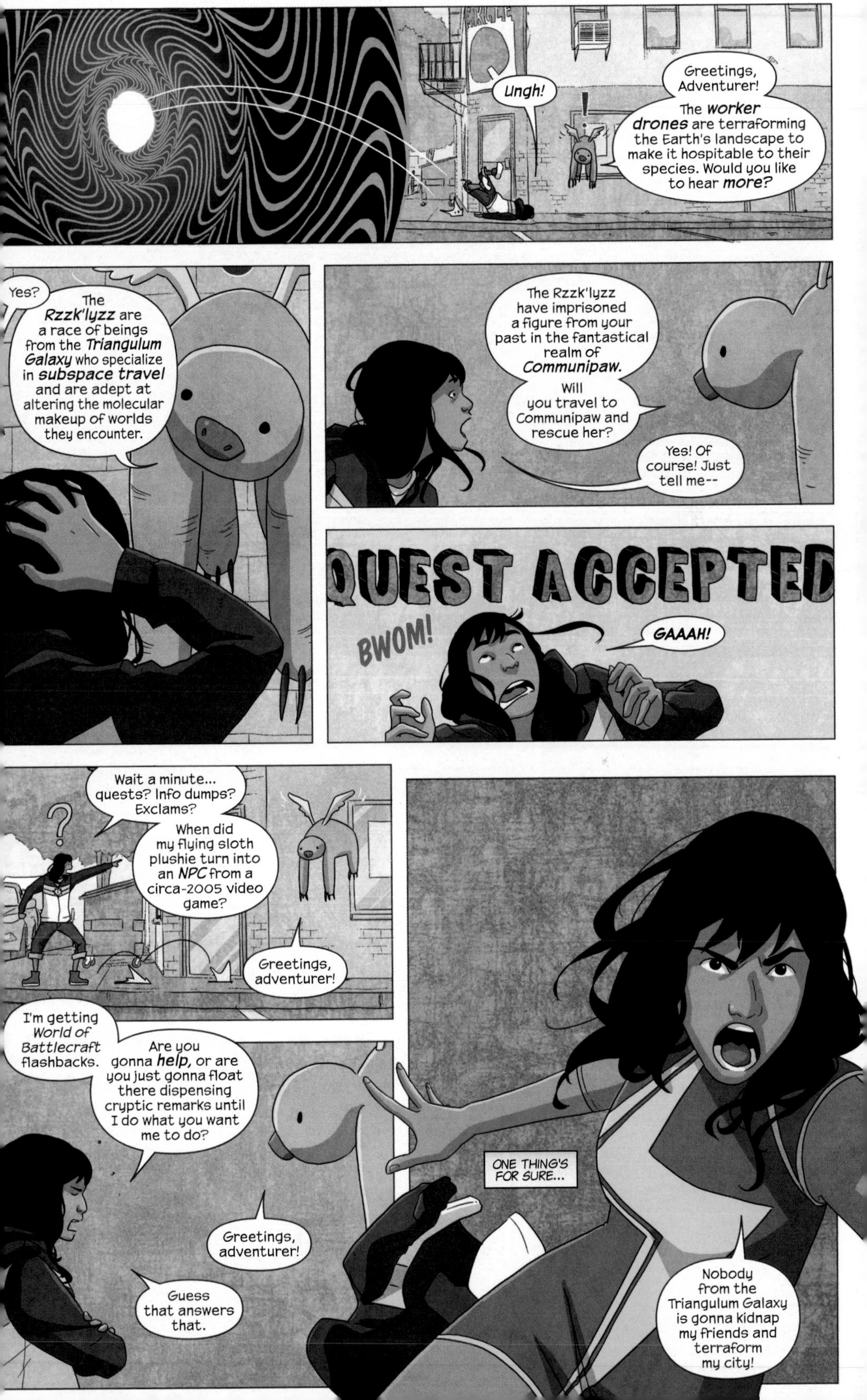
Ungh!
Greetings, Adventurer!
The worker drones are terraforming the Earth's landscape to make it hospitable to their species. Would you like to hear more?
Yes?
The Rzzk'lyzz are a race of beings from the Triangulum Galaxy who specialize in subspace travel and are adept at altering the molecular makeup of worlds they encounter.
The Rzzk'lyzz have imprisoned a figure from your past in the fantastical realm of Communipaw.
Will you travel to Communipaw and rescue her?
Yes! Of course! Just tell me--
QUEST ACCEPTED
BWOM!
GAAAH!
Wait a minute... quests? Info dumps? Exclams?
When did my flying sloth plushie turn into an NPC from a circa-2005 video game?
Greetings, adventurer!
I'm getting World of Battlecraft flashbacks.
Are you gonna help, or are you just gonna float there dispensing cryptic remarks until I do what you want me to do?
Greetings, adventurer!
Guess that answers that.
ONE THING'S FOR SURE...
Nobody from the Triangulum Galaxy is gonna kidnap my friends and terraform my city!

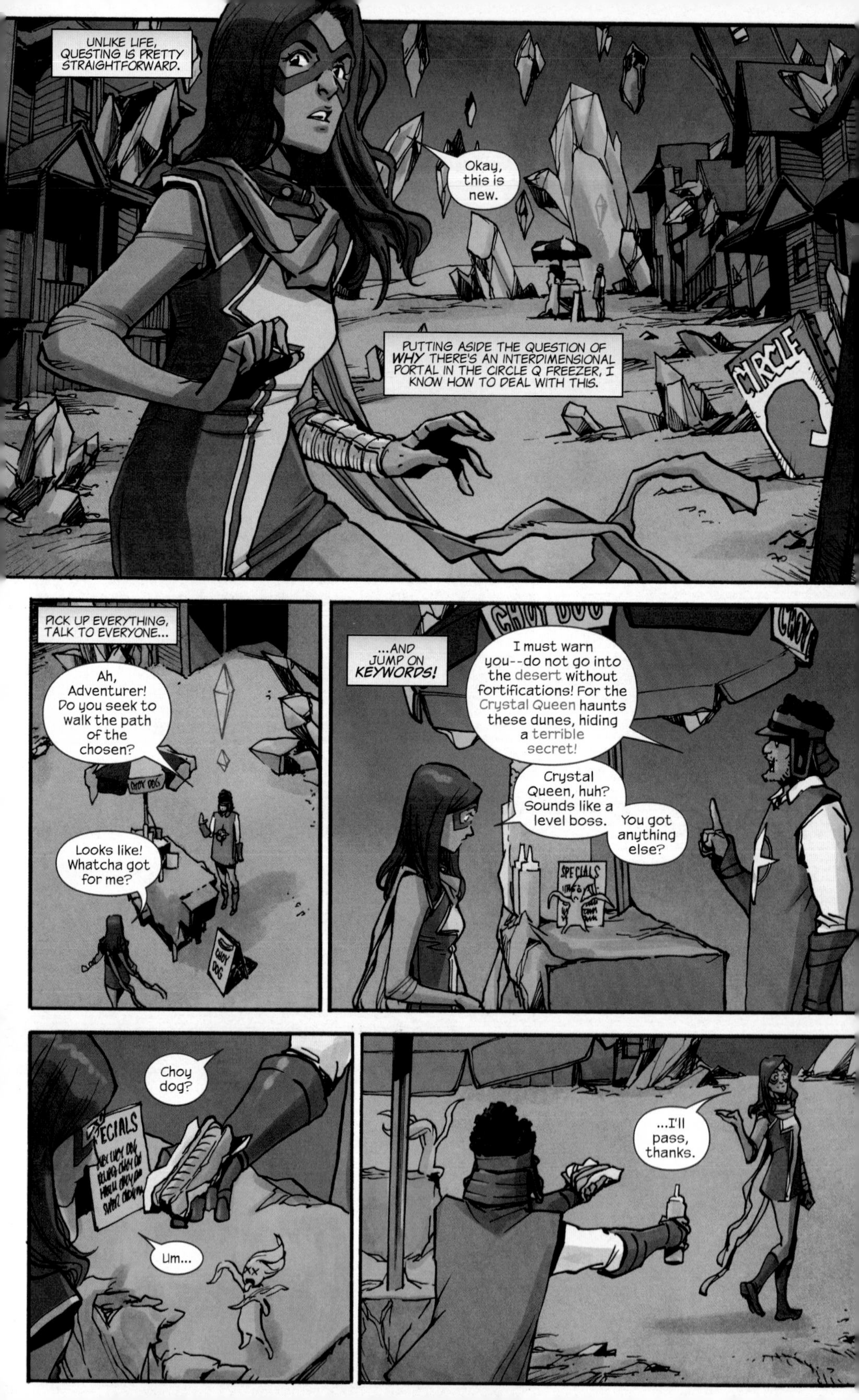
UNLIKE LIFE, QUESTING IS PRETTY STRAIGHTFORWARD.
Okay, this is new.
PUTTING ASIDE THE QUESTION OF *WHY* THERE'S AN INTERDIMENSIONAL PORTAL IN THE CIRCLE Q FREEZER, I KNOW HOW TO DEAL WITH THIS.
CIRCLE
PICK UP EVERYTHING, TALK TO EVERYONE...
Ah, Adventurer! Do you seek to walk the path of the chosen?
Looks like! Whatcha got for me?
CHOY DOG
...AND JUMP ON *KEYWORDS!*
I must warn you--do not go into the desert without fortifications! For the Crystal Queen haunts these dunes, hiding a terrible secret!
Crystal Queen, huh? Sounds like a level boss.
You got anything else?
SPECIALS
Choy dog?
Um...
...I'll pass, thanks.

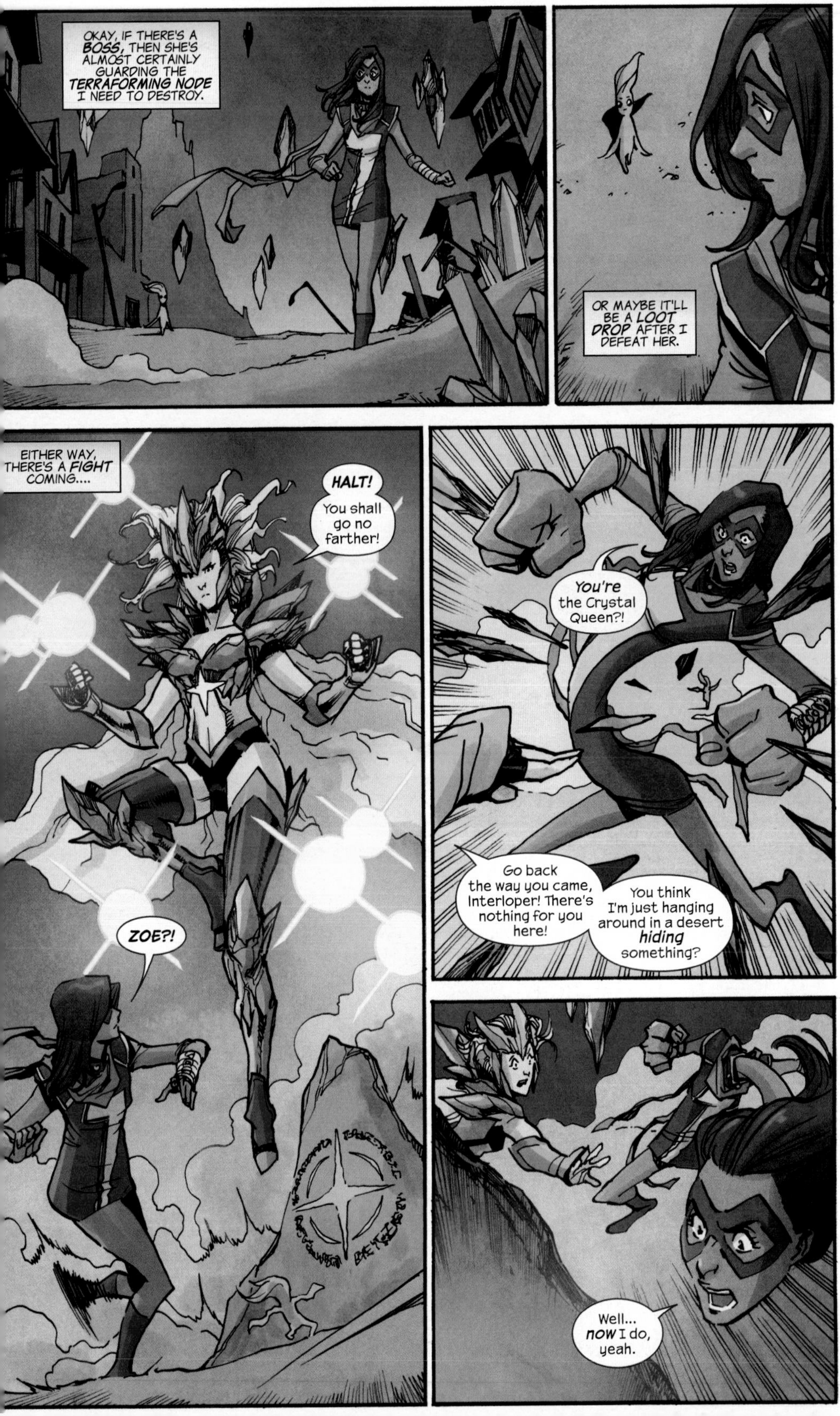
OKAY, IF THERE'S A BOSS, THEN SHE'S ALMOST CERTAINLY GUARDING THE TERRAFORMING NODE I NEED TO DESTROY.
OR MAYBE IT'LL BE A LOOT DROP AFTER I DEFEAT HER.
EITHER WAY, THERE'S A FIGHT COMING....
HALT!
You shall go no farther!
ZOE?!
You're the Crystal Queen?!
Go back the way you came, Interloper! There's nothing for you here!
You think I'm just hanging around in a desert hiding something?
Well... now I do, yeah.

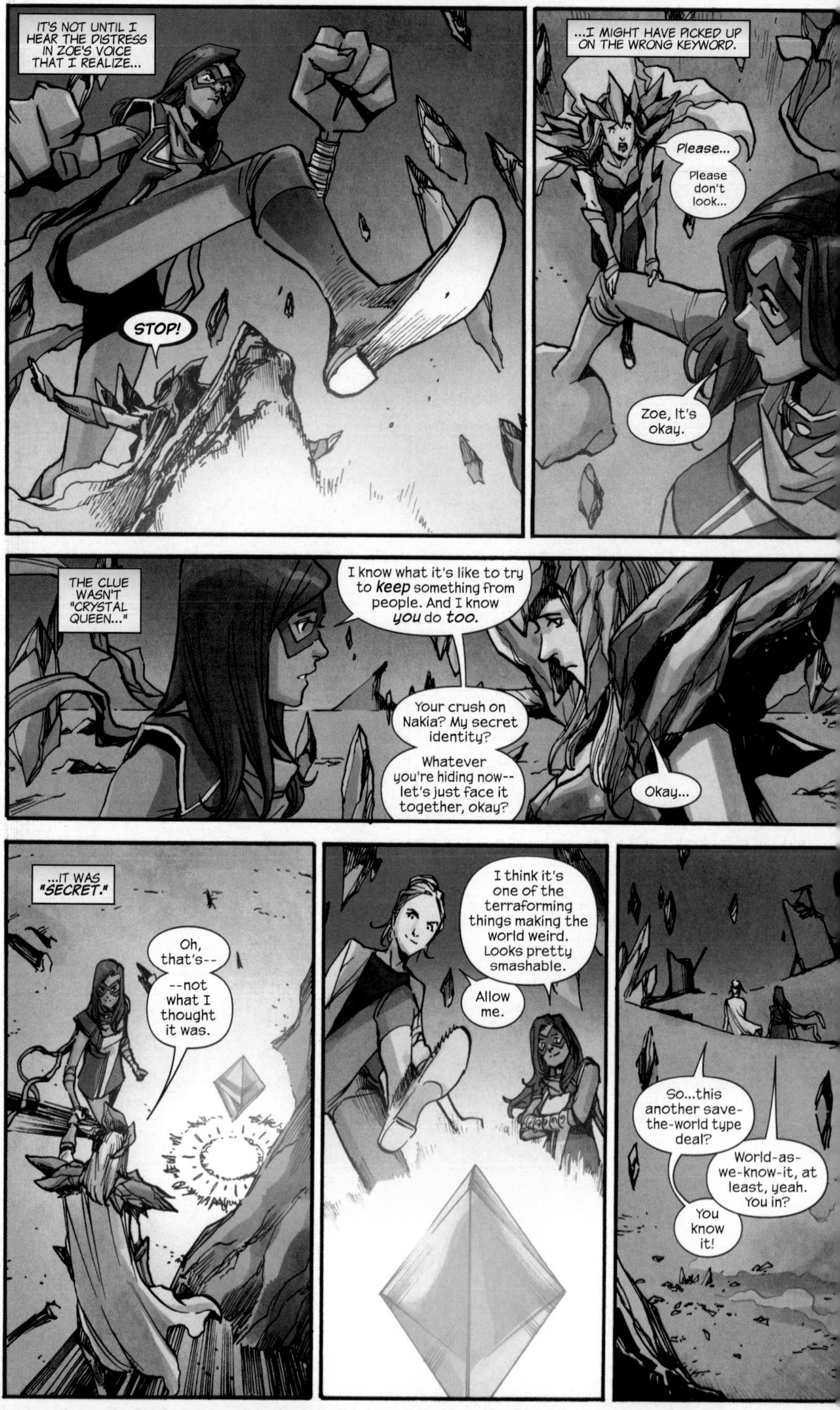
IT'S NOT UNTIL I HEAR THE DISTRESS IN ZOE'S VOICE THAT I REALIZE...
STOP!
...I MIGHT HAVE PICKED UP ON THE WRONG KEYWORD.
Please...
Please don't look...
Zoe, It's okay.
THE CLUE WASN'T "CRYSTAL QUEEN..."
I know what it's like to try to keep something from people. And I know you do too.
Your crush on Nakia? My secret identity?
Whatever you're hiding now--let's just face it together, okay?
Okay...
...IT WAS "SECRET."
Oh, that's--
--not what I thought it was.
I think it's one of the terraforming things making the world weird. Looks pretty smashable.
Allow me.
So...this another save-the-world type deal?
World-as-we-know-it, at least, yeah. You in?
You know it!

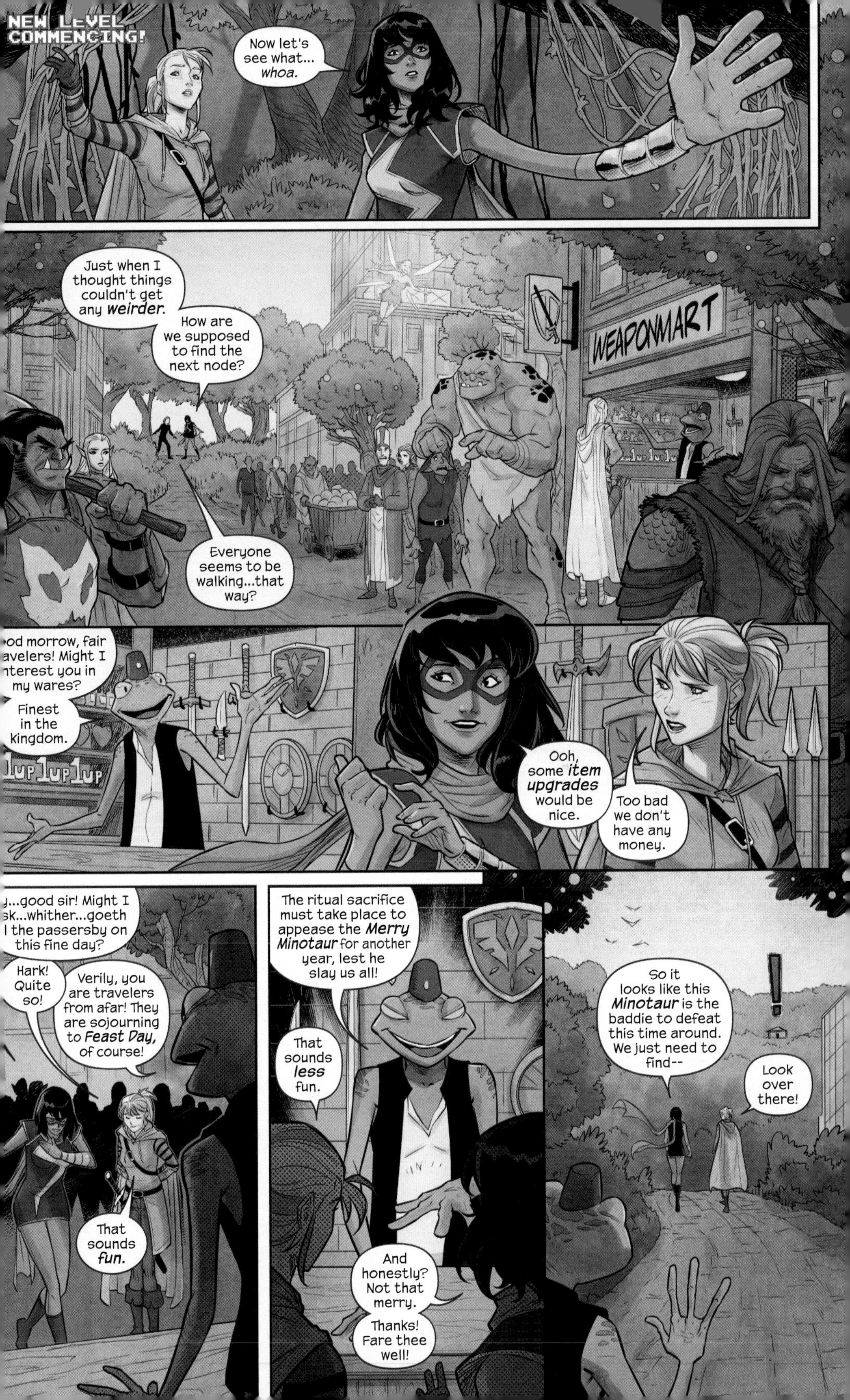
NEW LEVEL COMMENCING!
Now let's see what... whoa.
Just when I thought things couldn't get any weirder.
How are we supposed to find the next node?
Everyone seems to be walking...that way?
WEAPONMART
ood morrow, fair avelers! Might I nterest you in my wares?
Finest in the kingdom.
1UP 1UP 1UP
Ooh, some item upgrades would be nice.
Too bad we don't have any money.
y...good sir! Might I sk...whither...goeth l the passersby on this fine day?
Hark! Quite so!
Verily, you are travelers from afar! They are sojourning to Feast Day, of course!
That sounds fun.
The ritual sacrifice must take place to appease the Merry Minotaur for another year, lest he slay us all!
That sounds less fun.
And honestly? Not that merry.
Thanks! Fare thee well!
So it looks like this Minotaur is the baddie to defeat this time around. We just need to find--
Look over there!

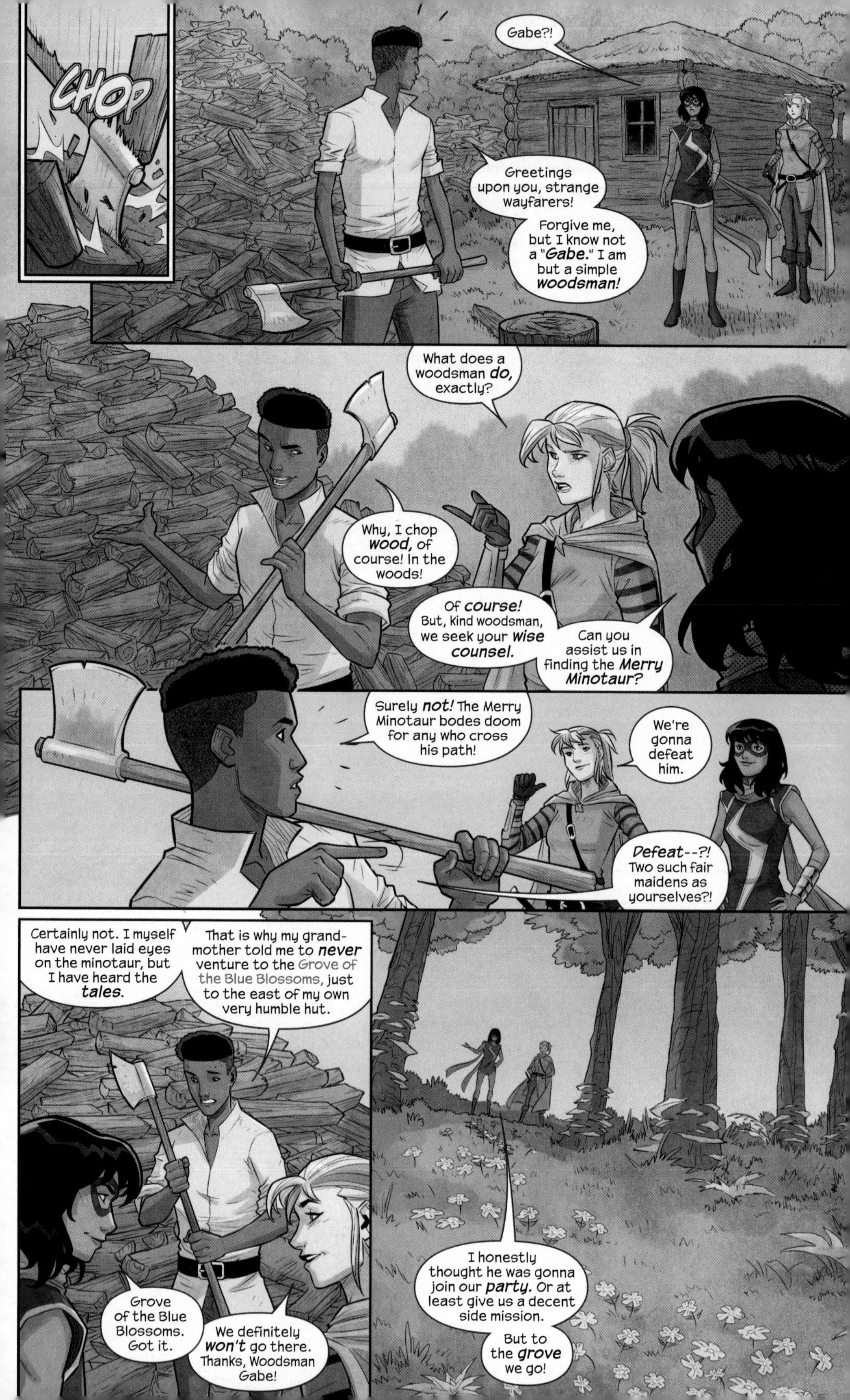
CHOP
Gabe?!
Greetings upon you, strange wayfarers!
Forgive me, but I know not a "Gabe." I am but a simple woodsman!
What does a woodsman do, exactly?
Why, I chop wood, of course! In the woods!
Of course! But, kind woodsman, we seek your wise counsel.
Can you assist us in finding the Merry Minotaur?
Surely not! The Merry Minotaur bodes doom for any who cross his path!
We're gonna defeat him.
Defeat--?! Two such fair maidens as yourselves?!
Certainly not. I myself have never laid eyes on the minotaur, but I have heard the tales.
That is why my grand-mother told me to never venture to the Grove of the Blue Blossoms, just to the east of my own very humble hut.
Grove of the Blue Blossoms. Got it.
We definitely won't go there. Thanks, Woodsman Gabe!
I honestly thought he was gonna join our party. Or at least give us a decent side mission.
But to the grove we go!

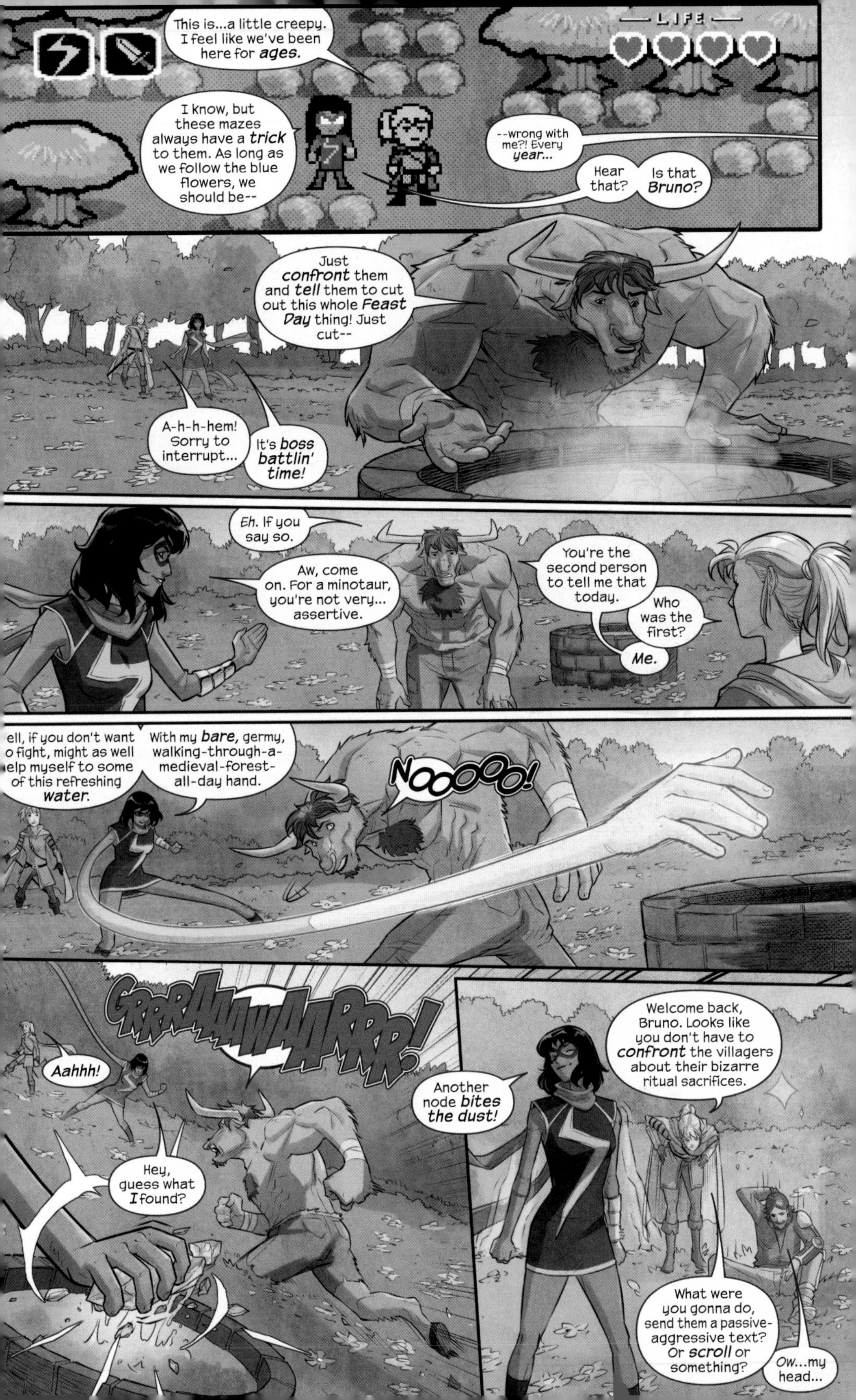

LIFE
This is...a little creepy. I feel like we've been here for ages.
I know, but these mazes always have a trick to them. As long as we follow the blue flowers, we should be--
--wrong with me?! Every year...
Hear that?
Is that Bruno?
Just confront them and tell them to cut out this whole Feast Day thing! Just cut--
A-h-h-hem! Sorry to interrupt...
It's boss battlin' time!
Eh. If you say so.
Aw, come on. For a minotaur, you're not very... assertive.
You're the second person to tell me that today.
Who was the first?
Me.
ell, if you don't want o fight, might as well elp myself to some of this refreshing water.
With my bare, germy, walking-through-a-medieval-forest-all-day hand.
NOOOOOO!
GRRRAAAWAARRRR!
Aahhh!
Hey, guess what I found?
Another node bites the dust!
Welcome back, Bruno. Looks like you don't have to confront the villagers about their bizarre ritual sacrifices.
What were you gonna do, send them a passive-aggressive text? Or scroll or something?
Ow...my head...

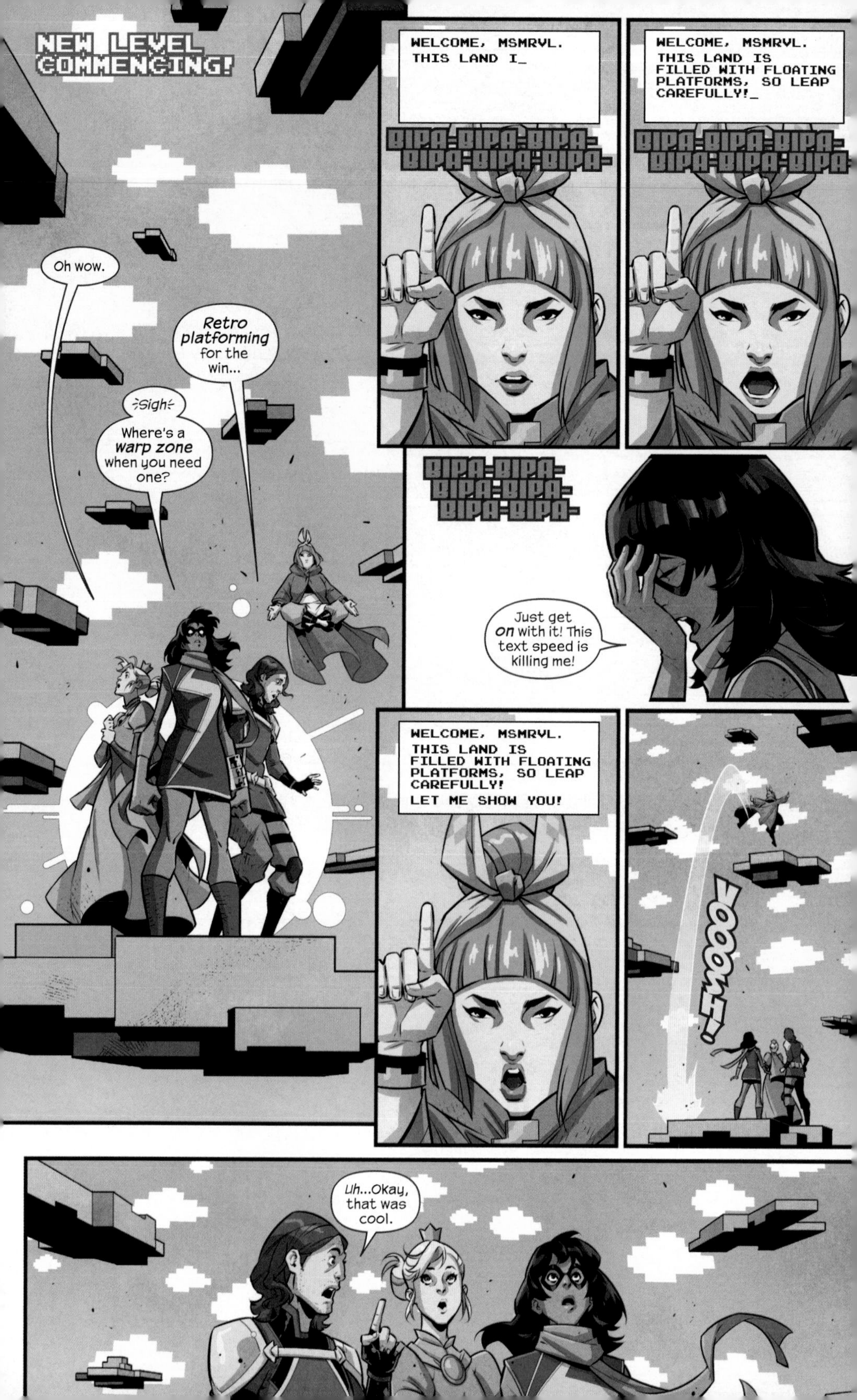
NEW LEVEL COMMENCING!
Oh wow.
Retro platforming for the win...
~Sigh~
Where's a warp zone when you need one?
WELCOME, MSMRVL.
THIS LAND I_
BIPA-BIPA-BIPA-BIPA-BIPA-BIPA-
WELCOME, MSMRVL.
THIS LAND IS FILLED WITH FLOATING PLATFORMS, SO LEAP CAREFULLY!_
BIPA-BIPA-BIPA-BIPA-BIPA-BIPA
BIPA-BIPA-BIPA-BIPA-BIPA-BIPA-
Just get on with it! This text speed is killing me!
WELCOME, MSMRVL.
THIS LAND IS FILLED WITH FLOATING PLATFORMS, SO LEAP CAREFULLY!
LET ME SHOW YOU!
VOOOOSH!
Uh...Okay, that was cool.

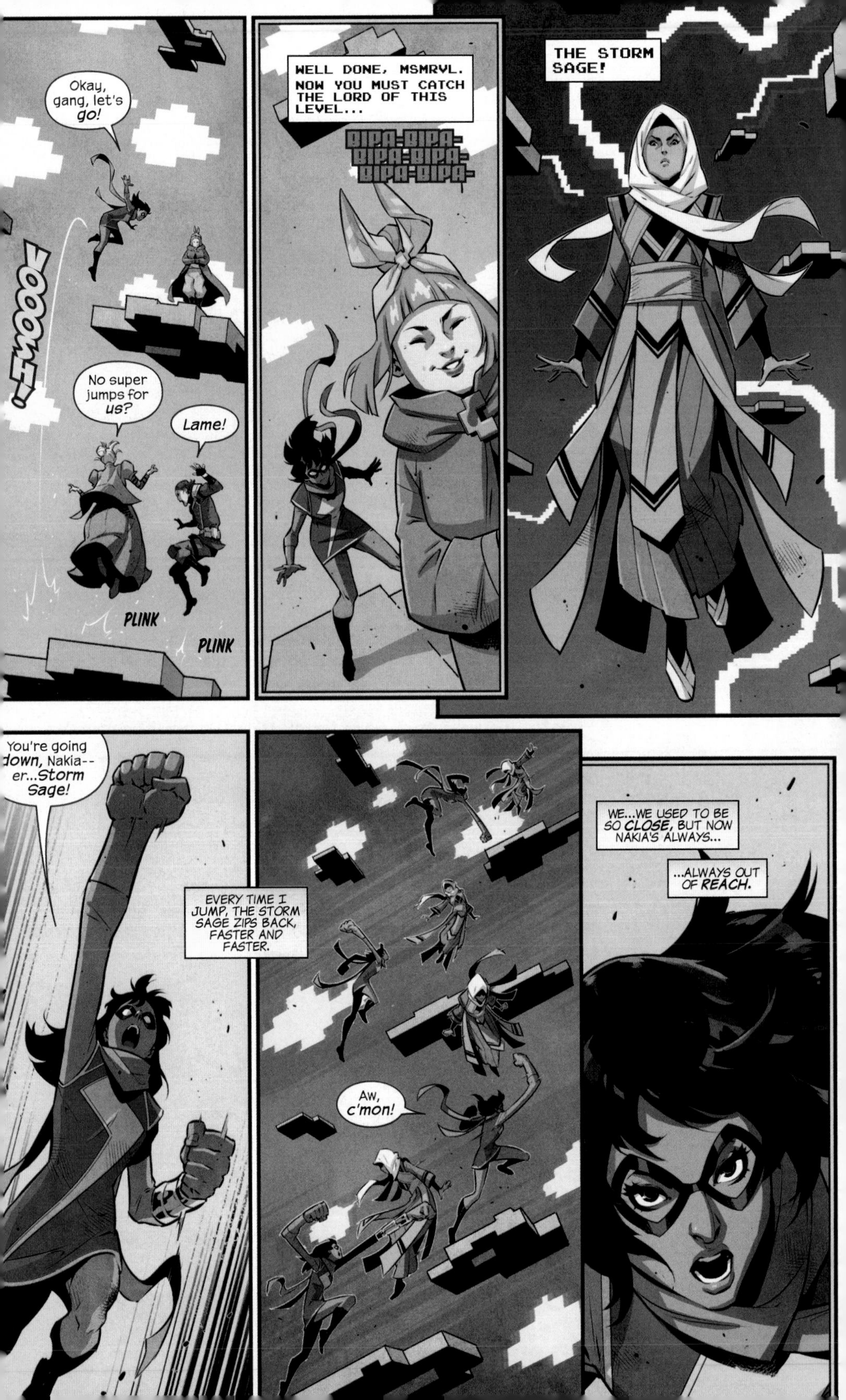
Okay, gang, let's go!
VOOOOM!
No super jumps for us?
Lame!
PLINK
PLINK
WELL DONE, MSMRVL. NOW YOU MUST CATCH THE LORD OF THIS LEVEL...
BIPA-BIPA-BIPA-BIPA-BIPA-BIPA-
THE STORM SAGE!
You're going down, Nakia-- er...Storm Sage!
EVERY TIME I JUMP, THE STORM SAGE ZIPS BACK, FASTER AND FASTER.
Aw, c'mon!
WE...WE USED TO BE SO CLOSE, BUT NOW NAKIA'S ALWAYS...
...ALWAYS OUT OF REACH.

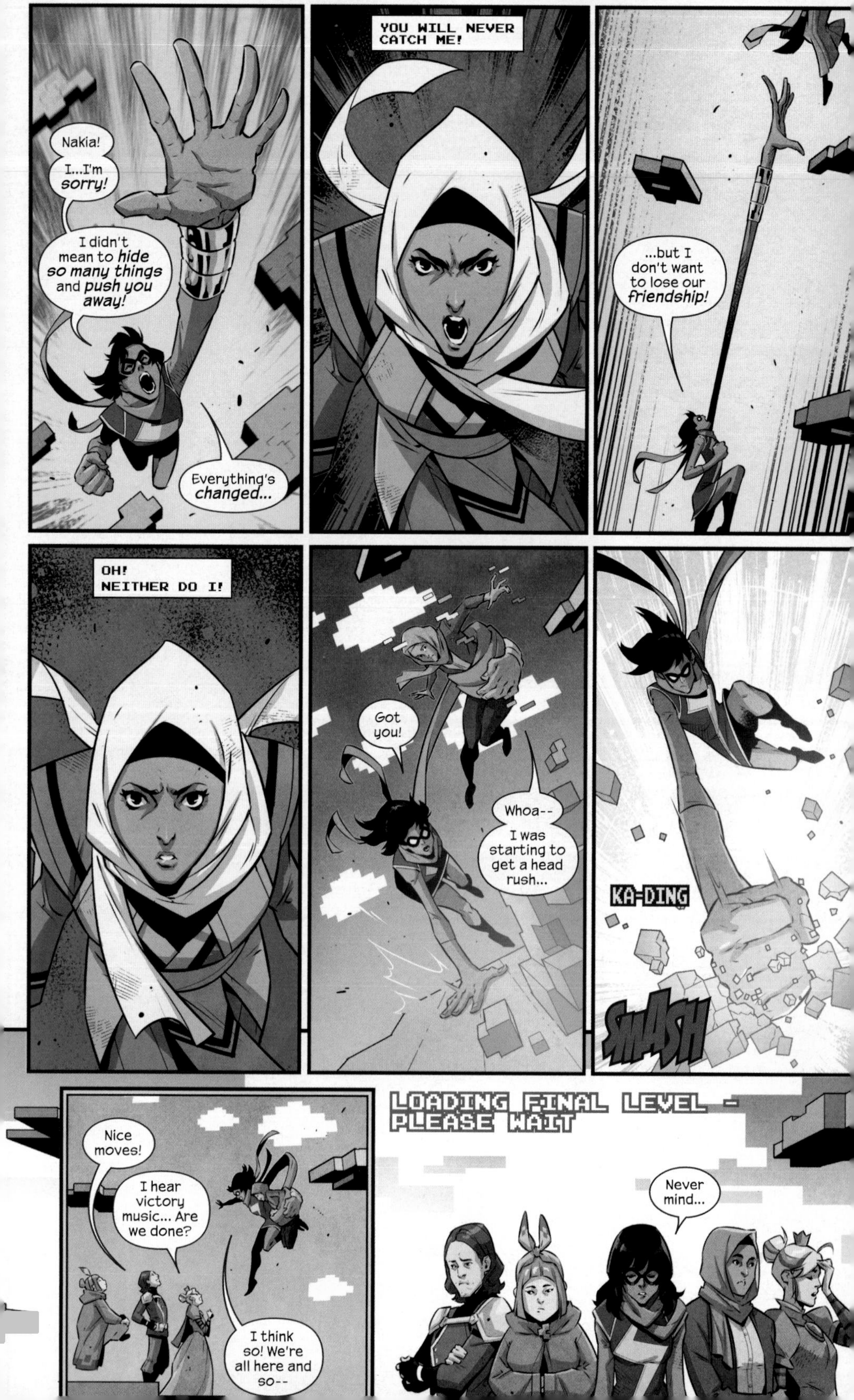
Nakia!
I...I'm sorry!
I didn't mean to hide so many things and push you away!
Everything's changed...
YOU WILL NEVER CATCH ME!
...but I don't want to lose our friendship!
OH! NEITHER DO I!
Got you!
Whoa--
I was starting to get a head rush...
KA-DING
SMASH
Nice moves!
I hear victory music... Are we done?
I think so! We're all here and so--
LOADING FINAL LEVEL - PLEASE WAIT
Never mind...

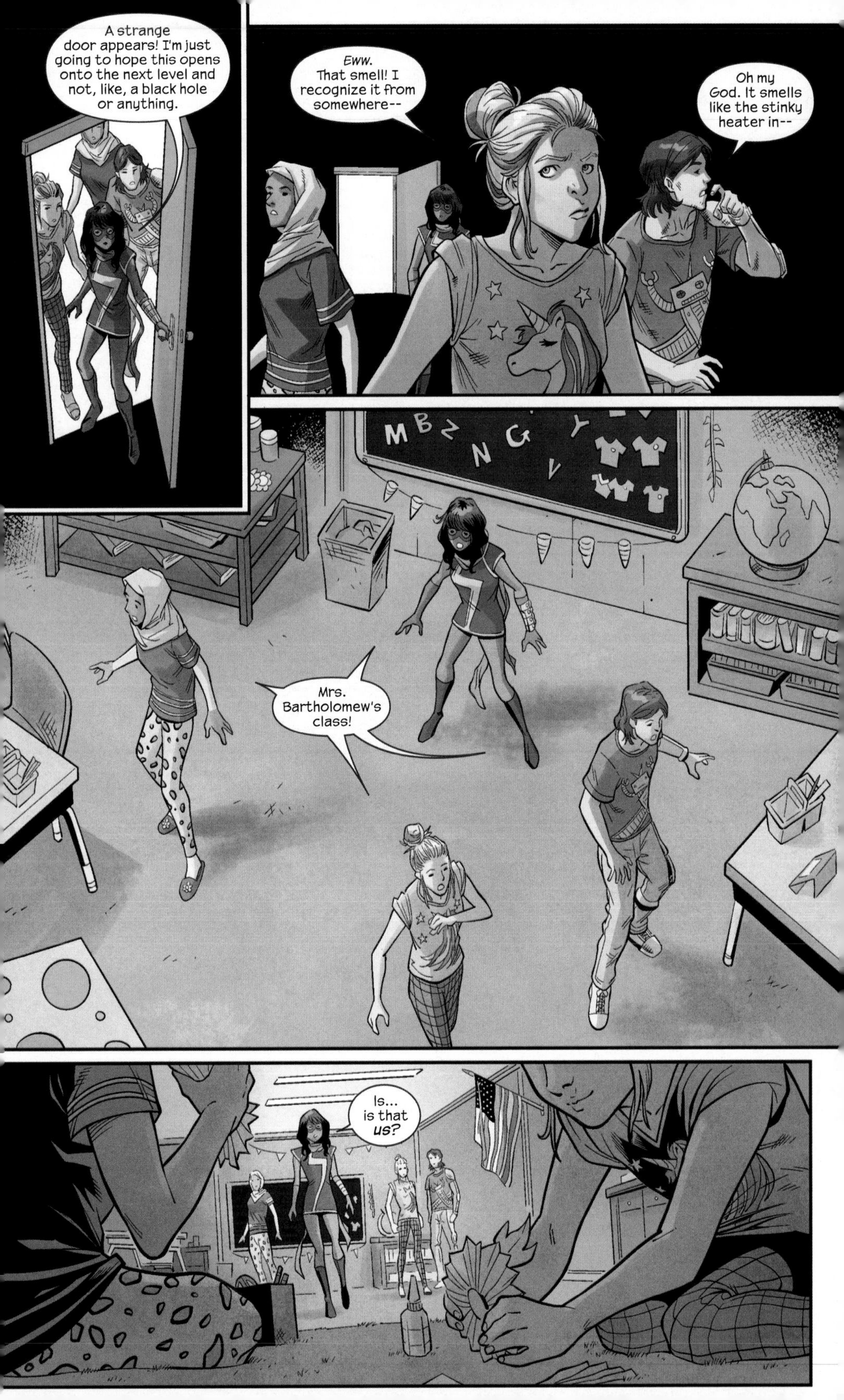
A strange door appears! I'm just going to hope this opens onto the next level and not, like, a black hole or anything.
Eww. That smell! I recognize it from somewhere--
Oh my God. It smells like the stinky heater in--
Mrs. Bartholomew's class!
Is... is that us?

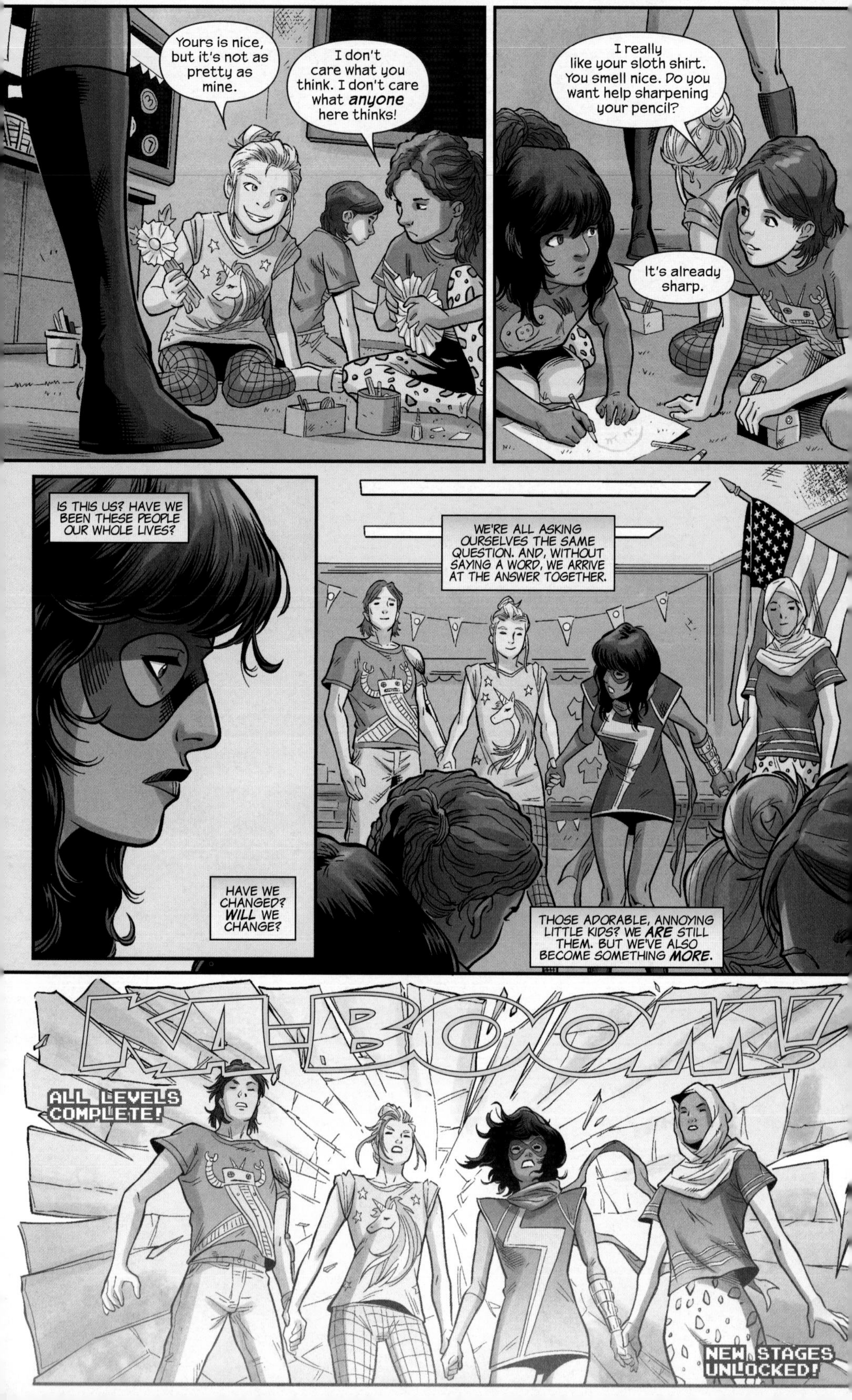
Yours is nice, but it's not as pretty as mine.
I don't care what you think. I don't care what **anyone** here thinks!
I really like your sloth shirt. You smell nice. Do you want help sharpening your pencil?
It's already sharp.
IS THIS US? HAVE WE BEEN THESE PEOPLE OUR WHOLE LIVES?
HAVE WE CHANGED? **WILL** WE CHANGE?
WE'RE ALL ASKING OURSELVES THE SAME QUESTION. AND, WITHOUT SAYING A WORD, WE ARRIVE AT THE ANSWER TOGETHER.
THOSE ADORABLE, ANNOYING LITTLE KIDS? WE **ARE** STILL THEM. BUT WE'VE ALSO BECOME SOMETHING **MORE**.
KA-BOOM!
ALL LEVELS COMPLETE!
NEW STAGES UNLOCKED!

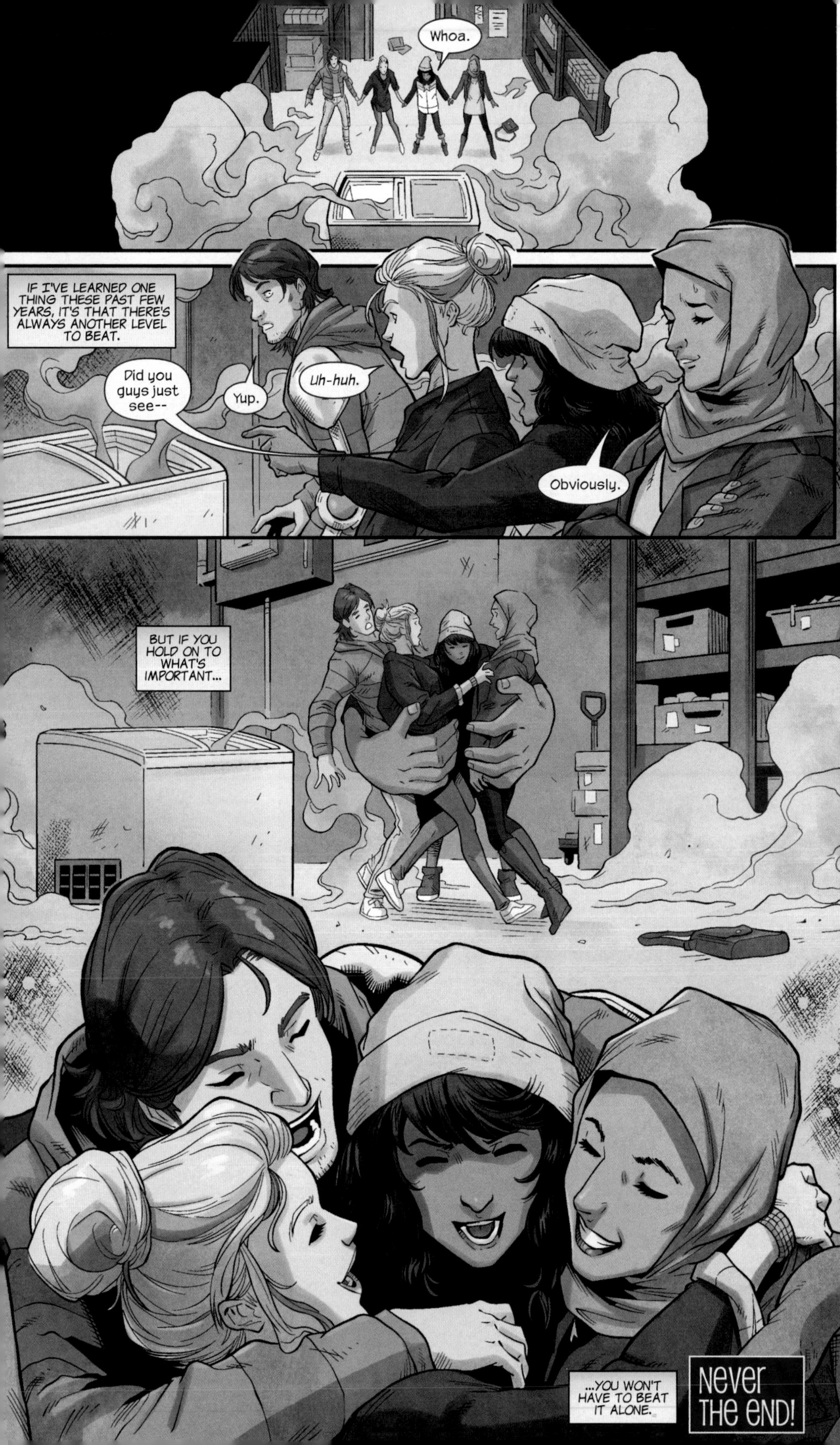
Whoa.
IF I'VE LEARNED ONE THING THESE PAST FEW YEARS, IT'S THAT THERE'S ALWAYS ANOTHER LEVEL TO BEAT.
Did you guys just see--
Yup.
Uh-huh.
Obviously.
BUT IF YOU HOLD ON TO WHAT'S IMPORTANT...
...YOU WON'T HAVE TO BEAT IT ALONE.
Never THE END!

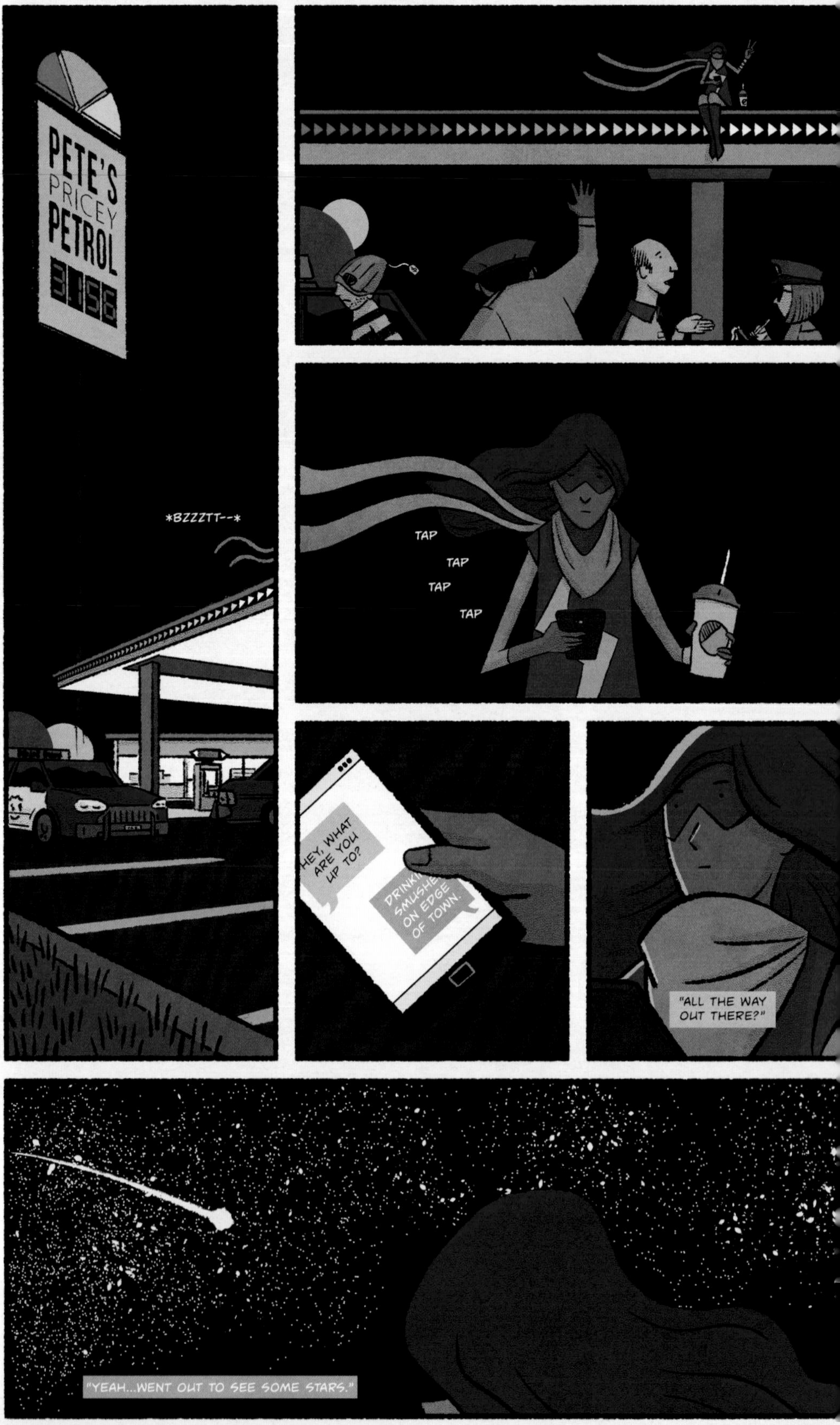
PETE'S
PRICEY
PETROL
3.156
BZZZTT--
TAP
TAP
TAP
TAP
HEY, WHAT ARE YOU UP TO?
DRINKI SMUSHE ON EDGE OF TOWN.
"ALL THE WAY OUT THERE?"
"YEAH...WENT OUT TO SEE SOME STARS."

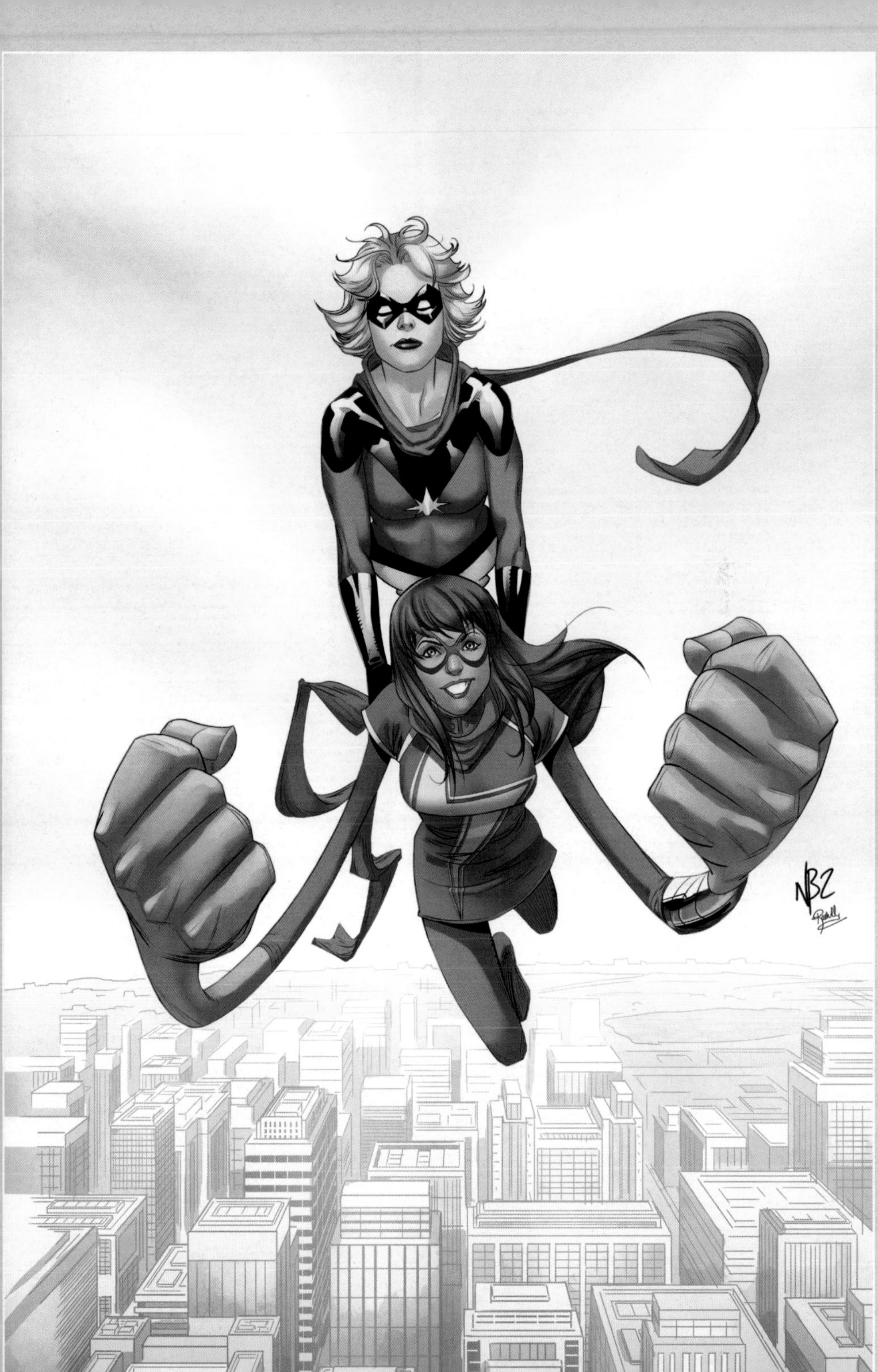
NBZ

GENERATIONS: MS. MARVEL & MS. MARVEL #1

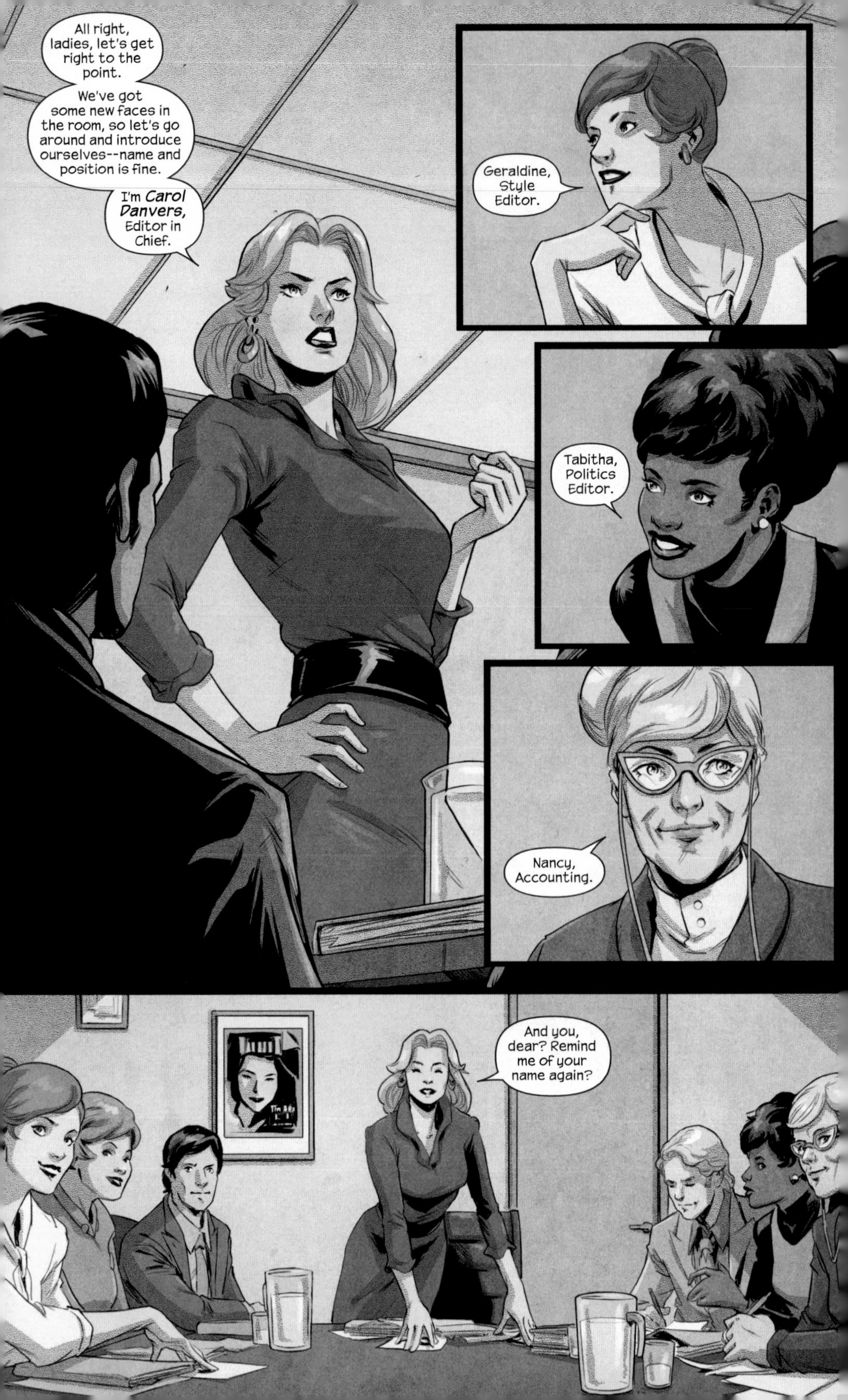

All right, ladies, let's get right to the point.
We've got some new faces in the room, so let's go around and introduce ourselves--name and position is fine.
I'm *Carol Danvers,* Editor in Chief.
Geraldine, Style Editor.
Tabitha, Politics Editor.
Nancy, Accounting.
And you, dear? Remind me of your name again?

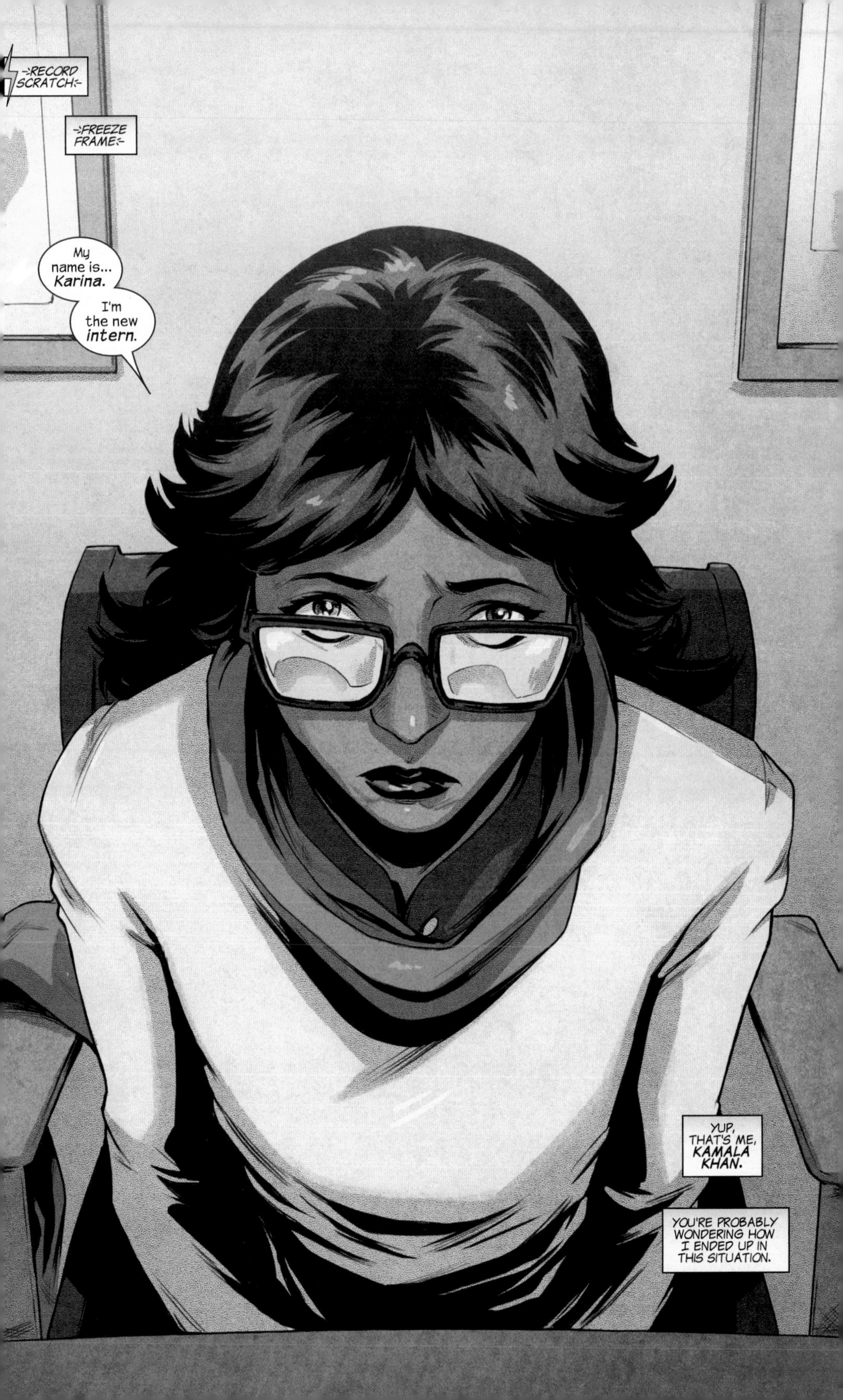

-RECORD SCRATCH-
-FREEZE FRAME-
My name is... Karina.
I'm the new intern.
YUP, THAT'S ME, KAMALA KHAN.
YOU'RE PROBABLY WONDERING HOW I ENDED UP IN THIS SITUATION.

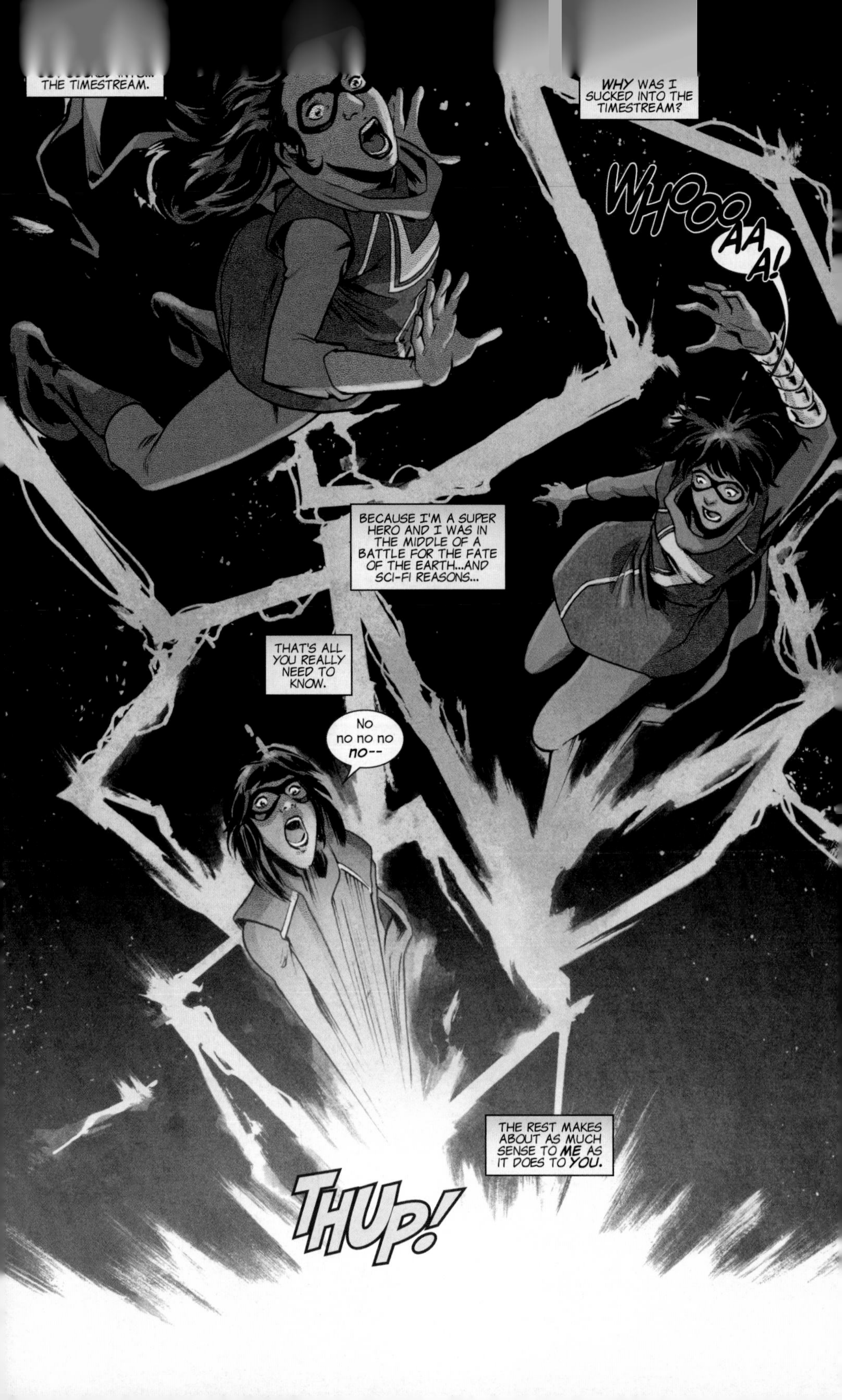
THE TIMESTREAM.
WHY WAS I SUCKED INTO THE TIMESTREAM?
WHOOOAAAA!
BECAUSE I'M A SUPER HERO AND I WAS IN THE MIDDLE OF A BATTLE FOR THE FATE OF THE EARTH...AND SCI-FI REASONS...
THAT'S ALL YOU REALLY NEED TO KNOW.
No no no no no--
THE REST MAKES ABOUT AS MUCH SENSE TO ME AS IT DOES TO YOU.
THUP!

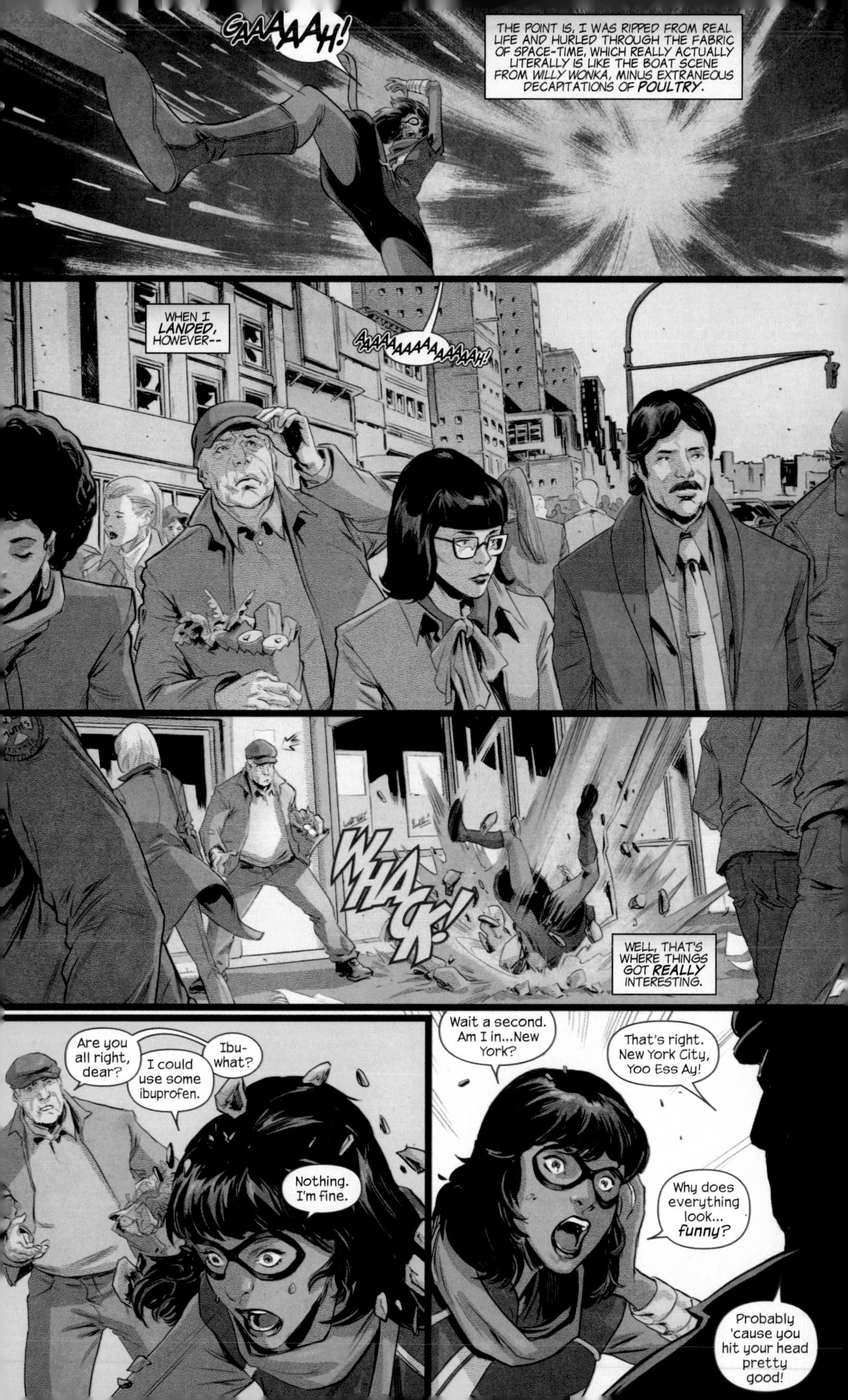
GAAAAAH!
THE POINT IS, I WAS RIPPED FROM REAL LIFE AND HURLED THROUGH THE FABRIC OF SPACE-TIME, WHICH REALLY ACTUALLY LITERALLY IS LIKE THE BOAT SCENE FROM WILLY WONKA, MINUS EXTRANEOUS DECAPITATIONS OF POULTRY.
WHEN I LANDED, HOWEVER--
AAAAAAAAAAAAAH!
WHACK!
WELL, THAT'S WHERE THINGS GOT REALLY INTERESTING.
Are you all right, dear?
I could use some ibuprofen.
Ibu-what?
Nothing. I'm fine.
Wait a second. Am I in...New York?
That's right. New York City, Yoo Ess Ay!
Why does everything look... funny?
Probably 'cause you hit your head pretty good!

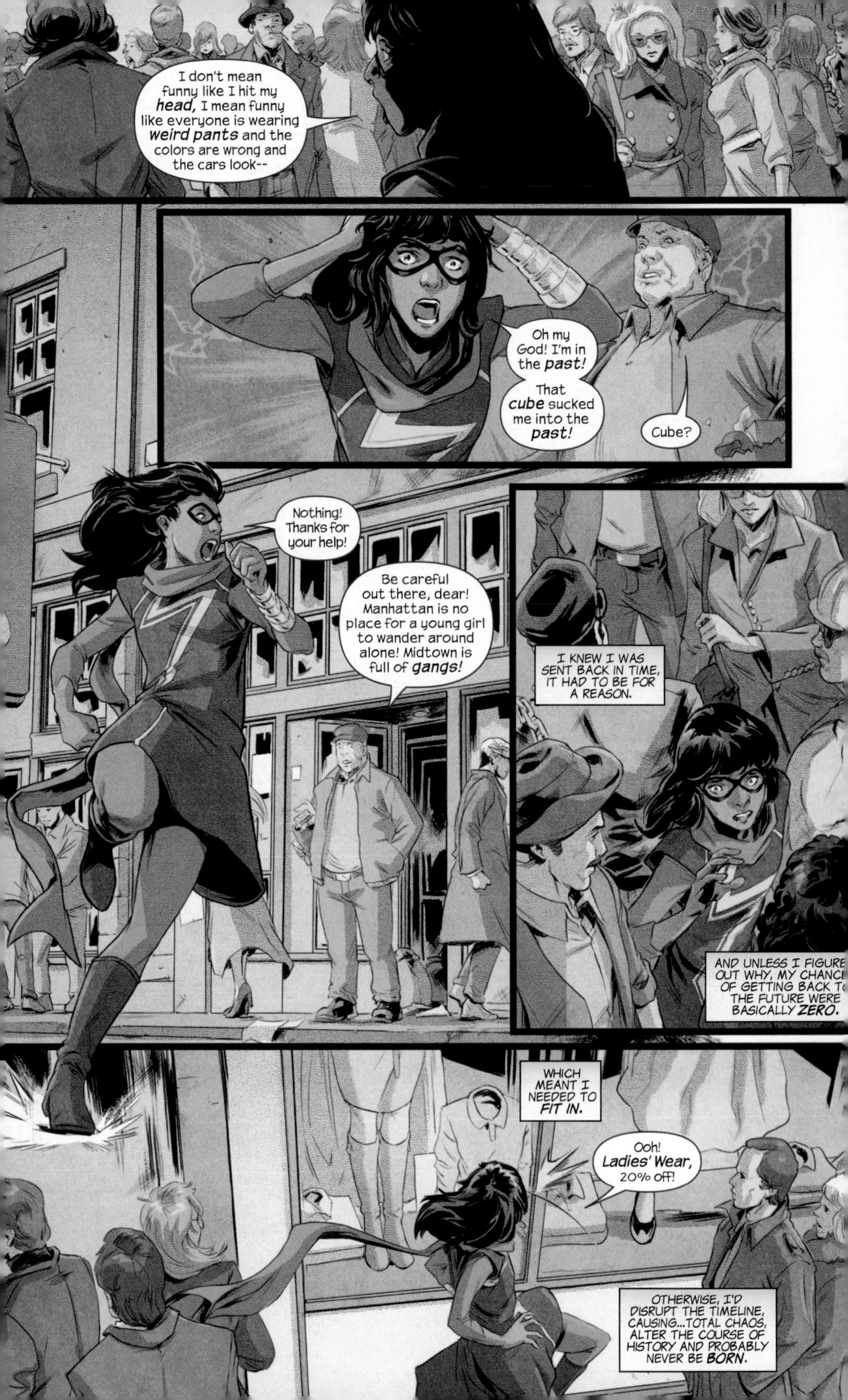
I don't mean funny like I hit my head, I mean funny like everyone is wearing weird pants and the colors are wrong and the cars look--
Oh my God! I'm in the past!
That cube sucked me into the past!
Cube?
Nothing! Thanks for your help!
Be careful out there, dear! Manhattan is no place for a young girl to wander around alone! Midtown is full of gangs!
I KNEW I WAS SENT BACK IN TIME, IT HAD TO BE FOR A REASON.
AND UNLESS I FIGURE OUT WHY, MY CHANCE OF GETTING BACK TO THE FUTURE WERE BASICALLY ZERO.
WHICH MEANT I NEEDED TO FIT IN.
Ooh! Ladies' Wear, 20% off!
OTHERWISE, I'D DISRUPT THE TIMELINE, CAUSING...TOTAL CHAOS, ALTER THE COURSE OF HISTORY AND PROBABLY NEVER BE BORN.

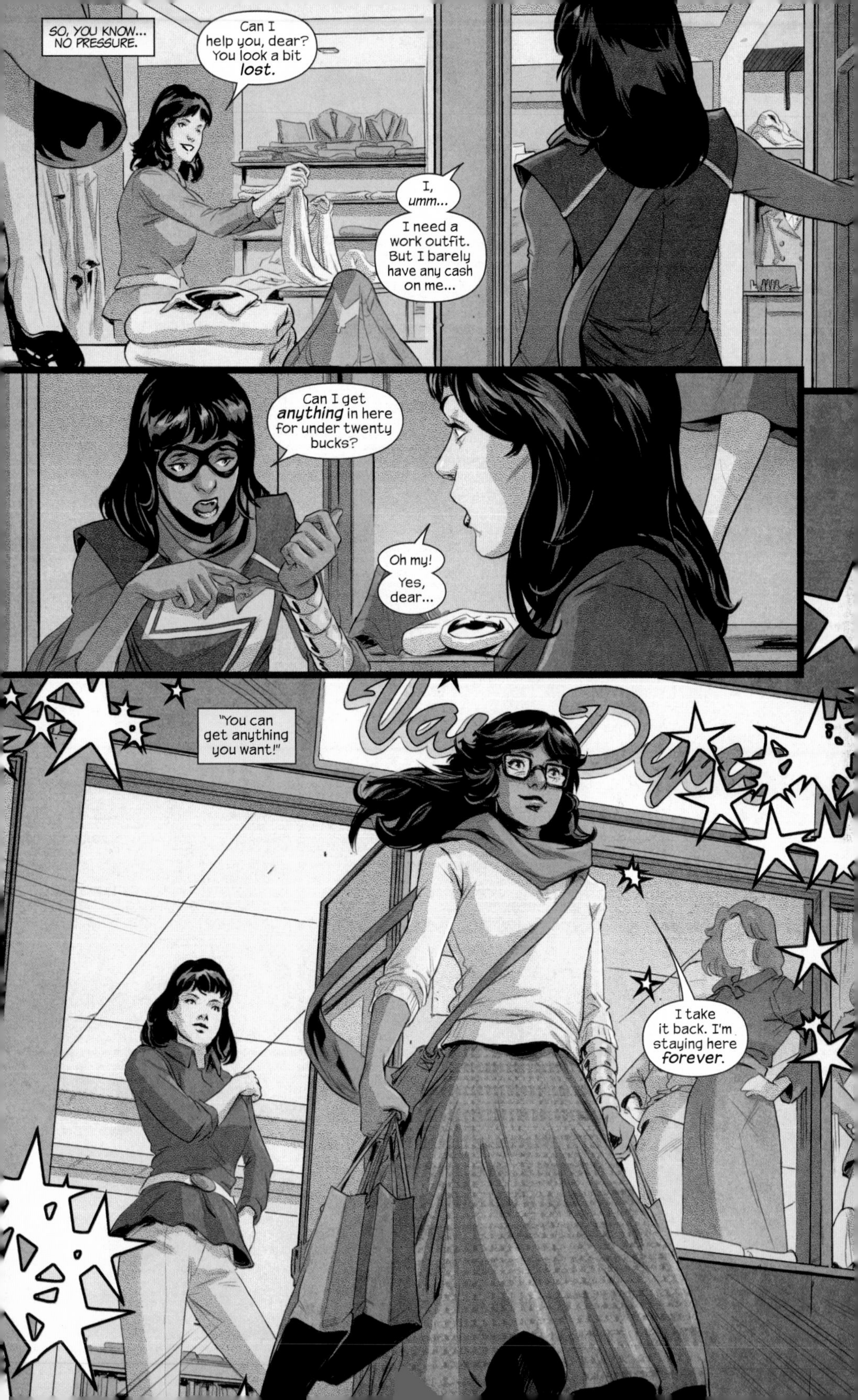
SO, YOU KNOW... NO PRESSURE.
Can I help you, dear? You look a bit lost.
I, umm...
I need a work outfit. But I barely have any cash on me...
Can I get anything in here for under twenty bucks?
Oh my!
Yes, dear...
"You can get anything you want!"
I take it back. I'm staying here forever.

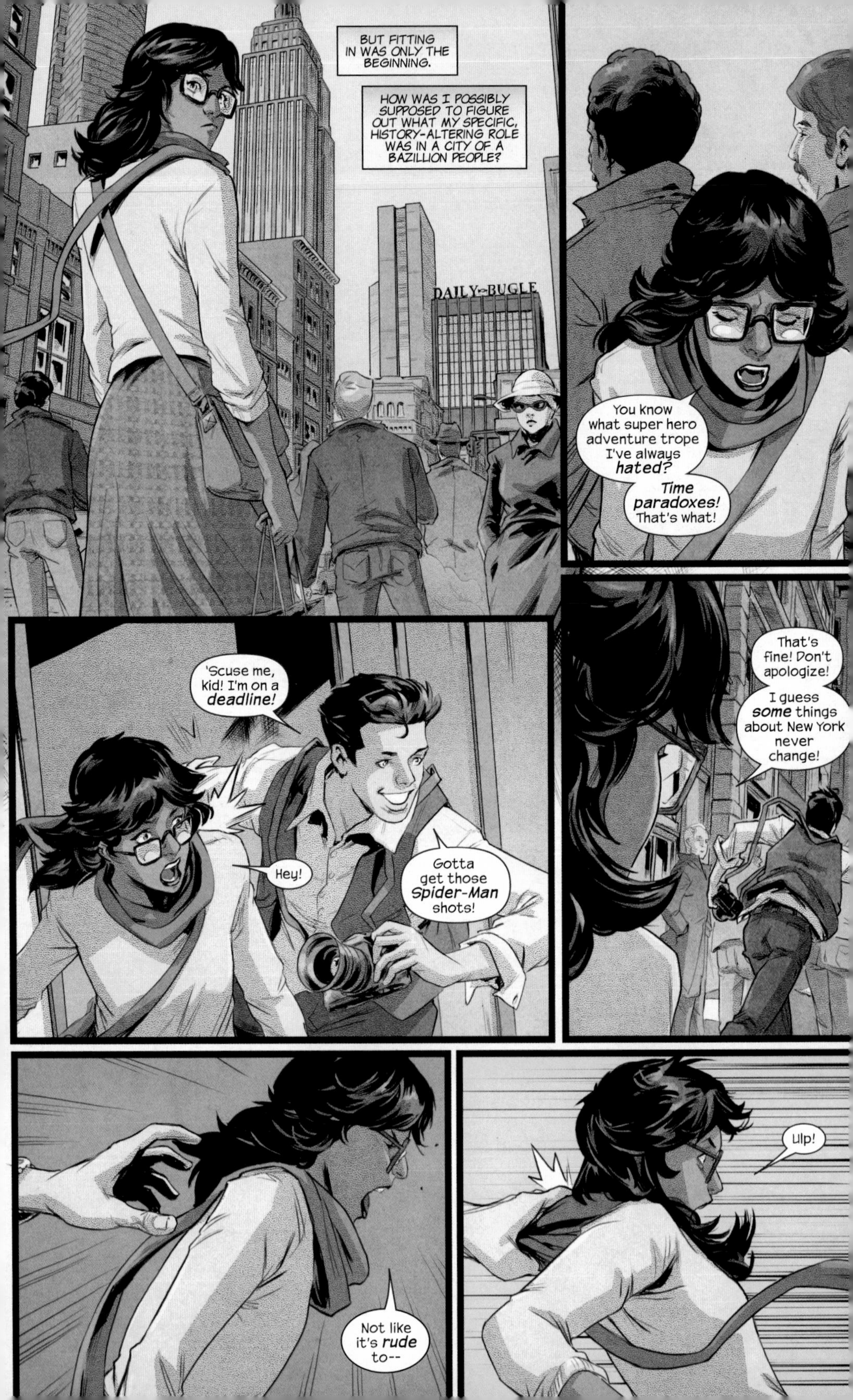
BUT FITTING IN WAS ONLY THE BEGINNING.
HOW WAS I POSSIBLY SUPPOSED TO FIGURE OUT WHAT MY SPECIFIC, HISTORY-ALTERING ROLE WAS IN A CITY OF A BAZILLION PEOPLE?
DAILY BUGLE
You know what super hero adventure trope I've always *hated?*
Time paradoxes! That's what!
'Scuse me, kid! I'm on a *deadline!*
Hey!
Gotta get those *Spider-Man* shots!
That's fine! Don't apologize!
I guess *some* things about New York never change!
Not like it's *rude* to--
Ulp!

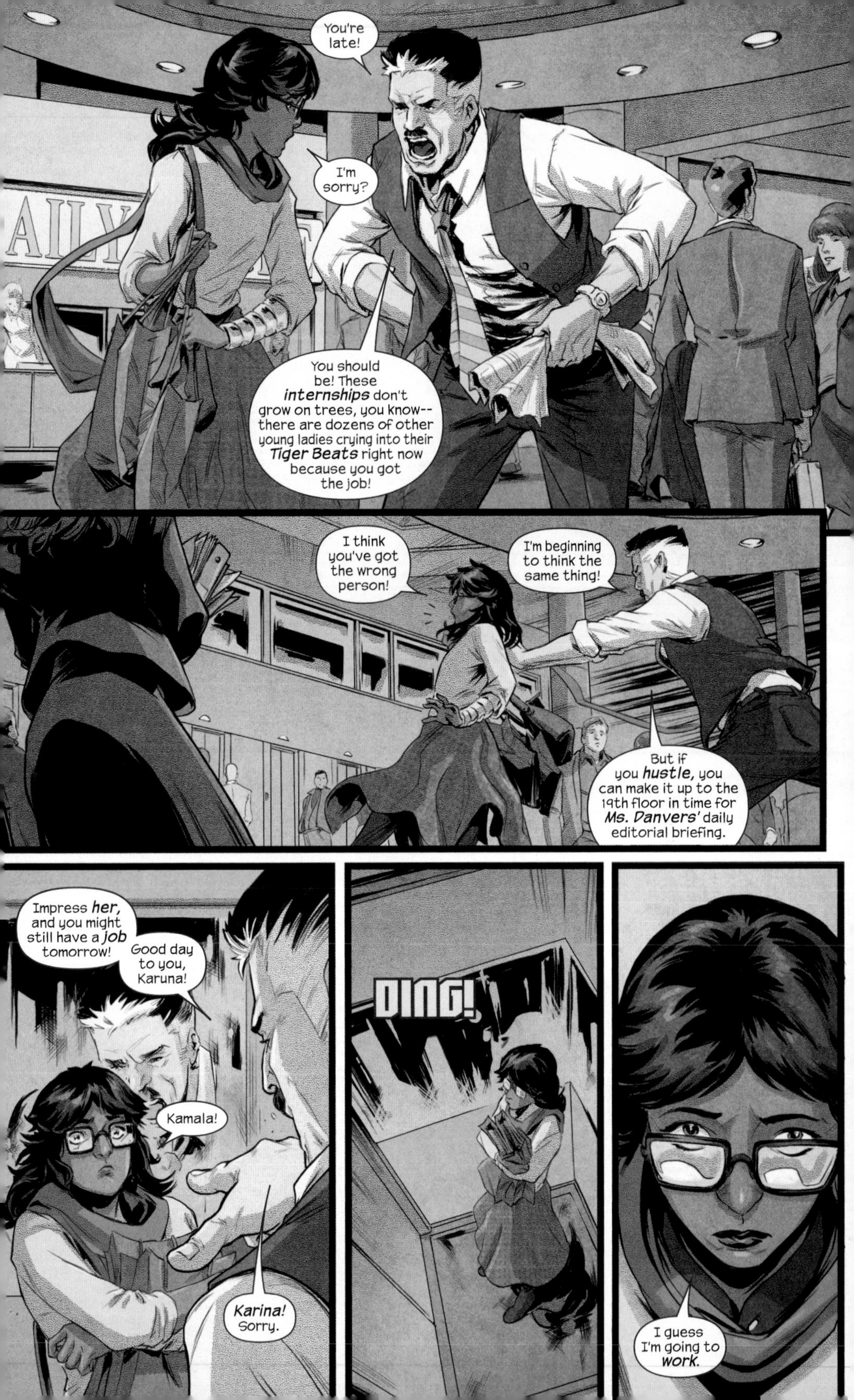
You're late!
I'm sorry?
You should be! These *internships* don't grow on trees, you know-- there are dozens of other young ladies crying into their *Tiger Beats* right now because you got the job!
I think you've got the wrong person!
I'm beginning to think the same thing!
But if you *hustle*, you can make it up to the 19th floor in time for *Ms. Danvers'* daily editorial briefing.
Impress *her*, and you might still have a *job* tomorrow!
Good day to you, Karuna!
Kamala!
Karina! Sorry.
DING!
I guess I'm going to *work*.

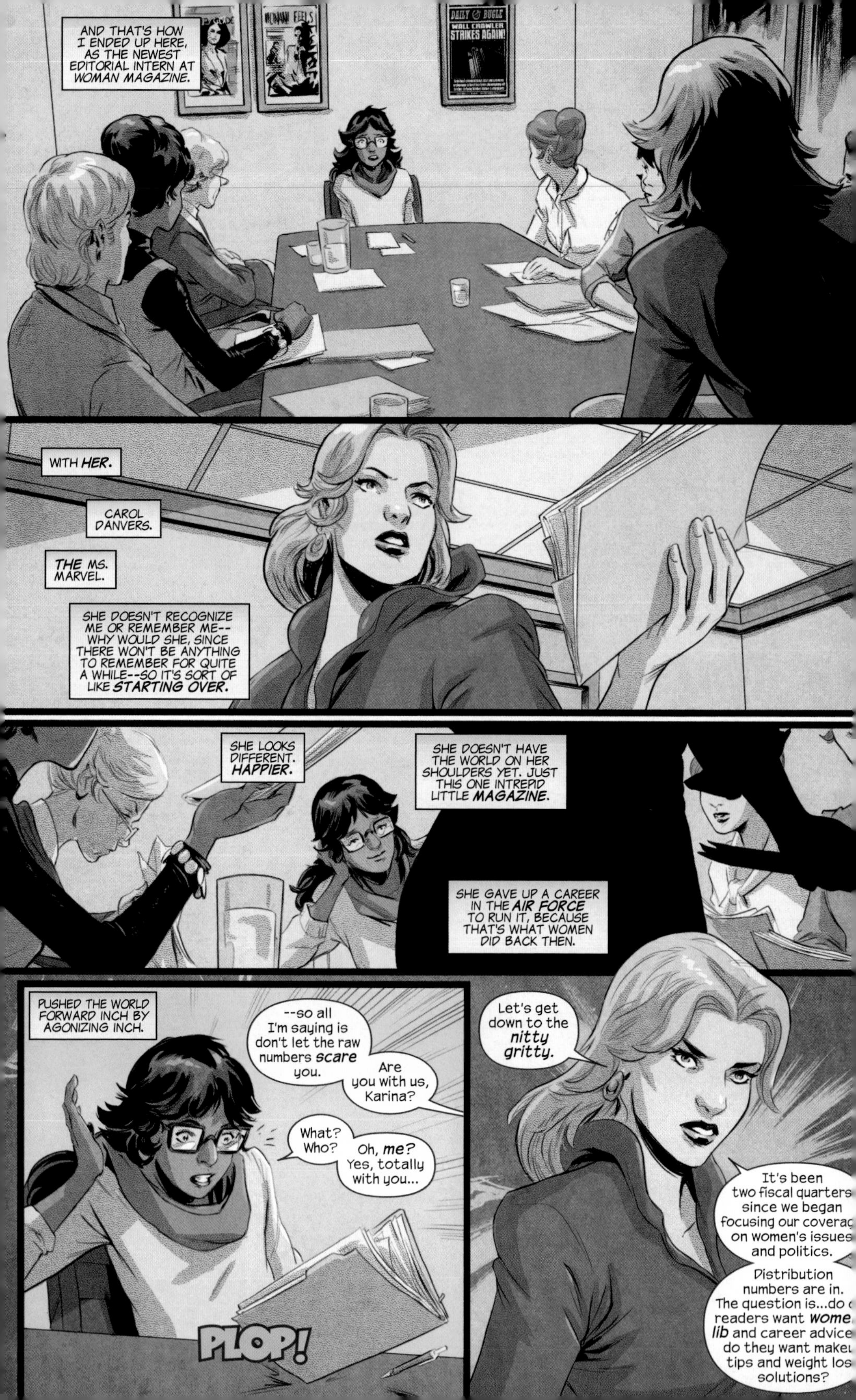
AND THAT'S HOW I ENDED UP HERE, AS THE NEWEST EDITORIAL INTERN AT WOMAN MAGAZINE.
WOMAN FEELS
DAILY BUGLE
WALL CRAWLER STRIKES AGAIN!
WITH HER.
CAROL DANVERS.
THE MS. MARVEL.
SHE DOESN'T RECOGNIZE ME OR REMEMBER ME--WHY WOULD SHE, SINCE THERE WON'T BE ANYTHING TO REMEMBER FOR QUITE A WHILE--SO IT'S SORT OF LIKE STARTING OVER.
SHE LOOKS DIFFERENT. HAPPIER.
SHE DOESN'T HAVE THE WORLD ON HER SHOULDERS YET. JUST THIS ONE INTREPID LITTLE MAGAZINE.
SHE GAVE UP A CAREER IN THE AIR FORCE TO RUN IT, BECAUSE THAT'S WHAT WOMEN DID BACK THEN.
PUSHED THE WORLD FORWARD INCH BY AGONIZING INCH.
--so all I'm saying is don't let the raw numbers scare you.
Are you with us, Karina?
What? Who?
Oh, me? Yes, totally with you...
PLOP!
Let's get down to the nitty gritty.
It's been two fiscal quarters since we began focusing our coverag on women's issues and politics.
Distribution numbers are in. The question is...do readers want wome lib and career advice do they want makeu tips and weight los solutions?

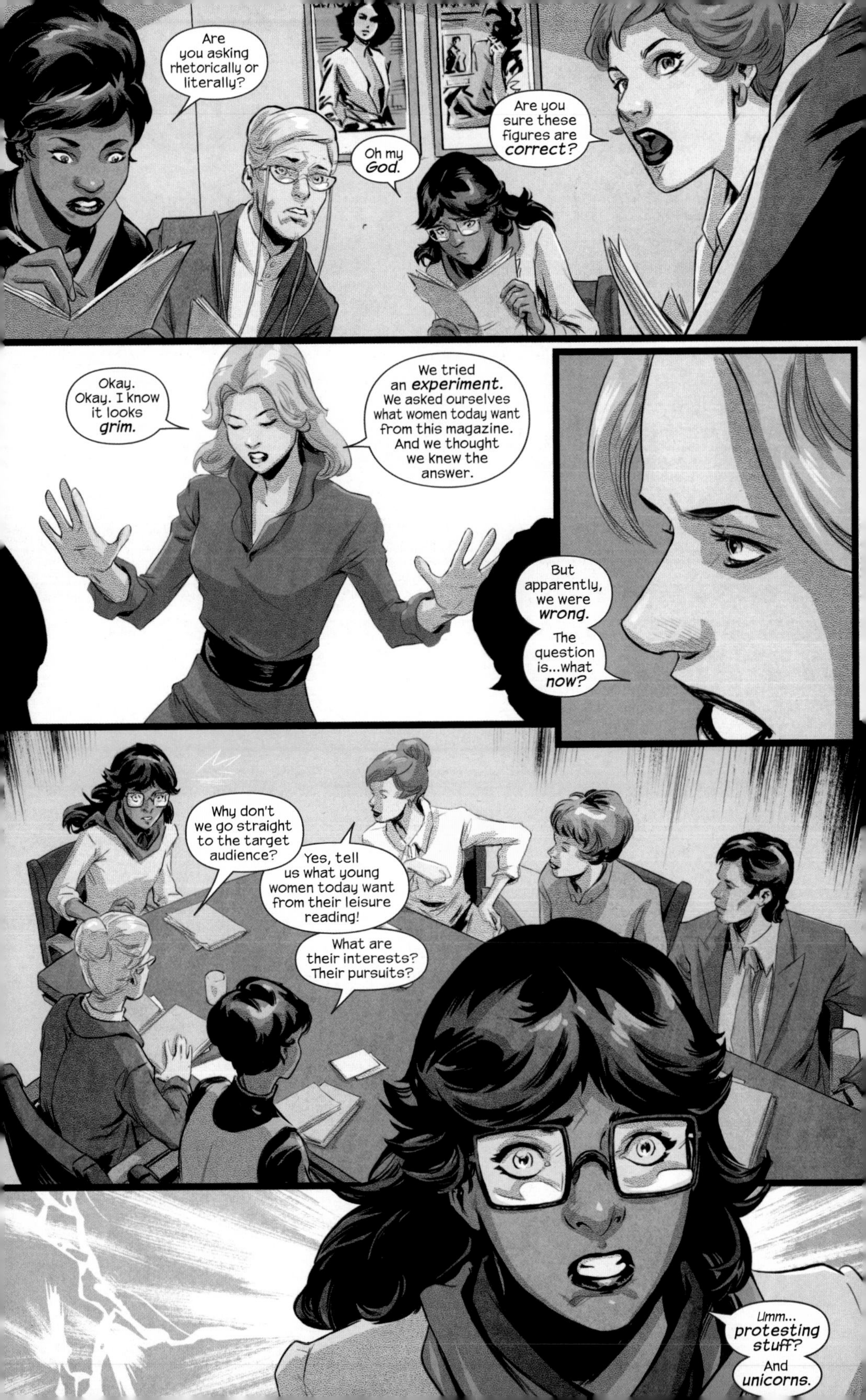

Are you asking rhetorically or literally?
Oh my God.
Are you sure these figures are correct?
Okay. Okay. I know it looks grim.
We tried an experiment. We asked ourselves what women today want from this magazine. And we thought we knew the answer.
But apparently, we were wrong.
The question is...what now?
Why don't we go straight to the target audience?
Yes, tell us what young women today want from their leisure reading!
What are their interests? Their pursuits?
Umm... protesting stuff?
And unicorns.

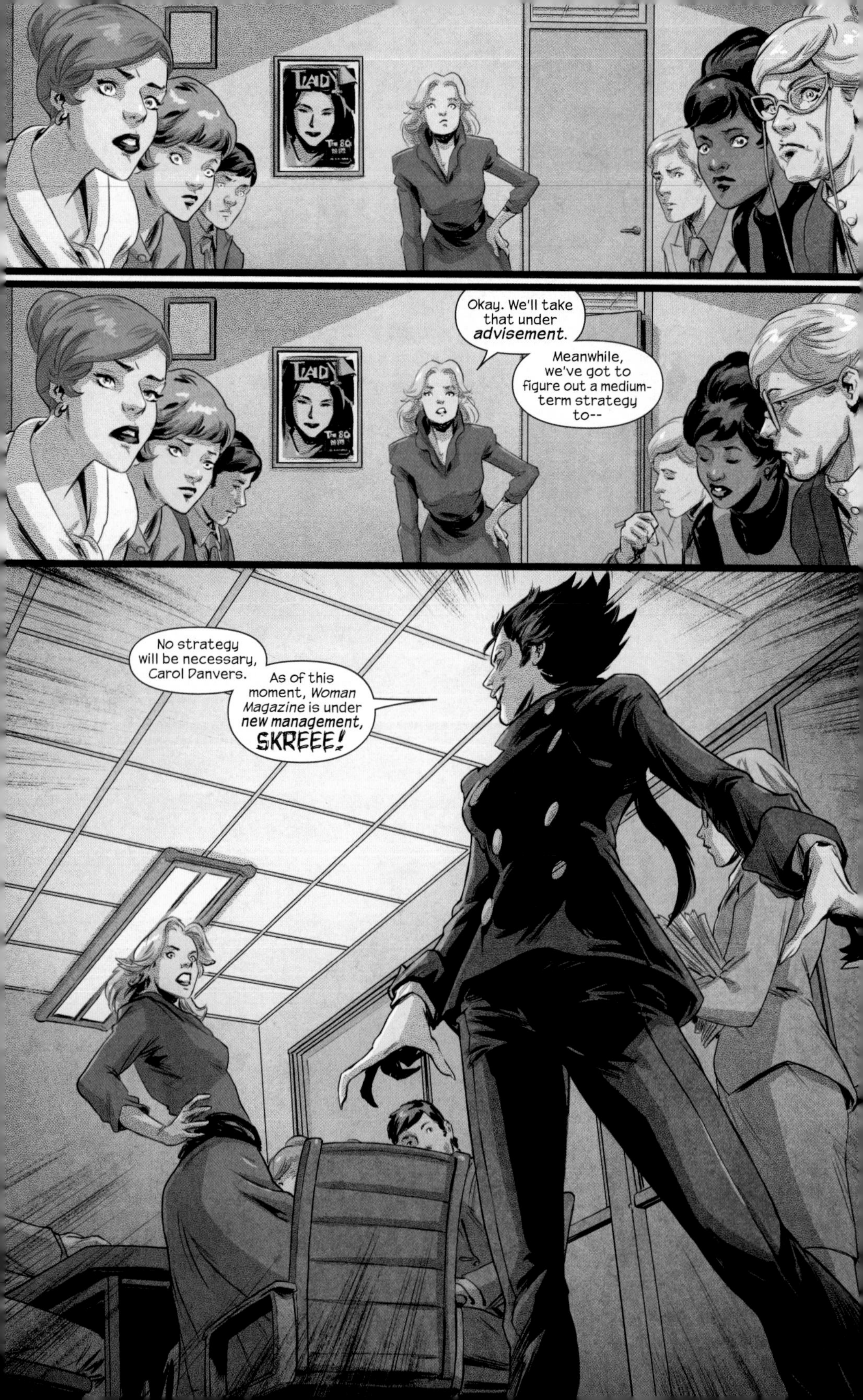
Okay. We'll take that under *advisement*.
Meanwhile, we've got to figure out a medium-term strategy to--
No strategy will be necessary, Carol Danvers.
As of this moment, *Woman Magazine* is under *new management*, SKREEE!

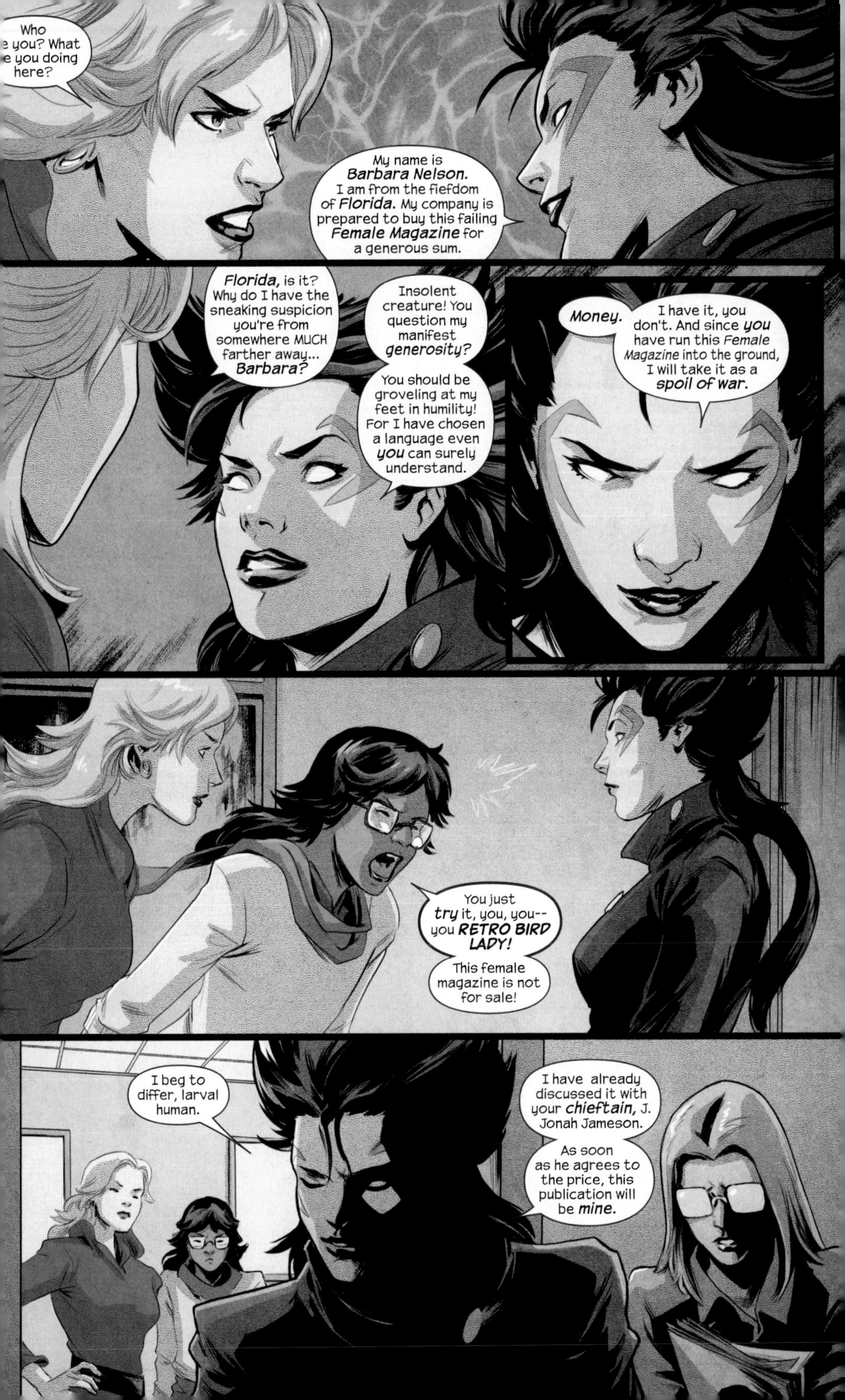
Who
e you? What
e you doing
here?
My name is Barbara Nelson. I am from the fiefdom of Florida. My company is prepared to buy this failing Female Magazine for a generous sum.
Florida, is it? Why do I have the sneaking suspicion you're from somewhere MUCH farther away... Barbara?
Insolent creature! You question my manifest generosity?
You should be groveling at my feet in humility! For I have chosen a language even you can surely understand.
Money.
I have it, you don't. And since you have run this Female Magazine into the ground, I will take it as a spoil of war.
You just try it, you, you-- you RETRO BIRD LADY!
This female magazine is not for sale!
I beg to differ, larval human.
I have already discussed it with your chieftain, J. Jonah Jameson.
As soon as he agrees to the price, this publication will be mine.

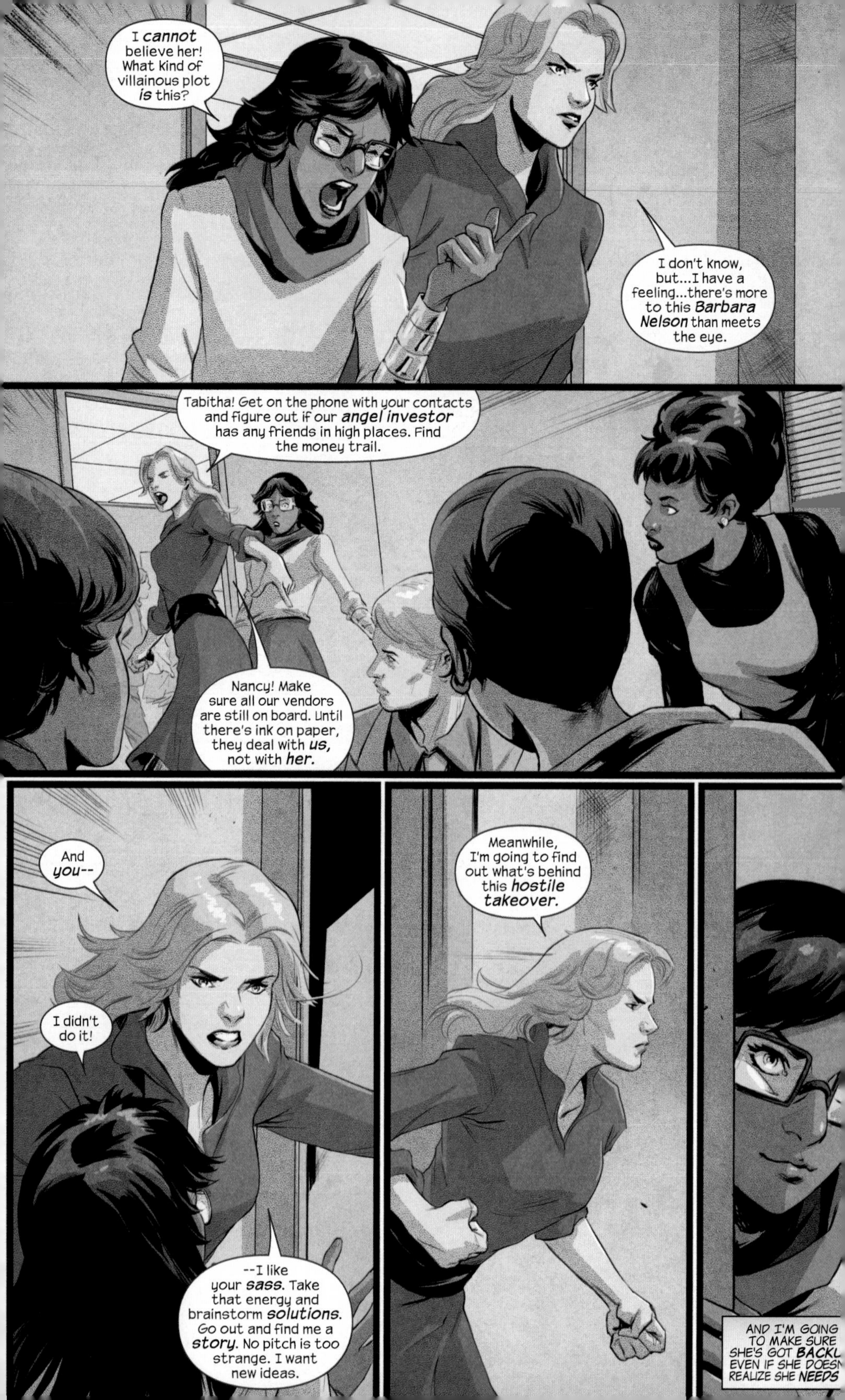

I cannot believe her! What kind of villainous plot is this?
I don't know, but...I have a feeling...there's more to this Barbara Nelson than meets the eye.
Tabitha! Get on the phone with your contacts and figure out if our angel investor has any friends in high places. Find the money trail.
Nancy! Make sure all our vendors are still on board. Until there's ink on paper, they deal with us, not with her.
And you--
I didn't do it!
--I like your sass. Take that energy and brainstorm solutions. Go out and find me a story. No pitch is too strange. I want new ideas.
Meanwhile, I'm going to find out what's behind this hostile takeover.
AND I'M GOING TO MAKE SURE SHE'S GOT BACKU
EVEN IF SHE DOESN
REALIZE SHE NEEDS

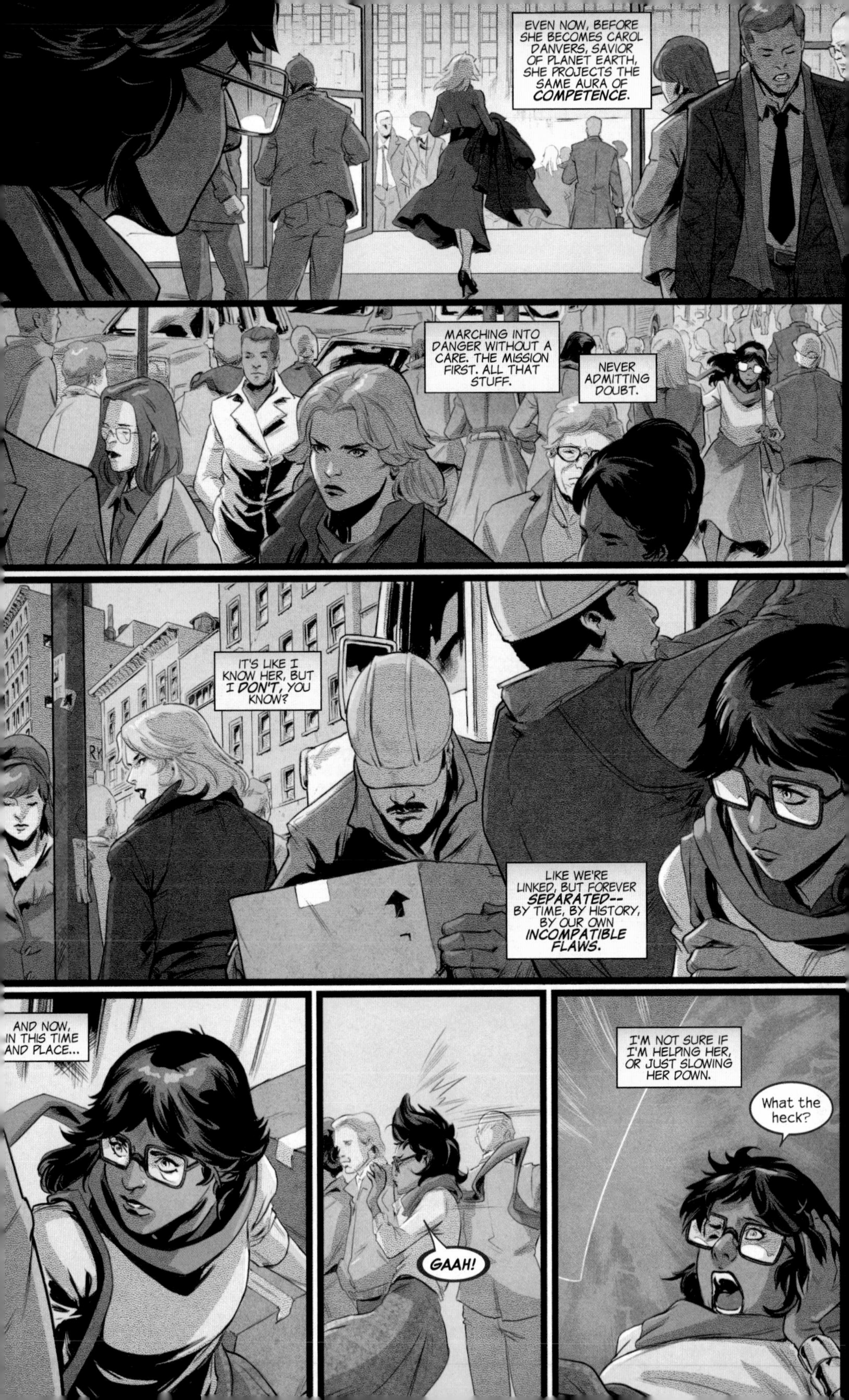

EVEN NOW, BEFORE SHE BECOMES CAROL DANVERS, SAVIOR OF PLANET EARTH, SHE PROJECTS THE SAME AURA OF COMPETENCE.
MARCHING INTO DANGER WITHOUT A CARE. THE MISSION FIRST. ALL THAT STUFF.
NEVER ADMITTING DOUBT.
IT'S LIKE I KNOW HER, BUT I DON'T, YOU KNOW?
LIKE WE'RE LINKED, BUT FOREVER SEPARATED-- BY TIME, BY HISTORY, BY OUR OWN INCOMPATIBLE FLAWS.
AND NOW, IN THIS TIME AND PLACE...
GAAH!
I'M NOT SURE IF I'M HELPING HER, OR JUST SLOWING HER DOWN.
What the heck?

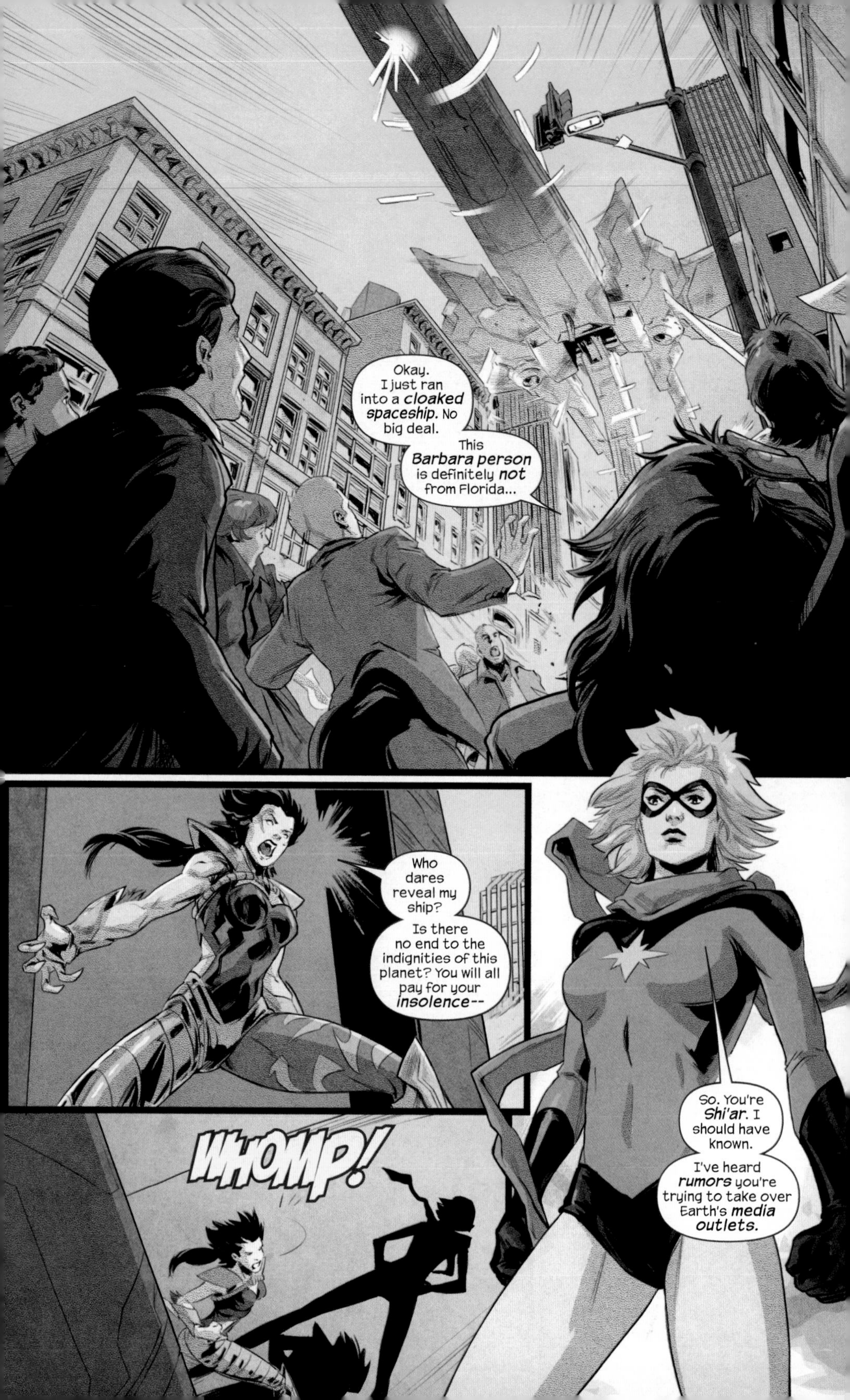
Okay. I just ran into a cloaked spaceship. No big deal.
This Barbara person is definitely not from Florida...
Who dares reveal my ship?
Is there no end to the indignities of this planet? You will all pay for your insolence--
WHOMP!
So. You're Shi'ar. I should have known.
I've heard rumors you're trying to take over Earth's media outlets.

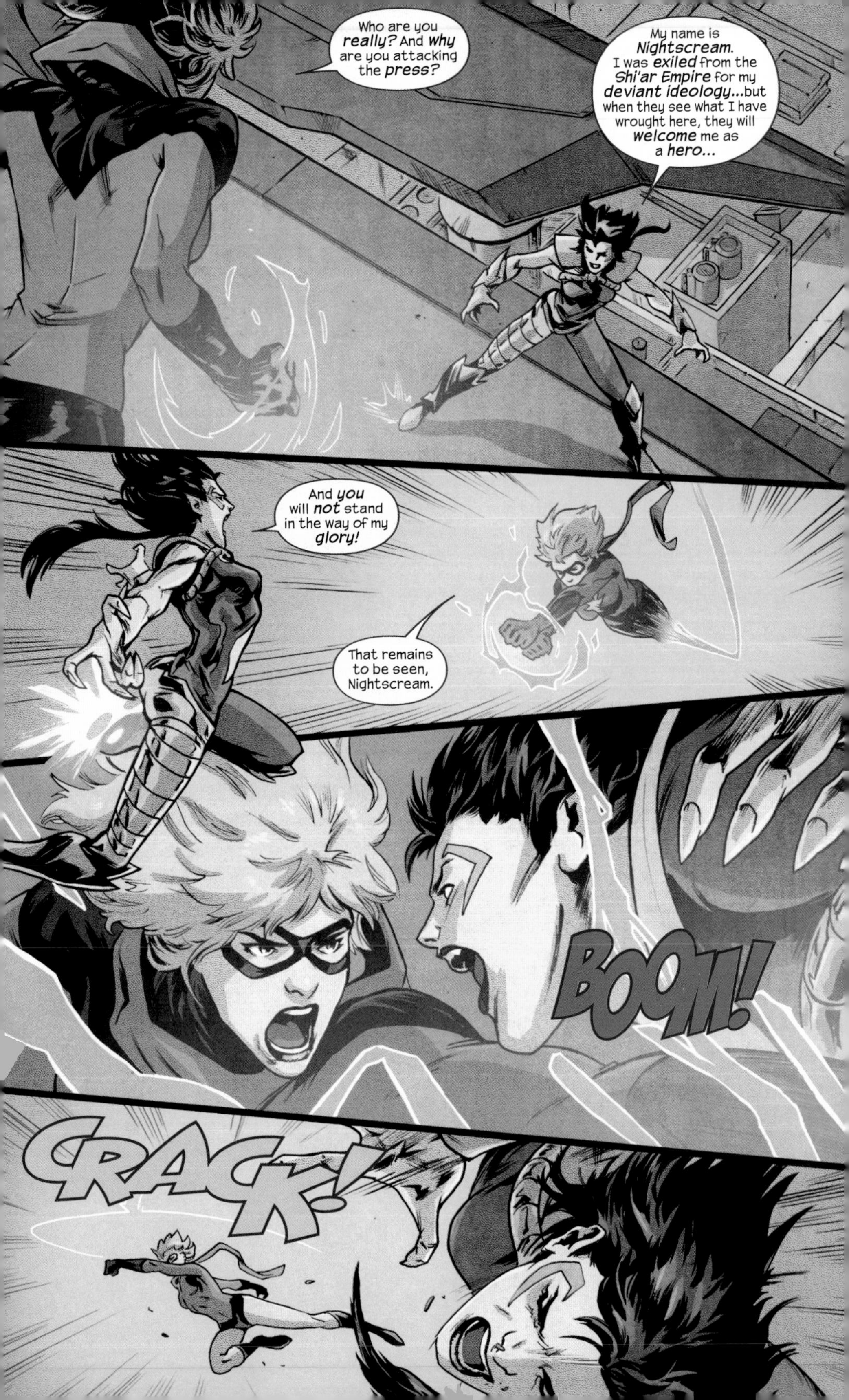
Who are you really? And why are you attacking the press?
My name is Nightscream. I was exiled from the Shi'ar Empire for my deviant ideology...but when they see what I have wrought here, they will welcome me as a hero...
And you will not stand in the way of my glory!
That remains to be seen, Nightscream.
BOOM!
CRACK!

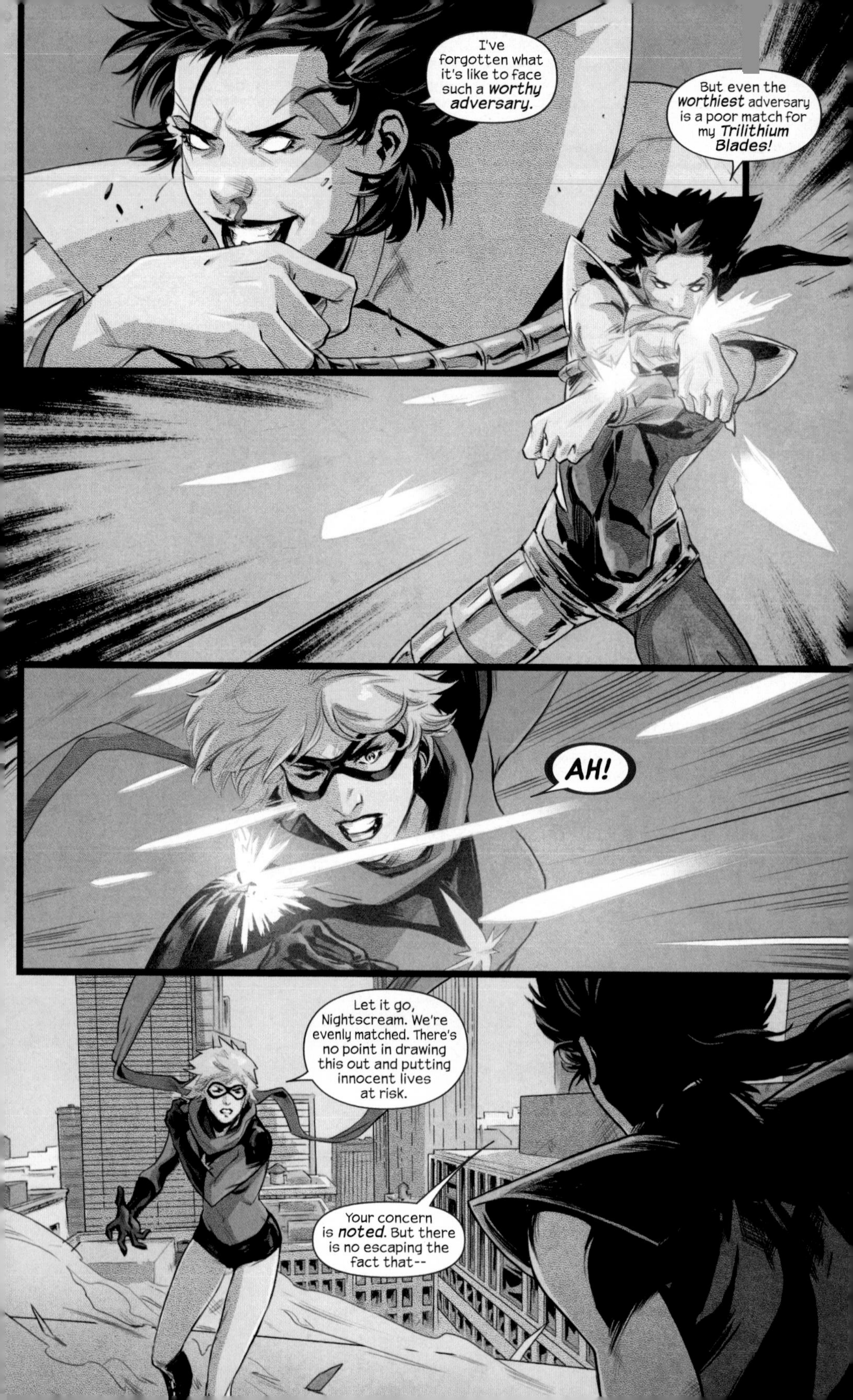

I've forgotten what it's like to face such a *worthy adversary.*
But even the *worthiest* adversary is a poor match for my *Trilithium Blades!*
AH!
Let it go, Nightscream. We're evenly matched. There's no point in drawing this out and putting innocent lives at risk.
Your concern is *noted*. But there is no escaping the fact that--

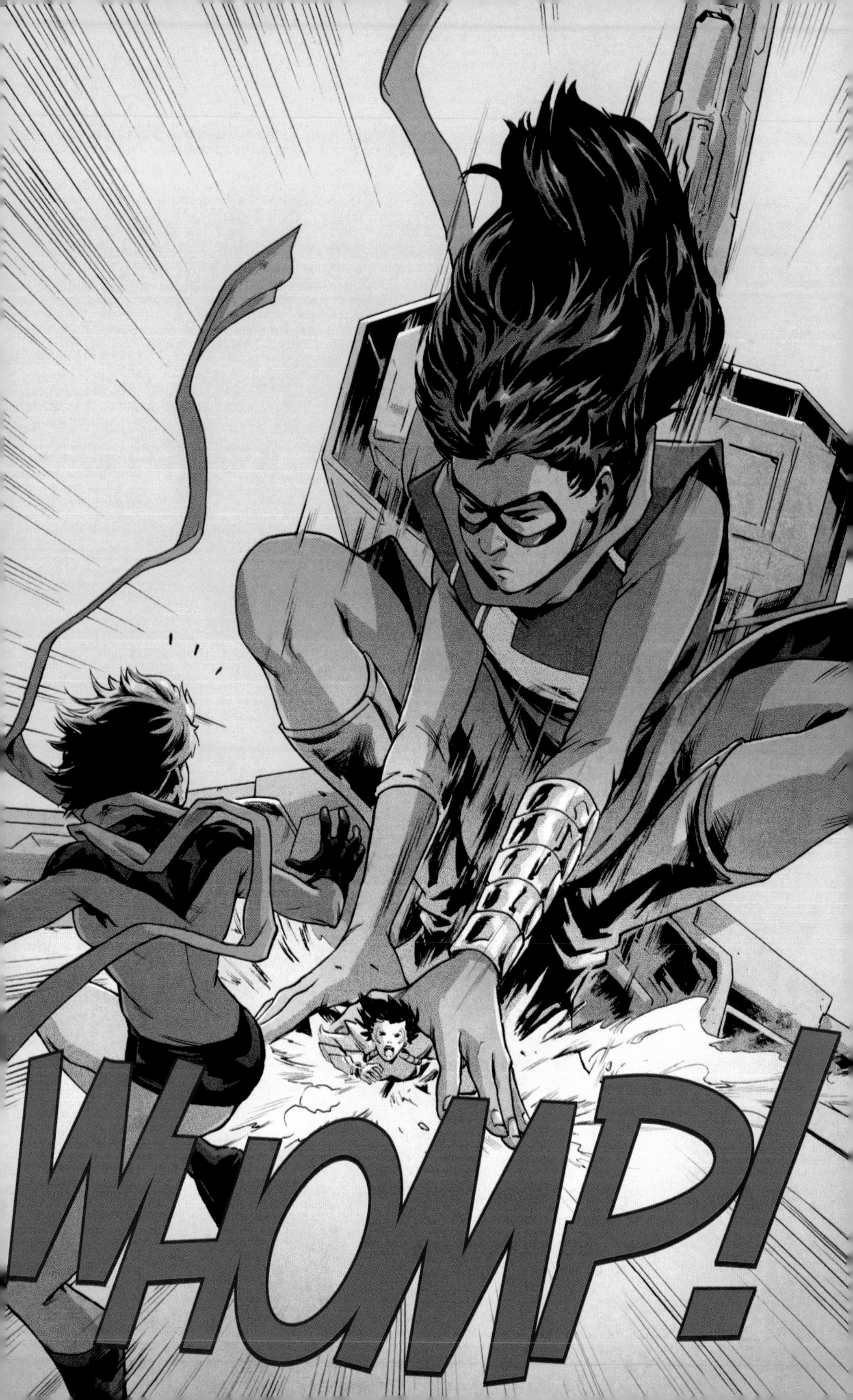
WHOMP!

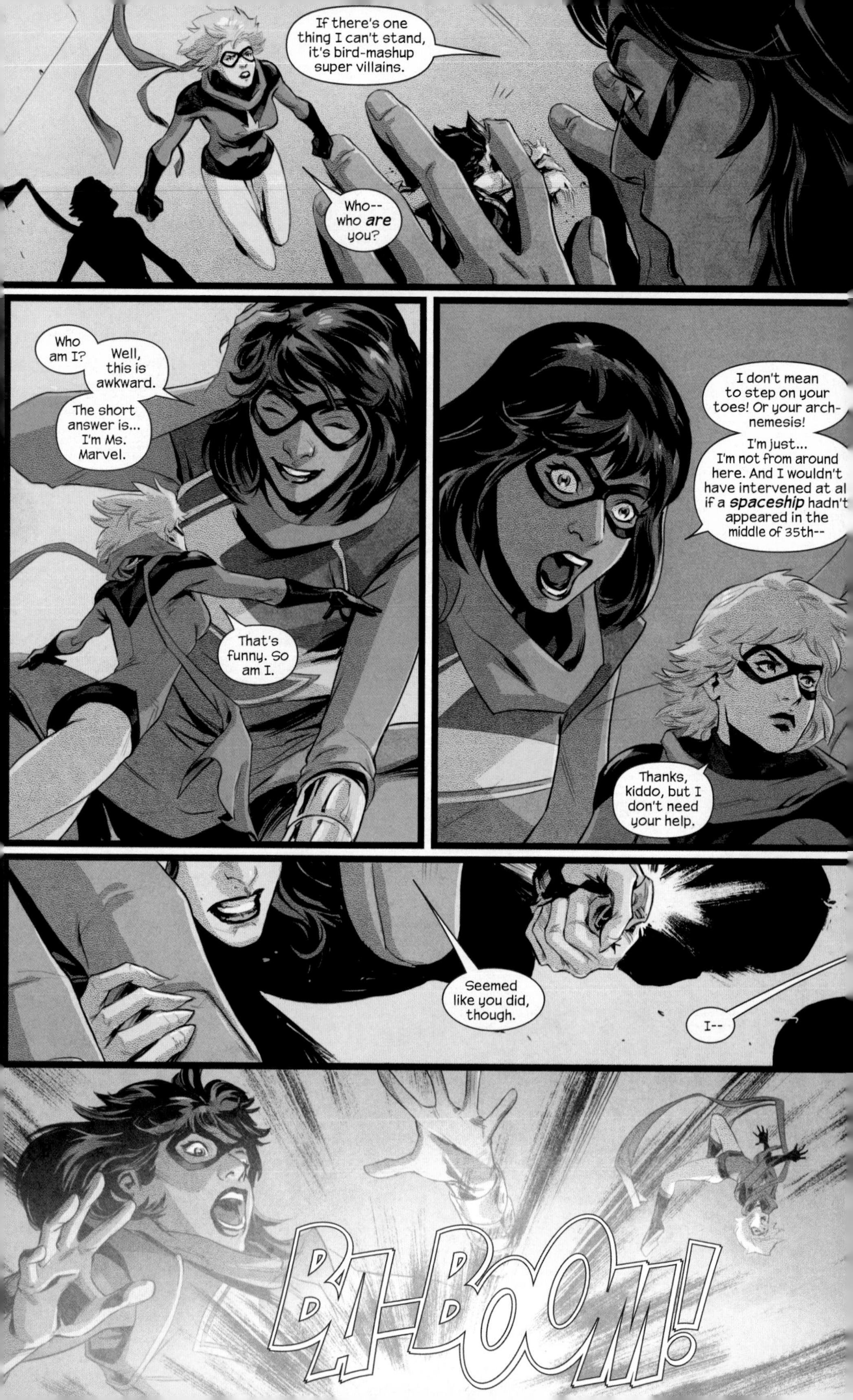
If there's one thing I can't stand, it's bird-mashup super villains.
Who-- who *are* you?
Who am I?
Well, this is awkward.
The short answer is... I'm Ms. Marvel.
That's funny. So am I.
I don't mean to step on your toes! Or your arch-nemesis!
I'm just... I'm not from around here. And I wouldn't have intervened at al if a *spaceship* hadn't appeared in the middle of 35th--
Thanks, kiddo, but I don't need your help.
Seemed like you did, though.
I--
BA-BOOM!

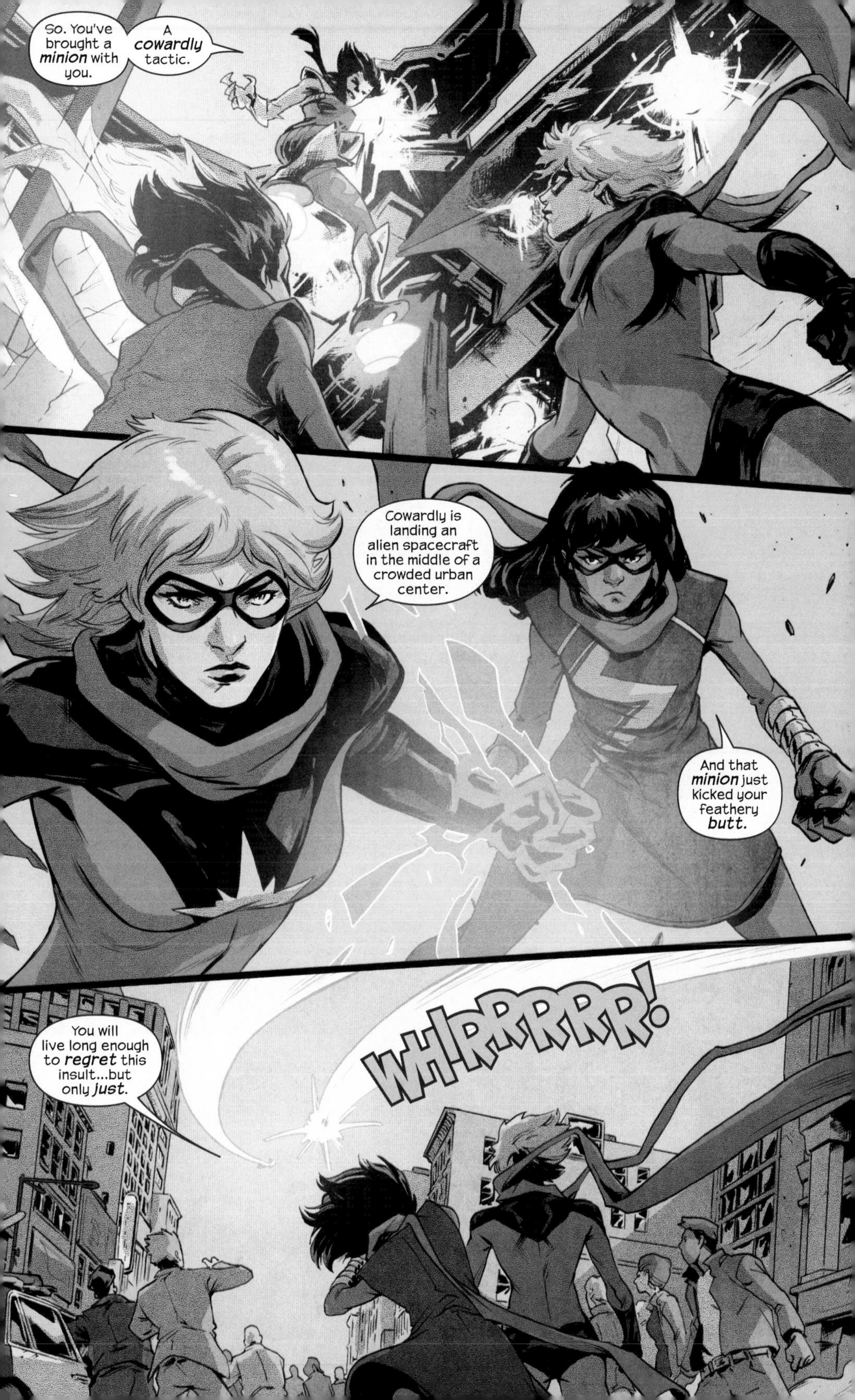
So. You've brought a *minion* with you.
A *cowardly* tactic.
Cowardly is landing an alien spacecraft in the middle of a crowded urban center.
And that *minion* just kicked your feathery *butt.*
You will live long enough to *regret* this insult...but only *just*.
WHIRRRRR!

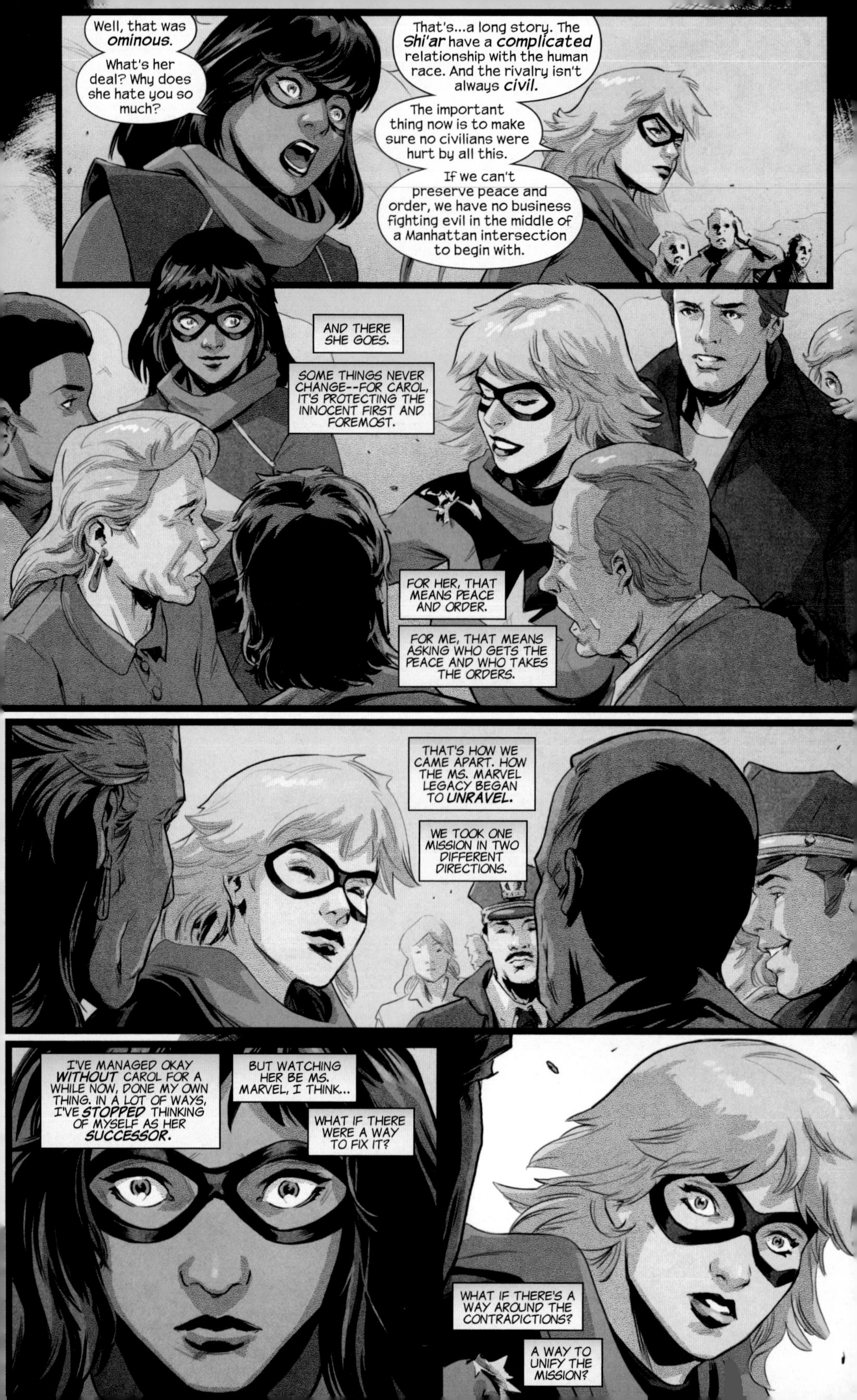
Well, that was ominous.
What's her deal? Why does she hate you so much?
That's...a long story. The Shi'ar have a complicated relationship with the human race. And the rivalry isn't always civil.
The important thing now is to make sure no civilians were hurt by all this.
If we can't preserve peace and order, we have no business fighting evil in the middle of a Manhattan intersection to begin with.
AND THERE SHE GOES.
SOME THINGS NEVER CHANGE--FOR CAROL, IT'S PROTECTING THE INNOCENT FIRST AND FOREMOST.
FOR HER, THAT MEANS PEACE AND ORDER.
FOR ME, THAT MEANS ASKING WHO GETS THE PEACE AND WHO TAKES THE ORDERS.
THAT'S HOW WE CAME APART. HOW THE MS. MARVEL LEGACY BEGAN TO UNRAVEL.
WE TOOK ONE MISSION IN TWO DIFFERENT DIRECTIONS.
I'VE MANAGED OKAY WITHOUT CAROL FOR A WHILE NOW, DONE MY OWN THING. IN A LOT OF WAYS, I'VE STOPPED THINKING OF MYSELF AS HER SUCCESSOR.
BUT WATCHING HER BE MS. MARVEL, I THINK...
WHAT IF THERE WERE A WAY TO FIX IT?
WHAT IF THERE'S A WAY AROUND THE CONTRADICTIONS?
A WAY TO UNIFY THE MISSION?

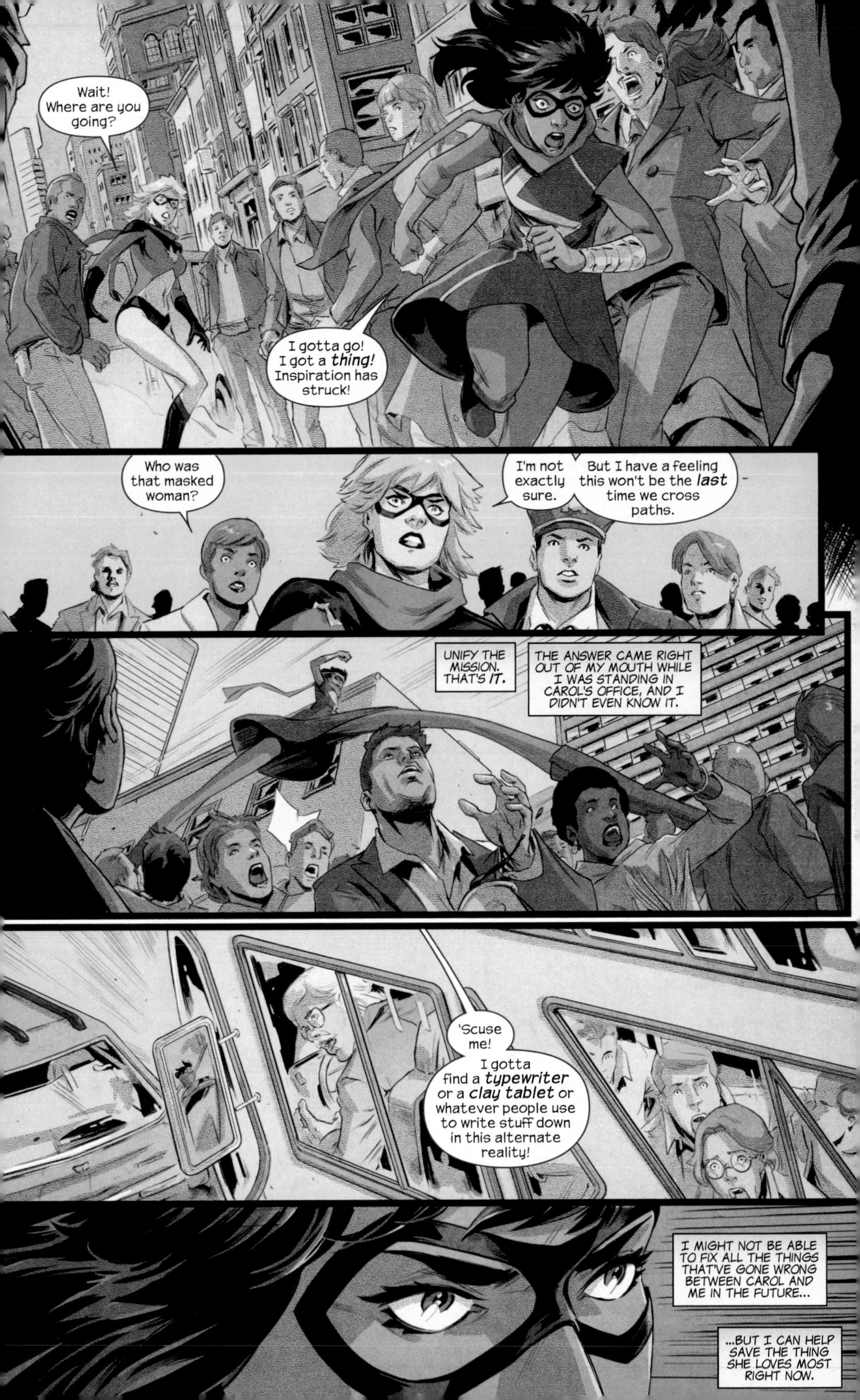
Wait! Where are you going?
I gotta go! I got a thing! Inspiration has struck!
Who was that masked woman?
I'm not exactly sure.
But I have a feeling this won't be the last time we cross paths.
UNIFY THE MISSION. THAT'S IT.
THE ANSWER CAME RIGHT OUT OF MY MOUTH WHILE I WAS STANDING IN CAROL'S OFFICE, AND I DIDN'T EVEN KNOW IT.
'Scuse me!
I gotta find a typewriter or a clay tablet or whatever people use to write stuff down in this alternate reality!
I MIGHT NOT BE ABLE TO FIX ALL THE THINGS THAT'VE GONE WRONG BETWEEN CAROL AND ME IN THE FUTURE...
...BUT I CAN HELP SAVE THE THING SHE LOVES MOST RIGHT NOW.

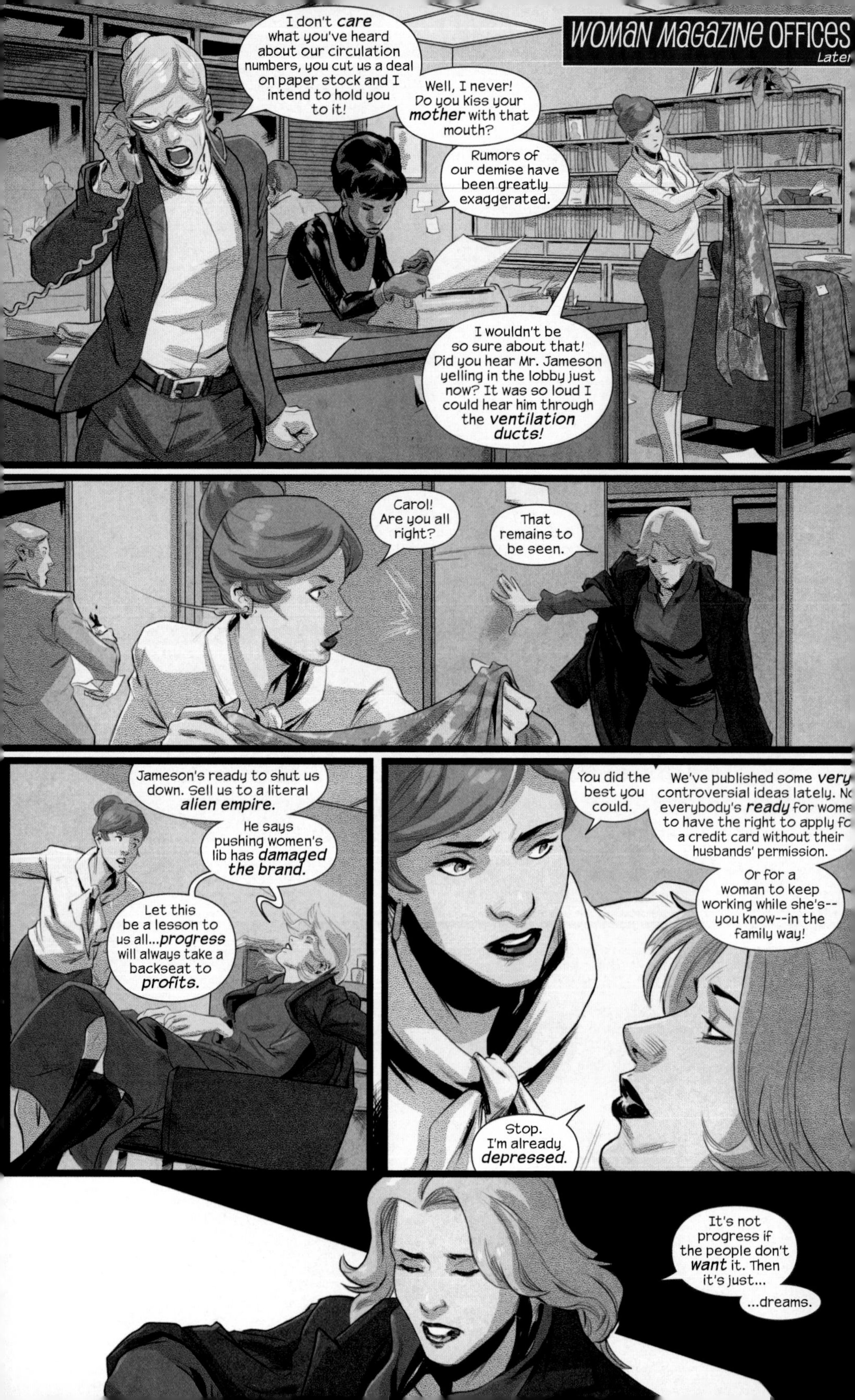
WOMAN MAGAZINE OFFICES
Later
I don't care what you've heard about our circulation numbers, you cut us a deal on paper stock and I intend to hold you to it!
Well, I never! Do you kiss your mother with that mouth?
Rumors of our demise have been greatly exaggerated.
I wouldn't be so sure about that! Did you hear Mr. Jameson yelling in the lobby just now? It was so loud I could hear him through the ventilation ducts!
Carol! Are you all right?
That remains to be seen.
Jameson's ready to shut us down. Sell us to a literal alien empire.
He says pushing women's lib has damaged the brand.
Let this be a lesson to us all...progress will always take a backseat to profits.
You did the best you could.
We've published some very controversial ideas lately. No everybody's ready for wome to have the right to apply fo a credit card without their husbands' permission.
Or for a woman to keep working while she's--you know--in the family way!
Stop. I'm already depressed.
It's not progress if the people don't want it. Then it's just...
...dreams.

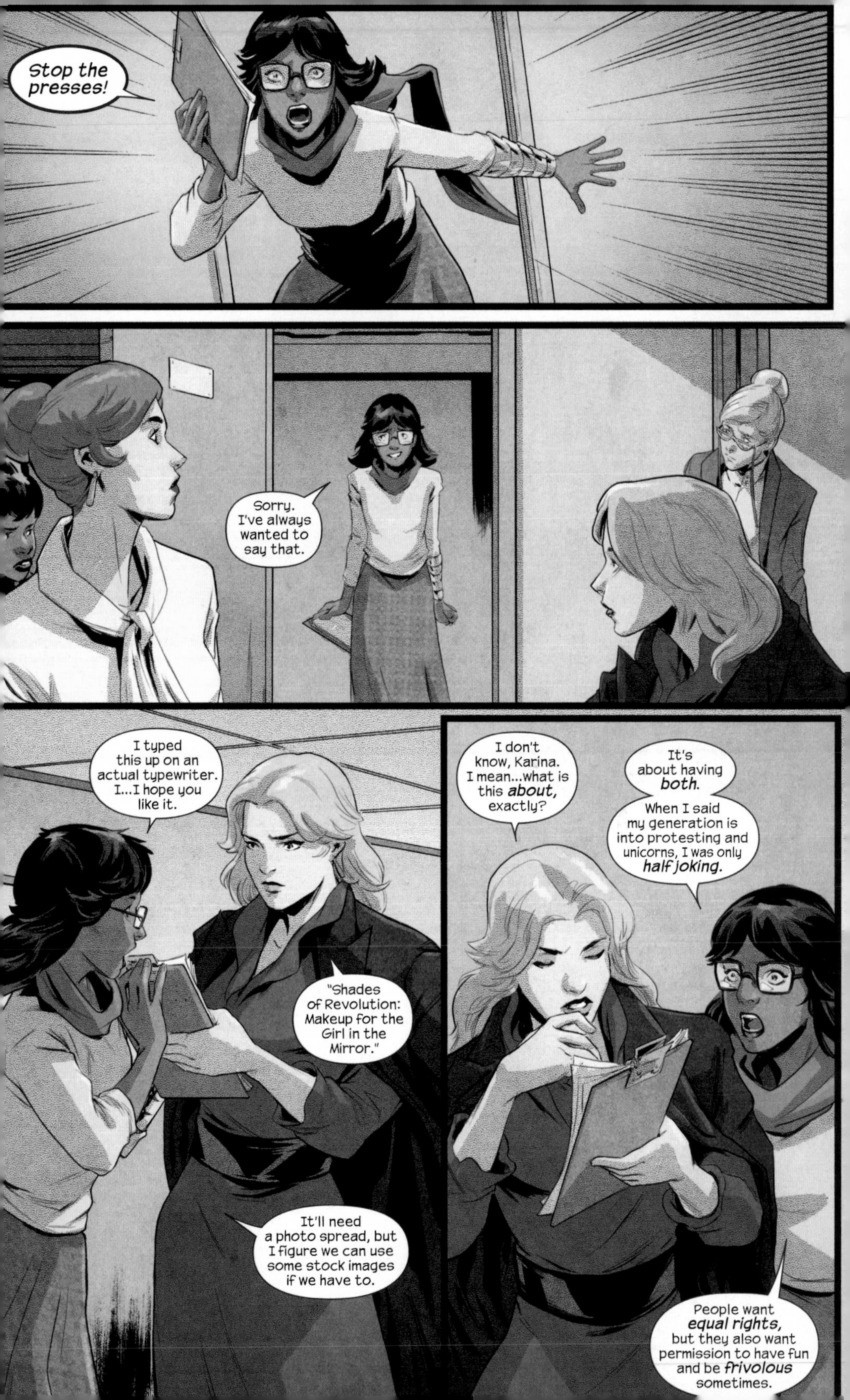
Stop the presses!
Sorry. I've always wanted to say that.
I typed this up on an actual typewriter. I...I hope you like it.
"Shades of Revolution: Makeup for the Girl in the Mirror."
It'll need a photo spread, but I figure we can use some stock images if we have to.
I don't know, Karina. I mean...what is this *about,* exactly?
It's about having *both.*
When I said my generation is into protesting and unicorns, I was only *half joking.*
People want *equal rights,* but they also want permission to have fun and be *frivolous* sometimes.

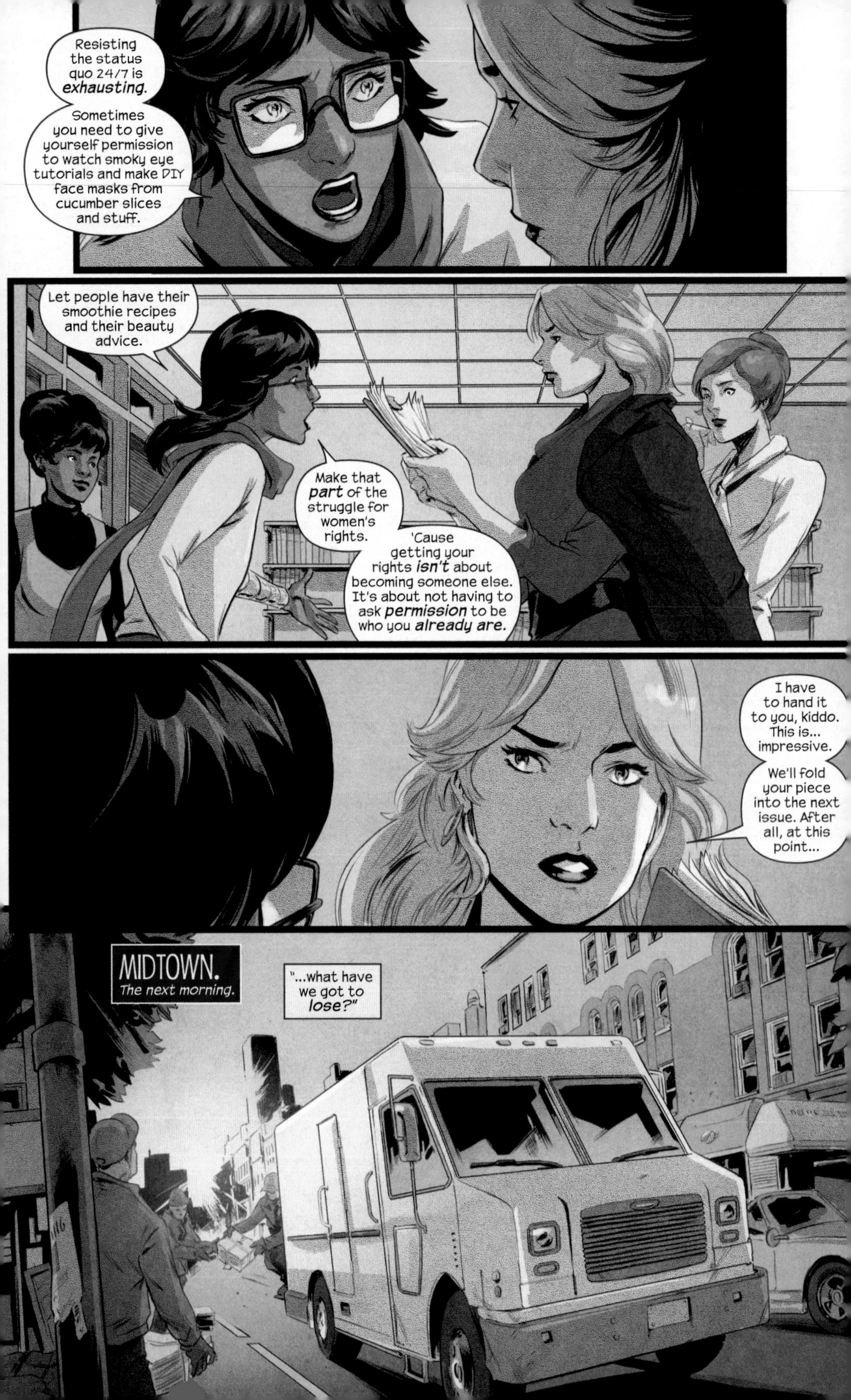

Resisting the status quo 24/7 is *exhausting*.
Sometimes you need to give yourself permission to watch smoky eye tutorials and make DIY face masks from cucumber slices and stuff.
Let people have their smoothie recipes and their beauty advice.
Make that *part* of the struggle for women's rights.
'Cause getting your rights *isn't* about becoming someone else. It's about not having to ask *permission* to be who you *already are*.
I have to hand it to you, kiddo. This is... impressive.
We'll fold your piece into the next issue. After all, at this point...
MIDTOWN. *The next morning.*
"...what have we got to *lose?*"

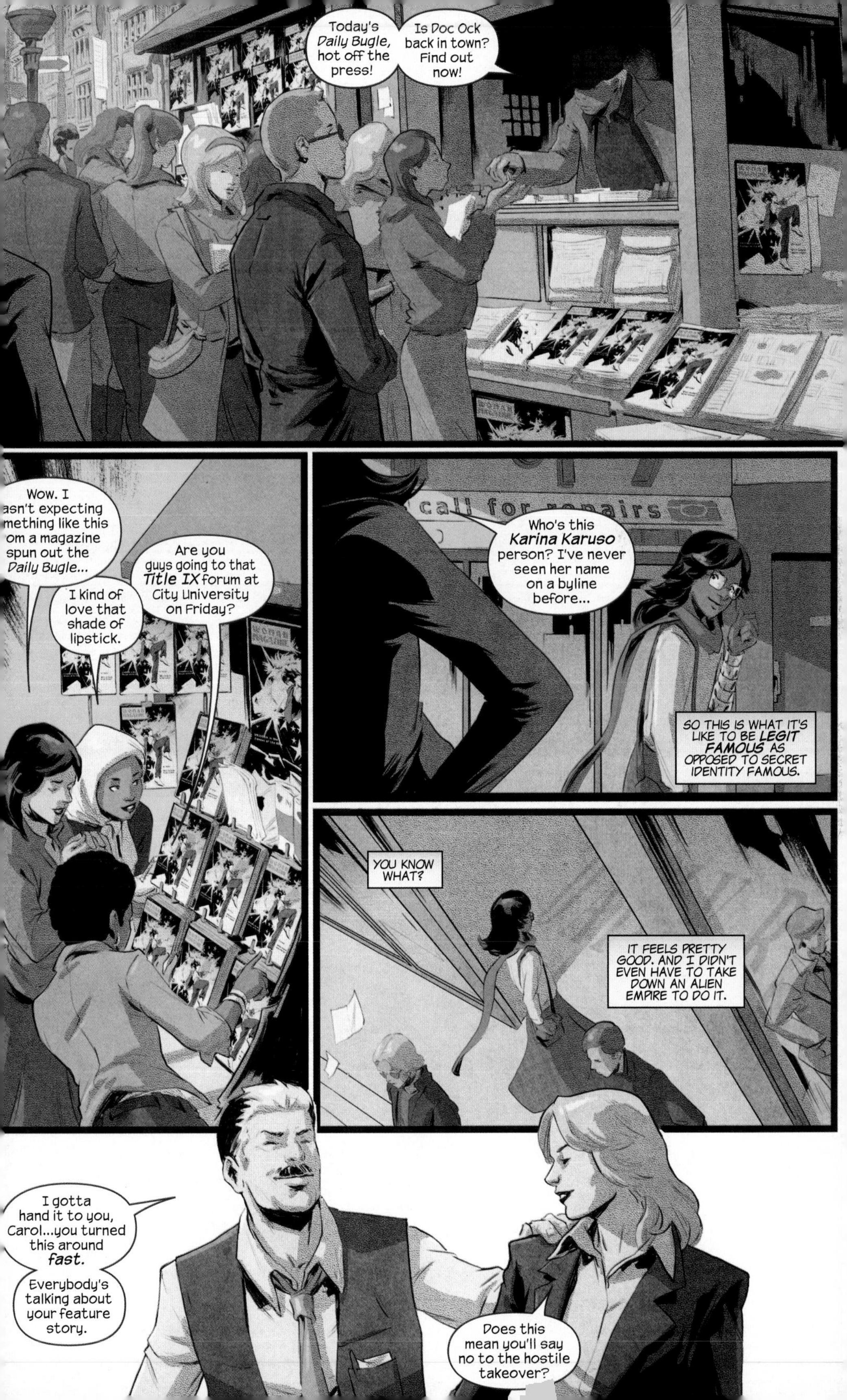
Today's Daily Bugle, hot off the press!
Is Doc Ock back in town? Find out now!
Wow. I asn't expecting mething like this om a magazine spun out the Daily Bugle...
I kind of love that shade of lipstick.
Are you guys going to that Title IX forum at City University on Friday?
call for repairs
Who's this Karina Karuso person? I've never seen her name on a byline before...
SO THIS IS WHAT IT'S LIKE TO BE LEGIT FAMOUS AS OPPOSED TO SECRET IDENTITY FAMOUS.
YOU KNOW WHAT?
IT FEELS PRETTY GOOD. AND I DIDN'T EVEN HAVE TO TAKE DOWN AN ALIEN EMPIRE TO DO IT.
I gotta hand it to you, Carol...you turned this around fast.
Everybody's talking about your feature story.
Does this mean you'll say no to the hostile takeover?

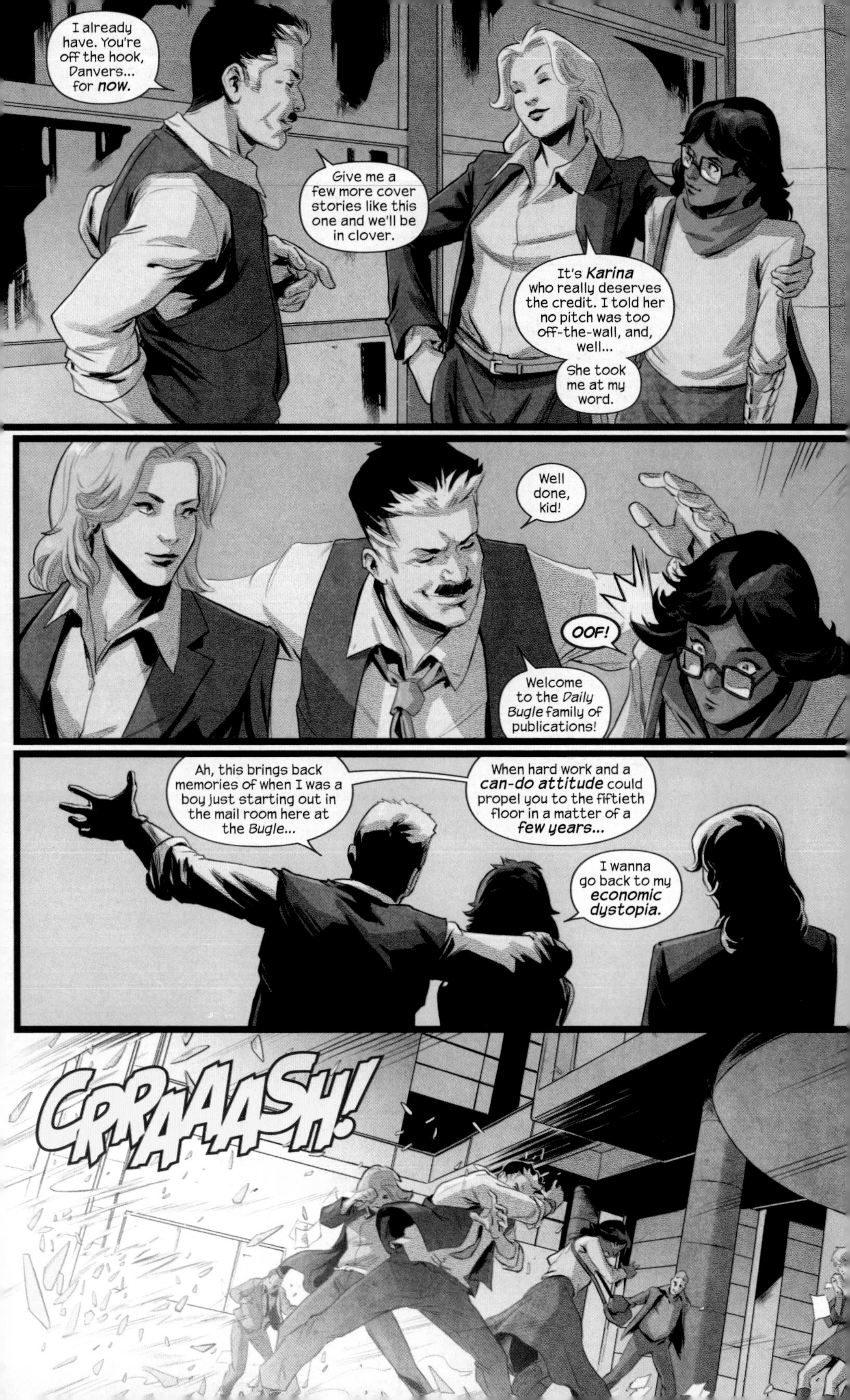

I already have. You're off the hook, Danvers... for *now.*
Give me a few more cover stories like this one and we'll be in clover.
It's *Karina* who really deserves the credit. I told her no pitch was too off-the-wall, and, well...
She took me at my word.
Well done, kid!
OOF!
Welcome to the *Daily Bugle* family of publications!
Ah, this brings back memories of when I was a boy just starting out in the mail room here at the *Bugle*...
When hard work and a *can-do attitude* could propel you to the fiftieth floor in a matter of a *few years...*
I wanna go back to my *economic dystopia.*
CRRAAASH!

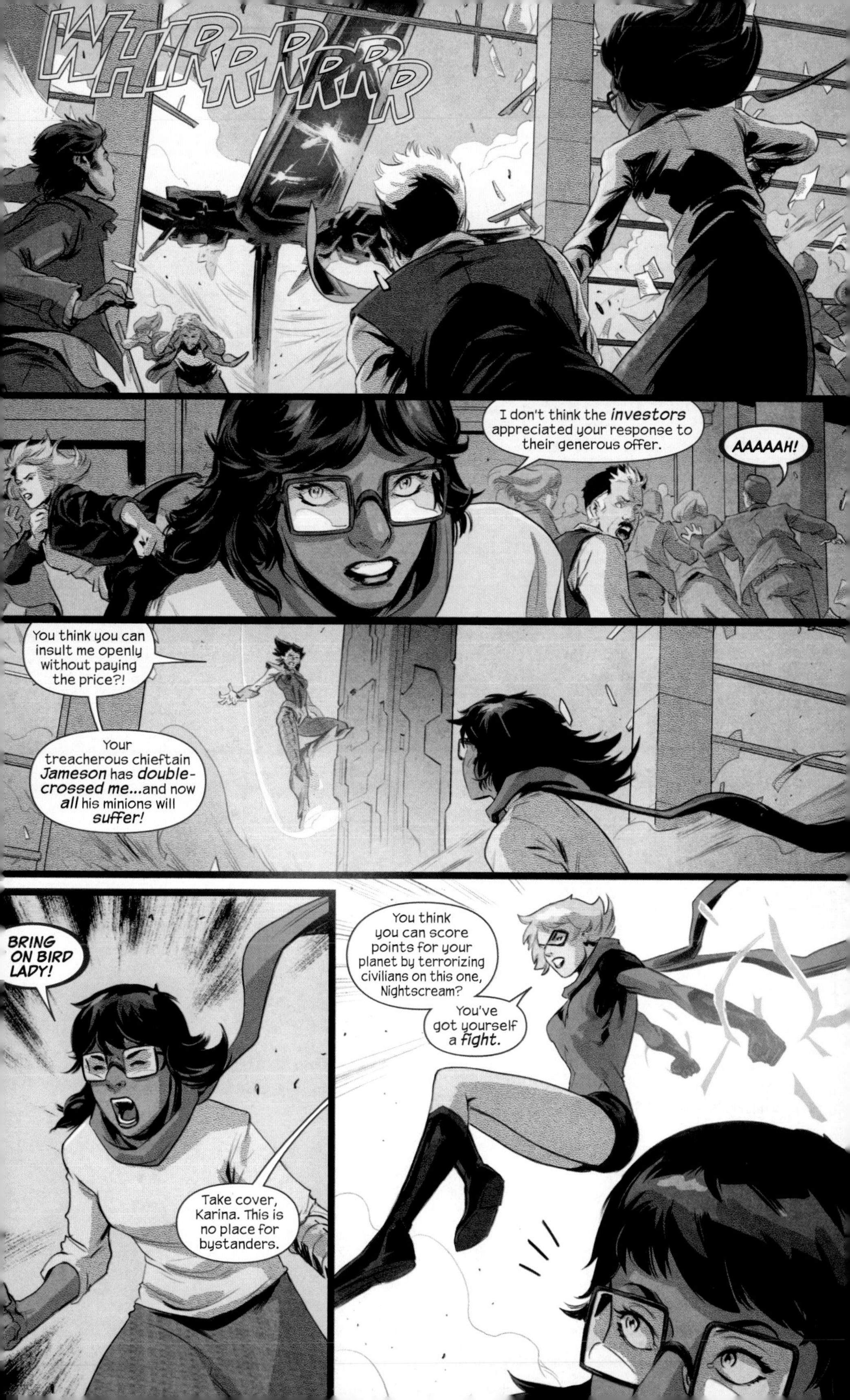
WHIRRRRRR
I don't think the *investors* appreciated your response to their generous offer.
AAAAAH!
You think you can insult me openly without paying the price?!
Your treacherous chieftain *Jameson* has *double-crossed me*...and now *all* his minions will *suffer!*
BRING ON BIRD LADY!
Take cover, Karina. This is no place for bystanders.
You think you can score points for your planet by terrorizing civilians on this one, Nightscream?
You've got yourself a *fight.*

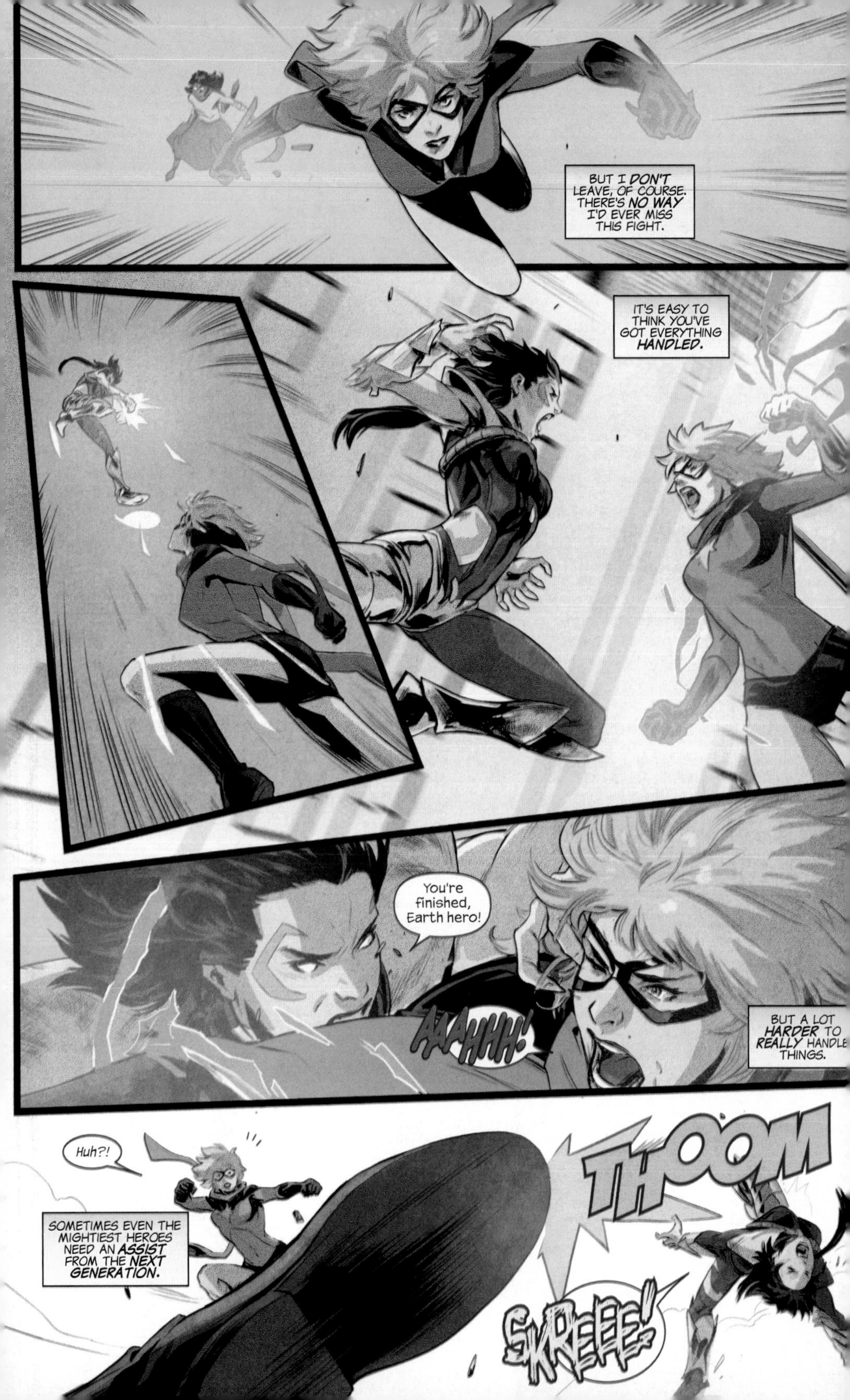
BUT I DON'T LEAVE, OF COURSE. THERE'S NO WAY I'D EVER MISS THIS FIGHT.
IT'S EASY TO THINK YOU'VE GOT EVERYTHING HANDLED.
You're finished, Earth hero!
AAAHHH!
BUT A LOT HARDER TO REALLY HANDLE THINGS.
Huh?!
THOOM
SOMETIMES EVEN THE MIGHTIEST HEROES NEED AN ASSIST FROM THE NEXT GENERATION.
SKREEE!

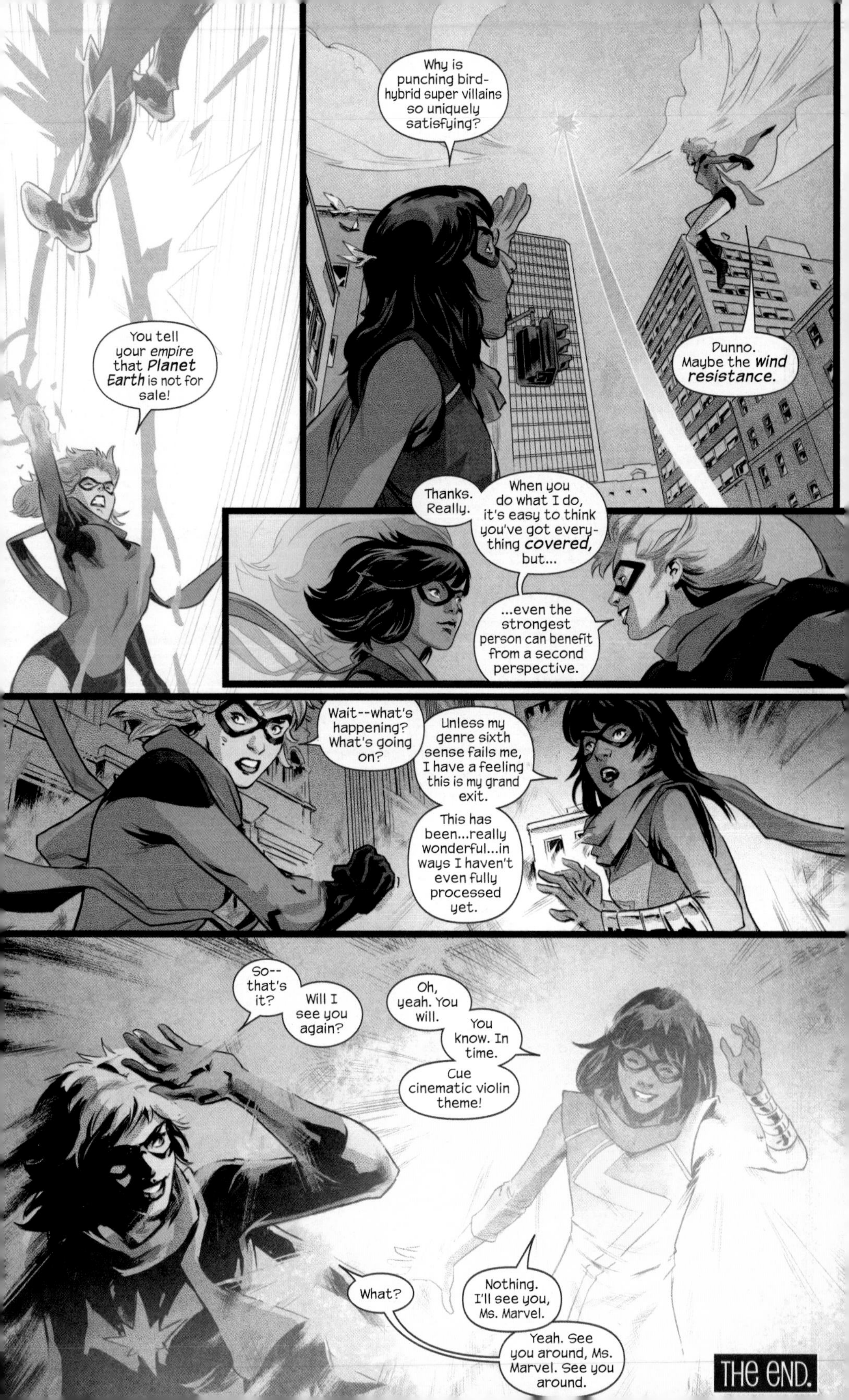

You tell your *empire* that *Planet Earth* is not for sale!
Why is punching bird-hybrid super villains so uniquely satisfying?
Dunno. Maybe the **wind resistance.**
Thanks. Really.
When you do what I do, it's easy to think you've got every-thing **covered,** but...
...even the strongest person can benefit from a second perspective.
Wait--what's happening? What's going on?
Unless my genre sixth sense fails me, I have a feeling this is my grand exit.
This has been...really wonderful...in ways I haven't even fully processed yet.
So--that's it?
Will I see you again?
Oh, yeah. You will.
You know. In time.
Cue cinematic violin theme!
What?
Nothing. I'll see you, Ms. Marvel.
Yeah. See you around, Ms. Marvel. See you around.
THE END.

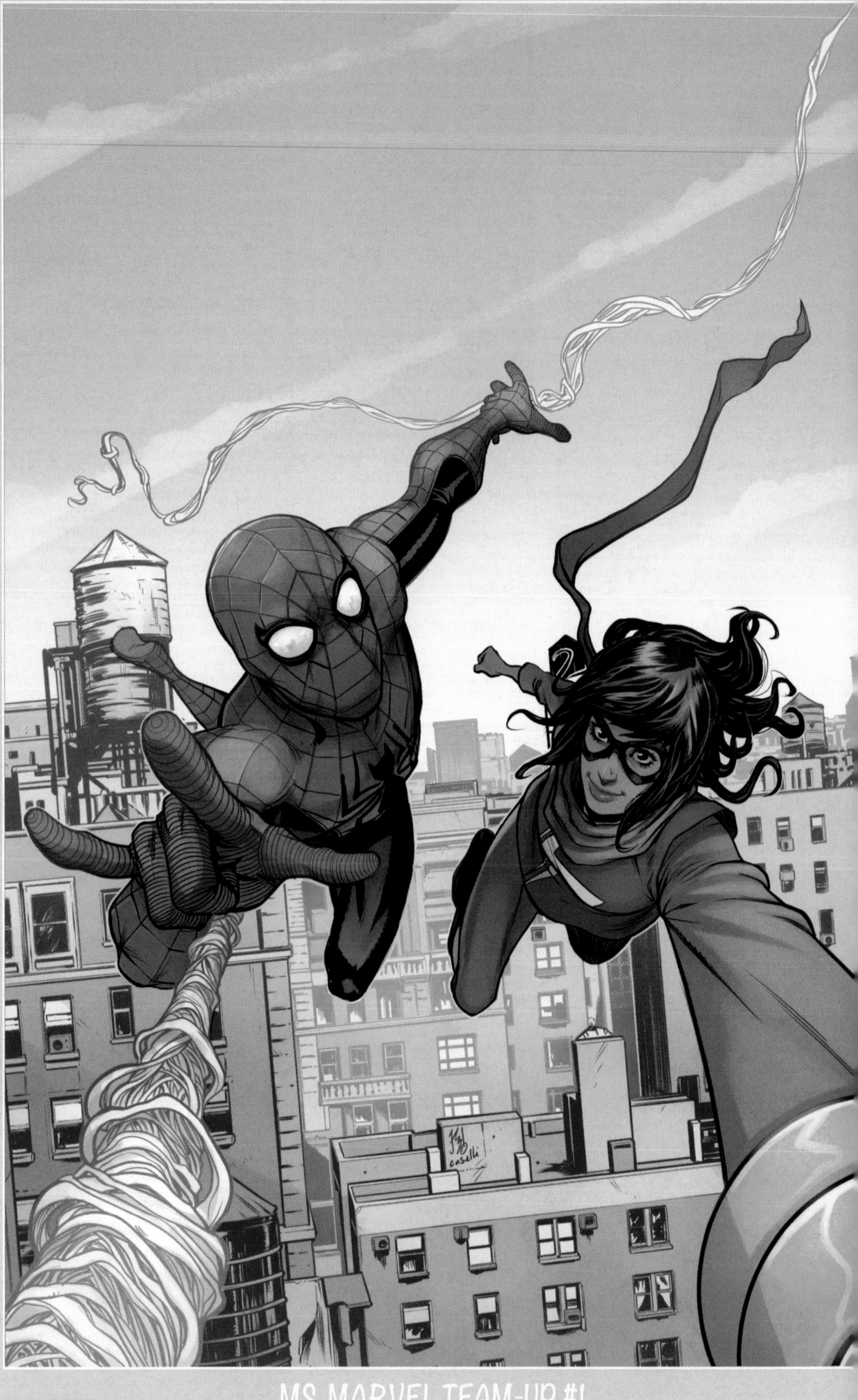

MS. MARVEL TEAM-UP #1

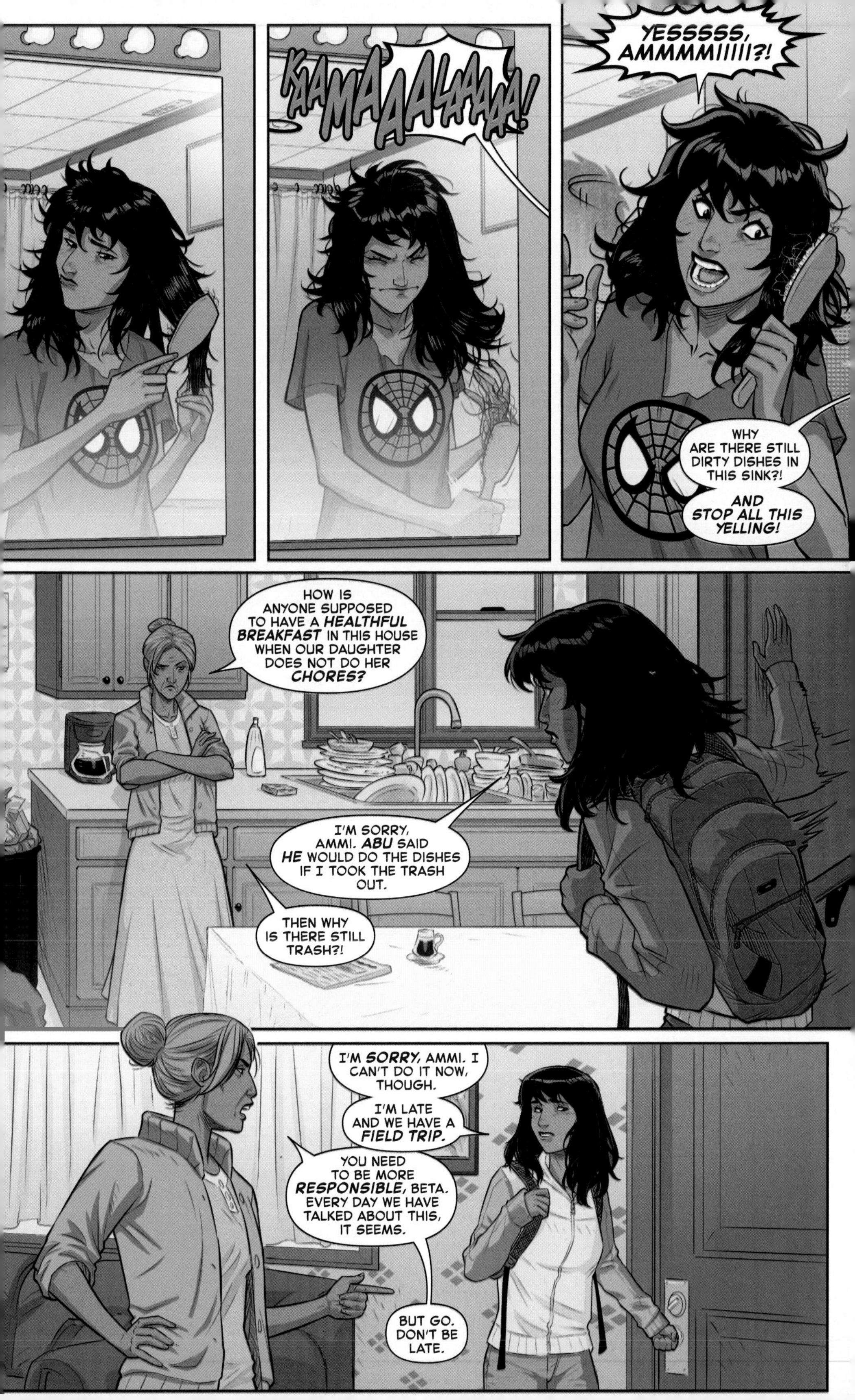
KAAMAAAALAAAAA!
YESSSSS, AMMMMIIIII?!
WHY ARE THERE STILL DIRTY DISHES IN THIS SINK?!
AND STOP ALL THIS YELLING!
HOW IS ANYONE SUPPOSED TO HAVE A HEALTHFUL BREAKFAST IN THIS HOUSE WHEN OUR DAUGHTER DOES NOT DO HER CHORES?
I'M SORRY, AMMI. ABU SAID HE WOULD DO THE DISHES IF I TOOK THE TRASH OUT.
THEN WHY IS THERE STILL TRASH?!
I'M SORRY, AMMI. I CAN'T DO IT NOW, THOUGH.
I'M LATE AND WE HAVE A FIELD TRIP.
YOU NEED TO BE MORE RESPONSIBLE, BETA. EVERY DAY WE HAVE TALKED ABOUT THIS, IT SEEMS.
BUT GO. DON'T BE LATE.

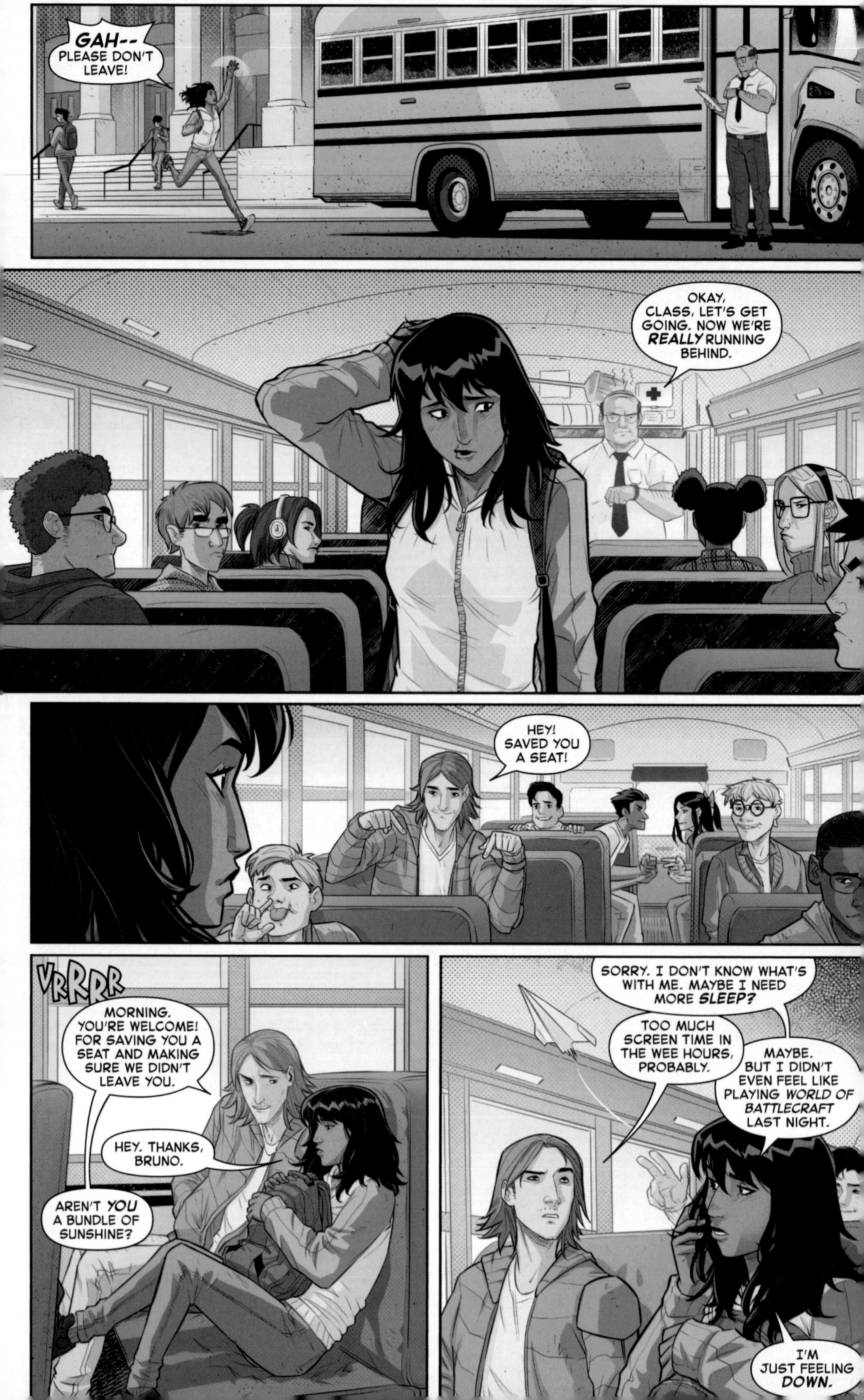
GAH-- PLEASE DON'T LEAVE!
OKAY, CLASS, LET'S GET GOING. NOW WE'RE REALLY RUNNING BEHIND.
HEY! SAVED YOU A SEAT!
VRRRR
MORNING. YOU'RE WELCOME! FOR SAVING YOU A SEAT AND MAKING SURE WE DIDN'T LEAVE YOU.
HEY. THANKS, BRUNO.
AREN'T YOU A BUNDLE OF SUNSHINE?
SORRY. I DON'T KNOW WHAT'S WITH ME. MAYBE I NEED MORE SLEEP?
TOO MUCH SCREEN TIME IN THE WEE HOURS, PROBABLY.
MAYBE. BUT I DIDN'T EVEN FEEL LIKE PLAYING WORLD OF BATTLECRAFT LAST NIGHT.
I'M JUST FEELING DOWN.

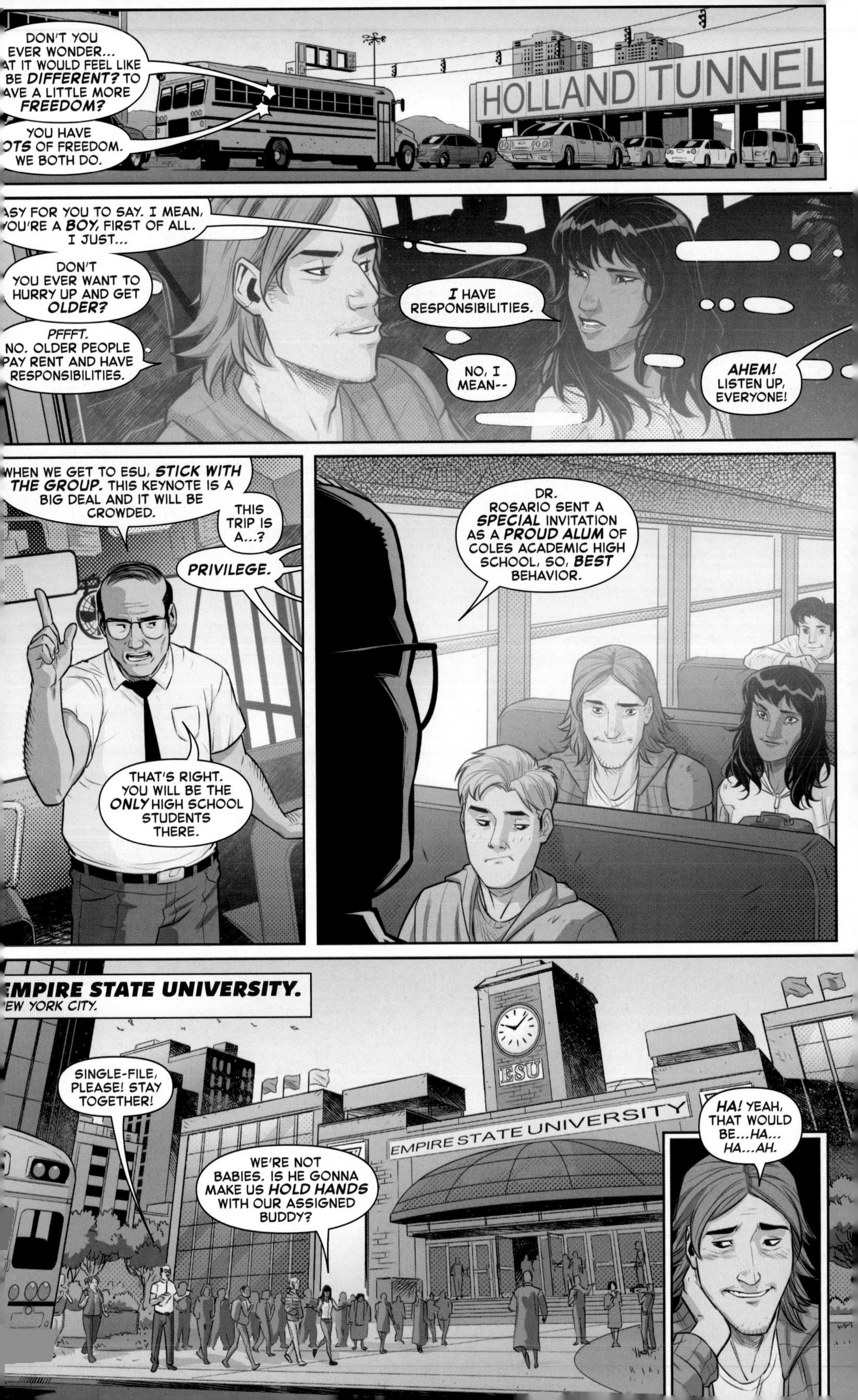
HOLLAND TUNNEL
DON'T YOU EVER WONDER... AT IT WOULD FEEL LIKE BE DIFFERENT? TO AVE A LITTLE MORE FREEDOM?
YOU HAVE OTS OF FREEDOM. WE BOTH DO.
ASY FOR YOU TO SAY. I MEAN, YOU'RE A BOY, FIRST OF ALL. I JUST...
DON'T YOU EVER WANT TO HURRY UP AND GET OLDER?
PFFFT. NO. OLDER PEOPLE PAY RENT AND HAVE RESPONSIBILITIES.
I HAVE RESPONSIBILITIES.
NO, I MEAN--
AHEM! LISTEN UP, EVERYONE!
WHEN WE GET TO ESU, STICK WITH THE GROUP. THIS KEYNOTE IS A BIG DEAL AND IT WILL BE CROWDED.
THIS TRIP IS A...?
PRIVILEGE.
THAT'S RIGHT. YOU WILL BE THE ONLY HIGH SCHOOL STUDENTS THERE.
DR. ROSARIO SENT A SPECIAL INVITATION AS A PROUD ALUM OF COLES ACADEMIC HIGH SCHOOL, SO, BEST BEHAVIOR.
EMPIRE STATE UNIVERSITY.
EW YORK CITY.
ESU
EMPIRE STATE UNIVERSITY
SINGLE-FILE, PLEASE! STAY TOGETHER!
WE'RE NOT BABIES. IS HE GONNA MAKE US HOLD HANDS WITH OUR ASSIGNED BUDDY?
HA! YEAH, THAT WOULD BE...HA... HA...AH.

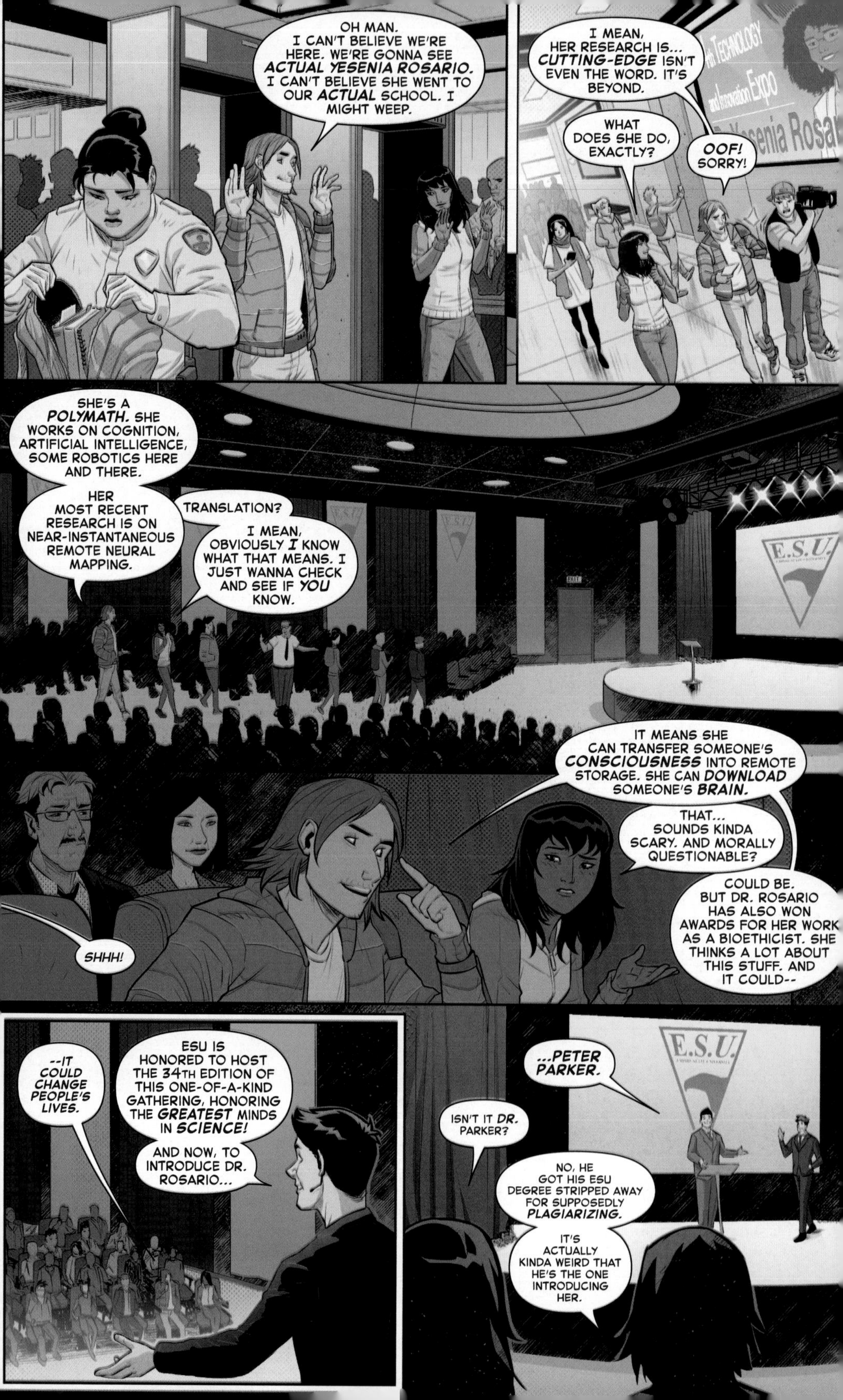
OH MAN. I CAN'T BELIEVE WE'RE HERE. WE'RE GONNA SEE ACTUAL YESENIA ROSARIO. I CAN'T BELIEVE SHE WENT TO OUR ACTUAL SCHOOL. I MIGHT WEEP.
I MEAN, HER RESEARCH IS... CUTTING-EDGE ISN'T EVEN THE WORD. IT'S BEYOND.
WHAT DOES SHE DO, EXACTLY?
OOF! SORRY!
SHE'S A POLYMATH. SHE WORKS ON COGNITION, ARTIFICIAL INTELLIGENCE, SOME ROBOTICS HERE AND THERE.
HER MOST RECENT RESEARCH IS ON NEAR-INSTANTANEOUS REMOTE NEURAL MAPPING.
TRANSLATION?
I MEAN, OBVIOUSLY I KNOW WHAT THAT MEANS. I JUST WANNA CHECK AND SEE IF YOU KNOW.
E.S.U.
IT MEANS SHE CAN TRANSFER SOMEONE'S CONSCIOUSNESS INTO REMOTE STORAGE. SHE CAN DOWNLOAD SOMEONE'S BRAIN.
THAT... SOUNDS KINDA SCARY. AND MORALLY QUESTIONABLE?
COULD BE. BUT DR. ROSARIO HAS ALSO WON AWARDS FOR HER WORK AS A BIOETHICIST. SHE THINKS A LOT ABOUT THIS STUFF. AND IT COULD--
SHHH!
--IT COULD CHANGE PEOPLE'S LIVES.
ESU IS HONORED TO HOST THE 34TH EDITION OF THIS ONE-OF-A-KIND GATHERING, HONORING THE GREATEST MINDS IN SCIENCE!
AND NOW, TO INTRODUCE DR. ROSARIO...
...PETER PARKER.
E.S.U.
ISN'T IT DR. PARKER?
NO, HE GOT HIS ESU DEGREE STRIPPED AWAY FOR SUPPOSEDLY PLAGIARIZING.
IT'S ACTUALLY KINDA WEIRD THAT HE'S THE ONE INTRODUCING HER.

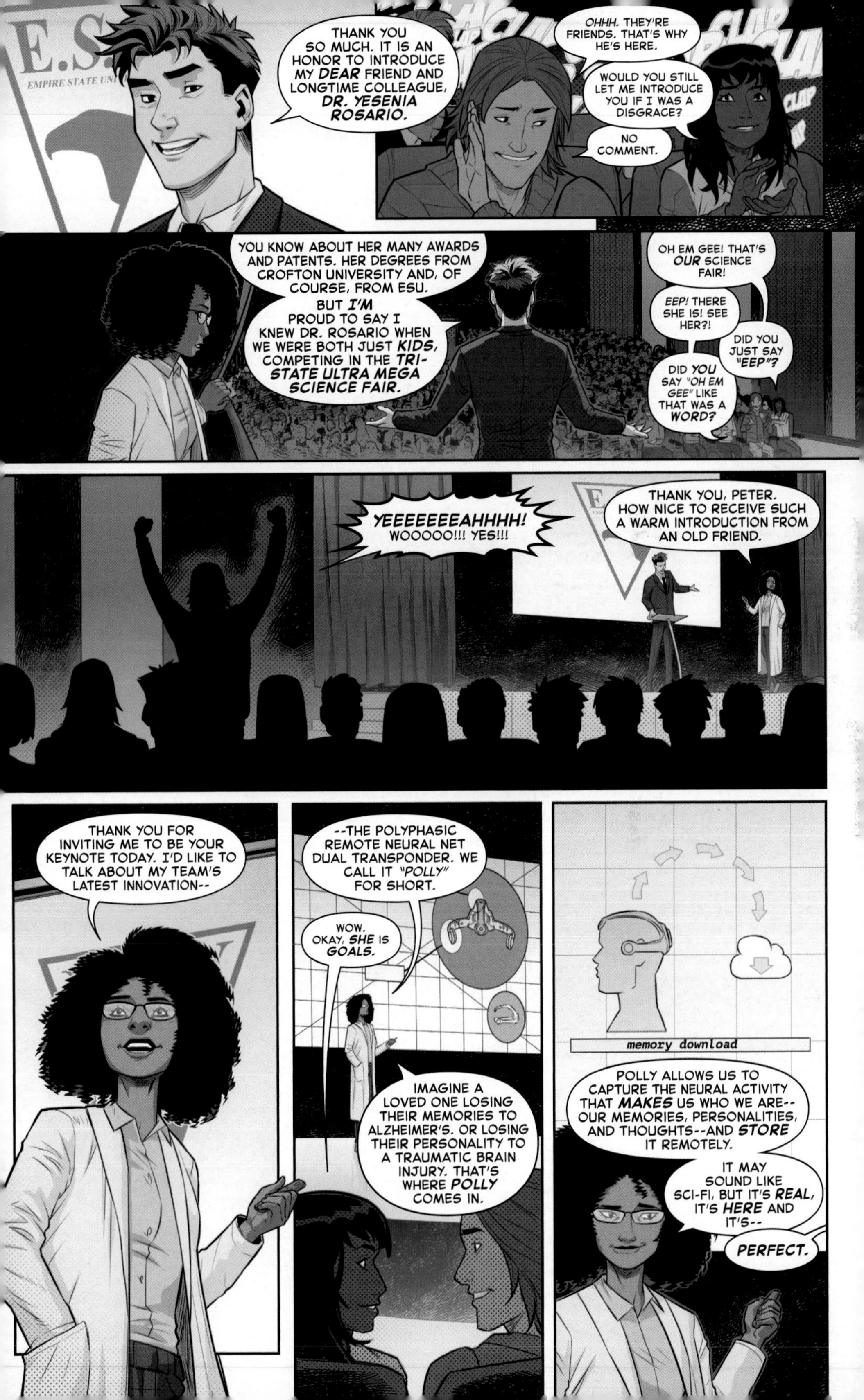
E.S.U.
EMPIRE STATE UNI
THANK YOU SO MUCH. IT IS AN HONOR TO INTRODUCE MY DEAR FRIEND AND LONGTIME COLLEAGUE, DR. YESENIA ROSARIO.
CLAP CLAP
OHHH. THEY'RE FRIENDS. THAT'S WHY HE'S HERE.
WOULD YOU STILL LET ME INTRODUCE YOU IF I WAS A DISGRACE?
NO COMMENT.
YOU KNOW ABOUT HER MANY AWARDS AND PATENTS. HER DEGREES FROM CROFTON UNIVERSITY AND, OF COURSE, FROM ESU.
BUT I'M PROUD TO SAY I KNEW DR. ROSARIO WHEN WE WERE BOTH JUST KIDS, COMPETING IN THE TRI-STATE ULTRA MEGA SCIENCE FAIR.
OH EM GEE! THAT'S OUR SCIENCE FAIR!
EEP! THERE SHE IS! SEE HER?!
DID YOU JUST SAY "EEP"?
DID YOU SAY "OH EM GEE" LIKE THAT WAS A WORD?
YEEEEEEEAHHHH! WOOOOO!!! YES!!!
THANK YOU, PETER. HOW NICE TO RECEIVE SUCH A WARM INTRODUCTION FROM AN OLD FRIEND.
THANK YOU FOR INVITING ME TO BE YOUR KEYNOTE TODAY. I'D LIKE TO TALK ABOUT MY TEAM'S LATEST INNOVATION--
--THE POLYPHASIC REMOTE NEURAL NET DUAL TRANSPONDER. WE CALL IT "POLLY" FOR SHORT.
WOW. OKAY, SHE IS GOALS.
IMAGINE A LOVED ONE LOSING THEIR MEMORIES TO ALZHEIMER'S. OR LOSING THEIR PERSONALITY TO A TRAUMATIC BRAIN INJURY. THAT'S WHERE POLLY COMES IN.
memory download
POLLY ALLOWS US TO CAPTURE THE NEURAL ACTIVITY THAT MAKES US WHO WE ARE--OUR MEMORIES, PERSONALITIES, AND THOUGHTS--AND STORE IT REMOTELY.
IT MAY SOUND LIKE SCI-FI, BUT IT'S REAL, IT'S HERE AND IT'S--
PERFECT.

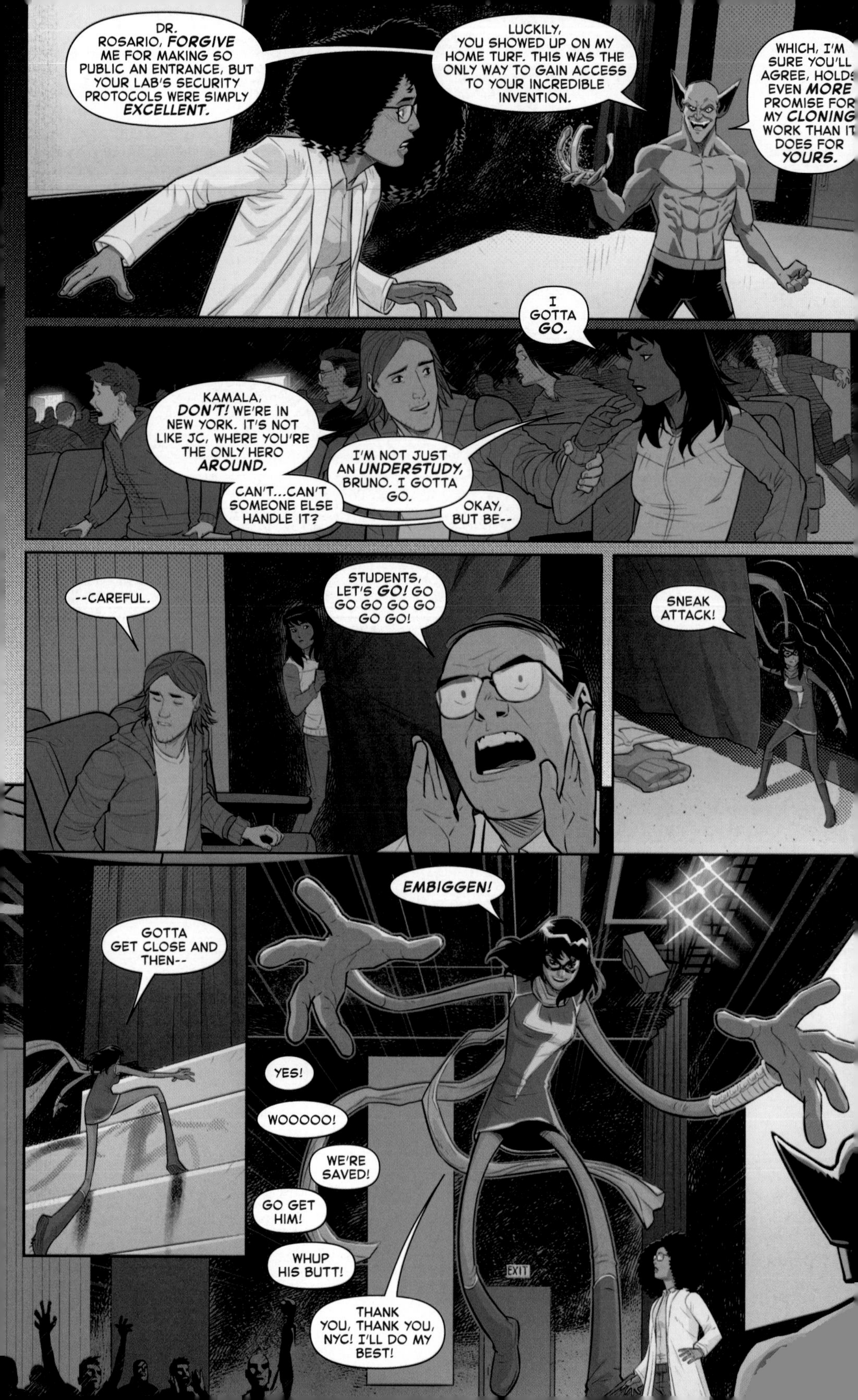
DR. ROSARIO, FORGIVE ME FOR MAKING SO PUBLIC AN ENTRANCE, BUT YOUR LAB'S SECURITY PROTOCOLS WERE SIMPLY EXCELLENT.
LUCKILY, YOU SHOWED UP ON MY HOME TURF. THIS WAS THE ONLY WAY TO GAIN ACCESS TO YOUR INCREDIBLE INVENTION.
WHICH, I'M SURE YOU'LL AGREE, HOLDS EVEN MORE PROMISE FOR MY CLONING WORK THAN IT DOES FOR YOURS.
I GOTTA GO.
KAMALA, DON'T! WE'RE IN NEW YORK. IT'S NOT LIKE JC, WHERE YOU'RE THE ONLY HERO AROUND.
I'M NOT JUST AN UNDERSTUDY, BRUNO. I GOTTA GO.
CAN'T...CAN'T SOMEONE ELSE HANDLE IT?
OKAY, BUT BE--
--CAREFUL.
STUDENTS, LET'S GO! GO GO GO GO GO GO GO!
SNEAK ATTACK!
GOTTA GET CLOSE AND THEN--
EMBIGGEN!
YES!
WOOOOO!
WE'RE SAVED!
GO GET HIM!
WHUP HIS BUTT!
THANK YOU, THANK YOU, NYC! I'LL DO MY BEST!
EXIT

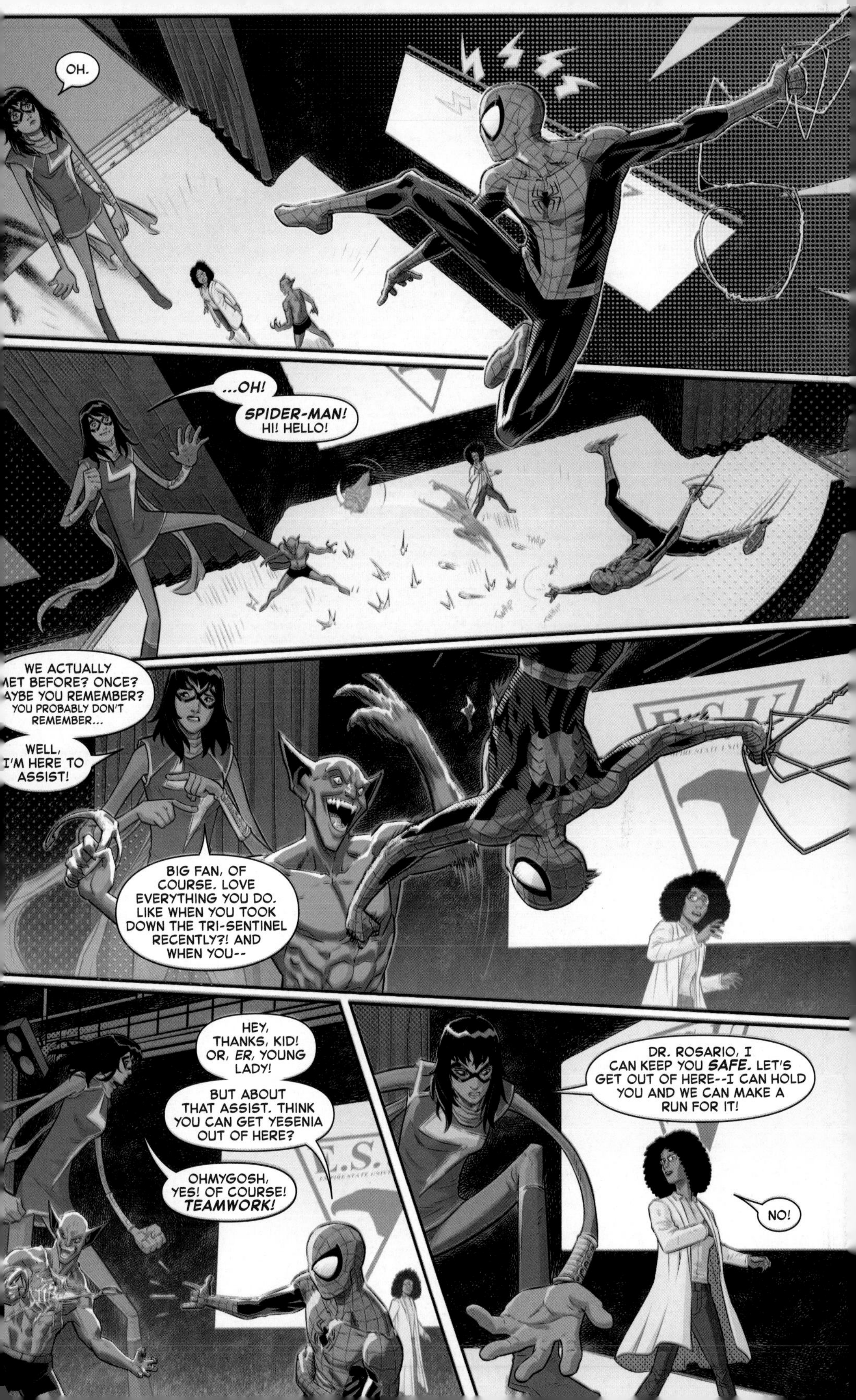
OH.
...OH! SPIDER-MAN! HI! HELLO!
THWIP
THWIP
THWIP
WE ACTUALLY MET BEFORE? ONCE? AYBE YOU REMEMBER? YOU PROBABLY DON'T REMEMBER...
WELL, I'M HERE TO ASSIST!
BIG FAN, OF COURSE. LOVE EVERYTHING YOU DO. LIKE WHEN YOU TOOK DOWN THE TRI-SENTINEL RECENTLY?! AND WHEN YOU--
HEY, THANKS, KID! OR, ER, YOUNG LADY!
BUT ABOUT THAT ASSIST. THINK YOU CAN GET YESENIA OUT OF HERE?
OHMYGOSH, YES! OF COURSE! TEAMWORK!
DR. ROSARIO, I CAN KEEP YOU SAFE. LET'S GET OUT OF HERE--I CAN HOLD YOU AND WE CAN MAKE A RUN FOR IT!
NO!

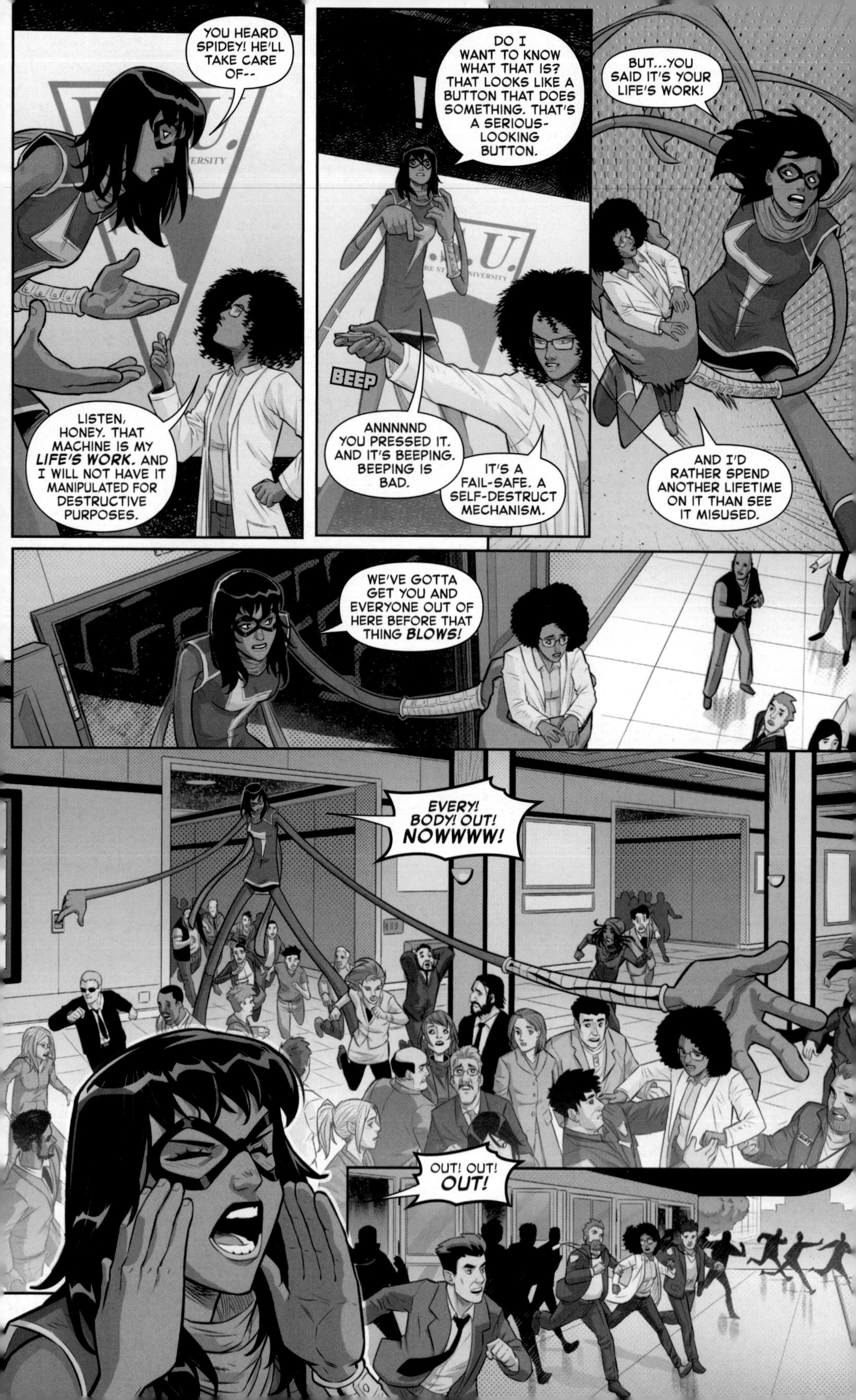
YOU HEARD SPIDEY! HE'LL TAKE CARE OF--
LISTEN, HONEY. THAT MACHINE IS MY LIFE'S WORK. AND I WILL NOT HAVE IT MANIPULATED FOR DESTRUCTIVE PURPOSES.
DO I WANT TO KNOW WHAT THAT IS? THAT LOOKS LIKE A BUTTON THAT DOES SOMETHING. THAT'S A SERIOUS-LOOKING BUTTON.
BEEP
ANNNNND YOU PRESSED IT. AND IT'S BEEPING. BEEPING IS BAD.
IT'S A FAIL-SAFE. A SELF-DESTRUCT MECHANISM.
BUT...YOU SAID IT'S YOUR LIFE'S WORK!
AND I'D RATHER SPEND ANOTHER LIFETIME ON IT THAN SEE IT MISUSED.
WE'VE GOTTA GET YOU AND EVERYONE OUT OF HERE BEFORE THAT THING BLOWS!
EVERY! BODY! OUT! NOWWWW!
OUT! OUT! OUT!

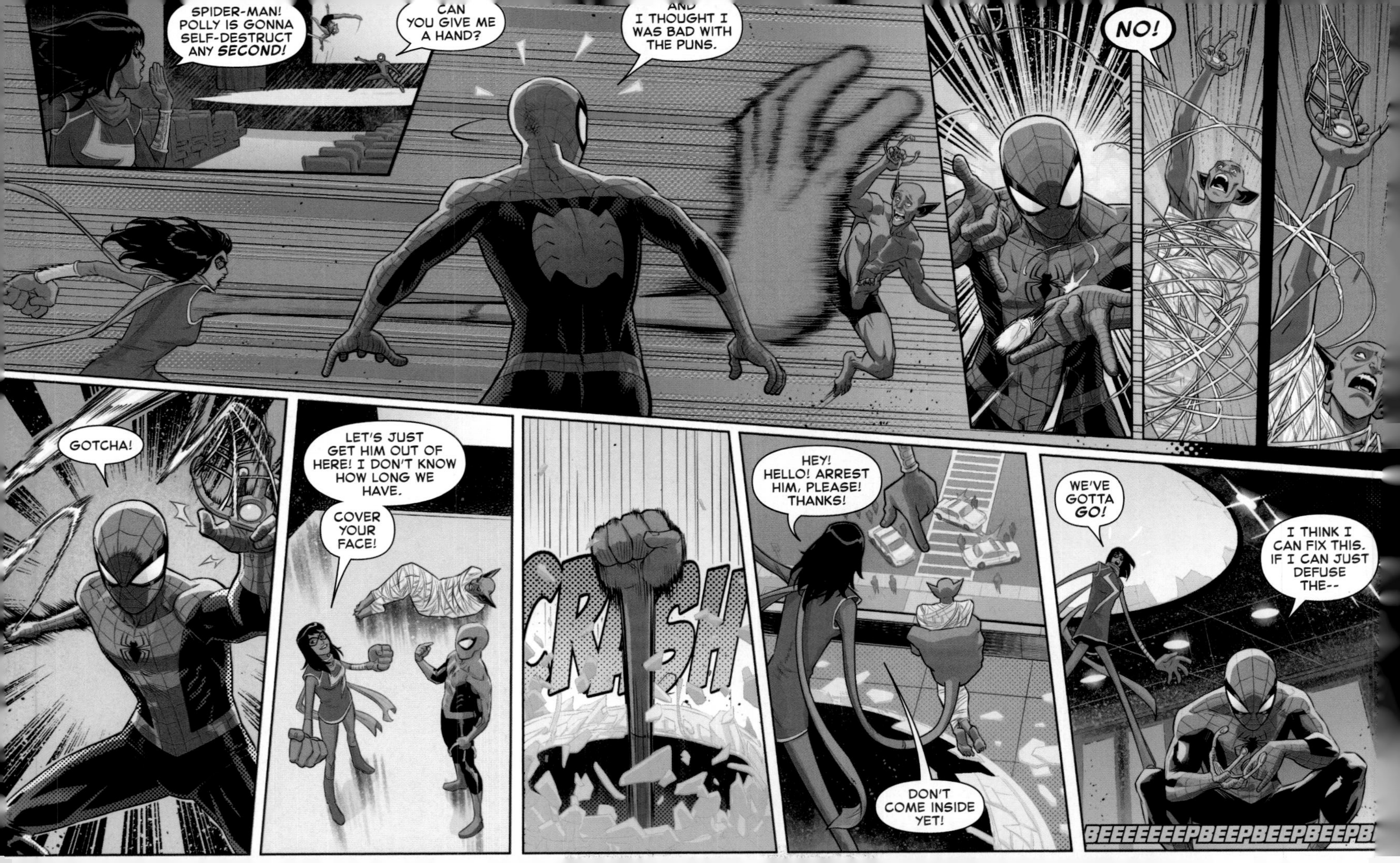
SPIDER-MAN! POLLY IS GONNA SELF-DESTRUCT ANY SECOND!
CAN YOU GIVE ME A HAND?
AND I THOUGHT I WAS BAD WITH THE PUNS.
NO!
GOTCHA!
LET'S JUST GET HIM OUT OF HERE! I DON'T KNOW HOW LONG WE HAVE.
COVER YOUR FACE!
CRASH
HEY! HELLO! ARREST HIM, PLEASE! THANKS!
DON'T COME INSIDE YET!
WE'VE GOTTA GO!
I THINK I CAN FIX THIS. IF I CAN JUST DEFUSE THE--
BEEEEEEEPBEEPBEEPBEEPB

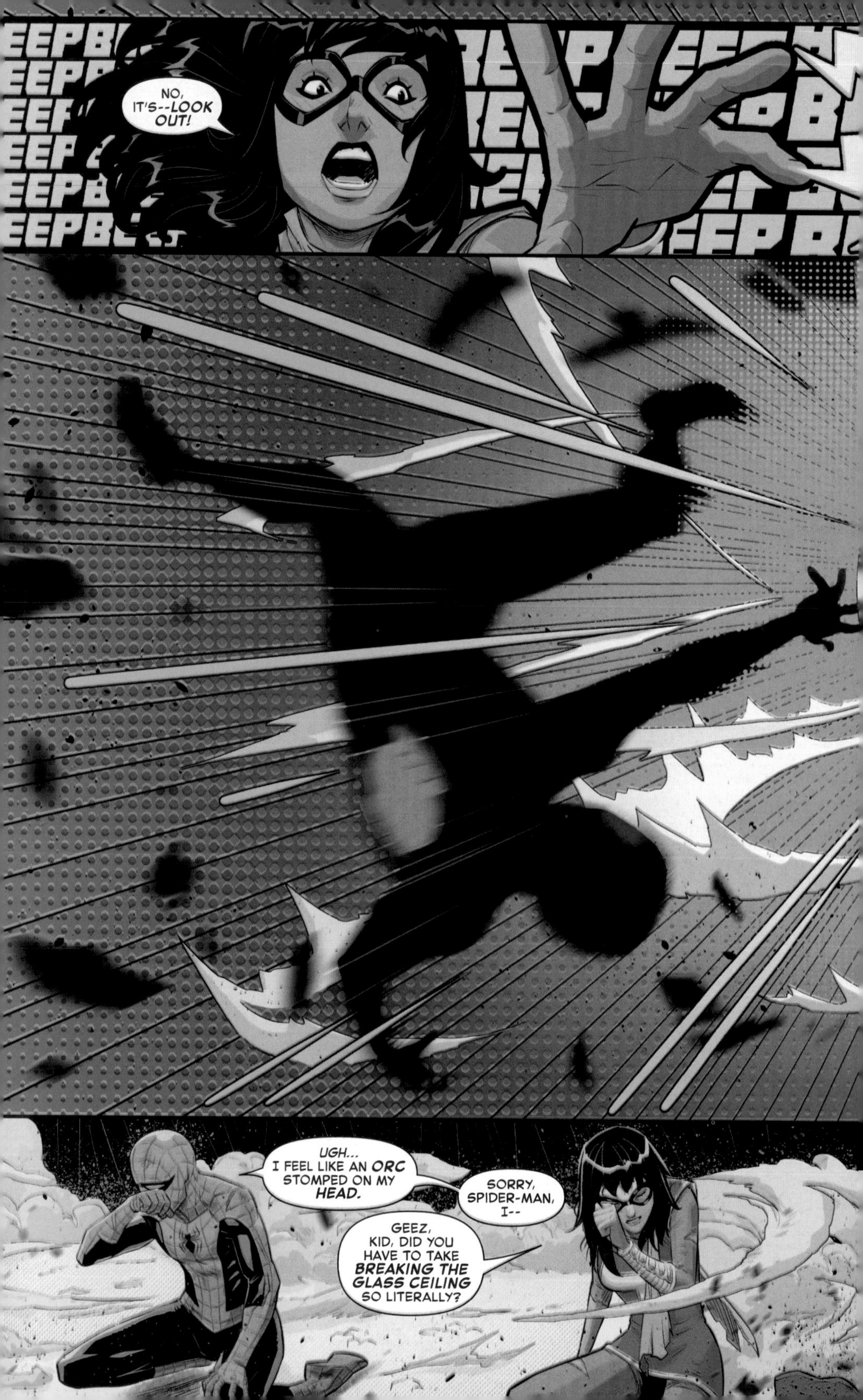
NO, IT'S--LOOK OUT!
UGH... I FEEL LIKE AN ORC STOMPED ON MY HEAD.
SORRY, SPIDER-MAN, I--
GEEZ, KID, DID YOU HAVE TO TAKE BREAKING THE GLASS CEILING SO LITERALLY?

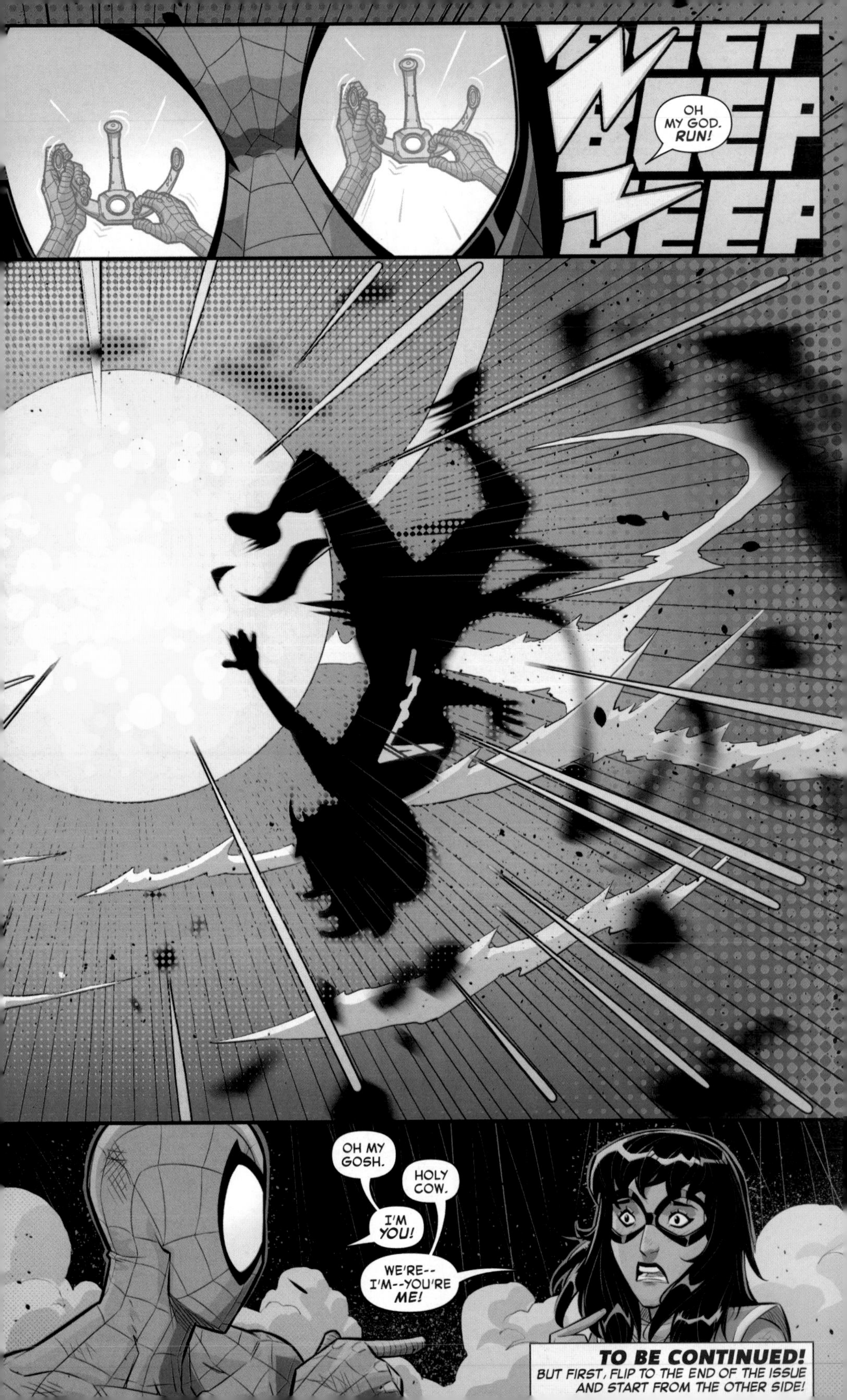
OH MY GOD. RUN!
OH MY GOSH.
HOLY COW.
I'M YOU!
WE'RE-- I'M--YOU'RE ME!
TO BE CONTINUED!
BUT FIRST, FLIP TO THE END OF THE ISSUE AND START FROM THE OTHER SIDE!

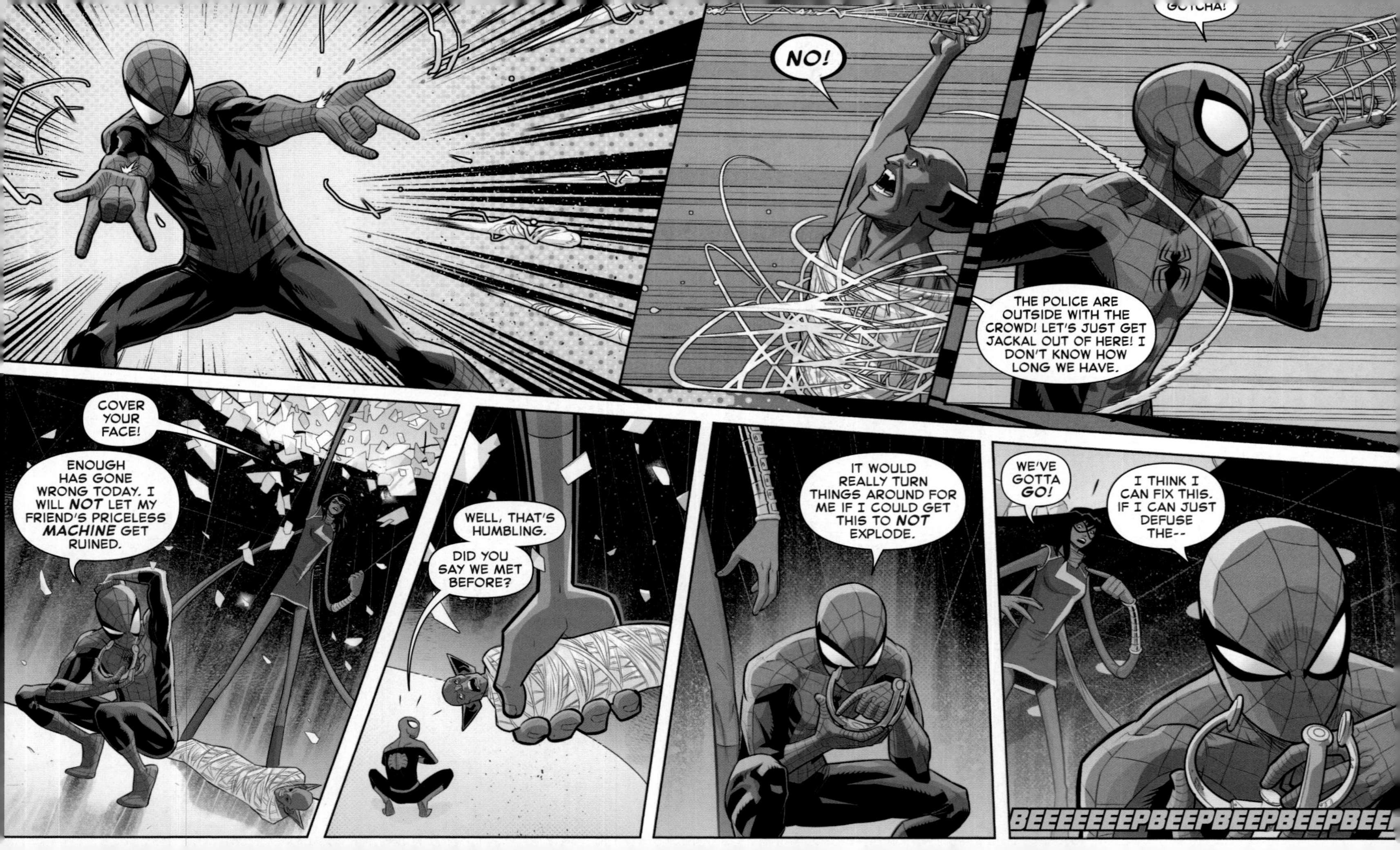
NO!
GOTCHA!
THE POLICE ARE OUTSIDE WITH THE CROWD! LET'S JUST GET JACKAL OUT OF HERE! I DON'T KNOW HOW LONG WE HAVE.
COVER YOUR FACE!
ENOUGH HAS GONE WRONG TODAY. I WILL **NOT** LET MY FRIEND'S PRICELESS ***MACHINE*** GET RUINED.
WELL, THAT'S HUMBLING.
DID YOU SAY WE MET BEFORE?
IT WOULD REALLY TURN THINGS AROUND FOR ME IF I COULD GET THIS TO **NOT** EXPLODE.
WE'VE GOTTA ***GO!***
I THINK I CAN FIX THIS. IF I CAN JUST DEFUSE THE--
BEEEEEEEPBEEPBEEPBEEPBEE

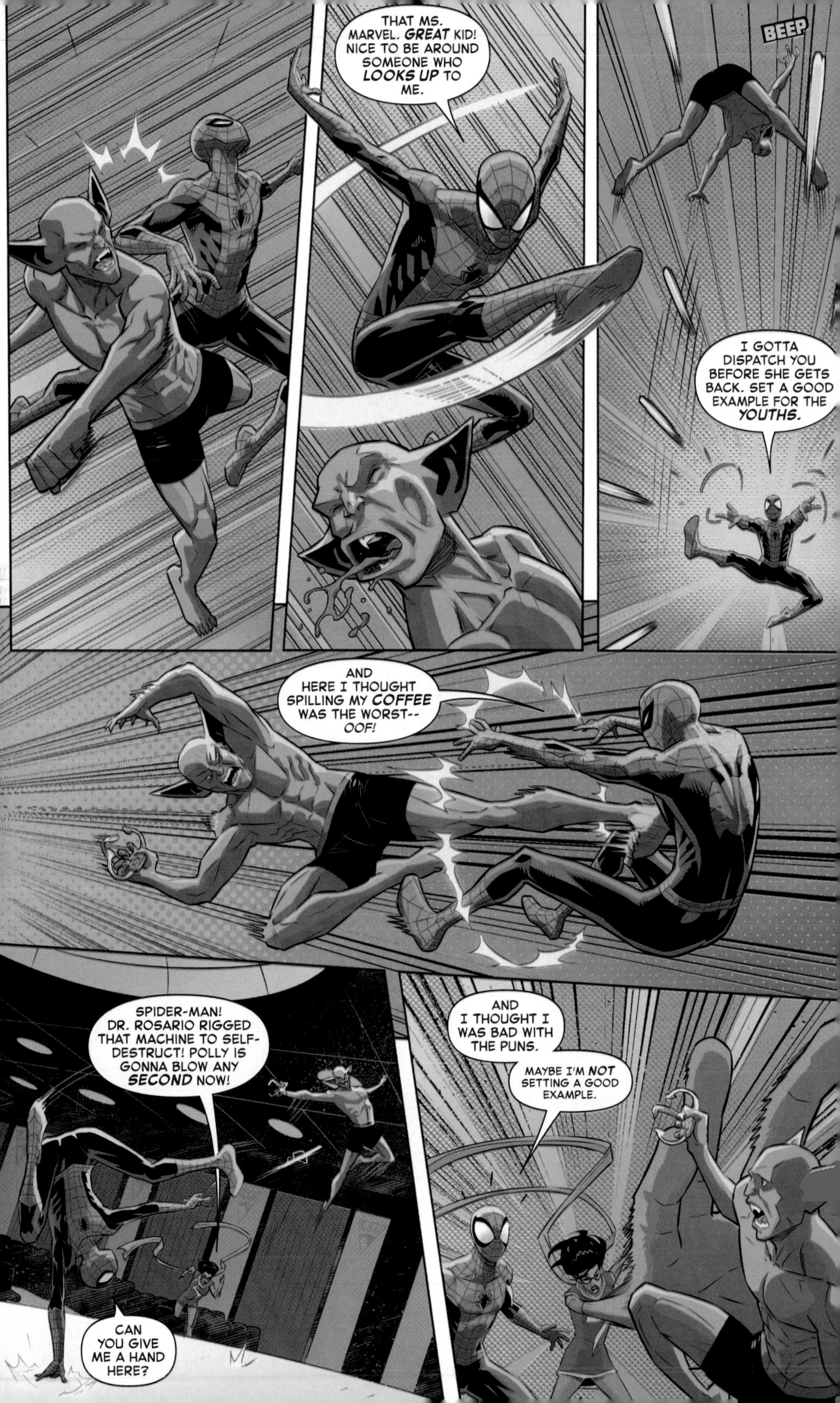
THAT MS. MARVEL. **GREAT** KID! NICE TO BE AROUND SOMEONE WHO **LOOKS UP** TO ME.
BEEP
I GOTTA DISPATCH YOU BEFORE SHE GETS BACK. SET A GOOD EXAMPLE FOR THE ***YOUTHS.***
AND HERE I THOUGHT SPILLING MY ***COFFEE*** WAS THE WORST-- *OOF!*
SPIDER-MAN! DR. ROSARIO RIGGED THAT MACHINE TO SELF-DESTRUCT! POLLY IS GONNA BLOW ANY ***SECOND*** NOW!
CAN YOU GIVE ME A HAND HERE?
AND I THOUGHT I WAS BAD WITH THE PUNS.
MAYBE I'M ***NOT*** SETTING A GOOD EXAMPLE.

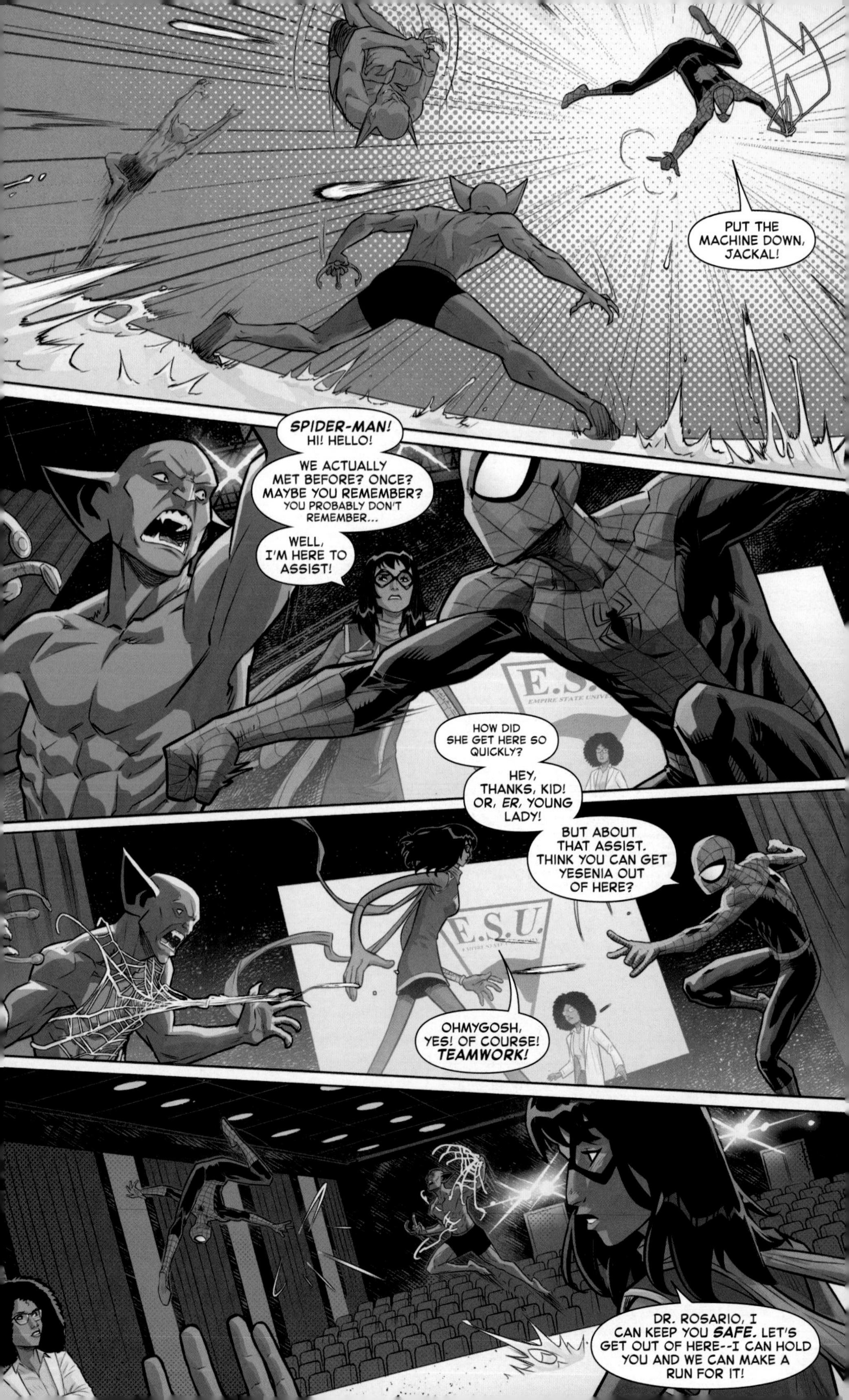
PUT THE MACHINE DOWN, JACKAL!
SPIDER-MAN! HI! HELLO!
WE ACTUALLY MET BEFORE? ONCE? MAYBE YOU REMEMBER? YOU PROBABLY DON'T REMEMBER...
WELL, I'M HERE TO ASSIST!
E.S.U.
EMPIRE STATE UNIV
HOW DID SHE GET HERE SO QUICKLY?
HEY, THANKS, KID! OR, ER, YOUNG LADY!
BUT ABOUT THAT ASSIST. THINK YOU CAN GET YESENIA OUT OF HERE?
E.S.U.
OHMYGOSH, YES! OF COURSE! TEAMWORK!
DR. ROSARIO, I CAN KEEP YOU SAFE. LET'S GET OUT OF HERE--I CAN HOLD YOU AND WE CAN MAKE A RUN FOR IT!

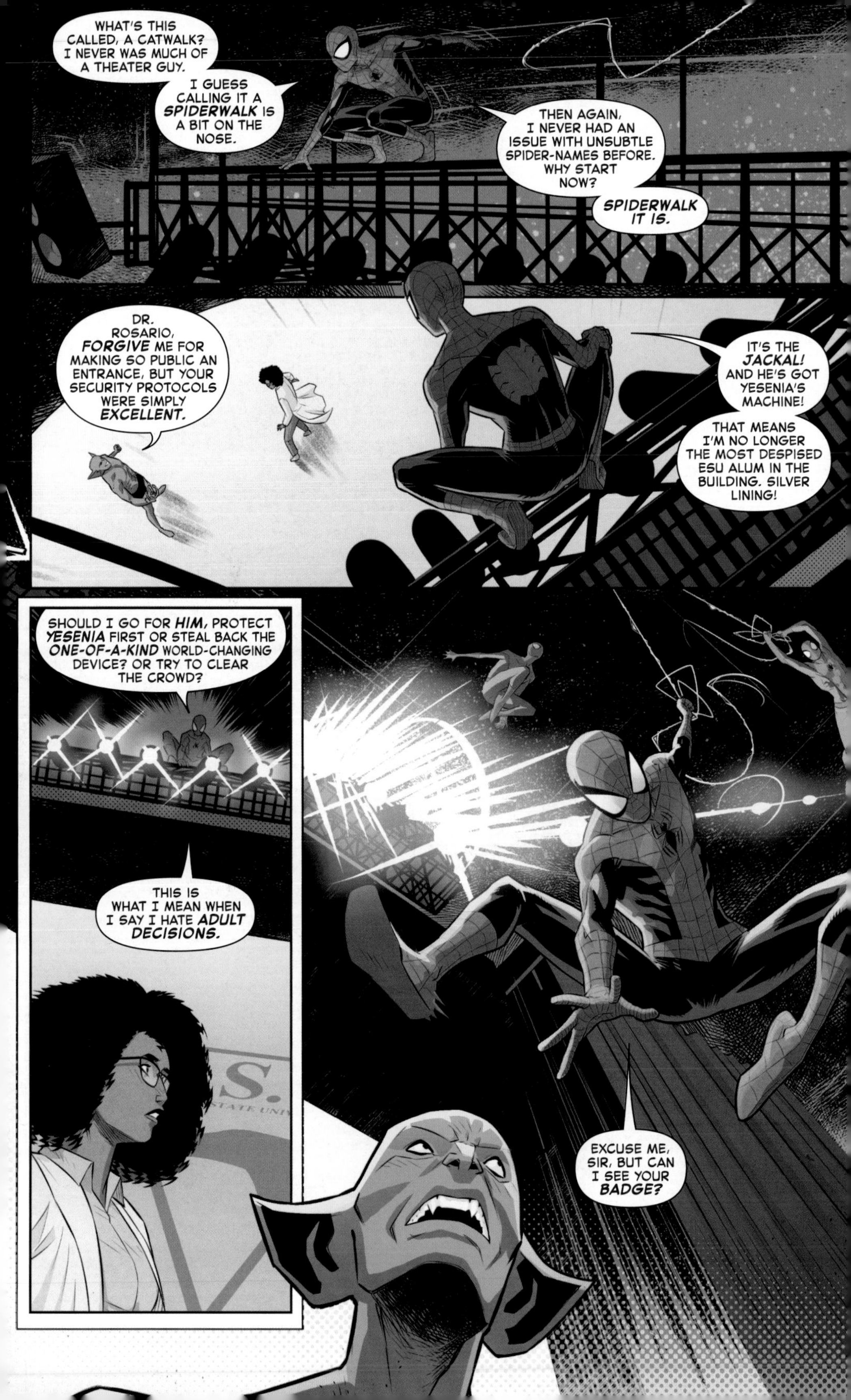
WHAT'S THIS CALLED, A CATWALK? I NEVER WAS MUCH OF A THEATER GUY.
I GUESS CALLING IT A **SPIDERWALK** IS A BIT ON THE NOSE.
THEN AGAIN, I NEVER HAD AN ISSUE WITH UNSUBTLE SPIDER-NAMES BEFORE. WHY START NOW?
SPIDERWALK IT IS.
DR. ROSARIO, **FORGIVE** ME FOR MAKING SO PUBLIC AN ENTRANCE, BUT YOUR SECURITY PROTOCOLS WERE SIMPLY **EXCELLENT.**
IT'S THE **JACKAL!** AND HE'S GOT YESENIA'S MACHINE!
THAT MEANS I'M NO LONGER THE MOST DESPISED ESU ALUM IN THE BUILDING. SILVER LINING!
SHOULD I GO FOR **HIM,** PROTECT **YESENIA** FIRST OR STEAL BACK THE **ONE-OF-A-KIND** WORLD-CHANGING DEVICE? OR TRY TO CLEAR THE CROWD?
THIS IS WHAT I MEAN WHEN I SAY I HATE **ADULT DECISIONS.**
EXCUSE ME, SIR, BUT CAN I SEE YOUR **BADGE?**

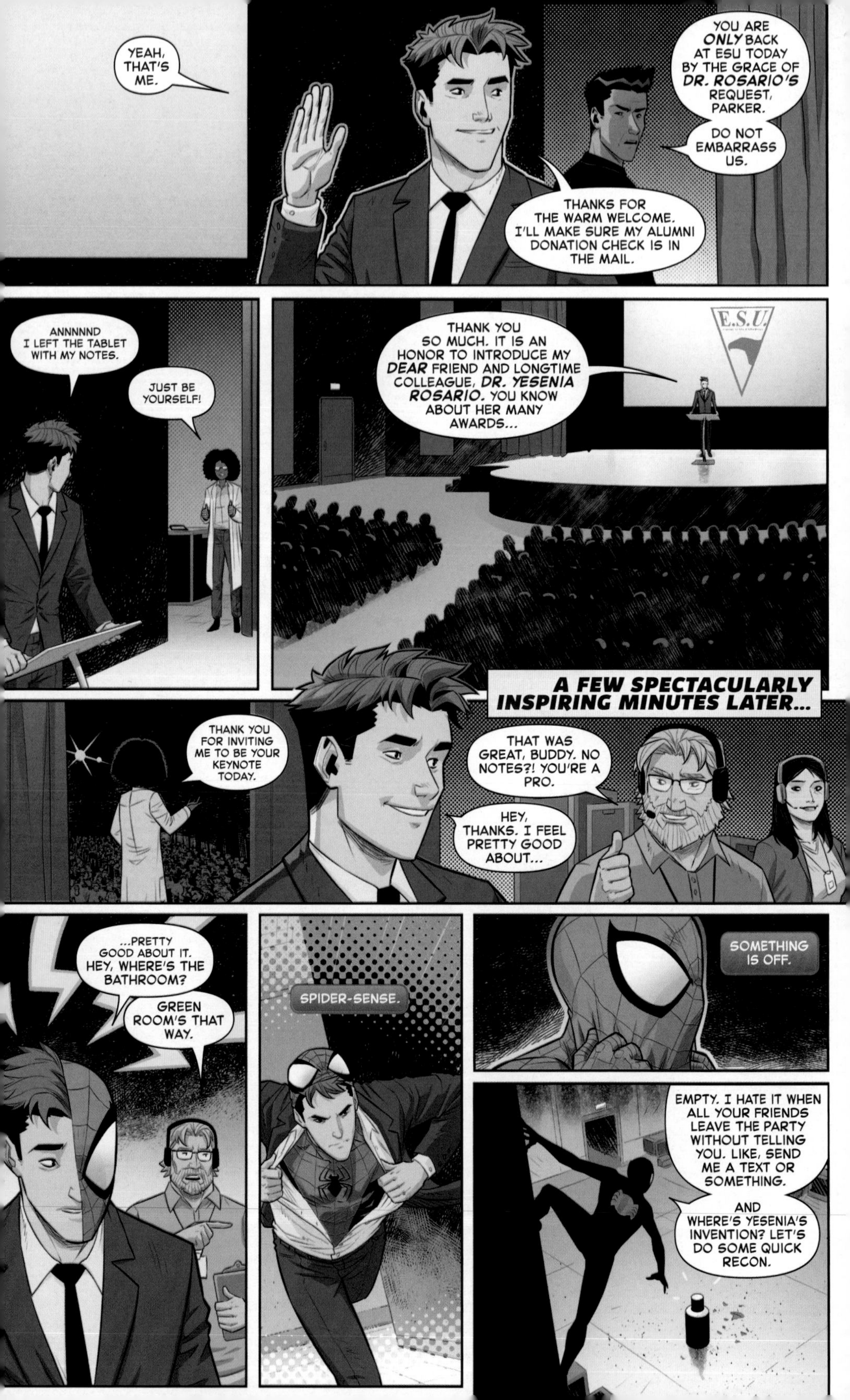
YEAH, THAT'S ME.
YOU ARE ONLY BACK AT ESU TODAY BY THE GRACE OF DR. ROSARIO'S REQUEST, PARKER.
DO NOT EMBARRASS US.
THANKS FOR THE WARM WELCOME. I'LL MAKE SURE MY ALUMNI DONATION CHECK IS IN THE MAIL.
ANNNNND I LEFT THE TABLET WITH MY NOTES.
JUST BE YOURSELF!
THANK YOU SO MUCH. IT IS AN HONOR TO INTRODUCE MY DEAR FRIEND AND LONGTIME COLLEAGUE, DR. YESENIA ROSARIO. YOU KNOW ABOUT HER MANY AWARDS...
E.S.U.
A FEW SPECTACULARLY INSPIRING MINUTES LATER...
THANK YOU FOR INVITING ME TO BE YOUR KEYNOTE TODAY.
THAT WAS GREAT, BUDDY. NO NOTES?! YOU'RE A PRO.
HEY, THANKS. I FEEL PRETTY GOOD ABOUT...
...PRETTY GOOD ABOUT IT. HEY, WHERE'S THE BATHROOM?
GREEN ROOM'S THAT WAY.
SPIDER-SENSE.
SOMETHING IS OFF.
EMPTY. I HATE IT WHEN ALL YOUR FRIENDS LEAVE THE PARTY WITHOUT TELLING YOU. LIKE, SEND ME A TEXT OR SOMETHING.
AND WHERE'S YESENIA'S INVENTION? LET'S DO SOME QUICK RECON.

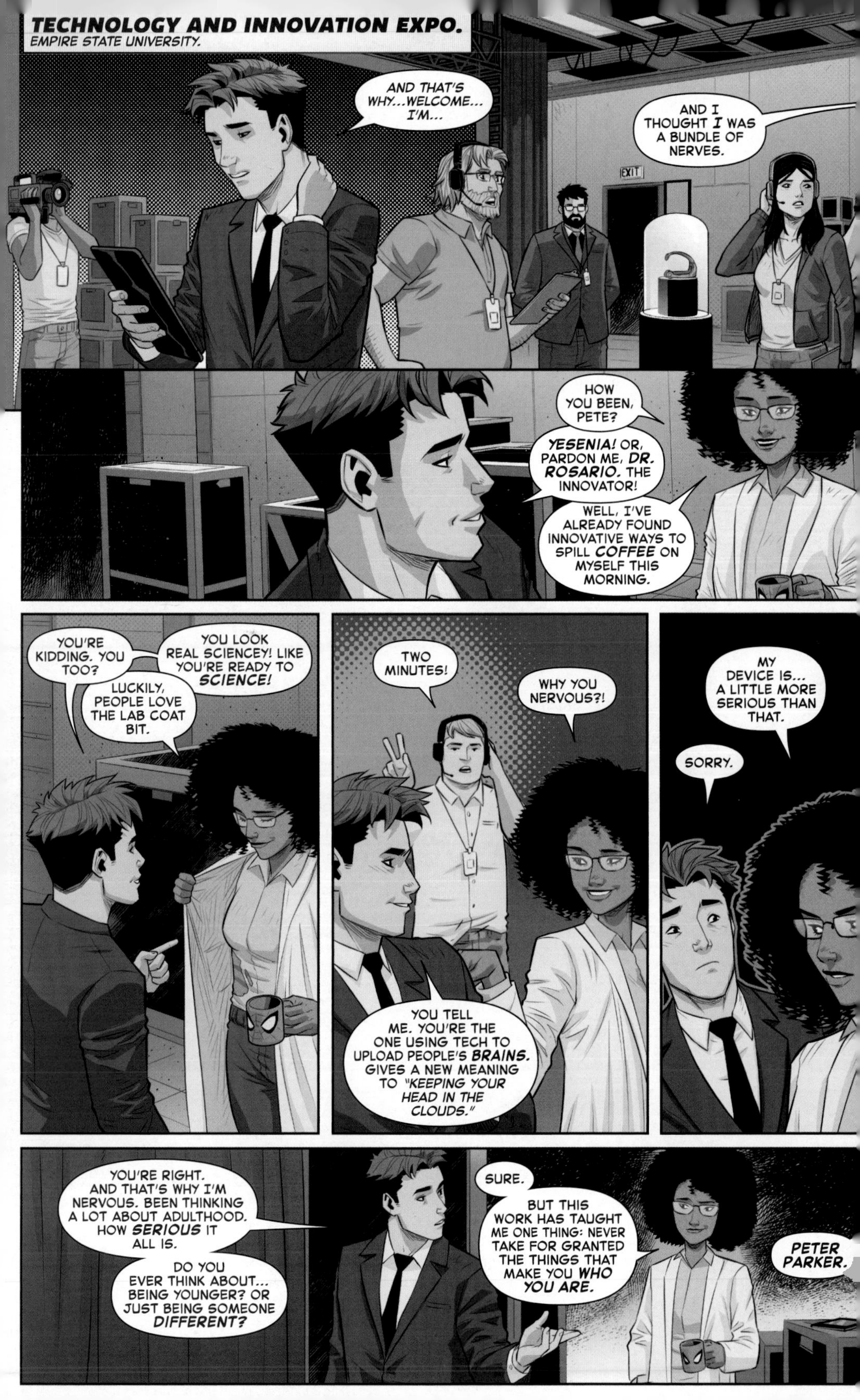
TECHNOLOGY AND INNOVATION EXPO.
EMPIRE STATE UNIVERSITY.
AND THAT'S WHY...WELCOME... I'M...
AND I THOUGHT I WAS A BUNDLE OF NERVES.
EXIT
HOW YOU BEEN, PETE?
YESENIA! OR, PARDON ME, DR. ROSARIO. THE INNOVATOR!
WELL, I'VE ALREADY FOUND INNOVATIVE WAYS TO SPILL COFFEE ON MYSELF THIS MORNING.
YOU'RE KIDDING. YOU TOO?
YOU LOOK REAL SCIENCEY! LIKE YOU'RE READY TO SCIENCE!
LUCKILY, PEOPLE LOVE THE LAB COAT BIT.
TWO MINUTES!
WHY YOU NERVOUS?!
YOU TELL ME. YOU'RE THE ONE USING TECH TO UPLOAD PEOPLE'S BRAINS. GIVES A NEW MEANING TO "KEEPING YOUR HEAD IN THE CLOUDS."
MY DEVICE IS... A LITTLE MORE SERIOUS THAN THAT.
SORRY.
YOU'RE RIGHT. AND THAT'S WHY I'M NERVOUS. BEEN THINKING A LOT ABOUT ADULTHOOD. HOW SERIOUS IT ALL IS.
DO YOU EVER THINK ABOUT... BEING YOUNGER? OR JUST BEING SOMEONE DIFFERENT?
SURE.
BUT THIS WORK HAS TAUGHT ME ONE THING: NEVER TAKE FOR GRANTED THE THINGS THAT MAKE YOU WHO YOU ARE.
PETER PARKER.

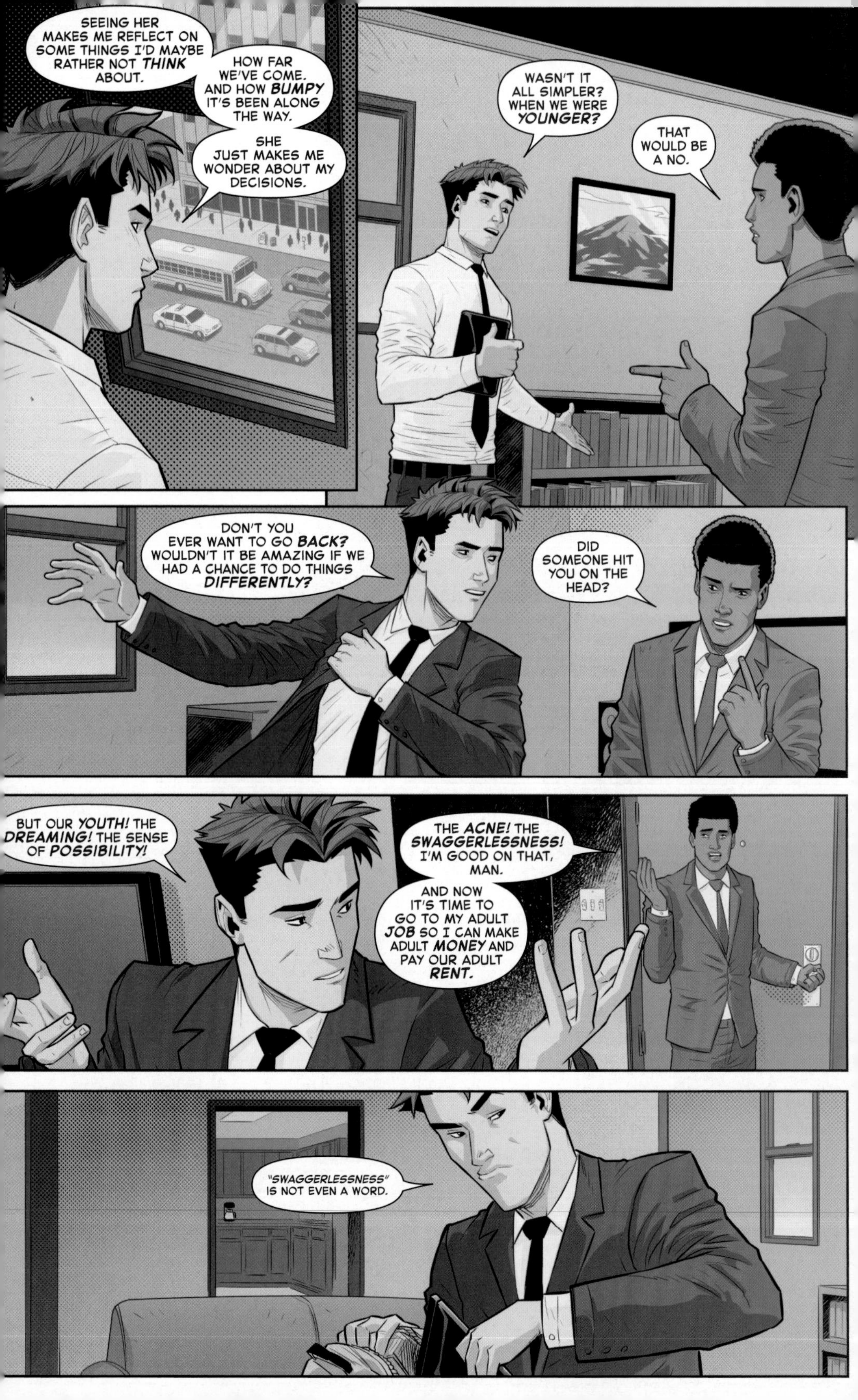
SEEING HER MAKES ME REFLECT ON SOME THINGS I'D MAYBE RATHER NOT *THINK* ABOUT.
HOW FAR WE'VE COME. AND HOW *BUMPY* IT'S BEEN ALONG THE WAY.
SHE JUST MAKES ME WONDER ABOUT MY DECISIONS.
WASN'T IT ALL SIMPLER? WHEN WE WERE *YOUNGER?*
THAT WOULD BE A NO.
DON'T YOU EVER WANT TO GO *BACK?* WOULDN'T IT BE AMAZING IF WE HAD A CHANCE TO DO THINGS *DIFFERENTLY?*
DID SOMEONE HIT YOU ON THE HEAD?
BUT OUR *YOUTH!* THE *DREAMING!* THE SENSE OF *POSSIBILITY!*
THE *ACNE!* THE *SWAGGERLESSNESS!* I'M GOOD ON THAT, MAN.
AND NOW IT'S TIME TO GO TO MY ADULT *JOB* SO I CAN MAKE ADULT *MONEY* AND PAY OUR ADULT *RENT.*
"*SWAGGERLESSNESS*" IS NOT EVEN A WORD.

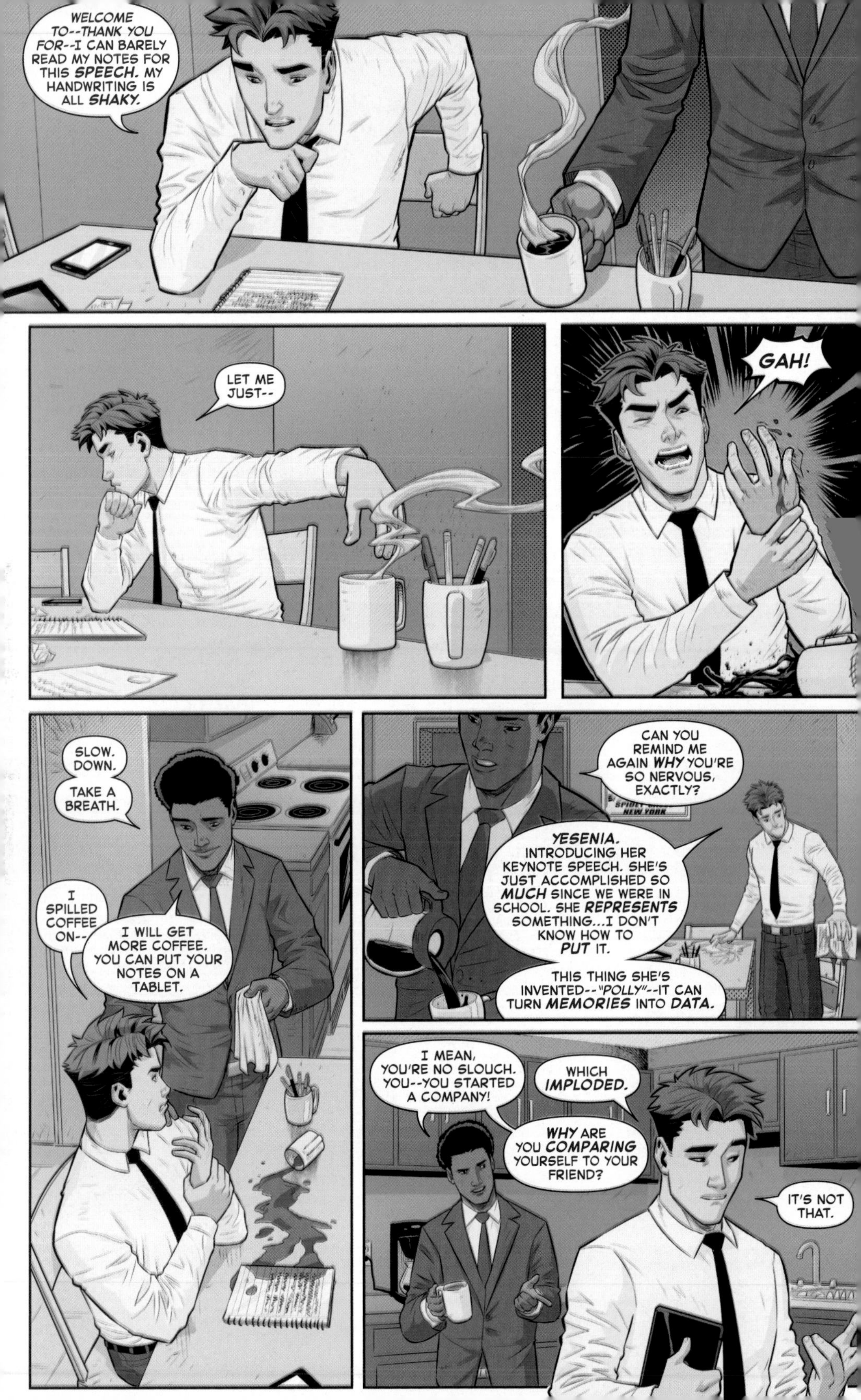

WELCOME TO--THANK YOU FOR--I CAN BARELY READ MY NOTES FOR THIS SPEECH. MY HANDWRITING IS ALL SHAKY.
LET ME JUST--
GAH!
SLOW. DOWN.
TAKE A BREATH.
I SPILLED COFFEE ON--
I WILL GET MORE COFFEE. YOU CAN PUT YOUR NOTES ON A TABLET.
CAN YOU REMIND ME AGAIN WHY YOU'RE SO NERVOUS, EXACTLY?
YESENIA. INTRODUCING HER KEYNOTE SPEECH. SHE'S JUST ACCOMPLISHED SO MUCH SINCE WE WERE IN SCHOOL. SHE REPRESENTS SOMETHING...I DON'T KNOW HOW TO PUT IT.
THIS THING SHE'S INVENTED--"POLLY"--IT CAN TURN MEMORIES INTO DATA.
I MEAN, YOU'RE NO SLOUCH. YOU--YOU STARTED A COMPANY!
WHICH IMPLODED.
WHY ARE YOU COMPARING YOURSELF TO YOUR FRIEND?
IT'S NOT THAT.

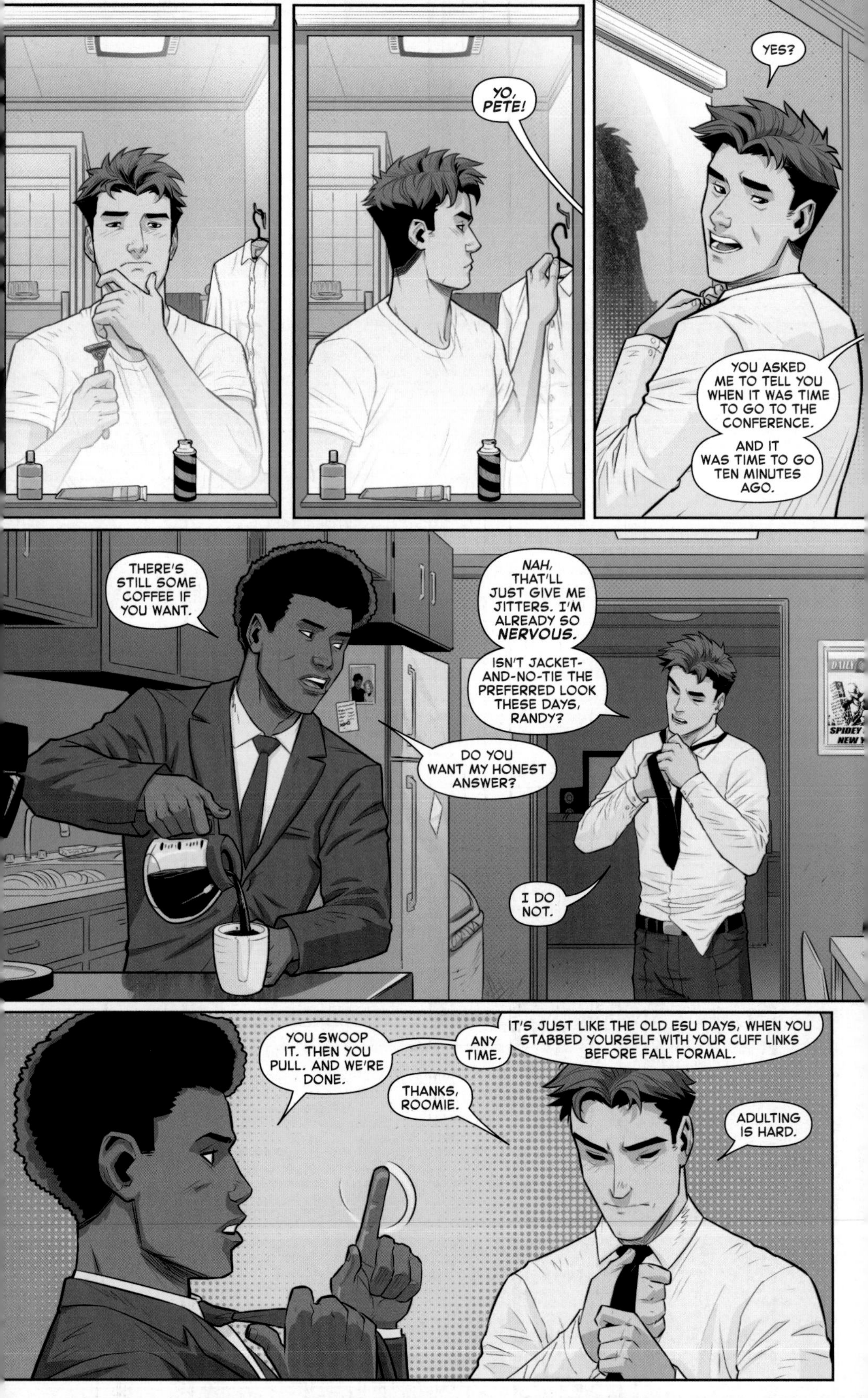
YO, PETE!
YES?
YOU ASKED ME TO TELL YOU WHEN IT WAS TIME TO GO TO THE CONFERENCE.
AND IT WAS TIME TO GO TEN MINUTES AGO.
THERE'S STILL SOME COFFEE IF YOU WANT.
NAH, THAT'LL JUST GIVE ME JITTERS. I'M ALREADY SO NERVOUS.
ISN'T JACKET-AND-NO-TIE THE PREFERRED LOOK THESE DAYS, RANDY?
DO YOU WANT MY HONEST ANSWER?
I DO NOT.
YOU SWOOP IT. THEN YOU PULL. AND WE'RE DONE.
THANKS, ROOMIE.
ANY TIME.
IT'S JUST LIKE THE OLD ESU DAYS, WHEN YOU STABBED YOURSELF WITH YOUR CUFF LINKS BEFORE FALL FORMAL.
ADULTING IS HARD.

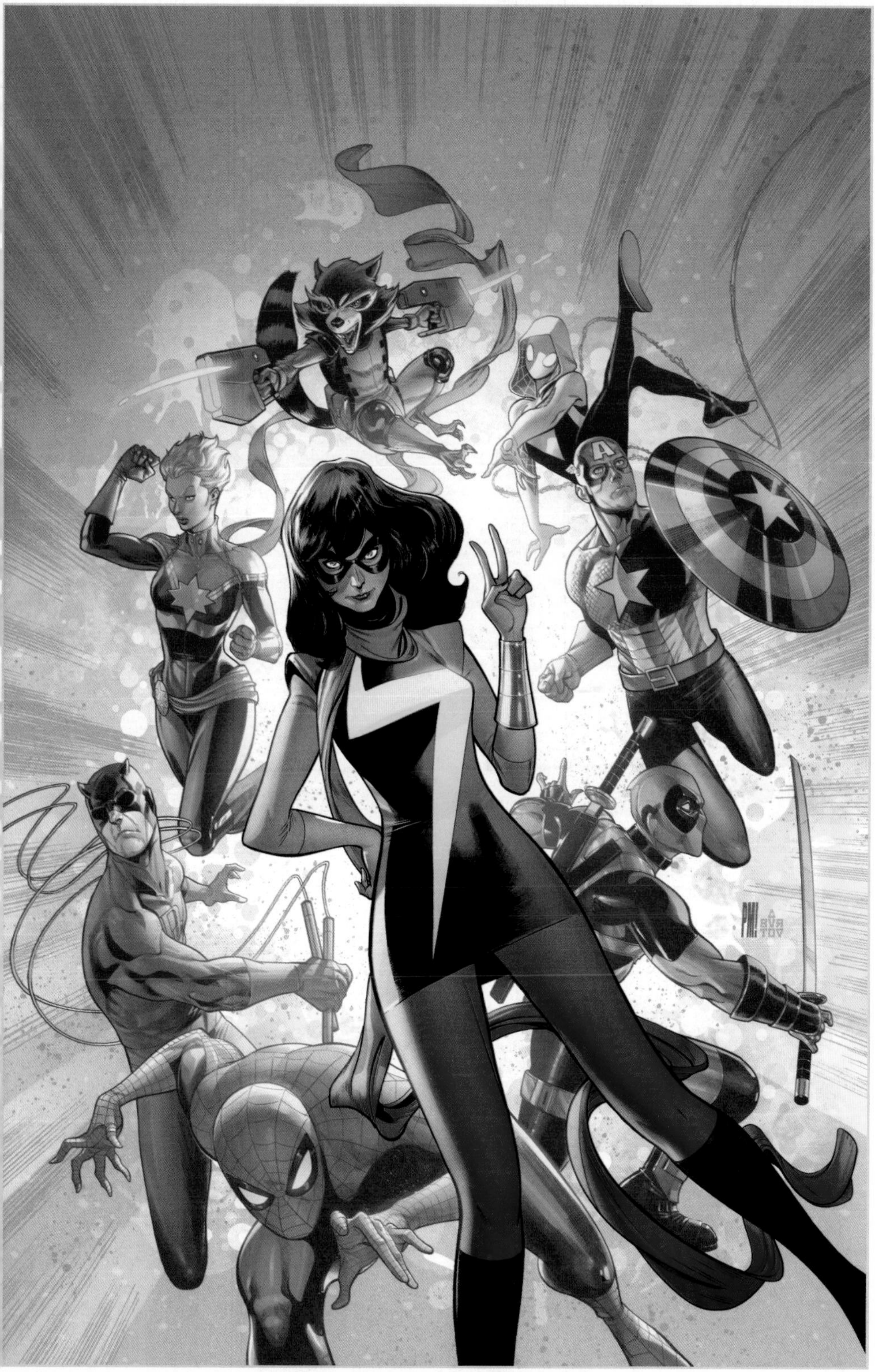

MS. MARVEL TEAM-UP #1 VARIANT
BY PACO MEDINA & JESUS ABURTOV

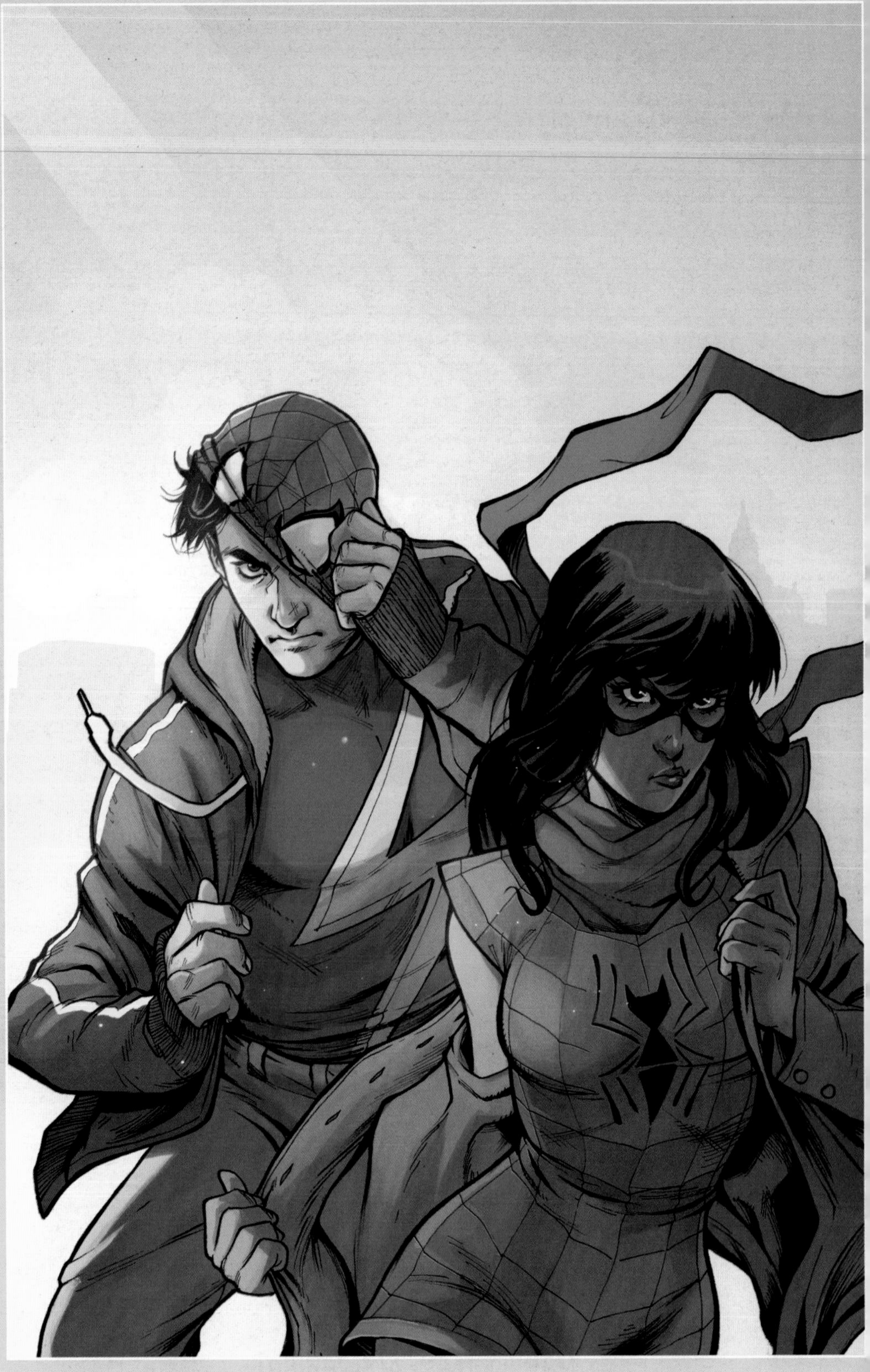

MS. MARVEL TEAM-UP #2

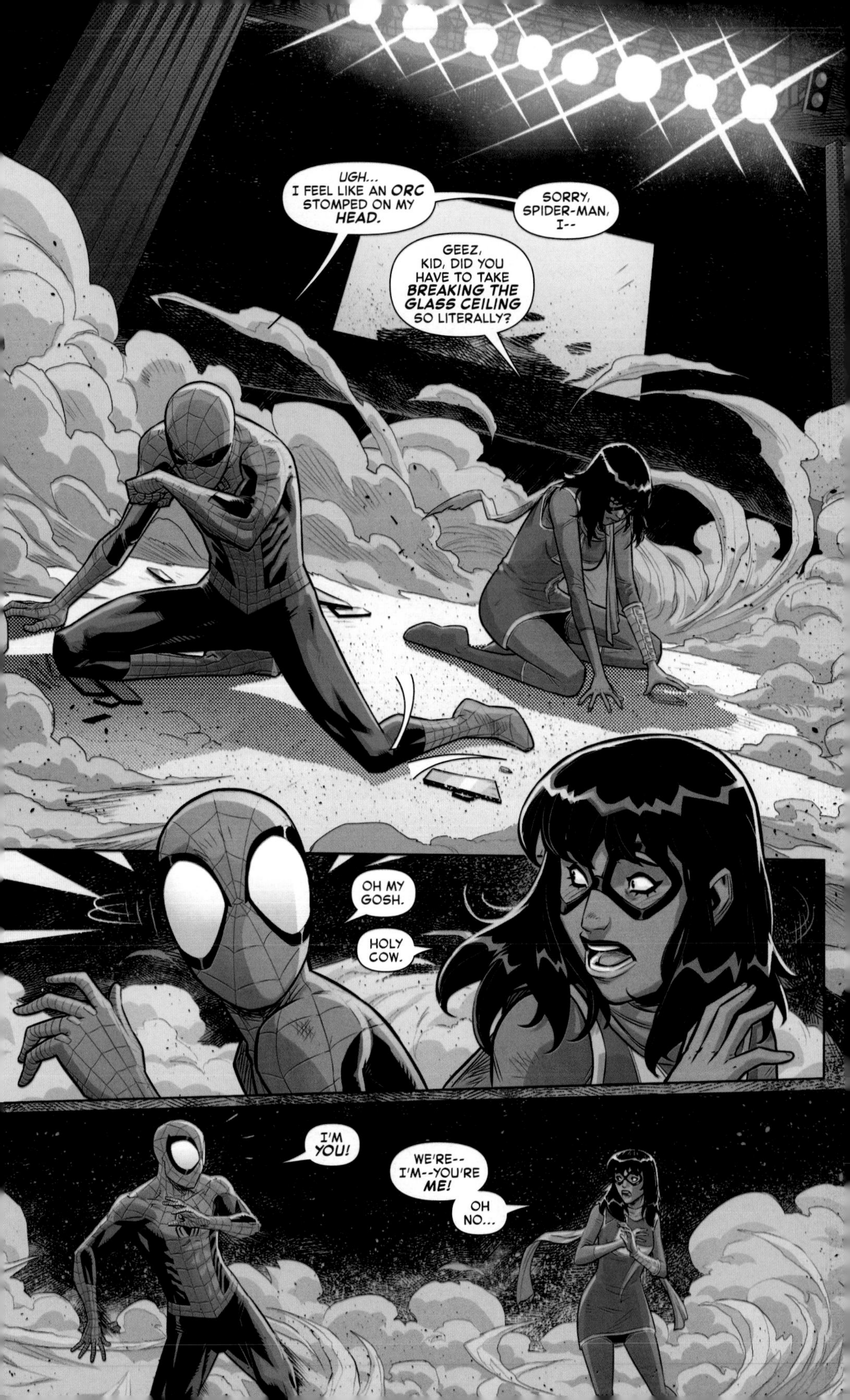
UGH... I FEEL LIKE AN ORC STOMPED ON MY HEAD.
SORRY, SPIDER-MAN, I--
GEEZ, KID, DID YOU HAVE TO TAKE BREAKING THE GLASS CEILING SO LITERALLY?
OH MY GOSH.
HOLY COW.
I'M YOU!
WE'RE-- I'M--YOU'RE ME!
OH NO...

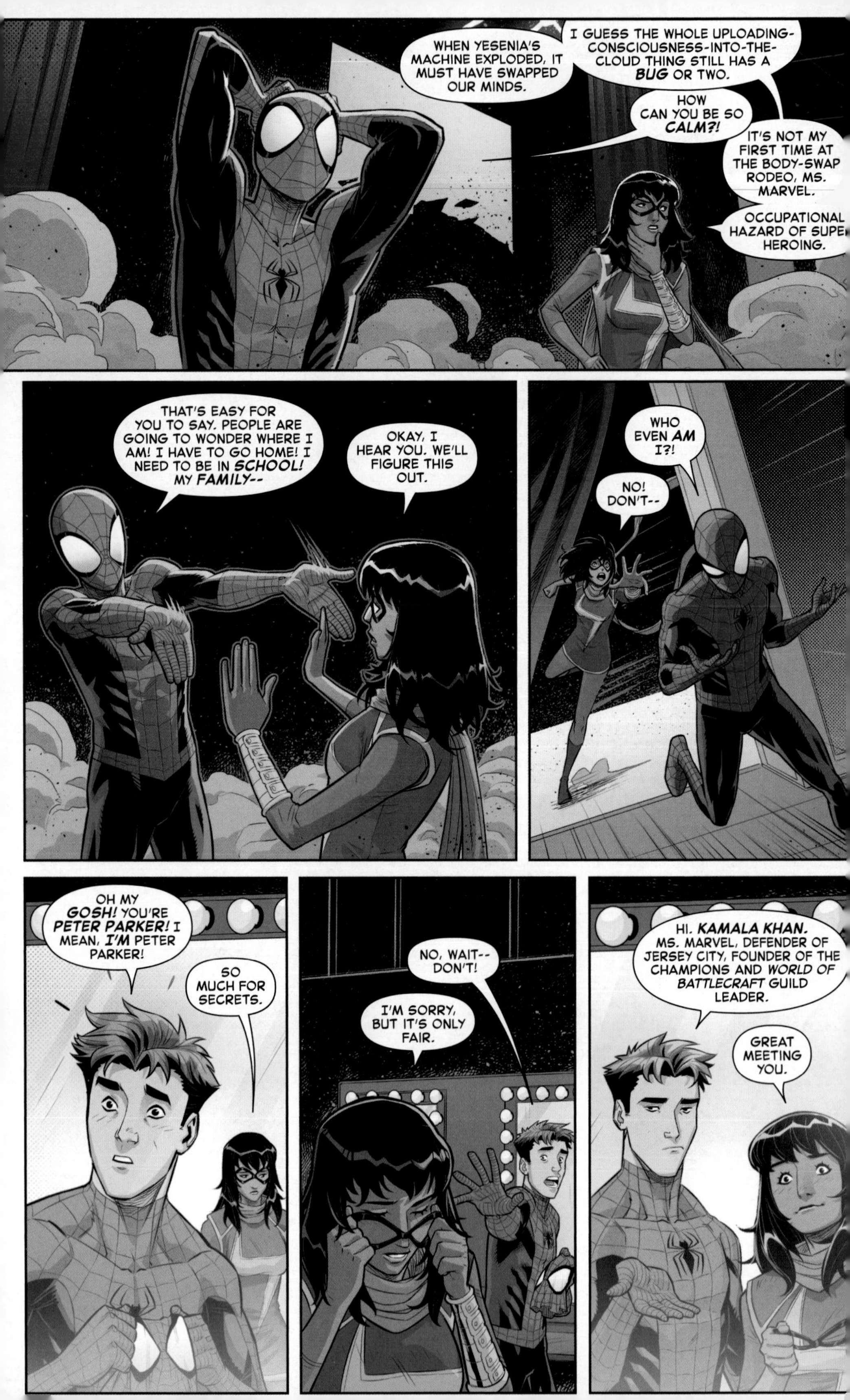

WHEN YESENIA'S MACHINE EXPLODED, IT MUST HAVE SWAPPED OUR MINDS.
I GUESS THE WHOLE UPLOADING-CONSCIOUSNESS-INTO-THE-CLOUD THING STILL HAS A BUG OR TWO.
HOW CAN YOU BE SO CALM?!
IT'S NOT MY FIRST TIME AT THE BODY-SWAP RODEO, MS. MARVEL.
OCCUPATIONAL HAZARD OF SUPE HEROING.
THAT'S EASY FOR YOU TO SAY. PEOPLE ARE GOING TO WONDER WHERE I AM! I HAVE TO GO HOME! I NEED TO BE IN SCHOOL! MY FAMILY--
OKAY, I HEAR YOU. WE'LL FIGURE THIS OUT.
WHO EVEN AM I?!
NO! DON'T--
OH MY GOSH! YOU'RE PETER PARKER! I MEAN, I'M PETER PARKER!
SO MUCH FOR SECRETS.
NO, WAIT-- DON'T!
I'M SORRY, BUT IT'S ONLY FAIR.
HI. KAMALA KHAN. MS. MARVEL, DEFENDER OF JERSEY CITY, FOUNDER OF THE CHAMPIONS AND WORLD OF BATTLECRAFT GUILD LEADER.
GREAT MEETING YOU.

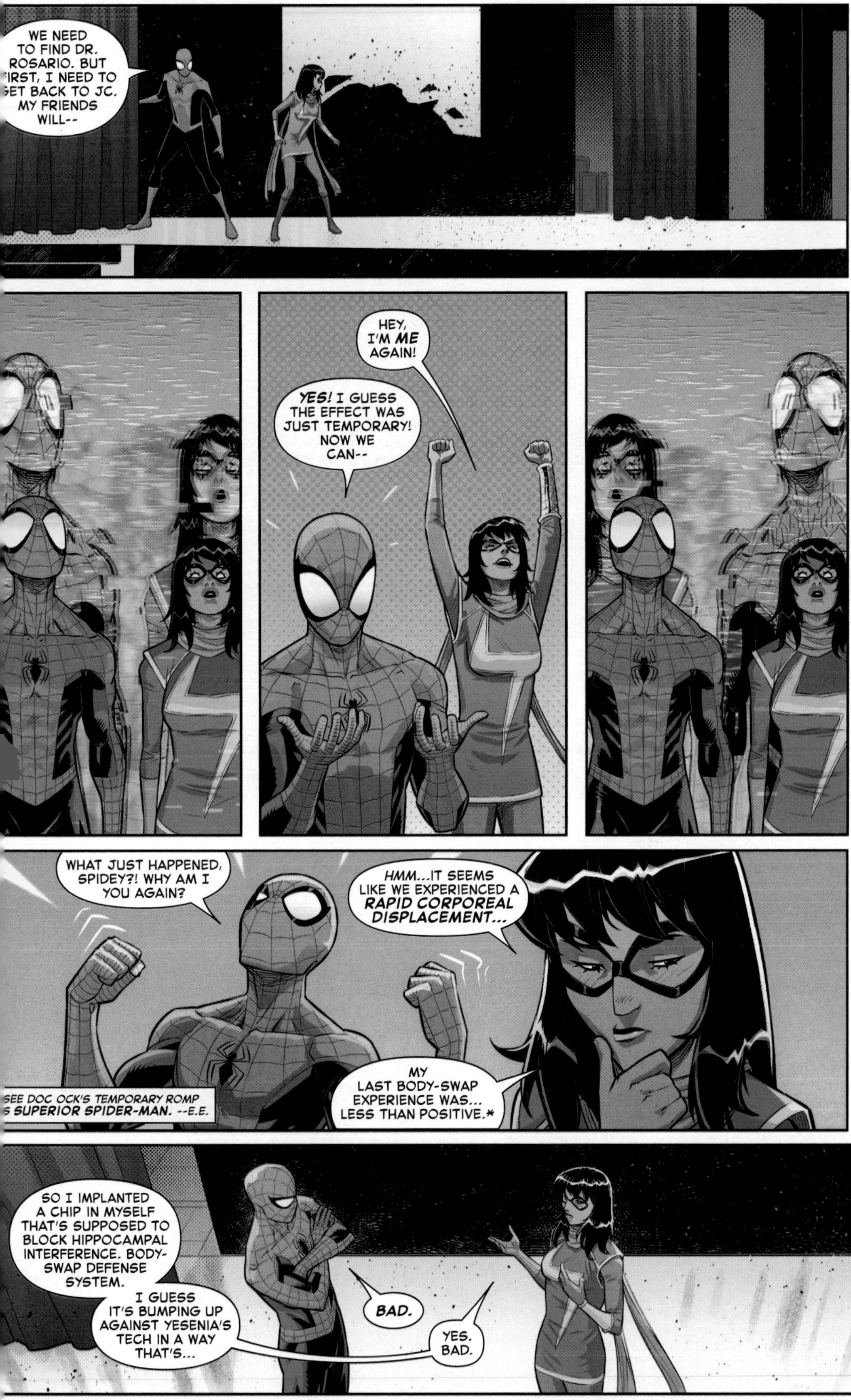
WE NEED TO FIND DR. ROSARIO. BUT FIRST, I NEED TO GET BACK TO JC. MY FRIENDS WILL--
HEY, I'M ME AGAIN!
YES! I GUESS THE EFFECT WAS JUST TEMPORARY! NOW WE CAN--
WHAT JUST HAPPENED, SPIDEY?! WHY AM I YOU AGAIN?
HMM...IT SEEMS LIKE WE EXPERIENCED A RAPID CORPOREAL DISPLACEMENT...
MY LAST BODY-SWAP EXPERIENCE WAS... LESS THAN POSITIVE.*
SEE DOC OCK'S TEMPORARY ROMP S SUPERIOR SPIDER-MAN. --E.E.
SO I IMPLANTED A CHIP IN MYSELF THAT'S SUPPOSED TO BLOCK HIPPOCAMPAL INTERFERENCE. BODY-SWAP DEFENSE SYSTEM.
I GUESS IT'S BUMPING UP AGAINST YESENIA'S TECH IN A WAY THAT'S...
BAD.
YES. BAD.

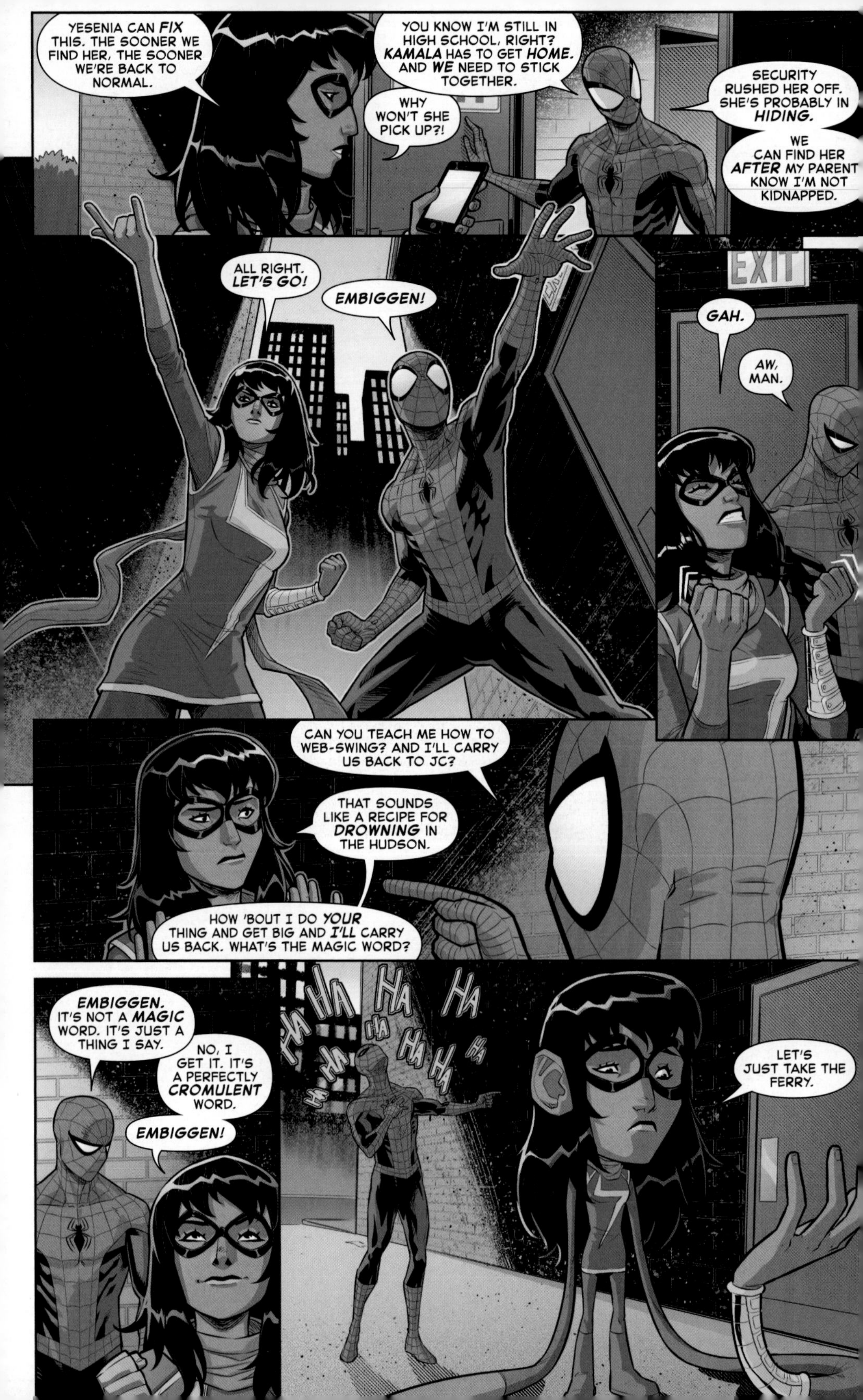

YESENIA CAN FIX THIS. THE SOONER WE FIND HER, THE SOONER WE'RE BACK TO NORMAL.
YOU KNOW I'M STILL IN HIGH SCHOOL, RIGHT? KAMALA HAS TO GET HOME. AND WE NEED TO STICK TOGETHER.
WHY WON'T SHE PICK UP?!
SECURITY RUSHED HER OFF. SHE'S PROBABLY IN HIDING.
WE CAN FIND HER AFTER MY PARENT KNOW I'M NOT KIDNAPPED.
ALL RIGHT. LET'S GO!
EMBIGGEN!
EXIT
GAH.
AW, MAN.
CAN YOU TEACH ME HOW TO WEB-SWING? AND I'LL CARRY US BACK TO JC?
THAT SOUNDS LIKE A RECIPE FOR DROWNING IN THE HUDSON.
HOW 'BOUT I DO YOUR THING AND GET BIG AND I'LL CARRY US BACK. WHAT'S THE MAGIC WORD?
EMBIGGEN. IT'S NOT A MAGIC WORD. IT'S JUST A THING I SAY.
NO, I GET IT. IT'S A PERFECTLY CROMULENT WORD.
EMBIGGEN!
HA HA HA HA HA HA HA HA HA HA HA
LET'S JUST TAKE THE FERRY.

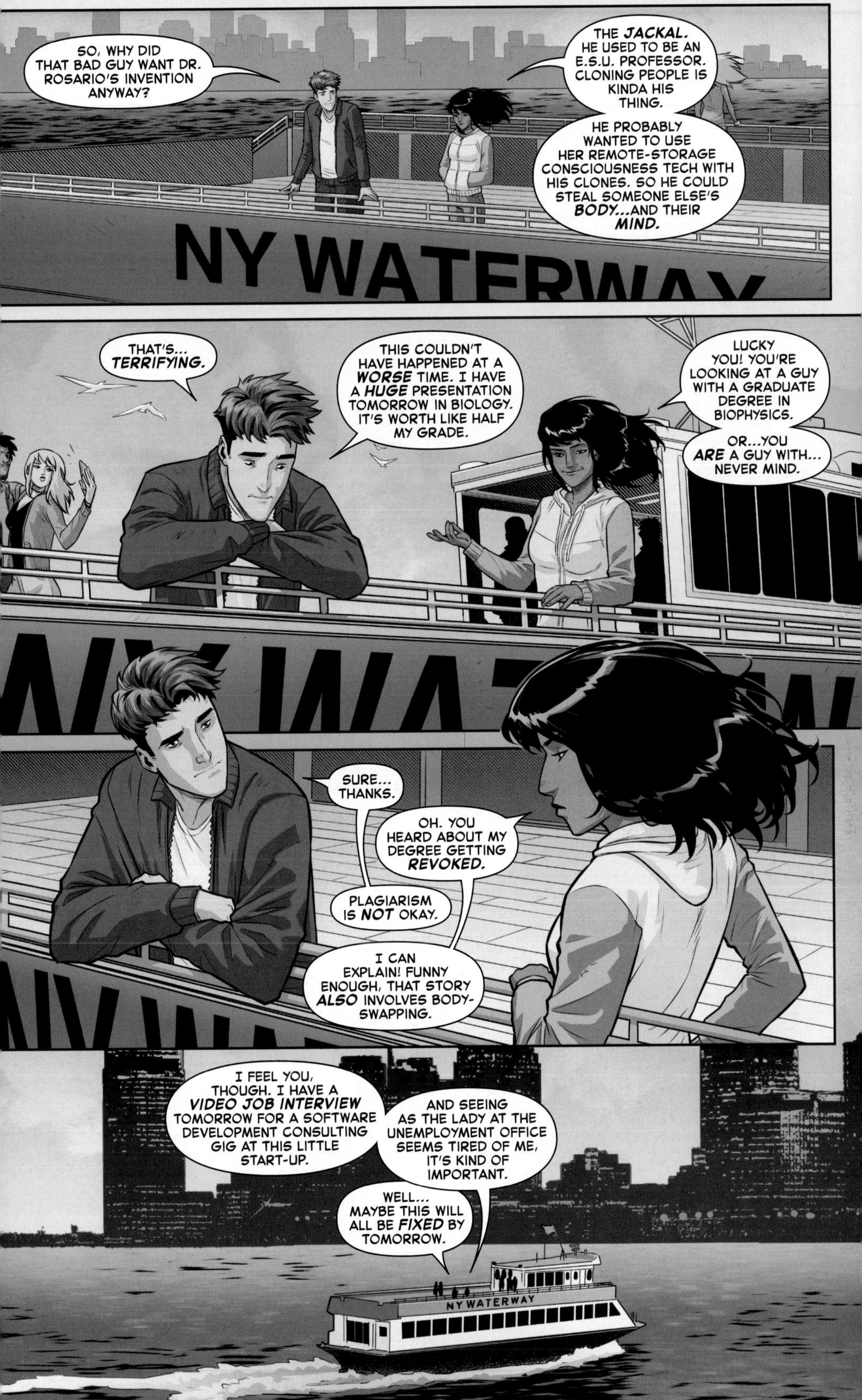
SO, WHY DID THAT BAD GUY WANT DR. ROSARIO'S INVENTION ANYWAY?
THE JACKAL. HE USED TO BE AN E.S.U. PROFESSOR. CLONING PEOPLE IS KINDA HIS THING.
HE PROBABLY WANTED TO USE HER REMOTE-STORAGE CONSCIOUSNESS TECH WITH HIS CLONES. SO HE COULD STEAL SOMEONE ELSE'S BODY...AND THEIR MIND.
NY WATERWAY
THAT'S... TERRIFYING.
THIS COULDN'T HAVE HAPPENED AT A WORSE TIME. I HAVE A HUGE PRESENTATION TOMORROW IN BIOLOGY. IT'S WORTH LIKE HALF MY GRADE.
LUCKY YOU! YOU'RE LOOKING AT A GUY WITH A GRADUATE DEGREE IN BIOPHYSICS.
OR...YOU ARE A GUY WITH... NEVER MIND.
SURE... THANKS.
OH. YOU HEARD ABOUT MY DEGREE GETTING REVOKED.
PLAGIARISM IS NOT OKAY.
I CAN EXPLAIN! FUNNY ENOUGH, THAT STORY ALSO INVOLVES BODY-SWAPPING.
I FEEL YOU, THOUGH. I HAVE A VIDEO JOB INTERVIEW TOMORROW FOR A SOFTWARE DEVELOPMENT CONSULTING GIG AT THIS LITTLE START-UP.
AND SEEING AS THE LADY AT THE UNEMPLOYMENT OFFICE SEEMS TIRED OF ME, IT'S KIND OF IMPORTANT.
WELL... MAYBE THIS WILL ALL BE FIXED BY TOMORROW.
NY WATERWAY

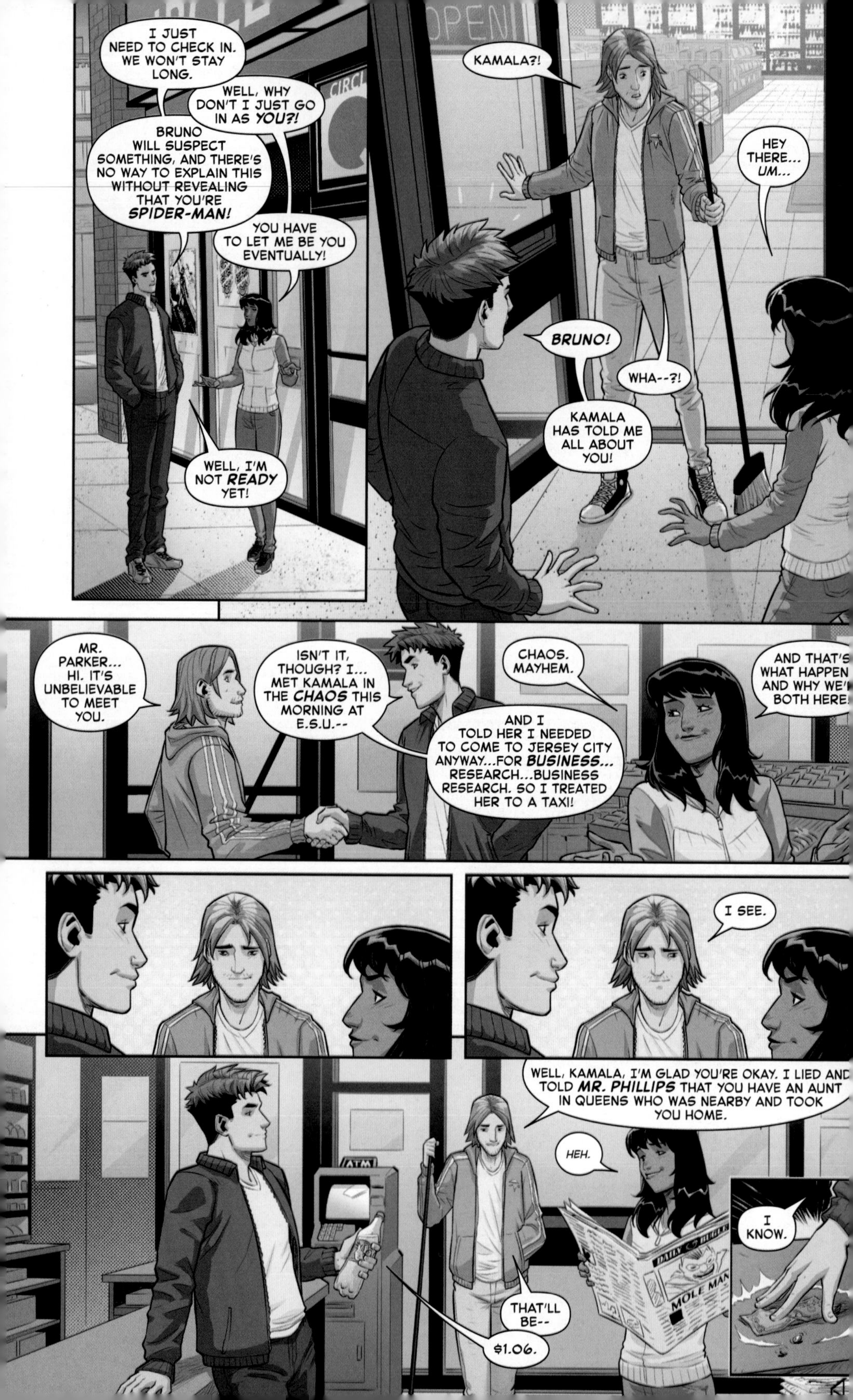

I JUST NEED TO CHECK IN. WE WON'T STAY LONG.
WELL, WHY DON'T I JUST GO IN AS YOU?!
BRUNO WILL SUSPECT SOMETHING, AND THERE'S NO WAY TO EXPLAIN THIS WITHOUT REVEALING THAT YOU'RE SPIDER-MAN!
YOU HAVE TO LET ME BE YOU EVENTUALLY!
WELL, I'M NOT READY YET!
OPEN
KAMALA?!
HEY THERE... UM...
BRUNO!
WHA--?!
KAMALA HAS TOLD ME ALL ABOUT YOU!
MR. PARKER... HI. IT'S UNBELIEVABLE TO MEET YOU.
ISN'T IT, THOUGH? I... MET KAMALA IN THE CHAOS THIS MORNING AT E.S.U.--
CHAOS. MAYHEM.
AND THAT'S WHAT HAPPEN AND WHY WE' BOTH HERE!
AND I TOLD HER I NEEDED TO COME TO JERSEY CITY ANYWAY...FOR BUSINESS... RESEARCH...BUSINESS RESEARCH. SO I TREATED HER TO A TAXI!
I SEE.
WELL, KAMALA, I'M GLAD YOU'RE OKAY. I LIED AND TOLD MR. PHILLIPS THAT YOU HAVE AN AUNT IN QUEENS WHO WAS NEARBY AND TOOK YOU HOME.
HEH.
ATM
MOLE MAN
I KNOW.
THAT'LL BE--
$1.06.

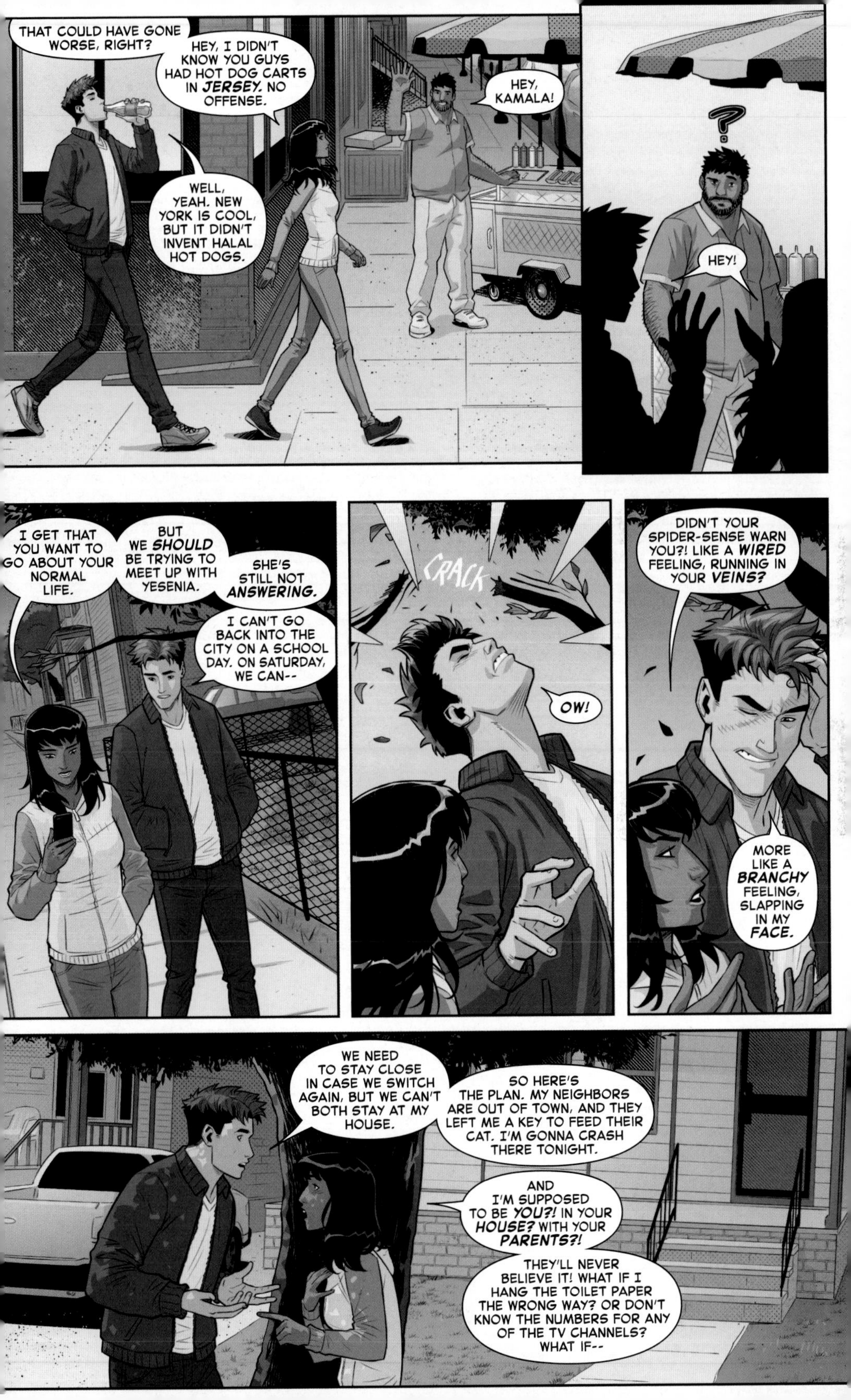
THAT COULD HAVE GONE WORSE, RIGHT?
HEY, I DIDN'T KNOW YOU GUYS HAD HOT DOG CARTS IN JERSEY. NO OFFENSE.
WELL, YEAH. NEW YORK IS COOL, BUT IT DIDN'T INVENT HALAL HOT DOGS.
HEY, KAMALA!
?
HEY!
I GET THAT YOU WANT TO GO ABOUT YOUR NORMAL LIFE.
BUT WE SHOULD BE TRYING TO MEET UP WITH YESENIA.
SHE'S STILL NOT ANSWERING.
I CAN'T GO BACK INTO THE CITY ON A SCHOOL DAY. ON SATURDAY, WE CAN--
CRACK
OW!
DIDN'T YOUR SPIDER-SENSE WARN YOU?! LIKE A WIRED FEELING, RUNNING IN YOUR VEINS?
MORE LIKE A BRANCHY FEELING, SLAPPING IN MY FACE.
WE NEED TO STAY CLOSE IN CASE WE SWITCH AGAIN, BUT WE CAN'T BOTH STAY AT MY HOUSE.
SO HERE'S THE PLAN. MY NEIGHBORS ARE OUT OF TOWN, AND THEY LEFT ME A KEY TO FEED THEIR CAT. I'M GONNA CRASH THERE TONIGHT.
AND I'M SUPPOSED TO BE YOU?! IN YOUR HOUSE? WITH YOUR PARENTS?!
THEY'LL NEVER BELIEVE IT! WHAT IF I HANG THE TOILET PAPER THE WRONG WAY? OR DON'T KNOW THE NUMBERS FOR ANY OF THE TV CHANNELS? WHAT IF--

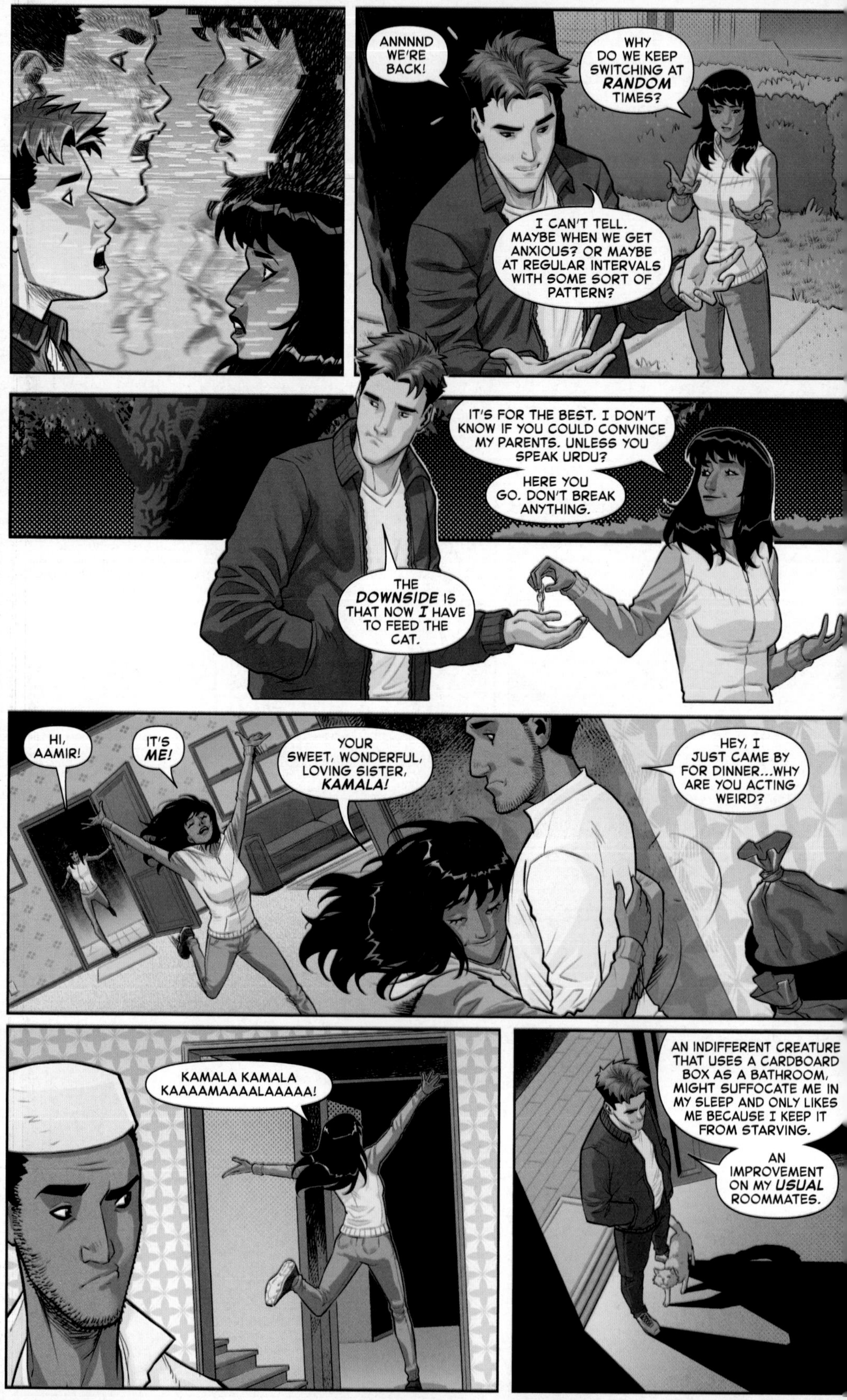
ANNNND WE'RE BACK!
WHY DO WE KEEP SWITCHING AT *RANDOM* TIMES?
I CAN'T TELL. MAYBE WHEN WE GET ANXIOUS? OR MAYBE AT REGULAR INTERVALS WITH SOME SORT OF PATTERN?
IT'S FOR THE BEST. I DON'T KNOW IF YOU COULD CONVINCE MY PARENTS. UNLESS YOU SPEAK URDU?
HERE YOU GO. DON'T BREAK ANYTHING.
THE *DOWNSIDE* IS THAT NOW *I* HAVE TO FEED THE CAT.
HI, AAMIR!
IT'S *ME!*
YOUR SWEET, WONDERFUL, LOVING SISTER, *KAMALA!*
HEY, I JUST CAME BY FOR DINNER...WHY ARE YOU ACTING WEIRD?
KAMALA KAMALA KAAAAMAAAALAAAAA!
AN INDIFFERENT CREATURE THAT USES A CARDBOARD BOX AS A BATHROOM, MIGHT SUFFOCATE ME IN MY SLEEP AND ONLY LIKES ME BECAUSE I KEEP IT FROM STARVING.
AN IMPROVEMENT ON MY *USUAL* ROOMMATES.

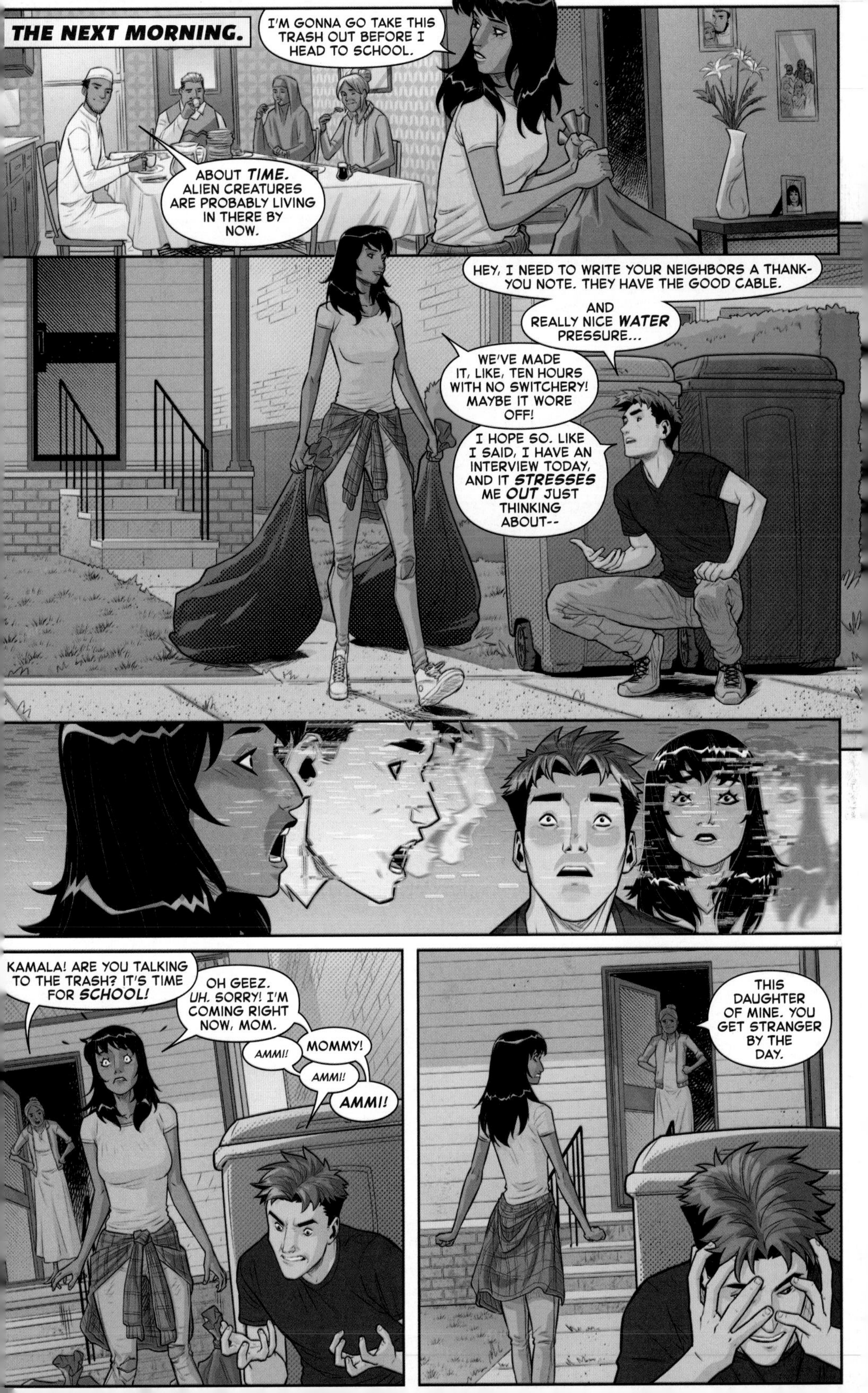
THE NEXT MORNING.
I'M GONNA GO TAKE THIS TRASH OUT BEFORE I HEAD TO SCHOOL.
ABOUT TIME. ALIEN CREATURES ARE PROBABLY LIVING IN THERE BY NOW.
HEY, I NEED TO WRITE YOUR NEIGHBORS A THANK-YOU NOTE. THEY HAVE THE GOOD CABLE.
AND REALLY NICE WATER PRESSURE...
WE'VE MADE IT, LIKE, TEN HOURS WITH NO SWITCHERY! MAYBE IT WORE OFF!
I HOPE SO. LIKE I SAID, I HAVE AN INTERVIEW TODAY, AND IT STRESSES ME OUT JUST THINKING ABOUT--
KAMALA! ARE YOU TALKING TO THE TRASH? IT'S TIME FOR SCHOOL!
OH GEEZ. UH. SORRY! I'M COMING RIGHT NOW, MOM.
MOMMY!
AMMI!
AMMI!
AMMI!
THIS DAUGHTER OF MINE. YOU GET STRANGER BY THE DAY.

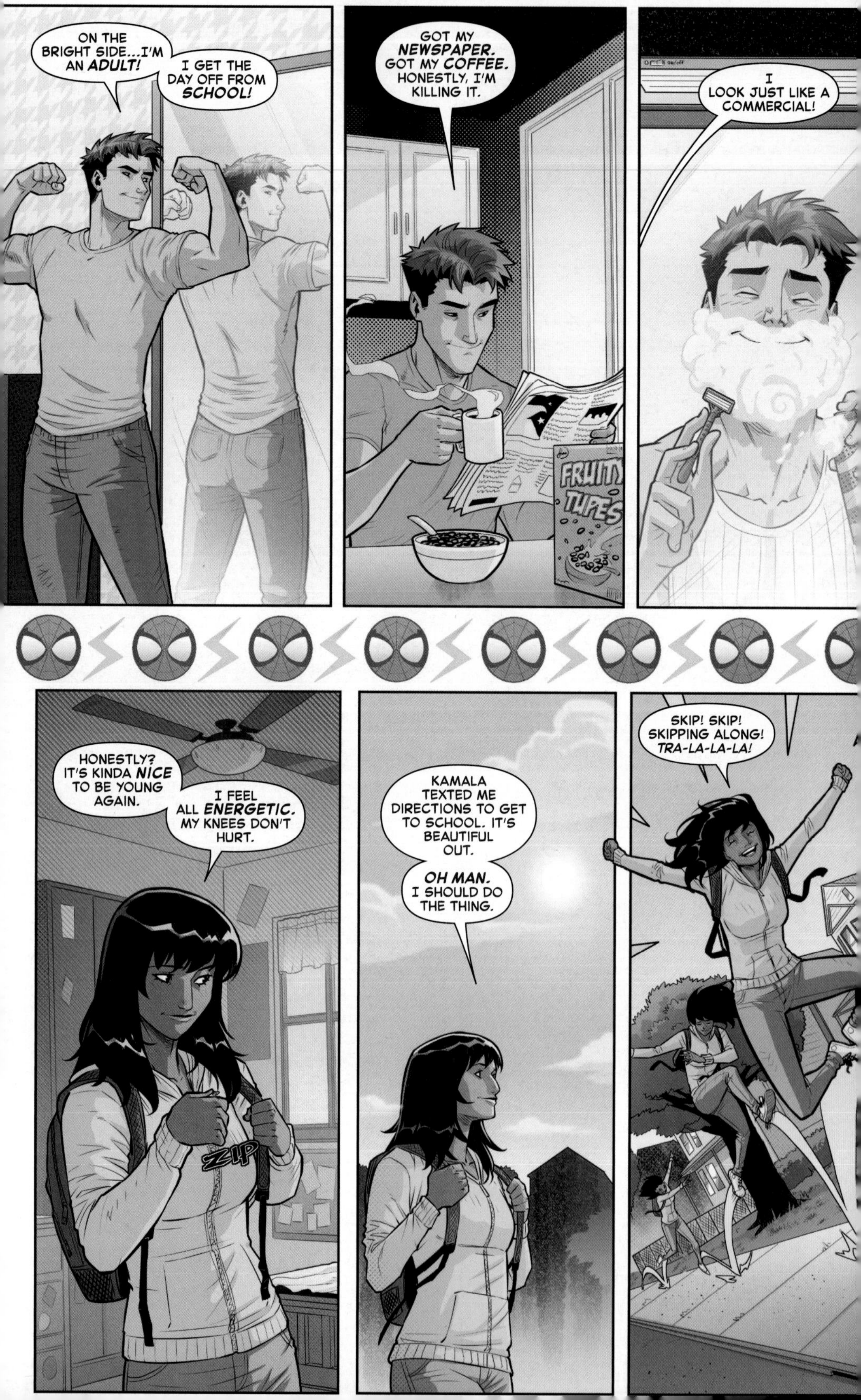
ON THE BRIGHT SIDE...I'M AN ADULT!
I GET THE DAY OFF FROM SCHOOL!
GOT MY NEWSPAPER. GOT MY COFFEE. HONESTLY, I'M KILLING IT.
FRUITY TUPES
I LOOK JUST LIKE A COMMERCIAL!
HONESTLY? IT'S KINDA NICE TO BE YOUNG AGAIN.
I FEEL ALL ENERGETIC. MY KNEES DON'T HURT.
ZIP
KAMALA TEXTED ME DIRECTIONS TO GET TO SCHOOL. IT'S BEAUTIFUL OUT.
OH MAN. I SHOULD DO THE THING.
SKIP! SKIP! SKIPPING ALONG! TRA-LA-LA-LA!

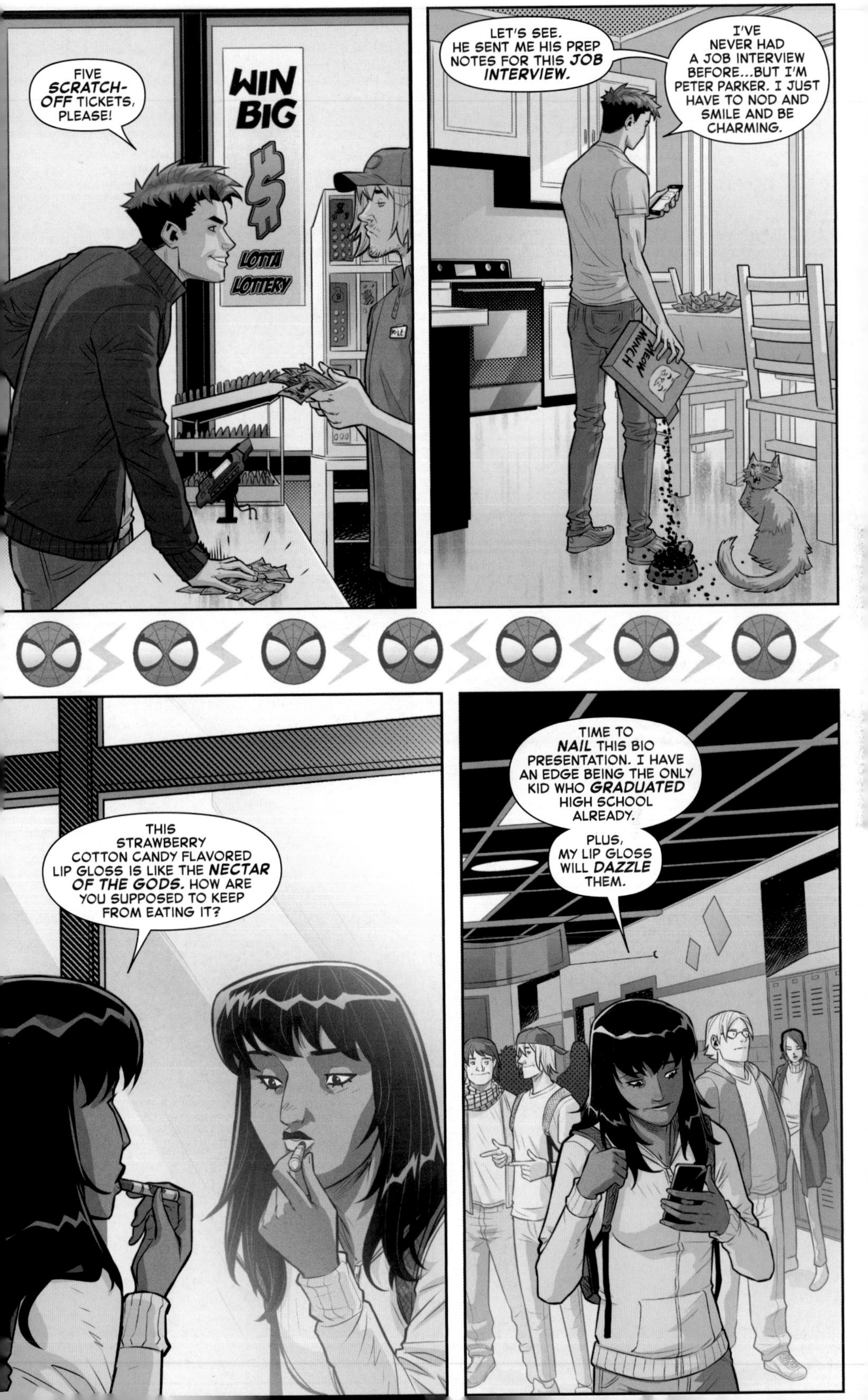
FIVE SCRATCH-OFF TICKETS, PLEASE!
WIN BIG
$
LOTTA LOTTERY
LET'S SEE. HE SENT ME HIS PREP NOTES FOR THIS JOB INTERVIEW.
I'VE NEVER HAD A JOB INTERVIEW BEFORE...BUT I'M PETER PARKER. I JUST HAVE TO NOD AND SMILE AND BE CHARMING.
MEOW MUNCH
THIS STRAWBERRY COTTON CANDY FLAVORED LIP GLOSS IS LIKE THE NECTAR OF THE GODS. HOW ARE YOU SUPPOSED TO KEEP FROM EATING IT?
TIME TO NAIL THIS BIO PRESENTATION. I HAVE AN EDGE BEING THE ONLY KID WHO GRADUATED HIGH SCHOOL ALREADY.
PLUS, MY LIP GLOSS WILL DAZZLE THEM.

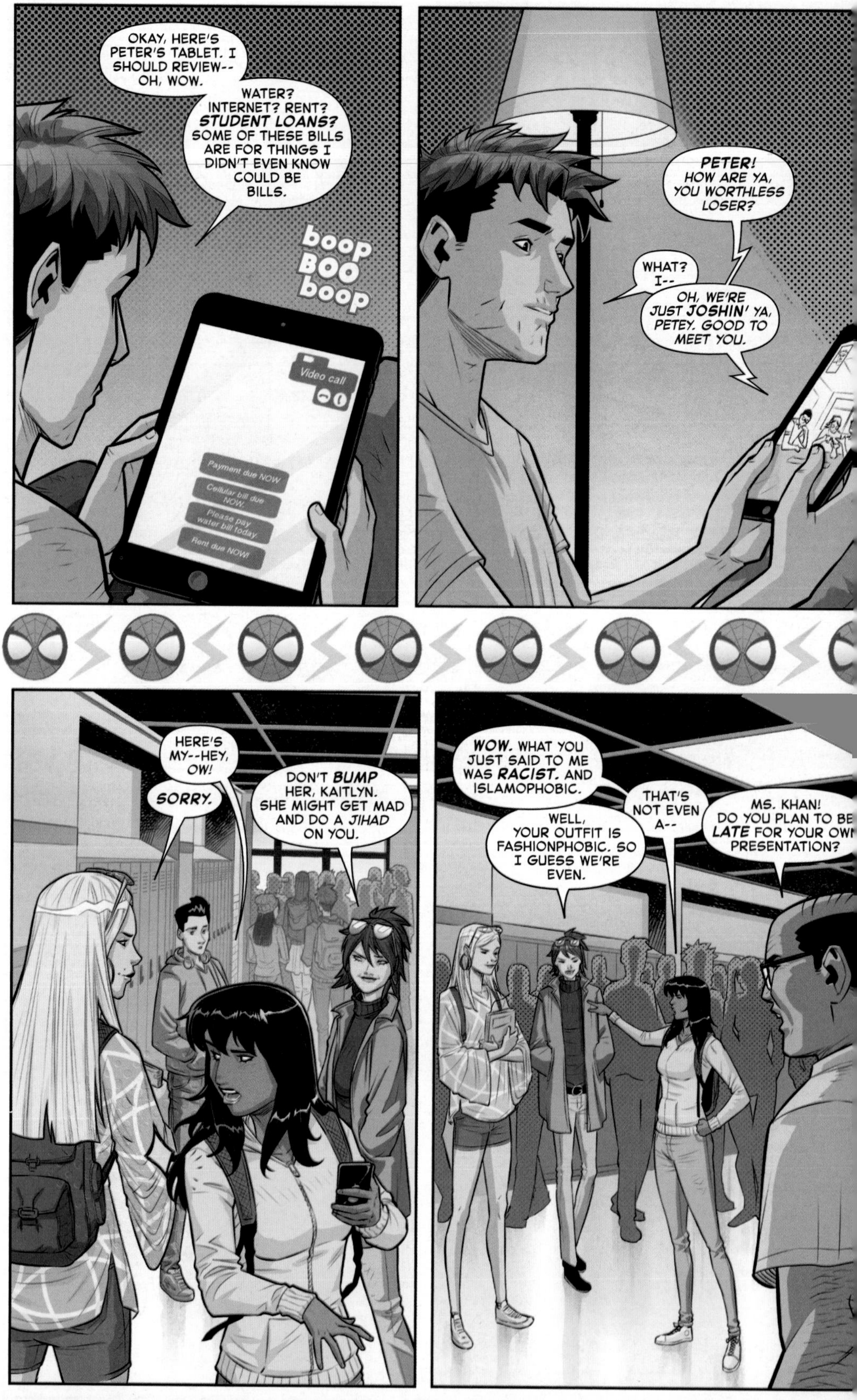
OKAY, HERE'S PETER'S TABLET. I SHOULD REVIEW-- OH, WOW.
WATER? INTERNET? RENT? STUDENT LOANS? SOME OF THESE BILLS ARE FOR THINGS I DIDN'T EVEN KNOW COULD BE BILLS.
boop BOO boop
Video call
Payment due NOW
Cellular bill due NOW.
Please pay water bill today.
Rent due NOW!
PETER! HOW ARE YA, YOU WORTHLESS LOSER?
WHAT? I--
OH, WE'RE JUST JOSHIN' YA, PETEY. GOOD TO MEET YOU.
HERE'S MY--HEY, OW!
SORRY.
DON'T BUMP HER, KAITLYN. SHE MIGHT GET MAD AND DO A JIHAD ON YOU.
WOW. WHAT YOU JUST SAID TO ME WAS RACIST. AND ISLAMOPHOBIC.
WELL, YOUR OUTFIT IS FASHIONPHOBIC. SO I GUESS WE'RE EVEN.
THAT'S NOT EVEN A--
MS. KHAN! DO YOU PLAN TO BE LATE FOR YOUR OWN PRESENTATION?

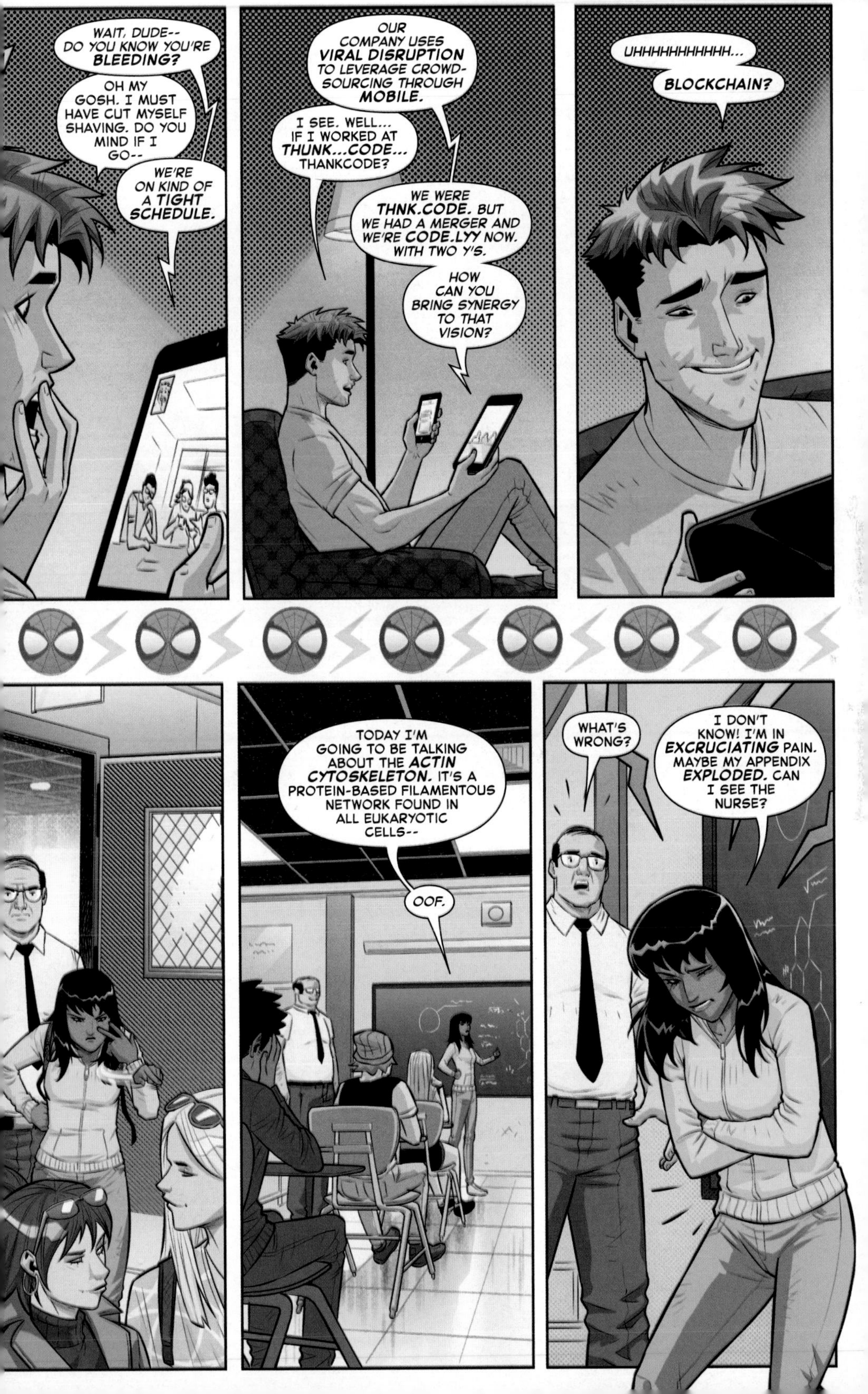
WAIT, DUDE-- DO YOU KNOW YOU'RE BLEEDING?
OH MY GOSH. I MUST HAVE CUT MYSELF SHAVING. DO YOU MIND IF I GO--
WE'RE ON KIND OF A TIGHT SCHEDULE.
OUR COMPANY USES VIRAL DISRUPTION TO LEVERAGE CROWD-SOURCING THROUGH MOBILE.
I SEE. WELL... IF I WORKED AT THUNK...CODE... THANKCODE?
WE WERE THNK.CODE. BUT WE HAD A MERGER AND WE'RE CODE.LYY NOW. WITH TWO Y'S.
HOW CAN YOU BRING SYNERGY TO THAT VISION?
UHHHHHHHHHHH...
BLOCKCHAIN?
TODAY I'M GOING TO BE TALKING ABOUT THE ACTIN CYTOSKELETON. IT'S A PROTEIN-BASED FILAMENTOUS NETWORK FOUND IN ALL EUKARYOTIC CELLS--
OOF.
WHAT'S WRONG?
I DON'T KNOW! I'M IN EXCRUCIATING PAIN. MAYBE MY APPENDIX EXPLODED. CAN I SEE THE NURSE?

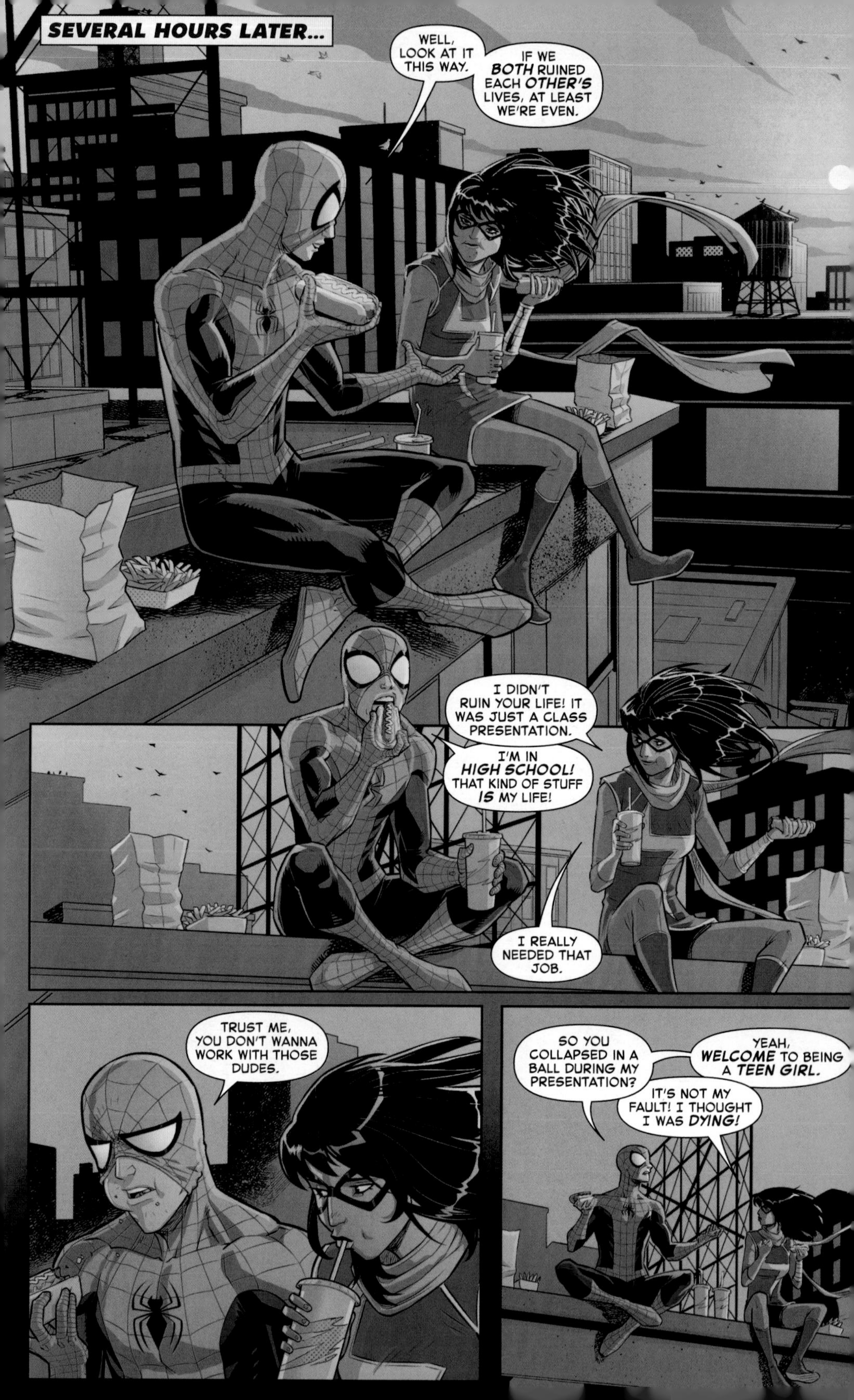
SEVERAL HOURS LATER...
WELL, LOOK AT IT THIS WAY.
IF WE BOTH RUINED EACH OTHER'S LIVES, AT LEAST WE'RE EVEN.
I DIDN'T RUIN YOUR LIFE! IT WAS JUST A CLASS PRESENTATION.
I'M IN HIGH SCHOOL! THAT KIND OF STUFF IS MY LIFE!
I REALLY NEEDED THAT JOB.
TRUST ME, YOU DON'T WANNA WORK WITH THOSE DUDES.
SO YOU COLLAPSED IN A BALL DURING MY PRESENTATION?
YEAH, WELCOME TO BEING A TEEN GIRL.
IT'S NOT MY FAULT! I THOUGHT I WAS DYING!

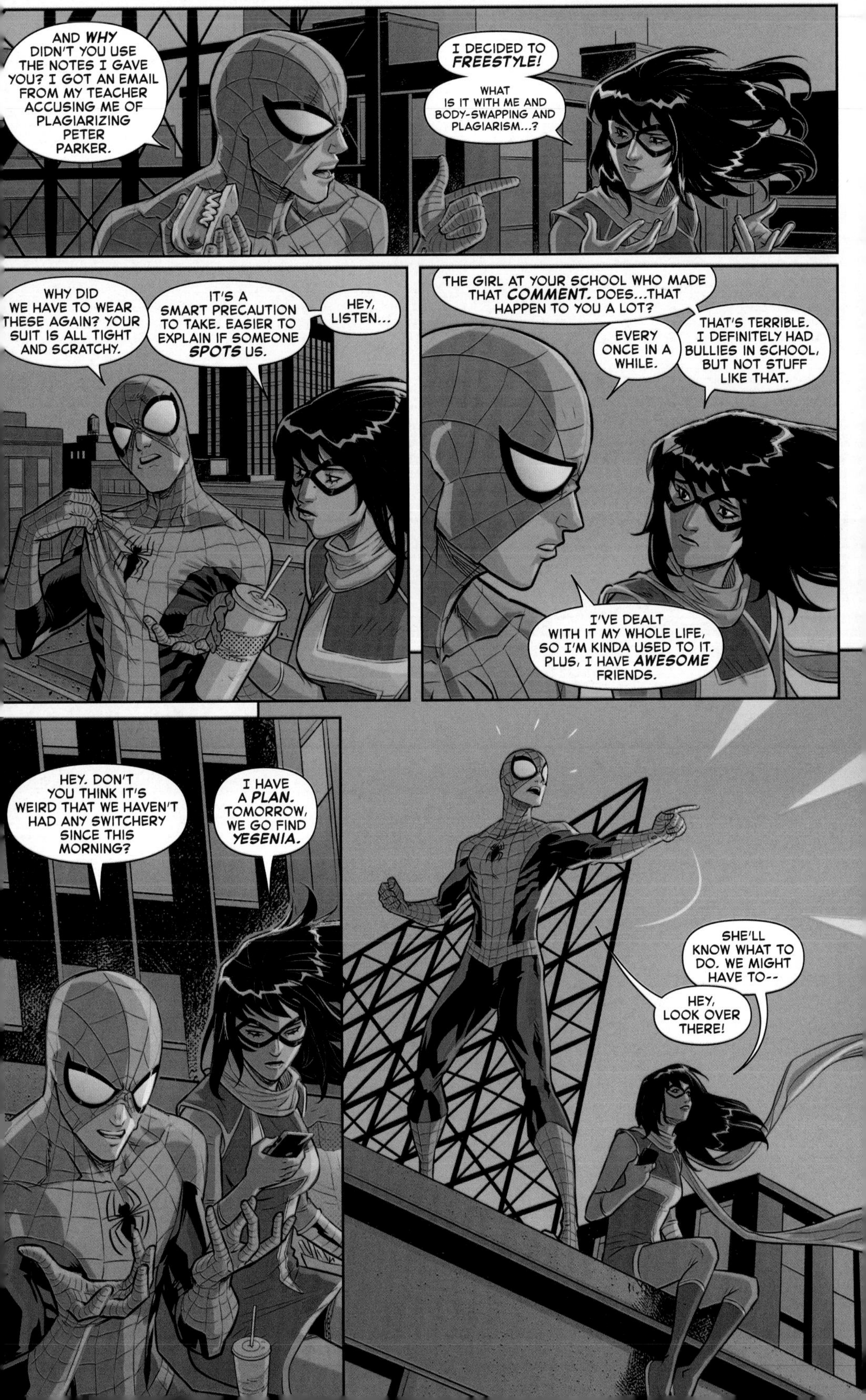
AND WHY DIDN'T YOU USE THE NOTES I GAVE YOU? I GOT AN EMAIL FROM MY TEACHER ACCUSING ME OF PLAGIARIZING PETER PARKER.
I DECIDED TO FREESTYLE!
WHAT IS IT WITH ME AND BODY-SWAPPING AND PLAGIARISM...?
WHY DID WE HAVE TO WEAR THESE AGAIN? YOUR SUIT IS ALL TIGHT AND SCRATCHY.
IT'S A SMART PRECAUTION TO TAKE. EASIER TO EXPLAIN IF SOMEONE SPOTS US.
HEY, LISTEN...
THE GIRL AT YOUR SCHOOL WHO MADE THAT COMMENT. DOES...THAT HAPPEN TO YOU A LOT?
EVERY ONCE IN A WHILE.
THAT'S TERRIBLE. I DEFINITELY HAD BULLIES IN SCHOOL, BUT NOT STUFF LIKE THAT.
I'VE DEALT WITH IT MY WHOLE LIFE, SO I'M KINDA USED TO IT. PLUS, I HAVE AWESOME FRIENDS.
HEY. DON'T YOU THINK IT'S WEIRD THAT WE HAVEN'T HAD ANY SWITCHERY SINCE THIS MORNING?
I HAVE A PLAN. TOMORROW, WE GO FIND YESENIA.
SHE'LL KNOW WHAT TO DO. WE MIGHT HAVE TO--
HEY, LOOK OVER THERE!

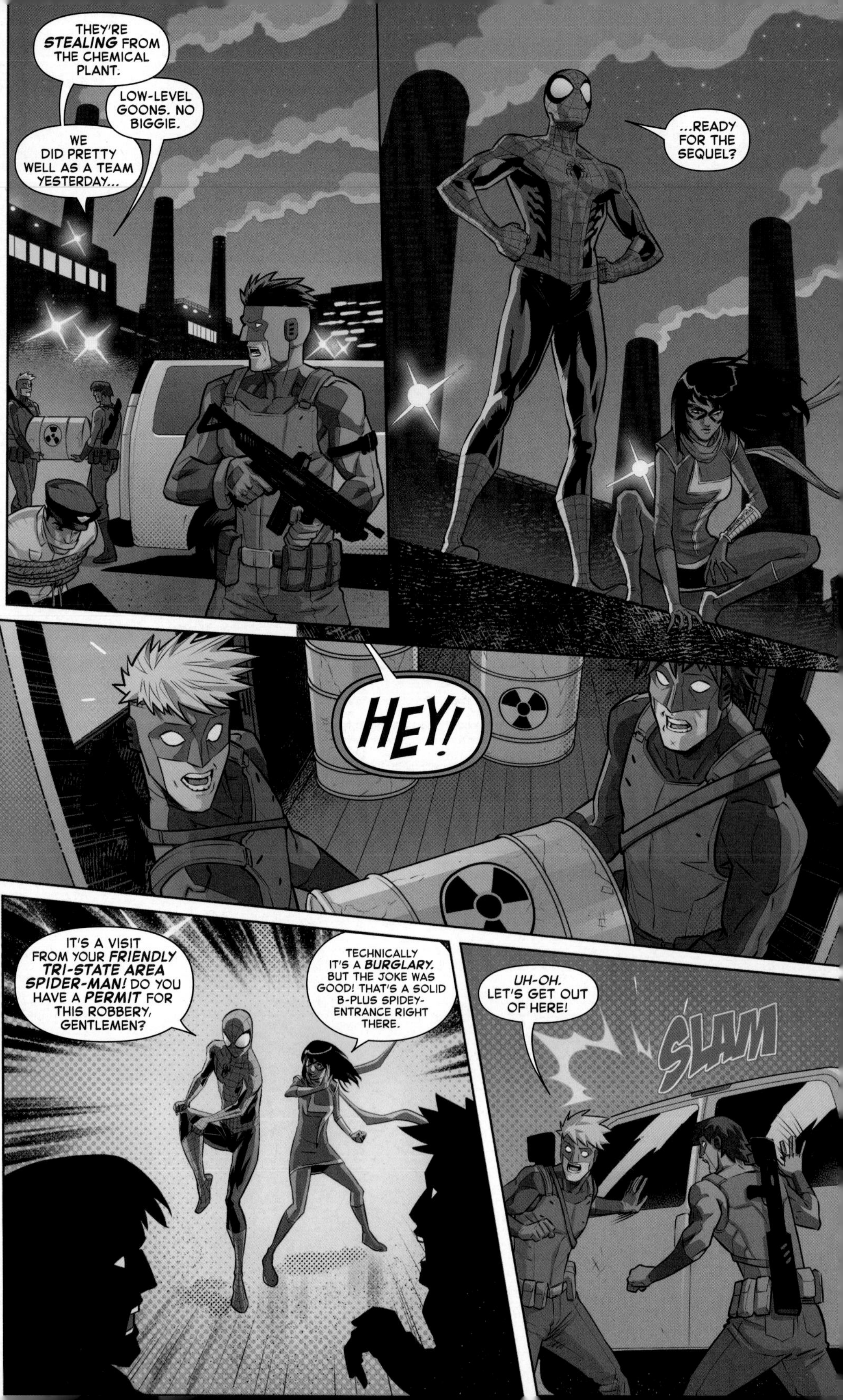
THEY'RE STEALING FROM THE CHEMICAL PLANT.
LOW-LEVEL GOONS. NO BIGGIE.
WE DID PRETTY WELL AS A TEAM YESTERDAY...
...READY FOR THE SEQUEL?
HEY!
IT'S A VISIT FROM YOUR FRIENDLY TRI-STATE AREA SPIDER-MAN! DO YOU HAVE A PERMIT FOR THIS ROBBERY, GENTLEMEN?
TECHNICALLY IT'S A BURGLARY. BUT THE JOKE WAS GOOD! THAT'S A SOLID B-PLUS SPIDEY-ENTRANCE RIGHT THERE.
UH-OH. LET'S GET OUT OF HERE!
SLAM

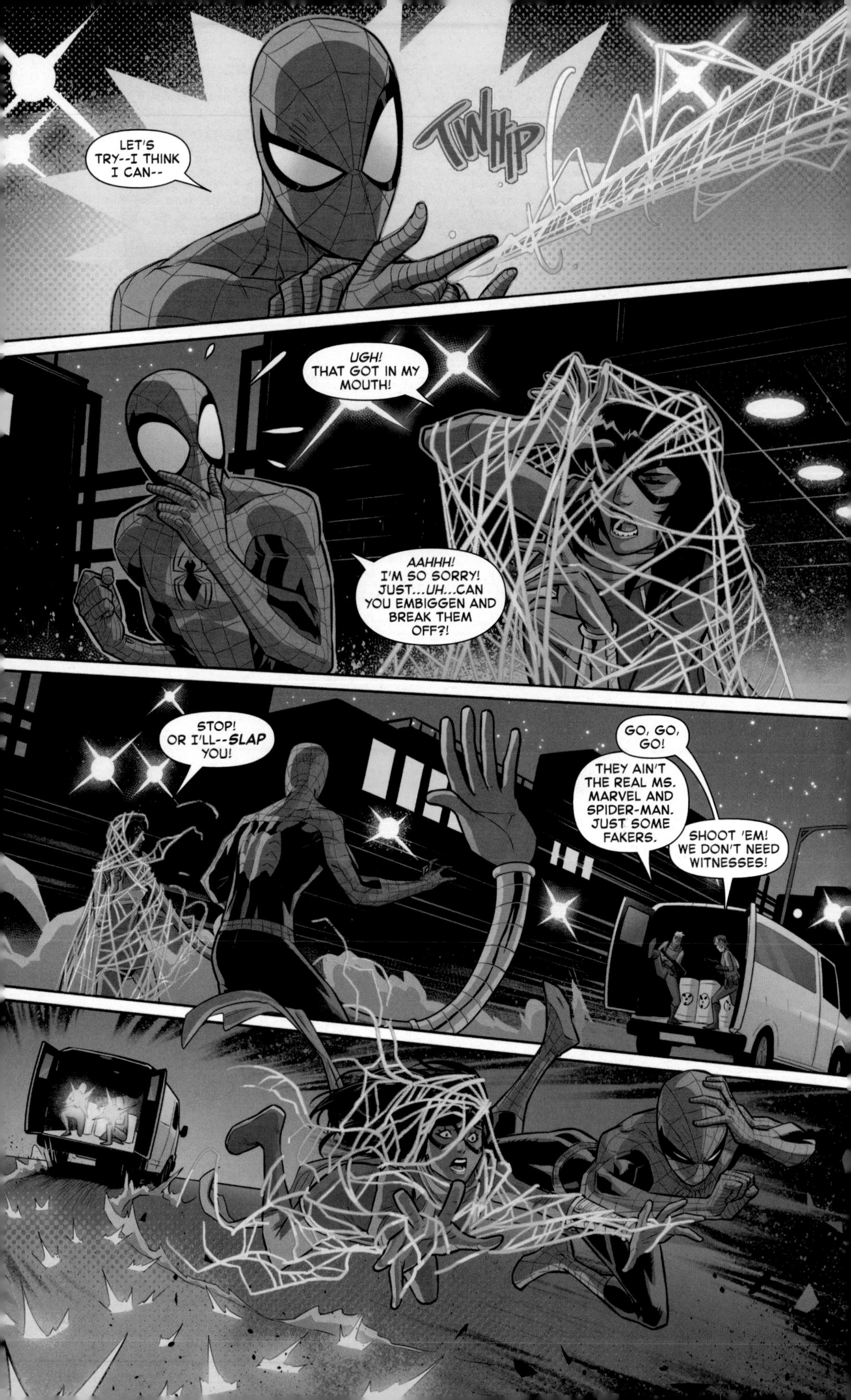
LET'S TRY--I THINK I CAN--
TWHIP
UGH! THAT GOT IN MY MOUTH!
AAHHH! I'M SO SORRY! JUST...UH...CAN YOU EMBIGGEN AND BREAK THEM OFF?!
STOP! OR I'LL--SLAP YOU!
GO, GO, GO!
THEY AIN'T THE REAL MS. MARVEL AND SPIDER-MAN. JUST SOME FAKERS.
SHOOT 'EM! WE DON'T NEED WITNESSES!

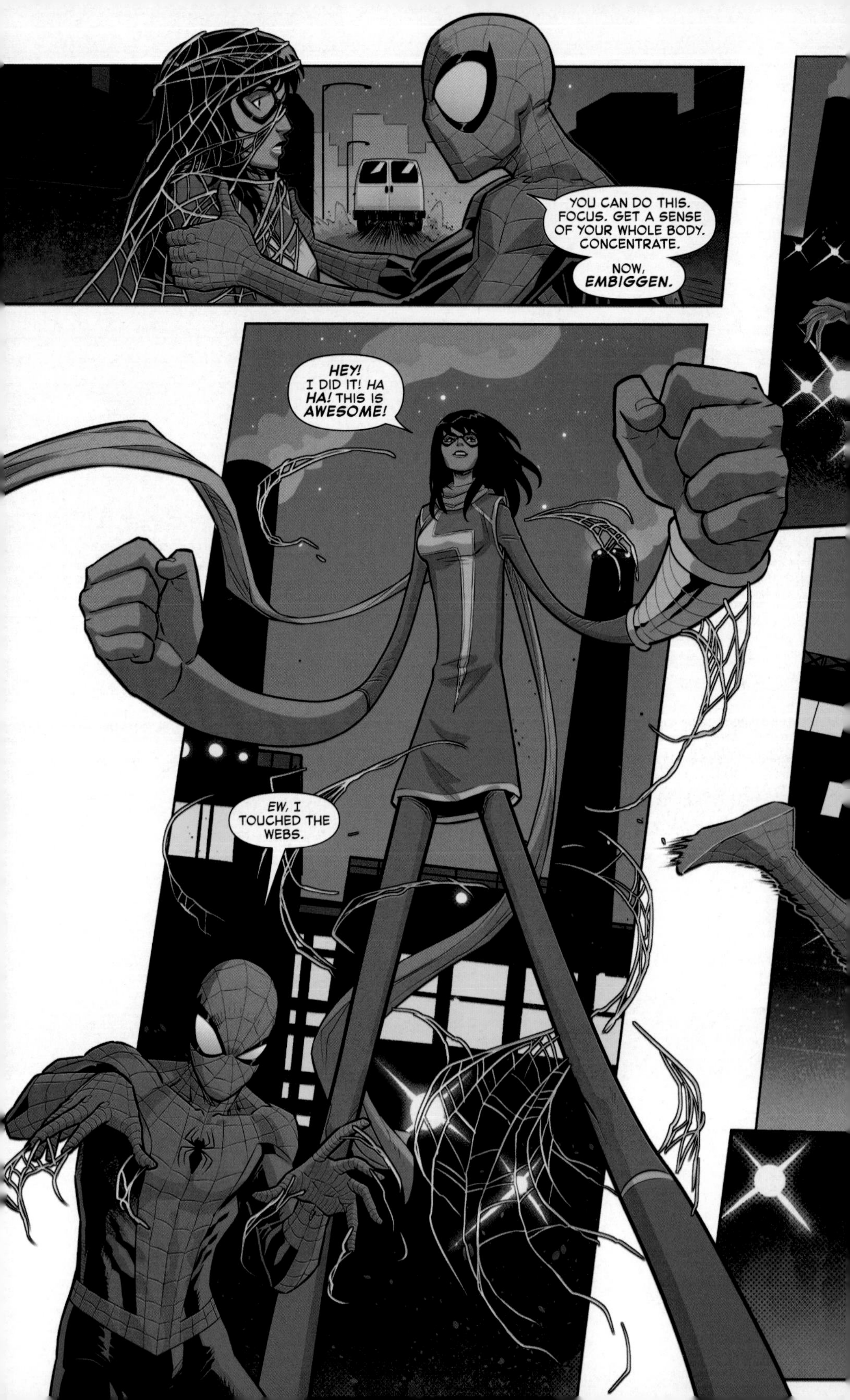
YOU CAN DO THIS. FOCUS. GET A SENSE OF YOUR WHOLE BODY. CONCENTRATE.
NOW, EMBIGGEN.
HEY! I DID IT! HA HA! THIS IS AWESOME!
EW, I TOUCHED THE WEBS.

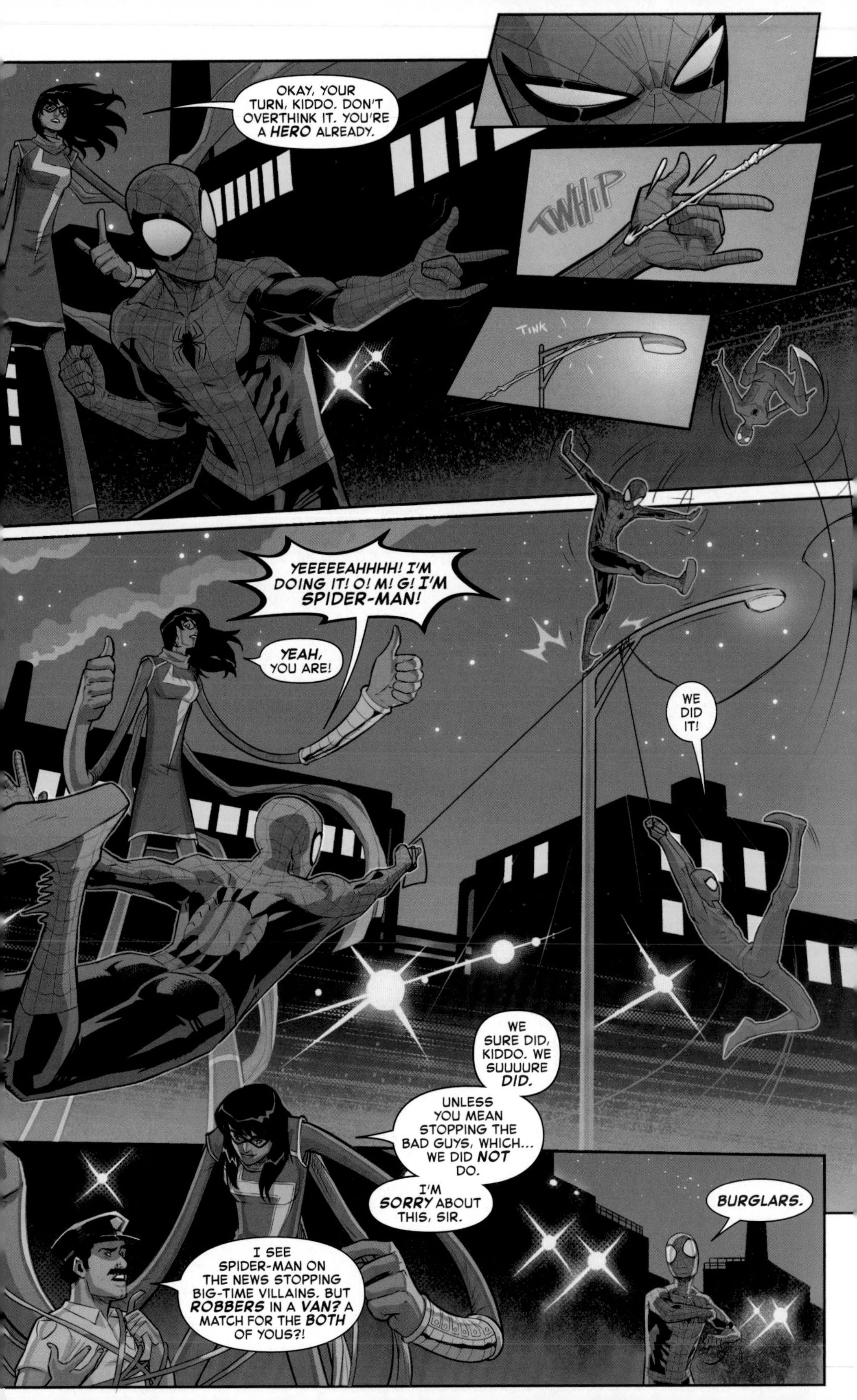
OKAY, YOUR TURN, KIDDO. DON'T OVERTHINK IT. YOU'RE A HERO ALREADY.
TWHIP
TINK
YEEEEEAHHHH! I'M DOING IT! O! M! G! I'M SPIDER-MAN!
YEAH, YOU ARE!
WE DID IT!
WE SURE DID, KIDDO. WE SUUUURE DID.
UNLESS YOU MEAN STOPPING THE BAD GUYS, WHICH... WE DID NOT DO.
I'M SORRY ABOUT THIS, SIR.
BURGLARS.
I SEE SPIDER-MAN ON THE NEWS STOPPING BIG-TIME VILLAINS. BUT ROBBERS IN A VAN? A MATCH FOR THE BOTH OF YOUS?!

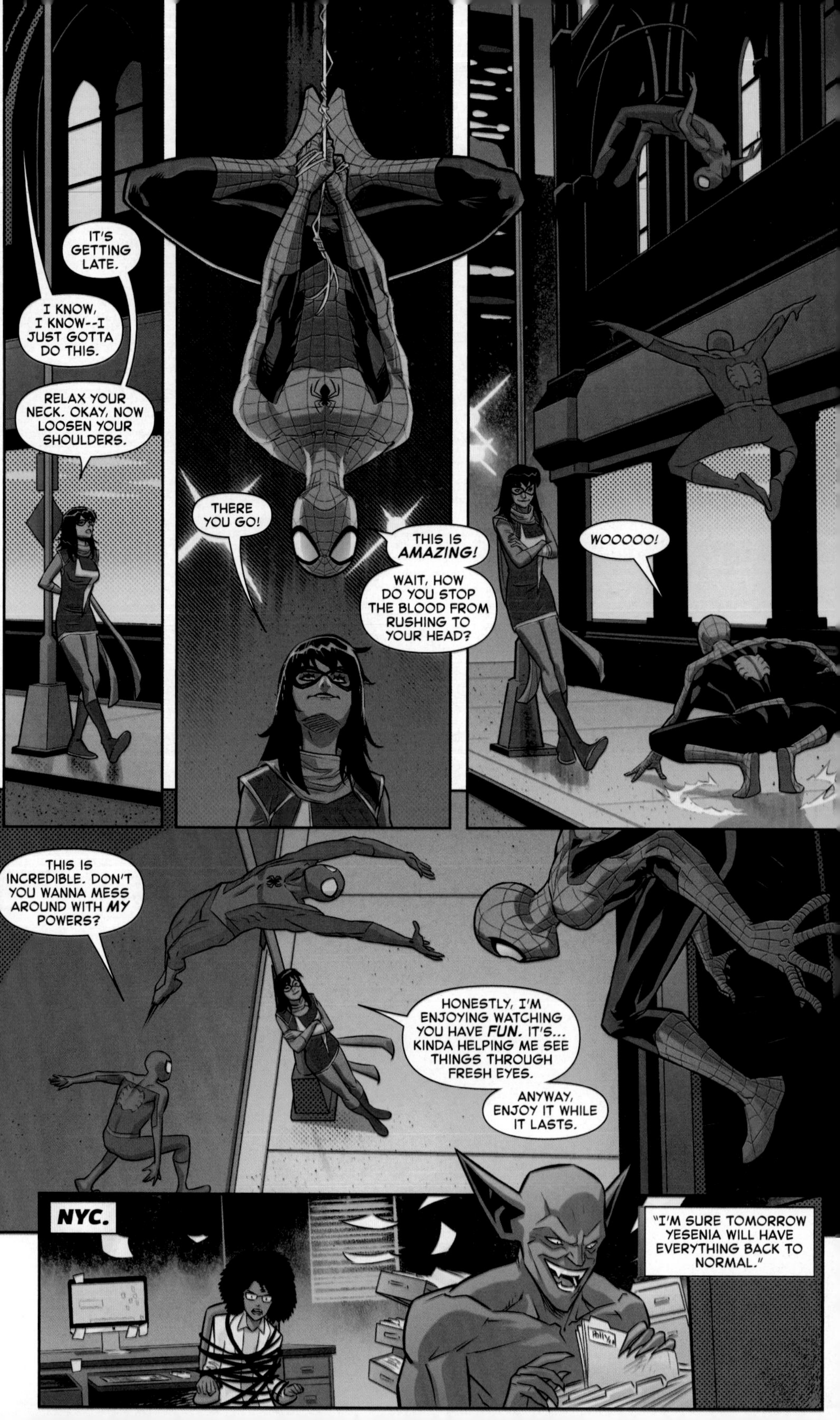
IT'S GETTING LATE.
I KNOW, I KNOW--I JUST GOTTA DO THIS.
RELAX YOUR NECK. OKAY, NOW LOOSEN YOUR SHOULDERS.
THERE YOU GO!
THIS IS AMAZING!
WAIT, HOW DO YOU STOP THE BLOOD FROM RUSHING TO YOUR HEAD?
WOOOOO!
THIS IS INCREDIBLE. DON'T YOU WANNA MESS AROUND WITH MY POWERS?
HONESTLY, I'M ENJOYING WATCHING YOU HAVE FUN. IT'S... KINDA HELPING ME SEE THINGS THROUGH FRESH EYES.
ANYWAY, ENJOY IT WHILE IT LASTS.
NYC.
"I'M SURE TOMORROW YESENIA WILL HAVE EVERYTHING BACK TO NORMAL."

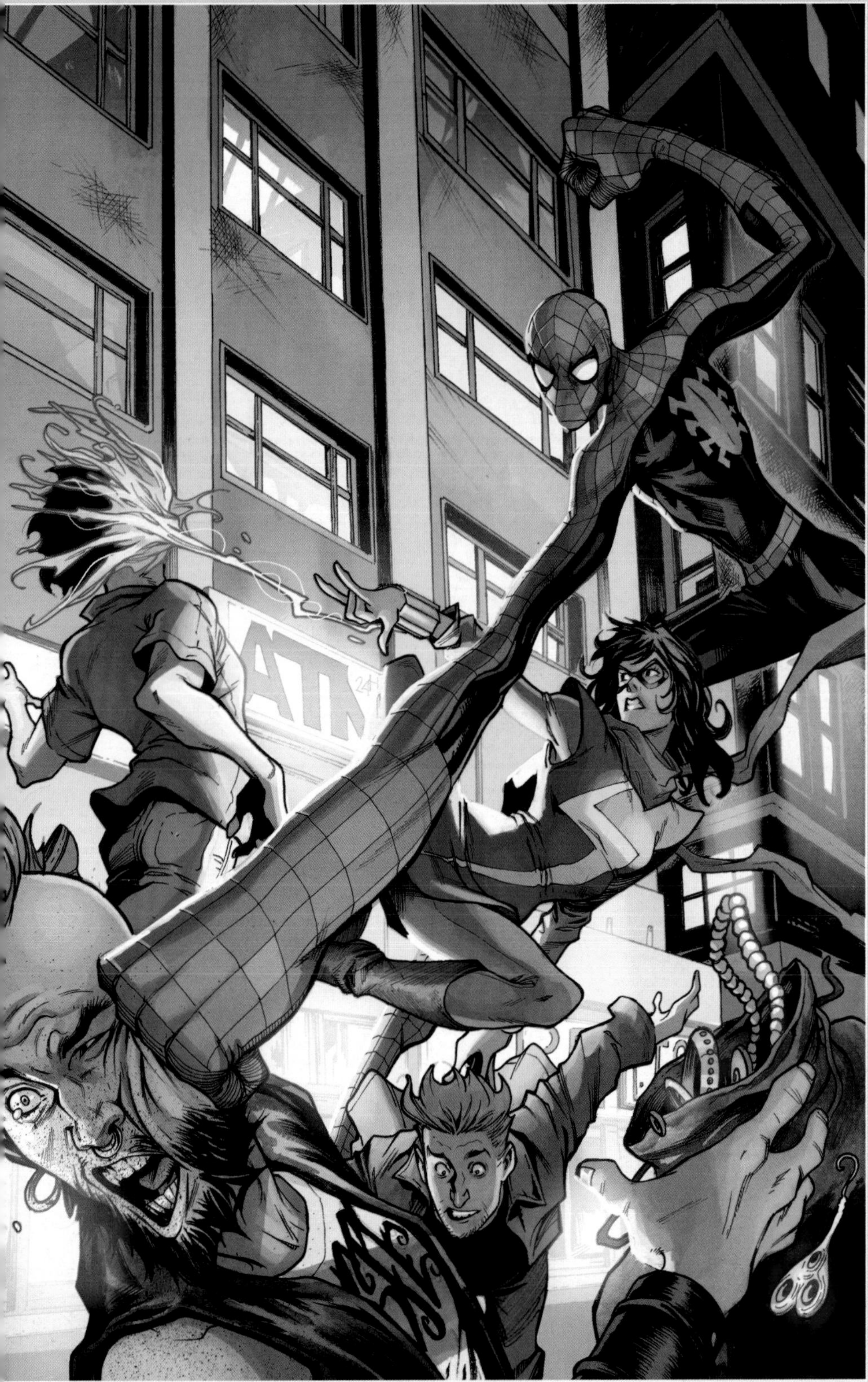
ATM
24

MS. MARVEL TEAM-UP #3

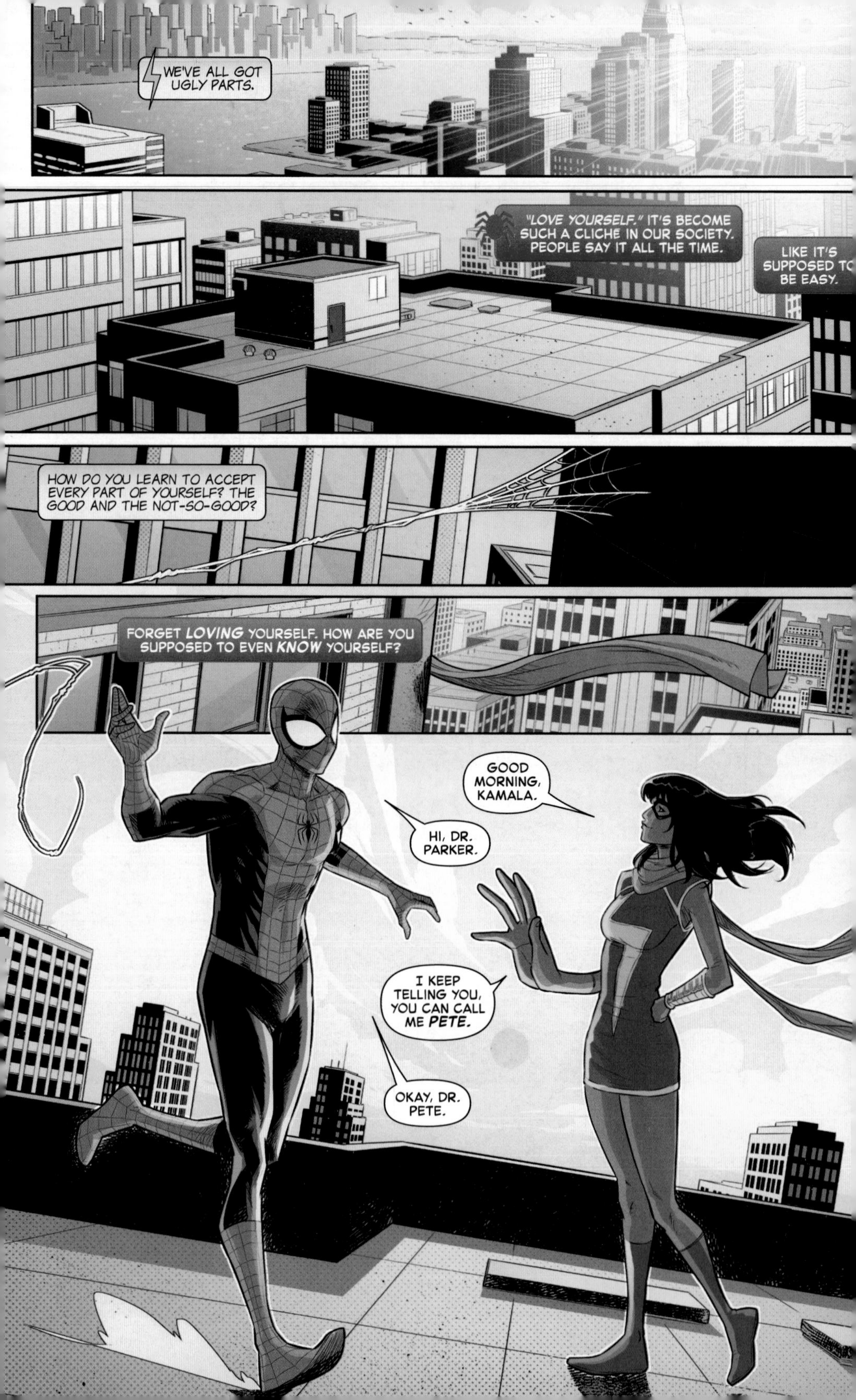
WE'VE ALL GOT UGLY PARTS.
"LOVE YOURSELF." IT'S BECOME SUCH A CLICHE IN OUR SOCIETY. PEOPLE SAY IT ALL THE TIME.
LIKE IT'S SUPPOSED TO BE EASY.
HOW DO YOU LEARN TO ACCEPT EVERY PART OF YOURSELF? THE GOOD AND THE NOT-SO-GOOD?
FORGET LOVING YOURSELF. HOW ARE YOU SUPPOSED TO EVEN KNOW YOURSELF?
GOOD MORNING, KAMALA.
HI, DR. PARKER.
I KEEP TELLING YOU, YOU CAN CALL ME PETE.
OKAY, DR. PETE.

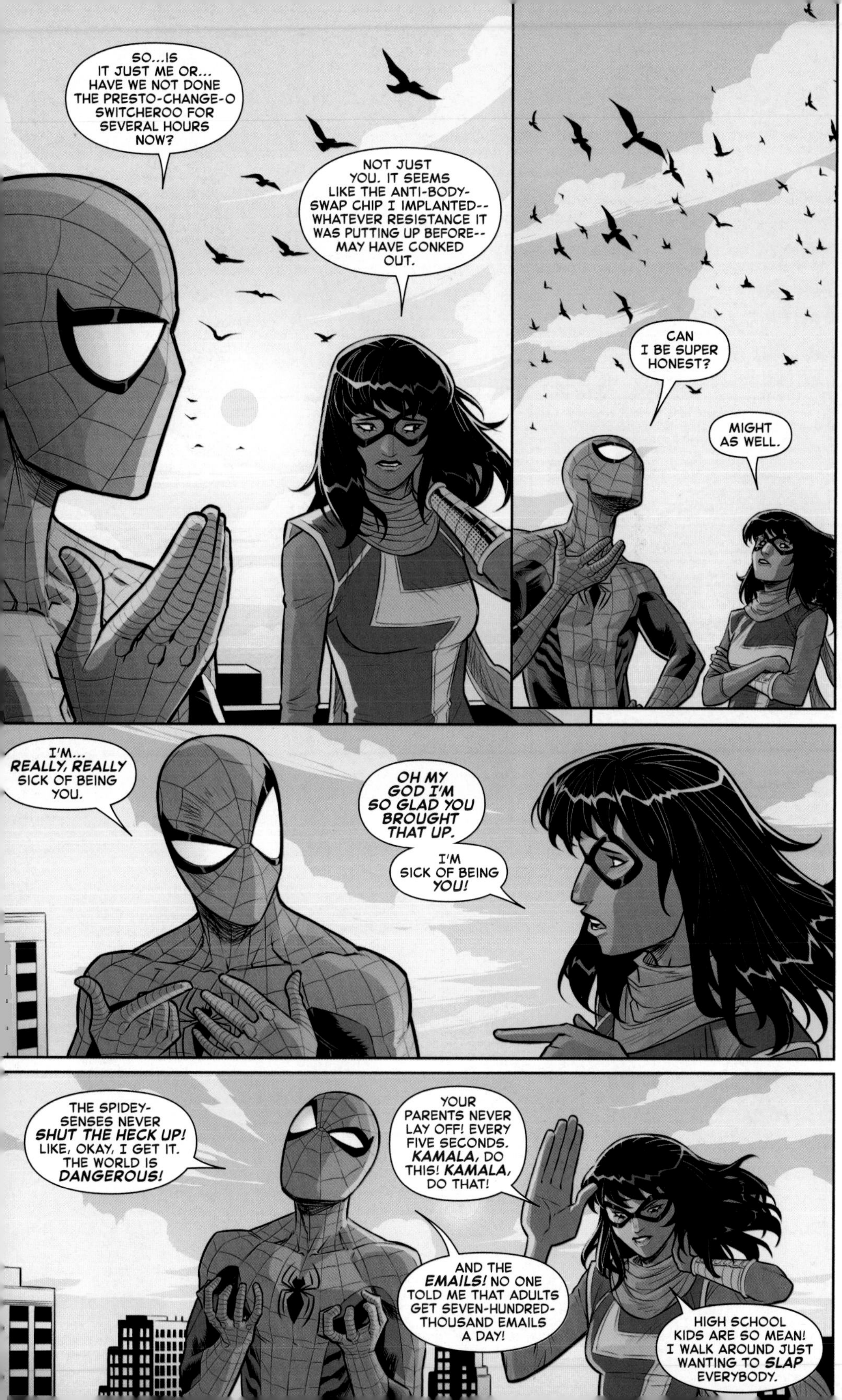
SO...IS IT JUST ME OR... HAVE WE NOT DONE THE PRESTO-CHANGE-O SWITCHEROO FOR SEVERAL HOURS NOW?
NOT JUST YOU. IT SEEMS LIKE THE ANTI-BODY-SWAP CHIP I IMPLANTED-- WHATEVER RESISTANCE IT WAS PUTTING UP BEFORE-- MAY HAVE CONKED OUT.
CAN I BE SUPER HONEST?
MIGHT AS WELL.
I'M... REALLY, REALLY SICK OF BEING YOU.
OH MY GOD I'M SO GLAD YOU BROUGHT THAT UP.
I'M SICK OF BEING YOU!
THE SPIDEY-SENSES NEVER SHUT THE HECK UP! LIKE, OKAY, I GET IT. THE WORLD IS DANGEROUS!
YOUR PARENTS NEVER LAY OFF! EVERY FIVE SECONDS. KAMALA, DO THIS! KAMALA, DO THAT!
AND THE EMAILS! NO ONE TOLD ME THAT ADULTS GET SEVEN-HUNDRED-THOUSAND EMAILS A DAY!
HIGH SCHOOL KIDS ARE SO MEAN! I WALK AROUND JUST WANTING TO SLAP EVERYBODY.

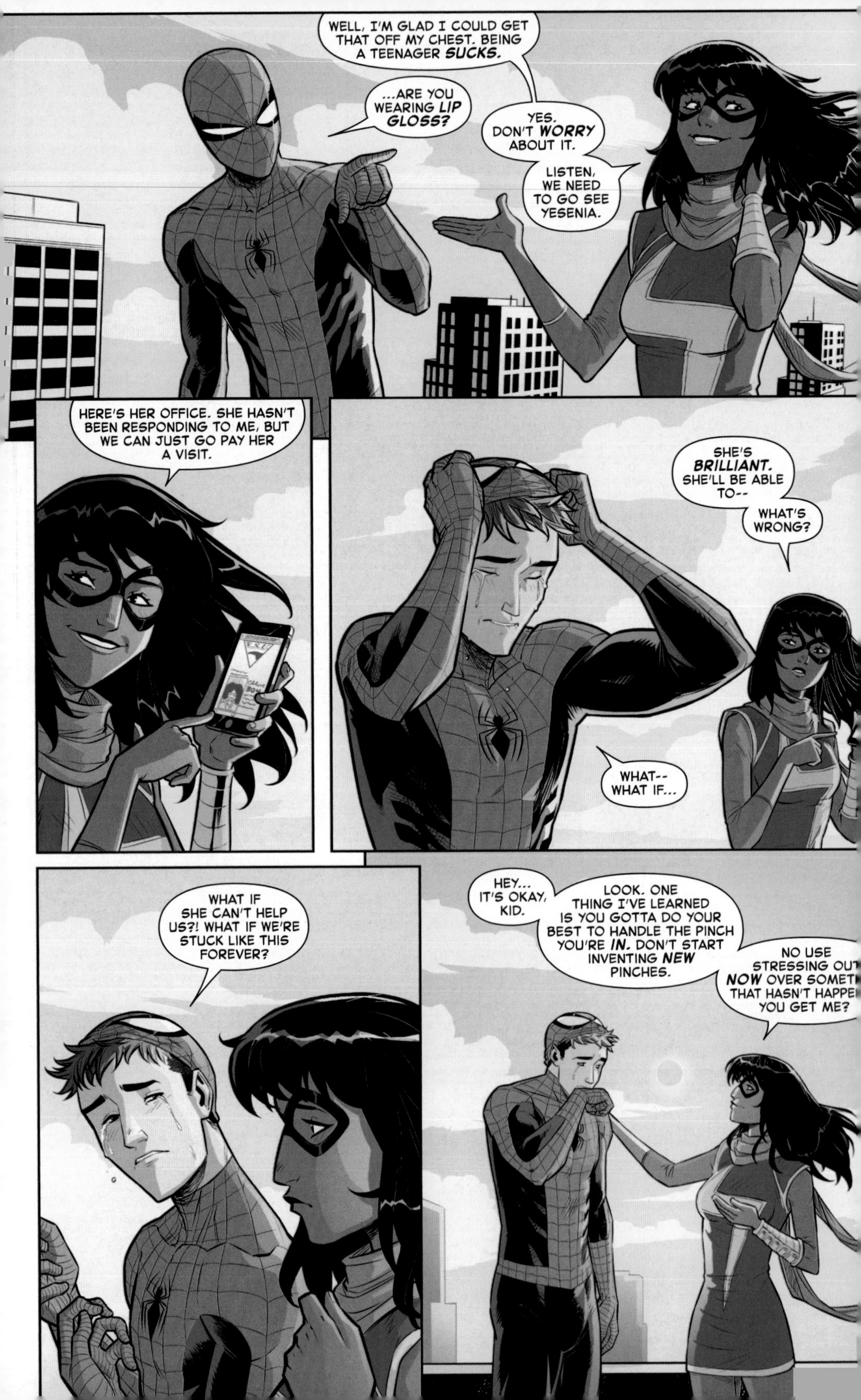

WELL, I'M GLAD I COULD GET THAT OFF MY CHEST. BEING A TEENAGER SUCKS.
...ARE YOU WEARING LIP GLOSS?
YES. DON'T WORRY ABOUT IT.
LISTEN, WE NEED TO GO SEE YESENIA.
HERE'S HER OFFICE. SHE HASN'T BEEN RESPONDING TO ME, BUT WE CAN JUST GO PAY HER A VISIT.
SHE'S BRILLIANT. SHE'LL BE ABLE TO--
WHAT'S WRONG?
WHAT-- WHAT IF...
WHAT IF SHE CAN'T HELP US?! WHAT IF WE'RE STUCK LIKE THIS FOREVER?
HEY... IT'S OKAY, KID.
LOOK. ONE THING I'VE LEARNED IS YOU GOTTA DO YOUR BEST TO HANDLE THE PINCH YOU'RE IN. DON'T START INVENTING NEW PINCHES.
NO USE STRESSING OUT NOW OVER SOMET THAT HASN'T HAPPE YOU GET ME?

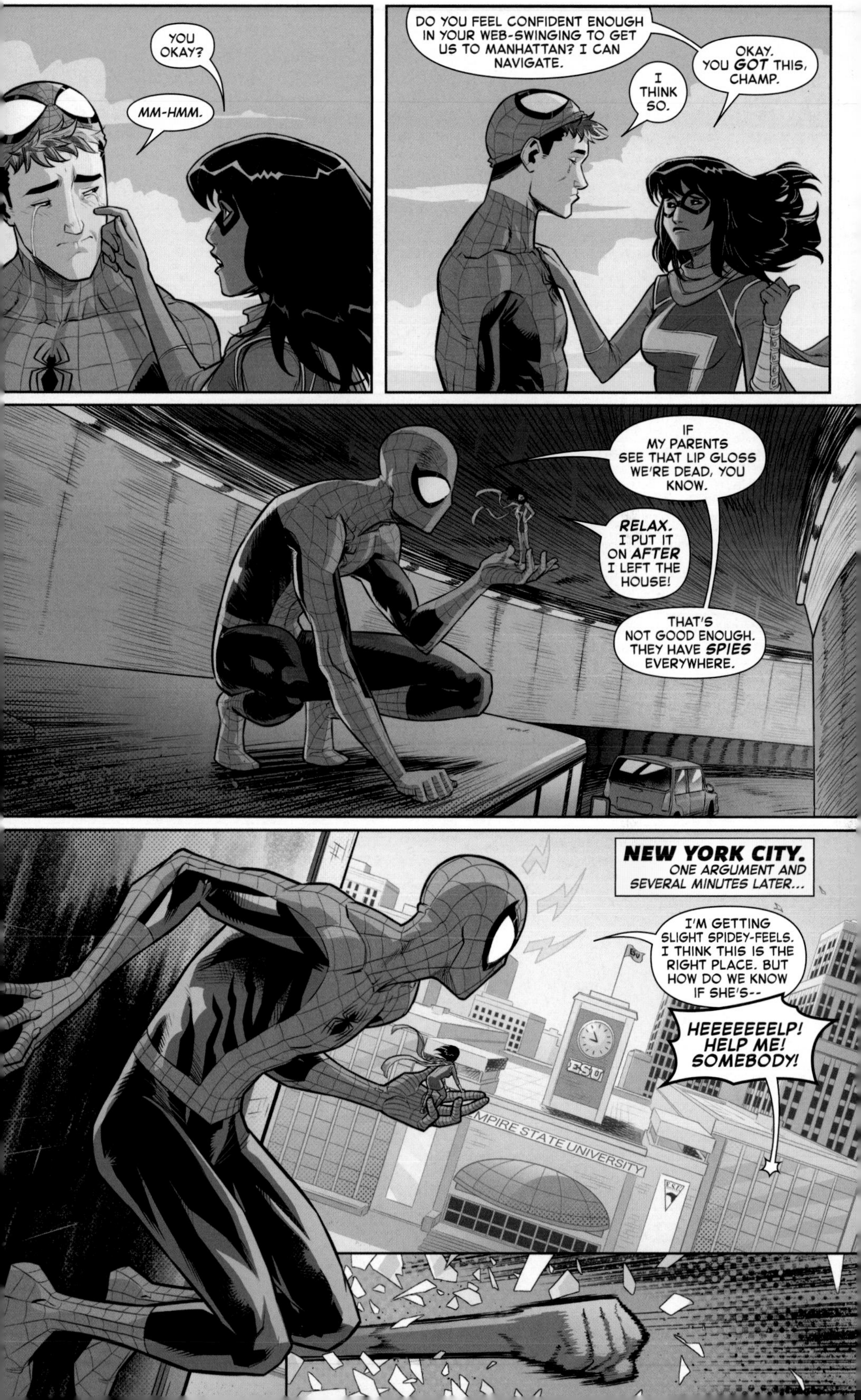
YOU OKAY?
MM-HMM.
DO YOU FEEL CONFIDENT ENOUGH IN YOUR WEB-SWINGING TO GET US TO MANHATTAN? I CAN NAVIGATE.
I THINK SO.
OKAY. YOU GOT THIS, CHAMP.
IF MY PARENTS SEE THAT LIP GLOSS WE'RE DEAD, YOU KNOW.
RELAX. I PUT IT ON AFTER I LEFT THE HOUSE!
THAT'S NOT GOOD ENOUGH. THEY HAVE SPIES EVERYWHERE.
NEW YORK CITY. ONE ARGUMENT AND SEVERAL MINUTES LATER...
I'M GETTING SLIGHT SPIDEY-FEELS. I THINK THIS IS THE RIGHT PLACE. BUT HOW DO WE KNOW IF SHE'S--
HEEEEEEELP! HELP ME! SOMEBODY!
ESU
EMPIRE STATE UNIVERSITY

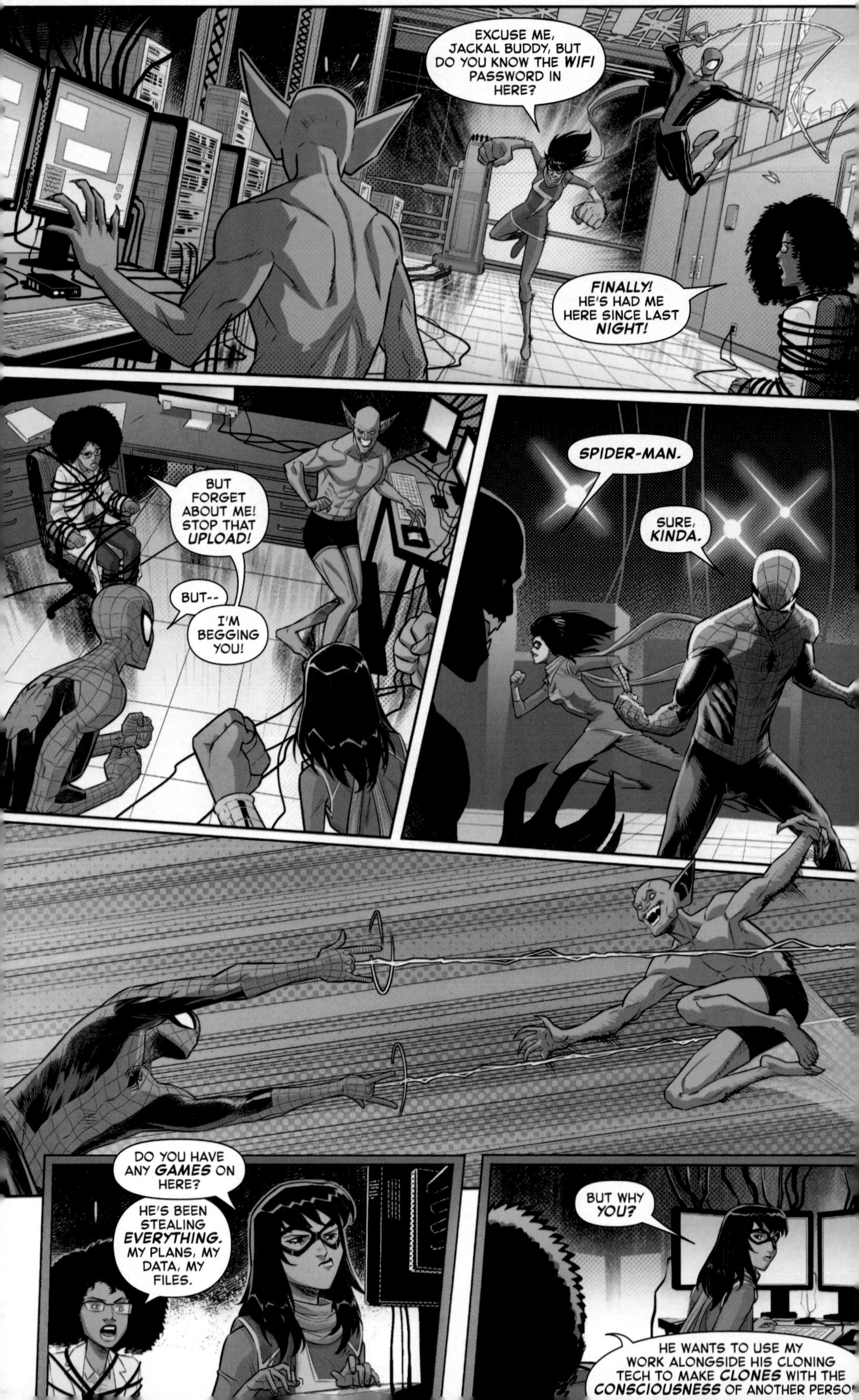
EXCUSE ME, JACKAL BUDDY, BUT DO YOU KNOW THE WIFI PASSWORD IN HERE?
FINALLY! HE'S HAD ME HERE SINCE LAST NIGHT!
BUT FORGET ABOUT ME! STOP THAT UPLOAD!
BUT--
I'M BEGGING YOU!
SPIDER-MAN.
SURE, KINDA.
DO YOU HAVE ANY GAMES ON HERE?
HE'S BEEN STEALING EVERYTHING. MY PLANS, MY DATA, MY FILES.
BUT WHY YOU?
HE WANTS TO USE MY WORK ALONGSIDE HIS CLONING TECH TO MAKE CLONES WITH THE CONSCIOUSNESS OF ANOTHER PERSO

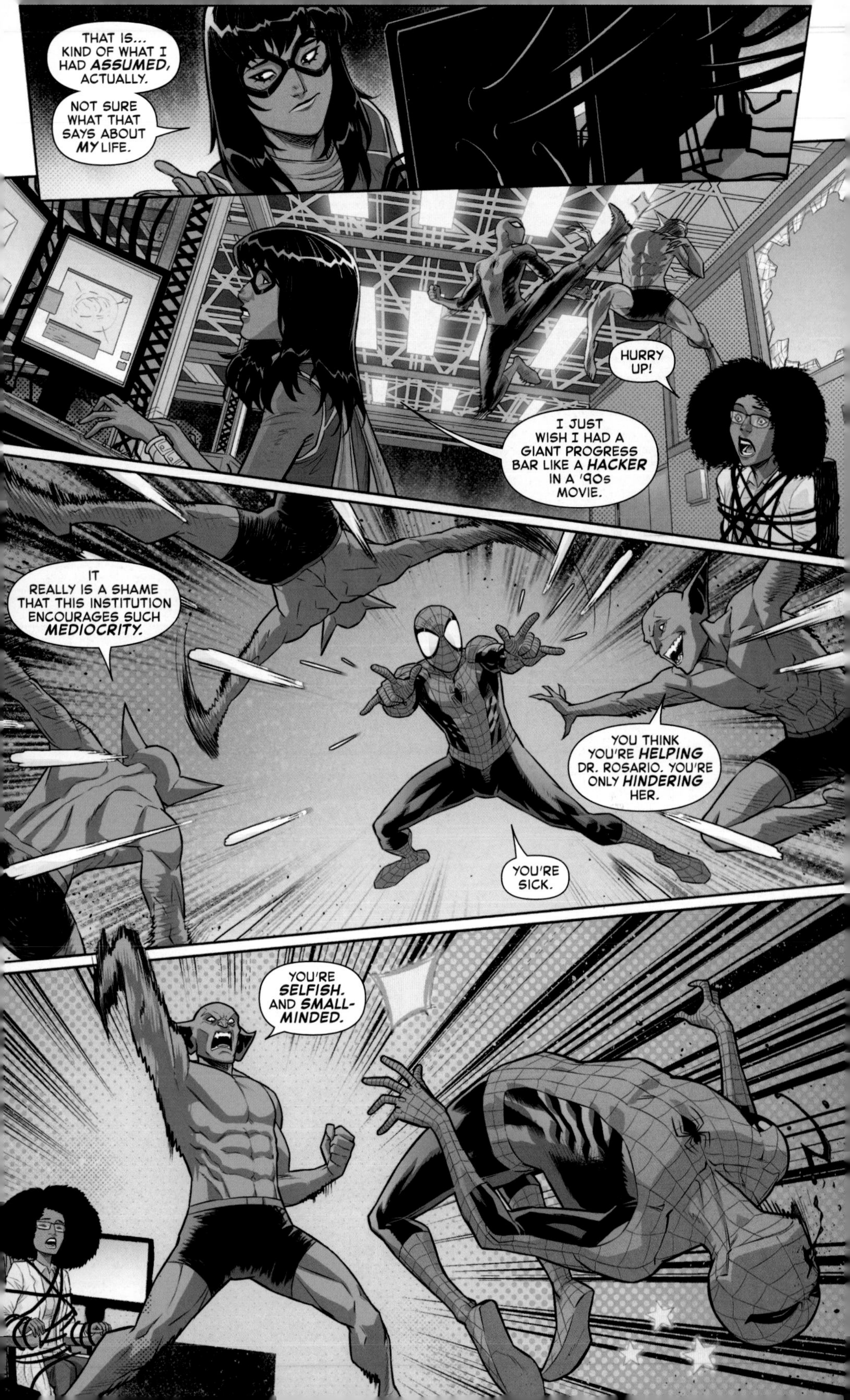
THAT IS... KIND OF WHAT I HAD ASSUMED, ACTUALLY.
NOT SURE WHAT THAT SAYS ABOUT MY LIFE.
HURRY UP!
I JUST WISH I HAD A GIANT PROGRESS BAR LIKE A HACKER IN A '90s MOVIE.
IT REALLY IS A SHAME THAT THIS INSTITUTION ENCOURAGES SUCH MEDIOCRITY.
YOU THINK YOU'RE HELPING DR. ROSARIO. YOU'RE ONLY HINDERING HER.
YOU'RE SICK.
YOU'RE SELFISH. AND SMALL-MINDED.

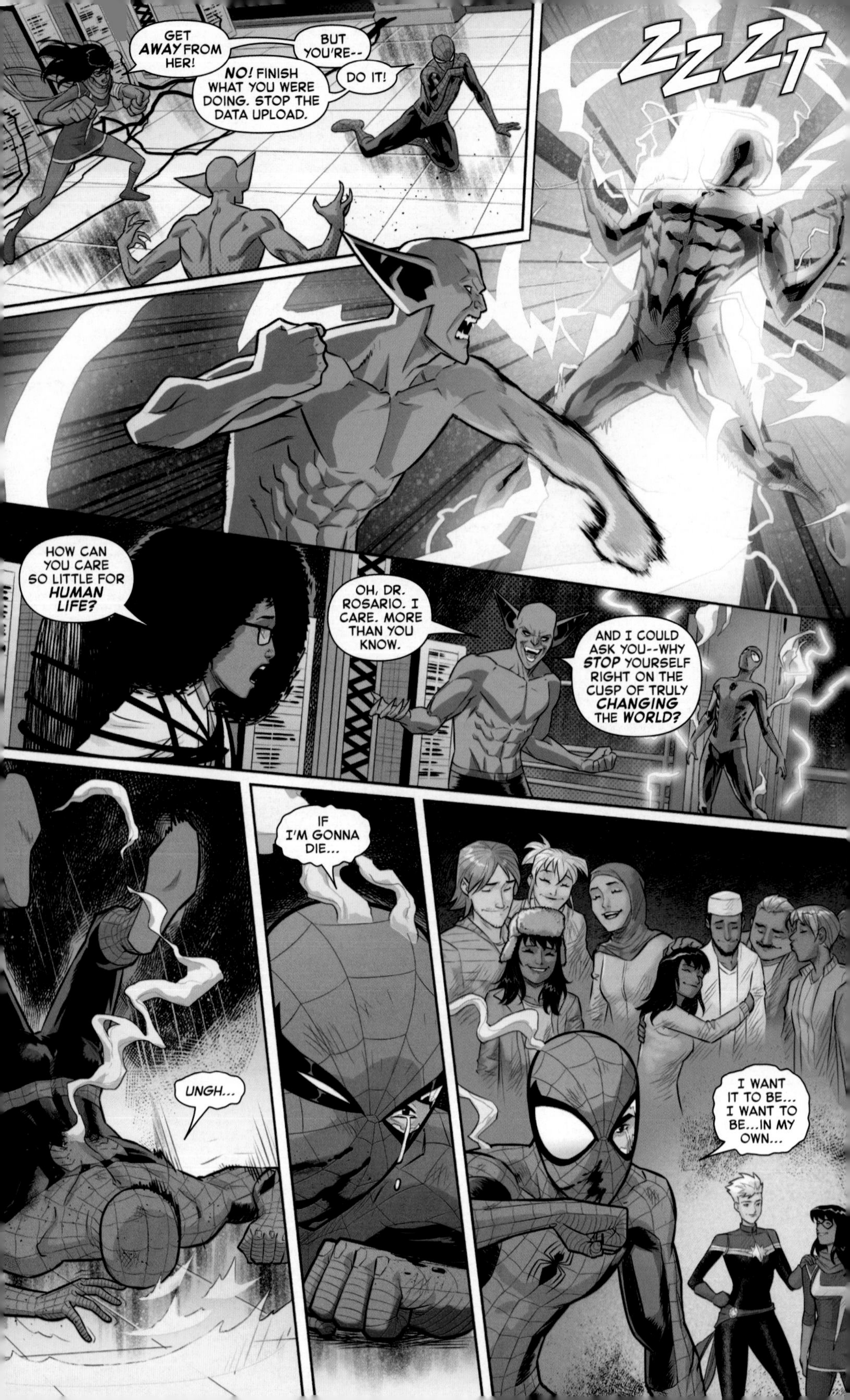
GET AWAY FROM HER!
BUT YOU'RE--
NO! FINISH WHAT YOU WERE DOING. STOP THE DATA UPLOAD.
DO IT!
ZZZT
HOW CAN YOU CARE SO LITTLE FOR HUMAN LIFE?
OH, DR. ROSARIO. I CARE. MORE THAN YOU KNOW.
AND I COULD ASK YOU--WHY STOP YOURSELF RIGHT ON THE CUSP OF TRULY CHANGING THE WORLD?
UNGH...
IF I'M GONNA DIE...
I WANT IT TO BE... I WANT TO BE...IN MY OWN...

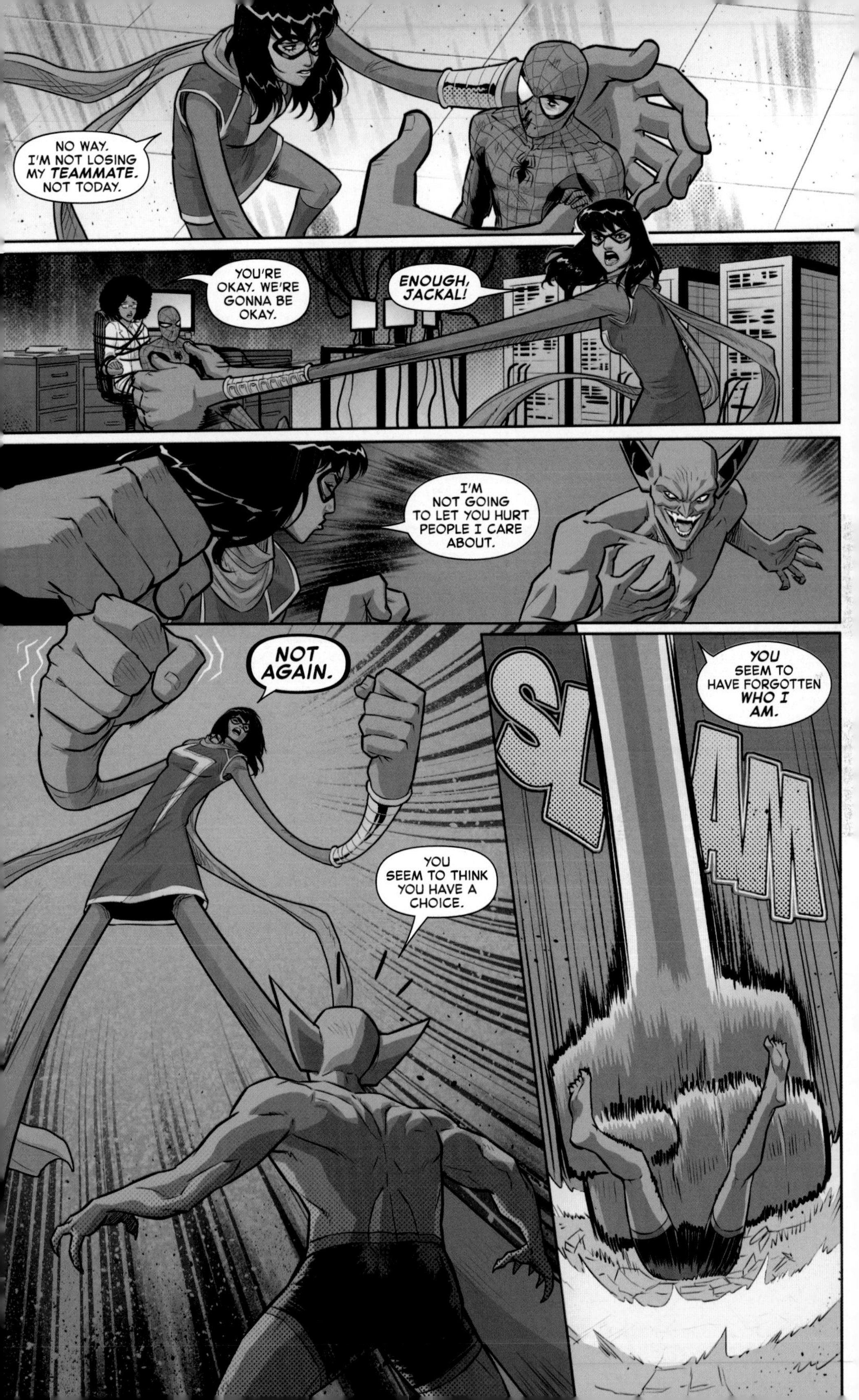
NO WAY. I'M NOT LOSING MY TEAMMATE. NOT TODAY.
YOU'RE OKAY. WE'RE GONNA BE OKAY.
ENOUGH, JACKAL!
I'M NOT GOING TO LET YOU HURT PEOPLE I CARE ABOUT.
NOT AGAIN.
YOU SEEM TO THINK YOU HAVE A CHOICE.
YOU SEEM TO HAVE FORGOTTEN WHO I AM.
SLAM

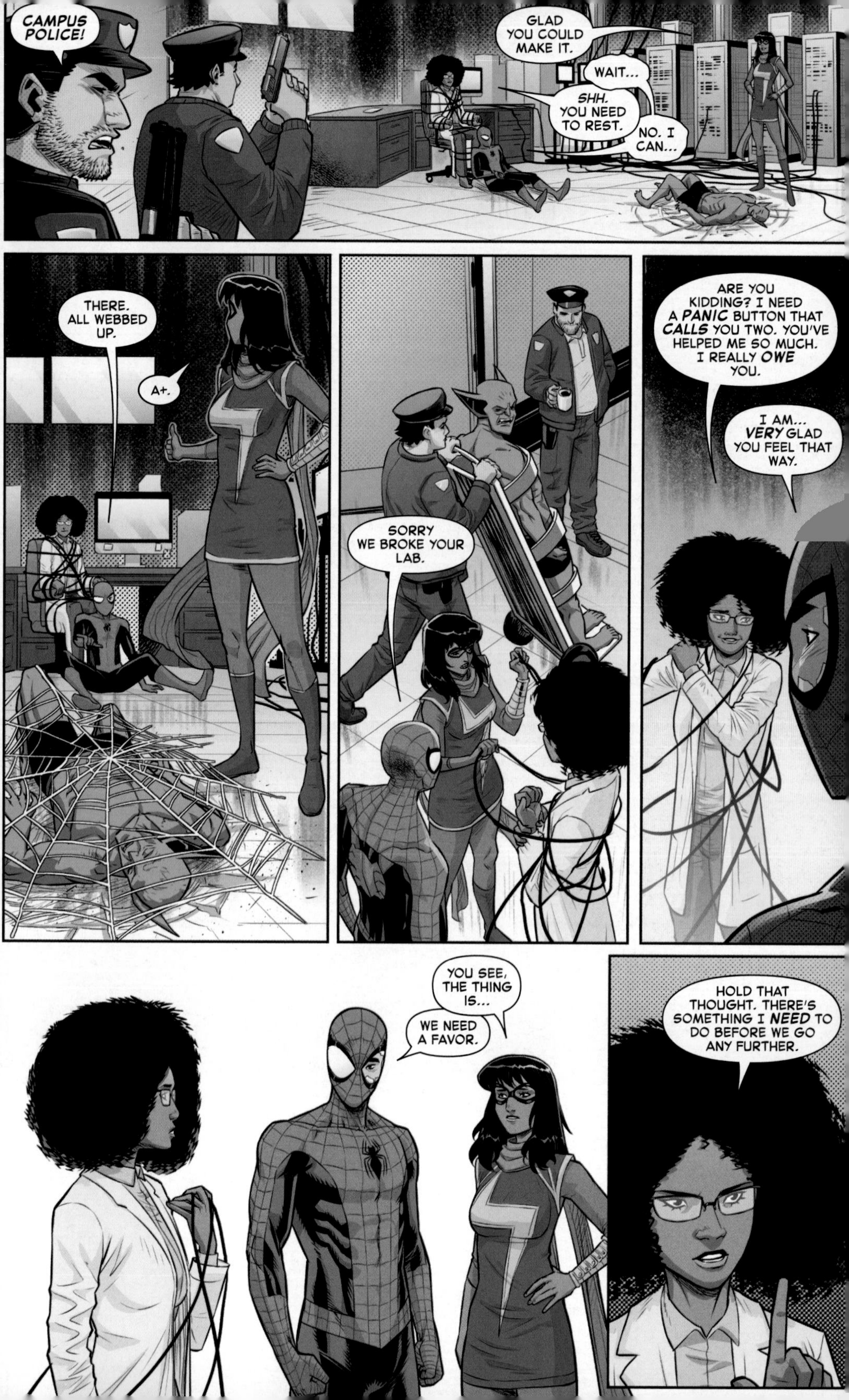
CAMPUS POLICE!
GLAD YOU COULD MAKE IT.
WAIT...
SHH. YOU NEED TO REST.
NO. I CAN...
THERE. ALL WEBBED UP.
A+.
SORRY WE BROKE YOUR LAB.
ARE YOU KIDDING? I NEED A PANIC BUTTON THAT CALLS YOU TWO. YOU'VE HELPED ME SO MUCH. I REALLY OWE YOU.
I AM... VERY GLAD YOU FEEL THAT WAY.
YOU SEE, THE THING IS...
WE NEED A FAVOR.
HOLD THAT THOUGHT. THERE'S SOMETHING I NEED TO DO BEFORE WE GO ANY FURTHER.

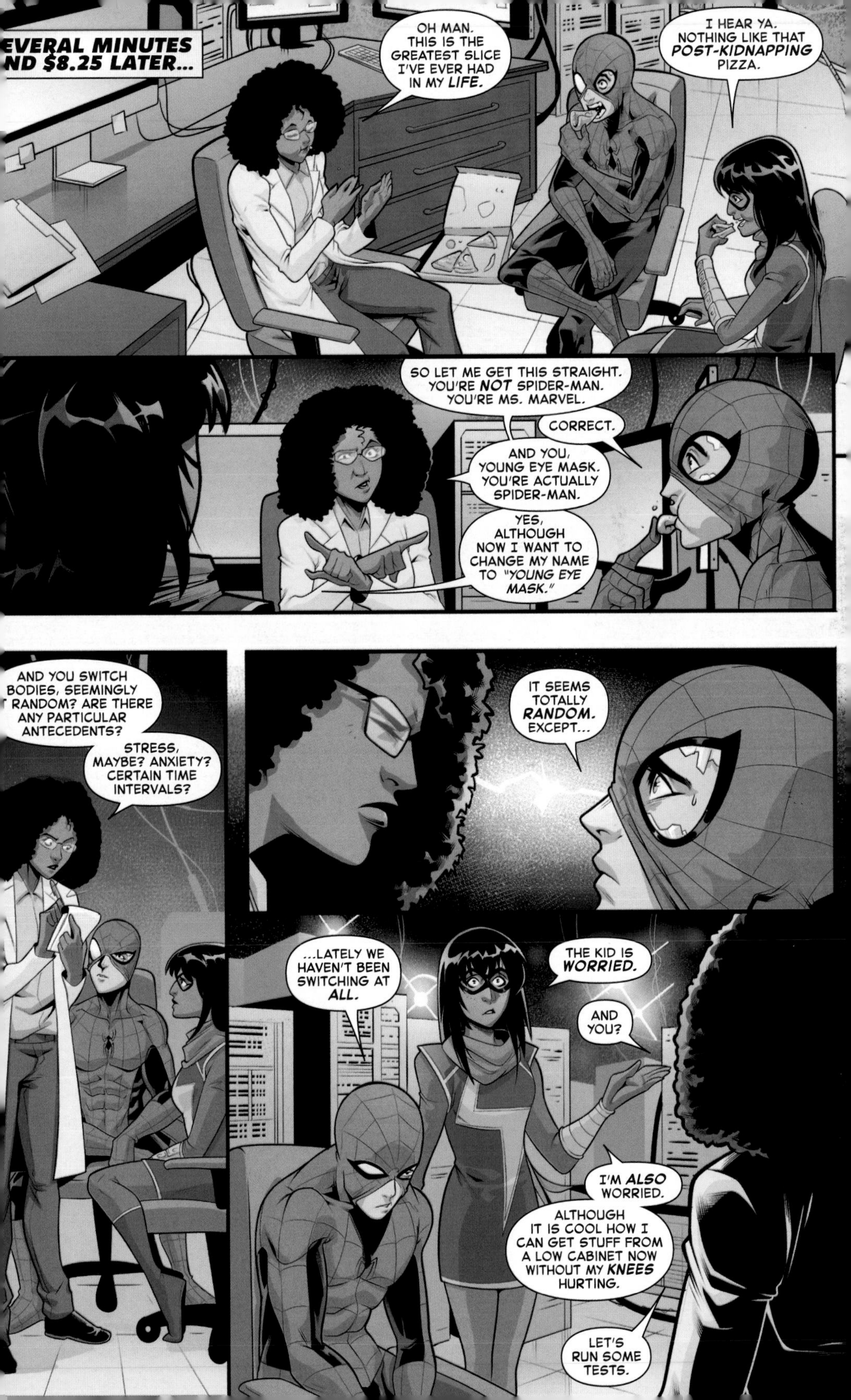
EVERAL MINUTES
ND $8.25 LATER...
OH MAN. THIS IS THE GREATEST SLICE I'VE EVER HAD IN MY *LIFE.*
I HEAR YA. NOTHING LIKE THAT *POST-KIDNAPPING* PIZZA.
SO LET ME GET THIS STRAIGHT. YOU'RE *NOT* SPIDER-MAN. YOU'RE MS. MARVEL.
CORRECT.
AND YOU, YOUNG EYE MASK. YOU'RE ACTUALLY SPIDER-MAN.
YES, ALTHOUGH NOW I WANT TO CHANGE MY NAME TO *"YOUNG EYE MASK."*
AND YOU SWITCH BODIES, SEEMINGLY RANDOM? ARE THERE ANY PARTICULAR ANTECEDENTS?
STRESS, MAYBE? ANXIETY? CERTAIN TIME INTERVALS?
IT SEEMS TOTALLY *RANDOM.* EXCEPT...
...LATELY WE HAVEN'T BEEN SWITCHING AT *ALL.*
THE KID IS *WORRIED.*
AND YOU?
I'M *ALSO* WORRIED.
ALTHOUGH IT IS COOL HOW I CAN GET STUFF FROM A LOW CABINET NOW WITHOUT MY *KNEES* HURTING.
LET'S RUN SOME TESTS.

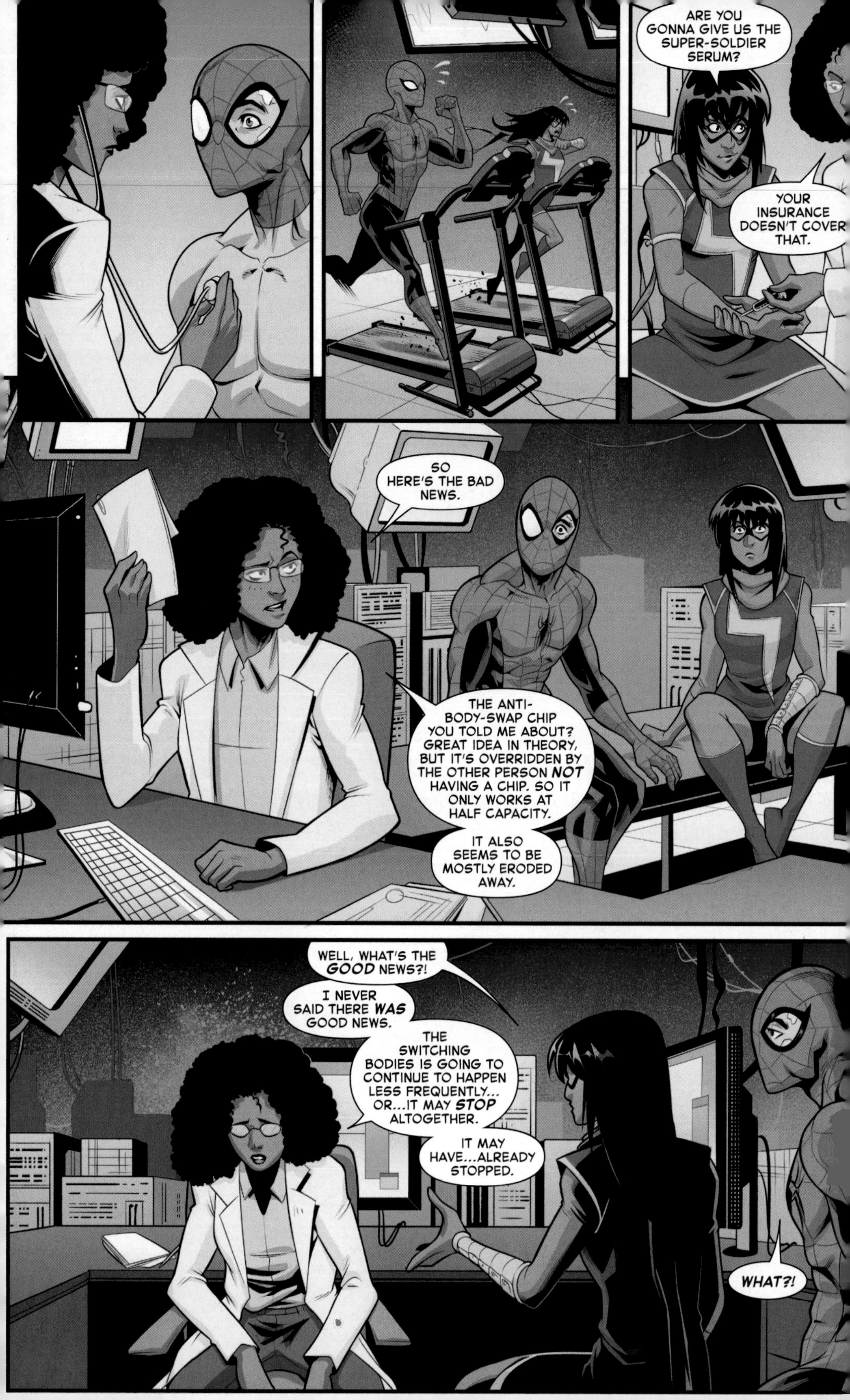
ARE YOU GONNA GIVE US THE SUPER-SOLDIER SERUM?
YOUR INSURANCE DOESN'T COVER THAT.
SO HERE'S THE BAD NEWS.
THE ANTI-BODY-SWAP CHIP YOU TOLD ME ABOUT? GREAT IDEA IN THEORY, BUT IT'S OVERRIDDEN BY THE OTHER PERSON NOT HAVING A CHIP. SO IT ONLY WORKS AT HALF CAPACITY.
IT ALSO SEEMS TO BE MOSTLY ERODED AWAY.
WELL, WHAT'S THE GOOD NEWS?!
I NEVER SAID THERE WAS GOOD NEWS.
THE SWITCHING BODIES IS GOING TO CONTINUE TO HAPPEN LESS FREQUENTLY... OR...IT MAY STOP ALTOGETHER.
IT MAY HAVE...ALREADY STOPPED.
WHAT?!

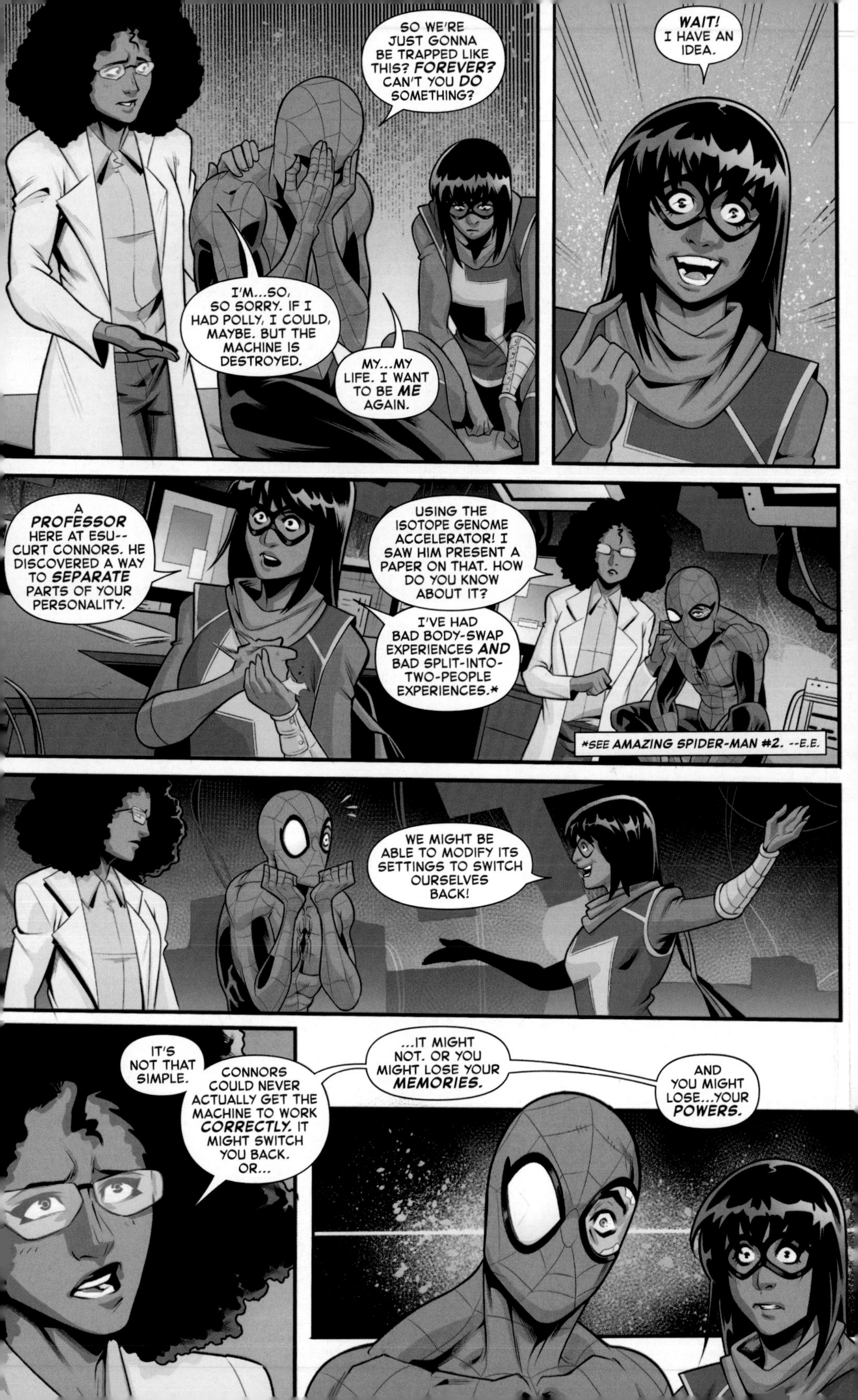
SO WE'RE JUST GONNA BE TRAPPED LIKE THIS? FOREVER? CAN'T YOU DO SOMETHING?
I'M...SO, SO SORRY. IF I HAD POLLY, I COULD, MAYBE. BUT THE MACHINE IS DESTROYED.
MY...MY LIFE. I WANT TO BE ME AGAIN.
WAIT! I HAVE AN IDEA.
A PROFESSOR HERE AT ESU-- CURT CONNORS. HE DISCOVERED A WAY TO SEPARATE PARTS OF YOUR PERSONALITY.
USING THE ISOTOPE GENOME ACCELERATOR! I SAW HIM PRESENT A PAPER ON THAT. HOW DO YOU KNOW ABOUT IT?
I'VE HAD BAD BODY-SWAP EXPERIENCES AND BAD SPLIT-INTO-TWO-PEOPLE EXPERIENCES.*
*SEE AMAZING SPIDER-MAN #2. --E.E.
WE MIGHT BE ABLE TO MODIFY ITS SETTINGS TO SWITCH OURSELVES BACK!
IT'S NOT THAT SIMPLE.
CONNORS COULD NEVER ACTUALLY GET THE MACHINE TO WORK CORRECTLY. IT MIGHT SWITCH YOU BACK. OR...
...IT MIGHT NOT. OR YOU MIGHT LOSE YOUR MEMORIES.
AND YOU MIGHT LOSE...YOUR POWERS.

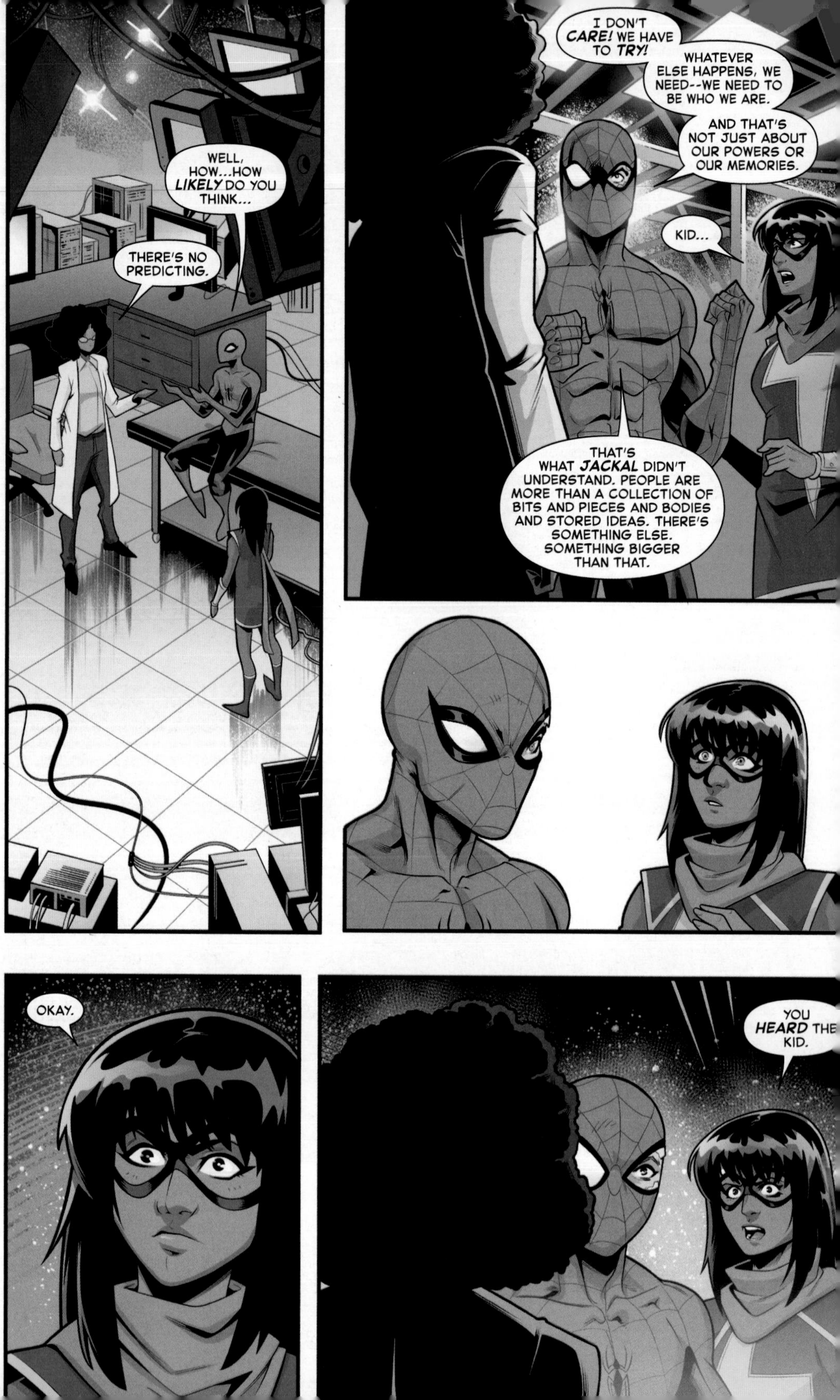

WELL, HOW...HOW LIKELY DO YOU THINK...
THERE'S NO PREDICTING.
I DON'T CARE! WE HAVE TO TRY!
WHATEVER ELSE HAPPENS, WE NEED--WE NEED TO BE WHO WE ARE.
AND THAT'S NOT JUST ABOUT OUR POWERS OR OUR MEMORIES.
KID...
THAT'S WHAT JACKAL DIDN'T UNDERSTAND. PEOPLE ARE MORE THAN A COLLECTION OF BITS AND PIECES AND BODIES AND STORED IDEAS. THERE'S SOMETHING ELSE. SOMETHING BIGGER THAN THAT.
OKAY.
YOU HEARD THE KID.

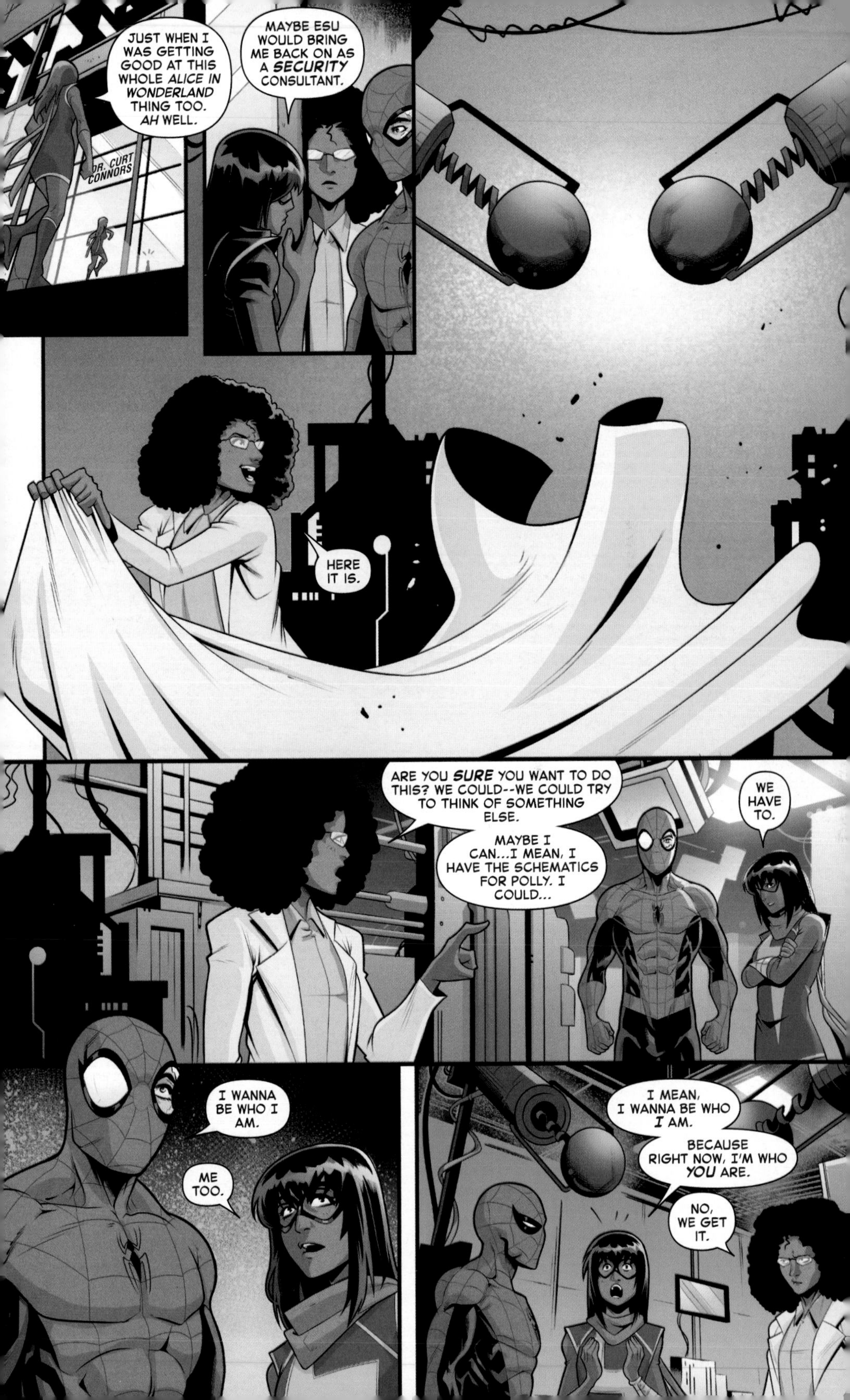
JUST WHEN I WAS GETTING GOOD AT THIS WHOLE ALICE IN WONDERLAND THING TOO. AH WELL.
DR. CURT CONNORS
MAYBE ESU WOULD BRING ME BACK ON AS A SECURITY CONSULTANT.
HERE IT IS.
ARE YOU SURE YOU WANT TO DO THIS? WE COULD--WE COULD TRY TO THINK OF SOMETHING ELSE.
MAYBE I CAN...I MEAN, I HAVE THE SCHEMATICS FOR POLLY. I COULD...
WE HAVE TO.
I WANNA BE WHO I AM.
ME TOO.
I MEAN, I WANNA BE WHO I AM.
BECAUSE RIGHT NOW, I'M WHO YOU ARE.
NO, WE GET IT.

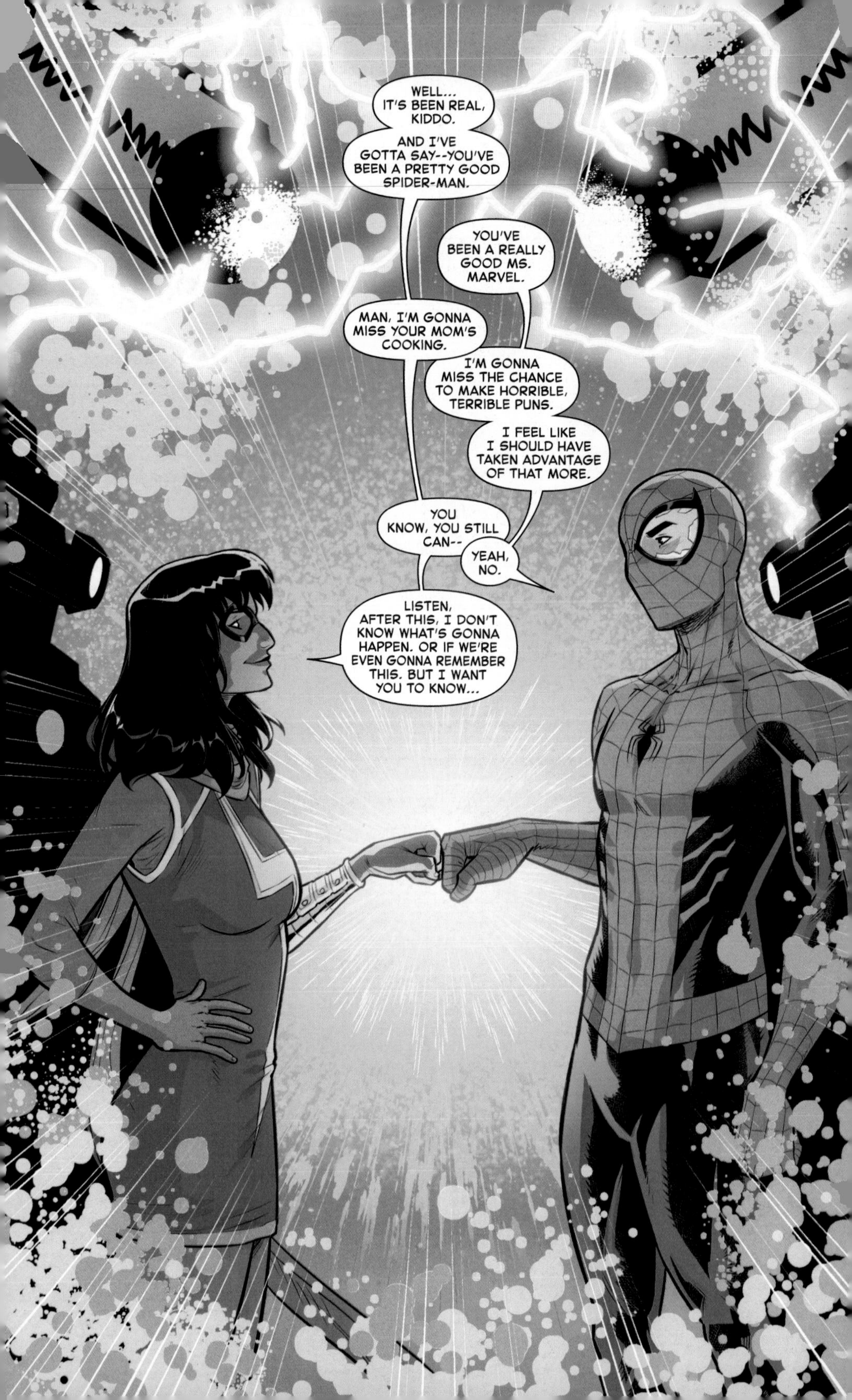
WELL... IT'S BEEN REAL, KIDDO.
AND I'VE GOTTA SAY--YOU'VE BEEN A PRETTY GOOD SPIDER-MAN.
YOU'VE BEEN A REALLY GOOD MS. MARVEL.
MAN, I'M GONNA MISS YOUR MOM'S COOKING.
I'M GONNA MISS THE CHANCE TO MAKE HORRIBLE, TERRIBLE PUNS.
I FEEL LIKE I SHOULD HAVE TAKEN ADVANTAGE OF THAT MORE.
YOU KNOW, YOU STILL CAN--
YEAH, NO.
LISTEN, AFTER THIS, I DON'T KNOW WHAT'S GONNA HAPPEN. OR IF WE'RE EVEN GONNA REMEMBER THIS. BUT I WANT YOU TO KNOW...

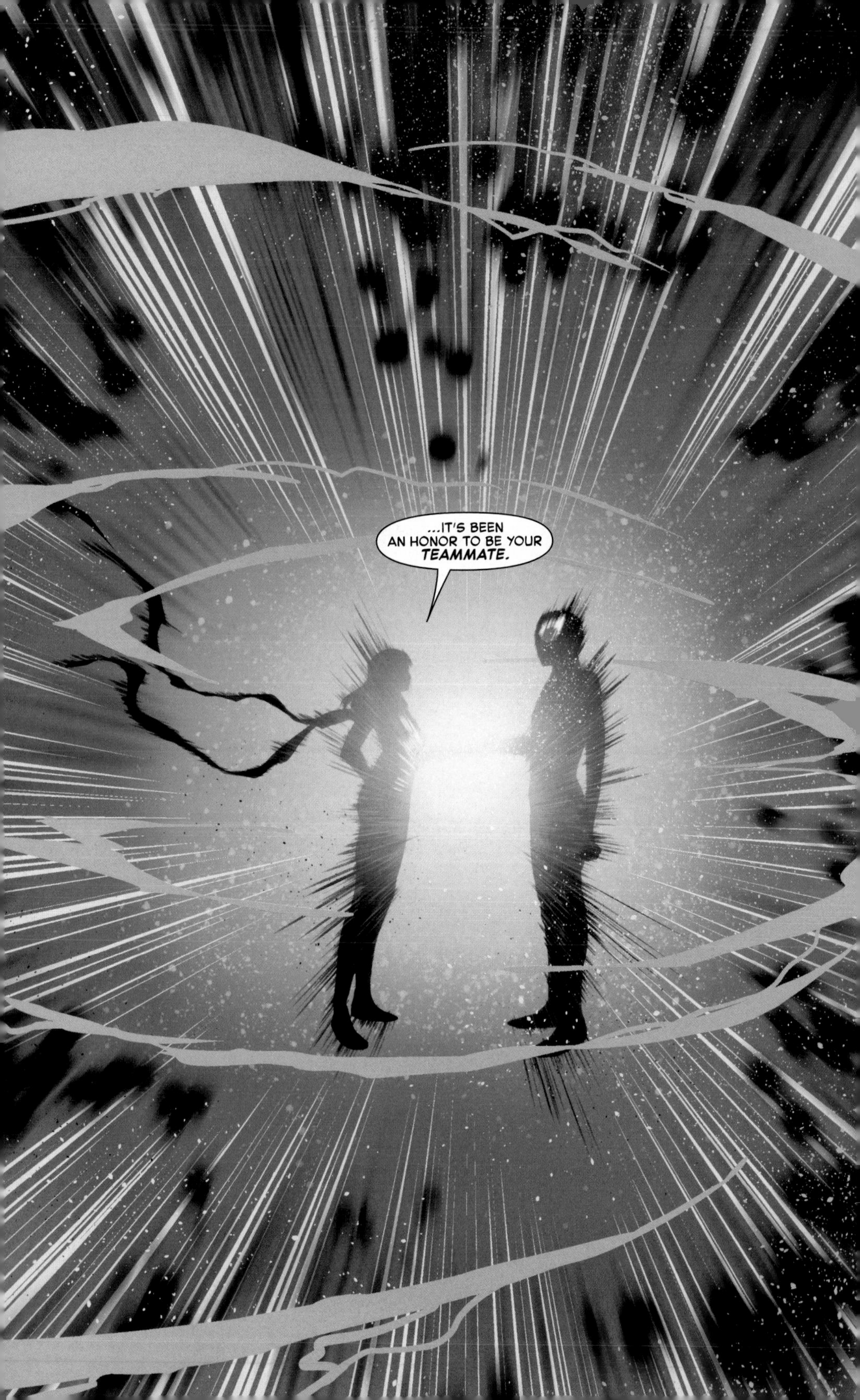
...IT'S BEEN AN HONOR TO BE YOUR TEAMMATE.

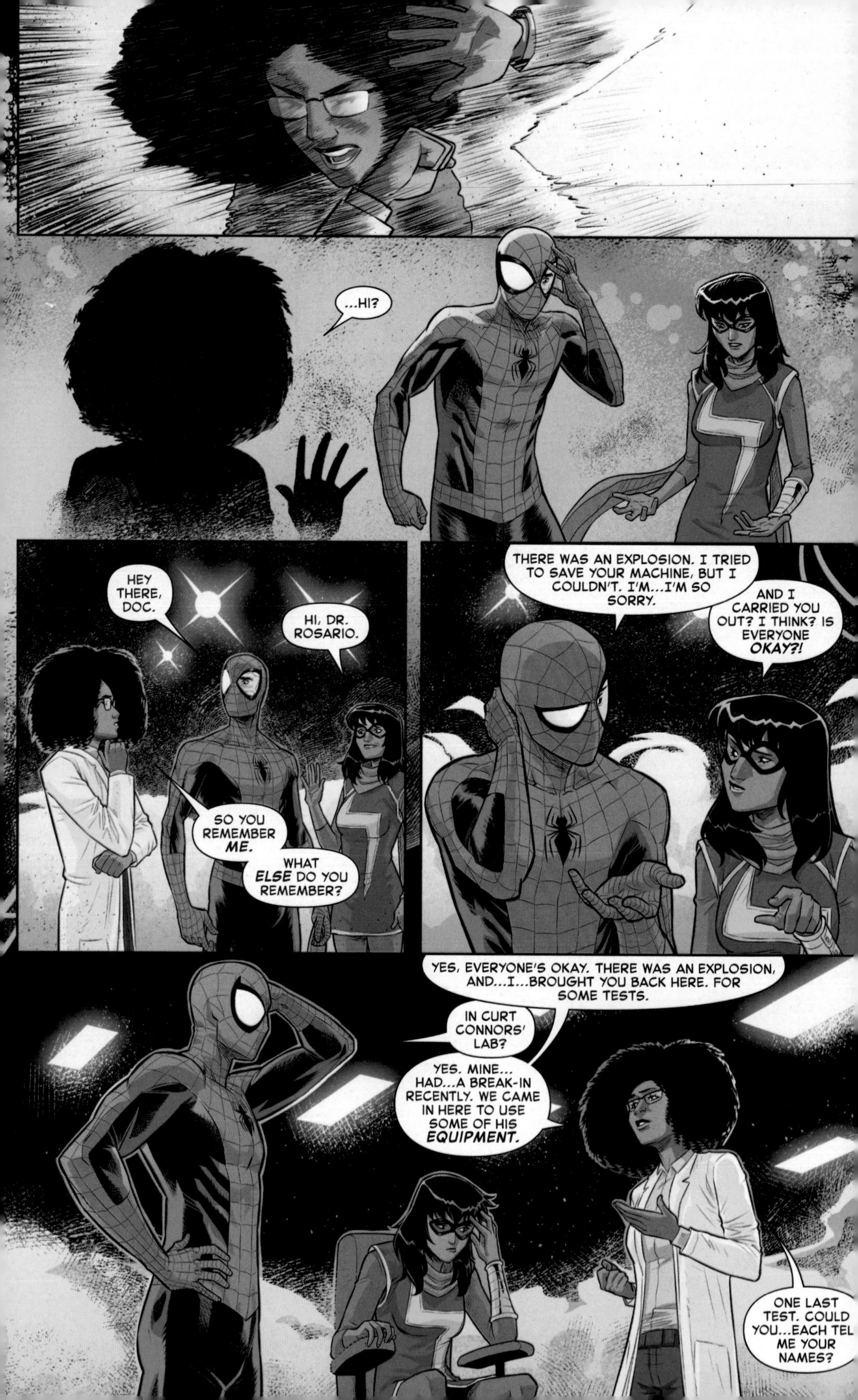

...HI?
HEY THERE, DOC.
HI, DR. ROSARIO.
SO YOU REMEMBER ME.
WHAT ELSE DO YOU REMEMBER?
THERE WAS AN EXPLOSION. I TRIED TO SAVE YOUR MACHINE, BUT I COULDN'T. I'M...I'M SO SORRY.
AND I CARRIED YOU OUT? I THINK? IS EVERYONE OKAY?!
YES, EVERYONE'S OKAY. THERE WAS AN EXPLOSION, AND...I...BROUGHT YOU BACK HERE. FOR SOME TESTS.
IN CURT CONNORS' LAB?
YES. MINE... HAD...A BREAK-IN RECENTLY. WE CAME IN HERE TO USE SOME OF HIS EQUIPMENT.
ONE LAST TEST. COULD YOU...EACH TEL ME YOUR NAMES?

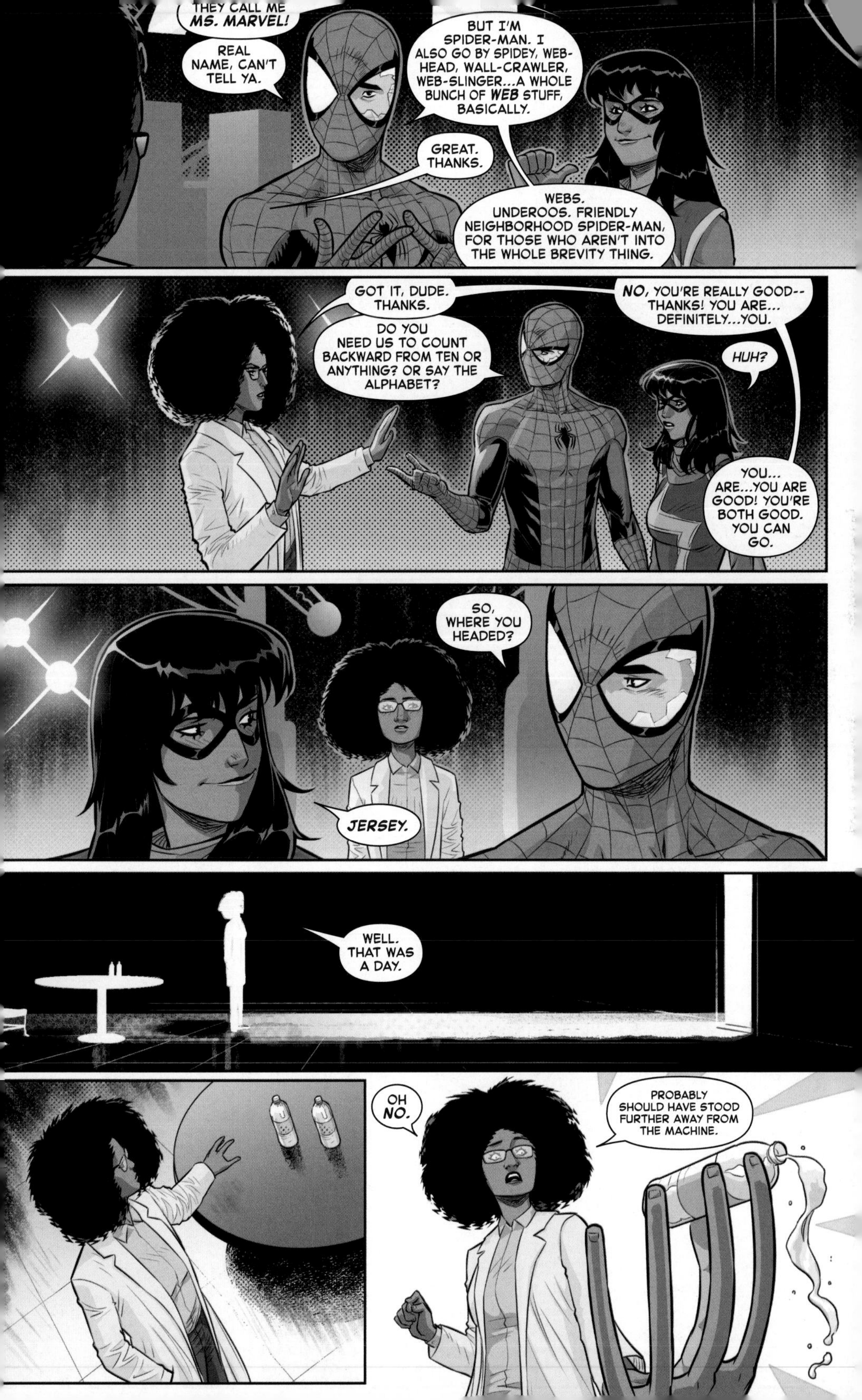
THEY CALL ME MS. MARVEL!
REAL NAME, CAN'T TELL YA.
BUT I'M SPIDER-MAN. I ALSO GO BY SPIDEY, WEB-HEAD, WALL-CRAWLER, WEB-SLINGER...A WHOLE BUNCH OF WEB STUFF, BASICALLY.
GREAT. THANKS.
WEBS. UNDEROOS. FRIENDLY NEIGHBORHOOD SPIDER-MAN, FOR THOSE WHO AREN'T INTO THE WHOLE BREVITY THING.
GOT IT, DUDE. THANKS.
DO YOU NEED US TO COUNT BACKWARD FROM TEN OR ANYTHING? OR SAY THE ALPHABET?
NO, YOU'RE REALLY GOOD--THANKS! YOU ARE... DEFINITELY...YOU.
HUH?
YOU... ARE...YOU ARE GOOD! YOU'RE BOTH GOOD. YOU CAN GO.
SO, WHERE YOU HEADED?
JERSEY.
WELL. THAT WAS A DAY.
OH NO.
PROBABLY SHOULD HAVE STOOD FURTHER AWAY FROM THE MACHINE.

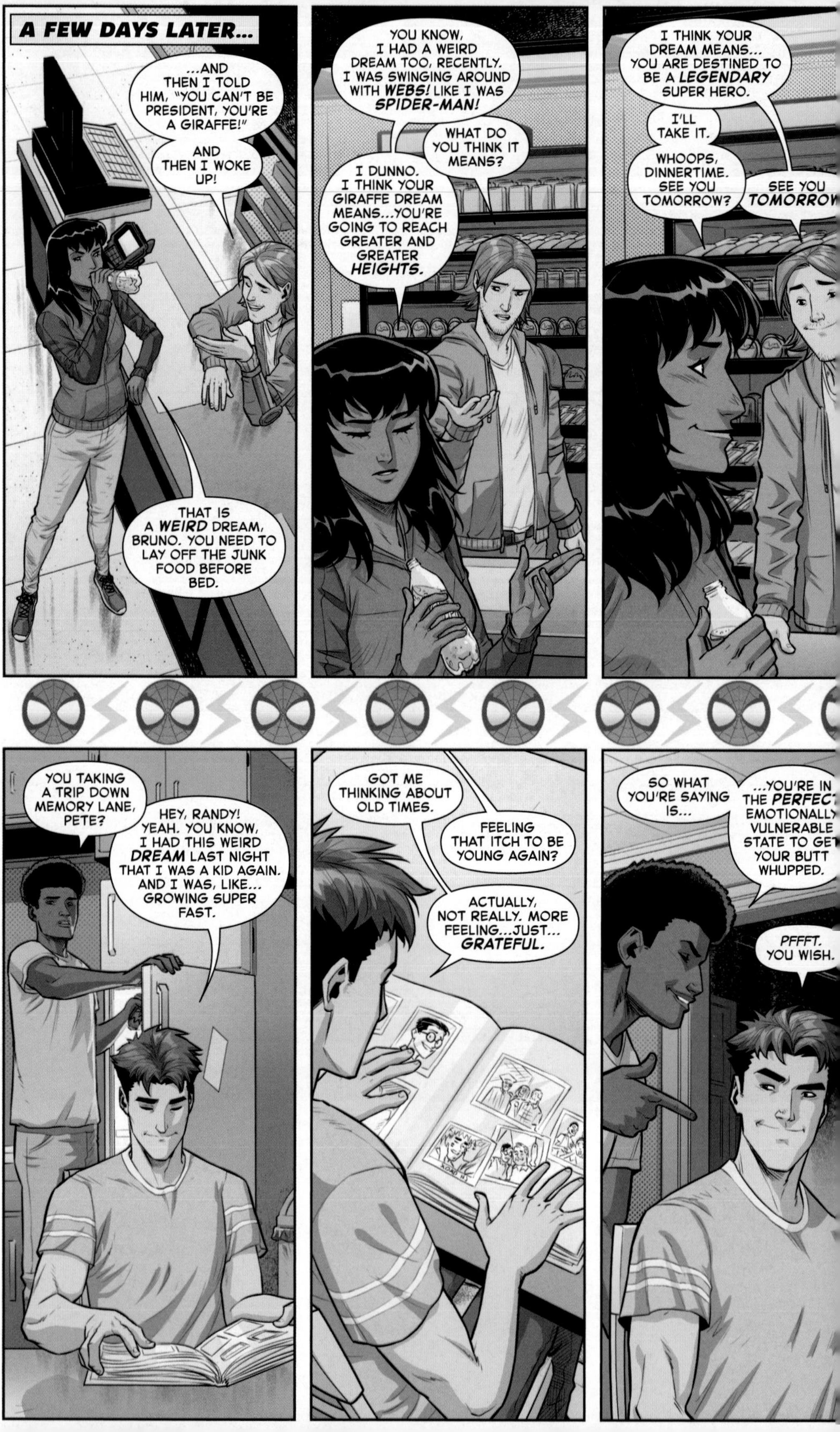
A FEW DAYS LATER...
...AND THEN I TOLD HIM, "YOU CAN'T BE PRESIDENT, YOU'RE A GIRAFFE!"
AND THEN I WOKE UP!
THAT IS A WEIRD DREAM, BRUNO. YOU NEED TO LAY OFF THE JUNK FOOD BEFORE BED.
YOU KNOW, I HAD A WEIRD DREAM TOO, RECENTLY. I WAS SWINGING AROUND WITH WEBS! LIKE I WAS SPIDER-MAN!
WHAT DO YOU THINK IT MEANS?
I DUNNO. I THINK YOUR GIRAFFE DREAM MEANS...YOU'RE GOING TO REACH GREATER AND GREATER HEIGHTS.
I THINK YOUR DREAM MEANS... YOU ARE DESTINED TO BE A LEGENDARY SUPER HERO.
I'LL TAKE IT.
WHOOPS, DINNERTIME. SEE YOU TOMORROW?
SEE YOU TOMORROW
YOU TAKING A TRIP DOWN MEMORY LANE, PETE?
HEY, RANDY! YEAH. YOU KNOW, I HAD THIS WEIRD DREAM LAST NIGHT THAT I WAS A KID AGAIN. AND I WAS, LIKE... GROWING SUPER FAST.
GOT ME THINKING ABOUT OLD TIMES.
FEELING THAT ITCH TO BE YOUNG AGAIN?
ACTUALLY, NOT REALLY. MORE FEELING...JUST... GRATEFUL.
SO WHAT YOU'RE SAYING IS...
...YOU'RE IN THE PERFECT EMOTIONALLY VULNERABLE STATE TO GET YOUR BUTT WHUPPED.
PFFFT. YOU WISH.

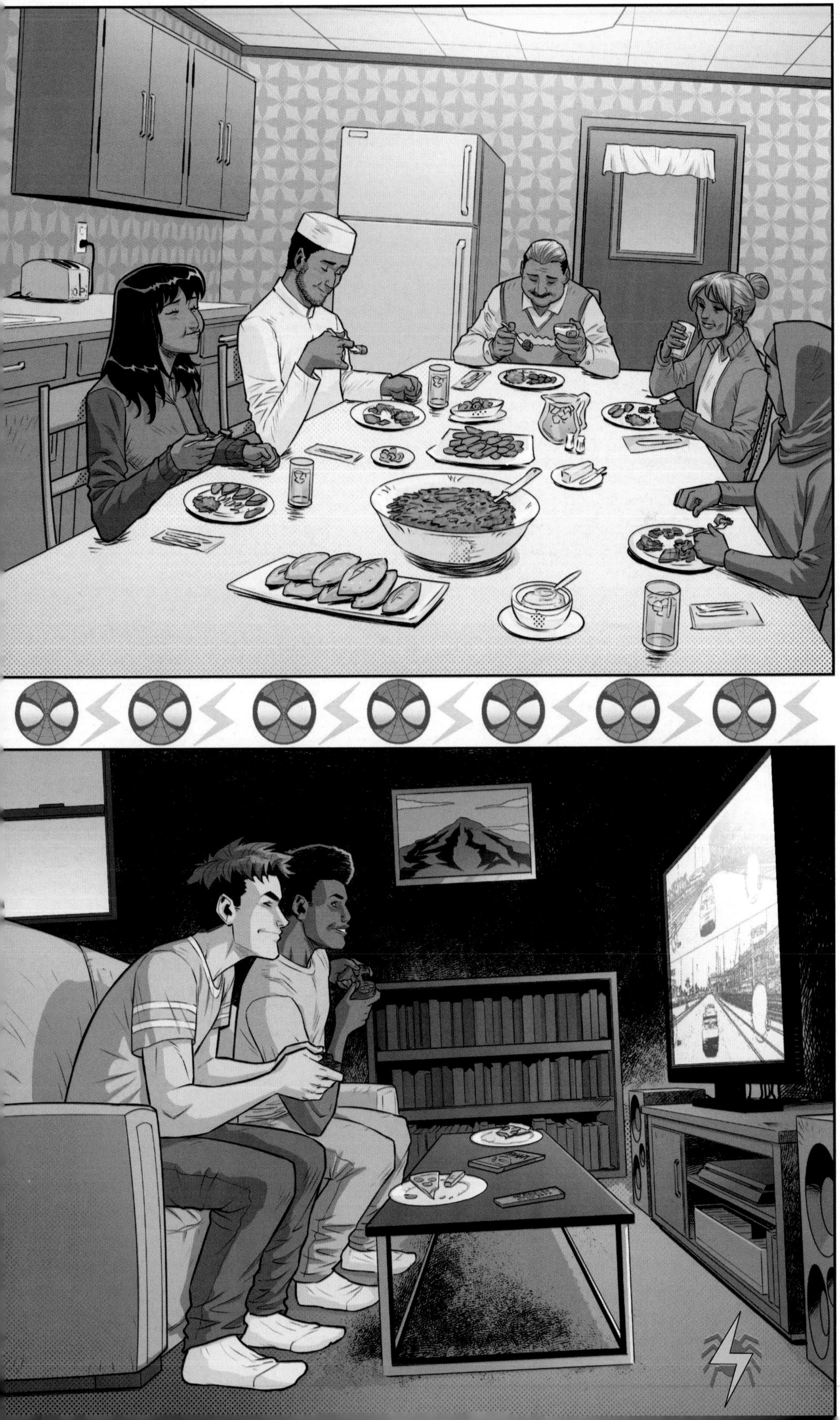

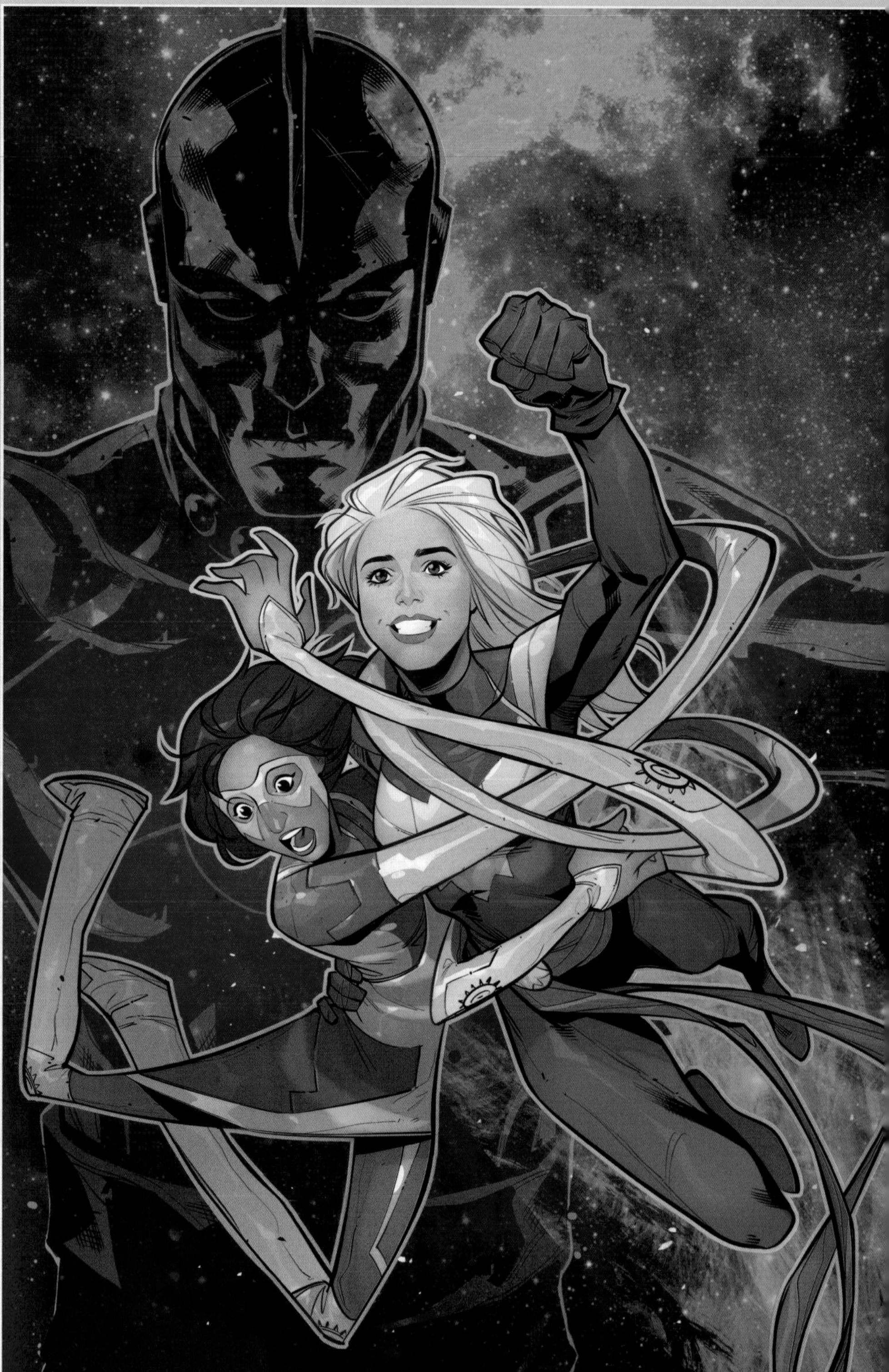

MS. MARVEL TEAM-UP #4

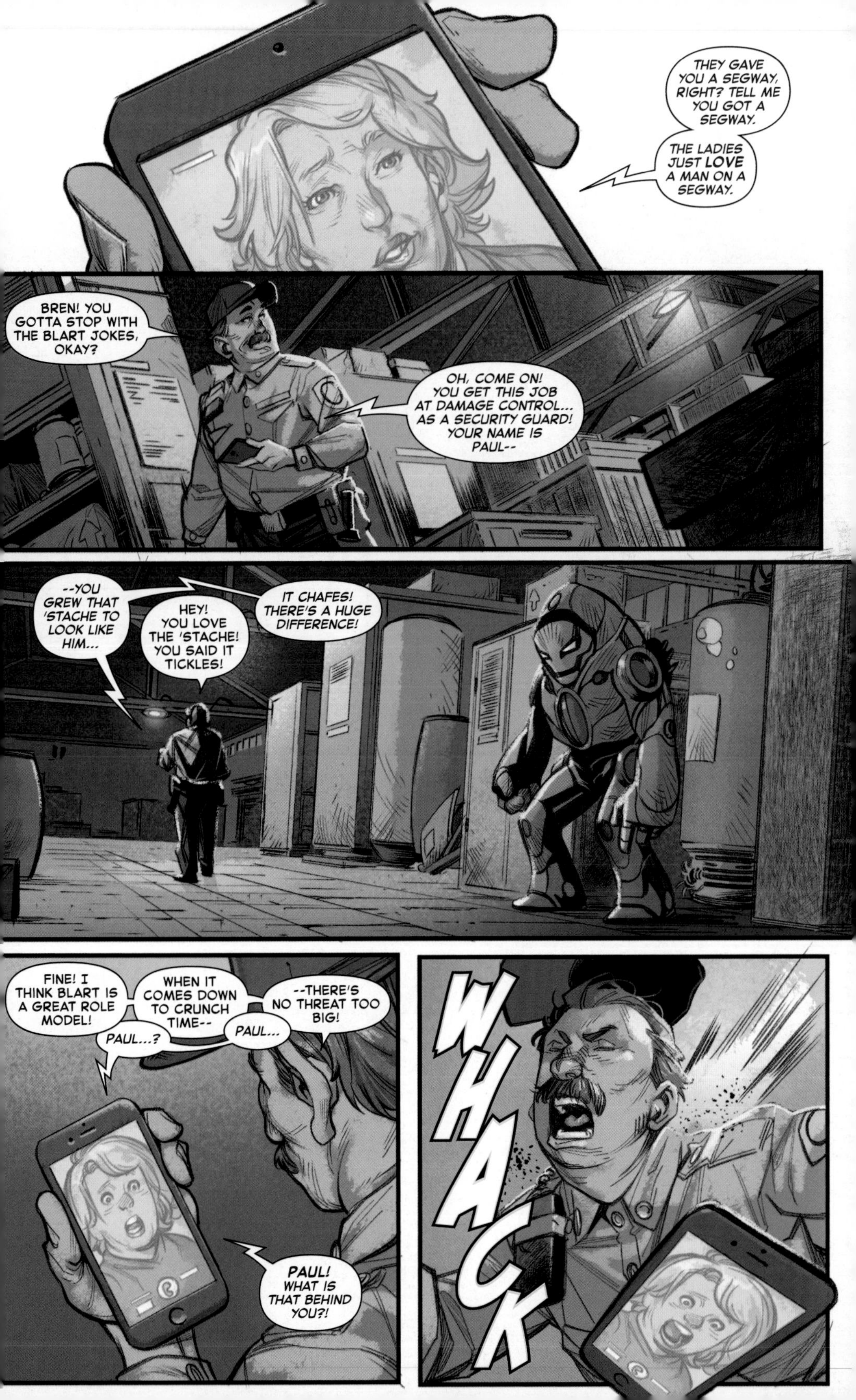
THEY GAVE YOU A SEGWAY, RIGHT? TELL ME YOU GOT A SEGWAY.
THE LADIES JUST **LOVE** A MAN ON A SEGWAY.
BREN! YOU GOTTA STOP WITH THE BLART JOKES, OKAY?
OH, COME ON! YOU GET THIS JOB AT DAMAGE CONTROL... AS A SECURITY GUARD! YOUR NAME IS PAUL--
--YOU GREW THAT 'STACHE TO LOOK LIKE HIM...
HEY! YOU LOVE THE 'STACHE! YOU SAID IT TICKLES!
IT CHAFES! THERE'S A HUGE DIFFERENCE!
FINE! I THINK BLART IS A GREAT ROLE MODEL!
WHEN IT COMES DOWN TO CRUNCH TIME--
--THERE'S NO THREAT TOO BIG!
PAUL...?
PAUL...
PAUL! WHAT IS THAT BEHIND YOU?!
WHACK

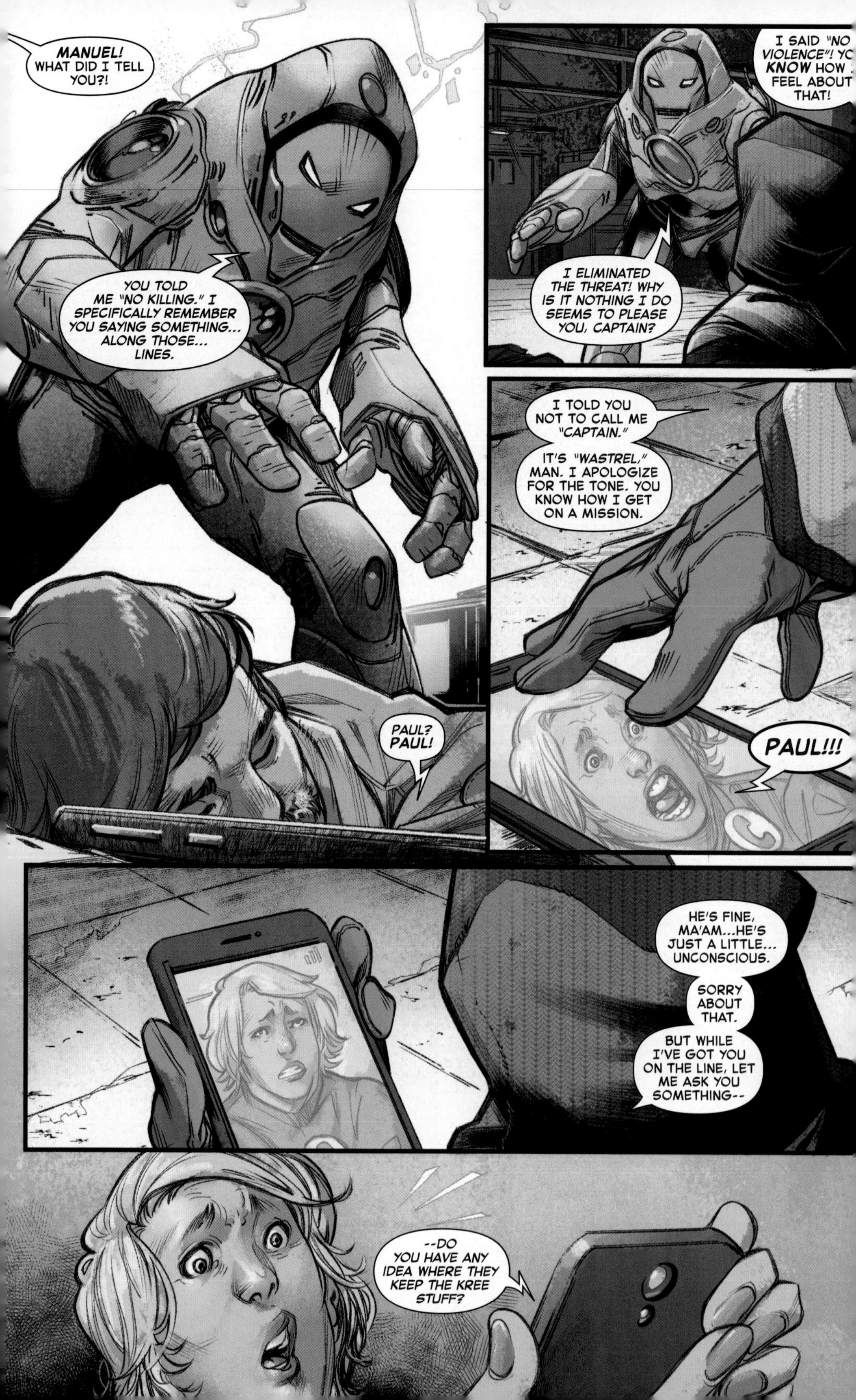
MANUEL! WHAT DID I TELL YOU?!
YOU TOLD ME "NO KILLING." I SPECIFICALLY REMEMBER YOU SAYING SOMETHING... ALONG THOSE... LINES.
I SAID "NO VIOLENCE"! YOU KNOW HOW I FEEL ABOUT THAT!
I ELIMINATED THE THREAT! WHY IS IT NOTHING I DO SEEMS TO PLEASE YOU, CAPTAIN?
PAUL? PAUL!
I TOLD YOU NOT TO CALL ME "CAPTAIN."
IT'S "WASTREL," MAN. I APOLOGIZE FOR THE TONE. YOU KNOW HOW I GET ON A MISSION.
PAUL!!!
HE'S FINE, MA'AM...HE'S JUST A LITTLE... UNCONSCIOUS.
SORRY ABOUT THAT.
BUT WHILE I'VE GOT YOU ON THE LINE, LET ME ASK YOU SOMETHING--
--DO YOU HAVE ANY IDEA WHERE THEY KEEP THE KREE STUFF?

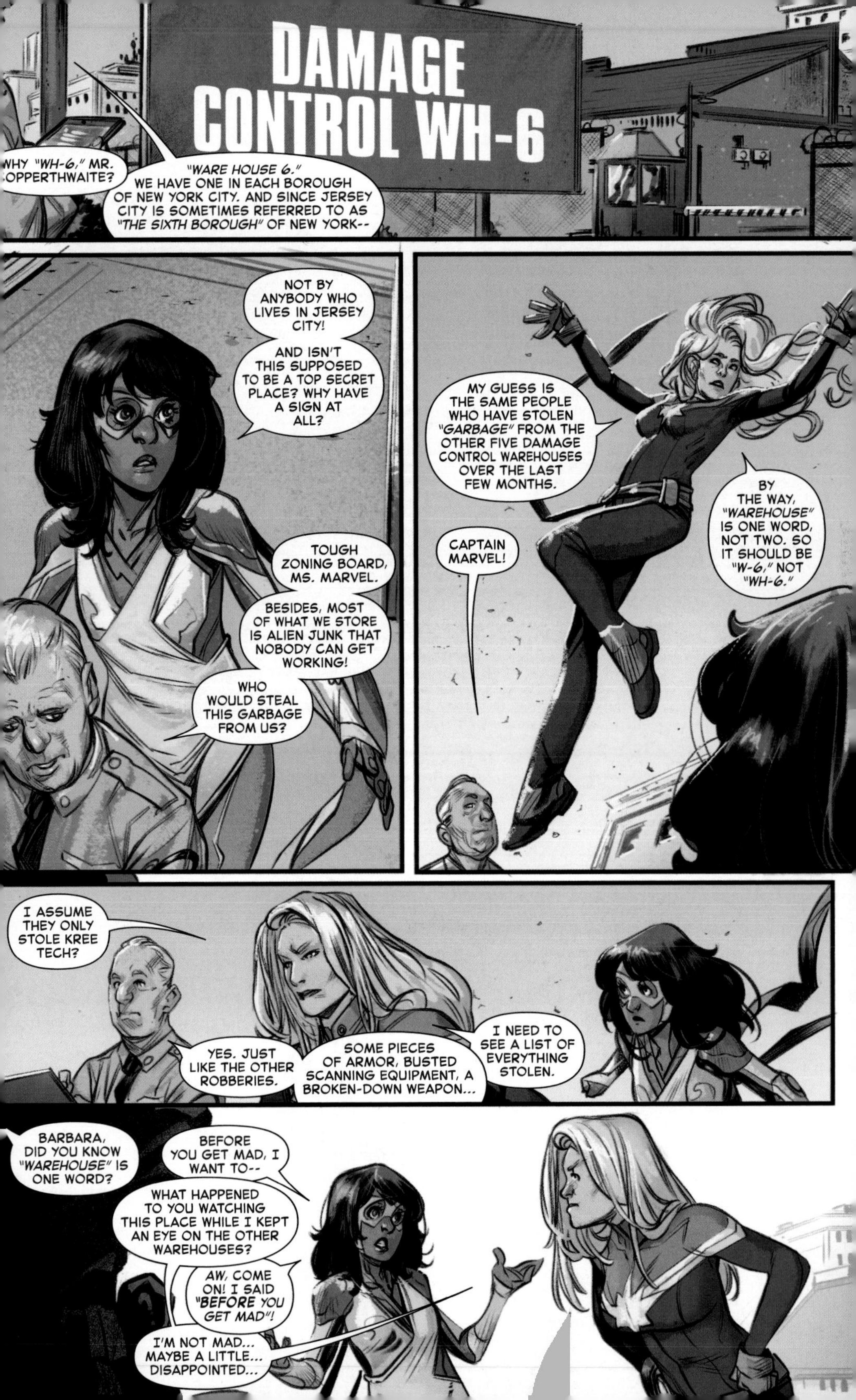
DAMAGE CONTROL WH-6
WHY "WH-6," MR. COPPERTHWAITE?
"WARE HOUSE 6." WE HAVE ONE IN EACH BOROUGH OF NEW YORK CITY. AND SINCE JERSEY CITY IS SOMETIMES REFERRED TO AS "THE SIXTH BOROUGH" OF NEW YORK--
NOT BY ANYBODY WHO LIVES IN JERSEY CITY!
AND ISN'T THIS SUPPOSED TO BE A TOP SECRET PLACE? WHY HAVE A SIGN AT ALL?
TOUGH ZONING BOARD, MS. MARVEL.
BESIDES, MOST OF WHAT WE STORE IS ALIEN JUNK THAT NOBODY CAN GET WORKING!
WHO WOULD STEAL THIS GARBAGE FROM US?
MY GUESS IS THE SAME PEOPLE WHO HAVE STOLEN "GARBAGE" FROM THE OTHER FIVE DAMAGE CONTROL WAREHOUSES OVER THE LAST FEW MONTHS.
CAPTAIN MARVEL!
BY THE WAY, "WAREHOUSE" IS ONE WORD, NOT TWO. SO IT SHOULD BE "W-6," NOT "WH-6."
I ASSUME THEY ONLY STOLE KREE TECH?
YES. JUST LIKE THE OTHER ROBBERIES.
SOME PIECES OF ARMOR, BUSTED SCANNING EQUIPMENT, A BROKEN-DOWN WEAPON...
I NEED TO SEE A LIST OF EVERYTHING STOLEN.
BARBARA, DID YOU KNOW "WAREHOUSE" IS ONE WORD?
BEFORE YOU GET MAD, I WANT TO--
WHAT HAPPENED TO YOU WATCHING THIS PLACE WHILE I KEPT AN EYE ON THE OTHER WAREHOUSES?
AW, COME ON! I SAID "BEFORE YOU GET MAD"!
I'M NOT MAD... MAYBE A LITTLE... DISAPPOINTED...

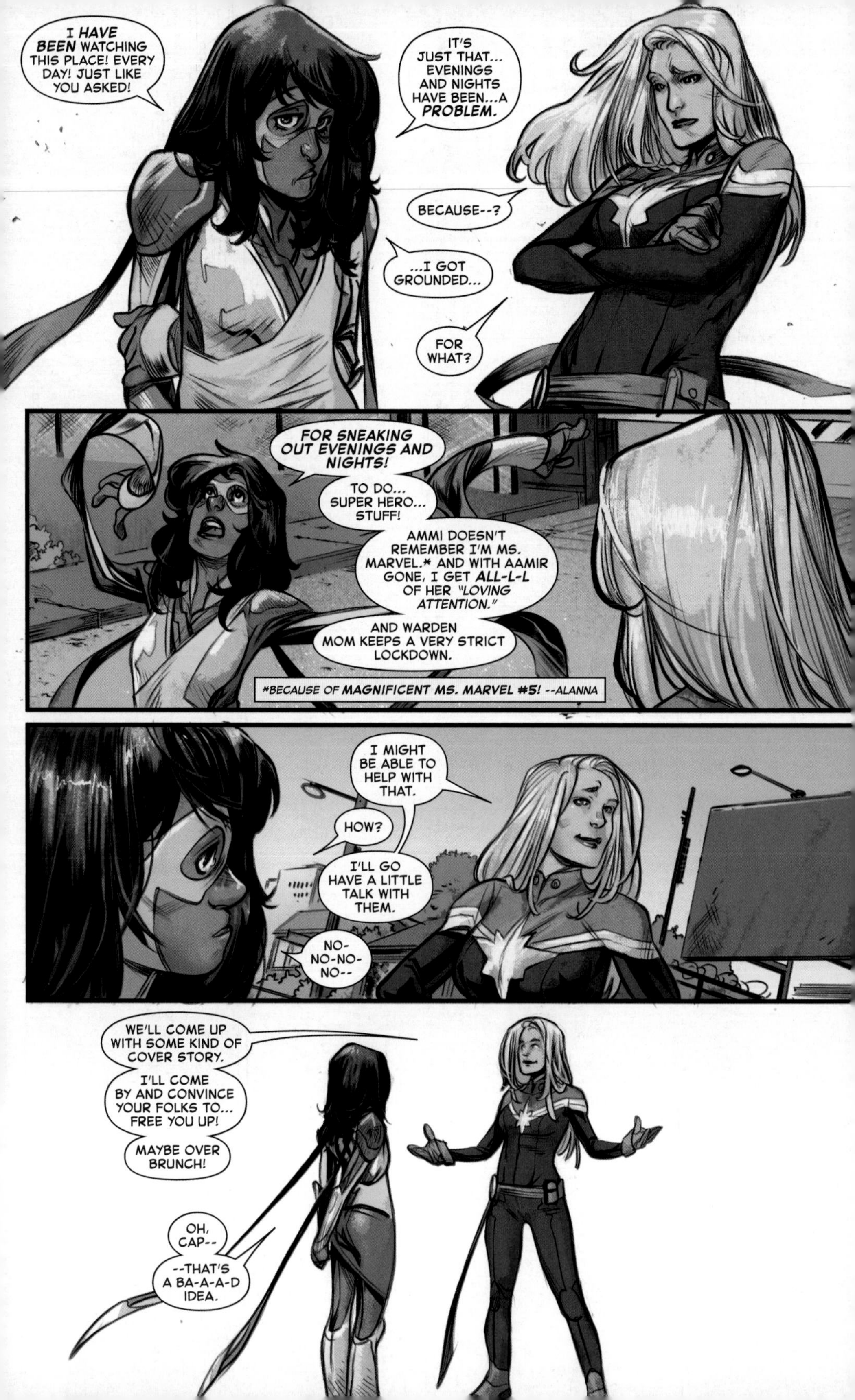
I HAVE BEEN WATCHING THIS PLACE! EVERY DAY! JUST LIKE YOU ASKED!
IT'S JUST THAT... EVENINGS AND NIGHTS HAVE BEEN...A PROBLEM.
BECAUSE--?
...I GOT GROUNDED...
FOR WHAT?
FOR SNEAKING OUT EVENINGS AND NIGHTS!
TO DO... SUPER HERO... STUFF!
AMMI DOESN'T REMEMBER I'M MS. MARVEL.* AND WITH AAMIR GONE, I GET ALL-L-L OF HER "LOVING ATTENTION."
AND WARDEN MOM KEEPS A VERY STRICT LOCKDOWN.
*BECAUSE OF MAGNIFICENT MS. MARVEL #5! --ALANNA
I MIGHT BE ABLE TO HELP WITH THAT.
HOW?
I'LL GO HAVE A LITTLE TALK WITH THEM.
NO-NO-NO-NO--
WE'LL COME UP WITH SOME KIND OF COVER STORY.
I'LL COME BY AND CONVINCE YOUR FOLKS TO... FREE YOU UP!
MAYBE OVER BRUNCH!
OH, CAP--
--THAT'S A BA-A-A-D IDEA.

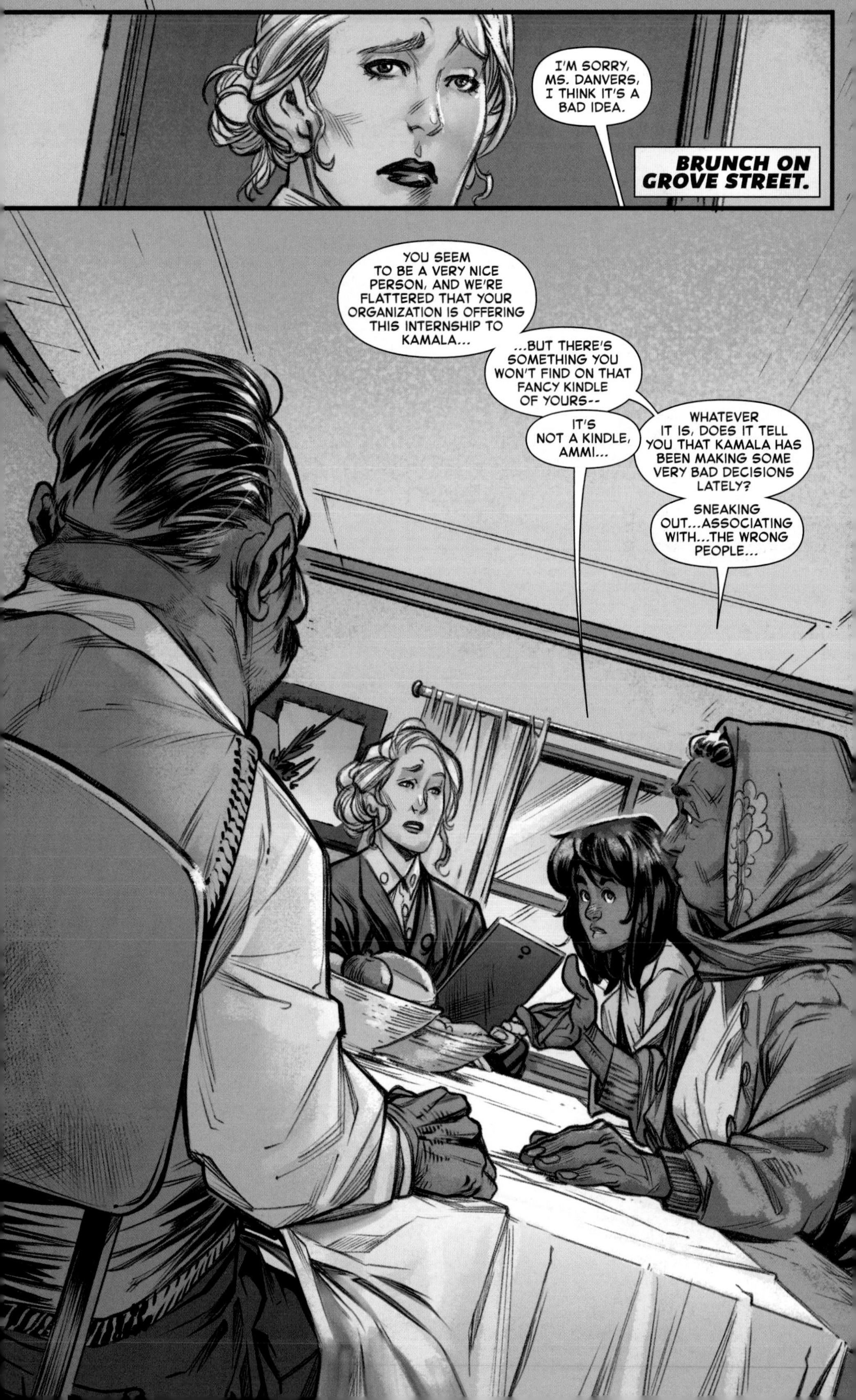
I'M SORRY, MS. DANVERS, I THINK IT'S A BAD IDEA.
BRUNCH ON GROVE STREET.
YOU SEEM TO BE A VERY NICE PERSON, AND WE'RE FLATTERED THAT YOUR ORGANIZATION IS OFFERING THIS INTERNSHIP TO KAMALA...
...BUT THERE'S SOMETHING YOU WON'T FIND ON THAT FANCY KINDLE OF YOURS--
IT'S NOT A KINDLE, AMMI...
WHATEVER IT IS, DOES IT TELL YOU THAT KAMALA HAS BEEN MAKING SOME VERY BAD DECISIONS LATELY?
SNEAKING OUT...ASSOCIATING WITH...THE WRONG PEOPLE...

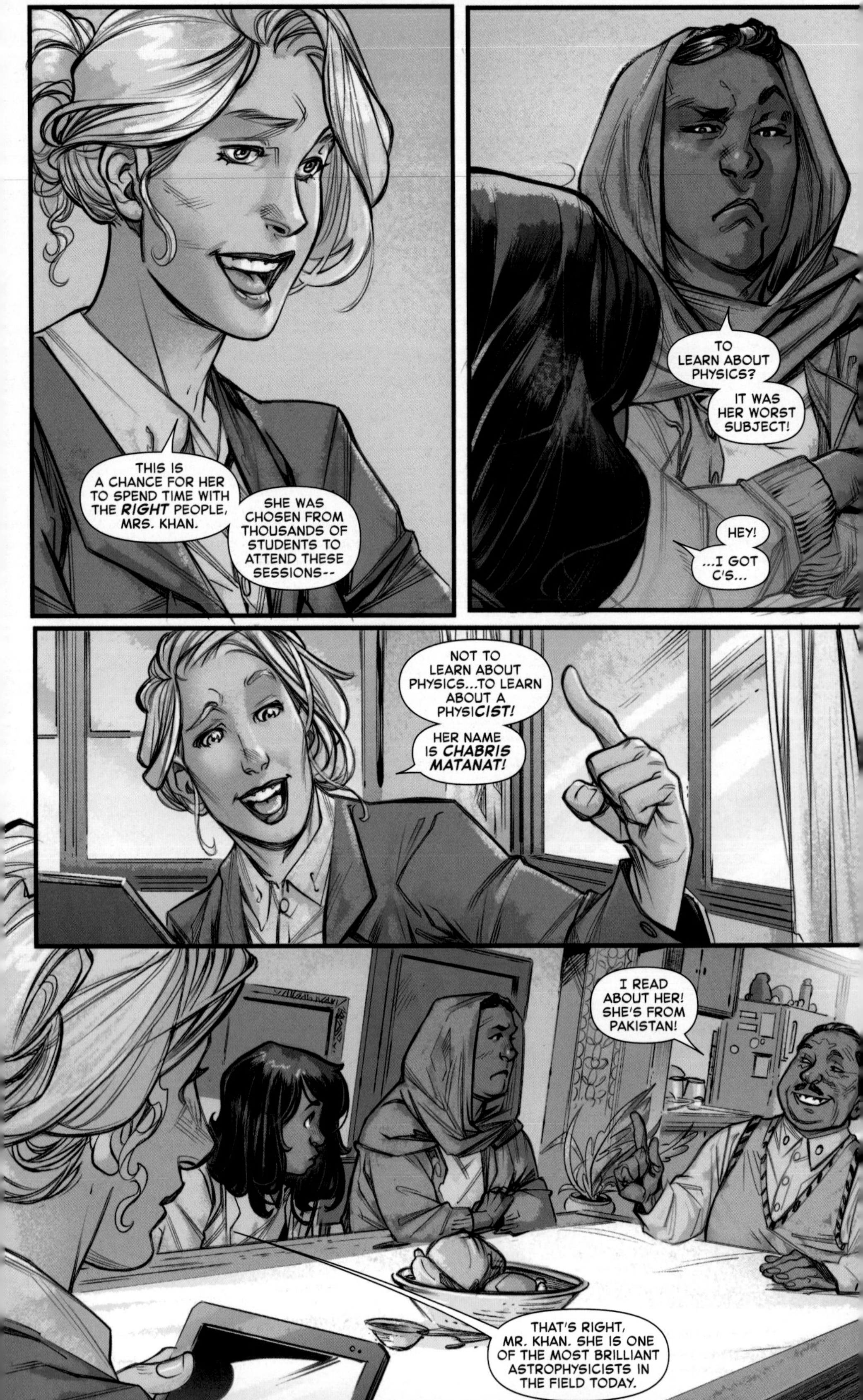
THIS IS A CHANCE FOR HER TO SPEND TIME WITH THE **RIGHT** PEOPLE, MRS. KHAN.
SHE WAS CHOSEN FROM THOUSANDS OF STUDENTS TO ATTEND THESE SESSIONS--
TO LEARN ABOUT PHYSICS?
IT WAS HER WORST SUBJECT!
HEY!
...I GOT C'S...
NOT TO LEARN ABOUT PHYSICS...TO LEARN ABOUT A PHYSI**CIST!**
HER NAME IS ***CHABRIS MATANAT!***
I READ ABOUT HER! SHE'S FROM PAKISTAN!
THAT'S RIGHT, MR. KHAN. SHE IS ONE OF THE MOST BRILLIANT ASTROPHYSICISTS IN THE FIELD TODAY.

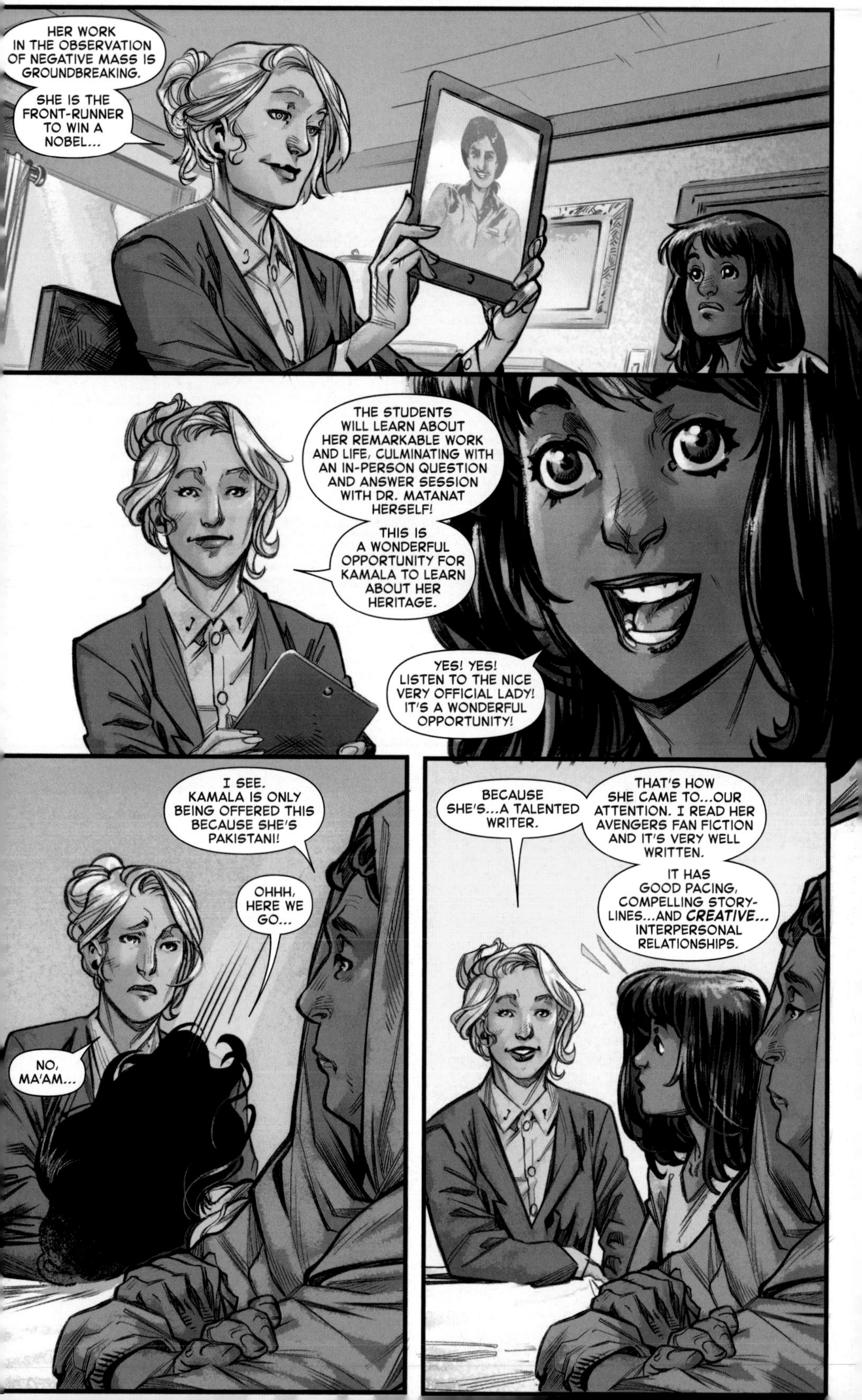
HER WORK IN THE OBSERVATION OF NEGATIVE MASS IS GROUNDBREAKING.
SHE IS THE FRONT-RUNNER TO WIN A NOBEL...
THE STUDENTS WILL LEARN ABOUT HER REMARKABLE WORK AND LIFE, CULMINATING WITH AN IN-PERSON QUESTION AND ANSWER SESSION WITH DR. MATANAT HERSELF!
THIS IS A WONDERFUL OPPORTUNITY FOR KAMALA TO LEARN ABOUT HER HERITAGE.
YES! YES! LISTEN TO THE NICE VERY OFFICIAL LADY! IT'S A WONDERFUL OPPORTUNITY!
I SEE. KAMALA IS ONLY BEING OFFERED THIS BECAUSE SHE'S PAKISTANI!
OHHH, HERE WE GO...
NO, MA'AM...
BECAUSE SHE'S...A TALENTED WRITER.
THAT'S HOW SHE CAME TO...OUR ATTENTION. I READ HER AVENGERS FAN FICTION AND IT'S VERY WELL WRITTEN.
IT HAS GOOD PACING, COMPELLING STORY-LINES...AND *CREATIVE...* INTERPERSONAL RELATIONSHIPS.

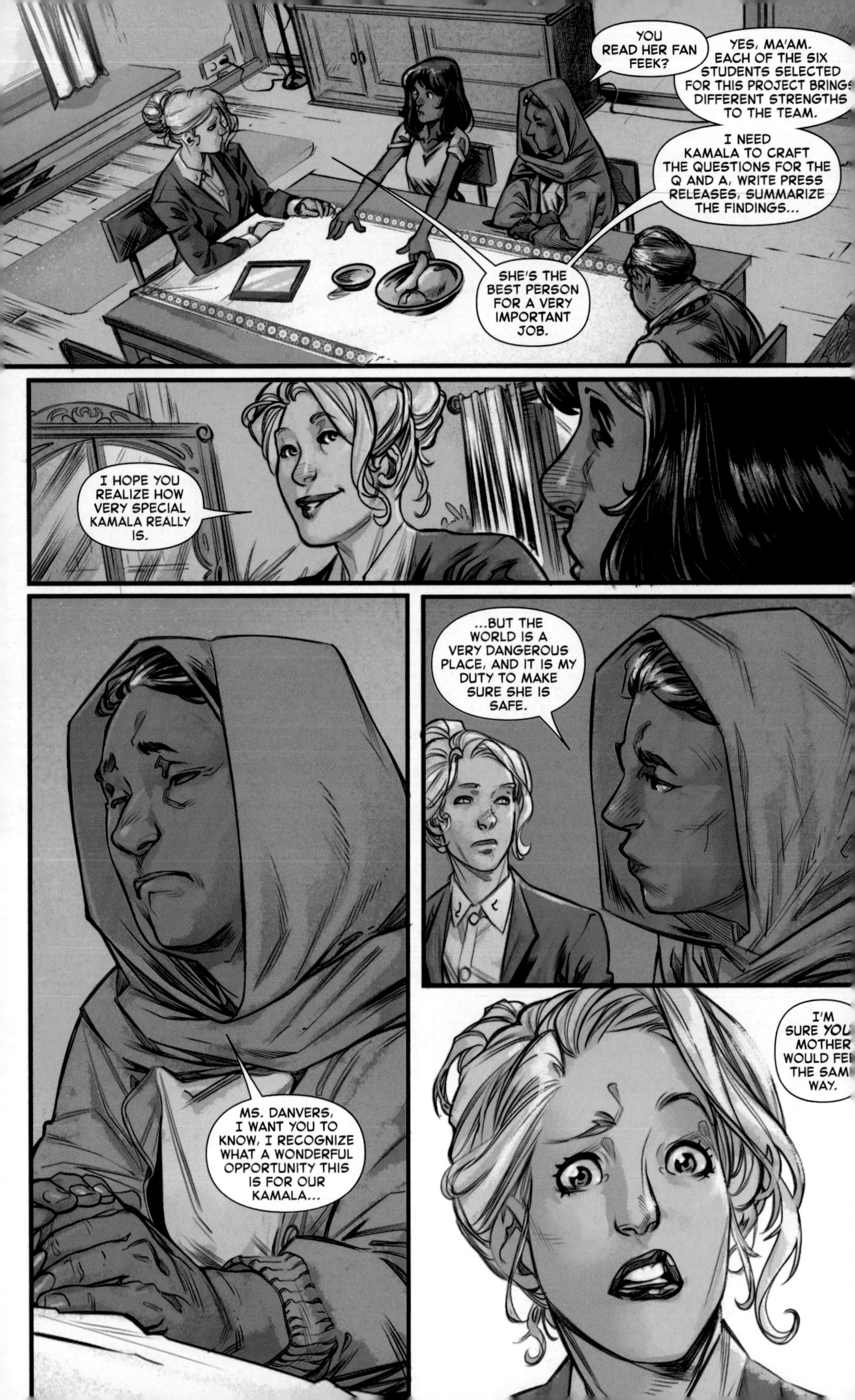

YOU READ HER FAN FEEK?
YES, MA'AM. EACH OF THE SIX STUDENTS SELECTED FOR THIS PROJECT BRINGS DIFFERENT STRENGTHS TO THE TEAM.
I NEED KAMALA TO CRAFT THE QUESTIONS FOR THE Q AND A, WRITE PRESS RELEASES, SUMMARIZE THE FINDINGS...
SHE'S THE BEST PERSON FOR A VERY IMPORTANT JOB.
I HOPE YOU REALIZE HOW VERY SPECIAL KAMALA REALLY IS.
MS. DANVERS, I WANT YOU TO KNOW, I RECOGNIZE WHAT A WONDERFUL OPPORTUNITY THIS IS FOR OUR KAMALA...
...BUT THE WORLD IS A VERY DANGEROUS PLACE, AND IT IS MY DUTY TO MAKE SURE SHE IS SAFE.

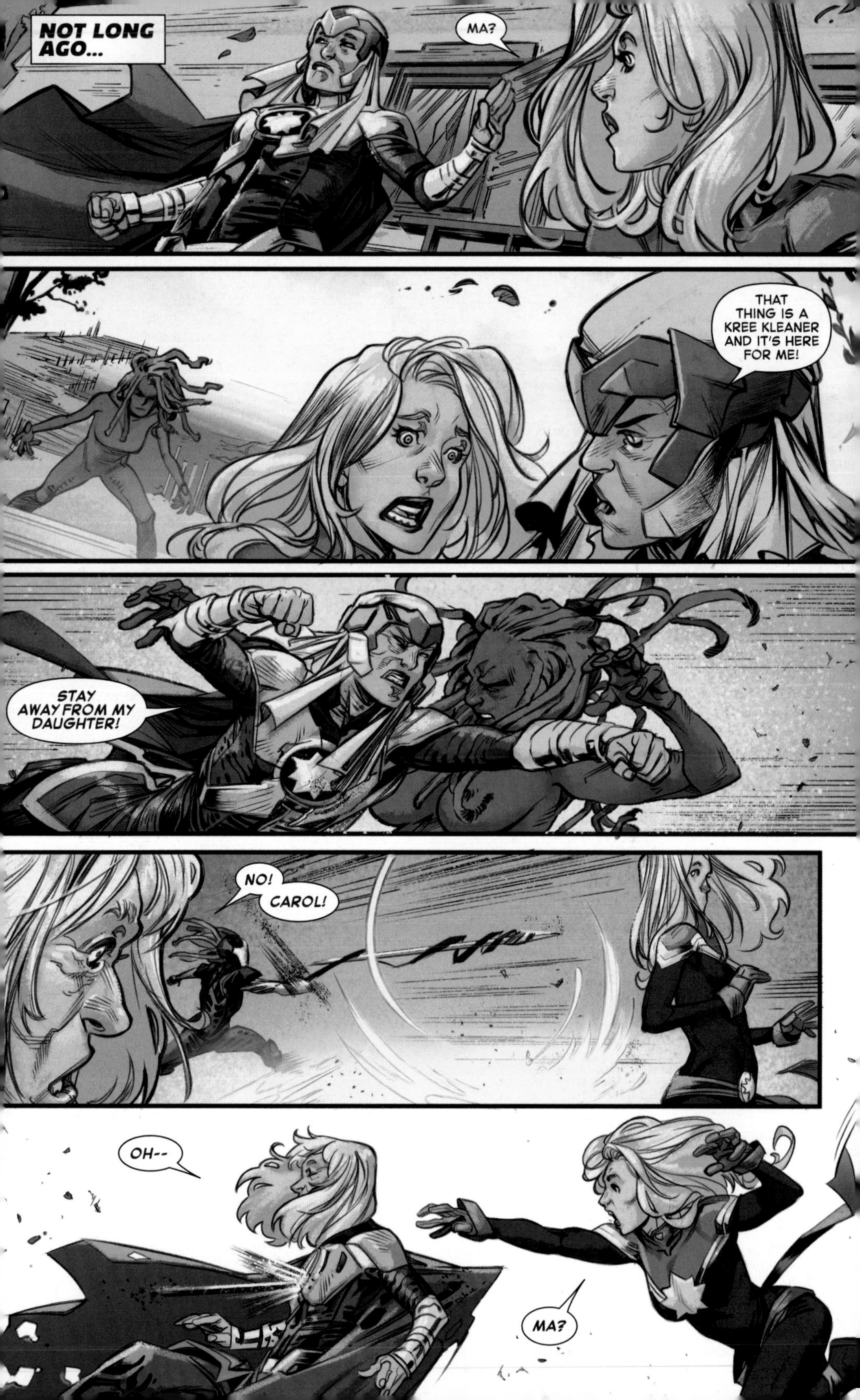
NOT LONG AGO...
MA?
THAT THING IS A KREE KLEANER AND IT'S HERE FOR ME!
STAY AWAY FROM MY DAUGHTER!
NO! CAROL!
OH--
MA?

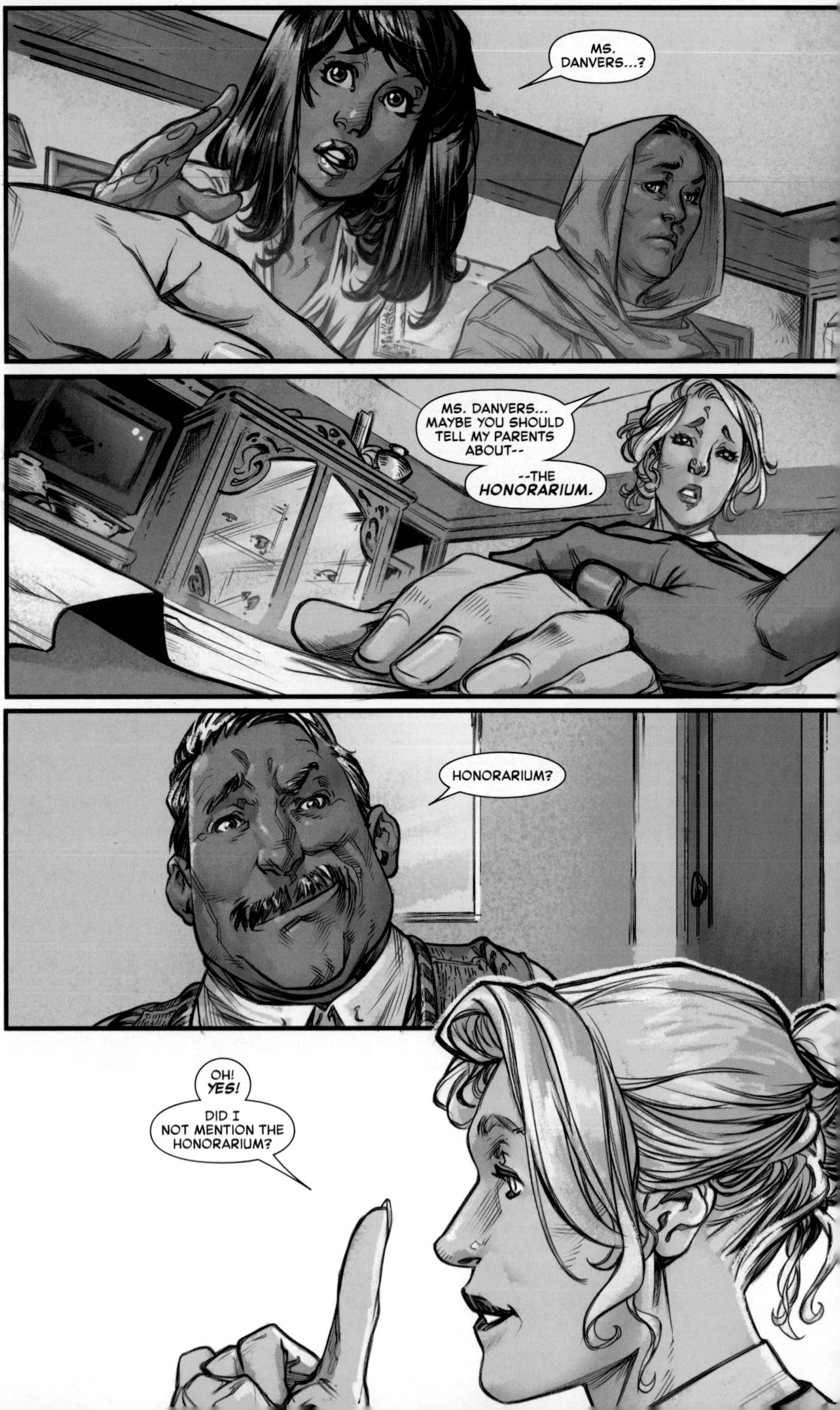
MS. DANVERS...?
MS. DANVERS... MAYBE YOU SHOULD TELL MY PARENTS ABOUT--
--THE *HONORARIUM.*
HONORARIUM?
OH! *YES!*
DID I NOT MENTION THE HONORARIUM?

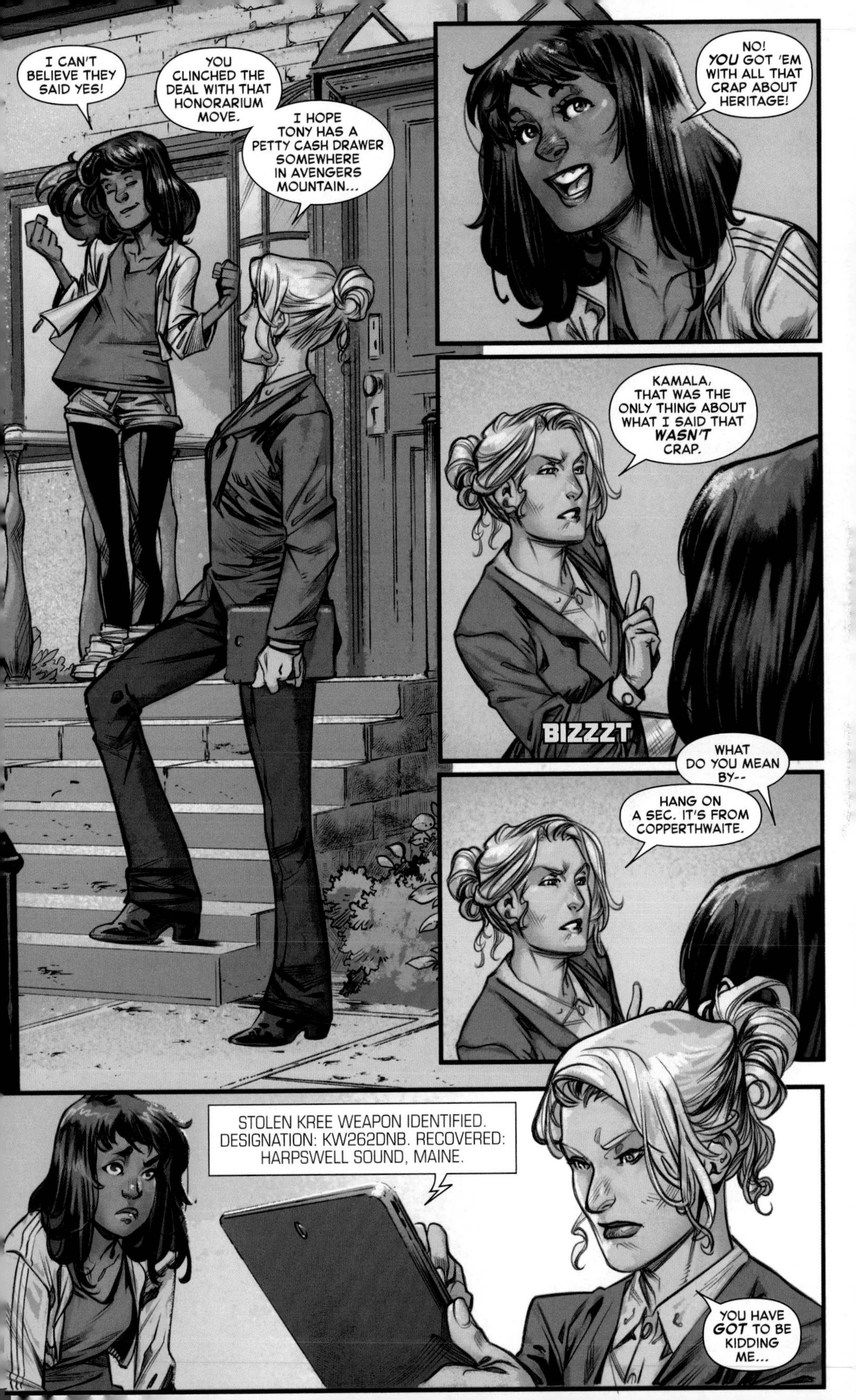
I CAN'T BELIEVE THEY SAID YES!
YOU CLINCHED THE DEAL WITH THAT HONORARIUM MOVE.
I HOPE TONY HAS A PETTY CASH DRAWER SOMEWHERE IN AVENGERS MOUNTAIN...
NO! YOU GOT 'EM WITH ALL THAT CRAP ABOUT HERITAGE!
KAMALA, THAT WAS THE ONLY THING ABOUT WHAT I SAID THAT WASN'T CRAP.
BIZZZT
WHAT DO YOU MEAN BY--
HANG ON A SEC. IT'S FROM COPPERTHWAITE.
STOLEN KREE WEAPON IDENTIFIED. DESIGNATION: KW262DNB. RECOVERED: HARPSWELL SOUND, MAINE.
YOU HAVE GOT TO BE KIDDING ME...

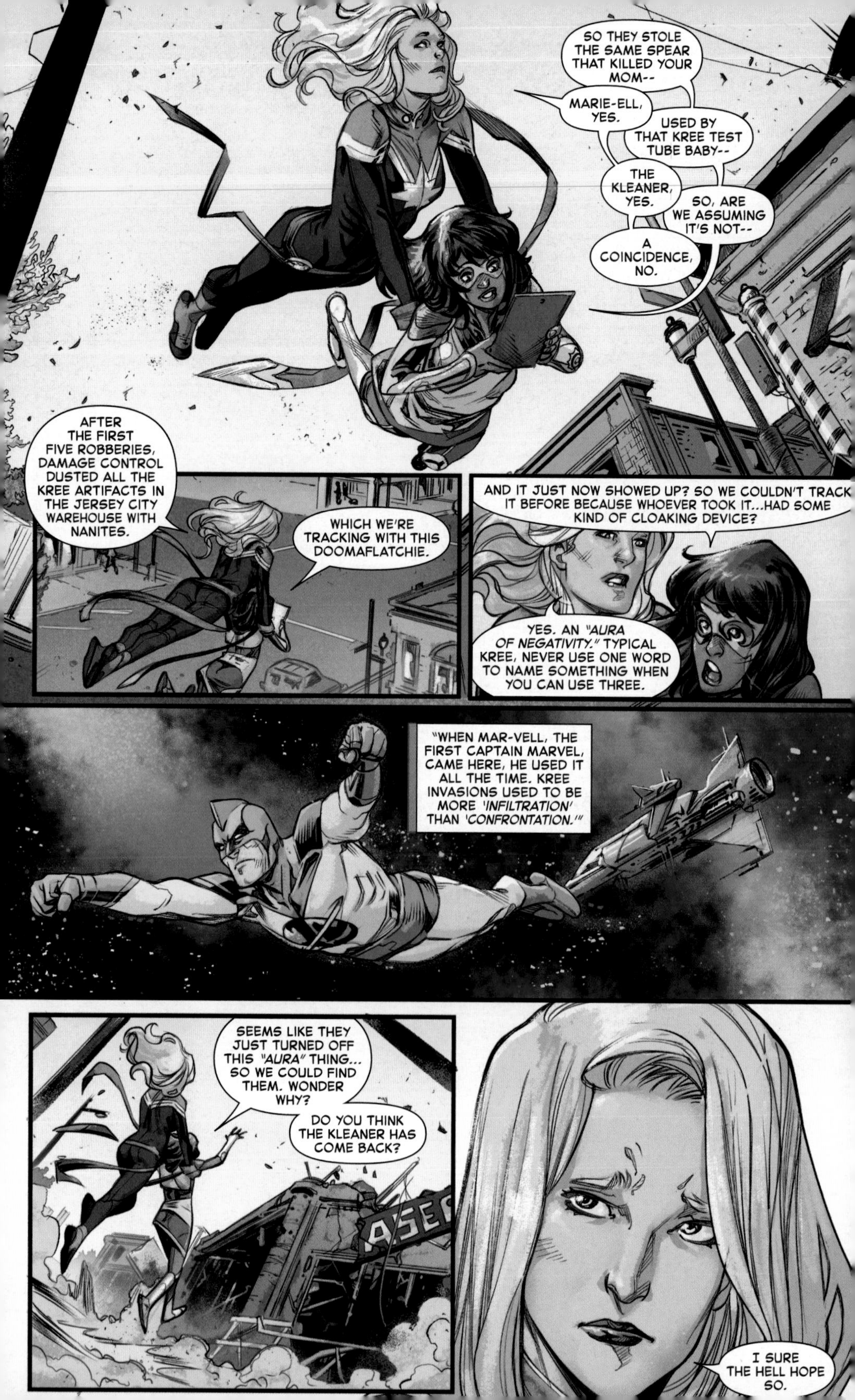
SO THEY STOLE THE SAME SPEAR THAT KILLED YOUR MOM--
MARIE-ELL, YES.
USED BY THAT KREE TEST TUBE BABY--
THE KLEANER, YES.
SO, ARE WE ASSUMING IT'S NOT--
A COINCIDENCE, NO.
AFTER THE FIRST FIVE ROBBERIES, DAMAGE CONTROL DUSTED ALL THE KREE ARTIFACTS IN THE JERSEY CITY WAREHOUSE WITH NANITES.
WHICH WE'RE TRACKING WITH THIS DOOMAFLATCHIE.
AND IT JUST NOW SHOWED UP? SO WE COULDN'T TRACK IT BEFORE BECAUSE WHOEVER TOOK IT...HAD SOME KIND OF CLOAKING DEVICE?
YES. AN *"AURA OF NEGATIVITY."* TYPICAL KREE, NEVER USE ONE WORD TO NAME SOMETHING WHEN YOU CAN USE THREE.
"WHEN MAR-VELL, THE FIRST CAPTAIN MARVEL, CAME HERE, HE USED IT ALL THE TIME. KREE INVASIONS USED TO BE MORE *'INFILTRATION'* THAN *'CONFRONTATION.'"*
SEEMS LIKE THEY JUST TURNED OFF THIS *"AURA"* THING... SO WE COULD FIND THEM. WONDER WHY?
DO YOU THINK THE KLEANER HAS COME BACK?
I SURE THE HELL HOPE SO.

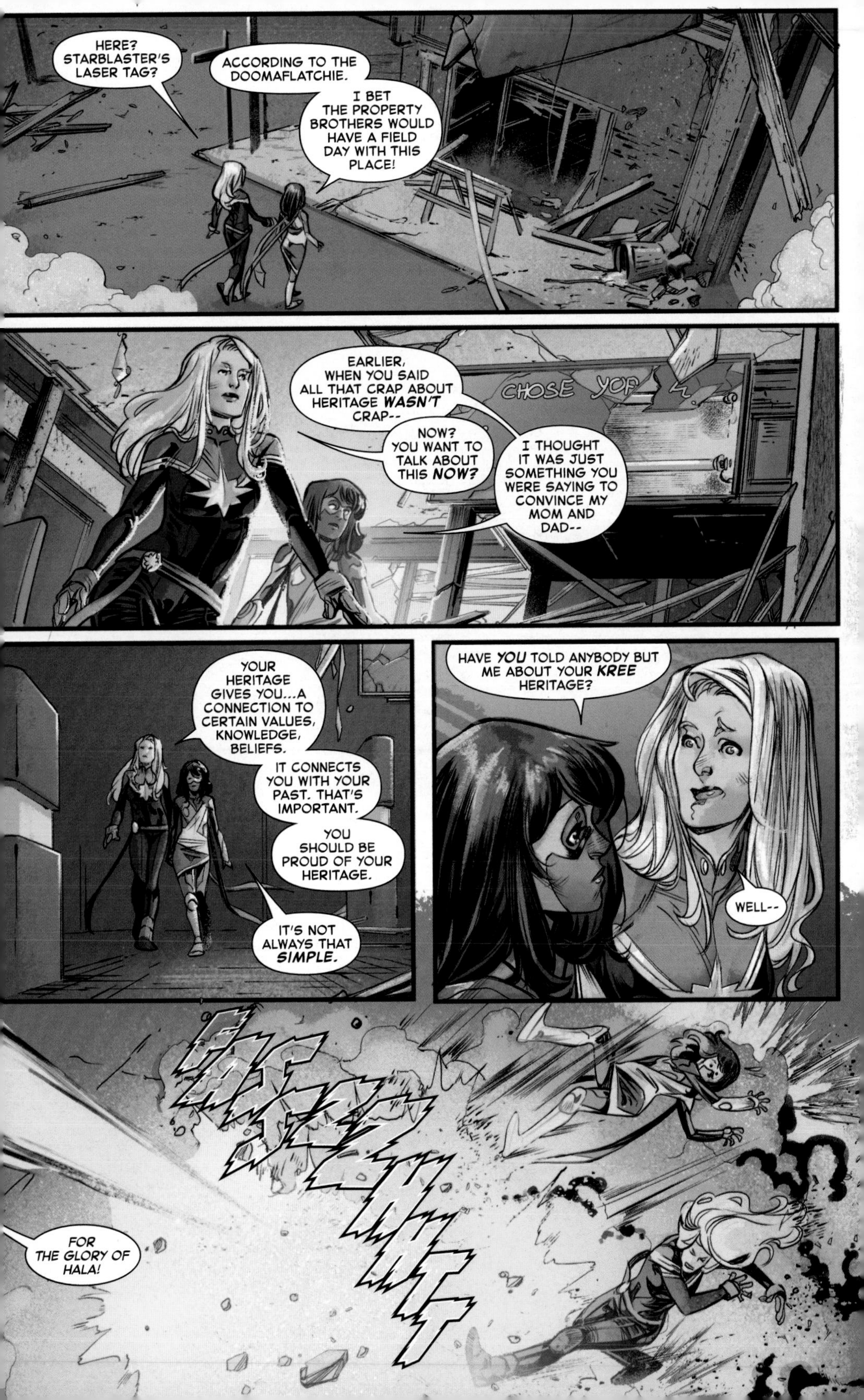
HERE? STARBLASTER'S LASER TAG?
ACCORDING TO THE DOOMAFLATCHIE.
I BET THE PROPERTY BROTHERS WOULD HAVE A FIELD DAY WITH THIS PLACE!
EARLIER, WHEN YOU SAID ALL THAT CRAP ABOUT HERITAGE WASN'T CRAP--
NOW? YOU WANT TO TALK ABOUT THIS NOW?
I THOUGHT IT WAS JUST SOMETHING YOU WERE SAYING TO CONVINCE MY MOM AND DAD--
YOUR HERITAGE GIVES YOU...A CONNECTION TO CERTAIN VALUES, KNOWLEDGE, BELIEFS.
IT CONNECTS YOU WITH YOUR PAST. THAT'S IMPORTANT.
YOU SHOULD BE PROUD OF YOUR HERITAGE.
IT'S NOT ALWAYS THAT SIMPLE.
HAVE YOU TOLD ANYBODY BUT ME ABOUT YOUR KREE HERITAGE?
WELL--
FOR THE GLORY OF HALA!

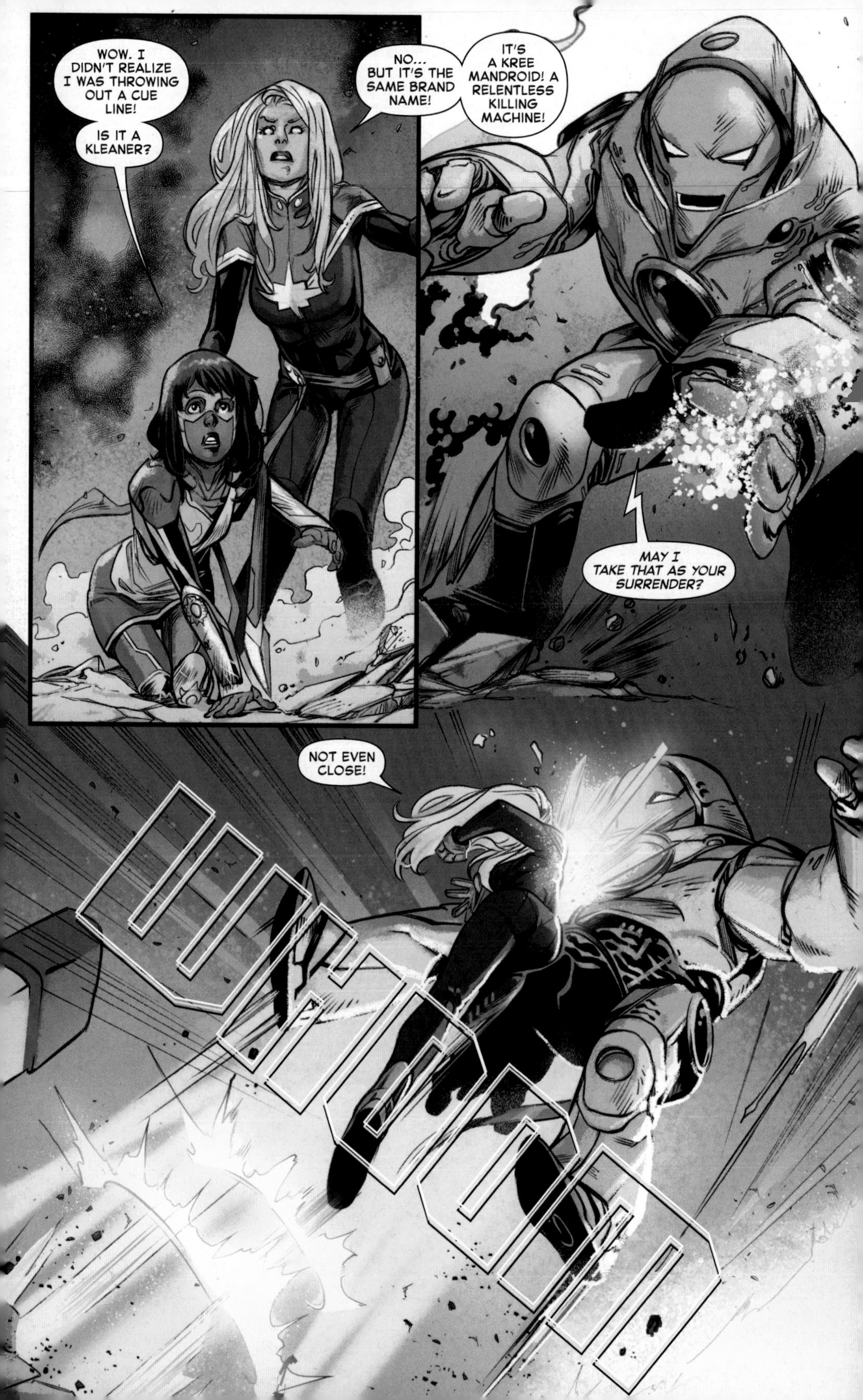
WOW. I DIDN'T REALIZE I WAS THROWING OUT A CUE LINE!
IS IT A KLEANER?
NO... BUT IT'S THE SAME BRAND NAME!
IT'S A KREE MANDROID! A RELENTLESS KILLING MACHINE!
MAY I TAKE THAT AS YOUR SURRENDER?
NOT EVEN CLOSE!

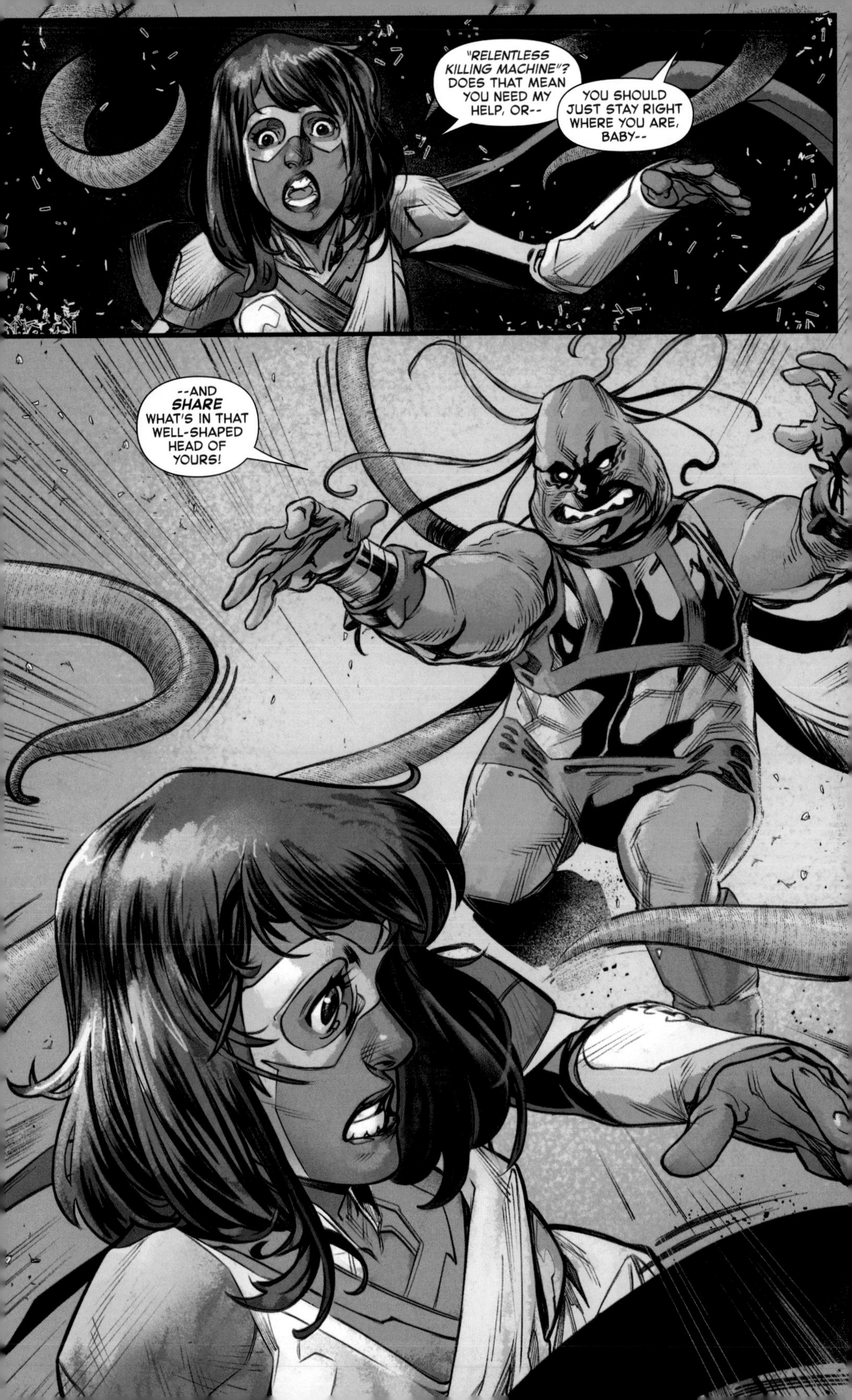
"RELENTLESS KILLING MACHINE"? DOES THAT MEAN YOU NEED MY HELP, OR--
YOU SHOULD JUST STAY RIGHT WHERE YOU ARE, BABY--
--AND SHARE WHAT'S IN THAT WELL-SHAPED HEAD OF YOURS!

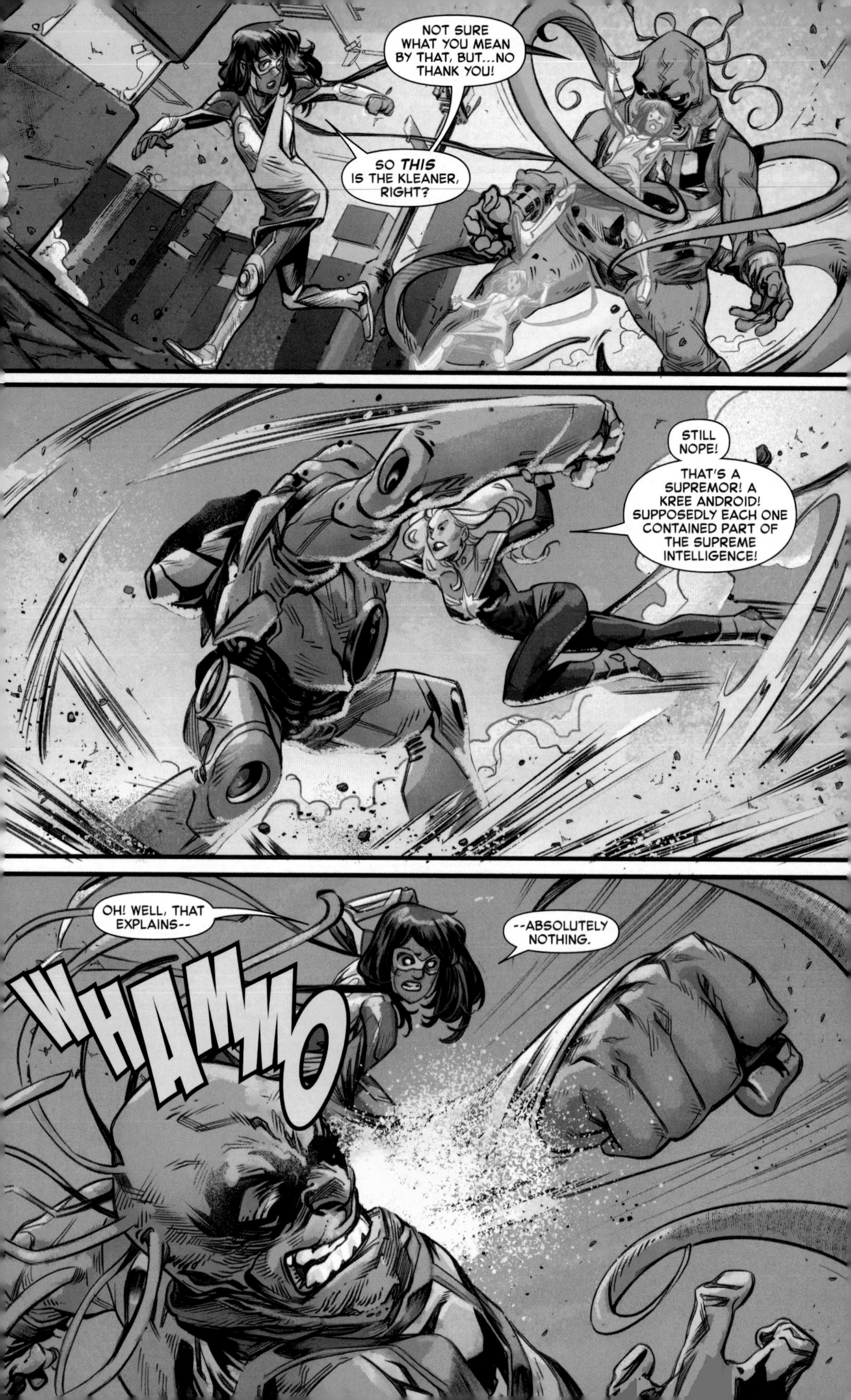
SO THIS IS THE KLEANER, RIGHT?
NOT SURE WHAT YOU MEAN BY THAT, BUT...NO THANK YOU!
STILL NOPE!
THAT'S A SUPREMOR! A KREE ANDROID! SUPPOSEDLY EACH ONE CONTAINED PART OF THE SUPREME INTELLIGENCE!
OH! WELL, THAT EXPLAINS--
--ABSOLUTELY NOTHING.
WHAMMO

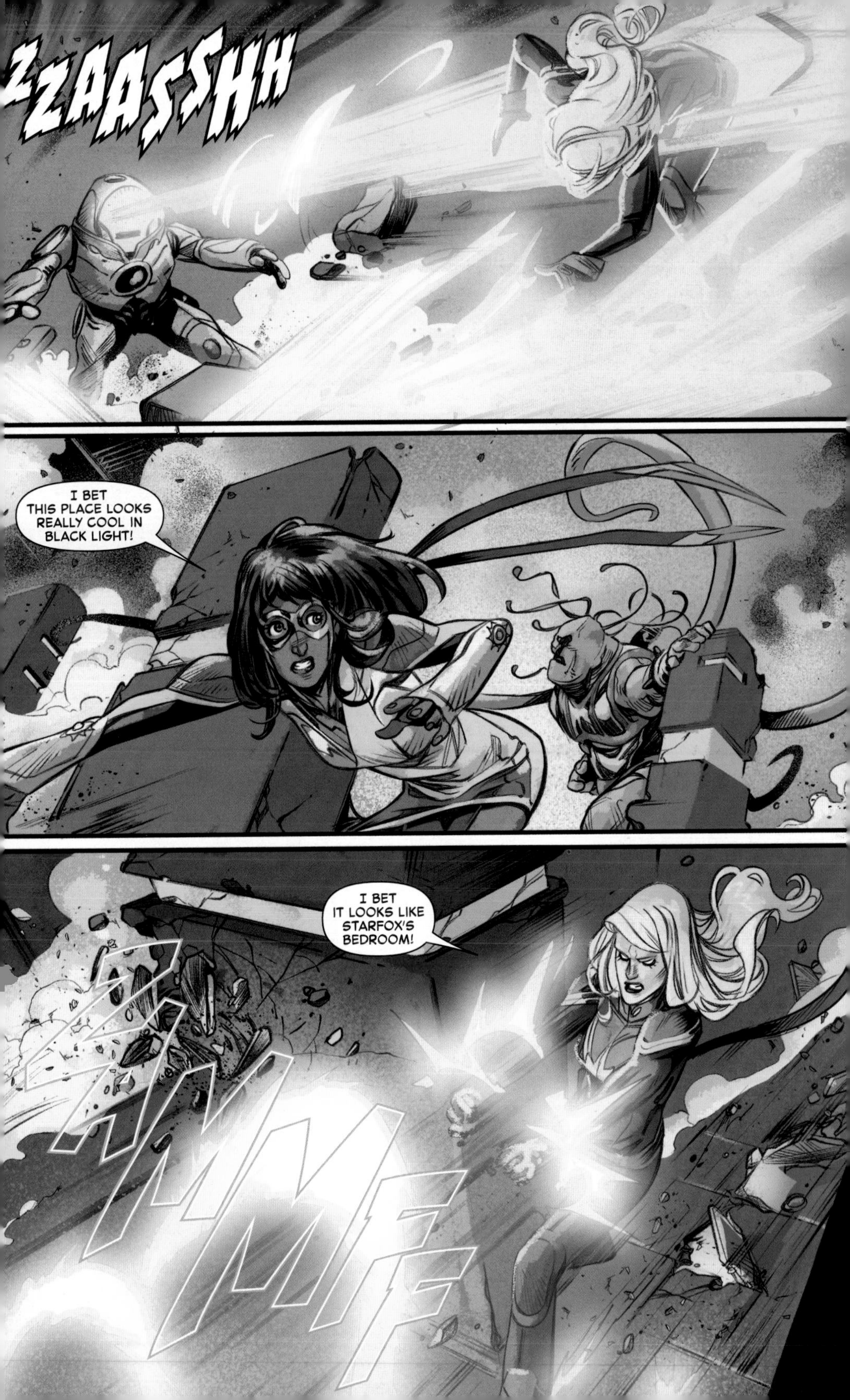
ZZAASSHH
I BET THIS PLACE LOOKS REALLY COOL IN BLACK LIGHT!
I BET IT LOOKS LIKE STARFOX'S BEDROOM!
ZUMF

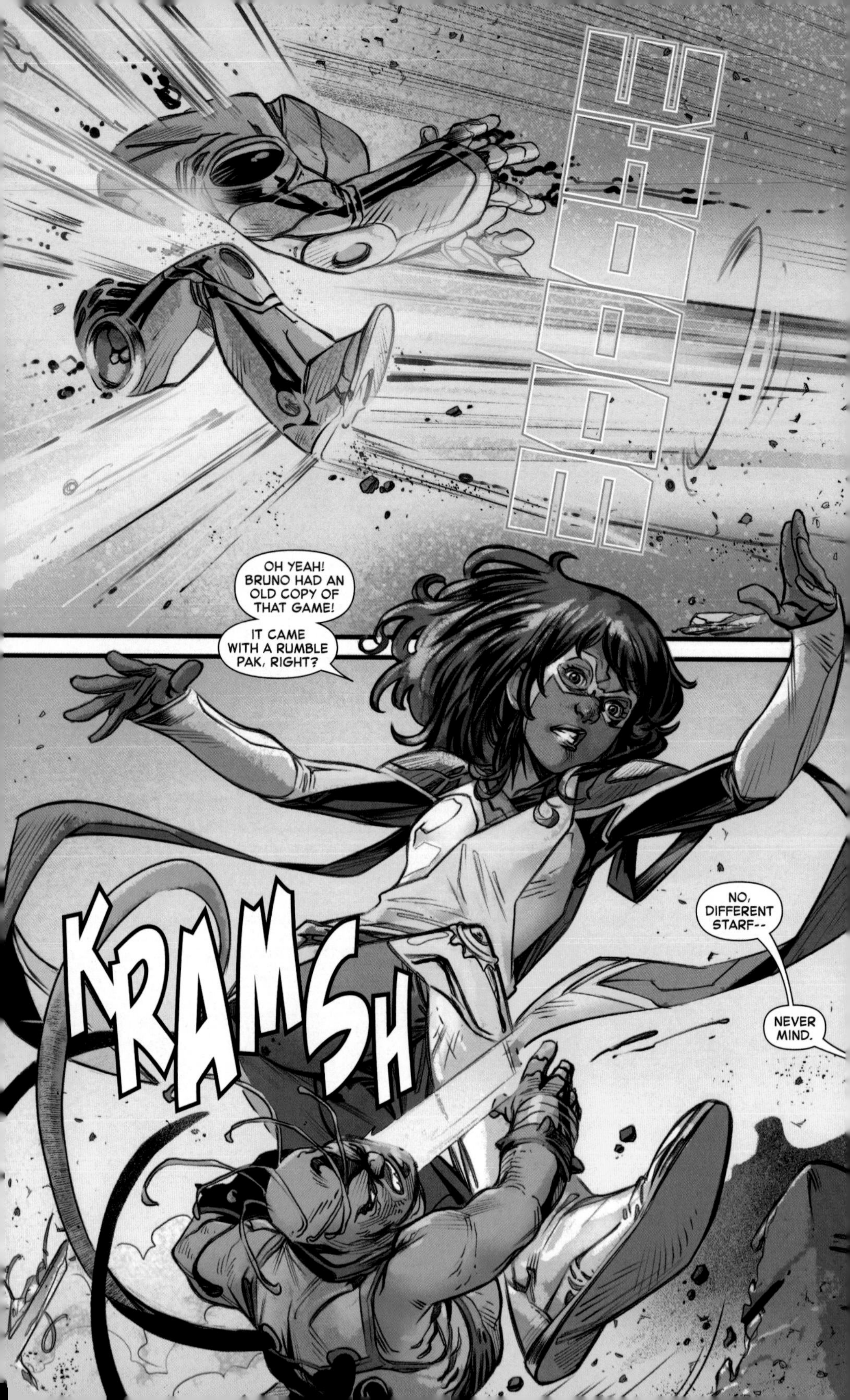
SHOOOM
OH YEAH! BRUNO HAD AN OLD COPY OF THAT GAME!
IT CAME WITH A RUMBLE PAK, RIGHT?
NO, DIFFERENT STARF--
NEVER MIND.
KRAMSH

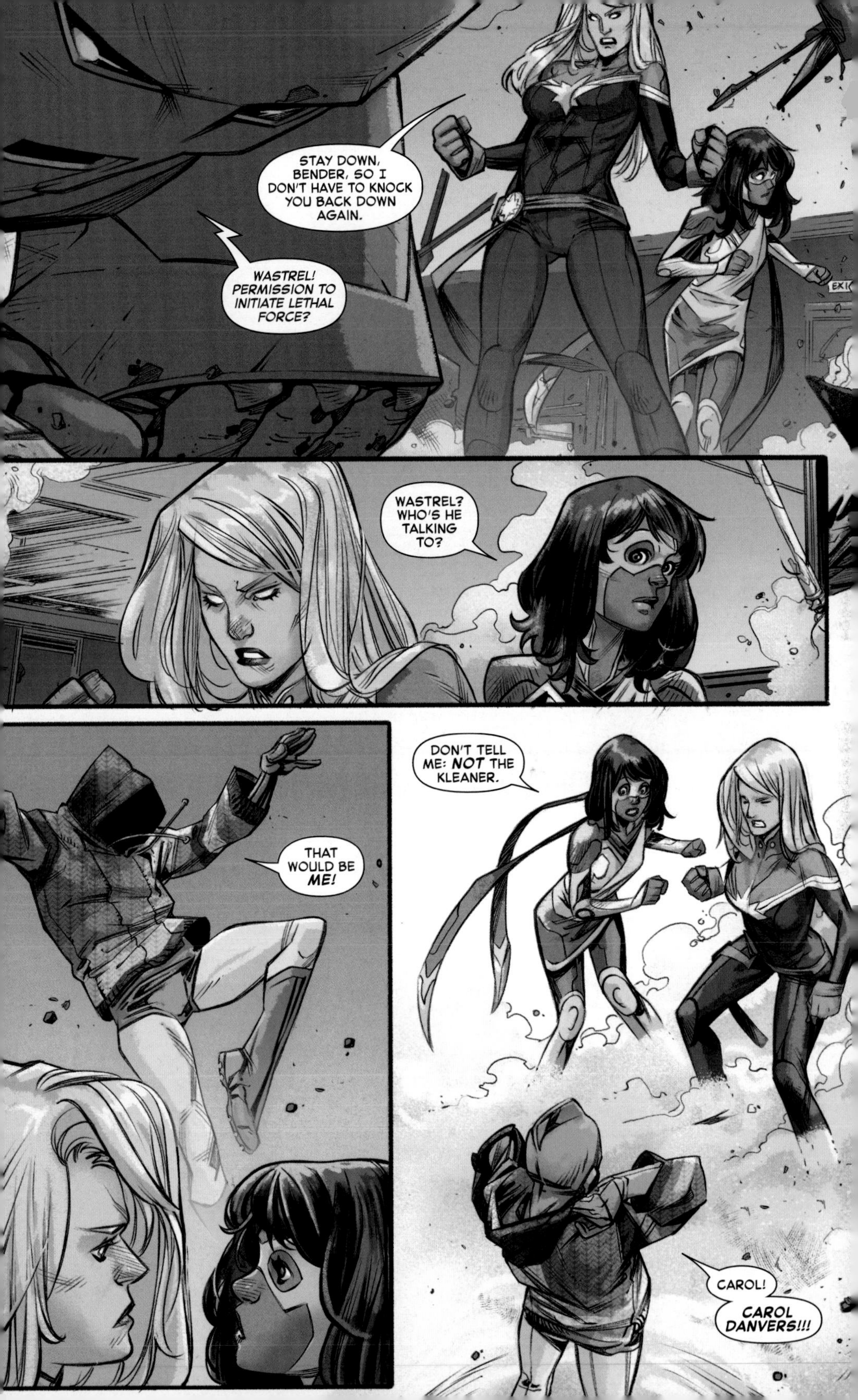
STAY DOWN, BENDER, SO I DON'T HAVE TO KNOCK YOU BACK DOWN AGAIN.
WASTREL! PERMISSION TO INITIATE LETHAL FORCE?
WASTREL? WHO'S HE TALKING TO?
DON'T TELL ME: *NOT* THE KLEANER.
THAT WOULD BE *ME!*
CAROL!
CAROL DANVERS!!!

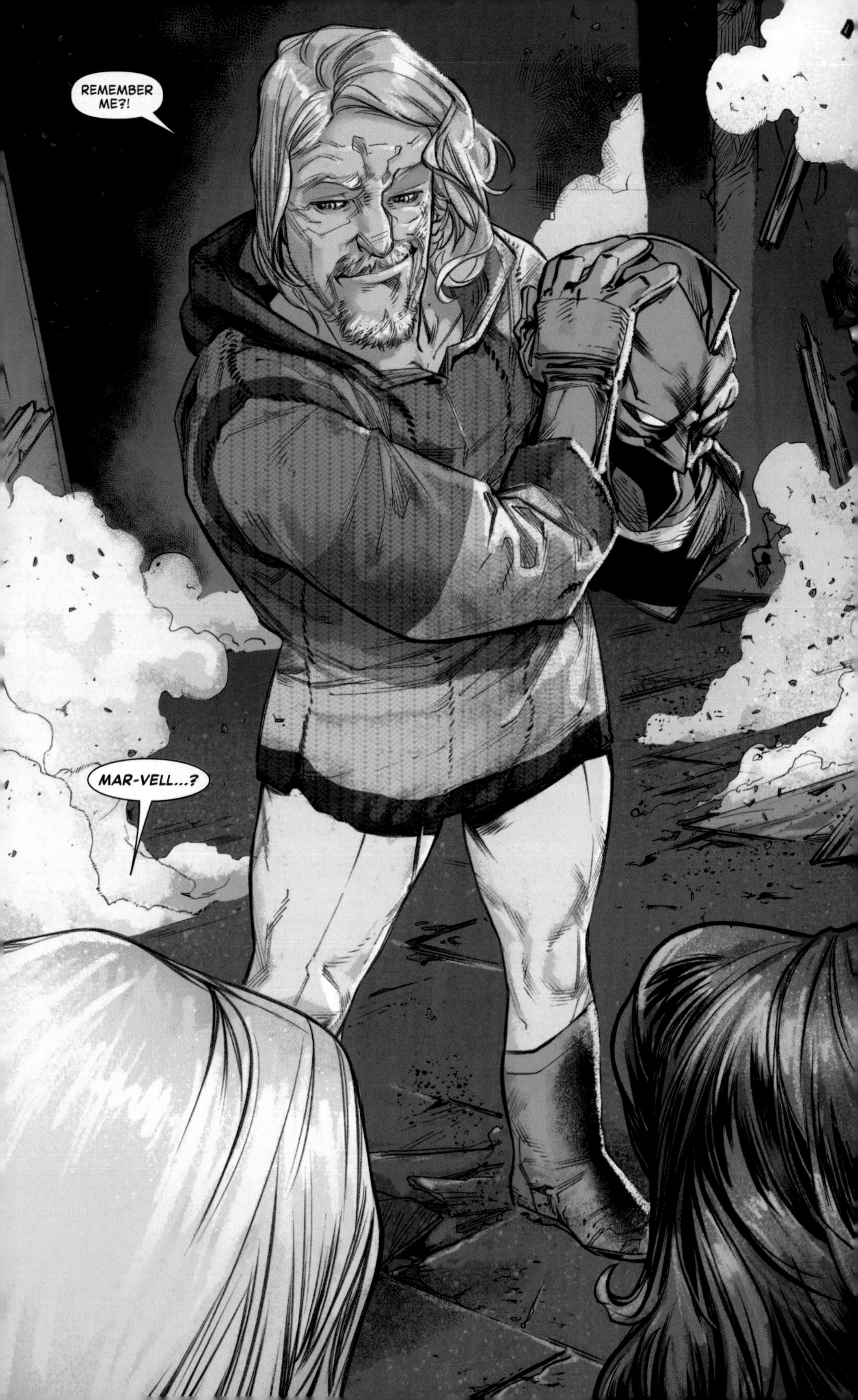
REMEMBER ME?!
MAR-VELL...?

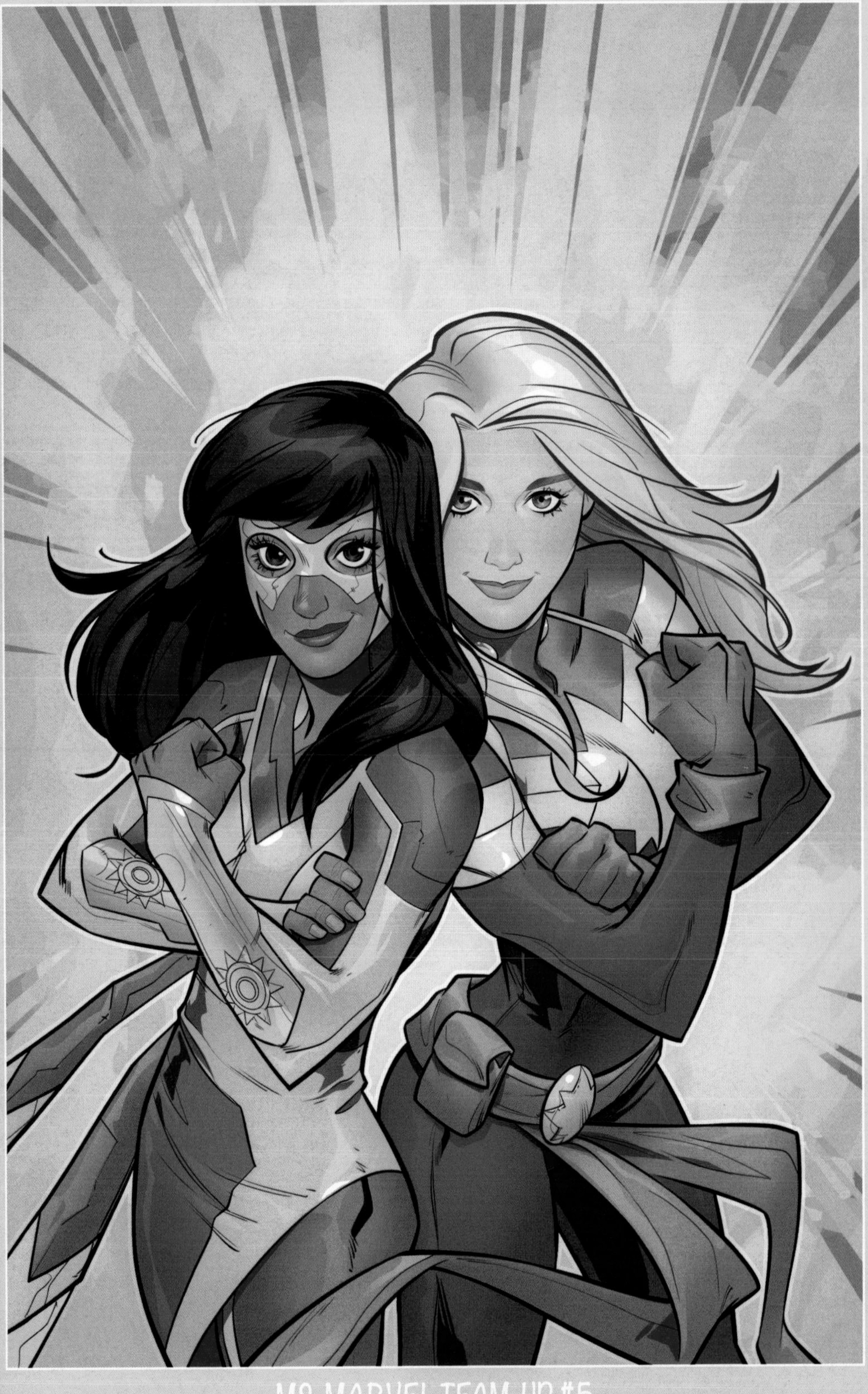

MS. MARVEL TEAM-UP #5

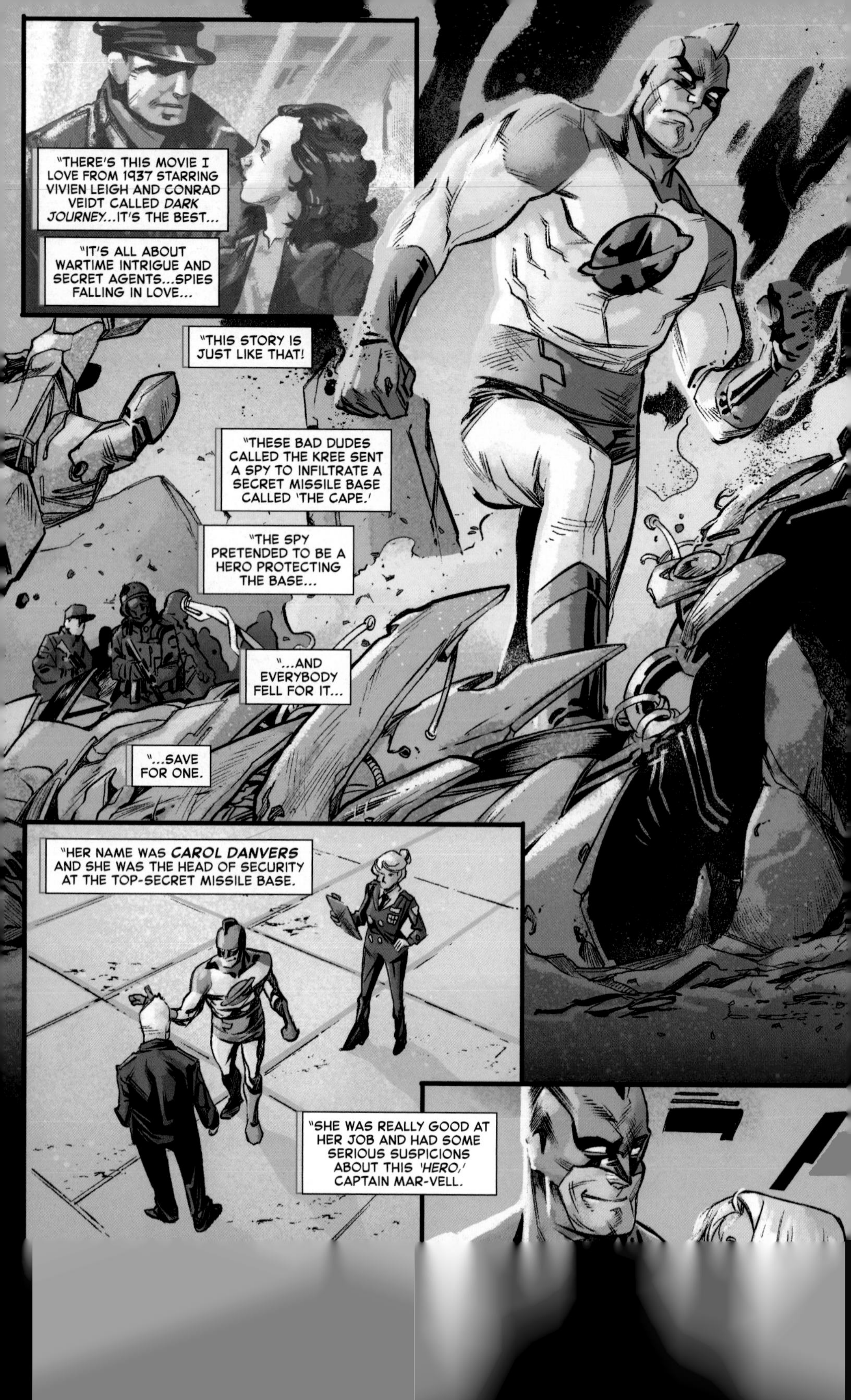
"THERE'S THIS MOVIE I LOVE FROM 1937 STARRING VIVIEN LEIGH AND CONRAD VEIDT CALLED *DARK JOURNEY*...IT'S THE BEST...
"IT'S ALL ABOUT WARTIME INTRIGUE AND SECRET AGENTS...SPIES FALLING IN LOVE...
"THIS STORY IS JUST LIKE THAT!
"THESE BAD DUDES CALLED THE KREE SENT A SPY TO INFILTRATE A SECRET MISSILE BASE CALLED 'THE CAPE.'
"THE SPY PRETENDED TO BE A HERO PROTECTING THE BASE...
"...AND EVERYBODY FELL FOR IT...
"...SAVE FOR ONE.
"HER NAME WAS **CAROL DANVERS** AND SHE WAS THE HEAD OF SECURITY AT THE TOP-SECRET MISSILE BASE.
"SHE WAS REALLY GOOD AT HER JOB AND HAD SOME SERIOUS SUSPICIONS ABOUT THIS *'HERO,'* CAPTAIN MAR-VELL.

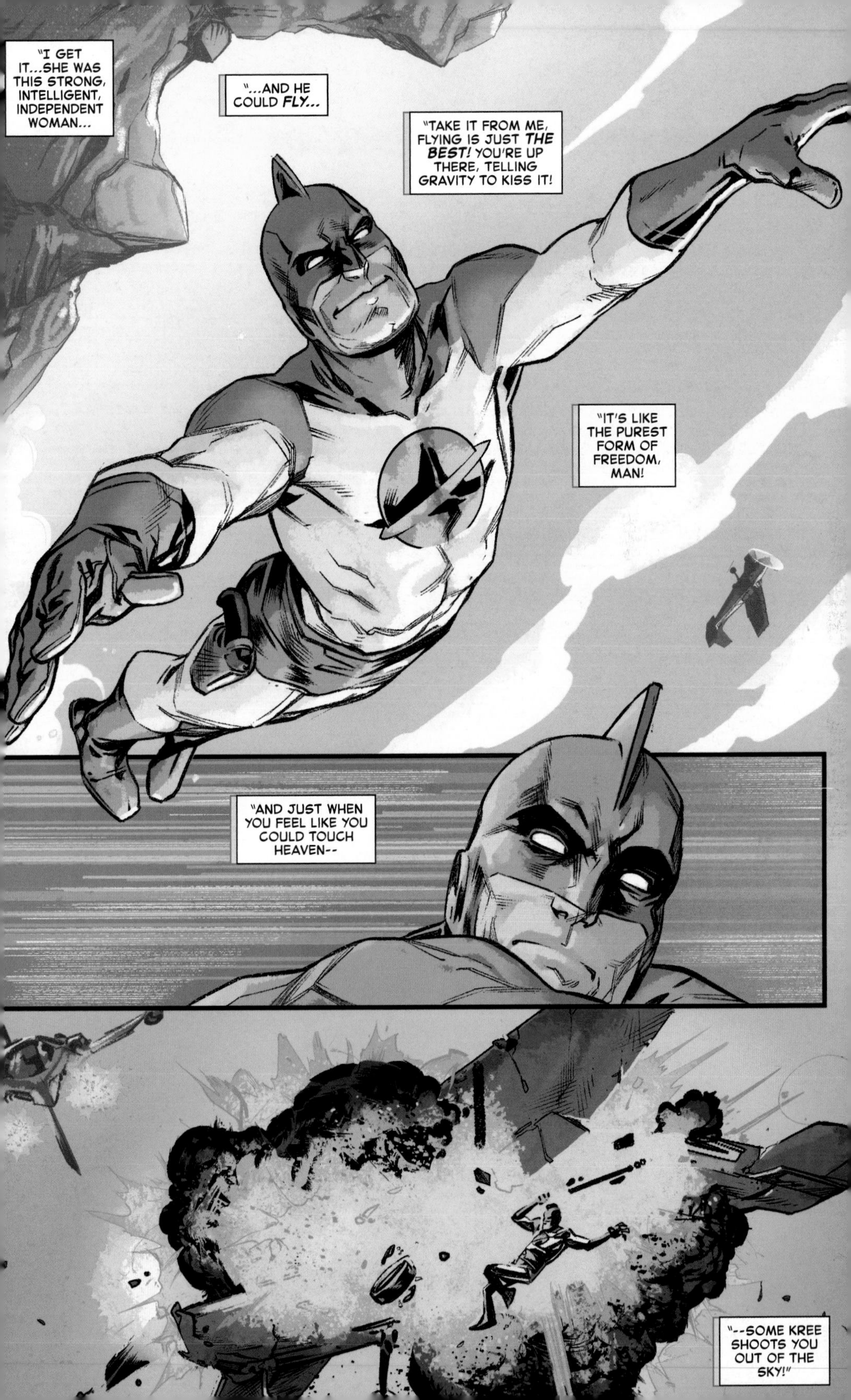

"I GET IT...SHE WAS THIS STRONG, INTELLIGENT, INDEPENDENT WOMAN...
"...AND HE COULD FLY...
"TAKE IT FROM ME, FLYING IS JUST THE BEST! YOU'RE UP THERE, TELLING GRAVITY TO KISS IT!
"IT'S LIKE THE PUREST FORM OF FREEDOM, MAN!
"AND JUST WHEN YOU FEEL LIKE YOU COULD TOUCH HEAVEN--
"--SOME KREE SHOOTS YOU OUT OF THE SKY!"

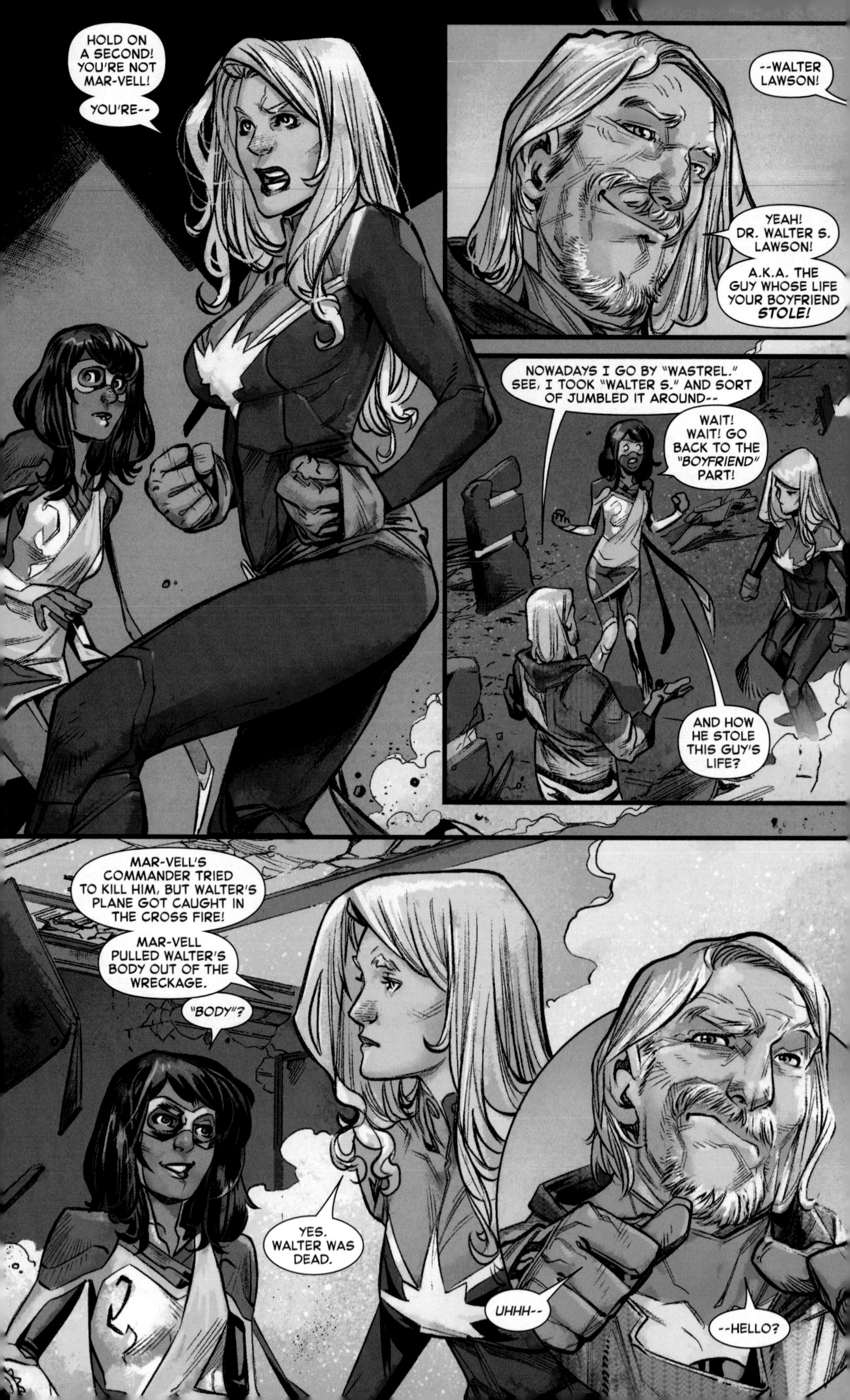
HOLD ON A SECOND! YOU'RE NOT MAR-VELL!
YOU'RE--
--WALTER LAWSON!
YEAH! DR. WALTER S. LAWSON!
A.K.A. THE GUY WHOSE LIFE YOUR BOYFRIEND STOLE!
NOWADAYS I GO BY "WASTREL." SEE, I TOOK "WALTER S." AND SORT OF JUMBLED IT AROUND--
WAIT! WAIT! GO BACK TO THE "BOYFRIEND" PART!
AND HOW HE STOLE THIS GUY'S LIFE?
MAR-VELL'S COMMANDER TRIED TO KILL HIM, BUT WALTER'S PLANE GOT CAUGHT IN THE CROSS FIRE!
MAR-VELL PULLED WALTER'S BODY OUT OF THE WRECKAGE.
"BODY"?
YES. WALTER WAS DEAD.
UHHH--
--HELLO?

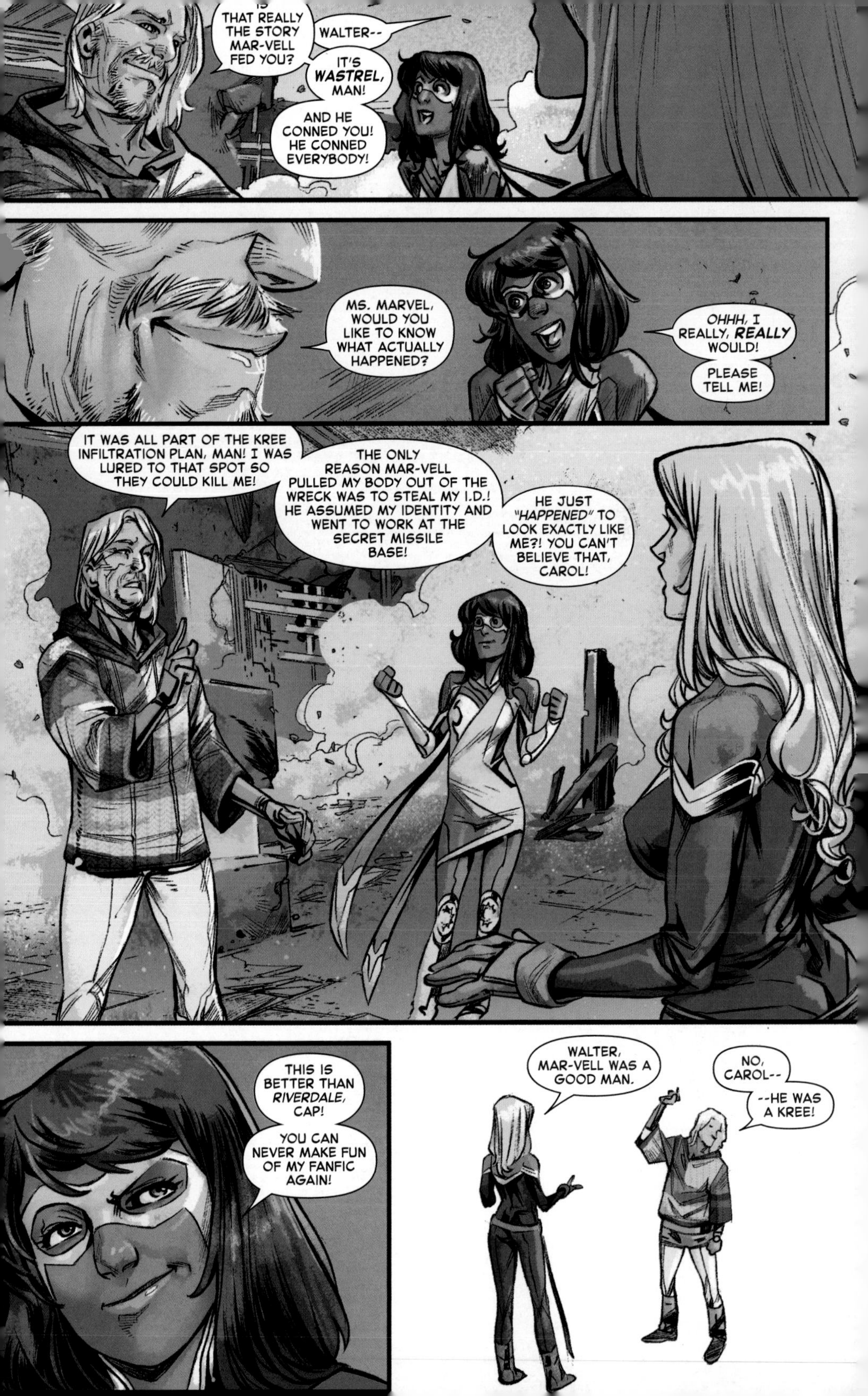
THAT REALLY THE STORY MAR-VELL FED YOU?
WALTER--
IT'S *WASTREL,* MAN!
AND HE CONNED YOU! HE CONNED EVERYBODY!
MS. MARVEL, WOULD YOU LIKE TO KNOW WHAT ACTUALLY HAPPENED?
OHHH, I REALLY, ***REALLY*** WOULD!
PLEASE TELL ME!
IT WAS ALL PART OF THE KREE INFILTRATION PLAN, MAN! I WAS LURED TO THAT SPOT SO THEY COULD KILL ME!
THE ONLY REASON MAR-VELL PULLED MY BODY OUT OF THE WRECK WAS TO STEAL MY I.D.! HE ASSUMED MY IDENTITY AND WENT TO WORK AT THE SECRET MISSILE BASE!
HE JUST *"HAPPENED"* TO LOOK EXACTLY LIKE ME?! YOU CAN'T BELIEVE THAT, CAROL!
THIS IS BETTER THAN *RIVERDALE,* CAP!
YOU CAN NEVER MAKE FUN OF MY FANFIC AGAIN!
WALTER, MAR-VELL WAS A GOOD MAN.
NO, CAROL--
--HE WAS A KREE!

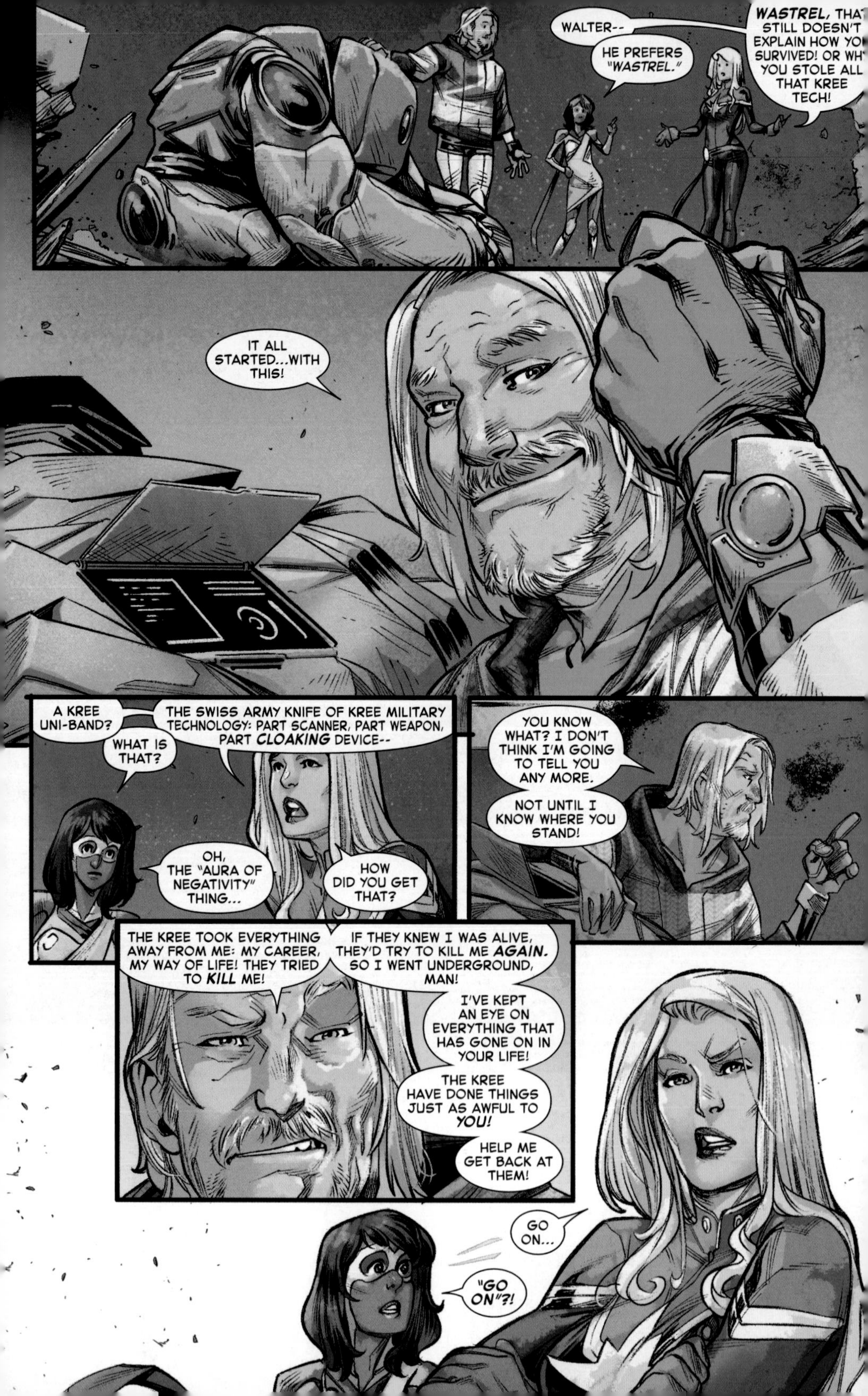
WALTER--
HE PREFERS "WASTREL."
WASTREL, THAT STILL DOESN'T EXPLAIN HOW YOU SURVIVED! OR WHY YOU STOLE ALL THAT KREE TECH!
IT ALL STARTED...WITH THIS!
A KREE UNI-BAND?
WHAT IS THAT?
THE SWISS ARMY KNIFE OF KREE MILITARY TECHNOLOGY: PART SCANNER, PART WEAPON, PART CLOAKING DEVICE--
OH, THE "AURA OF NEGATIVITY" THING...
HOW DID YOU GET THAT?
YOU KNOW WHAT? I DON'T THINK I'M GOING TO TELL YOU ANY MORE.
NOT UNTIL I KNOW WHERE YOU STAND!
THE KREE TOOK EVERYTHING AWAY FROM ME: MY CAREER, MY WAY OF LIFE! THEY TRIED TO KILL ME!
IF THEY KNEW I WAS ALIVE, THEY'D TRY TO KILL ME AGAIN. SO I WENT UNDERGROUND, MAN!
I'VE KEPT AN EYE ON EVERYTHING THAT HAS GONE ON IN YOUR LIFE!
THE KREE HAVE DONE THINGS JUST AS AWFUL TO YOU!
HELP ME GET BACK AT THEM!
GO ON...
"GO ON"?!

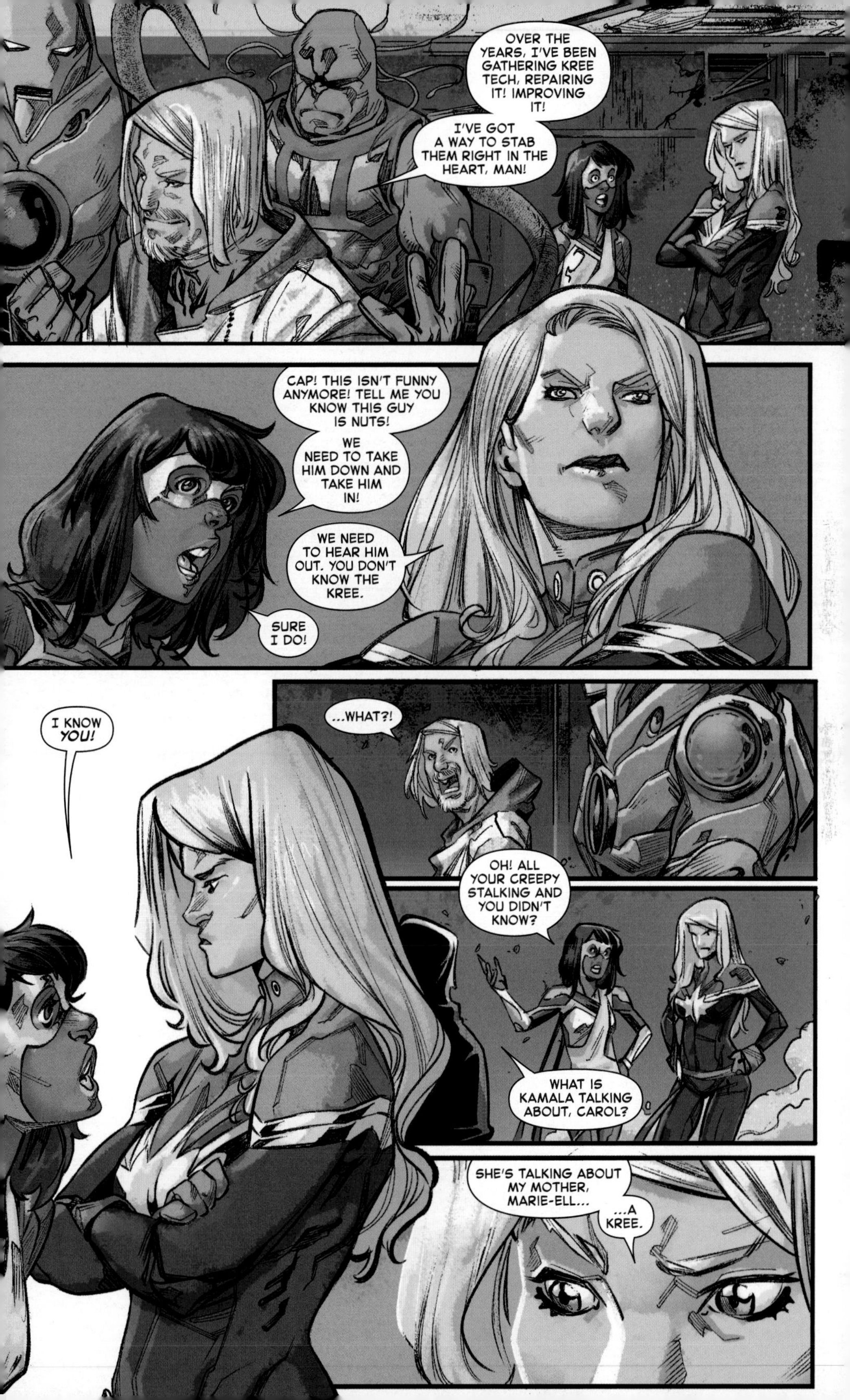
OVER THE YEARS, I'VE BEEN GATHERING KREE TECH, REPAIRING IT! IMPROVING IT!
I'VE GOT A WAY TO STAB THEM RIGHT IN THE HEART, MAN!
CAP! THIS ISN'T FUNNY ANYMORE! TELL ME YOU KNOW THIS GUY IS NUTS!
WE NEED TO TAKE HIM DOWN AND TAKE HIM IN!
WE NEED TO HEAR HIM OUT. YOU DON'T KNOW THE KREE.
SURE I DO!
I KNOW YOU!
...WHAT?!
OH! ALL YOUR CREEPY STALKING AND YOU DIDN'T KNOW?
WHAT IS KAMALA TALKING ABOUT, CAROL?
SHE'S TALKING ABOUT MY MOTHER, MARIE-ELL...
...A KREE.

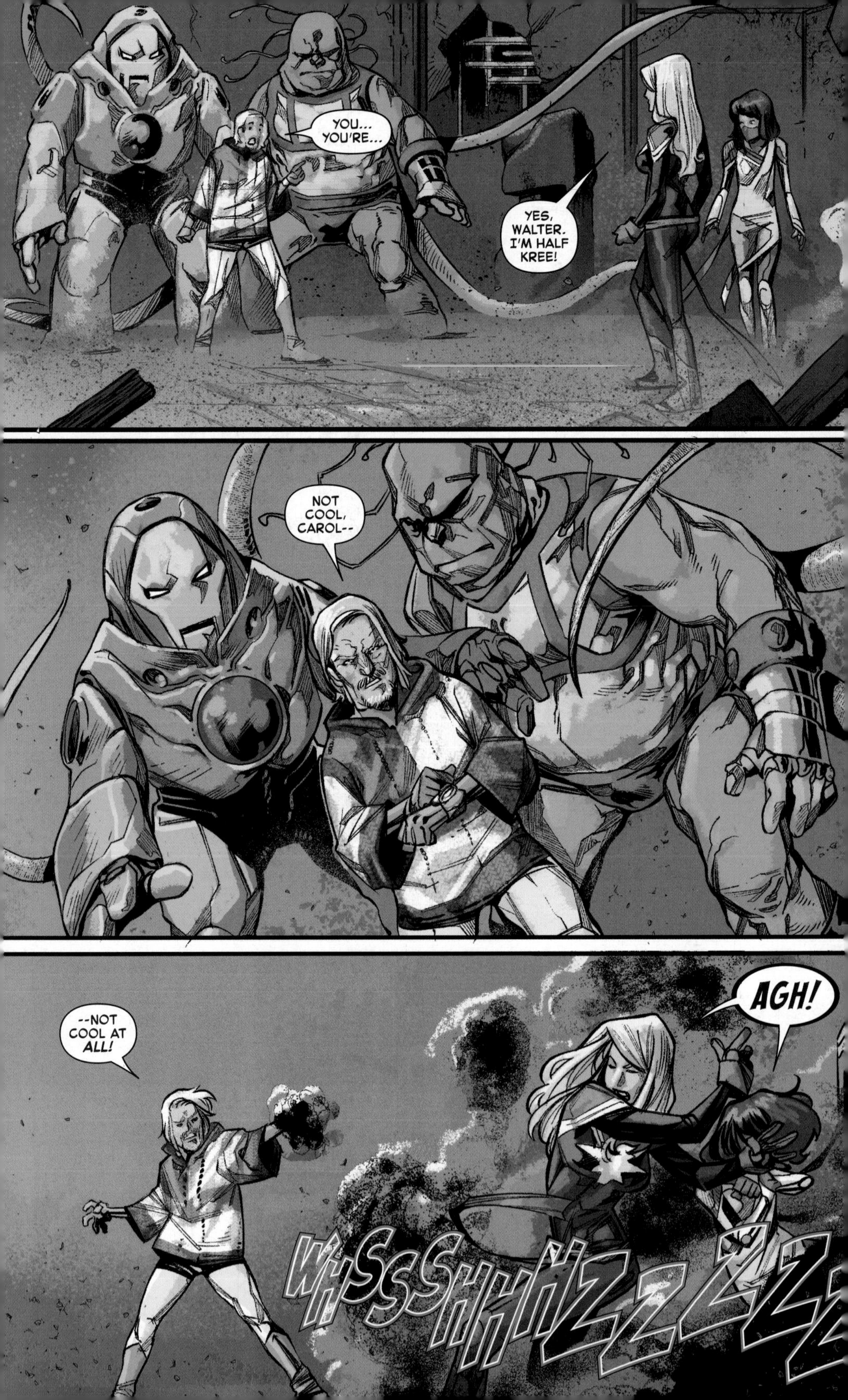
YOU... YOU'RE...
YES, WALTER. I'M HALF KREE!
NOT COOL, CAROL--
--NOT COOL AT ALL!
AGH!
WHSSSHHHZZZZZ

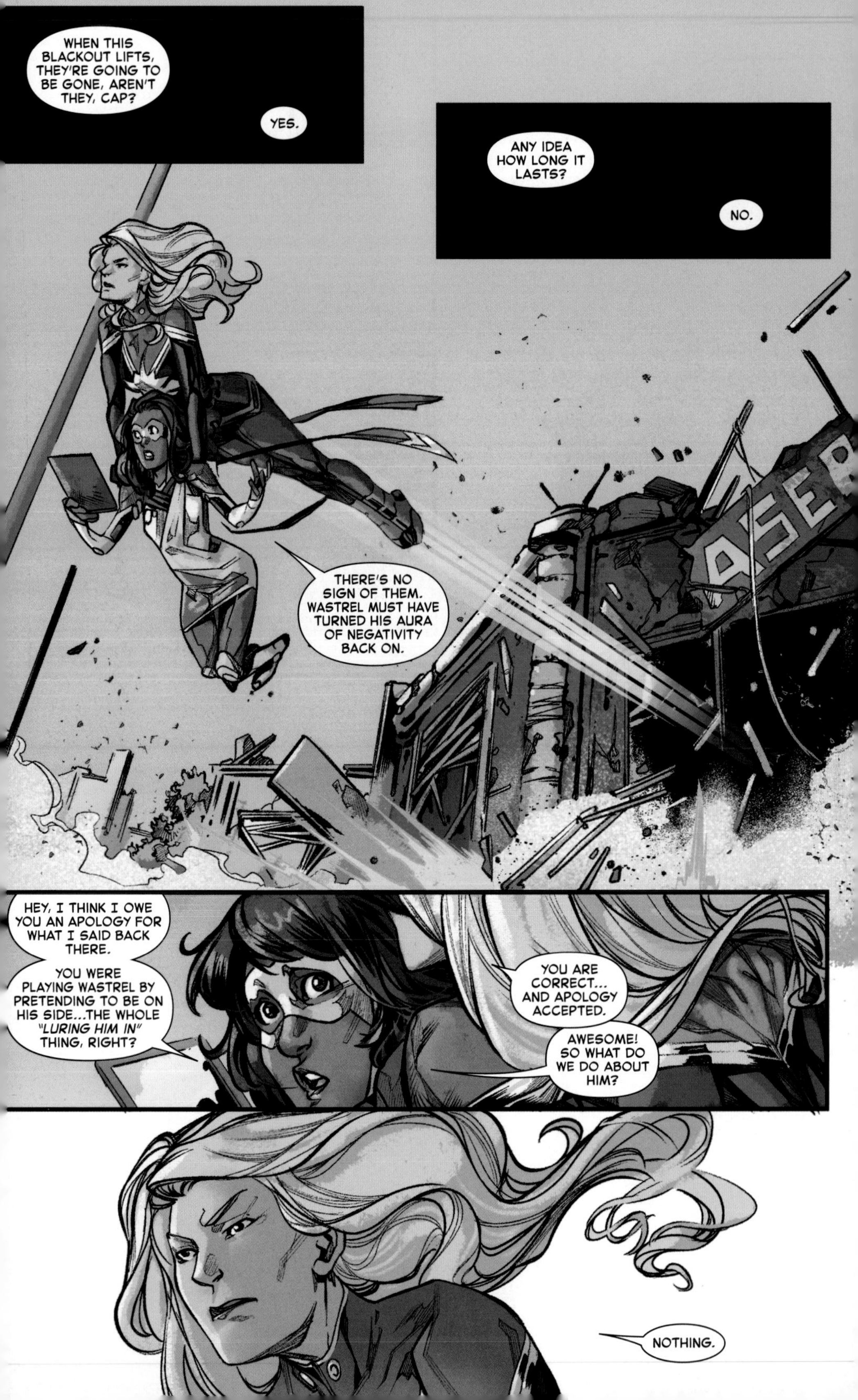
WHEN THIS BLACKOUT LIFTS, THEY'RE GOING TO BE GONE, AREN'T THEY, CAP?
YES.
ANY IDEA HOW LONG IT LASTS?
NO.
THERE'S NO SIGN OF THEM. WASTREL MUST HAVE TURNED HIS AURA OF NEGATIVITY BACK ON.
HEY, I THINK I OWE YOU AN APOLOGY FOR WHAT I SAID BACK THERE.
YOU WERE PLAYING WASTREL BY PRETENDING TO BE ON HIS SIDE...THE WHOLE *"LURING HIM IN"* THING, RIGHT?
YOU ARE CORRECT... AND APOLOGY ACCEPTED.
AWESOME! SO WHAT DO WE DO ABOUT HIM?
NOTHING.

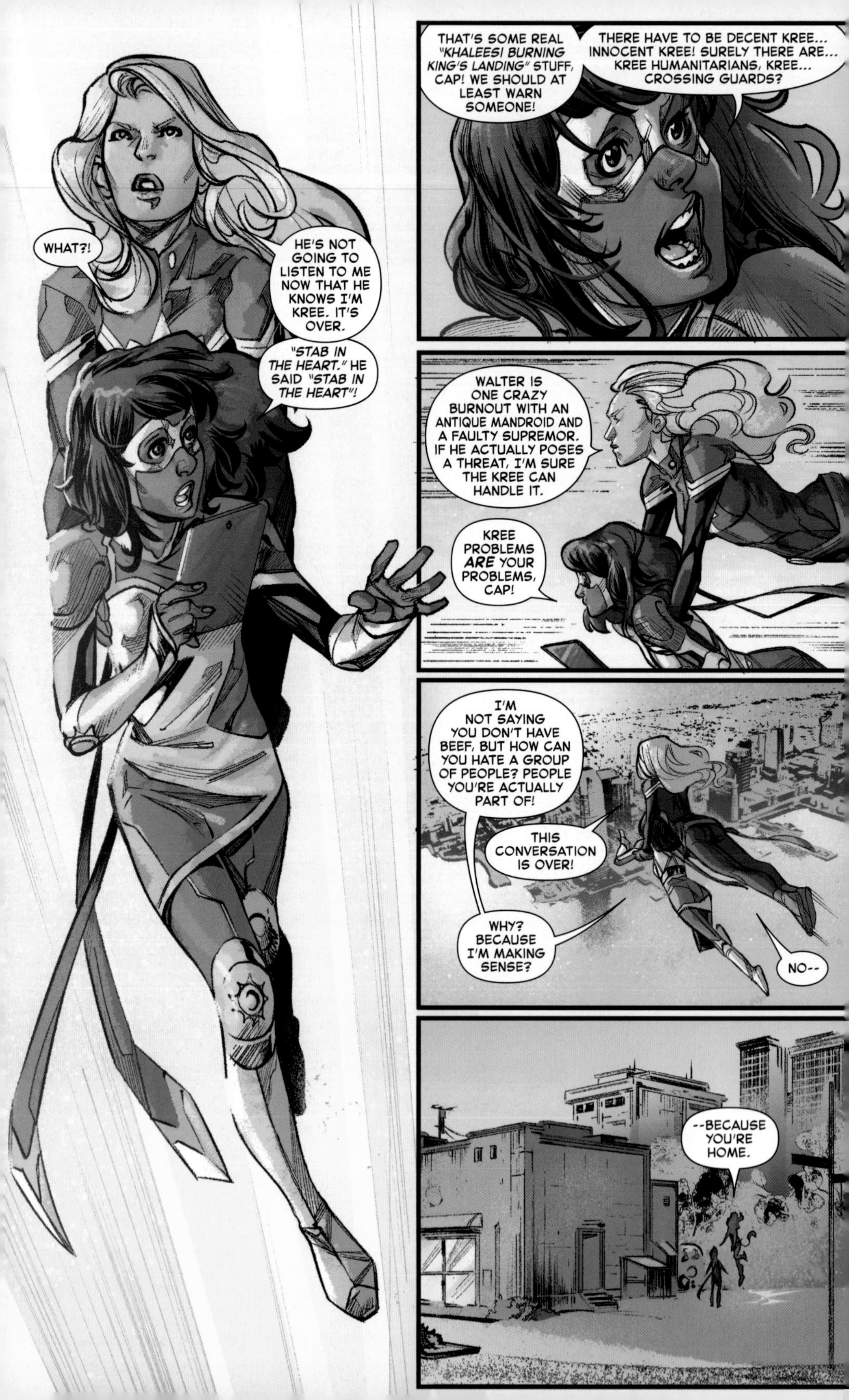
WHAT?!
HE'S NOT GOING TO LISTEN TO ME NOW THAT HE KNOWS I'M KREE. IT'S OVER.
"STAB IN THE HEART." HE SAID "STAB IN THE HEART"!
THAT'S SOME REAL "KHALEESI BURNING KING'S LANDING" STUFF, CAP! WE SHOULD AT LEAST WARN SOMEONE!
THERE HAVE TO BE DECENT KREE... INNOCENT KREE! SURELY THERE ARE... KREE HUMANITARIANS, KREE... CROSSING GUARDS?
WALTER IS ONE CRAZY BURNOUT WITH AN ANTIQUE MANDROID AND A FAULTY SUPREMOR. IF HE ACTUALLY POSES A THREAT, I'M SURE THE KREE CAN HANDLE IT.
KREE PROBLEMS ARE YOUR PROBLEMS, CAP!
I'M NOT SAYING YOU DON'T HAVE BEEF, BUT HOW CAN YOU HATE A GROUP OF PEOPLE? PEOPLE YOU'RE ACTUALLY PART OF!
THIS CONVERSATION IS OVER!
WHY? BECAUSE I'M MAKING SENSE?
NO--
--BECAUSE YOU'RE HOME.

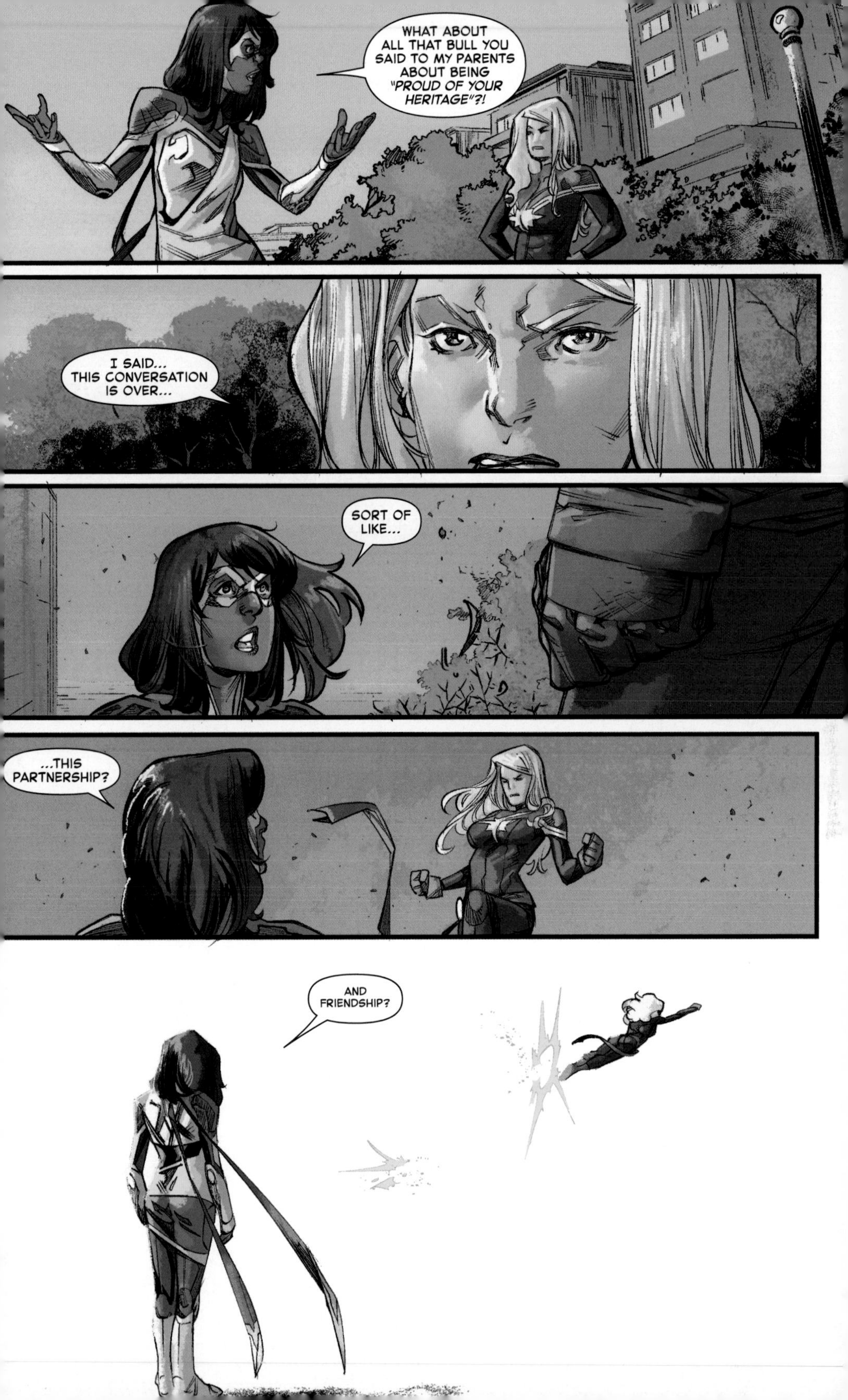
WHAT ABOUT ALL THAT BULL YOU SAID TO MY PARENTS ABOUT BEING *"PROUD OF YOUR HERITAGE"*?!
I SAID... THIS CONVERSATION IS OVER...
SORT OF LIKE...
...THIS PARTNERSHIP?
AND FRIENDSHIP?

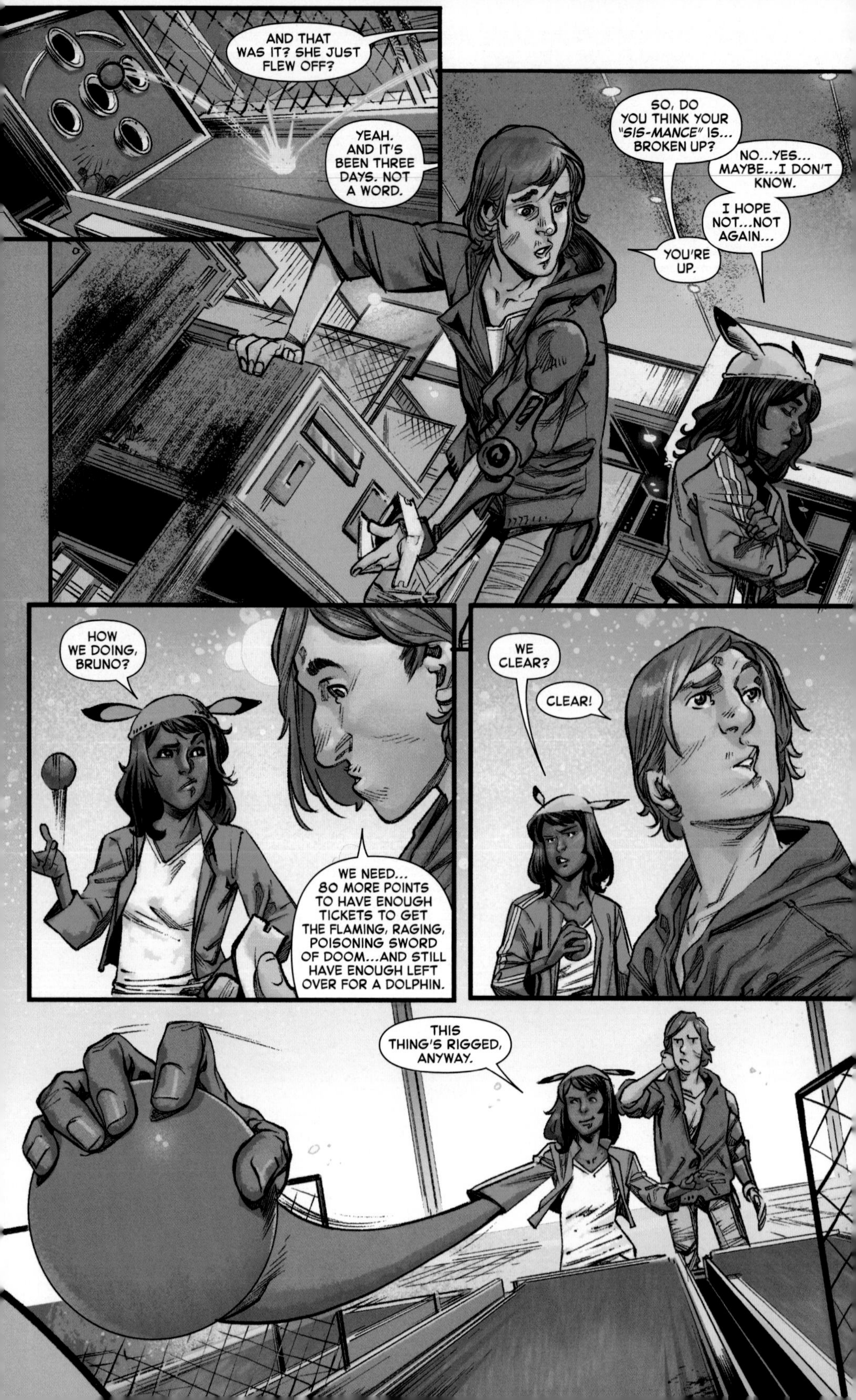
AND THAT WAS IT? SHE JUST FLEW OFF?
YEAH. AND IT'S BEEN THREE DAYS. NOT A WORD.
SO, DO YOU THINK YOUR "SIS-MANCE" IS... BROKEN UP?
NO...YES... MAYBE...I DON'T KNOW.
I HOPE NOT...NOT AGAIN...
YOU'RE UP.
HOW WE DOING, BRUNO?
WE NEED... 80 MORE POINTS TO HAVE ENOUGH TICKETS TO GET THE FLAMING, RAGING, POISONING SWORD OF DOOM...AND STILL HAVE ENOUGH LEFT OVER FOR A DOLPHIN.
WE CLEAR?
CLEAR!
THIS THING'S RIGGED, ANYWAY.

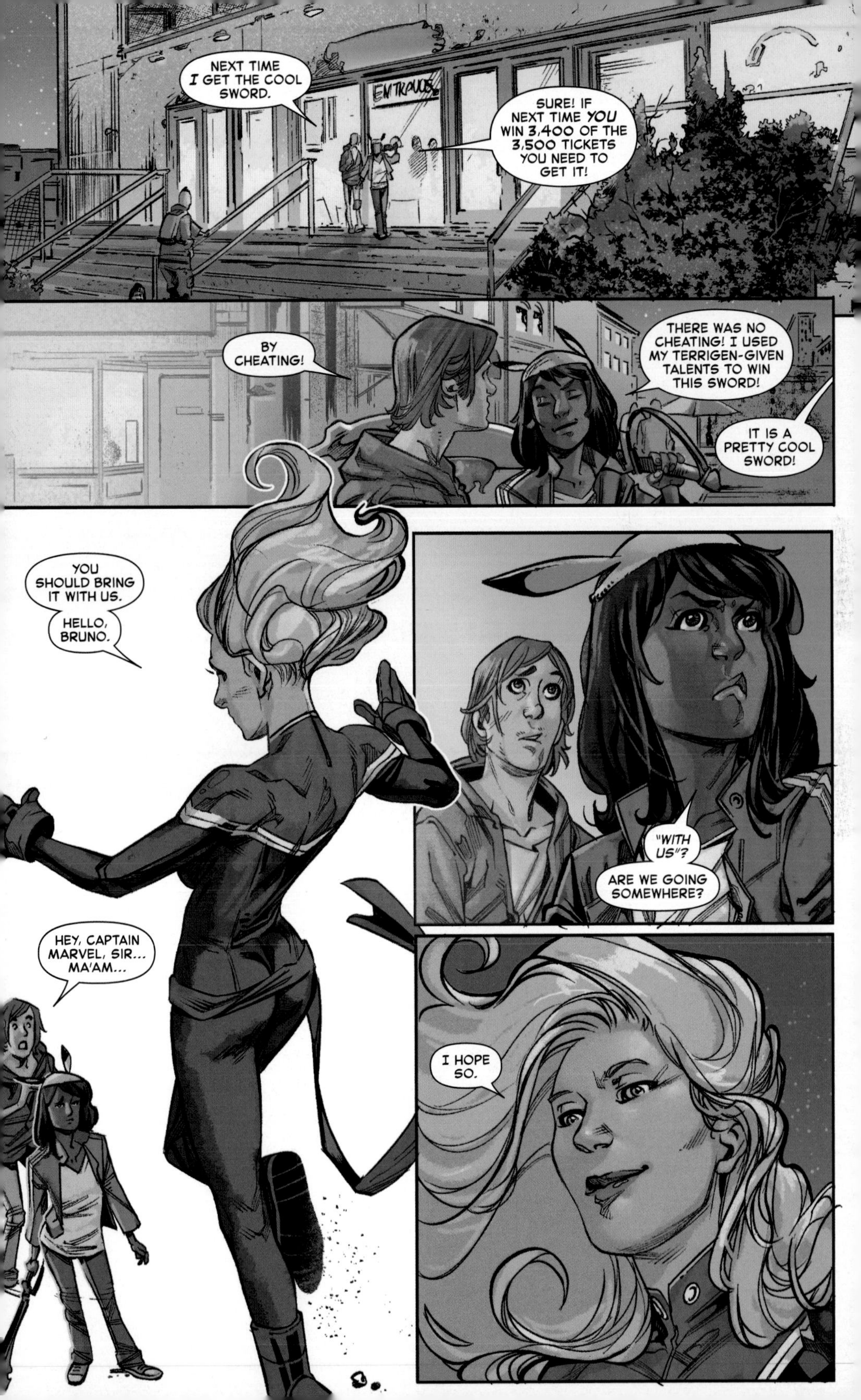
NEXT TIME I GET THE COOL SWORD.
SURE! IF NEXT TIME YOU WIN 3,400 OF THE 3,500 TICKETS YOU NEED TO GET IT!
ENTRANCE
BY CHEATING!
THERE WAS NO CHEATING! I USED MY TERRIGEN-GIVEN TALENTS TO WIN THIS SWORD!
IT IS A PRETTY COOL SWORD!
YOU SHOULD BRING IT WITH US.
HELLO, BRUNO.
"WITH US"?
ARE WE GOING SOMEWHERE?
HEY, CAPTAIN MARVEL, SIR... MA'AM...
I HOPE SO.

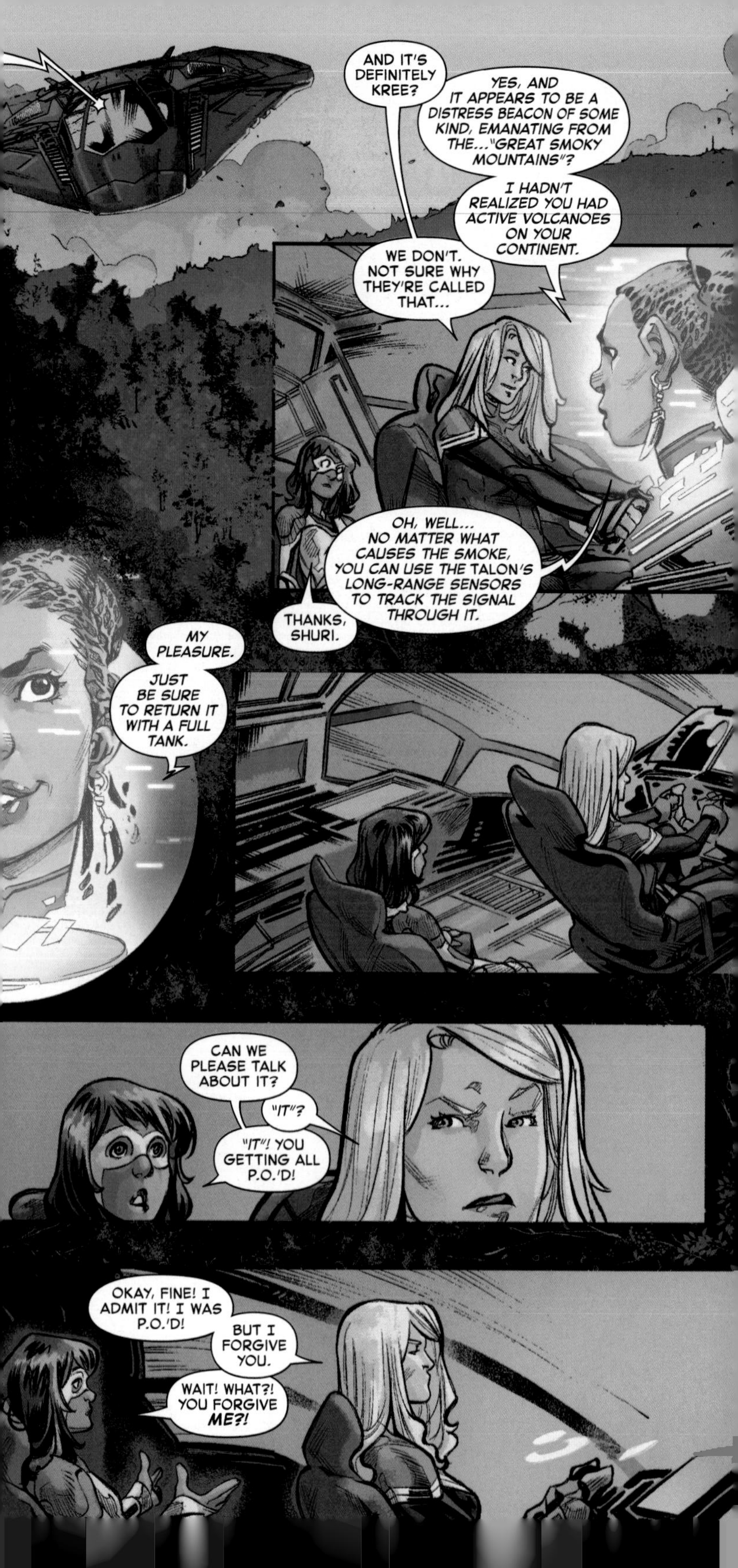
AND IT'S DEFINITELY KREE?
YES, AND IT APPEARS TO BE A DISTRESS BEACON OF SOME KIND, EMANATING FROM THE..."GREAT SMOKY MOUNTAINS"?
I HADN'T REALIZED YOU HAD ACTIVE VOLCANOES ON YOUR CONTINENT.
WE DON'T. NOT SURE WHY THEY'RE CALLED THAT...
OH, WELL... NO MATTER WHAT CAUSES THE SMOKE, YOU CAN USE THE TALON'S LONG-RANGE SENSORS TO TRACK THE SIGNAL THROUGH IT.
THANKS, SHURI.
MY PLEASURE.
JUST BE SURE TO RETURN IT WITH A FULL TANK.
CAN WE PLEASE TALK ABOUT IT?
"IT"?
"IT"! YOU GETTING ALL P.O.'D!
OKAY, FINE! I ADMIT IT! I WAS P.O.'D!
BUT I FORGIVE YOU.
WAIT! WHAT?! YOU FORGIVE *ME*?!

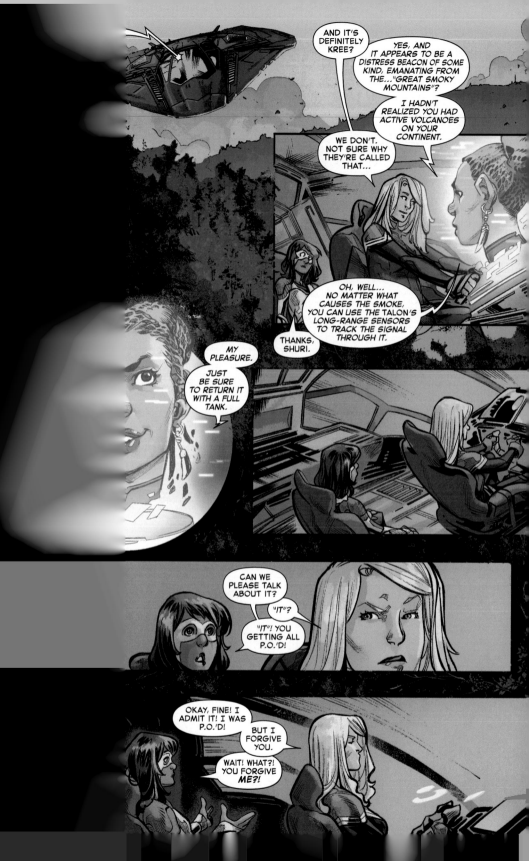

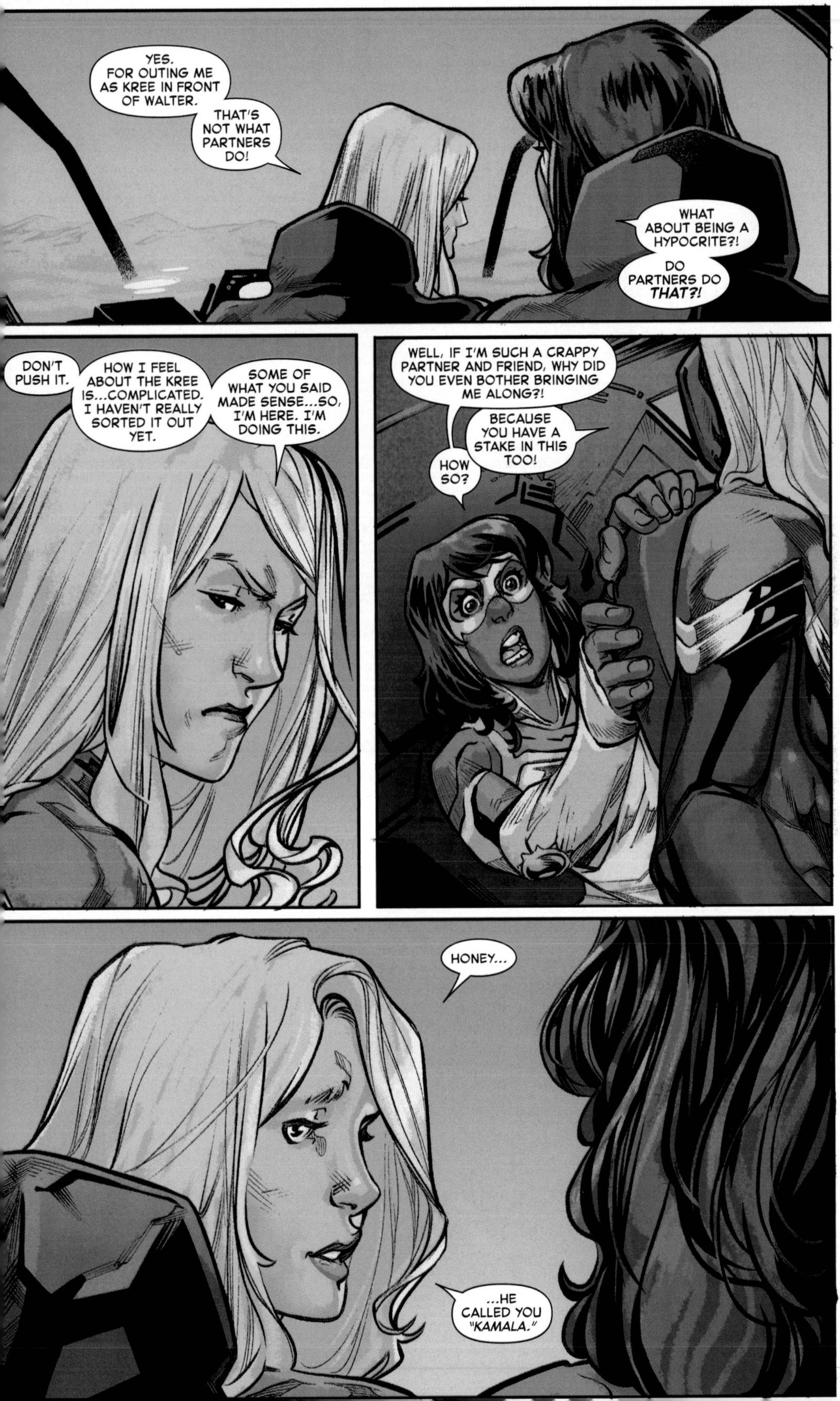
YES. FOR OUTING ME AS KREE IN FRONT OF WALTER.
THAT'S NOT WHAT PARTNERS DO!
WHAT ABOUT BEING A HYPOCRITE?!
DO PARTNERS DO *THAT?!*
DON'T PUSH IT.
HOW I FEEL ABOUT THE KREE IS...COMPLICATED. I HAVEN'T REALLY SORTED IT OUT YET.
SOME OF WHAT YOU SAID MADE SENSE...SO, I'M HERE. I'M DOING THIS.
WELL, IF I'M SUCH A CRAPPY PARTNER AND FRIEND, WHY DID YOU EVEN BOTHER BRINGING ME ALONG?!
BECAUSE YOU HAVE A STAKE IN THIS TOO!
HOW SO?
HONEY...
...HE CALLED YOU *"KAMALA."*

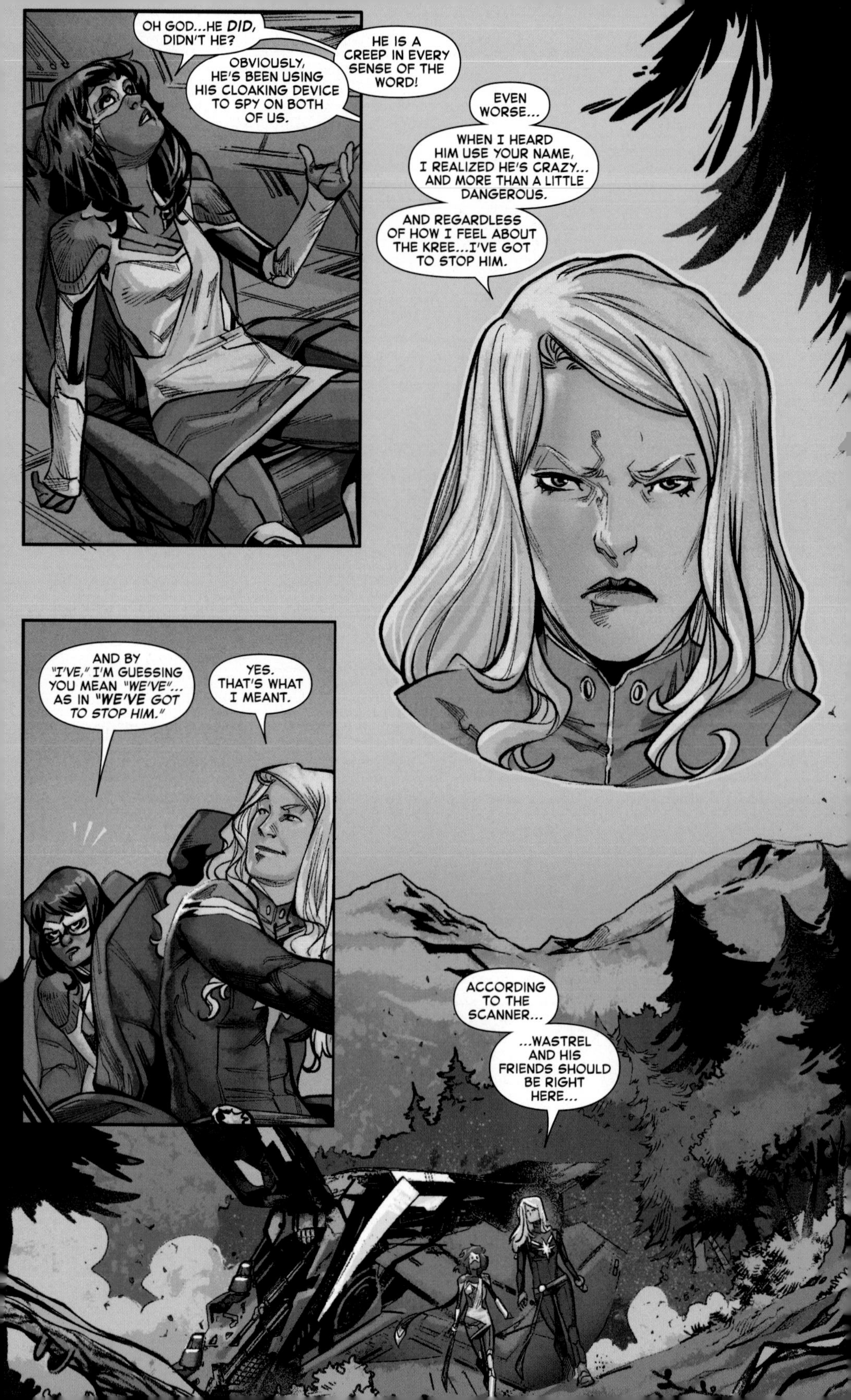
OH GOD...HE *DID*, DIDN'T HE?
OBVIOUSLY, HE'S BEEN USING HIS CLOAKING DEVICE TO SPY ON BOTH OF US.
HE IS A CREEP IN EVERY SENSE OF THE WORD!
EVEN WORSE...
WHEN I HEARD HIM USE YOUR NAME, I REALIZED HE'S CRAZY... AND MORE THAN A LITTLE DANGEROUS.
AND REGARDLESS OF HOW I FEEL ABOUT THE KREE...I'VE GOT TO STOP HIM.
AND BY *"I'VE,"* I'M GUESSING YOU MEAN *"WE'VE"*... AS IN ***"WE'VE** GOT TO STOP HIM."*
YES. THAT'S WHAT I MEANT.
ACCORDING TO THE SCANNER...
...WASTREL AND HIS FRIENDS SHOULD BE RIGHT HERE...

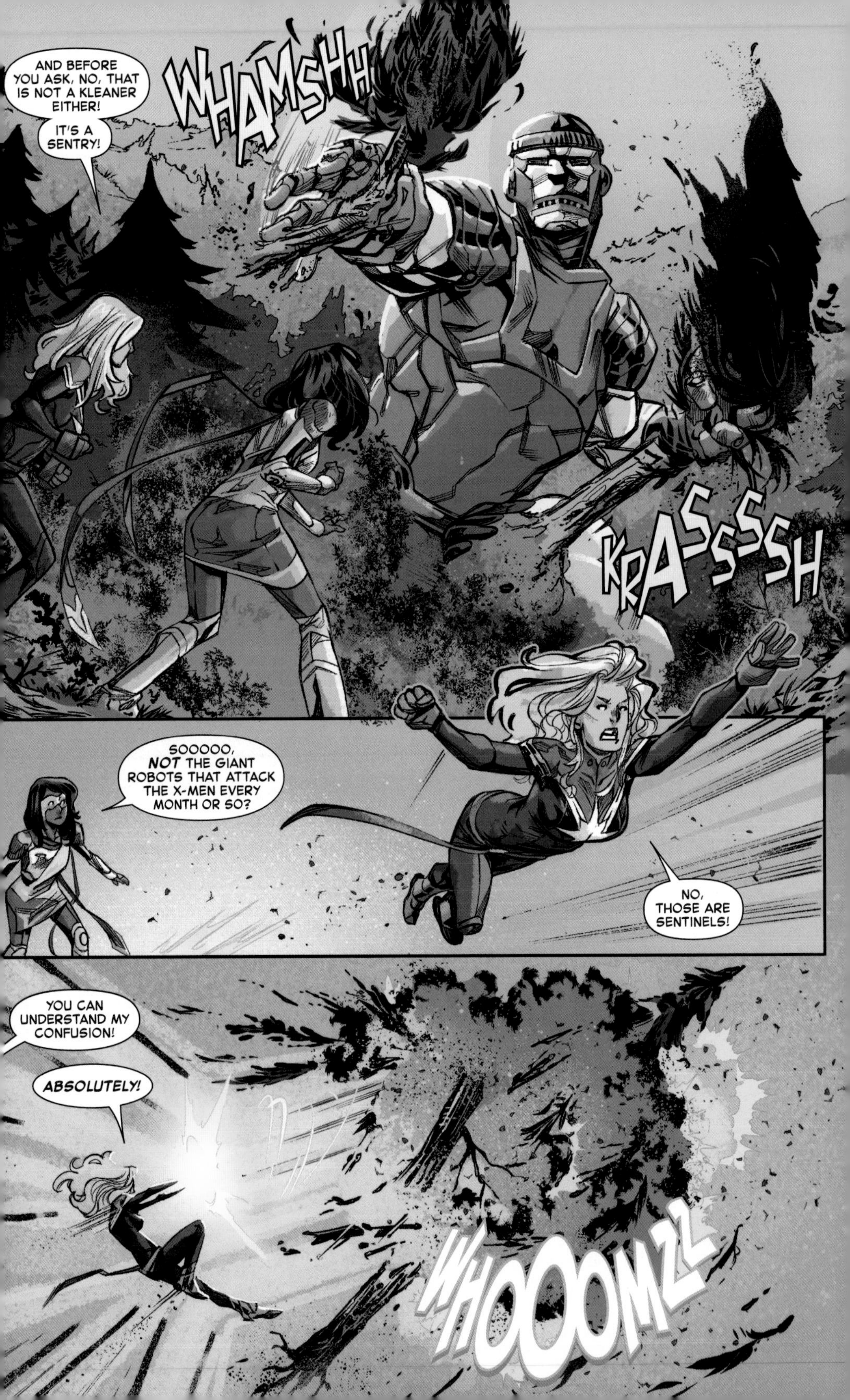
AND BEFORE YOU ASK, NO, THAT IS NOT A KLEANER EITHER!
IT'S A SENTRY!
WHAMSHH
KRASSSSH
SOOOOO, *NOT* THE GIANT ROBOTS THAT ATTACK THE X-MEN EVERY MONTH OR SO?
NO, THOSE ARE SENTINELS!
YOU CAN UNDERSTAND MY CONFUSION!
ABSOLUTELY!
WHOOOMZZ

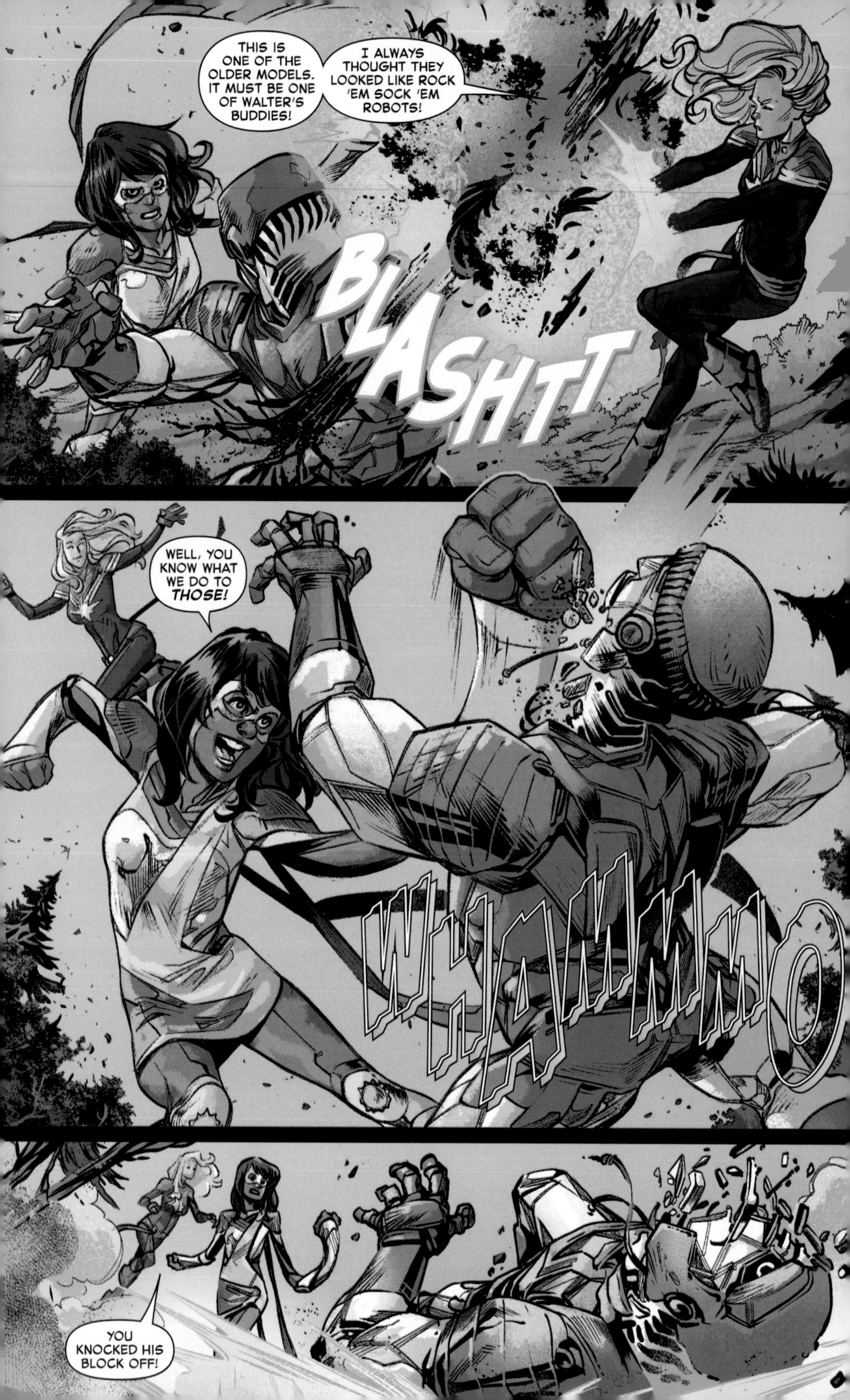
THIS IS ONE OF THE OLDER MODELS. IT MUST BE ONE OF WALTER'S BUDDIES!
I ALWAYS THOUGHT THEY LOOKED LIKE ROCK 'EM SOCK 'EM ROBOTS!
BLASHTT
WELL, YOU KNOW WHAT WE DO TO *THOSE!*
WHAMMMO
YOU KNOCKED HIS BLOCK OFF!

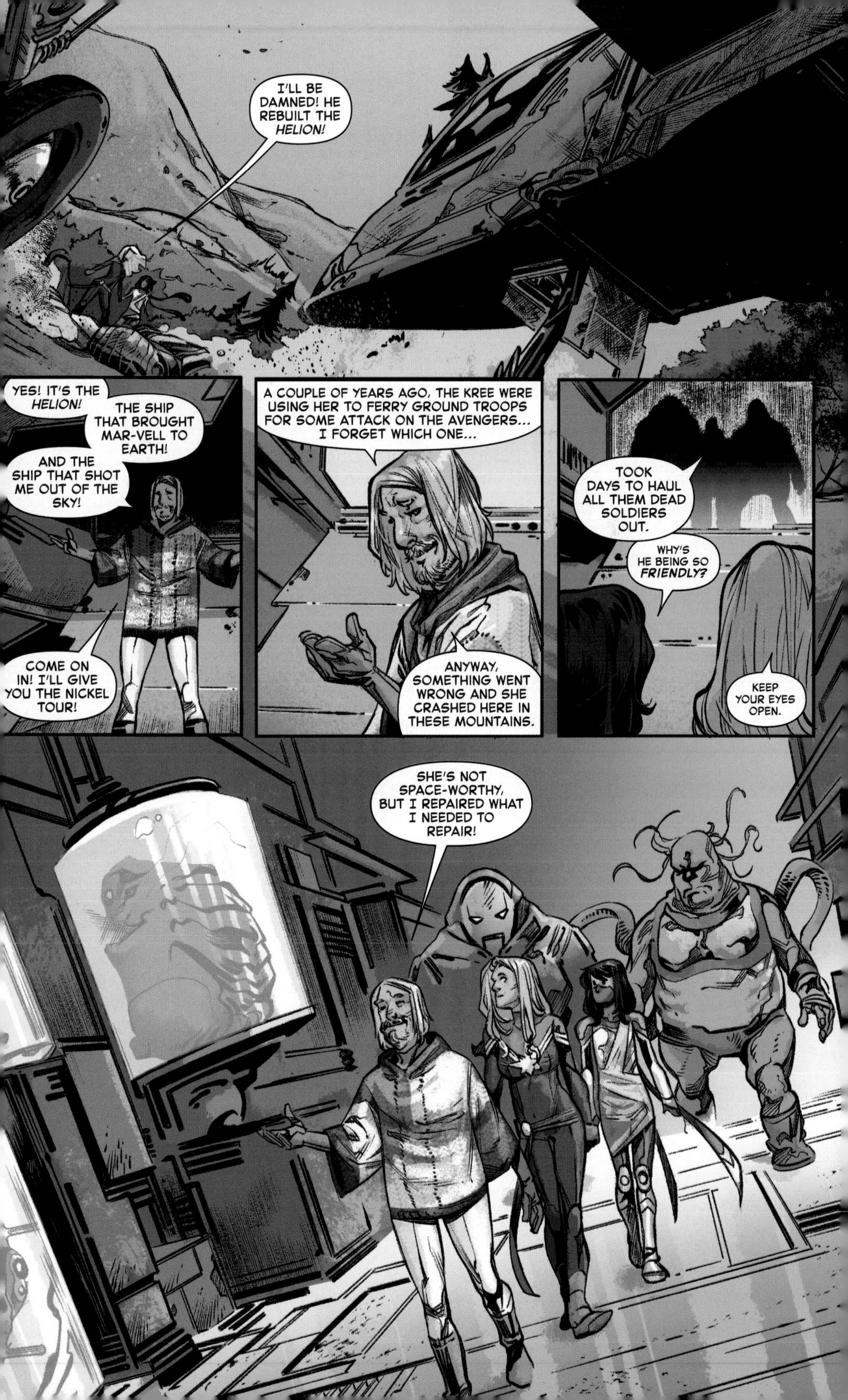
I'LL BE DAMNED! HE REBUILT THE *HELION!*
YES! IT'S THE *HELION!*
THE SHIP THAT BROUGHT MAR-VELL TO EARTH!
AND THE SHIP THAT SHOT ME OUT OF THE SKY!
COME ON IN! I'LL GIVE YOU THE NICKEL TOUR!
A COUPLE OF YEARS AGO, THE KREE WERE USING HER TO FERRY GROUND TROOPS FOR SOME ATTACK ON THE AVENGERS... I FORGET WHICH ONE...
ANYWAY, SOMETHING WENT WRONG AND SHE CRASHED HERE IN THESE MOUNTAINS.
TOOK DAYS TO HAUL ALL THEM DEAD SOLDIERS OUT.
WHY'S HE BEING SO *FRIENDLY?*
KEEP YOUR EYES OPEN.
SHE'S NOT SPACE-WORTHY, BUT I REPAIRED WHAT I NEEDED TO REPAIR!

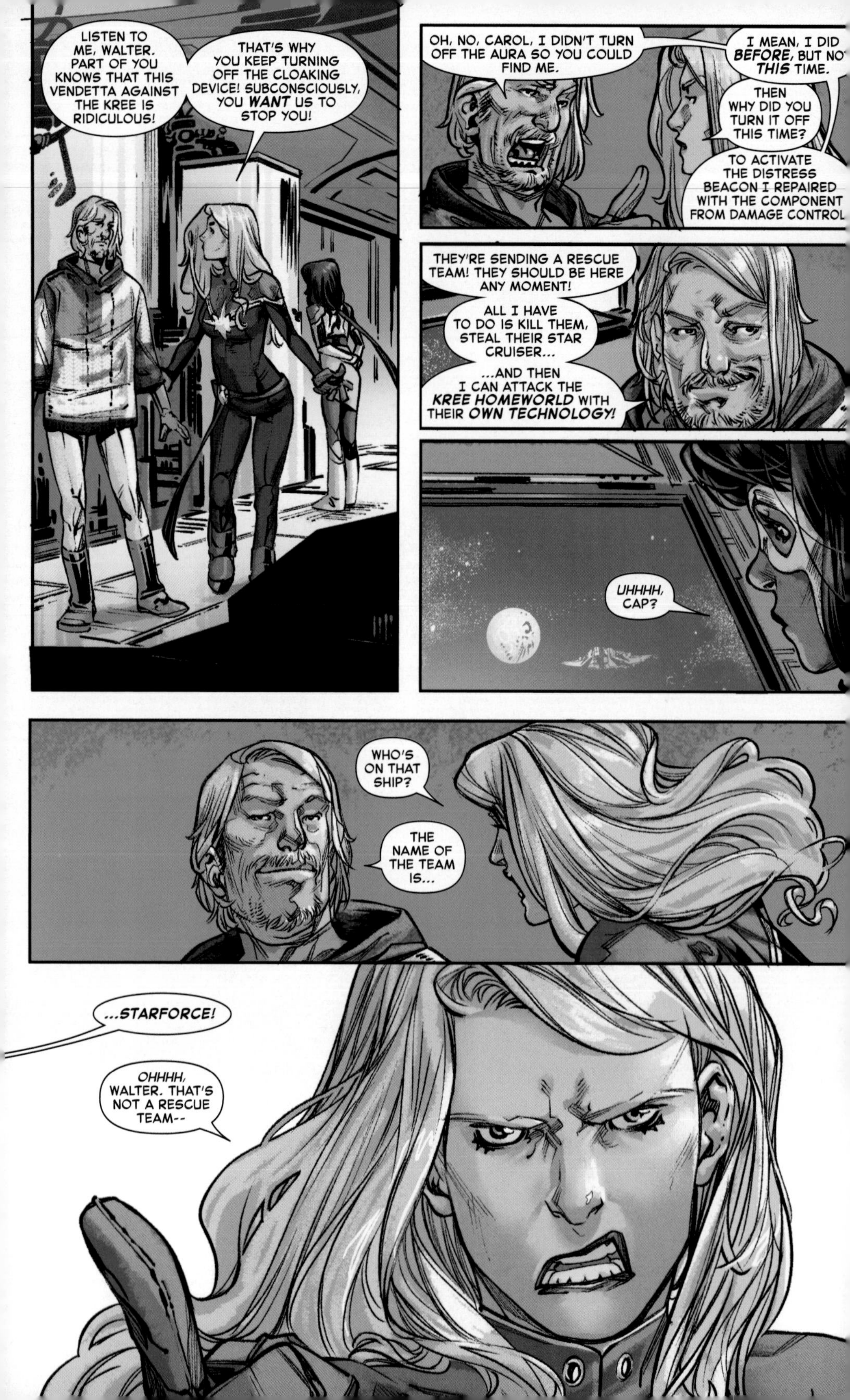

LISTEN TO ME, WALTER. PART OF YOU KNOWS THAT THIS VENDETTA AGAINST THE KREE IS RIDICULOUS!
THAT'S WHY YOU KEEP TURNING OFF THE CLOAKING DEVICE! SUBCONSCIOUSLY, YOU *WANT* US TO STOP YOU!
OH, NO, CAROL, I DIDN'T TURN OFF THE AURA SO YOU COULD FIND ME.
I MEAN, I DID *BEFORE,* BUT NOT *THIS* TIME.
THEN WHY DID YOU TURN IT OFF THIS TIME?
TO ACTIVATE THE DISTRESS BEACON I REPAIRED WITH THE COMPONENT FROM DAMAGE CONTROL
THEY'RE SENDING A RESCUE TEAM! THEY SHOULD BE HERE ANY MOMENT!
ALL I HAVE TO DO IS KILL THEM, STEAL THEIR STAR CRUISER...
...AND THEN I CAN ATTACK THE *KREE HOMEWORLD* WITH THEIR *OWN TECHNOLOGY!*
UHHHH, CAP?
WHO'S ON THAT SHIP?
THE NAME OF THE TEAM IS...
...STARFORCE!
OHHHH, WALTER. THAT'S NOT A RESCUE TEAM--

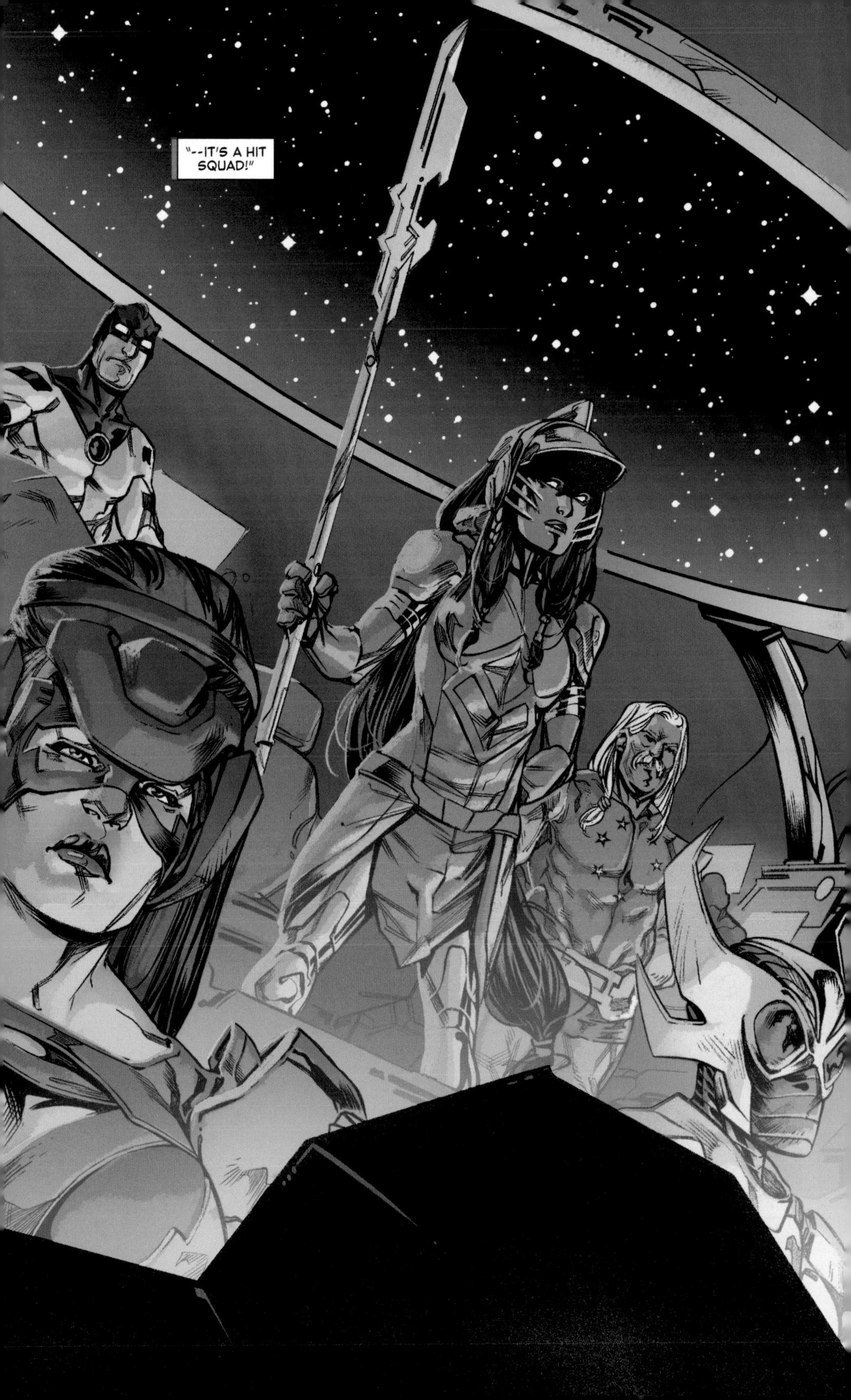
"--IT'S A HIT SQUAD!"

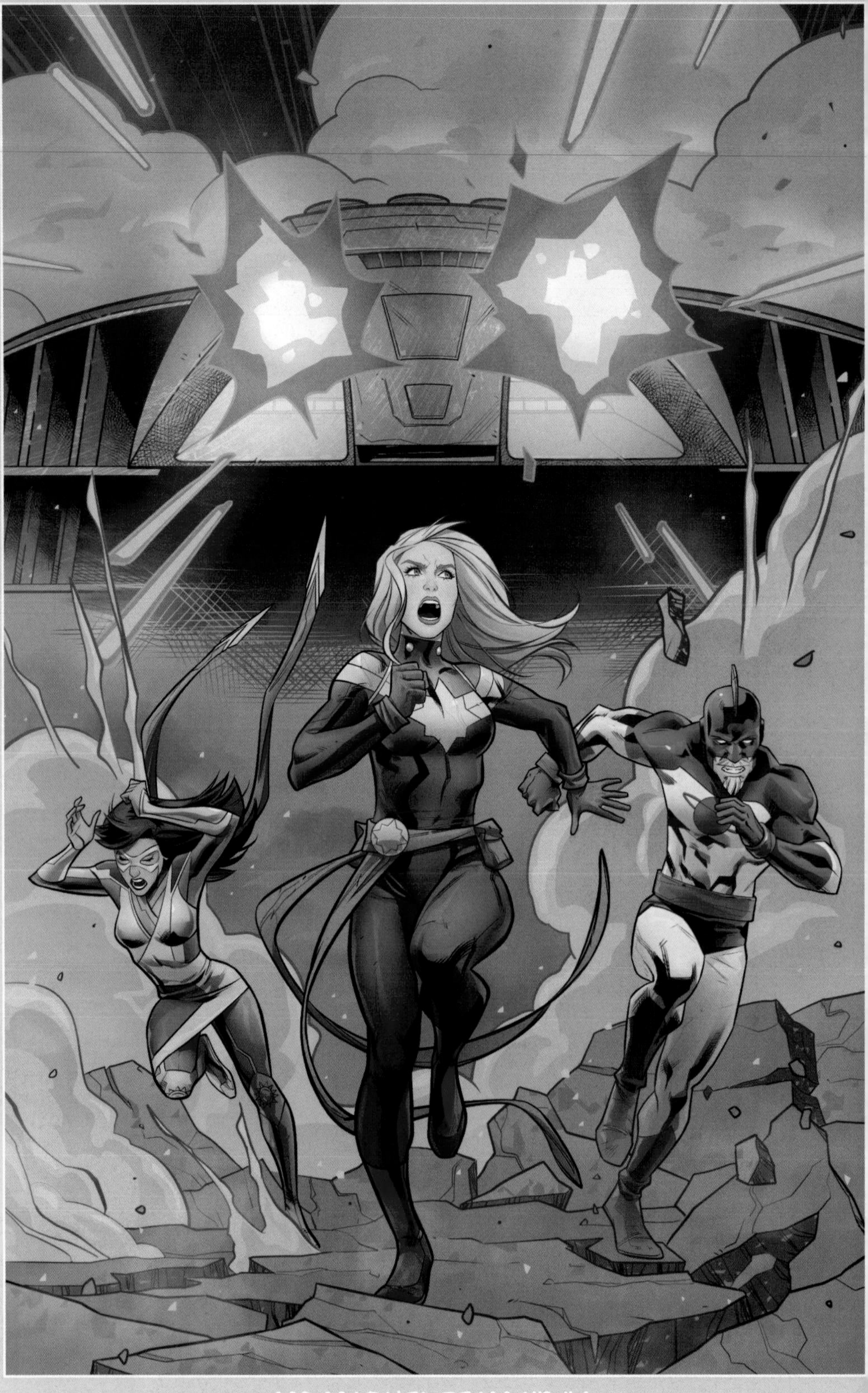

MS. MARVEL TEAM-UP #6

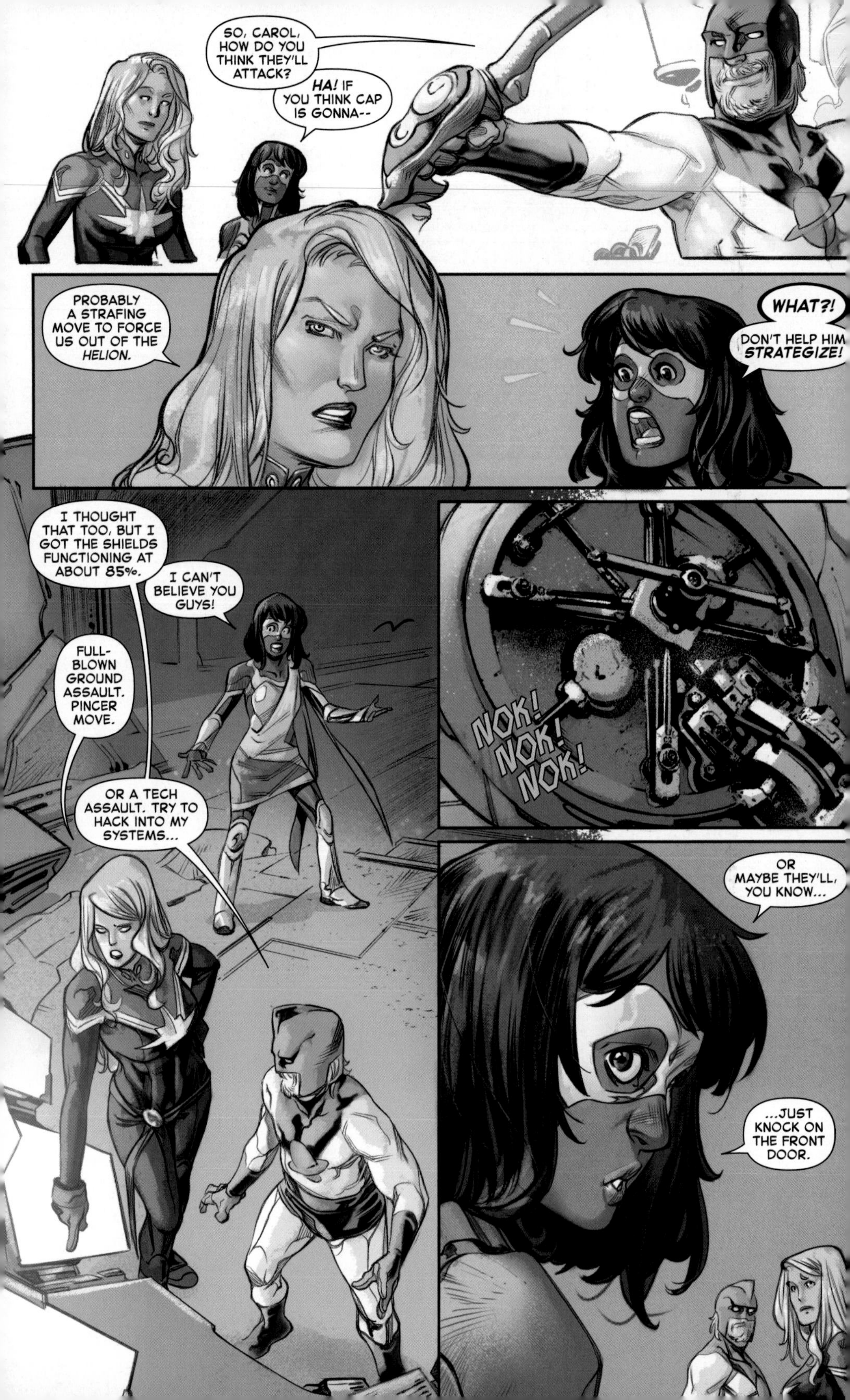
SO, CAROL, HOW DO YOU THINK THEY'LL ATTACK?
HA! IF YOU THINK CAP IS GONNA--
PROBABLY A STRAFING MOVE TO FORCE US OUT OF THE HELION.
WHAT?!
DON'T HELP HIM STRATEGIZE!
I THOUGHT THAT TOO, BUT I GOT THE SHIELDS FUNCTIONING AT ABOUT 85%.
I CAN'T BELIEVE YOU GUYS!
FULL-BLOWN GROUND ASSAULT. PINCER MOVE.
OR A TECH ASSAULT. TRY TO HACK INTO MY SYSTEMS...
NOK! NOK! NOK!
OR MAYBE THEY'LL, YOU KNOW...
...JUST KNOCK ON THE FRONT DOOR.

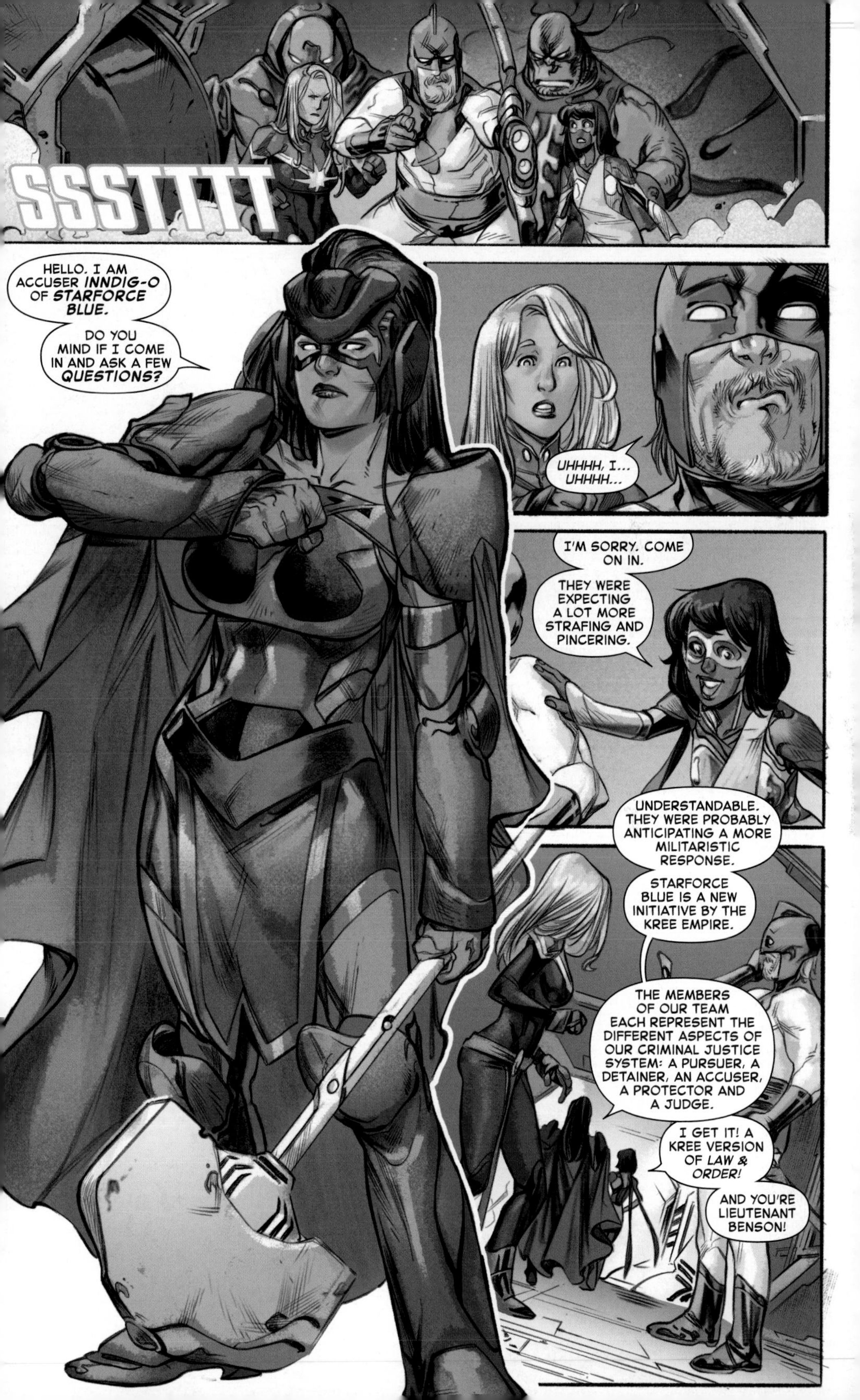
SSSTTTTT
HELLO. I AM ACCUSER INNDIG-O OF STARFORCE BLUE.
DO YOU MIND IF I COME IN AND ASK A FEW QUESTIONS?
UHHHH, I... UHHHH...
I'M SORRY. COME ON IN.
THEY WERE EXPECTING A LOT MORE STRAFING AND PINCERING.
UNDERSTANDABLE. THEY WERE PROBABLY ANTICIPATING A MORE MILITARISTIC RESPONSE.
STARFORCE BLUE IS A NEW INITIATIVE BY THE KREE EMPIRE.
THE MEMBERS OF OUR TEAM EACH REPRESENT THE DIFFERENT ASPECTS OF OUR CRIMINAL JUSTICE SYSTEM: A PURSUER, A DETAINER, AN ACCUSER, A PROTECTOR AND A JUDGE.
I GET IT! A KREE VERSION OF LAW & ORDER!
AND YOU'RE LIEUTENANT BENSON!

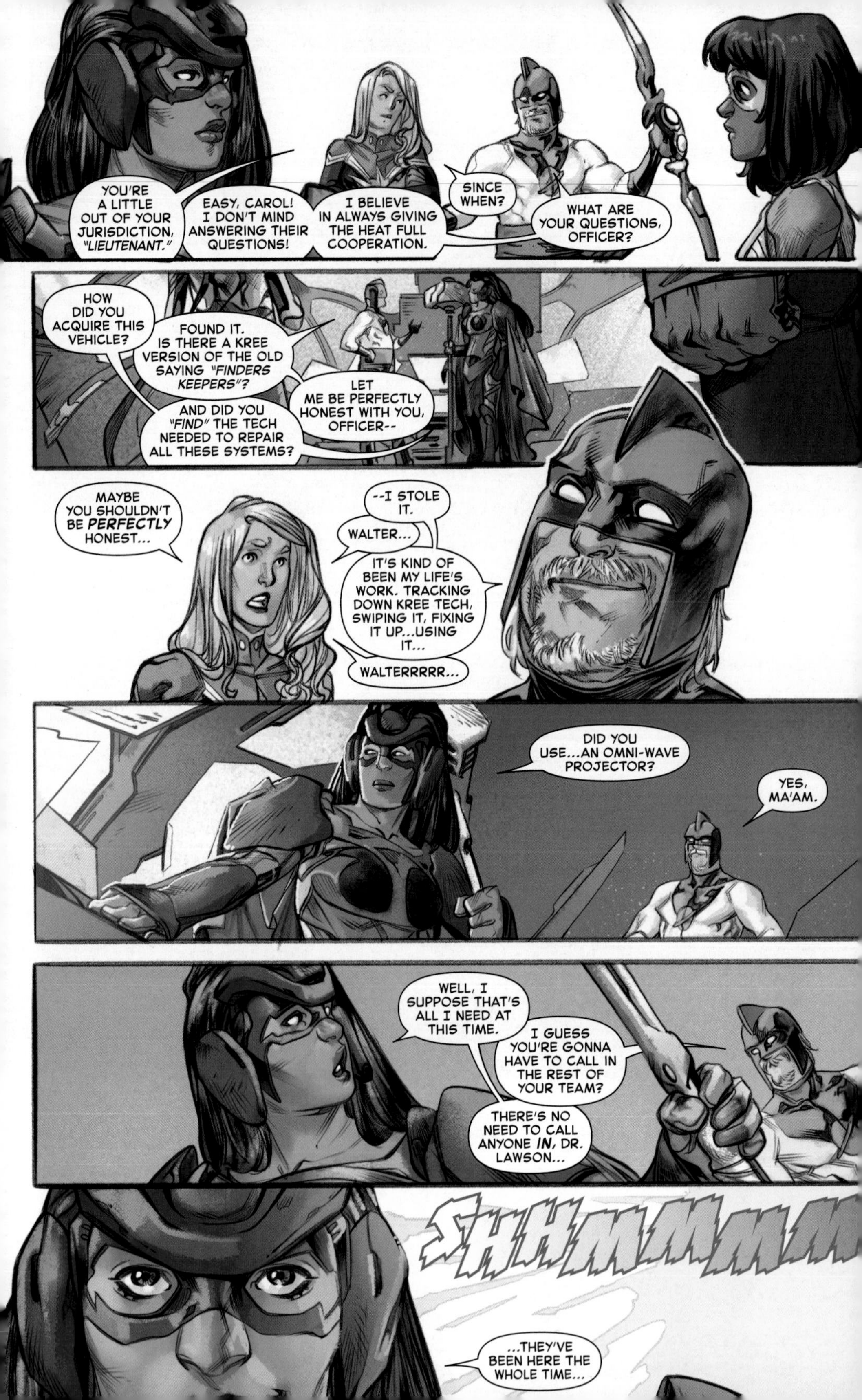
YOU'RE A LITTLE OUT OF YOUR JURISDICTION, "LIEUTENANT."
EASY, CAROL! I DON'T MIND ANSWERING THEIR QUESTIONS!
I BELIEVE IN ALWAYS GIVING THE HEAT FULL COOPERATION.
SINCE WHEN?
WHAT ARE YOUR QUESTIONS, OFFICER?
HOW DID YOU ACQUIRE THIS VEHICLE?
FOUND IT. IS THERE A KREE VERSION OF THE OLD SAYING "FINDERS KEEPERS"?
AND DID YOU "FIND" THE TECH NEEDED TO REPAIR ALL THESE SYSTEMS?
LET ME BE PERFECTLY HONEST WITH YOU, OFFICER--
MAYBE YOU SHOULDN'T BE PERFECTLY HONEST...
--I STOLE IT.
WALTER...
IT'S KIND OF BEEN MY LIFE'S WORK. TRACKING DOWN KREE TECH, SWIPING IT, FIXING IT UP...USING IT...
WALTERRRRR...
DID YOU USE...AN OMNI-WAVE PROJECTOR?
YES, MA'AM.
WELL, I SUPPOSE THAT'S ALL I NEED AT THIS TIME.
I GUESS YOU'RE GONNA HAVE TO CALL IN THE REST OF YOUR TEAM?
THERE'S NO NEED TO CALL ANYONE IN, DR. LAWSON...
SHHMMMMM
...THEY'VE BEEN HERE THE WHOLE TIME...

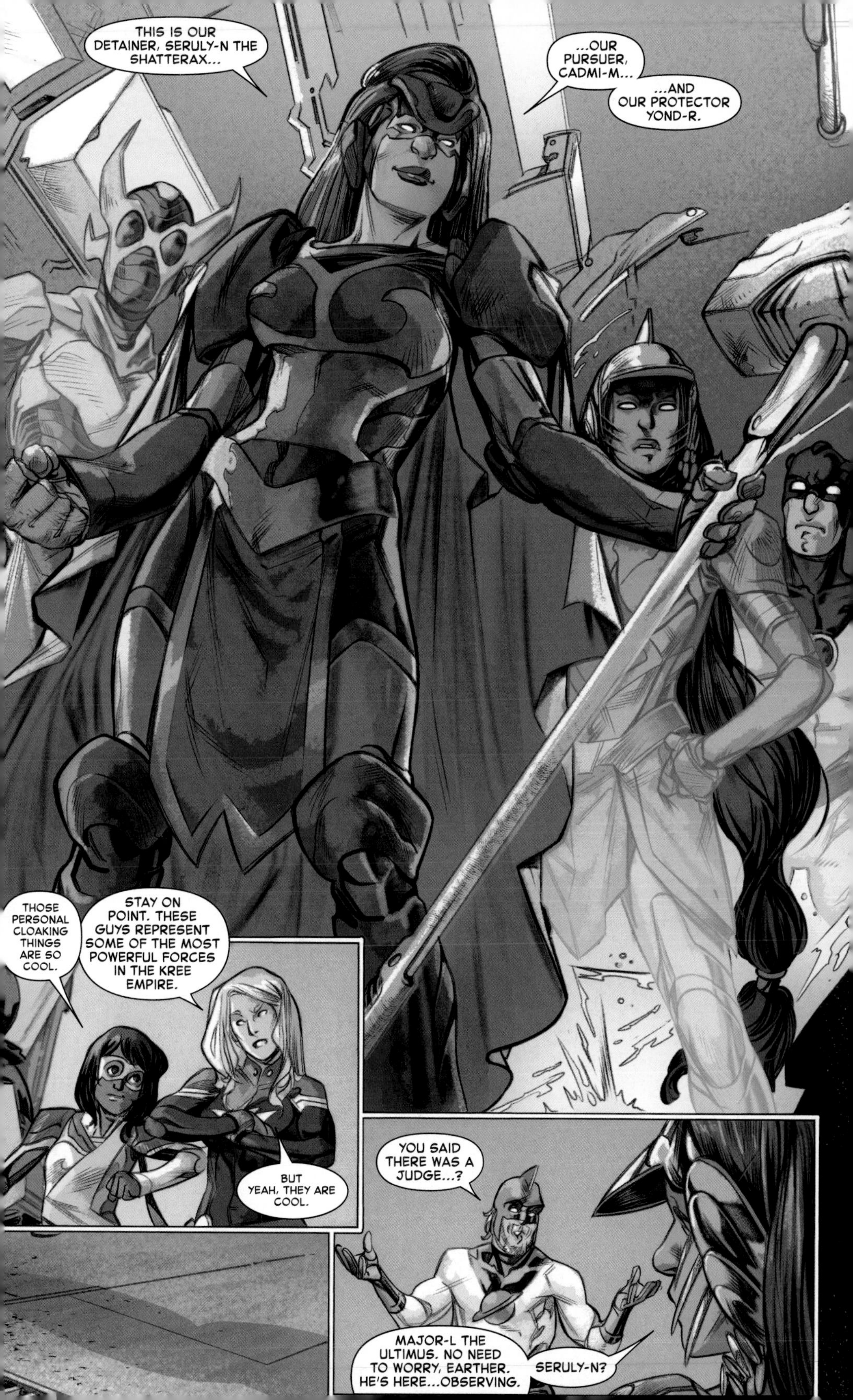
THIS IS OUR DETAINER, SERULY-N THE SHATTERAX...
...OUR PURSUER, CADMI-M...
...AND OUR PROTECTOR YOND-R.
THOSE PERSONAL CLOAKING THINGS ARE SO COOL.
STAY ON POINT. THESE GUYS REPRESENT SOME OF THE MOST POWERFUL FORCES IN THE KREE EMPIRE.
BUT YEAH, THEY ARE COOL.
YOU SAID THERE WAS A JUDGE...?
MAJOR-L THE ULTIMUS. NO NEED TO WORRY, EARTHER. HE'S HERE...OBSERVING.
SERULY-N?

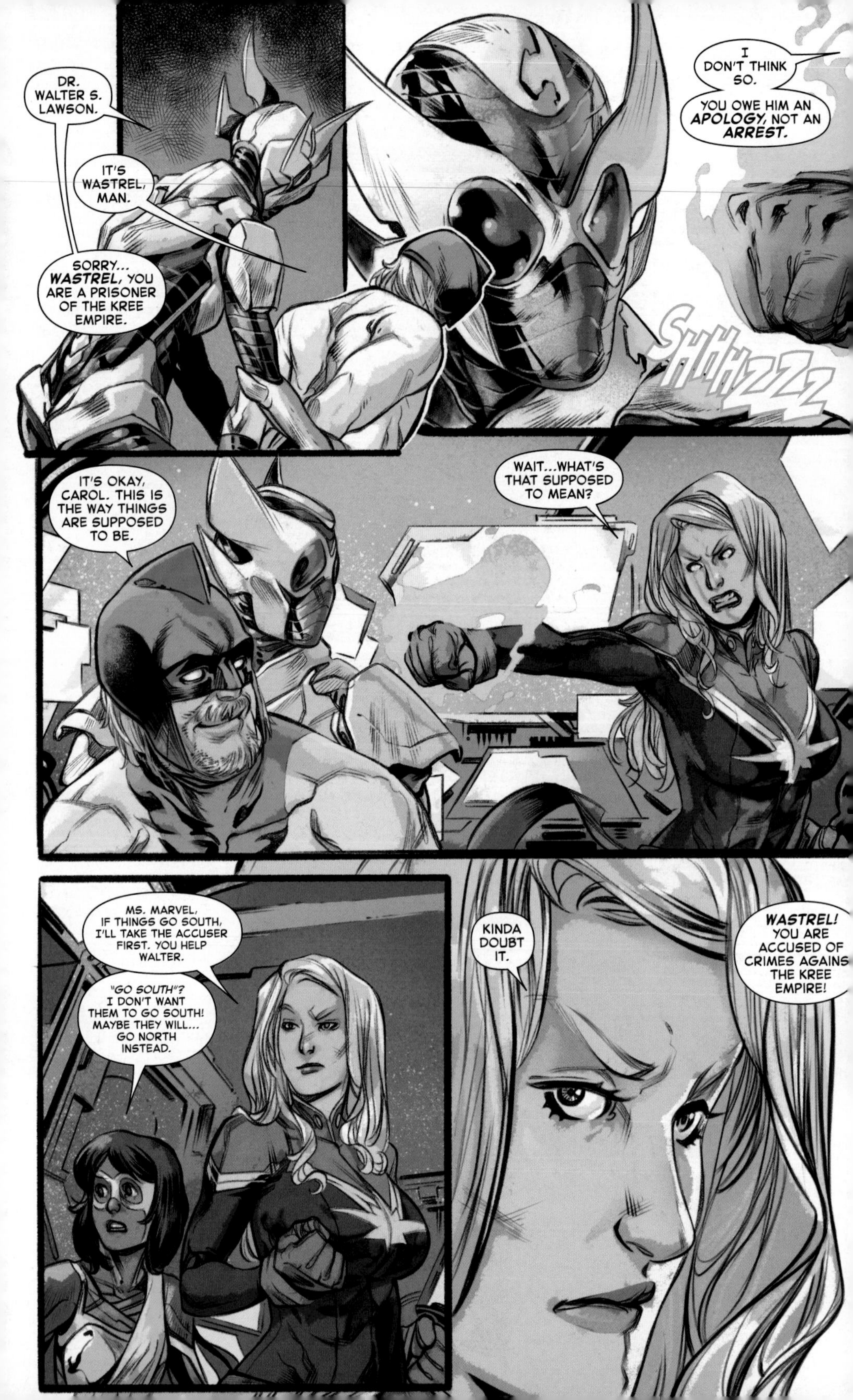
DR. WALTER S. LAWSON.
IT'S WASTREL, MAN.
SORRY... WASTREL, YOU ARE A PRISONER OF THE KREE EMPIRE.
I DON'T THINK SO.
YOU OWE HIM AN APOLOGY, NOT AN ARREST.
SHHHZZZz
IT'S OKAY, CAROL. THIS IS THE WAY THINGS ARE SUPPOSED TO BE.
WAIT...WHAT'S THAT SUPPOSED TO MEAN?
MS. MARVEL, IF THINGS GO SOUTH, I'LL TAKE THE ACCUSER FIRST. YOU HELP WALTER.
"GO SOUTH"? I DON'T WANT THEM TO GO SOUTH! MAYBE THEY WILL... GO NORTH INSTEAD.
KINDA DOUBT IT.
WASTREL! YOU ARE ACCUSED OF CRIMES AGAINS THE KREE EMPIRE!

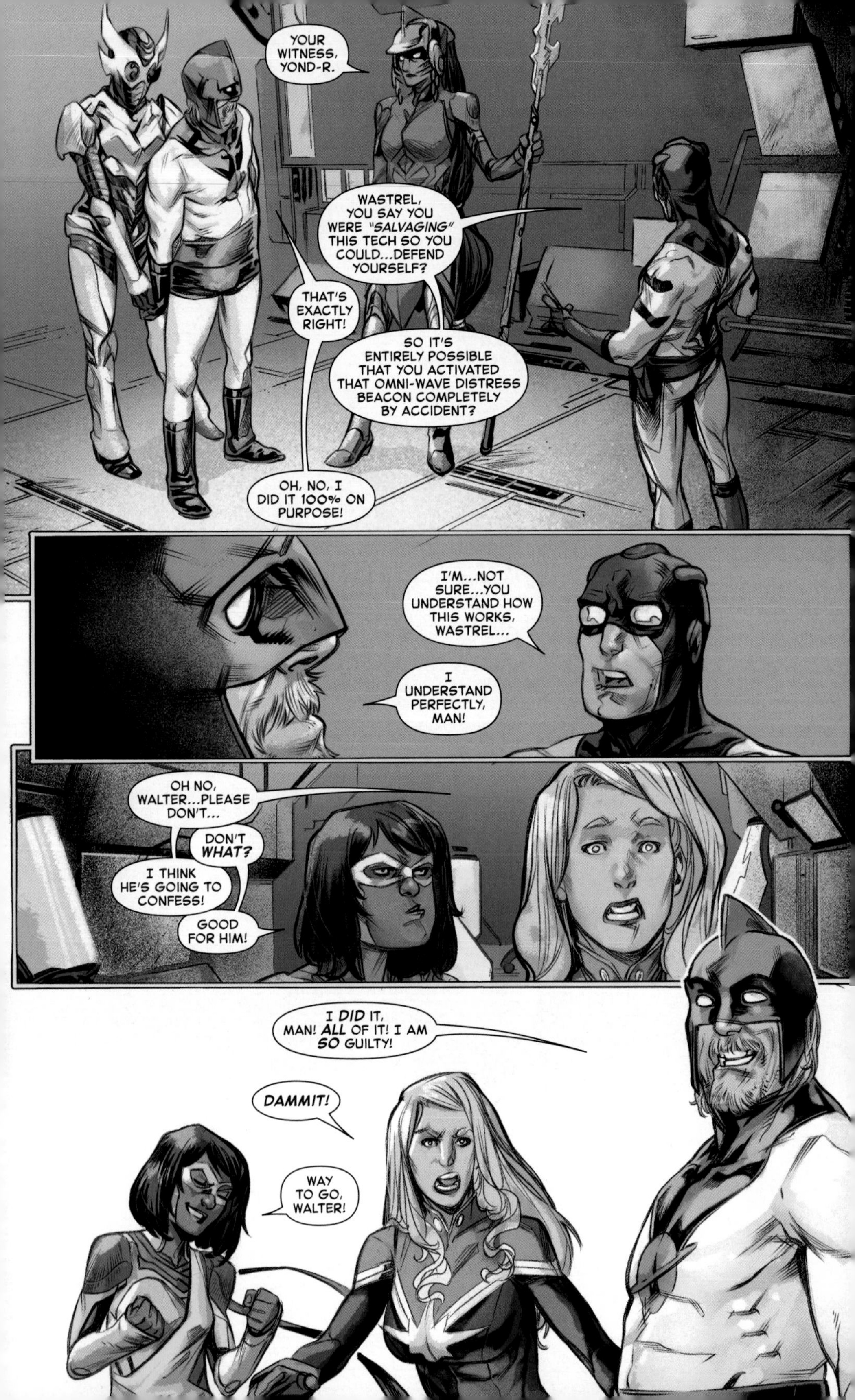
YOUR WITNESS, YOND-R.
WASTREL, YOU SAY YOU WERE "SALVAGING" THIS TECH SO YOU COULD...DEFEND YOURSELF?
THAT'S EXACTLY RIGHT!
SO IT'S ENTIRELY POSSIBLE THAT YOU ACTIVATED THAT OMNI-WAVE DISTRESS BEACON COMPLETELY BY ACCIDENT?
OH, NO, I DID IT 100% ON PURPOSE!
I'M...NOT SURE...YOU UNDERSTAND HOW THIS WORKS, WASTREL...
I UNDERSTAND PERFECTLY, MAN!
OH NO, WALTER...PLEASE DON'T...
DON'T *WHAT?*
I THINK HE'S GOING TO CONFESS!
GOOD FOR HIM!
I *DID* IT, MAN! *ALL* OF IT! I AM *SO* GUILTY!
DAMMIT!
WAY TO GO, WALTER!

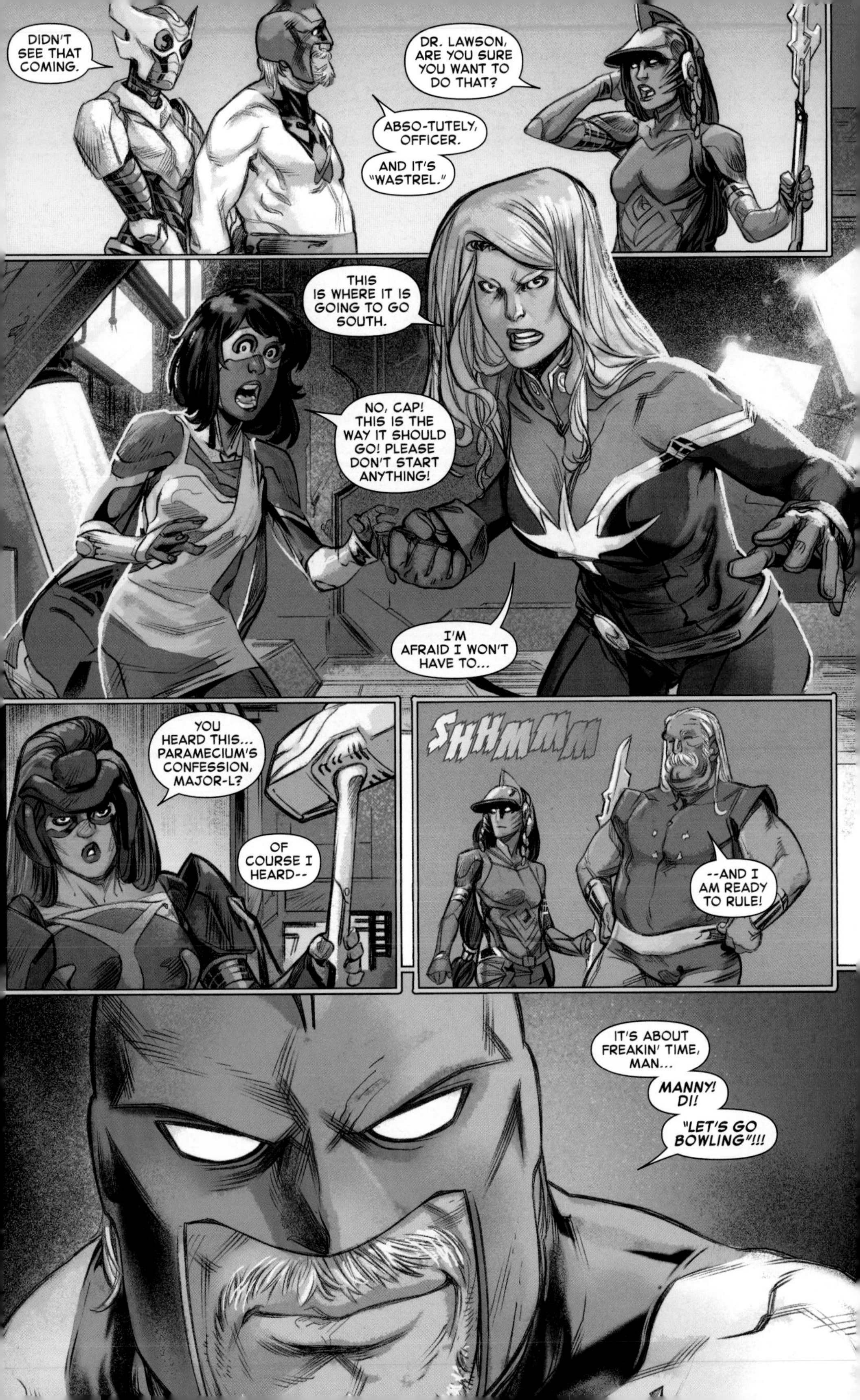
DIDN'T SEE THAT COMING.
DR. LAWSON, ARE YOU SURE YOU WANT TO DO THAT?
ABSO-TUTELY, OFFICER.
AND IT'S "WASTREL."
THIS IS WHERE IT IS GOING TO GO SOUTH.
NO, CAP! THIS IS THE WAY IT SHOULD GO! PLEASE DON'T START ANYTHING!
I'M AFRAID I WON'T HAVE TO...
YOU HEARD THIS... PARAMECIUM'S CONFESSION, MAJOR-L?
OF COURSE I HEARD--
SHHMMM
--AND I AM READY TO RULE!
IT'S ABOUT FREAKIN' TIME, MAN...
MANNY! DI!
"LET'S GO BOWLING"!!!

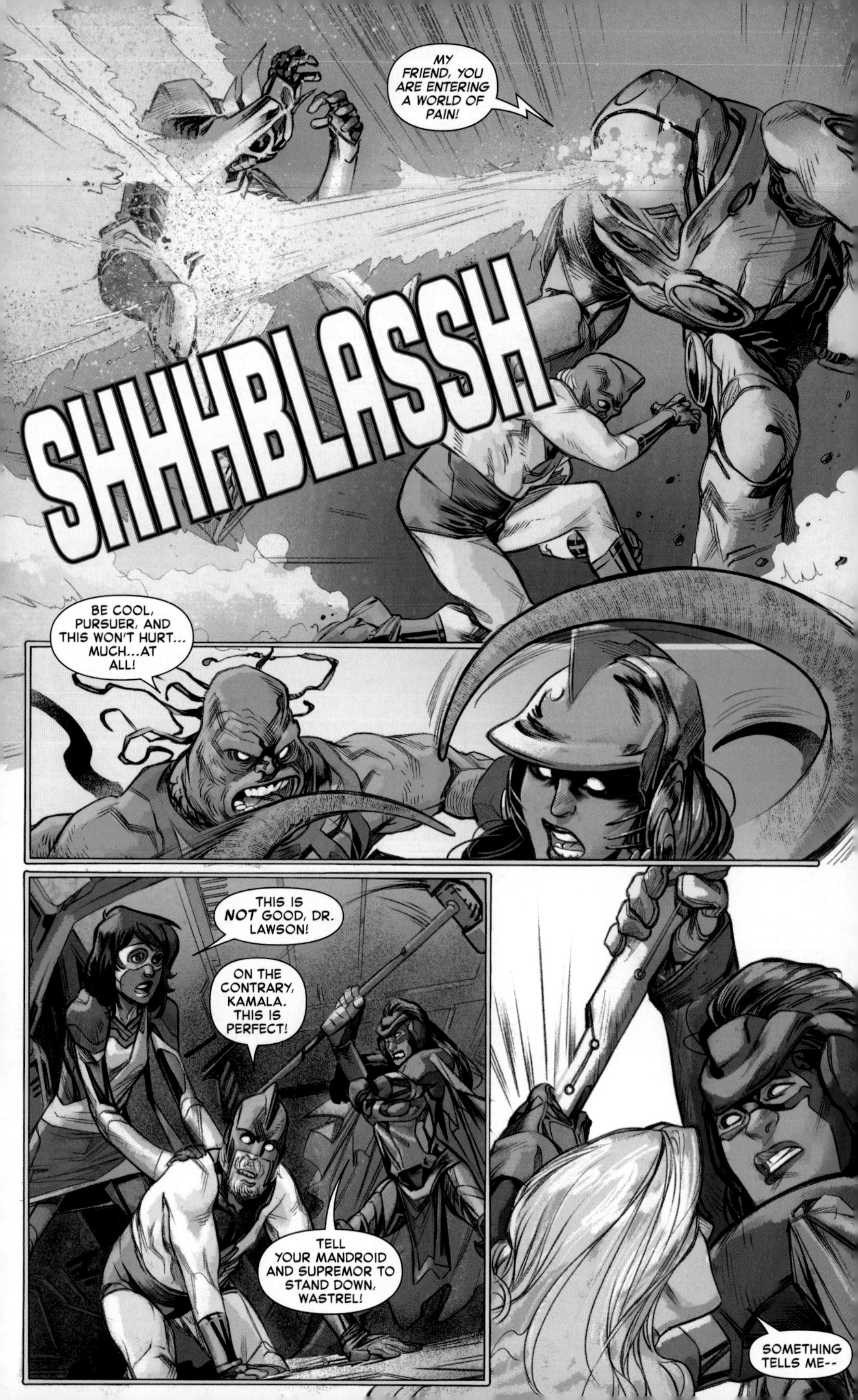
MY FRIEND, YOU ARE ENTERING A WORLD OF PAIN!
SHHHBLASSH
BE COOL, PURSUER, AND THIS WON'T HURT... MUCH...AT ALL!
THIS IS NOT GOOD, DR. LAWSON!
ON THE CONTRARY, KAMALA. THIS IS PERFECT!
TELL YOUR MANDROID AND SUPREMOR TO STAND DOWN, WASTREL!
SOMETHING TELLS ME--

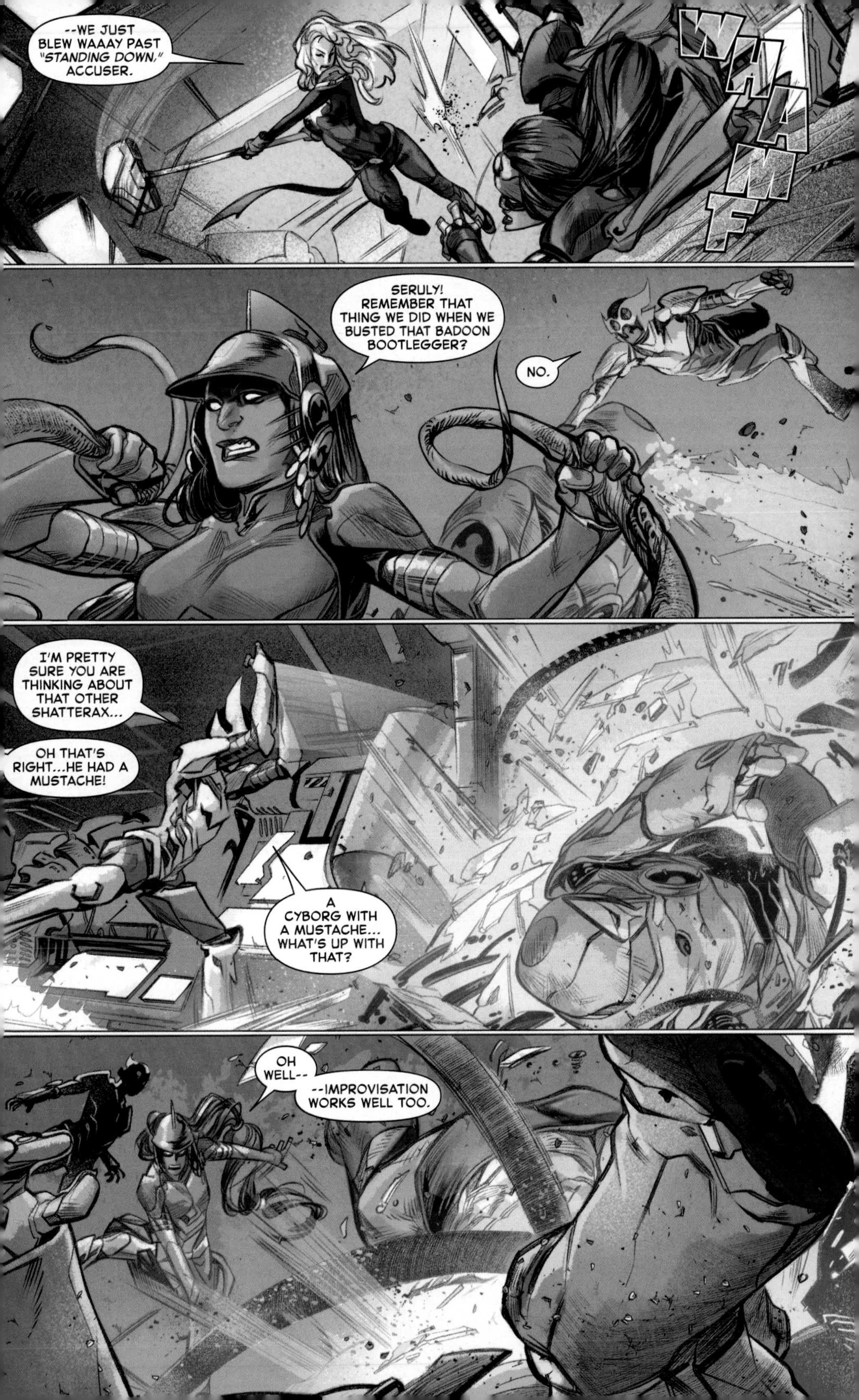
--WE JUST BLEW WAAAY PAST "STANDING DOWN," ACCUSER.
WHAMF
SERULY! REMEMBER THAT THING WE DID WHEN WE BUSTED THAT BADOON BOOTLEGGER?
NO.
I'M PRETTY SURE YOU ARE THINKING ABOUT THAT OTHER SHATTERAX...
OH THAT'S RIGHT...HE HAD A MUSTACHE!
A CYBORG WITH A MUSTACHE... WHAT'S UP WITH THAT?
OH WELL--
--IMPROVISATION WORKS WELL TOO.

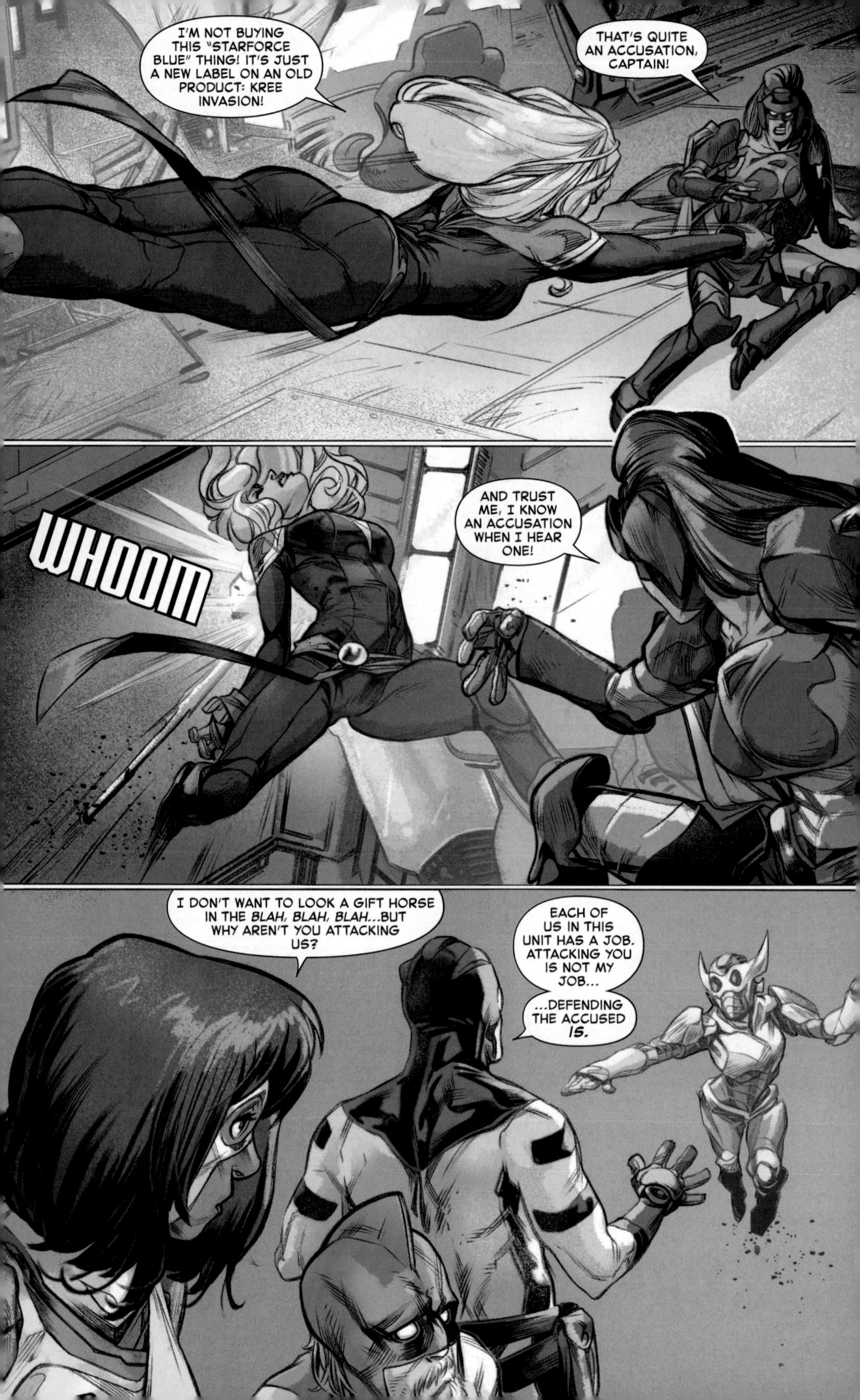
I'M NOT BUYING THIS "STARFORCE BLUE" THING! IT'S JUST A NEW LABEL ON AN OLD PRODUCT: KREE INVASION!
THAT'S QUITE AN ACCUSATION, CAPTAIN!
WHOOM
AND TRUST ME, I KNOW AN ACCUSATION WHEN I HEAR ONE!
I DON'T WANT TO LOOK A GIFT HORSE IN THE *BLAH, BLAH, BLAH*...BUT WHY AREN'T YOU ATTACKING US?
EACH OF US IN THIS UNIT HAS A JOB. ATTACKING YOU IS NOT MY JOB...
...DEFENDING THE ACCUSED *IS.*

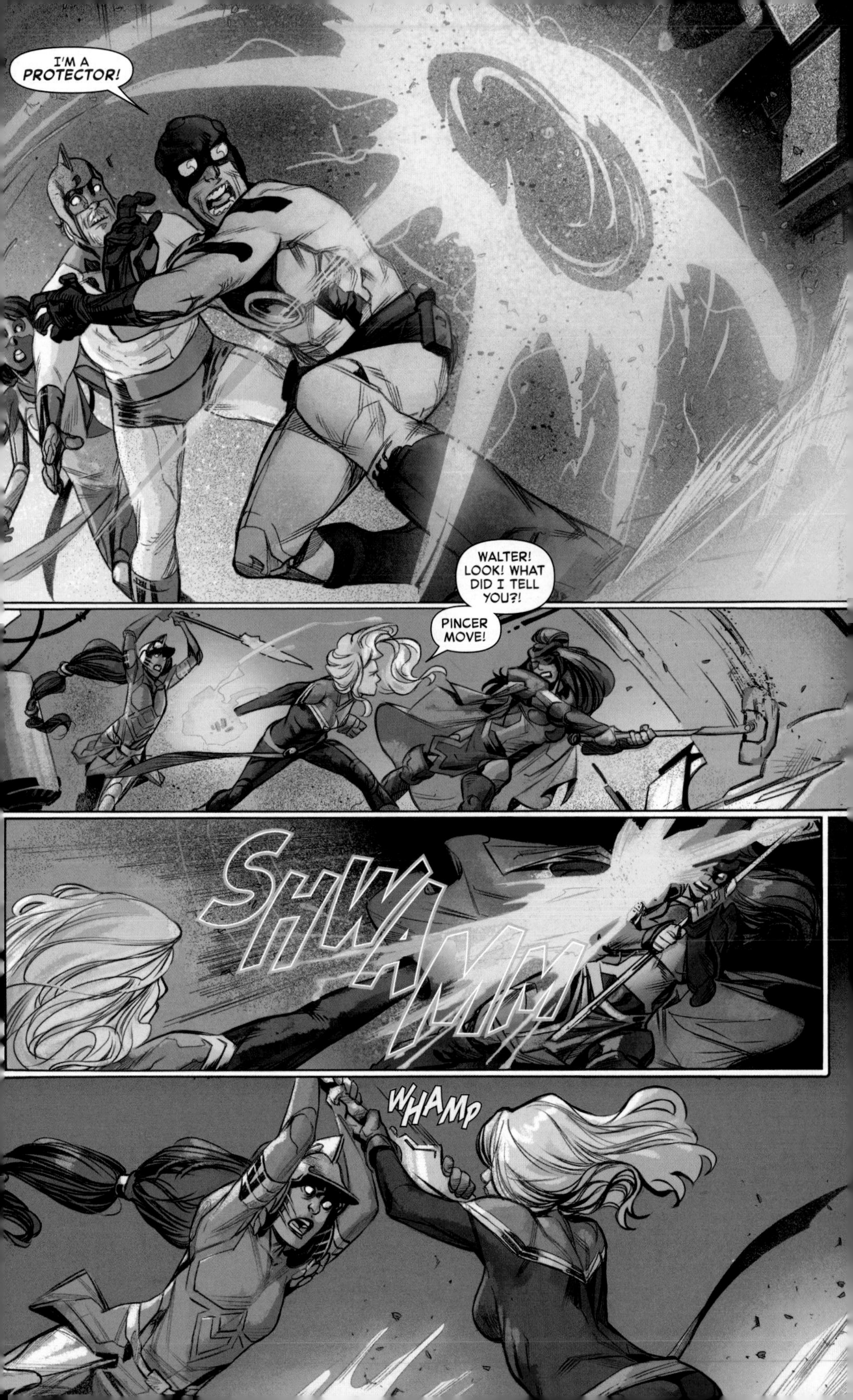
I'M A PROTECTOR!
WALTER! LOOK! WHAT DID I TELL YOU?!
PINCER MOVE!
SHWAMM
WHAMP

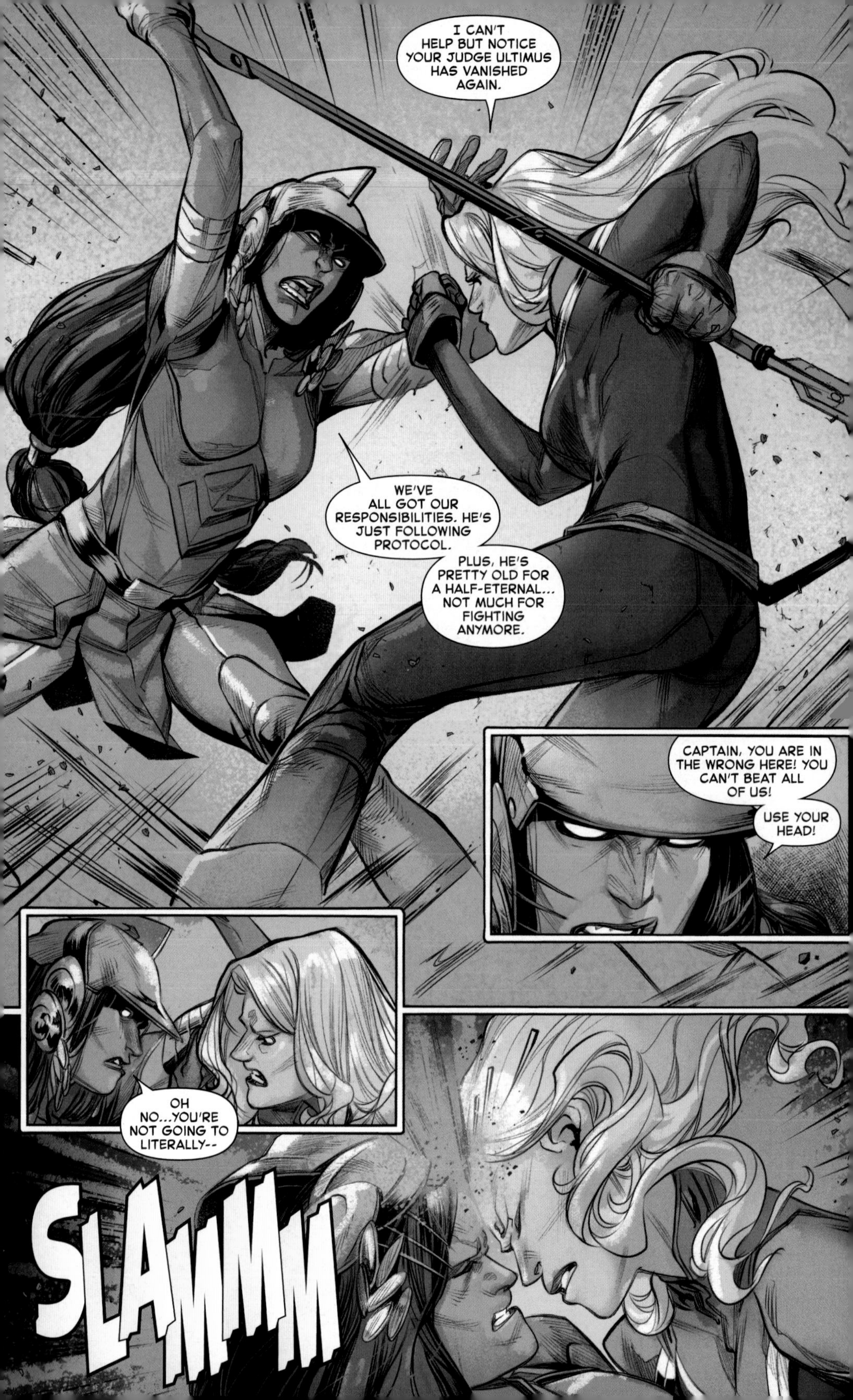
I CAN'T HELP BUT NOTICE YOUR JUDGE ULTIMUS HAS VANISHED AGAIN.
WE'VE ALL GOT OUR RESPONSIBILITIES. HE'S JUST FOLLOWING PROTOCOL.
PLUS, HE'S PRETTY OLD FOR A HALF-ETERNAL... NOT MUCH FOR FIGHTING ANYMORE.
CAPTAIN, YOU ARE IN THE WRONG HERE! YOU CAN'T BEAT ALL OF US!
USE YOUR HEAD!
OH NO...YOU'RE NOT GOING TO LITERALLY--
SLAMMM

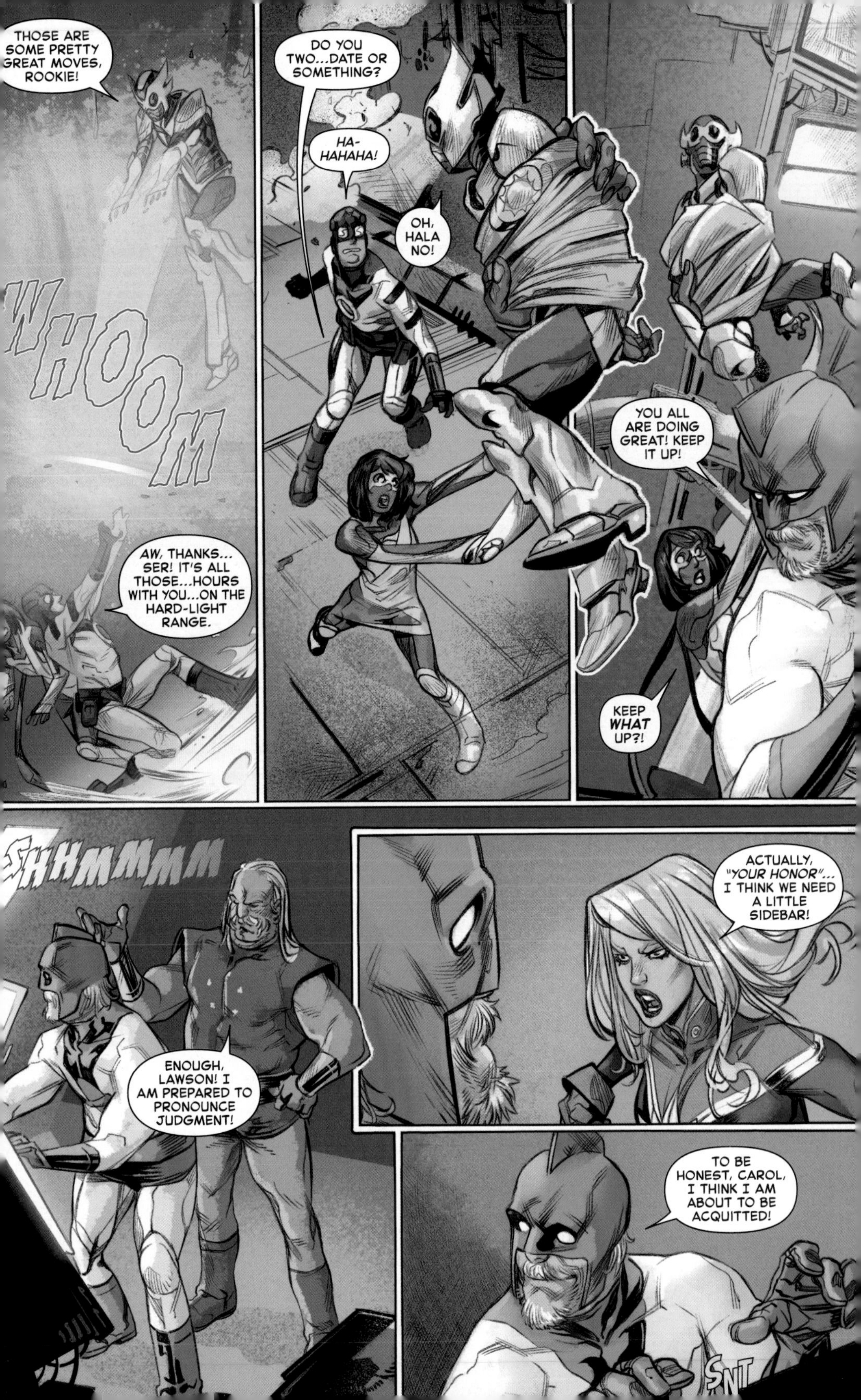
THOSE ARE SOME PRETTY GREAT MOVES, ROOKIE!
WHOOM
AW, THANKS... SER! IT'S ALL THOSE...HOURS WITH YOU...ON THE HARD-LIGHT RANGE.
DO YOU TWO...DATE OR SOMETHING?
HA-HAHAHA!
OH, HALA NO!
YOU ALL ARE DOING GREAT! KEEP IT UP!
KEEP WHAT UP?!
SHHMMMM
ENOUGH, LAWSON! I AM PREPARED TO PRONOUNCE JUDGMENT!
ACTUALLY, "YOUR HONOR"... I THINK WE NEED A LITTLE SIDEBAR!
TO BE HONEST, CAROL, I THINK I AM ABOUT TO BE ACQUITTED!
SNT

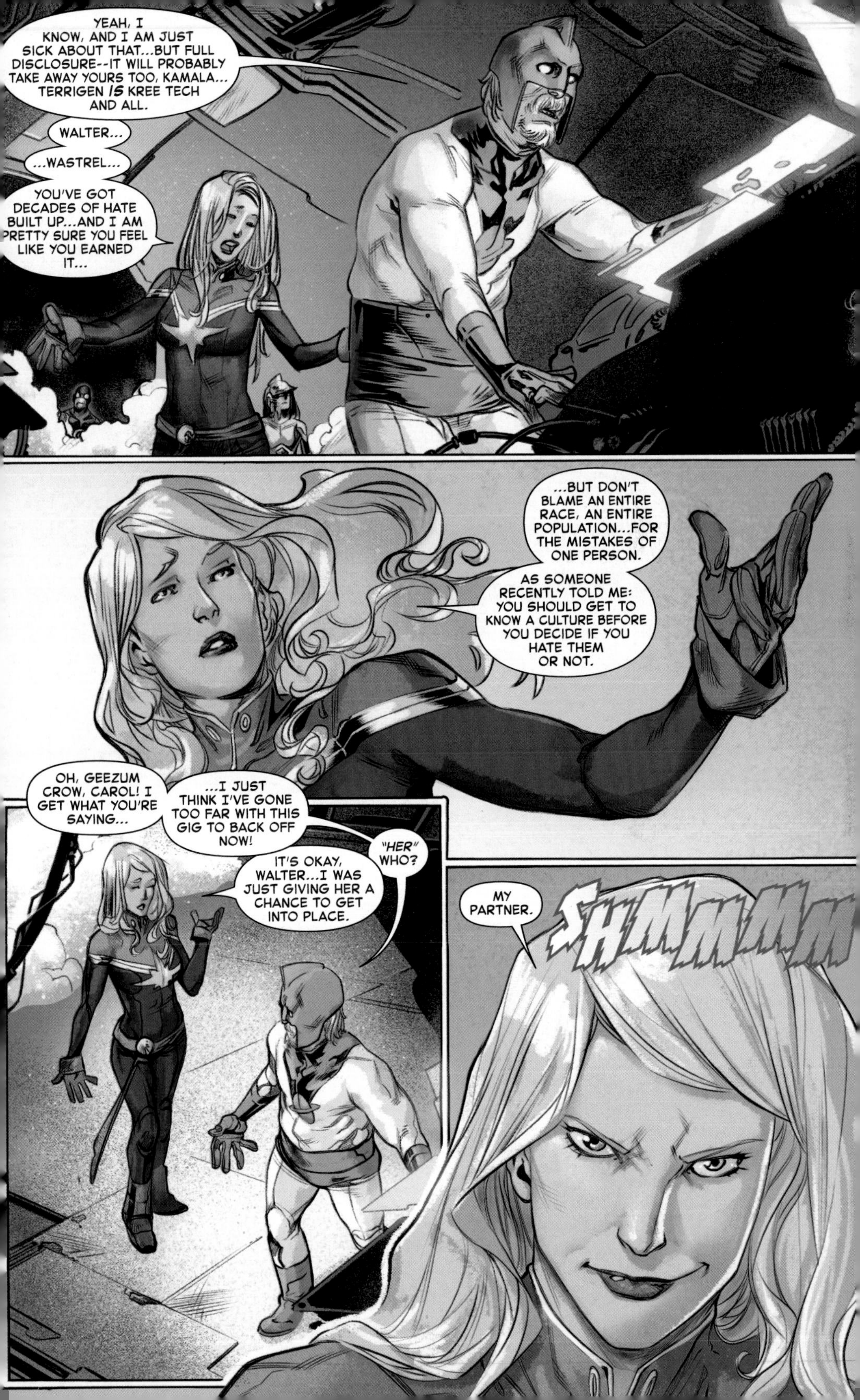
YEAH, I KNOW, AND I AM JUST SICK ABOUT THAT...BUT FULL DISCLOSURE--IT WILL PROBABLY TAKE AWAY YOURS TOO, KAMALA... TERRIGEN *IS* KREE TECH AND ALL.
WALTER...
...WASTREL...
YOU'VE GOT DECADES OF HATE BUILT UP...AND I AM PRETTY SURE YOU FEEL LIKE YOU EARNED IT...
...BUT DON'T BLAME AN ENTIRE RACE, AN ENTIRE POPULATION...FOR THE MISTAKES OF ONE PERSON.
AS SOMEONE RECENTLY TOLD ME: YOU SHOULD GET TO KNOW A CULTURE BEFORE YOU DECIDE IF YOU HATE THEM OR NOT.
OH, GEEZUM CROW, CAROL! I GET WHAT YOU'RE SAYING...
...I JUST THINK I'VE GONE TOO FAR WITH THIS GIG TO BACK OFF NOW!
IT'S OKAY, WALTER...I WAS JUST GIVING HER A CHANCE TO GET INTO PLACE.
"*HER*" WHO?
MY PARTNER.
SHMMMM

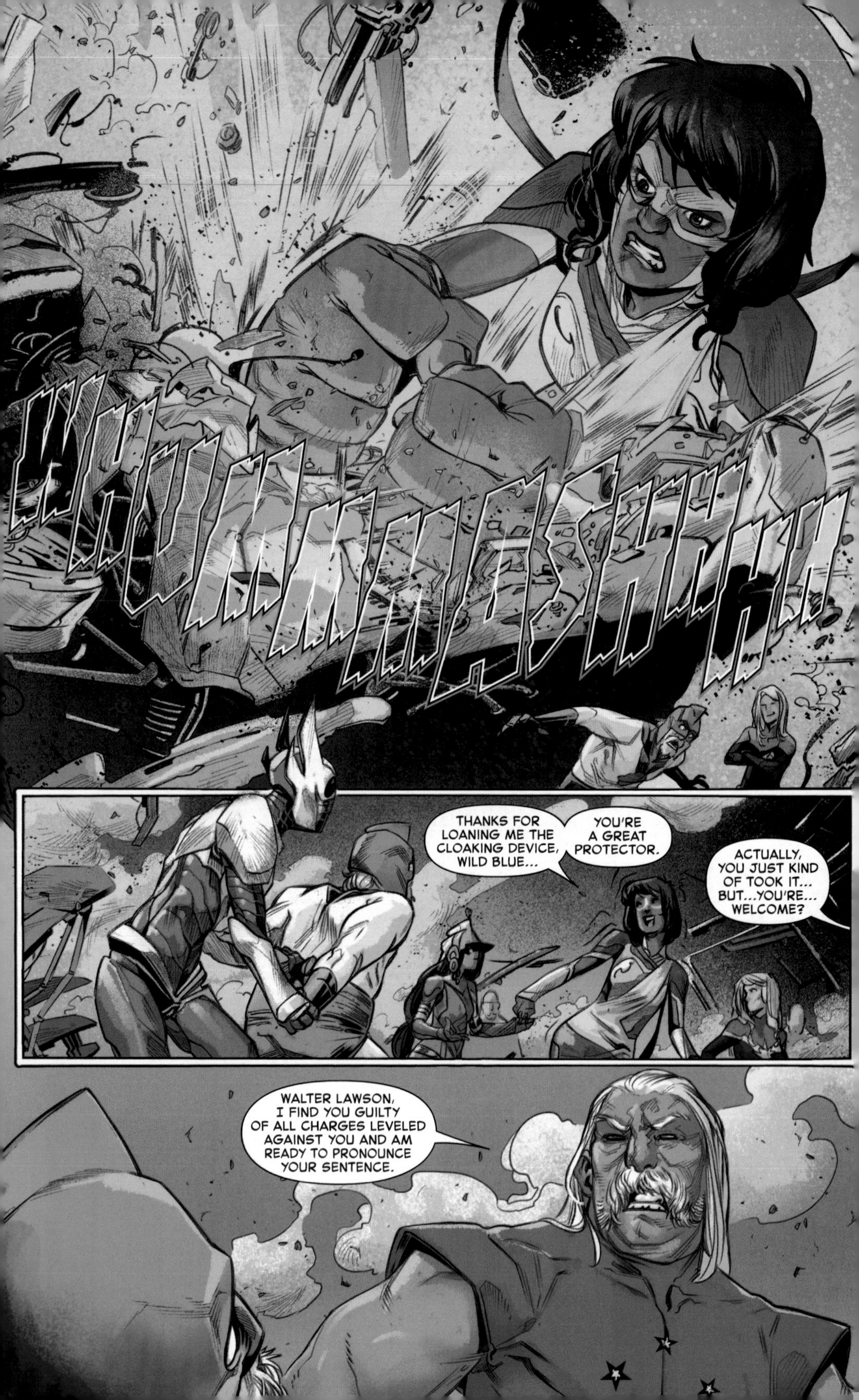

WHOOMMMMMASHHHH
THANKS FOR LOANING ME THE CLOAKING DEVICE, WILD BLUE...
YOU'RE A GREAT PROTECTOR.
ACTUALLY, YOU JUST KIND OF TOOK IT... BUT...YOU'RE... WELCOME?
WALTER LAWSON, I FIND YOU GUILTY OF ALL CHARGES LEVELED AGAINST YOU AND AM READY TO PRONOUNCE YOUR SENTENCE.

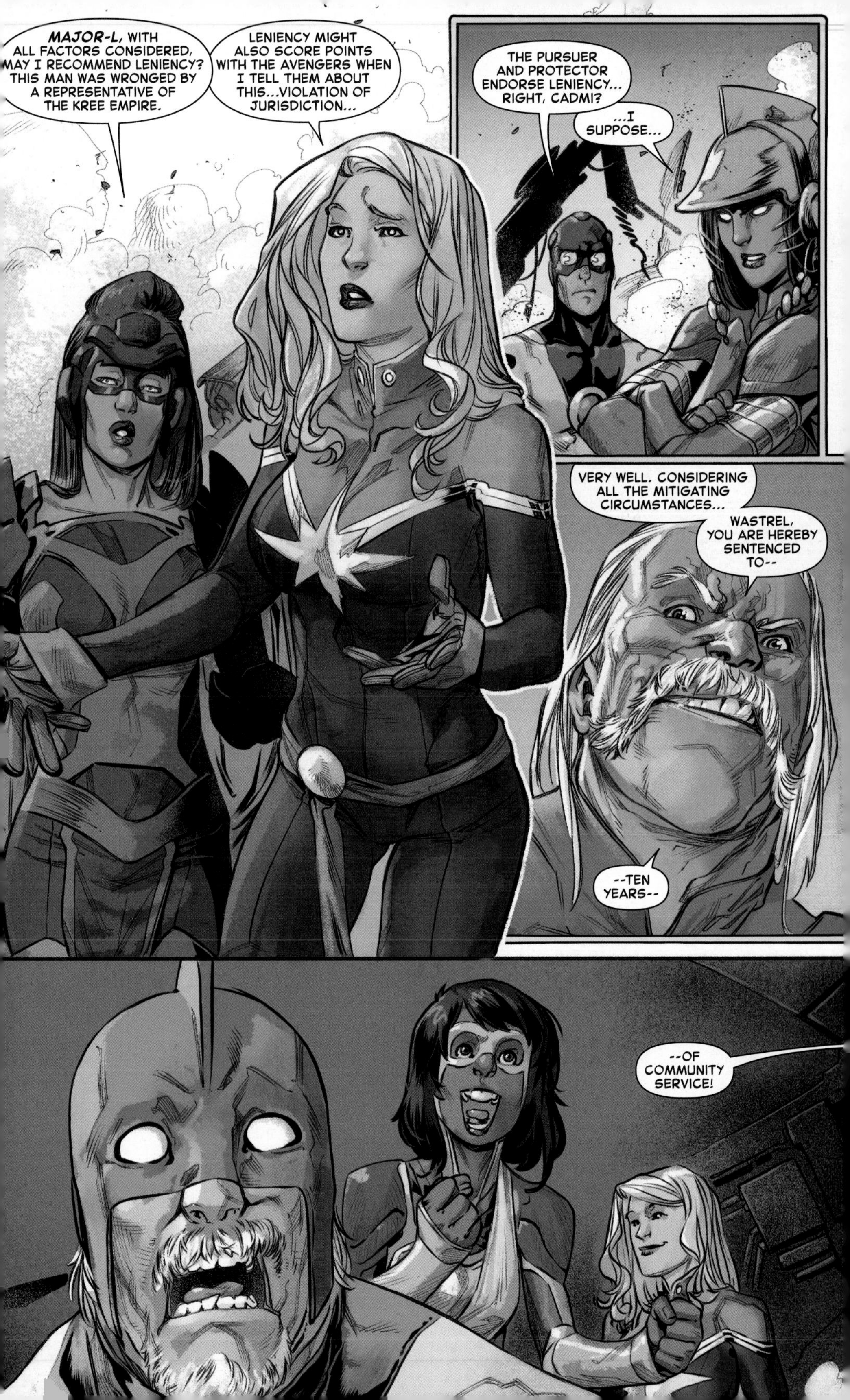

MAJOR-L, WITH ALL FACTORS CONSIDERED, MAY I RECOMMEND LENIENCY? THIS MAN WAS WRONGED BY A REPRESENTATIVE OF THE KREE EMPIRE.
LENIENCY MIGHT ALSO SCORE POINTS WITH THE AVENGERS WHEN I TELL THEM ABOUT THIS...VIOLATION OF JURISDICTION...
THE PURSUER AND PROTECTOR ENDORSE LENIENCY... RIGHT, CADMI?
...I SUPPOSE...
VERY WELL. CONSIDERING ALL THE MITIGATING CIRCUMSTANCES...
WASTREL, YOU ARE HEREBY SENTENCED TO--
--TEN YEARS--
--OF COMMUNITY SERVICE!

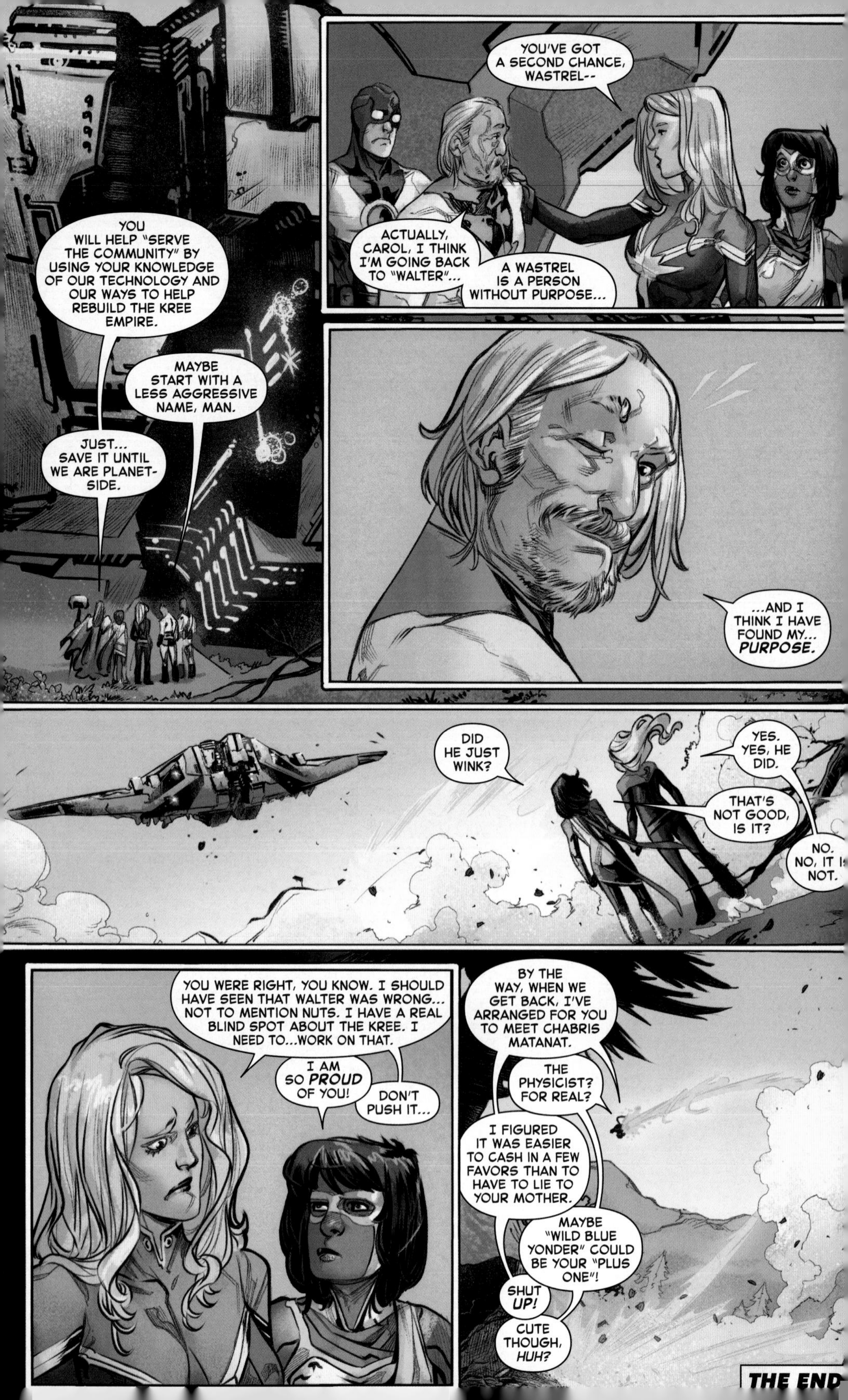
YOU WILL HELP "SERVE THE COMMUNITY" BY USING YOUR KNOWLEDGE OF OUR TECHNOLOGY AND OUR WAYS TO HELP REBUILD THE KREE EMPIRE.
MAYBE START WITH A LESS AGGRESSIVE NAME, MAN.
JUST... SAVE IT UNTIL WE ARE PLANET-SIDE.
YOU'VE GOT A SECOND CHANCE, WASTREL--
A WASTREL IS A PERSON WITHOUT PURPOSE...
ACTUALLY, CAROL, I THINK I'M GOING BACK TO "WALTER"...
...AND I THINK I HAVE FOUND MY... *PURPOSE.*
DID HE JUST WINK?
YES. YES, HE DID.
THAT'S NOT GOOD, IS IT?
NO. NO, IT IS NOT.
YOU WERE RIGHT, YOU KNOW. I SHOULD HAVE SEEN THAT WALTER WAS WRONG... NOT TO MENTION NUTS. I HAVE A REAL BLIND SPOT ABOUT THE KREE. I NEED TO...WORK ON THAT.
I AM SO *PROUD* OF YOU!
DON'T PUSH IT...
BY THE WAY, WHEN WE GET BACK, I'VE ARRANGED FOR YOU TO MEET CHABRIS MATANAT.
THE PHYSICIST? FOR REAL?
I FIGURED IT WAS EASIER TO CASH IN A FEW FAVORS THAN TO HAVE TO LIE TO YOUR MOTHER.
MAYBE "WILD BLUE YONDER" COULD BE YOUR "PLUS ONE"!
SHUT *UP!*
CUTE THOUGH, *HUH?*
THE END

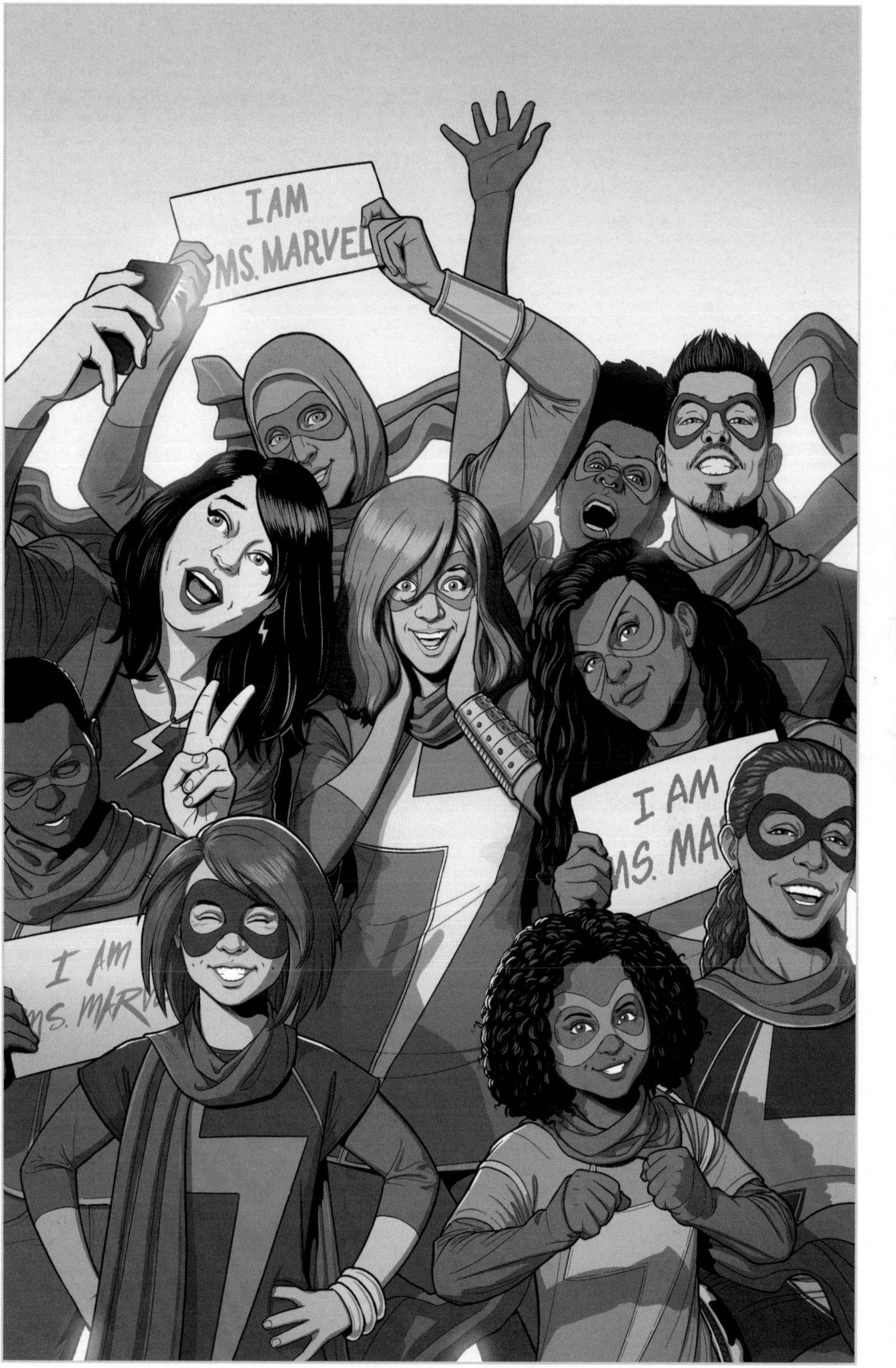
I AM
MS. MARVEL
I AM
MS. MA
I AM

MS. MARVEL #37 VARIANT
BY JAMIE McKELVIE

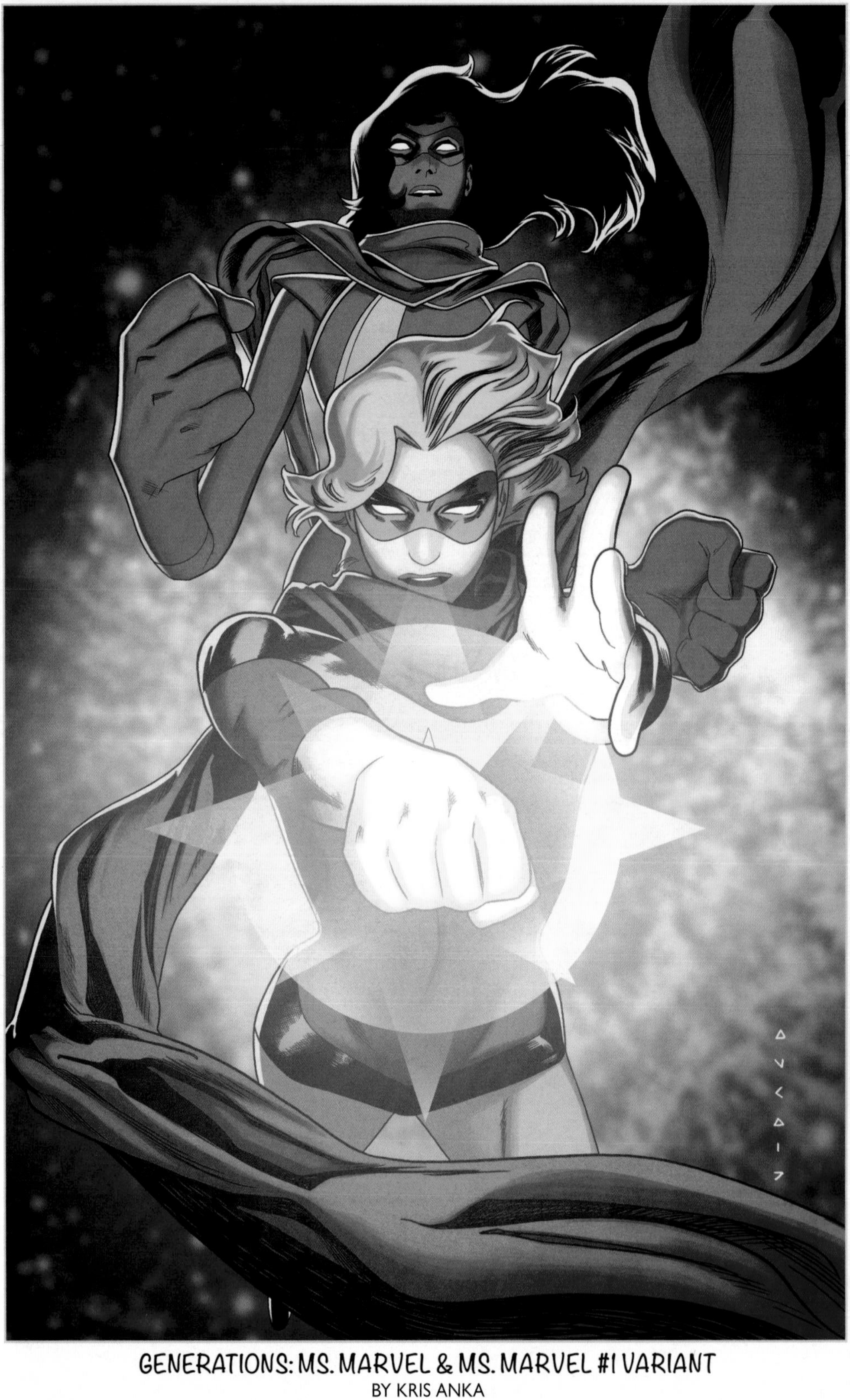

GENERATIONS: MS. MARVEL & MS. MARVEL #1 VARIANT
BY KRIS ANKA

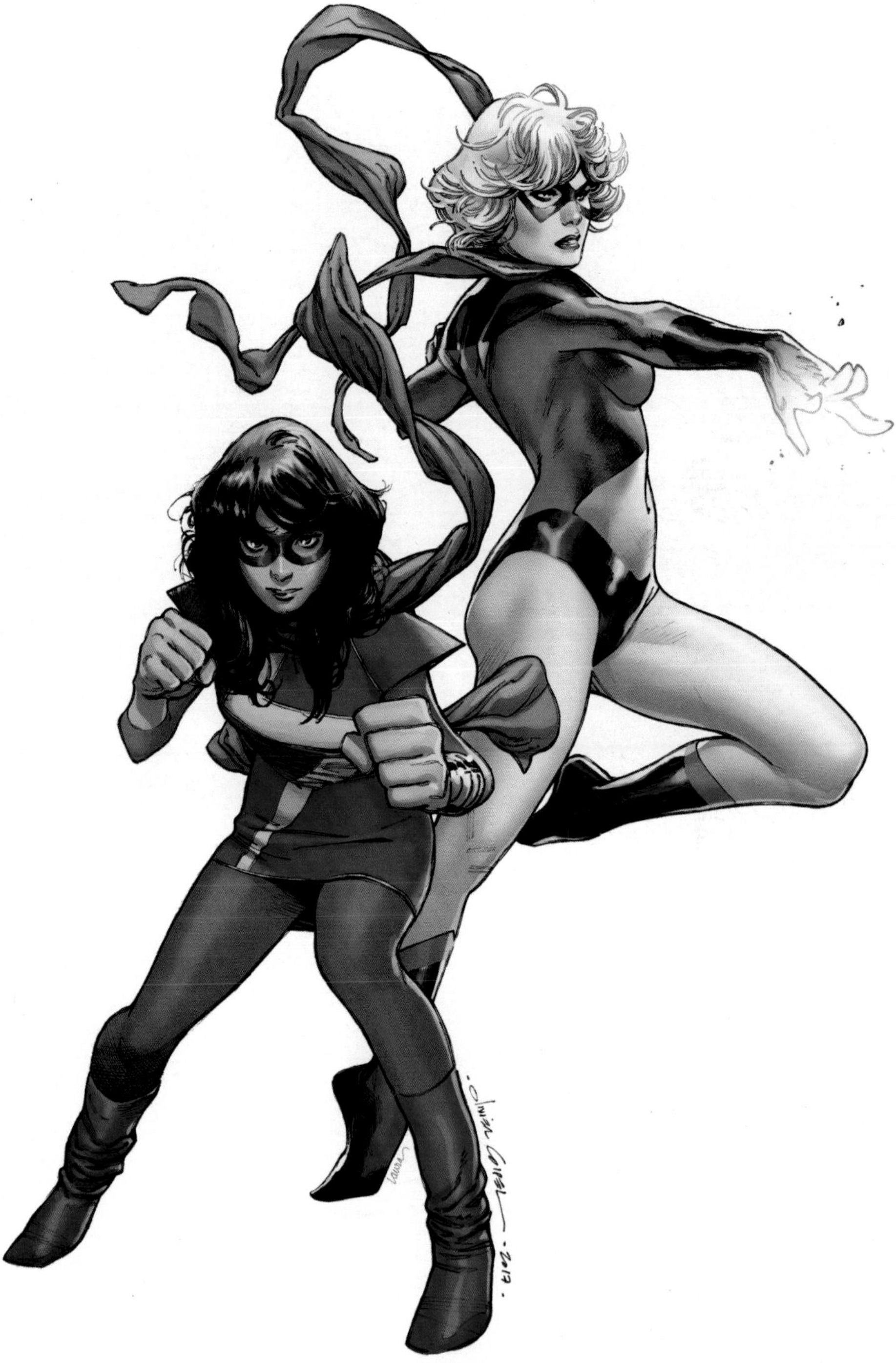

GENERATIONS: MS. MARVEL & MS. MARVEL #1 VARIANT

BY OLIVIER COIPEL & LAURA MARTIN

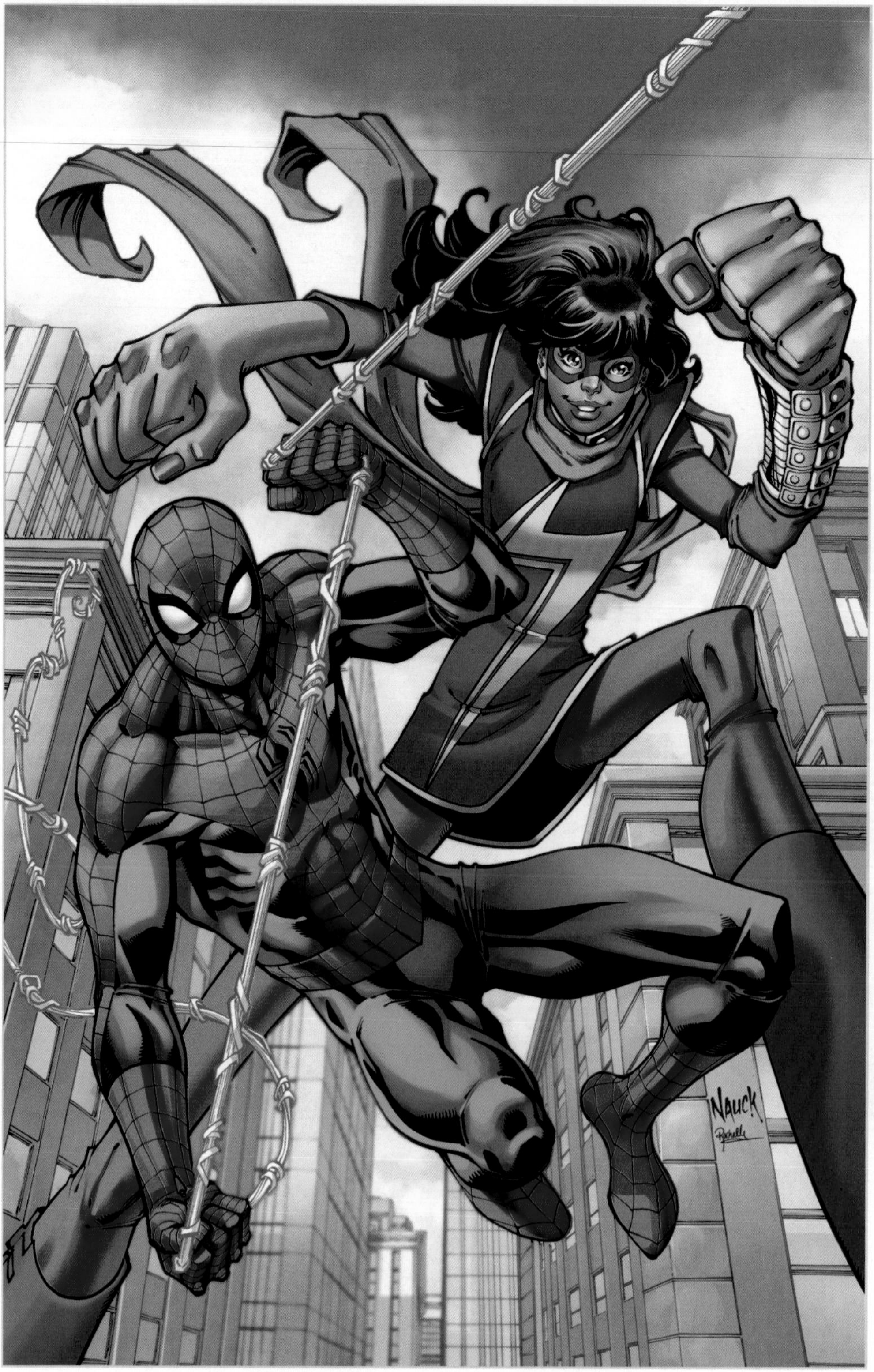
NAUCK

MS. MARVEL TEAM-UP #1 VARIANT
BY TODD NAUCK & RACHELLE ROSENBERG

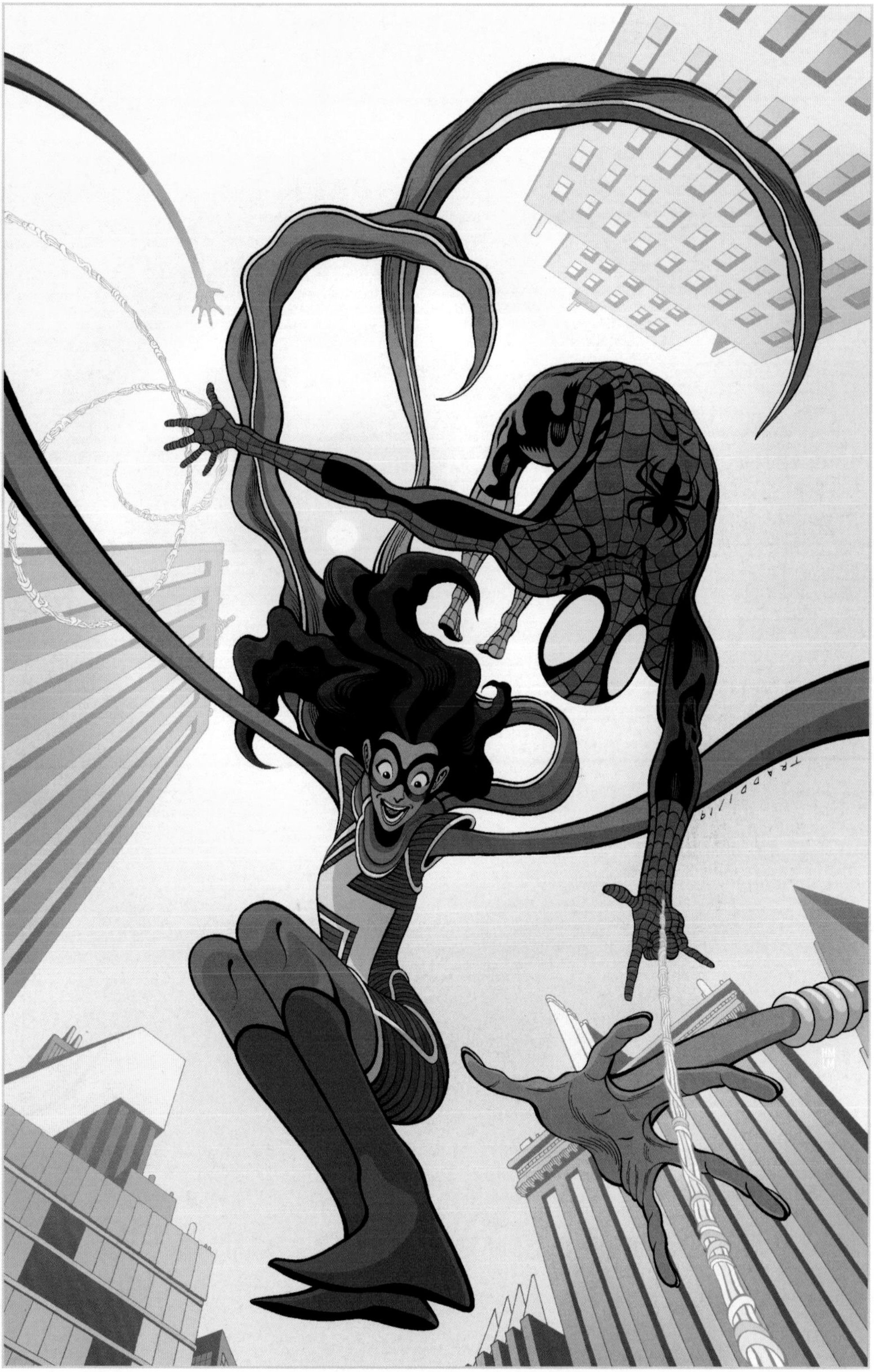

MS. MARVEL TEAM-UP #2 VARIANT
BY TRADD MOORE & HEATHER MOORE

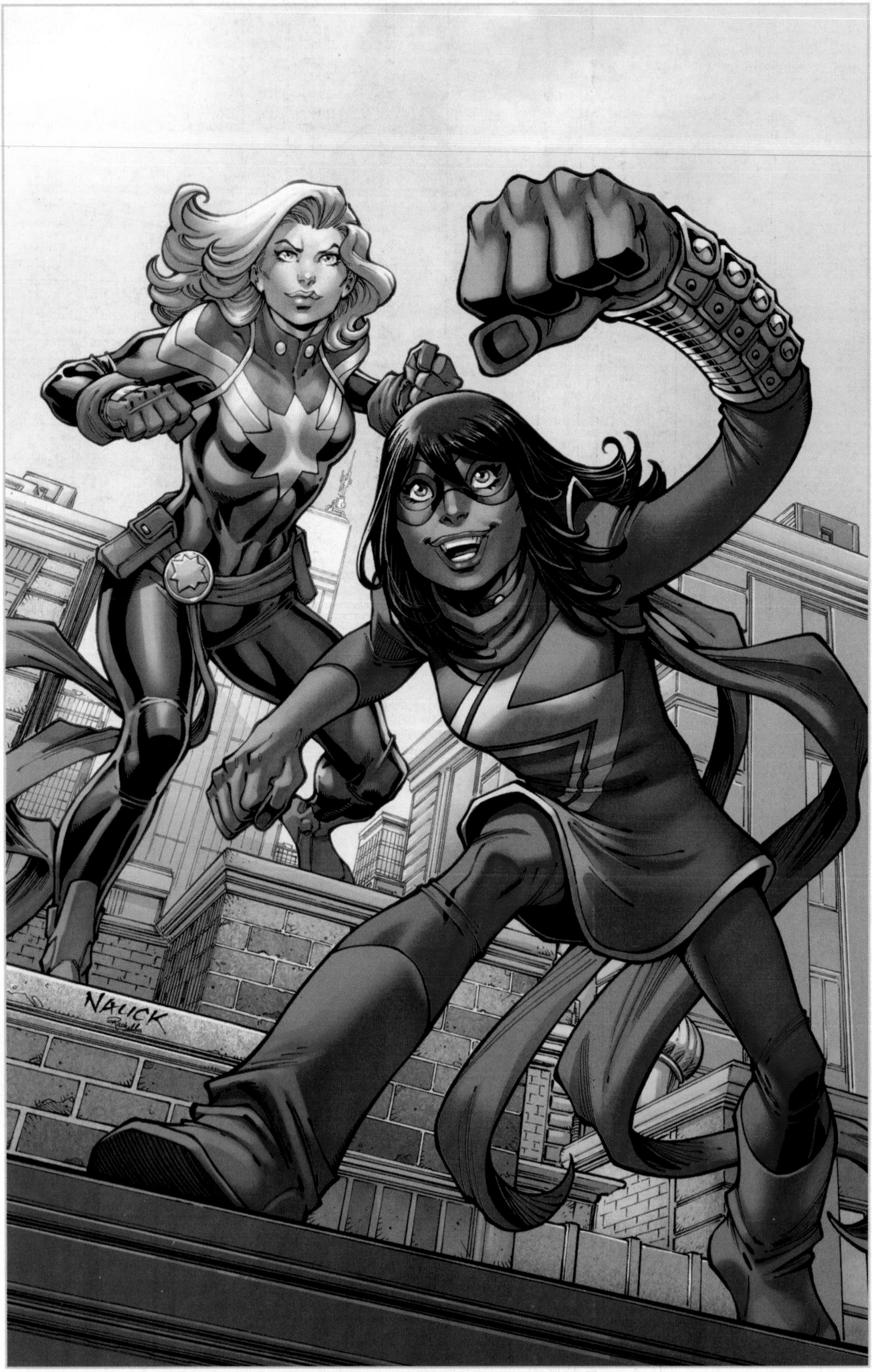
NAUCK

MS. MARVEL TEAM-UP #4 VARIANT
BY TODD NAUCK & RACHELLE ROSENBERG